Sean Wallace is the fou[...] of Prime Books. In his sp[...] number of projects, incl[...] *Magazine*, *The Dark*, and *Fantasy Magazine*, and a number of anthologies, including *Best New Fantasy*, *Japanese Dreams*, *The Mammoth Book of Steampunk*, *People of the Book*, *Robots: Recent A.I.*, and *War & Space: Recent Combat*. He has been nominated a number of times by both the Hugo Awards and the World Fantasy Awards, won three Hugo Awards and two World Fantasy Awards, and has served as a World Fantasy Award judge. He lives in Germantown, MD, with his wife, Jennifer, and their twin daughters, Cordelia and Natalie.

Recent Mammoth titles

The Mammoth Book of New Sherlock Holmes Adventures
The Mammoth Book of the Lost Chronicles
of Sherlock Holmes
The Mammoth Book of Historical Crime Fiction
The Mammoth Book of Best New SF 24
The Mammoth Book of Really Silly Jokes
The Mammoth Book of Undercover Cops
The Mammoth Book of Weird News
The Mammoth Book of Muhammad Ali
The Mammoth Book of Best British Crime 9
The Mammoth Book of Conspiracies
The Mammoth Book of Lost Symbols
The Mammoth Book of Steampunk
The Mammoth Book of New CSI
The Mammoth Book of Gangs
The Mammoth Book of SF Wars
The Mammoth Book of One-Liners
The Mammoth Book of Ghost Romance
The Mammoth Book of Best New SF 25
The Mammoth Book of Jokes 2
The Mammoth Book of New Horror 23
The Mammoth Book of Street Art
The Mammoth Book of Ghost Stories by Women
The Mammoth Book of Best British Crime 11

The Mammoth Book of Dieselpunk

Sean Wallace

ROBINSON

RUNNING PRESS
PHILADELPHIA · LONDON

ROBINSON

First published in Great Britain in 2015 by Robinson

Copyright © Sean Wallace, 2015

1 3 5 7 9 8 6 4 2

The moral right of the author has been asserted.

A CIP catalogue record for this book
is available from the British Library.

ISBN 978-1-47211-875-2 (paperback)
ISBN 978-1-47211-946-9 (ebook)

Typeset in Plantin Light by Hewer Text UK Ltd, Edinburgh
Printed and bound in Great Britain by CPI Group (UK) Ltd., Croydon, CR0 4YY

Robinson
is an imprint of
Constable & Robinson Ltd
100 Victoria Embankment
London EC4Y 0DY

An Hachette UK Company
www.hachette.co.uk

www.constablerobinson.com

First published in the United States in 2015 by Running Press Book Publishers,
A Member of the Perseus Books Group

Books published by Running Press are available at special discounts for bulk
purchases in the United States by corporations, institutions and other organizations.
For more information, please contact the Special Markets Department at the
Perseus Books Group, 2300 Chestnut Street, Suite 200, Philadelphia, PA 19103,
or call (800) 810-4145, ext. 5000, or email special.markets@perseusbooks.com.

US ISBN: 978-0-7624-5616-1
US Library of Congress Control Number: 2014956654

9 8 7 6 5 4 3 2 1
Digit on the right indicates the number of this printing

Running Press Book Publishers
2300 Chestnut Street
Philadelphia, PA 19103-4371

Visit us on the web!
www.runningpress.com

Contents

Introduction by Tobias S. Buckell vii

"Rolling Steel: A Pre-Apocalyptic Love Story"
by Jay Lake and Shannon Page 1

"Don Quixote" by Carrie Vaughn 19

"The Little Dog Ohori" by Anatoly Belilovsky 31

"Vast Wings Across Felonious Skies"
by E. Catherine Tobler 41

"Instead of a Loving Heart" by Jeremiah Tolbert 80

"Steel Dragons of a Luminous Sky" by Brian Trent 89

"Tunnel Vision" by Rachel Nussbaum 105

"Thief of Hearts" by Trent Hergenrader 139

"In Lieu of a Thank You" by Gwynne Garfinkle 161

"This Evening's Performance" by Genevieve Valentine 168

"Into the Sky" by Joseph Ng 219

"The Double Blind" by A. C. Wise 241

"Black Sunday" by Kim Lakin-Smith 258

"We Never Sleep" by Nick Mamatas 300

"Cosmobotica" by Costi Gurgu and Tony Pi 323

"Act of Extermination" by Cirilo S. Lemos
(translated by Christopher Kastensmidt) 340

"Blood and Gold" by Erin M. Hartshorn   389

"Floodgate" by Dan Rabarts   398

"Dragonfire is Brighter than the Ten Thousand Stars"
by Mark Robert Philps   414

"Mountains of Green" by Catherine Schaff-Stump   468

"The Wings The Lungs, The Engine The Heart"
by Laurie Tom   480

Acknowledgments   498

About the Contributors   500

Introduction

Science-fiction editor Gardner Dozois popularized the word "cyberpunk" in the 1980s to define a new subgenre making waves. Ever since then, readers and critics have been fond of adding "punk" as a modifier to call out interesting subgenres. Bio-punk for the cloning and nanotechnology-focused 1990s, and in the late 2000s, and on, Steampunk became a catchall for a wider movement of fashion, cosplay, and literature taking aesthetics cues from Victorian and Edwardian periods.

So it's not a surprise to see the word "Dieselpunk" appear on the scene.

But what is Dieselpunk?

It certainly conjures up images of belching engines, massive crankshafts revving up, and the thunderous roar of fuel-powered machines the likes of which I could imagine my grandfather working on in his youth. This isn't the hiss of steam and manners and corsets. It's grease and noise and "We Can Do It" posters.

One simple definition is that, while Steampunk normally uses a time period from the Victorian or Edwardian periods, Dieselpunk simply advances the clock forward to the interwar period. After World War I and before World War II (although, as with many categories, there are plenty of gray areas).

This is the time of the Art Deco movement, an aesthetic that tried to wrap itself around the increasingly powerful impact of machinery, industry, and factories. It contained contradictions in that attempt; it married strong, clean rectilinear lines with aerodynamic shapes. But from that frisson came art that is still admired today: the Chrysler Building with its iconic arches and clean lines, 30 Rockefeller Plaza, and the smooth flowing

Introduction

lines of the 1937 Delahaye Roadster, or any of the 1930s Cord automobiles. Even in cheap dollar stores, today, you can buy prints of jazz or governmental information posters from the era that are still striking in their marriage of simple form, economy, and composition.

But what kind of science fiction does this almost brutalist aesthetic create? Is it fiction just trying to emulate a technology from a very specific time period and that's it? Or is Dieselpunk trying to grapple with the same core problem that Art Deco was?

Dieselpunk, with its science fictional roots married to an Art Deco inspiration, is a perfect fit. Science fiction has long spent time trying to understand the impact technology has on the human psyche, and on our future. Is it any surprise that a subgenre of science fiction would look to inspiration from an aesthetic that tried to incorporate the mechanically modern, the engineer, to modern art?

While retro-futurist, Dieselpunk's Art Deco roots expressed in fiction allow the writers you'll find in this anthology to explore the length and breadth of the best genre fiction has to offer. The authors explore the impact of the factory on the people who are fed into it, or wonder what happens when technology can replace our very jobs – all too familiar concerns to those of us in the modern world . . . no matter which modern world it is we're living in. But the optimism of the interwar period isn't lost, as plenty of the stories here harken back to one of the defining moments of the literature of the time: pulp adventure, when magazines were filled with stories of derring-do and fantastic achievements. You'll find a lot of high-octane, fast-revving fun here.

So I hope you'll join me in flipping past these diesel-tinged pages to dig deeper into the all-too-human stories at their heart, and I also hope that you'll find these stories as fascinating and full of flair as I have.

Tobias S. Buckell

Rolling Steel:
A Pre-Apocalyptic Love Story

Jay Lake and Shannon Page

Rough Beast slouched toward the Bethlehem steel mill. Tons of fresh hot metal in there, every cobber and new chum from the Allegheny to the Delaware knew that. Even Topper, the old cat-eyed bastard with steel cables for fingers and a brain stewed in barium-laced æther, knew which way the good stuff lay, for all that he couldn't tell up from down on days ending with a /y/.

He's a bad man, our Topper. Used to run child-soldiers over the St Lawrence to the Froggies during the Quebec-and-Michigan War. *La troisième mutinerie*, the Quebecoise called it in one of their endless prayers to St Jude, for if ever a cause was lost surely it is theirs. Wolfe had put paid to their ambitions at the Plains of Abraham two centuries earlier, but no Frenchman ever born minded much dying for the romance of a shattered heart.

And there was no heart so shattered as that of a patriot whose country has been brought to ground.

And so we have Topper, driven bird-mad in the trenches of the Somme when it would have been kinder for him to have just died. Came home he did to the quack attentions of the New Friends of Sweet Reason, got caught up in the Technocracy movement as exhibit A, and finally fell apart as the country itself did in Roosevelt's dying days.

Now there's Wehrmacht units on the loose from Nova Scotia to New Jersey, the South has risen again (and again), the Federals are barely hanging on in the Mississippi basin, issuing wireless dispatches from Washington-on-the-Rails while the Great Madness takes anyone stupid enough to be caught outside at night anywhere between the Wabash and Pamlico Sound.

Only those who started mad can stand the stuff, and move faster by night than any prayerful man might by day. Especially Topper in his *Rough Beast*, which once upon a time was a machine meant to kill other machines before he made so much more of it, oh so much more.

"Metal, my pretty," he whispered, patting with a clattering crackle of steel the crawler's upholstered dashboard between the engraving of Percy Bysshe Shelley and the platinum-dipped weasel skull with the rhinestone eyes. Only one of those two had he killed, Topper, and some days he knew the difference. He squinted into the depths of night through the prism that made up *Rough Beast*'s forward vision block, watching for the mill which loomed close, its fires never banked.

Fate and fortune walked on the greased knuckles of Topper's war machine, as never they had since Poland's borders collapsed in the first of the lightning wars.

I patrolled the unquiet streets south of the steel mill, cussing as I walked back and forth in my own precious allotted square block of turf, practically wearing channels in the concrete with my steel-heeled stilettos. "Bastards," I muttered, thinking of the Best Sister and her Little Chums. Well, "bitches", technically, but I didn't fancy using such a term of endearment when referring to their ilk.

"Bastards," I growled, as I turned the corner for the seventeen-thousand-and-thirty-second time, only this time I was thinking of my crib mates, the ones who had sniffed out some sort of rupture in my soul and handed me this godforsaken turf as my undue reward.

"Bastard!" I screamed, jamming to a halt as the ferocious machine loomed before me. Hadn't heard the fucker coming at all. My NKVD surplus large-bore riot gun was already raised and trained on the madman coming up from a top hatch, red-lacquered nail rattling against the trigger as my finger trembled with desire. Then I saw it was Topper.

Which didn't change my assessment of the situation, or my epithet. But I did lower the gun, and hike up my leather mini-skirt an inch or two.

The gibbering fool grinned down at me, leaning over the console in a halo of actinic light to stare down the front of my corset. I set my shoulders back to improve his view and leered right back up at him.

"Going my way, big boy?" I called out.

"Bethlehem, Bethlehem, Bethlehem!" he chanted, his eyes rolling in his head.

Oops, there went the tiny whisper of sanity I'd detected a moment ago. I danced back a step, just in case the worms in his brain told him to gas up that monstrous vehicle and put paid to the sexiest thing he was likely to see all day – any day.

My heels tapped on the sidewalk as I leaned against the wall of the foundry behind me. "And what are you going to do when you get there, hmm?"

"Steal," Topper said, letting the word do its double duty. "Stable." Another word doing double duty. He stared down at the woman. Someone from another lifetime, Topper knows with animal cunning and vestiges of functional memory.

He has had many lifetimes, our Topper. Lived them all together inside one much-mended head, until his name has become legion because he is many. Swine out of Garaden could not be more multiplicitous than this man. But even through the palimpsest of his personality, this woman emerges like a slave ship out of an African fog bank.

"Coming with?" Topper asked. He gunned his twinned diesels for emphasis. *Rough Beast* shivered like a dog about to piss. The woman looked scared but determined, a combination which even Topper cannot ignore.

He locked down the upper hatch, set the brakes, pegged the clutches, disarmed the antipersonnel charges on the outer hull, and crawled back between the ammo cans and the fuel bags to undog the ventral hatch. As he twisted the clamps, Topper hoped the woman hadn't run away or been jumped or something. He can't protect her from up here. *Rough Beast* is made for salvage runs and fighting heavy metal, not personnel escort.

Topper is confused about a lot of things, but he's not confused about what his crawler does.

The woman was still outside, armed and dangerous. And that was just her looks. Dark hair swept back from an aristocratic face. Pretty teeth, which Topper remembers from white rooms full of screams. She had a big gun, too, a riot weapon meant for stopping dogs or people caught in the Great Madness.

"You're going to the plant," she said.

It was not a question.

"In," Topper ordered by way of a non-answer.

Indecision flicked across her face like a trout in a mountain stream, then she climbed the metal steps he'd dropped down for her. *Rough Beast* had ground clearance that would give an arborist's ladder a bad case of envy.

Distant gunfire echoed as Topper dogged the hatch, but the incoming wasn't to their address. He wormed back up to the driver's station, leaving the woman to follow or not as she chose.

The crawler got moving with a shuddering lurch which foretold trouble for the portside throw bearings. He could rebuild. He just needed some high-grade ingots to trade out for the finished parts. That was how he took care of everything on this monster.

A single man wasn't meant to maintain and operate something like *Rough Beast*. Not even a single man as profoundly unalone as Topper.

The woman squirmed into the radio operator's seat behind him. That surprised Topper, he'd already forgotten about her. No radio, never had been one, but there was part of a sandwich rack out of an automat right in front of her face, as if she could plot their course in egg salad and bologna and trimmed crusts.

"So." Her gun thumped briefly against the floor. He noted she was smart enough to clip it to the seat pedestal. "When did they let you out?"

Topper had to think that one over for a while. Finally he said, "Ain't sure they have yet."

Call it boredom if you like. I won't dispute it if you do, not at all. Boredom, ennui, a sense of adventure left unaddressed for far too long – any of that could explain why I left my post and crawled up into that oil-dripping beastie with the lunatic pilot.

When I'm summoned before Best Friend and her bitches to explain myself, though – and you know I will be – we won't be talking about any ennui bullshit. No, I'll be spinning some tale about surveillance and undercover and getting on the inside of the enemy camp and all that sort of yak.

To support this notion, and also because I was damned curious, I slithered up the ladder at the behest of the grisly creature. (Hey, don't let it be said I never plan ahead.) I'd known Topper before, of course; knew him before he was the raving lunatic we'd all come to know and love in the Madness. Not that he was ever entirely sane.

Who is, anymore?

I knew him because I'd been part of the crew that had taken him down, during the last round of the world-shifting adventures. We'd taken him hard, real hard, even before handing him over to the New Friends for, shall we say, readjustment therapy. I'd never expected to see him again. Which was shame, in its way.

So here he was, grinding up my street on his way to god-knows-what kind of tomfoolery down at the plant. Didn't even bother to deny it. Invited me aboard.

How could I resist?

I settled in behind him, looking around everywhere, trying to take it all in before he came to whatever shred of senses might have been left him by the New Friends and booted me out of there. Because, right, surveillance. Remember? I kept my right hand close to the NKVD riot gun in case Mr Topper decided to get cute. But he had already started the monster rolling again, ignoring me completely.

He answered my question well enough, I suppose. All things being equal, you never really do get out, do you?

I fell silent after that, wishing the asylum refugee had thought to put windows back at my seat. What was I supposed to do with A-4 and D-0? I'd had a lovely lunch already, thank you very much. The rats are fat and sassy, this part of town.

Oh, Jesus, just kidding. What do I look like? I don't eat rats. You think this figure comes from eating street sludge like rats?

Feral cats, now: that's where it's at. Yum yum, meow yum. Excellent diced and stir-fried, with tree ears and a sprinkling of hoisin sauce right at the end.

After a particularly difficult highway crossing, Topper's mind wanders back to the woman. She was muttering under her breath now. Something about rats and cats and someone named Hawser Ann. He could smell her breath even in the diesel-and-metal reek of the crawler.

Cats was right in there. Topper cackled. He'd had a cat once, lived in the bed with him in the pale green room with the telephone that whispered secret vices in his ear-of-virtue, and blessings in his ear-of-vice. He knew what had happened to that cat too, every time he blinked his eye.

Our Topper spent some quality time under the close personal care of Doctor Sergei S. Bryukhonenko, after the good Dr B. had fled the collapse of the Eastern Front and wound up under a New Friends of Sweet Reason ban working out of a former mental hospital in the quiet fields near Yellow Springs, Ohio. The fields were quiet then because of the gas pooling in the low-lying watersheds which killed off everything with a central nervous system.

Dr Bryukhonenko had been the beneficiary of good pressure seals and a number of human canaries chained to stakes in a three-mile radius around the hilltop facility. Our Topper had been the beneficiary of Dr Bryukhonenko's newfound health and safety.

Until the psychosurgeries began.

Now he saw in strange shades of gray, a world of movement and chiaroscuro, relying on childhood memories of paintboxes and flower gardens to fill in the colors. Topper still knows the curve of a woman's breast from the rounded nose of a bullet – he's not *that* far gone – but so much else slides past the greased corners of memory, electroshock therapy and deep conditioning, as if he were a human carpet afflicted with flea's eggs.

"Food?" he asked the woman. A gap yawned before the crawler, smoke crawling up out of some nether hole in the Pennsylvania soil. Mine fire? Enemy attack? Wrath of God?

He navigated around it while one of his inner selves listened to her answer.

"Is that a request or an offer?" she began suggestively, polishing the barrel of her riot gun.

"Dunno," Topper said. "Thought you might have some catsmeat." He felt vaguely like a cannibal for asking. Then his attention was distracted by the towering stacks of the mill, his destination. Someone flew a small aircraft close above them. He resisted the urge to jump up into the air and swat at it.

For all Topper knows, he might be able to do just that. Muscles he didn't know he had creaked at the thought.

"Rowr," the woman growled.

He wondered if she would purr, as well.

"You don't remember me, do you?" I asked the lunatic, after he'd failed to respond to my clever sally about the cat. I'd even growled to remind him. Good times. But I'm not even going to tell you about the look on his face when I did that, now.

Suffice it to say, crazy or not, the man had a strange charisma. And not because I was hard up, either. Not that I was ready to hop into the sack with him. Not right then. Not even the floor of this machine, or up against the wall of the mill. Not me.

The mill! A squinting straining gaze through what I could see of the forward view told me we were almost there, though Topper hadn't even been paying attention to the road. "Road" – such as it was, of course. The route, more like.

"Harridan Three, Harridan Three, do you copy?" a small voice crackled from my satchel. Damn, it must be one of the bitches in that plane buzzing overhead. Checking up on me. They don't trust me to wipe my own ass any more.

Of course I couldn't respond, not overtly. But if I didn't send her on her merry way, she'd land that overgrown horse-fly right in our path, and . . . well, let's just say I didn't fancy being two feet behind Topper when he was suddenly beset by Sisters in a well-armed aircraft, attempting to halt his forward progress.

"Nice rig you got here, Topper," I said instead. "I especially like the seats. Ooh, comfy."

He tore his attention away from peering up at the sky and

stared at me. A droplet of slobber formed in the V at the lowest point of his lip and hung there. "Seats?" he finally asked.

"Yep," I said loudly, patting the foul cracked vinyl next to me. "These seats right here, in this here vehicle you're driving me around in. Yep. Love it."

"Harridan Three, we copy," came the voice in my bag. It was Lena: bad news. And she was clearly pissed.

But the drone of the plane engine faded, and then the mill loomed large.

Too large.

"Stop!" I screamed, just as this abortion of a tank crashed through the wall.

Topper came round to paying attention to what he should be doing just after a few dozen tons of masonry bounced off the roof. That plane had buzzed off, but it had dropped him a present on the way out.

He spun *Rough Beast* left, just to confuse anyone who might be sighting in on him. From the sound of things, the crawler was now taking out another portion of the mill's outer wall. The hull pounded and shuddered, a brick rain.

"Where's the map?" he screamed over the deafening war.

She shook her head. *Useless bitch*, he thought. Bring a girl on a picnic, she doesn't even remember napkins. Topper keyed off the antipersonnel charges ringing the upper hatch and jacked his chair for a look. He let his feet do the driving.

Thing about a cat's eye is it sees in darkness. Not the pitch black of coal mines or a politician's soul, but places where a human being would stand blinking and wondering which way to the egress. The very bad Dr Bryukhonenko had built a neural jumper block so the input from the cat's eyes jammed swollen and dry into Topper's skull could be made sensible – sense-in-light for a man who lives in the endless nonsense of his own head.

All of which meant that with the Bethlehem mill running on blackout except for the glow from the Bessemers further down the compound, only Topper could see what was going on. The defenders had to rely on triangulation and their own knowledge of the terrain. Topper was ignoring the terrain in favor of the direct approach.

"Damned loading yard ought to be down here somewhere."

Rails had been torn up a long time ago – their fixed routes were useless in this age of rolling borders and continuous sabotage – but the rail yard was still useful space.

Having gotten something resembling his bearings, Topper spun *Rough Beast* around. The wide open area had been *behind* him.

A woman was screaming from down near his waist. She sounded familiar. He jacked the chair low and looked around.

"Marie," Topper said, pleased as hell to see her. "What are you doing here in San Diego?"

The look on Marie's face was almost frightening. The gun in her hand worried him more, though. When had she learned to shoot?

Outside, the aircraft buzz had come back. *Fucking spotters*, he thought. "Whoops, gotta go," he said, "bad guys up above. Hold that fire till we need it, kiddo."

By the time Topper was back out of the hatch and heating up the solenoids in the remotely-operated turrets, he'd forgotten what he'd gone down for. Until a gunshot echoed from inside the hull of his crawler.

Bastard flipped completely out on me after the impact. I mean, I shouldn't have been surprised, but it wasn't like I'd been having a peaceful day up till then, so I was a bit, well, off guard.

Hey. It happens.

Once the machine (not to mention Lena's bomb) rendered the wall of the mill into so many smithereens, it lurched but didn't stop, instead simply veering off to the left a bit. Or maybe that was Topper, yanking on the wheel. Anyway, that's the part that rattled me more than anything else. I was airborne a good two seconds, then crashed to the slimy floor of the tank-thing at his feet.

At least I held onto my gun.

Which stood me in good stead once I'd recovered enough to think again. The freak was looming over me, again paying no attention to the road, or corridor, or whatever it was we were driving down at the moment . . . yeah, another wall, I think . . .

interior wall. It was hard to tell, jammed underneath two hundred and fifty pounds of insane manflesh.

I waved the gun at him. "Back off, Topper, I mean it!"

He called me Marie.

Oh god.

Waving the gun again, I tried to look sufficiently menacing. This was no doubt undermined by his view down the front of the corset. He grinned, and mumbled something about San Diego. What the fuck?

Maybe I was still screaming or something, because just then Lena decided she'd had enough. "Harridan three, we're coming in. You're relieved from duty effective immediately. Surrender your weapon to the personnel who will be approaching the tank once we bring it to a halt."

I almost laughed. How exactly were they expecting to do that?

A burst of machine gun fire came from above, mixed in with the aircraft engine. Oh, that's how. At least it got Topper's attention. He yanked his eyeballs away from my girls and scrabbled up top.

Unfortunately, I didn't want Lena to take his attention. Nor did I want to "surrender" anything to any goddamned "personnel" inside Bethlehem. "Topper!" I yelled, but he was beyond hearing me.

I took a shot in his general direction, careful not to aim for anything vital. Like around the middle. Riot loads weren't *supposed* to be fatal.

What? Just thinking ahead here. He'd cleaned up nicely once before. Who's to say it couldn't happen again? Girl can't be too picky these days.

Good. That got his fleeting attention once more. He slithered back down below and stood before me. "Marie?"

"Not Marie," I said. Then I reached down and toggled my radio to blessed silence so we could talk privately. "Grace, and don't you forget it, you moron."

"Grace . . ." The name slid off his pink tongue, making it sound dirty. "Graaace."

Oh good lord. We were in for a long night.

★ ★ ★

Topper stuttered. That's what the doctor had called it – not Bryukhonenko the surgeon, but that New Friends woman with three moles on her chin that always made him think of H. G. Wells's *War of the Worlds* for some reason.

Threes, all evil things came in threes. That's why men and women stayed in pairs. That's why a woman had two tits, a man had two nuts, everyone had two eyes, two ears, two hands, two legs, two nostrils, two lungs for the love of God.

Threes. And the stutters always came in threes. Dr Roseglove, that was her name, like she had thorns turned inward to her hands, tiny red-brown spikes to pierce the skin, an Orchidglove would have been a very different doctor indeed, or a Lily-of-the-valleyglove, and when he stuttered he lost *time*, he lost *control*, he lost his *marker* in the place of life.

Bad things. Threes. A woman named Marie, not Grace. But he'd known Marie? Had she been a twin? Or worse, a triplet? Was Grace her middle name, her secret name, her confirmation name, her gang name, her spymaster's handle?

She was shouting. Outside something was bombing. His thigh hurt like fucking hell where something bad had happened.

Adrenaline, he thought, a moment of clarity amid the stutter. *Adrenaline and a pressure bandage, before I die of assassination.*

Why would anyone want to kill our Topper? Even he cannot answer that. Well, other than all the people he's killed over the years, of course, but very few of them have anything to say about it now. Dead is dead, and no one's got relatives no more, not in this fragged world.

She's still yelling, this woman, but he's ignoring her in single-minded pursuit of his wound. He doesn't worry so much about the scattered pellets embedded in the flesh of his leg. They will either kill him or they won't.

Topper jacked up into his open hatch. *Rough Beast* wasn't equipped for anti-air operations. An angry woman loose with a riot gun down below was a problem. Amplified voices and high explosives outside were a bigger problem.

He left his stutter behind when he realized that his enemies had come to ground. Obliging of them. *Rough Beast* was very well equipped for anti-personnel operations.

A beefy woman stood in the red glare between shadows cast by his own arc lights, shouting for someone named Jason Adair to stand down. Topper didn't know any Jason Adair, not since before the wars began when he might once have answered to that name, so he activated the electrically controlled chin turret that looked like a fuel junction and could surprise an unwary, beefy woman and turned this one into a spray of blood and cloth.

Then he ground the crawler straight toward the ducted fan aircraft grounded before him. Topper admired the engineering of the thing – innovative, frightening, probably stolen from the Germans – until *Rough Beast* crushed it to scrap.

He wasn't sure which was more annoying: Marie screaming from below or some woman screaming from the crushed cockpit of the aircraft. In either case it didn't matter. The metal yard was ahead, and that was his purpose here.

Okay.

Fuck.

Breathe. Just get hold of yourself: breathe, bitch.

'Cause when Topper took out Lena and her bodyguard du jour, *not to mention the whole fucking aircraft* thank you very much, well, okay, it sent me into a bit of a spin.

So maybe I shot him again. Just a little bit. I'm really not sure, frankly. Everything got kind of crazy and blurry there for a few minutes. Like maybe there were psychotic drugs floating in the air around Topper.

No, I didn't mean anti-psychotic drugs. That would have helped. I meant what I said. Pay attention, I'm not going to say it again.

It didn't make a damn bit of difference to his apparent sanity, or lack thereof. I mean the shooting-him-again part, if it happened. The drugs, I have no idea. That was just a metaphor kind of thing. I was making a comparison, one thing to another.

Although who knows?

Anyway, my sanity, however. Well . . . like I said, I lost a few minutes there. Once everything was tracking again, I saw that the aircraft was a pile of oily rubble behind us, and Topper was rolling the tank forward, muttering about Germans.

He never stopped with the verbiage, that one. If only any of it made the smallest bit of sense. I'd love to see him across a poker table. Looked like every thought was immediately broadcast.

Not that I was likely to be playing poker again any time soon. Anyway, Lena had my deck of cards. Probably they were ground into the mud behind us, too.

Mud and oil and blood and . . .

Don't think about it. *Don't think about it!*

I clipped my riot gun back into the rack beside the seat, just in case I was tempted to use it again. Because the part of my brain that had been functioning throughout the little misadventure of the past few minutes had just presented me with the irrefutable fact that my fate was now tied to that of this overgrown monkey, the one now drooling and gibbering and steering this massive bit of machinery toward what had to be the biggest metal yard I'd ever seen.

In other words: no more Sisters, not for me, not here, not now. By climbing aboard this contraption. I'd thrown my lot in with Topper.

God, I *hoped* he still cleaned up nicely.

I sidled forward in the cab, or at least something reasonably approximating sidling. Tough to do when the thing was rolling and grinding and rocking back and forth, throwing me from side to side like a hamster in a blender.

"Marie!" he said, catching sight of me. He gave me a delighted smile.

I fell into the co-pilot's seat beside him, or whatever you'd call it. Jump seat. Small bit of cushioning in a vast expanse of well lubricated metal parts and pieces. "Grace," I said, in a friendly and conversational tone.

"Marie-Grace?"

"Just Grace. Remember, sweetheart, how we went over this?" He kept staring at me. "Well – never mind that, anyway. Just watch where you're driving, okay?"

"Driving, doing, zooming, duckling," he said. But his head wafted back in the general direction of forward.

"Good boy," I said. "Just keep doing what you're doing." Sooner or later, some of this was going to make sense. For now, he just had to keep us alive.

"W-74," Topper sang out. "Tungsten steel. Hard as a shield, cuts like a blade, keep it sharp, never be late . . . Burma Shave!"

Marie-Grace Just Grace snorted at him. He was pretty sure she'd shot him a bit earlier, but she had a nice smile. Maybe he'd been wounded by one of the dizzy bitches from that airplane.

Bullets fell on *Rough Beast*'s hull like lead rain. The locals were getting to it. But now he was in the metal yard, the El Dorado of this Pennsylvania hellhole.

"Here, Missy Marie-Grace Just Grace," Topper said, handing her down a gas mask. "Wear this a while and don't get nothing on your skin." He paused, solicitous as a fragment from some long-forgotten safety briefing (back when "safety" and "briefing" were applicable concepts) emerged into his forebrain like pack ice on a midnight river. "You weren't planning to have no children, were you?"

"Not right *now*," she squealed.

Topper wasn't sure that Marie-Grace Just Grace had taken the real point of the question, but duty had been discharged. He pressed the big red button labeled "DO NOT PRESS." It was wired just below a portrait of Bing Crosby with a Hitler moustache.

Several loud, ominous thumps echoed from the outside of the crawler's hull. This was followed by a hissing noise. Topper belatedly remembered to pull on his own gas mask, then wondered what he'd done with the chemical suit.

The part of him that was sane enough to keep the rest of the traveling circus alive watched the sweep second hand on the dashboard clock – Swiss timing in a genuine hand-carved Chinese ivory casing, and possibly the most valuable thing aboard *Rough Beast*. Topper liked his treasures portable. He was a man who'd left more towns under more clouds than Seattle saw in a year.

One hundred and eighty seconds later he bailed out into the dissipating yellow fog. Defending fire had stopped, except for the occasional stutter of a weapon discharged as a finger shriveled too tightly in death. That hardly counted, though Topper knew a bullet was a bullet no matter who had fired it.

He wasn't moving right. The dizzy bitch really *had* shot him. Couldn't have been something too fierce, or his leg would be shattered. Riot gun with rubber loads, maybe? Who the hell would hang around a Pennsylvania mill town at night armed with sublethal munitions? That was like bringing a housewife to a bullfight.

Ahead of Topper were thirty-six pallets of high-grade tungsten steel. Finest kind, ready for shipment to the manufactories of Detroit and Fort Wayne. Or ripe for the jacking by an enterprising man with good intelligence and solid orders.

Or woman, he reminded himself. Topper turned to stare at *Rough Beast*, wondering what he'd been thinking and which part of him had been thinking it. Her head poked up now, insect-eyed and blank-faced in the gas mask.

An electric turret whined as she brought one of the Bofors to bear on him.

"Screw you," Topper shouted, and began dragging the cargo chains out. It was hijacking time. He didn't have what it took to die again right now.

After monkey-boy propositioned me a few times, I knew we were getting somewhere. Excellent. I could work with that.

The discussion of children, however, was a tad premature. I almost said something, but then he pressed some big goddamn red button and all manner of excitement began.

No, the other kind of excitement.

That all changed once he'd killed everyone within a ten-mile radius of the tank. Or so it seemed, anyway, given the swath of destruction all around us. After that, he turned back to me, with a terrible, deeply insane look about him.

I mean, he'd been insane all along. I knew that. You might have even said it was part of his charm. But I'd just watched him kill everyone I worked for, lived with, fucked and fought. Then I'd watched him kill everyone at the mill I was supposedly defending. Then he turned and looked at me.

"Now or never, baby," I said to myself, cranking one of his cannon turrets to point at him. That ought to put the fear into him.

All he did was proposition me a third time, then turn away and start fooling with a tangle of chains.

I threw my riot gun at him. Insane I can handle. Inconsistency: that makes me crazy.

"Marie-Grace Just Grace," he babbled on, as he started spreading the chains out on the gravel in front of us. He ignored the riot gun completely, after glancing at it. I clambered down out of the tank and retrieved it, but it was too big to hold if I was going to help him get the pallets aboard.

Sure, I helped him. He could barely move the damn things. I was in far too deep to back out now. Might as well get our business done in here and get the hell out. Then we could talk about children, or whatever the fuck he wanted.

Men. Can't live with 'em, can't stake 'em out for the vultures. Though some of them might be improved. Including this crazy old bastard.

He was my last ticket.

Topper yanked the cold steel out of the charnel house of the mill one-quarter-ton ingot at a time. The winches could handle the load, no problem – they were made for much heavier work than this, naval-grade hardware salvaged off a captured Kriegsmarine surface raider which had been broken in a gray-market yard hidden up the Rappahannock.

The girl helped. She was small, and weak, and not half-rebuilt out of spare parts and Soviet medicine, but she was tough and smart. Topper wondered how he knew her. Good-looking, too, and not just in an any-woman-in-a-war-zone way.

Somehow having his hands on all this hard-case metal was bringing him back into himself. Memories spiraled in kaleidoscope paths to land in partially assembled chiaroscuros somewhere deep in our Topper's head. Like how a real person might think, it occurred to him, coherent images and more than a little bit of focused recall stitching together into timelines.

He wanted to turn away from some of them – deeply unpleasant, unpleasantly deep, or just infused with a stunning sadness for the boy and man someone with his name and face might once of have been.

It was her, he realized. Not the metal. Not the dead. Not the distant thump of artillery and first drone of engines gone raiding in the cold, smoky sky. Not the screaming cats and bleeding eye sockets of memory. Not the white coats and wire-rimmed spectacles which had dominated so much of the intervening years.

Her.

Topper stepped closer, subtle as a pork roast in a synagogue, and sniffed.

"What the hell are you doing, you cre—" she shouted, then stopped when she got a good look at his face.

"M . . . Grace," Topper said, and looked her full in the eyes. He could fall into that pooled, dark amber forever, he realized.

Something was waiting to be born here beneath the shadow of *Rough Beast*, behind the walls of Bethlehem. He could feel it stirring inside him.

A soul. Hope. Affection.

Love?

He closed his eyes and breathed her in. She struck him all the way down into the lizard brain, scent and smell wired by million years of evolution and a hundred thousand generations of hairless apes dropping from the trees to say, *this one. This is the one.*

Before he could open his eyes again, she kissed him.

Somewhere inside the shattered Japanese puzzle box of his head, he was made whole.

"Let's get the last of this stuff on board," Topper said, rough but gentle as he drew her into his arms. "Then we're gonna say screw it to the Sisterhood and the New Friends and the Federals and the Wehrmacht and go be alone together. There's freemen in the Alleghenies would pay good money for our cargo, and hire us to raid for them."

His mind was dancing with visions of a quiet cabin, an open sky and skin exposed for no purpose more sinister than a long slow trail of the tongue.

God, it was like being a kid again.

For the first time in his life, Topper had woken up.

★   ★   ★

Yeah. So. Okay, I kissed him. Like I said, I'd kind of run out of options at that point.

But it was more than that. Much more.

When Topper turned and looked at me, really looked at me; when he got my name right; when the man that lived somewhere underneath all the layers of insanity our world had thrust at him suddenly bled through and took charge . . . I kissed him.

And when he pulled me into his arms and I caught the scent of him – the real, true scent, beyond the oil and blood and gasoline and the rank sweat of fear and battle – it hit me right below the belt.

Yeah, there. I meant what I said. How do you think things *become* clichés, anyway?

"Right," I said. "Last load and we're out of here."

And we rumbled off into the sunset. Sunrise. Whatever: I'm telling the story here, okay? The light changed and took us with it into a different world.

Don Quixote

Carrie Vaughn

The distant thunder and subtle earthquake of a bombardment
shouldn't have bothered me. I'd stayed in Madrid through the
siege, three years starting in 'thirty-six, and a man didn't forget
a thing like that. My gut didn't turn over at the noise, but at its
implications. The war was supposed to be all but over now. So
why the bombing?

Joe and I had left the main army to drive a truck along the
river, looking for a vantage where we could watch the defenders' last stand. Most of the other reporters had already fled the
country. I imagined I'd follow soon enough. As soon as I got
that one great story. There had to be some kind of nobility in
the face of defeat. Some kind of lesson for the future.

We stopped at a ridge and looked out over the river valley,
trying to guess Franco's army's next move. Without getting too
close, of course. I shaded my eyes. Another rumble of thunder
rolled over us, and columns of smoke rose up from around the
next hill.

Joe squinted into the sky. "Where're those bombs coming
from? I don't see any planes—"

"It's not planes."

"Then what is it, artillery?"

It didn't feel like artillery; the ground wasn't thumping with
every report. "Want to find out?"

"You drive, I'll get my camera."

We left the overlook and drove until we found a turn off
leading toward all that smoke.

I gripped the steering wheel; the truck lurched over potholes,
the shocks squealing. Joe held the dash with one hand and his

camera with the other, waiting for his shot. Not that there was anything to see – the landscape was barren of trees and vegetation. Not a spot of green. The battle had passed by here already, some time ago.

When we circled the next hill and came into an open stretch, the world changed. The battle here had been recent. Battle – more like a rout. Evidence suggested a massive aerial bombardment: tanks broken into pieces, treads shattered and turrets ripped from chassis; craters dotting the field like paint spatters; platoons reduced to scattered body parts. Vegetation still smoldered, and smoke rose up from wrecked ground. If I didn't know better, I'd have said this was someplace on the Western Front, twenty years ago. It's what happened when you took a thousand pounds of explosives and used them to scrape the land clean.

We had expected to find the crumpled remains of a defeated army. The fascists had pushed the Republican defenders back to the edges of their territory. The war was just about over, with Franco the victor. Everyone said so. Without outside aid, the Republicans didn't have a chance. But any potential allies had just turned their backs by making peace with Hitler. So-called peace, however long it lasted.

Somehow, I couldn't turn away from the disaster.

"Something's not right," I said finally.

"You just now noticed?"

"No – look at those rifles, the markings. These guys are Nationalists. Franco's army."

"Wait – aren't they supposed to be winning?"

"Yeah."

Joe got excited. "Then it's true – the loyalists came up with some secret weapon. They're going to turn it around after all."

I thought it really was too late – you had to have territory before you could defend it, and the loyalists didn't have much of that at all at this point. But if they did have a secret weapon – why wait until now to use it? "Something doesn't add up."

Crows circled. The air was starting to stink. There wasn't even anybody left to retrieve bodies, as if Franco's army hadn't yet figured out it had suffered such a defeat.

"Hank, let's get out of here—"

"Wait a minute." I grabbed binoculars from my bag on the seat next to me and peered out.

The road we were on hugged the hill and looped away from the plain where the battle had taken place. On the far side, beyond the destruction, another road stretched away: fresh, cut into the hard earth, an unpaved destructive swathe trammeling vegetation to pulp. It was as wide as two tanks driving abreast.

Of course we had to follow it.

We took the truck as far as we could across the battlefield, which wasn't far at all. Weaving around debris, we avoided most obstacles but got stalled in a deep-cut rut. Ten minutes of spinning our tires in mud didn't get us anywhere. After an argument, we decided to continue on, to follow the story.

What I figured: the weapon was mobile – the rectangular sections of treads had dug into the ground, leaving an obvious path to follow. It was big, heavy. And it had to be pretty fast, because even through the binoculars, I couldn't find a sign of it ahead.

"It must be a tank," Joe said.

"Too big," I answered. "Too wide." I'd been a cub reporter in the Great War and had seen up close what tanks could do, which was quite a lot, but not this much. Unless, as Joe said, some genius had made improvements. "I don't know of any tank that carries enough shells to level a battalion like that."

"A couple of tanks maybe? A whole squad of them?"

But there was only one path leading out, one pair of treads traveling onwards, a helpful dotted line guiding the way.

The sun started toward the west. We had canteens of water, some bread and sardines stuffed in our packs, but no blankets, nothing for camping out. Not even a flashlight. I thought about suggesting we turn around, then decided to wait until Joe suggested it first.

"You hear that?" Joe said, in our second hour of slogging.

I stopped, and heard it: the metallic grinding of gears, the bass chortle of a diesel engine. If I'd been back in the states, close to a town, I'd have assumed I was near a construction site, jackhammers and cranes working at full capacity.

We had just a little further to scramble, over another tread-rutted rise, before we saw what it was.

A small camp had been set up: a fire, over which a pot hung from a tripod, containing boiling water. A canvas lean-to was propped on a set of rickety branches that must have been picked up from the side of the road. A bearded Spaniard in worn army fatigues sat by the fire, stirring whatever was in the pot. In the shadows outside the reach of the fire, another Spaniard worked at what looked like an armored-encased engine block mounted on a scaffold. The engine glowed, spat sparks and spewed a shroud of smoke into the air. Atop the engine block was a steel chassis; below it were the treads that had cut the road from the battlefield.

It was a tank, but not really. Rather, some Frankenstein's monster of tank parts. The war machine had been cobbled together and greatly expanded, drawing on the initial tank design for inspiration then taking it to an extreme. Wide treads on a hinged base performed the same motion as an ankle joint, bending as it climbed over obstacles, keeping the chassis level. The cannon stood in for arms, firing six-inch shells if I had my guess. A squadron's worth of bombing in a single go. Armored, mobile, crushing everything in its path. As if ten thousand years of warfare had led to this.

The glowing engine seemed like nothing so much as a beating heart, pounding in anger, atop a muscled body and stout legs. The red, yellow and purple stripes of the Republican flag were painted on its side.

Joe and I just stared, until the first Spaniard drew a pistol from a pouch on his belt and shouted at us in Spanish.

Joe put his arms up and yelled back, "*Somos Americanos! Americanos!*"

For a frozen moment I thought that wouldn't matter and we'd both get shot. I prepared to run. But the Spaniard lowered his pistol and laughed. "I don't believe it!" he said in accented English. "We thought you all left!"

He invited us to sit by the fire. The mechanic climbed off the machine and joined us. The man at the fire was Pedro; the mechanic, Enrique. Pedro was a nondescript soldier in worn fatigues, hat pressed over shaggy hair. Enrique was otherworldly:

his eyes were invisible behind tinted goggles, his head was bare – his hair appeared to have been singed off by the heart of the engine where he worked.

After exchanging names, we told our stories. But Joe and I couldn't stop looking at the modified tank. Pedro saw this and smiled. "What do you think?"

"It's—" I started, then shook my head. "I don't know what to think."

"We call it the *Don Quixote*."

"Because you're tilting at windmills?"

Pedro laughed and said to Enrique, "I told you people would understand!"

Enrique didn't say a word. He sat on the ground, arms around his knees. The firelight reflected off his goggles, so he could have been looking anywhere.

"But what is it?" Joe asked.

"It's a personal tank," Pedro said. "Enrique built it, but it was my idea. It's better than a tank – faster, more agile, simpler to operate. It only needs one man instead of a whole crew. You've seen what one person is able to do with a machine like this?"

"That battalion back there – you destroyed it?" I said. "It's amazing."

"Yes, it is," Pedro said.

"If you'd had this a year ago you might have made a difference," Joe said.

Pedro's smile fell, and he and his partner both looked at us, cold and searching. "Never too late," Pedro said, shoving another stick into the fire. "It took us years to build this one. But now that it's finished, we can build more, many more. An army of them. The Great War didn't end war – but this might. No one would dare stand against an army of Don Quixotes."

This gave me the image of a hundred wizened old men sitting astride broken horses, making a stand against Franco. I almost laughed. But then I glanced at the shadow of the war machine. This conversation should have taken place in a bar, over a third pitcher of beer. Then, I would have been able to laugh. But here, in the dark and cold, an hour's walk from a scene of slaughter, the firelight turning the faces into shadowed skulls, I thought I was looking at a new kind of warfare, and was terrified.

The Spaniards let Joe and I stay at their camp. They didn't have extra blankets, but the fire was warm and they shared the thin stew they'd cooked. Enrique slept in the machine, by the engine, which although it was shut down now, never stopped its subtle clicking, cooling noises. Like the beat of a heart.

"This is going to make a hell of a story," Joe said, whispering at me in the dark. "I can't wait to get pictures in the morning."

A hell of a story, yeah. "This isn't going to turn the war around for them, you know," I said.

"Of course not, with just the two of them. Even if they do have that monster. And I think they're a little crazy to boot. But that's not the point, is it? This thing – folks back home'll go gonzo for it. It'd be like King Kong. If we could get them to bring it to the states we could sell tickets."

There was an idea – if the two men would ever agree to it. More likely they'd prefer to stay and smash as much of Franco as they could before going down in flames. They wouldn't have a chance to build their army of personal tanks.

"What do you think, Hank? Can we talk them into giving up the fight and bringing that thing to New York? Get it to climb the Empire State Building?"

The fire was embers. Enrique's machine clicked like crickets, and Pedro seemed to be asleep. I shook my head. "I'm thinking about what the Germans would do with that thing. Scratch that – with a hundred of them." Pedro and Enrique couldn't build an army of them, but an industrialized war machine like Germany?

"What?"

"That armor might be able to stomp out a few battalions, but it can't win the war. They've got no allies, no outside support, while Franco's got Germany and Italy supplying him. As soon as the fascists cross the river, they've got Spain – and if they capture those two, they've got that thing, too. Then the Germans get a hold of it—"

"And what are the Germans going to do with it?"

"Boggles the mind, doesn't it?" I said.

*   *   *

Dawn came slowly, filtered through the haze of smoke and a sense of dread. Like the sky was a predator waiting to pounce.

In daylight, the tank looked even more anthropomorphic. The engine heart burned, the cannons could be raised and lowered like arms. The articulated treads had bolts above them that looked very much like knees. A single, slotted viewport in the chassis stared like a cyclopean eye. The machine even carried a bandolier of spare shells across its chest, just to drive the point home.

Pedro was stoking the fire back to life when an unmistakable, mechanical rumble shook in the distance – the sound of an army on the move. Enrique entered the personal tank through a hatch in the back of the chassis. The engine coughed back to life.

Joe knelt at the rise sheltering the camp and stared through the binoculars. "It's one of Franco's patrols, coming this way."

Following the path of destruction from the crushed battalion, looking for the enemy that had done such a thing.

Pedro laughed, as he seemed to in reaction to everything. "Now you can see first hand what *Don Quixote* can do!"

I had a thought. "Let me come along. Let me ride with that thing."

Pedro looked taken aback. Even Enrique poked his head out of the hatch to look, though his expression was blank.

"There's barely enough room for Enrique – you can't do anything there," Pedro said.

I talked fast. "I can write about it. Get you publicity back home – in American newspapers. Imagine if some big investor decided to make you an offer. You'd be famous – inventors of the most amazing war machine in history. Famous – and rich. But only if I'm able to write about it. *Really* write about it. First-hand testimony."

Pedro and Enrique regarded each other, and whatever secret signal passed between them, I didn't catch it.

"You can ride with Enrique," Pedro said finally. "But only if you write about it. Get us those investors, yes? The money?"

So much for the socialist ideals of the loyalists.

I shrugged on my jacket, checking for my pencil and notebook. Joe came over and grabbed my sleeve. "You know what you're doing?"

"Sure I do. Just remember to tell everyone how brave I was if I don't make it back."

"Brave? Is that what you're calling it?"

I grinned. "We can call it anything we want, we're the ones writing about it."

I knew exactly what I was doing. I climbed up to the back of the machine, where Enrique held out his hand to assist me through the hatch in the chassis.

Don Quixote had enough room for two – barely. Enrique settled onto a board that had been bolted in front of a control panel. There wasn't a seat for me, so I perched behind the driver in a narrow indentation left by the hatch. My knees were jammed up to my chest, and I had to reach up to hold on to a bar welded above my head. The air inside was thick, close, and full of the stink of burned oil. The thing didn't seem to have any ventilation – the armor was sealed up tight. The slit above the controls offered the driver the narrowest of views. I couldn't see a thing, only the metal interior, scarred with hammer blows and smeared with soot. Sweat broke out all over me, and I had trouble catching my breath.

Enrique didn't seem to notice the burning air. He pulled on several of a dozen levers and turned a handful of toggles. The vibrations rattling through the machine changed, growing more severe. The engine throbbed beneath my feet, a burning furnace ready to explode.

Then, the machine began to move. The chassis lurched straight up, like an elevator jerking hard to the next floor. Gears and drive belts squealed, treads rumbled, and the tank rolled forward. The motion was rough, jarring, like driving too fast over gravel, swaying this way and that as we passed over some rut or chunk of vegetation. Incredibly, we were moving. My teeth rattled in my jaw. Enrique sat calmly, his hands steady on the controls, moving levers in what seemed to be a random sequence. He was driver, gunner, mechanic, engineer and commander all in one. Any normal tank would have needed six men to do all those jobs. He turned another set of toggles, and a new set of gears engaged; the chassis tipped back, as if the machine was now looking skyward.

I opened the hatch a crack to steal a look. The side-mounted gun turrets had ratcheted into place, aiming toward the approaching enemy. I shut the hatch again.

By lifting myself up, I could see around Enrique's head and catch a glimpse of the outside through the slit in the metal. The view was like flashing on individual frames of film without seeing the whole picture: a tank motoring toward us, artillery guns lined up, trucks circling, troops moving into position, and among them all the red and gold of the fascist flag.

Enrique jumped up, throwing me against the back wall of the chassis. The driver pulled on a lever jutting above him, and an explosion burst, enveloping *Don Quixote* in a storm of thunder, the cannons firing. He pulled on a second lever, and a second shell launched. I ducked to try and glimpse what was happening through the slit, but I saw only smoke. I heard distant detonations, and screams.

The Spaniard kept pulling on the overhead levers, and shells kept firing. He must have had an automatic mechanism loading ammunition. And if the Germans got ahold of *that* bit of technology . . .

I tore a piece of paper out of my notebook, wadded up two small bits, and shoved them in my ears. That only cut out the sound a little; I could still feel every vibration in my bones. I was growing dizzy from it.

The cannon acted like Gatling guns. Firing six-inch explosive shells, over and over. Enrique's tank churned along the edge of the battlefield, swiveling the chassis to move the gun, raking the enemy with cannon fire. This second battalion didn't last long.

An occasional bullet pinged off *Don Quixote*'s armored chassis, but did no damage. The vulnerable bits of the mechanism were too well protected. Enemy artillery launched a few shells before *Don Quixote*'s cannon destroyed them, but the explosives detonated dozens of feet away. The personal tank's small size and mobility made it difficult to target.

This thing just kept getting more dangerous.

Then it was over. The tank stopped rolling and settled on its treads. Enrique powered down the engine, which softened to a low growl.

I opened the back hatch and tumbled out into the fresh air. Relatively fresh – the stink of gunpowder and blood rose around me. But at least there was a breeze. My ears kept rattling, seemed as if they would rattle for ages.

Pedro and Joe ran toward us. They must have seen the whole thing – they'd have had a better view than I'd had. Joe had probably gotten some splendid photos.

"Ha! You did it again, Enrique! *Bueno!*" Pedro called. Enrique was climbing down from the chassis more gracefully. "And you, Hank – did you get a good story?"

I hadn't written a word. But I had a good story.

"Guys, both of you, get over here. Let me get a picture of you in front of the battlefield," Joe said, gesturing the Spaniards together and pointing his camera.

I leaned against the tank, *Don Quixote*. I had a story, but I didn't know how to tell it. Or if I even could. Instead, I made a plan.

Finding footholds on leg joints, gripping bolts, gears, and the window slot on the front of the chassis, I climbed to the front of the tank. Balancing there, I reached to the bandolier of artillery shells and pulled out two left over from the battle, tucking them in the pockets of my jacket.

By following exhaust pipes, I found my way to the engine, and the fuel tank hidden behind armor plating under the chassis. A simple sliding door gave access to it for refueling. Enrique obviously wasn't expecting sabotage.

I jammed one of the shells between a set of pistons operating the tank's legs, and dropped the second in the fuel tank. I twisted up a handkerchief into a makeshift fuse and lodged it in the fuel tank door. Then I lit a match.

Wouldn't give me much time, but I didn't need much.

I tried not to look too nervous, to draw suspicions, when I marched over to Joe and grabbed his arm. "We have to get out of here."

Joe had been directing Pedro and Enrique toward a photograph against the backdrop of destruction, and dozens of shattered bodies. The two men were grinning like hunters who'd bagged an eight-point buck.

The photographer looked at me, confused.

"We *really* have to get out of here," I said.

"Hey!" Pedro said. "You're going write about *Don Quixote*, yes? You write about us? Tell everyone – we can win the war. They'll see that we're finally winning and send help!"

"That's right," I said, patting my notebook in my jacket pocket even as I dragged Joe away, back up the rise. "I've got it all down, you don't need to worry! In fact, we need to get back and phone this story to our editor right now. Can't waste any time!"

Pedro seemed to accept this explanation and waved us on our way, calling out blessings in Spanish. Enrique just watched us go, through glassy, goggled eyes; he'd never taken them off.

"Hank, what the hell are you doing?"

"Just keep walking."

The explosion came as we passed into the next bowl of a valley. Good timing, there. We missed the brunt of the shockwave. But the force of it still knocked us both to the ground.

"Christ, what was that?" Joe scrambled to look behind us. A dome of black smoke was rising into the air.

Maybe the two Spaniards had had a chance to get away. Maybe they'd been knocked clear by the initial blast. But probably not.

We watched as the cloud expanded and dissipated. "Maybe that thing wasn't as well built as they thought," I observed.

Joe looked at me. "Then we were lucky to get out of there," he said, deadpan.

"Yes, we were, I imagine."

We kept walking.

A winter breeze was blowing, and my jacket didn't seem able to hold off the chill. I wasn't sure we were walking toward the truck. For all I knew, that second battalion had confiscated or smashed it. It didn't matter. We just needed to dodge Franco's troops, get across the river, then get out of Spain. I listened for the sound of tank treads, truck motors, of a thousand marching bodies, but the world was silent. Wind rustling through dried brush, that was all.

"I think they could have done it," Joe said after a half an hour of walking. The Ebro River had appeared, a shining strip of water in the distance. "I think they could have beaten back Franco with that machine, if they'd had enough time."

"Then what? They build more, or sell the design to a real manufacturer, and then what? You really want to see those things stomping all over Europe in the next war?"

"What next war? There isn't going to be a next war, not after the Munich treaty."

I stared at him. Everyone kept telling themselves that. As if this whole debacle in Spain wasn't the opening salvo. "Let me see your camera a minute."

Joe, bless him, handed it right over. I popped the cover and yanked out the yard of film he'd shot, exposing the film, destroying the pictures.

"Hey!" Joe said, but that was all. I closed the cover and handed the camera back. Somehow, deep down, the photographer must have understood.

That was why we were all here, wasn't it? Doing our part to make the world a better place?

The Little Dog Ohori

Anatoly Belilovsky

The young soldier jumps to his feet, snaps to attention.

"At ease, Comrade Corporal," the officer says. "And please, sit down." A white coat hangs off the officer's shoulders; it hides her shoulder tabs, leaving visible only the caduceus in her lapel.

The soldier hesitates. The officer leans against the wall; her coat falls off one shoulder, revealing three small stars. The soldier's eyes widen.

"Begging Comrade Colonel's pardon," he says, and sits down. The movement is slow and uncertain, as if his body fights the very thought of sitting while an officer stands.

"Sit," the officer says, more firmly now. "This is an order."

"Thank you, Comrade Colonel," the soldier says, sees a small frown crease the officer's face, and adds, "I mean, Doctor."

The officer smiles and nods. A strand of graying hair escapes her knot and falls to her face; she sweeps it back with an impatient gesture.

"Carry on," she says.

The soldier hesitates again.

"That's an order, too," she says and points to the caduceus in her lapel. "A medical order."

"Thank you, Doctor," the soldier says. "I only came to visit; I'm not here as a patient."

"She is," the doctor says and tilts her head at the hospital bed.

The soldier turns to face the dying woman in the bed, leans toward her, takes her hand, and whispers to her in a language the doctor does not understand.

★   ★   ★

Cold.

Lying on the riverbank in a puddle of blood and melting snow, she listens for the sounds of gunfire, the roar of engines, the clatter of tank tracks, anything to say she is not alone. She no longer feels her hands, though she can see her right hand on the trigger of her Tokarev-40, the index finger frozen into a hook. She no longer feels pain where the shell splinter tore into her belly, only cold. Cold comfort, too, in the bodies scattered on the ice beyond the riverbank, eleven black specks against relentless white, eleven fewer *Waffen-SS*, eleven plus two hundred and three already in the killbook makes two hundred and fourteen fewer who could threaten . . .

Her mind's eye projects a glimpse of Selim's face against the night, then all is dark again.

She listens, and hears a friendly sound.

The little dog Ohori is barking.

"*Help* . . ." From a throat parched raw through desiccated lips, one of the last small drops of strength drains into the word.

The barking stops, but silence does not return. There is a noise like leaves fluttering in the wind.

No, wait. It's winter; a white cloak for camouflage in the snow. No grass to hide, no leaves to whisper.

Whisper.

"Is she . . . ?"

A woman's whisper, in Russian.

"I don't know."

Another voice, a woman, too, or a goddess.

"Please . . ." Another drop of strength, gone, but now she can see Selim again, him with his great happy crooked smile. She tries to touch it but it is out of reach. Could this be Ogushin, the taker of souls, or the nine-tailed were-fox Kumiho? She can no longer tell what is real and what is not. There is only strength enough to hope:

. . . Please, little dog Ohori who brings lost loves together . . .

The darkness deepens . . .

. . . please, angel Oneuli who watches over orphans, please, Sister Sun and Brother Moon . . .

. . . please. If only for a moment . . .

. . . please let me see my family again . . .

"Were you close, the two of you?" the doctor asks.

The soldier opens his mouth, closes it again. His eyes grow distant, focus far away.

"Sorry," the doctor says. "Stupid of me to ask."

The soldier nods. The doctor takes it as "Yes, we were close," not "Yes, stupid of you to ask."

The woman's breathing is becoming ragged: a burst of rapid gasps, then slow breaths, then rapid again.

"I'm sorry," the doctor says. "It won't be long now."

The soldier reaches into his tunic pocket, brings out a tattered notepad.

The doctor bends forward to look at it. "Her diary?"

"Her killbook," the soldier answers.

"Ah," the doctor says. "I see."

The captain's name, Kryviy, is Ukrainian.

"Age?" he says.

"Nineteen," she answers, a pang of guilt for lying.

"Ethnicity?"

"Uzbek," she says. A smaller pang.

"Why do you want to enlist?"

This is a question she does not expect. This question wouldn't ever be asked of a man. Or a Great Russian.

She rifles through a list of plausible lies, and settles on a partial truth: "I want to be a sniper."

The captain looks up from his notes. His ice-blue eyes aim at her face. "Sniper?" he says. "Can you see well enough, with those . . ." He squints in imitation of her features.

She looks out at the sunbaked desert beyond the open window. Some distance away, a truck approaches, raising a plume of dust behind it. She points in its direction.

"Truck number 43-11," she says, and looks at the captain again.

The captain stands up, approaches the window. He watches the truck approach, squints, this time in concentration, and leans out the window.

"I see the 11," he says slowly, then, after a pause: "Yes. 43-11." He returns to his chair, crosses a line off his notes, and writes another. "You'll do," he says, and shouts: "Next!"

The woman's hand tightens, just enough to see the tiny twitch. The soldier puts the killbook in her hand. Another twitch.

The doctor leans against the doorjamb. The wood plank creaks. The soldier looks up.

"It took an hour to pry her from that riverbank," the soldier says. "Two nurses from the Medical-Sanitary Battalion. In the dark. Under enemy fire." He shakes his head. "And then they dragged her back to the Division hospital, three kilometers away." He touches his chest; two of his medals ring together. "No matter what I do, I'll never be their equal."

The doctor's hands are in the pockets of her tunic. Her fingers itch for something – a cigarette, a scalpel – she worries at the knots in the pocket's seam, rolls specks of lint into a ball. *Surgery is easy*, she thinks. *Listening is hard.*

She looks at the killbook. "I'll remember her name. Heroes should never be forgotten."

The soldier raises his head, looks straight at her. She sees the hesitation in his eyes, and the crystallization at a decision.

"That's not her real name," he says slowly, and looks at the dying woman again.

The doctor does, too. She compares the dying woman's features with the soldier's, her trained mind catalogs the differences.

She reaches for the killbook, turns its pages with reverence. Places: Stalingrad, Kursk, Smolensk. Dates: last in December, 1943. Ranks: *Scharführer SS, Feldwebel, Hauptmann*. And on the last page, a stick figure of a dog, and writing in neither Cyrillic nor Arabic nor Latin. She looks up for a moment, then turns to the soldier sharply.

"Korean?" she says.

The soldier nods.

"Passing for . . ." she hesitates. "Kazakh?"

"Uzbek," the soldier says quietly.

"Nineteen thirty-seven?" the doctor asks. Matching the

soldier's tone comes naturally; suppressing the urge to look behind her for eavesdroppers does not.

The soldier looks up. "Not many people know about that."

The doctor says nothing.

"My grandfather was selling lamb *samsa* at a train station," the soldier says. "A train carrying deportees stopped there one day. It had been traveling from Vladivostok for a month."

The doctor's fingers scramble in her pocket. She bites her lip.

"They stopped to bury the dead in the desert. Her mother was one of them. She was thirteen, and an orphan. Grandfather brought her back to our *qishlaq*. She became one of the family."

Selim comes out of the recruiting office, a happy grin on his face.

"I did it!" he says. "They are sending me to sniper school. And I have you to thank."

She draws a breath. "Did you tell them—"

He shakes his head. "I'm not that stupid. Can you imagine? 'Oh yes, Comrade Captain, a little girl taught me everything I know about hunting.' They would call a neuropathologist next, to have my head examined."

"I am not little, Selim," she says firmly. "I'll be eighteen come spring, and I'll enlist, too. I'll ask to join your unit, and we'll be together again."

His face grows somber. "They won't take you. I'm sorry."

"What are you talking about?" She puts her hand on her hips. "They take girls!"

"They don't take Koreans," he whispers. "They have a list of undesirables, only assigned to labor battalions: Tatars, Volga Germans, Chechens . . ." He looks down, spurns a clod of dirt with the toe of his boot, then looks at her again. "Koreans, too. I'm sorry."

She does not answer, except for a glint in her eyes: exactly, he thinks, like a reflection off the barrel of Grandfather's old Mosin Nagant .300.

Exactly like the glint she had on the first anniversary of her joining the clan when, returning to the *qishlaq* with an antelope and two hares in the back of their donkey-drawn *arba*, she turned to him and said, in too-precise Karakalpak Uzbek: "When I am old enough, Selim, we will be married."

The doctor is used to silences; the soldier is not.

"You might not believe this, but she taught me to shoot," the soldier says.

The doctor says nothing. She reaches for the killbook, turns its pages with reverence.

"What am I saying?" the soldier says. "Of course you believe it, Colonel. Most people—"

"Most people don't command a military hospital," the doctor says. "Most people haven't seen what soldiers are made of."

"You must have, as a surgeon," the soldier says.

"That, too," she whispers.

The train approaches, the smoke from its engine thinning, the chuffing slowing down.

"This makes no sense," says Uncle Tsoi. "First of all, there is no war now; the Japanese were beaten at Halhin-Gol, and they are not coming back. Secondly, even if they were, why would we help them? We left Korea to get away from the Japanese. And thirdly, why resettle all of us? They could just arrest the richer peasants, like the Pak family." He sighs. "No, I think it's a mistake. I think someone misunderstood what Comrade Stalin said, and when that becomes clear the train will turn around and bring us back here. I just hope it won't be too late for the apple harvest."

He looks up to find that his niece isn't looking at him. She is staring at the train in the distance.

"This isn't polite," Uncle Tsoi says. "You should pay attention when your elders are talking."

She nods absent-mindedly.

"Haven't you ever seen a train before?" Uncle Tsoi says, and follows her gaze.

His face drops. "This isn't a passenger train," he whispers. "We are going to travel ten thousand kilometers in cattle cars."

They wait for the train in silence.

A man approaches, a Great Russian by his appearance.

"Comrade Tsoi?" he calls. "Which of you is Comrade Tsoi?"

Uncle Tsoi stands up straighter. "See," he says. "Someone realized it's a mistake." He turns to the man and raises his hand. "I'm Tsoi," he says loudly.

"Please come with us," the man says softly.

Uncle Tsoi turns to her. "Go get your mother."

"Just you," the man says.

The train stops. The gates slide open with a clatter.

"All aboard!" a man shouts from the locomotive.

She watches Uncle Tsoi escorted away from the train, past a line of armed soldiers, until she feels her mother tug at her hand.

She turns. There are tears in her mother's coal-black eyes, rolling down her face that is the palest she had ever seen.

"Come. Have to go," her mother says. A cough escapes before she can cover her mouth.

They board the train in silence, find a spot to sit. More people come until there is no more room. Then some more. Then more.

Then, finally, there is a whistle, the gates clang shut, and the train departs.

"My brother," her mother whispers.

She leans closer to her mother. They are both too old to believe in little dog Ohori; but she decides she'll never be too old to hope.

"Do you see your target?" Uncle Tsoi says.

Her head tilted over the stock of Uncle Tsoi's Berdan rifle, she gives a tiny nod.

"What are you aiming at?" Uncle Tsoi asks.

"The big pine cone," she says.

"That is wrong," says Uncle Tsoi. "Pick a scale. One scale on the whole pine cone. Aim at that. Have you got that?"

She nods again.

"Now, breathe in, then out, and on the *out*, close your whole hand on the trigger."

She presses on the trigger, flinching just a bit before the rifle bucks and the shot explodes. The pine cone dances but does not fall.

"Two more things," says Uncle Tsoi. "First, squeeze the trigger slowly enough that the shot comes as a surprise to you. Understand?"

She nods. "And the second?" she says.

"Connect with your target," says Uncle Tsoi. "Some people imagine reaching out and touching it; some talk to the target in their minds. Some apologize in advance for hitting it. You have to care, in some way, about the target, to shoot true."

She aims again, breathes in and out, imagines the little dog Ohori running to the pine tree, leaping to sniff the pine cone, leave a wet print of its nose on one particular scale.

The shot rings out, startling her. The pine cone disintegrates into a cloud of chaff.

"She talked about her uncle so much, I felt like I knew him," the soldier says. "Sometimes I could almost hear his voice come out of her mouth. 'When Brother Moon and Sister Sun lived together on Mount Baekdu, they had a little dog named Ohori who loved them both. And when the supreme god Cheonjiwang sent each of them to a different part of the sky, Ohori ran from one to the other until he brought them together, but when they met, they shone light only on each other, leaving the Earth in pitch darkness, so Queen Baji petitioned Cheonjiwang to allow them only one meeting a month. So each new Moon, Ohori is free to roam the Earth, and when you hear barking on a moonless night it just might be Ohori searching for you, to bring you back to someone you miss very much.'"

The soldier's voice wavers on the last words. The doctor reaches to touch the soldier's shoulder. Her hand trembles an inch above his shoulder board, then pulls back to wipe her tears. She blinks, and hopes her eyes have time to dry before he sees them.

Colonels don't cry. Not with a corporal present.

Is it a starshell, or dawn already? It is light: light enough to see green grass, birch trees in leaf – it can't be spring – or does it matter? The rhythmic footfalls she hears – pulsing blood, or boots measuring time? And – faces, smiling faces she never thought she'd see again, and voices she never hoped to hear cry, once more, just one more time: "Hurrah! Hurrah! Hurrah!"

And, nipping at their feet, the little dog Ohori, his barking mixing with laughter and with the shouts of welcome.

The hand gives one more twitch; the chest rises, falls, never to rise again. The soldier frees his hand from the lifeless grasp, smooths the dead woman's hair, stands up, face to face with the doctor.

"Thank you," he says.

"For what?" the doctor says.

"We got to see each other, she and I," the soldier says.

"It's worth so much to you?" the doctor says.

"To me?" the soldier raises his eyebrows. "It does not matter what it's worth to me. It's what *she* wanted. She was worth a million of me, you know." He pats his pockets, takes out his cap, places on his head, draws to attention and salutes. "Goodbye . . ." he begins, but then his voice gives out.

The doctor reaches for a carafe on a bedside table, looks for a glass, finds none, and hands the carafe to the soldier.

"Here. Drink from that. Go ahead, drink."

The soldier brings the carafe to his mouth, takes a long swallow.

"Thank you," he says. "And thank you for bringing her here. I know you bent the rules—"

"We take care of our own," the doctor interrupts. "Which includes you. Go get some sleep. Stop by my office in the morning, I'll have my clerk process a leave extension."

The soldier shakes his head. He steps past the doctor through the door, takes another step in the corridor, stops, turns around and faces the dead woman again.

"Goodbye, Grandmother," he says. "Give my regards to Grandpa Selim. And to all of your old comrades." He takes a breath. "And a few of mine."

He turns to the doctor. "Please, Comrade Colonel, don't order me to stay. We, too, take care of our own. My unit is short a man till I come back, and . . ." he checks his watch ". . . an Antonov-24 is scheduled to lift off for Kandahar in an hour."

He draws to attention and salutes again. "I beg the Colonel's permission to be dismissed," he says, in crisp militarese.

"Granted," the doctor says, and watches him march away. It isn't lost on her that his cadence is the same as for the change-of-watch before the Monument to the Unknown Soldier.

The doctor waits until she hears his footfalls no more before she covers the dead woman's face.

Vast Wings Across Felonious Skies

E. Catherine Tobler

"Sakura?"

"I see . . . it."

A mile out, the void coalescing within a burgeoning bank of storm clouds above the Nevada desert resembled a tornado tipped on its side. Dorothy Sakata plotted a route for the XD-2 Black Dragon she was piloting for delivery, taking them away from the storm, but she couldn't drag her gaze away. It was unlike anything she'd seen before, enormous and unknown. Her mother would have loved the barely contained energy of it, her father not so much.

The void's whirling length vanished into the growing thunderhead while lightning crackled tendrils across a widening, cavernous mouth. The energy did not dissipate or reach for the ground; the lightning circled the entry, a wreath hung upon a door no one wanted to enter. It did nothing to brighten the fathomless darkness within.

A brief glance at the desert floor showed no rain, the dry storm kicking up swirls of dirt and tumbleweed, but then Dorothy's eyes came back to the disruption; in that brief span, it had moved, grown. Rain started to spackle the Black Dragon's windshield, but the experimental plane wasn't buffeted by turbulence. The air was smooth, untroubled, despite the storm vomiting itself into life.

"You have radar on that thing, Avery?"

"It's not showing anything. Not a goddamn *thing*." Stress didn't enter the woman's voice, it rarely did. Dorothy heard only confusion from the radar operator over the radio.

From the gunner's seat behind Dorothy came a third voice, carrying a little more stress, a little more depth of feeling. "What in the holy—"

"Zip it, Bochanek."

Dorothy bit the inside of her cheek, willing herself to calm even as the hair on her arms stood up. Surely it was just a storm. It was not an *ōkubi* prophesying doom, nor any other mythological creature come to warn them. It was surely nothing like the thing that swallowed a plane from Mines Field a month prior. Nothing like the thing the other pilots had claimed to see from here to the Mexico border. No way in hell.

Dorothy banked the XD-2 toward the ever-growing storm, feeling the first jolt of turbulence as she did. The twin engines remained steady, growling a warning to the skies at large. Closing in, near enough that the rain splatter-hammered the windows in a steady rhythm, the drone of the engines was eclipsed by another sound, an eerie moan that called to mind the buckling of metal. Dorothy raised a hand, pressing fingers to the thunder-rattled windows that arced over her.

"Hold together, baby," she whispered.

"Sakura—"

"I see that, too."

A tendril of lightning-encased cloud crept from the void's outermost edge, reaching not toward the plane, but skimming across the horizon. Another joined it, dipping for the first time toward the ground. It didn't get far before the lightning sparked an explosion; the cloud, as if a living thing, drew back into the swirling mass, stung and swallowed.

"That ain't normal."

Dorothy's mouth lifted in a smile at the assessment from Avery at radar. She couldn't argue the point.

"You think the Germans . . ." Bochanek trailed off.

Dorothy didn't know the answer to that, either. The storm looked natural, even as it didn't. No tornado tipped itself on its side high in the desert skies. On either side of the storm, more clouds pulled in close, as if the entire thing meant to double or triple in size before it was done. As fresh arms of lightning emerged, sparking from end to end, Dorothy shook her head.

"Whatever it is, we are not this thing's lunch," she muttered.

But before she could prove the storm entirely wrong and break off, the tendrils of crackling energy whipped chaotically and snagged the plane within its sparking grasp. Dorothy's grip tightened on the stick, trying to turn the plane out of the energy's hold, but the void pulled the tendrils back inward, bringing the Black Dragon with them. Dorothy only became aware of the amount of struggle between plane and storm when the muscles in her arms snapped, elbows locking as she fought to keep the plane in the air. She leaned into the tension, trying to angle the plane any way she might; not even the back and forth rocking motion of a Dutch roll loosened the plane from the storm's influence.

"You want guns on this thing, Sakata?"

Dorothy very much wanted Bochanek to empty her guns on it, but what could bullets do against clouds and rain? "Hold, Bochanek."

Rain sheeted off the windows, the daylight evaporating as the plane was drawn deeper into the storm. Dorothy refused to ease her hold on the stick, trying again and again to pull the plane out of the roiling clouds, but when she glimpsed the crescent of distant sky above them, she realized exactly how far down they had already been drawn. Would there be *any* getting out? She hadn't made a lick of difference yet.

She was never clear on how much time passed, or when exactly her hands came off of the stick; there was the sensation of weightlessness, coupled with a bone-deep nausea, and then there was simply nothing. Dorothy was not aware of the plane or the storm, nor of colors or scents. She was not even aware of a darkness, only of a general *lack*. There was nothing, though she breathed and felt her hair had come loose from its knot, brushing against her cheeks as she floated. Floated?

Dorothy opened her eyes to find herself where she had always been, the Black Dragon's cockpit, buckled into her chair. Her hands rested palm up on her thighs, the ache in her arms giving proof to the fight against the storm. One palm was reddened, the struggle burned into her very skin. She lifted her head, heavy and aching, and began the seemingly impossible work of unbuckling her belt.

"Ruth? Ina?"

She called to her crew, but there was no reply. Cold air flooded down on her, her flight suit overly thin in the chill, and her eyes snapped to the canopy above; the paned glass was unbroken, showing walls arcing beyond, all traced in metal scaffolding. No clouds, no sky. The plane itself sat motionless, no longer in flight, and Dorothy slid out of her chair. She dropped to the floor, but the hatch was already open, the ladder down. Had Ina left this way after being unable to wake her?

Dorothy dropped from the ladder, trusting the ground would hold her if it held the plane. The floor beneath her boots was solid and, judging from the sound, just as metallic as it appeared. She gave it another kick and it rang hollow, a taut drum. It was no material she knew, though; when she pressed a hand to the floor, it nearly writhed under her touch, the way a dog might. She drew her hand back and shuddered.

Beyond the familiar shape of the Black Dragon, the air remained clouded, but the space in which she found herself could be nothing other than a hangar, designed to hold more aircraft than only her own. The walls were bare metal, stained and streaked with rust, rising above her in a bulging A-frame arc. Shape and function were vaguely familiar, but Dorothy climbed back into the plane to grab a wrench from the toolkit. She wanted a proper weapon, something of use from a distance, but America hadn't been invaded and how many times had she been told that they weren't military pilots, no matter that they delivered military aircraft. The military was desperate for their skills, but wouldn't make women part of their core, and while the world was going to war, it was a distant thing, not on these shores.

"Never on these shores," Dorothy whispered, fingers tight around the wrench's comforting weight.

"Ruth Avery?"

She tried again, but there was no response to the name. Her voice didn't so much as echo within the hangar. Dorothy turned a slow circle, lifting a hand to stroke the only familiar thing in the room, the solid metal of the Black Dragon.

She walked a slow, assessing circle around the plane, to ensure the craft was whole. However the plane had come to be here, its nose pointed toward the far, clouded end of the hangar, not so much as a dent or scratch upon it. The brass at Mines didn't need a damaged plane delivered, and Dorothy was sure of one thing: she was going to deliver this plane, come hell or—

"High damn water," she said, ducking under the second wing. The plane showed no signs of weapon fire – receiving or delivering. The only thing she noted was the dropped rear entry hatch, proving a clue as to how Ruth had exited. Normally. That made no damn sense.

Dorothy rounded the Black Dragon's twin-boom tail and moved toward the nose. Beyond, the room dropped abruptly away and she walked to the very edge, waving a hand to dispel the fog. The clouds curled apart and across a wide metallic chasm, a space that could have held a dozen aircraft carriers, she saw more hangars lining the walls, each home to what appeared aircraft, though none of the designs were familiar to Dorothy.

Above the hangars, the walls swept up and away in dramatic geometric forms; other shapes descended from an unseen ceiling, hollow tubes and cubes, as if conduits leading deeper into the vessel. One glance down had Dorothy gasping; she could see forever, a world stretching into an endless vessel of metal and light. She picked out doorways and balconies, windows and narrow catwalks; some of the metal featured markings in bright colors, but if the marks were letters or numbers, they were neither English nor Japanese. Even German might have made more sense than what she saw.

From the ledge on which she stood, there seemed no climbing down; the walls were smooth metal, without hand or footholds. Three amber lights glowed up at her, but they were so far down, she didn't dare jump to the platform that supported them. Dorothy backtracked along the length of the Black Dragon, discovering that the back wall of the hangar curved into a hallway. Her wrench lifted, Dorothy continued along its gray length, jumping twice at her own shadow before she calmed. Only the sound of her footsteps accompanied her, until the small hall widened into another space of vast metal; there, she heard the low rumble of well-working machinery and in the near distance, voices.

She opened her mouth, to call to Ruth and Ina again, but abruptly realized the voices had something in common with the markings on the metal. If it was conversation – and there *were* two differently pitched voices – they were not speaking English. Nor was it any other language Dorothy recognized, not even Ina Bochanek's beloved Czech. This stopped her in her tracks, wondering where the hell she was, where the hell her crew had gone – or had been taken.

Her skin pricked with a new awareness, the second hallway warmer than the hangar had been. From this space, the hall-way stretched in either direction, coiling around what might have been the central core of the – vessel? It was the only appropriate word, but Dorothy couldn't say who owned the craft. The idea that it was German was staggering and terrify-ing; she couldn't allow herself to believe that, but who else might be capturing and cataloging aircraft? But how in the hell were they doing it – how was it that no one had noticed them? Hiding inside storms?

Nothing made any sense, so Dorothy kept on, creeping closer to the sound of voices. Down the hallway and around another curving wall of metal, the floor vibrated. It did nothing to set Dorothy at ease even if it reminded her of the way a plane's floorboards would rattle on takeoff. The walls here were etched, emblazoned with time-dark lines and sweeping arcs that looked like charts, but if they showed night skies, they were like none Dorothy had seen before. She reached out to touch the coal and silver lines, but drew her hand back before she actually could. Something about the wall repelled her, perhaps the memory of the way the floor had moved when she had touched it.

Her grip had grown slick around the wrench she carried, and she switched hands long enough to drag her palm down her pant leg. She was shifting the wrench back into her right hand as she came around another corner and discovered the two figures at the end of the corridor. She drew herself up short, unseen. She expected German officers in uniform, but what she saw was not that.

The two figures called to mind a painted landscape scroll in her grandmother's house, black figures drawn as if with a careless brush barely guided down the browned paper. They were unnaturally thin and bent, as if barren trees under snow. Hairless, oblong heads tapered into bone and branch shoulders without so much as a neck, their arms as long as their torsos. The figures were impossibly thin through their bodies, more lines on paper without specific curves signifying or refuting sex. They were barely there trees, no buds, no leaves, and while she saw fingers she could not discern toes, and wanted to turn away but for the play of color and light, silhouetted as they were against the chiaroscuro wall. She stared, much the way she had the first time she'd seen her grandmother's art. The figures were the ancient inked trees brought to life, but they moved without so much as a sound, their eyes burning as suns before going nova. Gaseous clouds of hydrogen and oxygen were ready to ignite as they spiraled outward from a central burning pinprick.

Suns about to—

Their eyes.

With a jolt, Dorothy realized they were watching her as much as she watched them. The figures moved as if under the guidance of a wind she could not feel. Their bodies bowed and unbowed with a slow fluidity as though they did not contain a single bone, as though they were made of only hard muscle bound beneath a skin that resembled—

Ink.

Oil slicks.

Molasses.

They moved like water in that moment, supernova eyes expanding to encompass everything Dorothy was, everything she knew. Instantly, she felt their black, watery hands inside her chest, scrabbling between her ribs, holding and weighing the most intimate parts of her anatomy, and on one level, this made perfect sense to her, given their own sleek bodies, their decided *lack* of everything she contained, but on another level, her mind screamed in terror, begging her to run, to get out before she vanished like Ruth and Ina, to swing her wrench and flee.

She swung. The wrench connected with the chin of one body, impossibly hard and solid, and promptly ricocheted into the temple of other. Both figures dropped to the floor as if felled with an axe and Dorothy ran, arms ringing from the blow. She sought solace in the part of her mind that wanted to flee, screaming for Ruth and Ina as she traced her way back to the Black Dragon, to the hangar where she would . . .

Would what? Her mind raced and came up empty, hands clutching fistfuls of her flight suit. She expected to find it ripped, her body bloodied, but she was whole and unbroken and couldn't logically sort what had just happened.

With a cry, Dorothy ran for the engines, stuffing her wrench into a pocket before she pulled each of the engine's propellers. She hated that the moment called for her to be careless – not ensuring the props had turned as far as they needed to turn, but she could almost *feel* time running out, as if it were a concrete substance leaking through her fingers.

She was vaguely aware of the way her legs shook as she pushed herself up the ladder and back into the pilot's compartment. There was no time for it, she told herself, pushing the panic to the side as she hauled the ladder back in, secured the hatch, and stumbled into her chair. She had to get out, and she worked automatically through the procedures she knew so well: throttle, flaps, oil pressure, mix controls, ignition.

She became aware of movement beyond the cockpit, the tree-bark figures moving without sound, like smoke or water, something not easily grasped. Dorothy stared longer than she should have, watching as they coiled in serpentine patterns around the plane, until one slithered into the propeller. The spinning metal was invisible at that speed – could they not hear the engine's roar in the hangar? – and the body fragmented under its violent force. Streaming, steaming black muck splattered the walls, the windshield, and Dorothy stared in wonder and horror both. The other figure had ceased its approach, casting wary eyes upon the plane now.

"That's right," Dorothy whispered. "I will take you apart."

She had no idea what she meant to do other than to get away. She'd be damned if she would stay, if she would let these . . . Her mind stuttered again at the thought of their hands inside her ribs. The hangar contained no proper runway, but Dorothy made use of the space as best she could. The remaining figure backed away from the Black Dragon as Dorothy released the brakes and loosed the plane into motion.

That she would never get the plane to speed was foremost in her mind. The faster she went, the quicker the hangar seemed to run out, the yawning mouth growing ever close. Beyond the room there was only a massive hangar-lined corridor, but there was nowhere else to go. With a shout, Dorothy did what she did best: she trusted the metal and the engines and engineering that made it all possible.

The plane dropped off the edge of the hangar. Dorothy was keenly aware of the weight of the plane around her, and she held her breath, expecting to plummet uncontrollably into the metallic chasm where she and the Black Dragon would erupt into a fireball. She tasted blood, cheek clenched between her teeth as the plane dropped, but the engines were strong, propelling the Black Dragon down the chasm with ease. Dorothy guided the plane into a roll, marveling at the effortless movement. For an experimental aircraft, it was a thing of beauty, hopefully something they would build for years and years to come, war or no.

Dorothy turned her attention to the landscape of the strange vessel around her: walkway tubes and over-arching structures she took for bridges, endless walls filled with more wide hangars. She saw no other flying craft within these other hangars, though.

Where was Ina . . . where was Ruth . . .

"Guns full, Bochanek," she whispered, and then, "There!" The sound of her own voice in the close cockpit was somehow reassuring, kept her from shaking out of her flight suit.

She saw the sliver of sky at the end of the chasm, much the way she had when they'd been sucked down. It was not the clouded sky she remembered, but a sliver of night, stars vomiting light against an endless black canvas. The stars recalled the eyes – eyes like supernova – and that twist of revulsion moved inside of her again. Where was Ina? Where was Ruth?

"Goddamn it, Sakata."

She spat the words, every part of her shaking as she guided the plane ever onwards. It was flying an obstacle course, up and down, over metal hurdles and between towering structures she could not properly name. Leaving her crew behind went against everything she knew and yet to stay was death, she felt certain of it. The scrabble of those hands in her ribs. The endless firelight inside their eyes.

Dorothy couldn't vomit and pilot at the same time, so chose the latter, taking comfort in the feel of the stick under her hands and the sure weight of the plane around her. As much as that weight had worried her coming off the edge of the hangar platform, it was a known element, nothing that would drag her to the ground. She knew this plane, she knew these skies, and it was with a triumphant shout that she burst out of the metal chasm, propelling the plane into a wide night sky.

But like fog in sunshine, the night evaporated around her. The darkness shredded away, consumed and replaced by the clouds she had known before; the clouds that had curled unnaturally on their side, sucking her in. She glanced back and up, but there was no tornado, no looming thunderhead. The blue sky was clear, but for the four fighters rising in formation behind her. Her radio burst to life with static and panicked, demanding voices.

"—agon, you will comply—"

Dorothy turned her attention ahead, wide open skies and Mines Field sudden and stark beneath the Black Dragon's wings, when it should have been Nevada desert. These pilots didn't know her, weren't expecting her, and she couldn't get the tremor out of her voice, couldn't make herself understood beyond the hammer of her heart.

When they touched down, the ground was blessedly firm and whole, and Dorothy exhaled, pressing her hands to the canopy above her. The glass was cold, almost frosted as if she'd flown much higher than she actually had.

"Good job, baby," she whispered.

But her hands wouldn't stop shaking as she taxied off the runway, applied the brakes and worked through post-flight procedures. She couldn't pull her eyes from the military police officers that had begun to circle the plane or the rifles they carried, and couldn't dismiss the idea that something had gone horribly wrong.

She unlatched the hatch in the floor and eased it open slowly, not surprised to find herself looking down a rifle barrel. "I'm going – I'm going to pop the l-ladder," she said, not wanting to alarm anyone with the ladder's sudden appearance. He gave her a sharp up-nod of understanding and took a single step backward.

"Ladder down, come out slow, hands on the rungs!"

Dorothy moved slow, certain she couldn't have done differently. Her legs felt like water and every rung down the short ladder like a lifetime. She glanced at the police officer and his eyes widened.

"I'm Dorothy Sakata," she said, "and there's—"

The rifle lifted again, trained now on her face. "On the ground, Jap! Hands behind your head!"

She froze half way off the final rung, his words registering like an unexpected fist to the face. The word was worse than the rifle, akin to those strange hands inside her ribs, prying her bones apart. For a long while, she could only stare at the man, wanting to ask what had happened, why they were treating her like an enemy agent. But the look in his eyes brooked no reply; he was in no mood for a question and answer session, this confirmed by the way he struck the back of her knee with the butt of his rifle to take her off the ladder.

Dorothy spilled to the ground, lifting her hands in surrender as more police officers closed in around her, rifles trained at her head. But one of the officers was studying the plane with keen eyes.

"Sir, this plane is . . . it's . . ."

Dorothy watched a broad hand press against the Black Dragon's black metal hull and she flinched at the sight of someone else touching what she'd come to think of as *her* plane.

"Spit it out."

". . . eight months overdue."

The MPs hauled Dorothy from the asphalt and given the threat of the rifles pointed at her, she stopped trying to explain herself or her appearance as they cuffed her and hauled her toward a waiting jeep. Inside, she was pressed between two MPs, their guns pointed at the roof, their eyes heavy on her.

This wasn't the world it had been only an hour before and Dorothy didn't know what had happened. Everything looked ordinary – the men in uniforms, the airfield, the sunshine spilling to the streets as they headed toward the brig. She had never spent time within a brig, but as they walked her toward a small cell with two thinly-padded narrow cots, it all looked normal. Nothing was as strange as the other vessel she had encountered, not even the sparkling Christmas garland spread over the desks. A small decorated tree sat on the floor, oversized glass lights of all colors blinking in a mindless rhythm against the drying, tinsel-draped branches.

The MPs didn't remove her cuffs before locking the cell and Dorothy opened her mouth to protest, but seeing the look on the officer's face, she swallowed the complaint whole. She sank onto the cot and waited, arms beginning to ache, but rather from swinging the wrench at the tree-like figures, not yet because of the cuffs confining her.

"Figures" was an imprecise word when it came to thinking of the beings on that vessel. Neither did "people" seem appropriate, but . . . gremlins? Dorothy shivered despite the close air of the cell. She didn't like that word, either, because it implied entirely too much.

"Sakata, is it? Dorothy?"

She looked up sharply at the man beyond the cell's bars. He was tall, and tall enough that it gave Dorothy a jolt because it reminded her of the . . . figures . . . on the strange vessel. His hair was dark and closely cropped against his head, doing nothing to conceal the scar that traced a path down his temple and cheek. She wondered at it, even as part of her mind whispered *wrench*, but he hadn't been there; she hadn't hit him because he was . . . human. Her throat tightened, but she stood and nodded.

"Yes, Ser— Master Sergeant."

A cigar would have looked right at home wedged in the corner of his broad mouth, but it was a pen he drew out, its length long since broken in two. He made a short note in the file he carried, blue eyes flicking back to Dorothy a second later. They were calm eyes, not hostile or narrowed, and she wondered what he saw, if he had taken the time to read her file, if he knew anything about her. The name patch on his chest read "Minsky".

"They call you Sakura in the skies?"

She flinched at her call sign, wondering if her fellow pilots would ever call her that again. Ruth and Ina were foremost in her mind, even given her current surroundings. Even so, she nodded.

"Yes."

"And you've been flying for us how long?"

"Not even a year, but—" The question hovered in her mind, but remained unspoken. She had the feeling Minsky would have let her ask it, given the patience within his eyes, but she shook her head. She took a step back from the cell door and sank onto the cot once more. "It wasn't like this."

Keys rattled in the well-worn lock and Minsky stepped into the cell. The door closed behind him and the space seemed impossibly small with him a part of it. He sat on the cot opposite her own, her file spread open on his thighs. He smelled like a smokehouse and looked like he should have been bench-pressing tanks rather than questioning pilots. He tucked the pen back into the corner of his mouth and regarded her for a long while before he spoke again.

"Tell me what you know of Pearl Harbor."

"Pearl . . ." She clasped her hands together, palm to palm, shoulders beginning to ache now given the range of motion the cuffs allowed. She shook her head a little, trying to make sense of what he was asking. "Can you . . . Can *you* tell *me* what the date is?" Her eyes were drawn to the Christmas décor once more.

Her question seemed to stir the first bit of unease she saw in his eyes, a stone thrown into water. "Fifth of January."

"It's *May*," she whispered, unable to stop the words. "We left Tonopah and it was *May*." Had no one missed her? Had no one wondered when the Black Dragon hadn't been delivered? She met his eyes and swallowed hard, forcing herself to remember what he had asked of her. "There is a naval station at Pearl Harbor, but I've never been there. Our routes are all mainland, usually solo and I'm out of Alamogordo, but this plane . . . She's . . ." She wanted to tell him how well the Black Dragon flew, but fell to silence. January!

"You failed to deliver your plane, Miss Sakata. They believed you and your crew stole it, sold it, possibly to the Germans, yeah?" Minsky chewed his pen as he regarded her.

Fuming, Dorothy clasped her hands together and thumped their combined weight against her thigh. The Germans. She wasn't buying *that*, but the idea that a pilot might take the plane they meant to deliver was one she and other pilots always speculated over; how easy, to just fly into the wide sky and not look back.

She told him then, about the cloud, about the way it had pulled the Black Dragon inside. Told him about the vessel and how she had woken, alone; said someone needed to send a plane back up there for Ina and Ruth. The more she talked, the more the disquiet in his eyes grew, his jaw tightening.

"Mines Field lost a plane to this thing in April, didn't they?" she asked. She realized she had slid to the edge of the cot and was leaning toward Minsky, daring him to admit something had gone wrong and had been going wrong for a long while now. "There have been all kinds of reports of strange clouds in the sky – huge storms. They're not storms, Master Sergeant, least not as we know them."

And then he told her, about the war, about the Imperial Japanese Navy and their attack on Pearl Harbor. One hundred and eighty-three planes in the skies, Minsky said, and twenty-four hundred dead. The navy destroyed, the world on fire, and Dorothy could say nothing for the shock that paralyzed her. The way they'd trained the guns on her, the slur in the officer's mouth, came into slow focus. She stared at Minsky, her mouth gaping open, but she couldn't find the words for a long while.

"This . . . this thing," Dorothy eventually managed. "It's not Japanese. It's not even German if I had to guess. There were these . . ." A shudder rolled through her; she couldn't say gremlins to him, couldn't. "Beings . . . and they are . . . It's not—"

"It won't matter," Minsky said. He drew the pen from his mouth and closed it into her file as he stood from the cot. "As a Japanese-American, you have been designated an enemy alien, your flight status revoked. They'll be sending you to a camp, Sakata, where they've herded up the rest of your kind for . . . safe keeping."

The venom in his voice couldn't be concealed. As much as he might have wanted to listen to her, he wouldn't – couldn't – because orders were orders. Dorothy stood from the cot, her gaze not wavering on Minsky.

"With all due respect, that *thing* is probably still out there! Swallowing planes, keeping them, studying them – who knows what, but it's – I lost eight *months* inside that thing and two of my crew and you—"

"*Enough*." Minsky cut her protest short with a single word.

Dorothy sank back to the cot, staring at the floor beyond her cuffed wrists. Seven months lost, the world entirely changed, and what of her family? At the idea of what had become of her mother, father and grandparents, it seemed those gremlin hands moved inside her again, but now they squeezed her heart until it might burst.

She always watched the skies.

Fair weather or foul, Dorothy assessed the skies morning, noon, and night, but in the fourteen months that followed her transfer to the internment camp on the eastern plains of Colorado, she saw nothing resembling what she had encountered in the skies above Nevada and began to wonder if it wouldn't be making a repeat performance. Reliable news of the outside world was infrequent within the camp, not that the military would have told its prisoners anything, be it regarding strange storms in the sky or otherwise, Dorothy supposed. The ghosts of Ina and Ruth haunted her dreams, but there was nothing she could do for them behind these walls.

They were kept inside a mile-square enclosure, on land formerly populated by the Cheyenne. It wasn't uncommon to find arrowheads in the clay dirt as they dug new gardens; Dorothy had a small collection of them now, surprised that no one had been by to collect them, labeling them forbidden goods. The walls that enclosed the city – if it could be called such – were patrolled by hulking automatons, and at regular intervals, towers sporting machine guns that discouraged anyone from taking a stroll beyond the stone. The camp had barracks, a cemetery, a dump, and even a hospital, where the morning found Dorothy studying the skies, while the Dragon Yamamoto decided if he'd trade medicine for a nugget of gold.

Yamamoto, possibly the oldest person Dorothy had ever seen, pressed the nugget between his teeth, eyes narrowed to slits as if the process were the most difficult he had ever experienced. Dorothy waited, having learned how to swallow impatience. Yamamoto knew her mother was not well, never having adjusted to Colorado's altitude, and that the doctors could prescribe nothing to help, save for the advice she live closer to the sea. Transferring her to another camp was impossible, so the doctors wrote her off as a lost cause, surprised she hadn't already died. Dorothy refused to give up so easily, seeking out the wisest within the camp to procure something, anything, to help her mother breathe. But even the wisest was not without his own rituals and antics. Yamamoto liked to perform for those who sought him out. Dorothy could not help but look at the sky, though; today, the blue vault was absolutely flawless, as if the sky had never had the idea of clouds.

"Take this."

The old man pressed a linen pouch into Dorothy's hands, drawing her attention from the cloudless day. The pouch was light as though empty, and the color of Mrs Watanabe's best eggs. Yamamoto nodded, the gold nugget resting as a lump in his cheek.

"Will ease her breathing, that. Manticore scales, you tell her. Brew the tea." Yamamoto shuffled across the small courtyard and settled into the lounge chair he usually occupied. "Tell Jun his presents are coming, probably here by Friday." His mouth split in a bright grin. "I never get to the other side of the city these days – Jun keeps the rickshaw?"

Dorothy wanted to laugh at the question of the rickshaw, but mention of Jun's "presents" tempered her mood. Had Yamamoto actually acquired the weapons Jun sought? "Painted it orange and white, calls it the Tank," she answered of the rickshaw. She glanced up at the camp's water tower, also painted orange and white. It towered over everything, gleaming in the day's sun.

"*Domo arigatou gozaimasu*," Dorothy said and made a bow to Yamamoto. His mouth lifted in a smile and he waved her off. "Go, *onēsan*. Go."

Dorothy went. Some days, Yamamoto was prone to stories, but too often liked to dwell on how the military had roused he and his family from their homes, when they had done nothing suspicious. None of them had, Dorothy knew, but given the tensions with Japan . . .

No, that didn't excuse it. She had tried to understand, but could not. She cast a glance at the sky as she walked toward their family dwelling; the entire complex was built well enough and if one didn't look beyond the innermost structures, one might not see the walls, the guns, the hulking automatons that moved against anyone who came near or stepped out of line. But Dorothy had not been able to live that way, not with the wide open sky above them and the ache of flying in her bones.

She was grateful to have been assigned to the same camp as her own family, her father and mother and grandmother. Many families had not been so lucky, separated at the time of the transfers. Dorothy was certain she would not forget the look on her mother's face when Minsky brought her to the camp – that mixture of sorrow and relief flooding her eyes.

That Minsky had brought her told Dorothy something, too. He hadn't been able to act on the information she had given him regarding the strange storm and its vessel, but he believed her. Seeing her placed with her family was – well, it wasn't an apology, but it was something.

Belief was something, too, and one reason Dorothy kept watching the skies. Every time planes passed overhead, she looked, and every time thunderstorms gathered, she looked. When the moon was new and hidden, she looked, fearing that such a storm could creep up upon them in the dark of night and swallow them whole. It was a child's fear, but she could not shake it. There were still nights she woke from dreams wherein she felt her ribs being spread apart, her bones flooded by the viscous fluids that had splattered the hangar walls.

Dorothy found her mother on her knees in the garden at the end of the barracks. Her small body was bent over the soil, working to break up the thick clay that made most of the ground here. It was a wonder the vegetables grew as well as they did, but despite all conditions, the gardens of the city flourished. It was early in the growing season yet, but small hints of green had begun to shade the plots, lattices being hammered into place to support eventual vines.

"*Okaasan*, come rest, I have your tea."

Keiko came as bid, dirt cascading from her worn trousers. Her fingers were clotted with clay, which she rolled off and tossed back into the garden plot. A small patio of their own making edged against the barracks, a space of shade, stone, and a variety of padded chairs that had been acquired from neighbors. All were welcome to come, but few did, still not entirely trusting Dorothy. Hadn't she flown for the Americans? Perhaps she was a spy, sent to watch over them and report to the white men. Denying the suspicions only gained her more.

"Have you ever seen such a clear sky?" Keiko murmured as she sat in her favorite chair, the metal frame padded with fabric decorated with yellow birds and blue morning glories. Dorothy liked to imagine it was a scene her mother remembered from her childhood in Japan, just as the wind chime her mother had made and her grandmother's paintings within their rooms touched back on the quiet life she had led there.

Dorothy looked up at the familiar blue. "No," she said, and it was true. Perhaps the afternoon would bring storms to study, but this sky was strangely clear and calm, endless. She turned her attention to the tea she was preparing for her mother, trying to keep her hands steady. What she withdrew from the pouch was not manticore scales, but leaves. They possessed a sheen to them that made them look like small dragon scales, recently plucked from a snoozing beast.

"*Okaasan*, have you seen Jun today?" The idea of the "presents" Yamamoto was bringing still made Dorothy twitch. Jun couldn't be serious about blowing a hole in the camp's outer wall, he just couldn't. The landscape beyond the walls was flat, endless. He would never get out and if he did get out, he'd never get away.

"No," Keiko said. She rolled the last of the clay from her fingers then dunked her hands into the bucket of water nearby;

she washed her hands the way she often washed her paint-brushes, eyes on Dorothy. "You don't think he means—"

Whatever else Keiko meant to say was lost in the sudden rumble of an aircraft passing over; nothing so strange as the storm Dorothy kept an eye out for, but unusual nonetheless. Carrying high-level personnel, Dorothy thought, and that coupled with Jun's "presents" made her meet her mother's gaze.

"Oh, I think he means it." She settled a few leaves into her mother's favorite cup, then went inside to put the kettle on. She prayed for the ritual of tea to take her mind to a calmer place, but it never did; she stared out the small kitchen window at the sky, wondering what else it would bring.

It brought nothing until nightfall, when the camp began to settle for sleep. Dorothy finished the last of their dishes and prepared to brew her mother another cup of tea that might help ease her breathing. She was listening to her parents soft murmur of Japanese from the sitting room when she saw from the kitchen window the spark of light against the dark sky. Her stomach knotted and she couldn't breathe, watching a long trail of light draw itself upon the night's otherwise blank canvas. It was perfectly white, like a flare gun, and when Dorothy stepped outside, she could smell the faint tang of gunpowder on the air.

"Jun," she whispered.

She looked back once, considering that she should tell her parents where she meant to go, but they would only worry if she did. If anything happened, she knew they were smart enough to not run into the middle of it, and so without a word she left the building. Her boots moved silent over the dry, fallow ground between barracks, as she made her way to the farthest edge of the gardens, where Jun had said he meant to stage his attack.

In this space, no light from the barracks fell and Jun was a shadow that resembled an overgrown pumpkin, hunched with arms sprawling as he worked to assemble the last of his weapons, bundles of dynamite. His hands were gentle in the work, steady, as if carrying his young niece and nephew had prepared him for such a delicate work. Children or explosives – Dorothy saw the similarities between them as she cleared her throat. Clearly the presents Yamamoto had promised were already here. Had Friday been code for something else?

"Heard you two plots back," Jun said without looking up. "Guess pilots don't need soft footfalls, eh Sakura?"

Dorothy was glad of the darkness, so Jun wouldn't see the way she flinched when he used her call sign. The comment was nearly an insult, touching on a beloved profession she could no longer pursue but still longed for. She swallowed every insult that rose to mind and looked at the nearby stone wall Jun thought he could take down. It rose like a sheet of black iron against the night sky, higher than she could estimate. It was two feet thick, they said, like a castle wall. Atop the battlements, the automatons patrolled. If Jun did manage to blast the wall open, he'd bring those things down on their heads, into the camps where they would hunt freely.

The automatons were metal giants, the latest in a line of constructed beings; their predecessors had been made of leather and glue, lacquer and wood, things easier to blow apart. These automatons were an upgrade, designed to quell further camp disruptions, and so far, they'd been worth whatever the military had paid for them; in twelve months, the camp had lain quiet, its citizens compliant. Metal, Jun insisted, would prove just as subservient to the whims of well-placed dynamite.

"In five minutes," Jun said, "the first will go." He lifted his head, to study Dorothy in the dark, the bundle of dynamite held carefully in his hands. "Have you come to help?"

There was no good answer to this question and Dorothy only looked into his eyes for a long while, remembering when she had met him on her first day in the camp. He had been brewing her mother's tea that day, having cared for her parents from the time they had arrived, bruised in spirit and flesh both. She felt that debt upon her shoulders even now, for Jun had no family of his own here, only that which he had made.

"There is no shame in saying no, Dorothy," Jun said. He cradled the dynamite in one arm, and reached for her with the other. His fingers were cool against her cheek. "I know you have your family to think of."

But Dorothy found herself shaking her head. "This is no way for them to live, but if the wall comes down, and those . . . things are let loose in here . . . I don't know which is worse, Jun. Waiting for them or having them come." She could have said the same of the strange storm cloud, feeling its lingering threat much as she did that of the automatons. "I have come to help."

Jun's smile was bright even in the night. "Thunderous Raijin comes to us in many forms and tonight, possesses yours." Jun handed Dorothy the bundle of dynamite then plucked another from the ground nearby. "Place that at the tower behind you and look for the double flare before the wall goes. After the wall, the automatons. Hiroshi saw them wired."

"Wired—"

Jun sprinted off and Dorothy looked up as an automaton passed on its regular patrol. It moved with a low sound of thunder. Jun's brother, Hiroshi, was part of the small crew allowed upon the wall to help service the great machines; they were often in need of oil and wrenching, subject to decay as everything in the world seemed to be. What had they done under the guise of normal repairs? Dorothy pictured their metallic bellies filled with explosives and as the world began to ignite around them, figured she was not far from wrong.

She placed her bundle of dynamite at the base of the tower, finding the end of the fuse Jun had been running. She tied the bundle in and ran for cover, through the gardens, aware of her shoes sticking in the damp clay, of the plants she trampled when the white double flare illuminated the night and the first explosions rocked the camp. The night turned to day as the dynamite ignited, shards of wall and tower and automaton blown throughout the camp. Dorothy was thrown to the ground under the force of one blast, knees hitting before the rest of her came down. Clouds of smoke and dust concealed the camp, but beyond that veil, she watched in amazement as the wall shattered, as each and every automaton atop the wall erupted in violent fireballs. She thought she saw human faces within the flames, *kechibi* come to swallow the wicked who remained upon the earth. Dorothy hoped they took each and every guard, each and every soldier, so that her people might live beyond walls once more, that she might fly the sky again.

She felt not so much possessed by the thunder god Raijin as she did a frightened child. The camp wall continued to fall, automatons exploding and dropping like shooting stars from its great height, and everywhere people emerged from the barracks, shrieking in delight and terror both. The delight was short-lived as Dorothy began to hear the weapons fire within the camp – not dynamite, but guns, pistols and, quick on their heels, machine guns. Dorothy's stomach sank.

They had no weapons, the barracks regularly searched. While they were encouraged to make their spaces as home-like as possible, the dwellings were searched to prevent people from possessing anything they should not. Given Yamamoto's long reach even within camp walls, one might procure anything, given enough time. But guns, no one had managed guns.

Inside the kitchen of a neighbor, Dorothy put her hands on a tire iron, having no idea where it would have come from. No one owned cars, but perhaps once they had. Perhaps the iron was a symbol for them, of what they had lost and what they hoped to one day reclaim. For now, the iron was a good weapon, and Dorothy put it to quick use, notching it into the face of the lieutenant who strode into the kitchen. Blood burst from his mouth and he didn't move once he'd gone down; she didn't know him, but took great pleasure in the way he dropped like a stone. Dorothy stepped over him and moved back into the night.

She moved toward her own dwelling, meaning to get her parents to some form of safety, but never reached it. Out of the smoke-cloaked night there emerged a figure, so large and hulking, she thought at first it was an automaton that had escaped detonation. Dorothy took an uneven step backward and lifted the tire iron, having no hope of taking such a thing down. It would be equipped with guns. It would take her down without so much as an independent thought.

But as the figure parted the smoke, she found herself face to face with someone familiar, one Master Sergeant Minsky, who looked considerably more put out than he had at their last encounter. His face was streaked with soot, his uniform burned around the edges, and he strode forward with the look of a man who would not be put off. Dorothy lowered the tire iron.

"Minsky?"

His paw of a hand closed around her arm, pulling her out of harm's way as another plummeting automation met its doom. The roof nearby crumbled under the automaton's exploding weight and debris scattered wide. "Sakata."

Minsky hauled her in the opposite direction of where she meant to go, and she tried to twist from his hold. Around them, night exploded with fire. "Minsky – my family—"

"Is the least of your concern." Minsky gave her a hard shake and hauled her against the barracks' wall.

Dorothy could not pry herself from his hold; his hand had fastened around her like an iron band, unmovable. As the sky above them erupted in more fire, she swung with her free hand, the one holding the tire iron. Minsky deflected it with a broad forearm, the makeshift weapon ricocheting into the stucco wall. Dorothy dropped it before the reverberations through the iron could rattle her arm off.

"You listen to me, Sakata," Minsky began.

Dorothy *did* listen and what she heard caught her off guard.

"I came here with a deal for you, and this . . ." He looked at the violent night sky, erupting in shades of fire and soot, then back to her. A muscle in his jaw leapt. "This was not in the plan."

Minsky's words were unsteady, but not due to the conflict around them. Something else had brought him here – she wondered if his had been the plane earlier that day – and this conflict had complicated his already complicated plans.

"What plan?" She tried again to free herself from his grip, but he wouldn't let her go. She became aware then of the shaking in his arm, of the unshed tears in his eyes. Maybe it was just the smoke, or maybe it was—

"Your storm cloud. It's back."

Dorothy didn't know until that moment how long she had been holding her breath. More than a year, she decided, because now that it had come, now that the storm that wasn't a storm had returned, she felt herself exhale. Something inside her let go. All this time, she had waited. She had wanted someone to believe her story, and now Minsky did. But—

"That's not all," she murmured, because he was more troubled than a single cloud would make a man of his years and military experience. "What happened?"

He released her arm, but didn't take a step back, and Dorothy didn't feel inclined to move. She felt rooted, her hair whipping in the exhalation of distant explosions as she waited for Minsky to deliver the rest of the news. He did this as capably as any military commander, giving her the cold, hard details without a trace of emotion.

The cloud had reappeared a month prior, in the skies over Nevada exactly where Dorothy had claimed an encounter with it. The storm hadn't done anything other than fume, spewing tentacles of cloud edged in lightning; it hadn't seemed to send out any communications or ships. All attempts at remote communication with it failed, and so they sent a plane inside – a plane that didn't return. This plane was followed by a second. And then fighters were deployed en masse.

The battle, if one could call it that, proved devastating. Every plane sent in was vomited back out in a tangle of metal and bodies. The sky around the cloud had grown thick with the disfigured aircraft, Minsky said; they never fell to the ground, but hovered in the sky as if in orbit of the cloud-storm. Though they hadn't sent any new craft in, the cloud continued to spit mangled planes out, as if to display its might while creeping closer toward California and Mines Field. At the same time, similar storms had been reported over London, Tokyo and Berlin.

Storms, Dorothy thought – no, *points of entry*.

"Command told me to get you," Minsky finished, his gaze dropping from the fiery skies to take in Dorothy once more. "Because *you* came out of that thing and might know what the hell to do."

Dorothy stared at him in disbelief, and then she laughed. She moved now, mostly because she wanted to shake the awful feeling that had crept into her, the feeling of those strange hands prying her ribs apart. She wrapped her arms around herself in an effort to remind herself that she was whole and unbroken, that those things hadn't gotten inside, but the memory was too clear and she couldn't shake it.

"Sakata, we need you. We are absolutely clueless against this thing."

She tried to enjoy his admission and that idea: that the military was baffled and that she, a civilian pilot, a Japanese-

American pilot, a *female* pilot, might be the one to save them all, but there was no joy. The memory of the storm terrified her, the ghosts of Ina and Ruth rarely allowing her to sleep in peace, and there was no joy, the camp around them still falling to dust.

"You came here with a deal for me," she reminded him softly. She hadn't forgotten those words.

Minsky nodded, his face shadowed by more than soot now. "I can get you out, get you flying regular again."

Dorothy's stomach flip-flopped at the very idea. Once, that would have been enough, a life outside walls, a life in all that sky, but now . . . She looked at the camp exploding to ruin around them, and by Minsky's face, she knew that he already knew.

"We won't live behind walls, Minsky. Any of us. You raze this and every other camp in this nation – how many are there? You burn them to the ground and let these people go."

"You know I don't have that kind of author—"

"Then I don't know what the hell you are talking about! Clouds that eat planes? As if." The anger that flooded Dorothy surprised even her. She strode back to the wall, picked up the tire iron, and pointed it at Minsky's face. "Maybe they'll put you in a camp for safe-keeping." She spat the words, recalling too clearly her last conversation with Minsky.

"All right!" Minsky lifted his hands, his expression absolutely hopeless as he stared at her.

"All right what?" Dorothy advanced on him, tire iron still lifted, but he didn't give up his position. He didn't back down or look away. Broad-shouldered and tall, Minsky stared her down, not flinching.

"None of you will live behind walls, Dor— Sakata," he said. "None."

Dorothy never lowered her eyes from his steady gaze, giving no ground as the camp around them continued to crumble, and, not knowing if she genuinely believed Minsky or if the lure of flying again was simply too much, lowered her tire iron.

Beyond the cockpit windows of the Corsair, the disturbance resembled a normal thunderhead, blossoming and bruised clouds spread across a bright blue sky. But contained within was the familiar anomaly, the tornado tipped on its side.

Dorothy tried not to flinch at the sight of it, but the response was automatic; she remembered too easily how the Black Dragon had been pulled inside, how she had woken with no memory of landing. How Ina and Ruth had never been found.

And those gremlin hands.

She flinched again at the memory, the violent spin of the storm spawning tentacles of black, lightning-cracked clouds. Scattered at the mouth of the storm, within the writhing tentacle clouds, dozens upon dozens of wrecked aircraft hung as if caught in the storm's gravity. Dorothy flew cautiously closer, noting the familiar shape of a broken Corsair wing, a shattered fuselage still showing remnants of its nose art, a pin-up girl cut cruelly in two by whatever power had taken the plane apart. She saw fragments of Mustangs and Black Widows, but as she circled again, she saw something even stranger. Amid the debris were wings and fuselages marked with the flags of Britain, Japan and Germany.

Despite the storm and the wreckage of armies strewn before it, a wave of happiness rose inside Dorothy. Being back in the sky and having a plane under her control were two things she had longed for. She hadn't forgotten the feel of the stick in her hands, or the way a cockpit rattled as the plane gained altitude, but she had forgotten the way a plane smelled in the air and the way the air crept inside to chill hands and cheeks.

Despite her best intentions to not think of it as such, Dorothy pictured the entire storm as the great and monstrous eye of an *ōkubi*, a face of cloud staring down upon the world, come to prophecy its doom. Dorothy pushed that nonsense to the side and banked around the storm.

She took another pass, conferring with Minsky on the radio all the while. They wanted a reconnaissance pass, didn't want her inside yet, but Dorothy suspected the storm wouldn't let her go. Whether truth or fancy, she knew it was aware of her; the cloud arms crackled through the Corsair's propeller, skimming the plane's long nose before butting against the windshield. There, the cloud broke into dozens of wriggling offshoots, all eagerly trying to press through the glass. Dorothy swallowed her nausea and turned the plane away, just as the storm grabbed hold.

Much as it had been the first time, Dorothy felt the plane spiraling downward, and nothing she did resulted in dislodging the craft from the lightning-grip. The radio sparked and cut out, Minsky fading to shouts of static as the cloud wall closed over the Corsair. It was like being pulled under water, so quickly did the day's light vanish. Shadow filled the cockpit, erased the world, and Dorothy fought to maintain consciousness even as the air grew thin as if she were being hauled into the oblivion of space. In her swimming vision, on the hazy outskirts of the plane, she thought she saw the fluid beings once more. They wrapped their liquid bodies around the plane the way morning glories wrapped themselves around poles. Under this force, the plane began to stall and Dorothy could do nothing as it rolled over on one wing. She envisioned it flipping, but the Corsair stayed steady and true, despite the creatures pulling it down.

She woke in a hangar, much as she had the first time, but this hangar was not empty. It was littered with other planes, most broken to bits, but three stood whole. Still, judging by the dust that coated them, they had been here a good long while.

"Minsky, you hear me?" She tried the radio a final time, but there was only a final burst of static before the entire thing went silent. She pulled her headset off, and wondered exactly how much time would pass inside this vessel before she got out this time. The idea of leaving *now* was attractive, but so was the notion that she might learn something, that she might—

"Find Ina and Ruth, goddamn it," she whispered. "Eight months lost in this thing, what're you going to do *this* time?"

She unbuckled her shoulder harness and cracked the cockpit open, the motions practiced, unforgotten despite the time in the camp. Before exiting the plane, her fingers ghosted over the pistol she wore in a sling holster over her flight suit. She didn't like the idea they'd given her a weapon this time around, because it meant they believed she might genuinely require it.

Dorothy climbed out of the cockpit and onto the broad, gray wing of the Corsair, legs more steady than she expected. The hangar was colder than she remembered, the ground crackling under her boots like ice on a lake might as she dropped from the wing. Just as last time, she made a slow circle of her aircraft, to ensure nothing strange had befallen it.

"Well," she murmured, and laughed to herself. "Perhaps we need to define strange, given the circumstances, Sakata."

As she rounded the tail of the Corsair, she noticed a body splayed in the hangar debris. Dorothy dropped to a crouch, one hand on the butt of her pistol. She didn't draw, only watched and listened to the hangar around her. She expected the strange gremlin creatures to appear, to slide their hands into and through that body, but all appeared still. Dorothy picked her way through the debris and under the wing of a still imposing B-24 Liberator; the plane was banged up, but still looked flyable. Where the hell was her pilot?

Dorothy reached for the body, discovering it was a woman – a woman with a pulse hammering in her neck. Dorothy waited for relief to flood through her, because surely it *should* have been relief at the sight of another living human being in this vessel. But there was no relief, because as she brushed the softly curling strawberry blonde hair away from the face, she saw the woman was more like a caricature than an actual woman of flesh and bone. She looked like she had been drawn – painted – into life. She was clad in a bright sapphire blue bathing suit, a large bow fashioned into a flower against her plump backside. Her feet sported illogically high heels, black and shiny, exactly like—

Dorothy looked back at the B-24, taking in the minor damage, the broad wings, but it was the nose art she took the most interest in. The lettering was still there, STRAWBERRY BITCH spelled out in gleaming red paint, but the pin-up that had once decorated the metal was gone. Unconscious in the debris before her, Dorothy thought.

She pressed her hand against the pin-up's flawless cheek. "Can you hear me?" The woman didn't stir and Dorothy patted the cheek with a little more force. "Hey." Her mouth twisted at the very idea of what she was about to do. "Strawberry?"

She didn't expect the woman to actually wake, but she did, blinking wide blue eyes in astonishment as she came upright. Then, she started screaming.

Dorothy didn't rein in the impulse to slap Strawberry. Her palm cracked across the flawless cheek and Strawberry took a stuttering breath, blinking tears from her eyes as she stared at Dorothy.

"Oh . . . It . . . You're not *them*."

A chill rolled through Dorothy. She didn't have to guess which "them" Strawberry meant and glanced around the hangar to be sure they we still alone. "Can you stand?" Dorothy asked, but Strawberry was already doing so, easily in those crazy heels, as if they were a part of her. "Them who?" It never hurt to ask.

Strawberry shuddered, her hair curling over her bare shoulders. "Those *things* that run this place. They . . ." Her eyes darted to the B-24 and back to Dorothy again, worried. "They took me and . . ."

If gremlins had actually peeled a painted woman from the fuselage of the Liberator and breathed life into her, Dorothy told herself. she would swallow a bullet whole. As it was, she just stared at the figure, somehow transfixed. She was as three dimensional as anything in this room, and yet . . .

Dorothy strode toward the end of the hangar, where it branched into hallways. "You got a name? Where are you from?" Dorothy looked into the empty halls, then back at Strawberry who was pressing her hands against the sides of the B-24.

"Says right here," she whispered. "Strawberry Bitch . . . what kind of name is that?" She looked down at herself and scoffed at her clothing. "I should be nothing more than paint and dreams, but I'm . . ." She lowered her hands from the plane and pressed them against her belly. "They made me so they could . . ." But she trailed off, unable to finish the sentence because she was staring in naked panic at something beyond Dorothy's shoulder.

Dorothy wheeled around, expecting the fluid gremlins, but no. Another pin-up approached them, seeming as baffled as Strawberry was.

Diamond Lil, if one judged by the lettering left on the fuselage behind her, wore a floor-length black gown, diamonds glittering in a trail between her high breasts. Her hair was a glossy waterfall of straight black, eyes as blue as the sky Dorothy had just flown through.

"This isn't possible, you realize," Dorothy said, more to herself than the two pin ups before her. "It's probably an effect of the . . . drowning . . . or however they brought me down . . ." She couldn't explain it beyond that because how, and why, would gremlins do such a thing? She didn't want to understand, didn't want . . .

Deep within the ship, down the empty hallway, something caused the ship to tremble. Dorothy braced one hand against the wall, drawing her pistol with the other. If she was hallucinating, nothing mattered, so she strode into the hallway and trusted the pin-ups would follow if they were so inclined.

The floor was terribly solid beneath her boots, telling Dorothy she wasn't hallucinating, and when the sound of Strawberry and Lil's heels came behind her, Dorothy felt as though she wanted to vomit. She couldn't unravel the game at play here, because nothing presently made sense. Her only hope was the idea that somewhere on this ship, other human beings lived and struggled to solve the same game.

And maybe Ruth, her heart whispered; and maybe Ina.

The source of the rumbling didn't make itself readily known to Dorothy; the hall curved into another wide space, showing Dorothy the same jumble of items she remembered from her first time inside. A massive corridor lined with conduits, hurdles, ports and tracks. A corridor much like the one she had flown to escape. She glanced back at the pin-ups, staring at them in confused silence. If she was hallucinating . . . How did one interrogate paint?

"Have you explored this ship?" she asked them. Diamond Lil shook her head, but Strawberry nodded.

"That's how I . . ." Strawberry wrapped her arms around herself as if she had gone cold. "After they . . . made me . . . and they . . ." She stuttered, squeezed her eyes shut, and bowed her chin to her chest.

"Strawberry. It's okay. Tell me."

"I woke in a small room," she said in a voice just above a whisper. "Dark, cold. Like a closet. I was alone so I . . . left. I wasn't going to stay, when I knew . . ." She looked back up at Dorothy. "It wasn't right. *I'm* not right. I'm paint, for god's sake. I thought if I . . . if I could get back to the Liberator." She looked back the way they had come. "I thought I could press myself back into the metal. Go back where . . . where I belonged."

A painted pin-up, thinking actual thoughts and breathing actual air. Dorothy supposed it didn't matter how such a thing was possible; it was, and they could only move forward.

"All right." Dorothy looked at Diamond Lil, whose eyes had gone wide with alarm at Strawberry's words. "All right."

They made a slow and thorough search of the hangars adjacent to that which held Dorothy's Corsair, discovering planes both broken and whole, and other pin-up girls peeled from their noses. The alarm Dorothy felt at the sight of them never lessened; each time was strange, new, because the girls should have been flat, without dimension, but they were not. They were wholly dimensional women, save for the lack of knowledge they possessed. No past, brought to life by the stroke of a brush, kindled into another form of life by the gremlins, but to what purpose?

The women proved up to any task Dorothy assigned them, as if they had been waiting for such a purpose; the hangars on the deck were so numerous the women easily could have continued searching without cease, but Dorothy was painfully reminded that the time spent here was passing more quickly on Earth. It might not matter for these painted caricatures, but it mattered to her, to her family, and Minsky. The first time Dorothy had lost an hour in here, Japan had attacked the United States. What might come this time? She shuddered to think.

The hangars appeared endless and Dorothy reminded herself this was but a fraction of one level. She was never not aware of the bulk of the vessel around them, of the number of hangars she had seen on her way out the first time through. How many planes, how many pin-up girls?

At the end of the main corridor, an inclined ramp curved down, into the level below. Given the soot and oil splatters on the floor, Dorothy wondered if planes had been brought through here, but it didn't make sense, given the way the gremlins had hauled her own on board.

From below came the creak of protesting metal and a barked curse.

She looked back at the pin-ups. "Wait here."

She watched with a little pride as the women flanked the ramp, guarding all access points behind her. Dorothy moved down the ramp, holding her pistol before her, and another curse echoed through the halls. She didn't dare hope the voice was one she knew, but it somehow was.

The nose of an aircraft was wedged into the corridor, as if someone had shared Dorothy's own thought, but the P-51 Mustang's wings were lodged into the wall, the ramp proving not wide enough after all. Under the broad wings stood Ruth Avery, hands wrapped around a wrench so that she could beat on the metal in frustration.

"Avery?"

The radar operator jumped at the sound of her name, whirling around with her wrench held high. Her face was streaked with oil and soot, but her plump cheeks still lifted in a smile, a smile that washed over Dorothy like sunshine.

"Just me, Avery."

"Sakata!" She lowered the wrench, but didn't move from her position under the wing. "Jesus, I thought—" Her voice broke. "I thought they got you, too. The Black Dragon was gone and Ina . . ."

Dorothy closed the distance between them, recalling the way she had woken the first time here, both Ina and Ruth taken from the experimental Black Dragon. Guessing from what Minsky had told her, Ruth had only been here three hours, when in the world beyond months had passed.

"Where's Ina?" Dorothy looked beyond the Mustang, into the corridor that sprawled away from the ramp they occupied; everything was dark, broken, and vast.

"Ina's—" Ruth's voice broke and Dorothy wasn't sure she'd ever heard such emotion from the woman. "Ina's gone."

The word was worse than "dead", or even "taken." Each conveyed something slightly different and "gone" was terrible, it kept too much hidden. Ina was simply no longer here, and Dorothy bowed her head, trying to be okay with this idea. She'd had more than a year to come to terms with leaving them behind, but never had. This loss was like a fresh blow in her gut, robbing her of breath.

"Did you find the Black Dragon, Sakata? Did you—" Ruth's mouth twisted and she shoved the wrench into a pocket. She closed her eyes, letting her head rock to the side, and a pained expression creased her filthy face. "They say they're stuck, can you hear that racket?"

Dorothy didn't hear anything, but for the distant rumble of what might have been an engine. "My plane is a level up, Ruth. We should—"

"Blow this thing sky-high," Ruth whispered. "It's the only way out, for everyone. Everyone." Her eyes rolled open and she stared at Dorothy. "How can you not hear that? Incessant sizzle in my head. They're close. Did you see them? Like black water and tree bark. Not Germans. You said—" Her brow creased. "You brought a plane? They're stuck and we can unstick 'em – c'mon!"

As Ruth grabbed Dorothy by the arm, Dorothy decided explanations about time discrepancies could wait. Ruth hauled her up the ramp, maintaining a swift pace until she saw the pin-up girls guarding the top. She startled at the sight of them, then hauled Dorothy right on through.

"Plane. Now. Tell me it's loaded."

"Tell me what you're hearing, Avery," Dorothy countered, pulling arm free of the woman's hold.

Ruth seemed unable to hold still. She paced a circle around Dorothy, watching the pin-up girls all the while. "Ever since we got here, crackling in my brain." She scrubbed her hands through her hair, eyes swinging back to Dorothy. "Ina heard it too – before they . . . They made her fall to pieces, Dorothy." Her voice hitched and she pressed the back of one hand against her mouth before continuing. "Made her crumple like an old mushroom, stretched her thin, tried to talk with her mouth, but—"

She broke off, her entire body heaving as though she meant to vomit. She strode away from the pin-ups and Dorothy, shaking. Dorothy glanced at the other girls, none of which seemed inclined to follow Ruth; they only watched in silent confusion. Dorothy followed Ruth, feeling time running out as they lingered here.

"Ruth, tell me."

"They're stuck!" Ruth spat the words and it was plain to Dorothy how difficult speech was becoming for her. Every word was forced, spittle wetting her lips. "Inside my head, inside our atmosphere, inside *them*." She cast a venomous look at the pin-ups as they began to walk closer. "The gremlins will be inside everything given long enough and they just want *out*. Tell me you have a loaded plane. Tell me."

Dorothy looked at the pin-ups with new eyes – the pin-ups *were* the gremlins? She watched the way they moved as a group, not seeing only Strawberry and only Diamond Lil, but the whole group of them. Throughout, every motion was mirrored, the flow of water and not the motion of individuals. Dorothy grasped Ruth's arm and pulled her closer, moving down the hall she and the pin-ups had cleared only minutes before.

"An explosion knocks them out?" Dorothy asked. Keeping hold of Ruth with one hand, she drew her pistol with the other. She recalled Strawberry's words, "Go back where . . . Where I belonged." Was that all the gremlins wanted?

"Blow it s-sky-high," Ruth said.

With the pin-ups closing in, Dorothy tightened her hold on Ruth's arm and ran, trusting she would keep the pace. She did. Behind them, the pin-ups moved with a whispering sound, water over leaves, and Dorothy tried to shut it out, even as she felt it creeping into her mind. The sound was cold fingers prying at the edges of her skull until she screamed out.

Out, the sound said.

Stuck, the sound said.

You abominations, the sound said.

Dorothy wheeled around and fired on the women.

As one, the women broke apart in an explosion of black water. Improbable gowns and hairstyles and heels burst apart as they flooded the deck, no more real than they ever had been. The water did not change form, did not rise up to confront Dorothy and Ruth, so Dorothy kept running toward the hangar where she'd left the Corsair.

"Sweet salvation," Ruth whispered when she saw the planes in the hangar. "I got the Mustang."

Dorothy let her go, running for the Corsair she'd brought in. And if the Mustang failed? Had been sitting too long? It was only three hours, Dorothy told herself. Only three. Beneath her feet, the deck rumbled and Dorothy launched herself at the Corsair's wing. The plane felt more steady, even if the craft around it was protesting.

Much as it had been the first time, Dorothy had no time for proper pre-fight checks and prayed the plane would do its job. "Hold together, baby," she whispered as if those words had become part of the ritual. She glanced out the windows to Ruth, and, with the radio still dead, gestured with two fingers toward the end of the hangar. They would taxi out the way she had before, but this time, they'd leave a souvenir. Or five.

The Corsair was fully loaded – she had insisted and Minsky hadn't balked – and Dorothy could see the Mustang was, too. Whatever the gremlins had tried to access in an attempt at communication or travel, they hadn't tried the countless weapons on the aircraft they'd swallowed. Perhaps it was easier to understand and manipulate hands and mouths, but as this idea crossed Dorothy's mind, the cold press against her skull returned and with it, the scramble of gremlin hands inside her.

Screaming did not dislodge the sensation; her awareness of the plane dwindled even as it began to taxi forward, and all that remained was the cold seep of black water against her bones. Inside her skull, every thought was buoyed by the brack.

Just out, the brack whispered.

Split the sky, the cold demanded.

Dorothy pushed the sensation away, as if sweeping back a blanket on a hot summer's night. It was heavy and clung, but she kicked free. Nausea drenched her and the world threatened to go black again.

"Y-you can vomit or you can f-fly this goddamn plane, Sakata," she said, if only to hear her own voice.

The familiarity erased the sibilant strangeness of the gremlins, the edge of the hangar sharp and abrupt, and the Corsair was falling – flying. She couldn't tell which until she felt the air as she had never felt it before, a living and breathing thing much as she was. A living and breathing thing that she knew how to move through. She dived down the corridors of metal, the Corsair steady under her control. At her side, Ruth followed her lead.

The gremlin vessel was as Dorothy remembered, an obstacle course of metal and peril. But her hands were steady on the stick, guiding the Corsair as if they had flown the course a hundred times before. She thought of Ina, of other possible pilots within the structure, but pressed these notions back; if she stopped to consider all the reasons for not blowing this thing to hell, they would never stop it from swallowing more and more aircraft.

Black tendrils of barely contained water made themselves known before Dorothy few much further. They obscured the windshield for a long breath before pulling themselves together into arms. Impossibly thin, oblong, naked; the gremlins Dorothy remembered from her first time aboard began to whisper their demands in chilled tones. She could not help but notice the way they avoided the propellers – as if they had learned a lesson from the first time.

Dorothy fought to follow the curving corridor, mindful of only that, of needing to drop the bombs before they exited. She could not yet see daylight around the curve, could see no end to the course, and told herself to stay steady, stay true. The gremlins swarmed in more numbers now, blackening her windshield until she could not see. She refused to let panic tighten her hands; instead, she let loose a missile, which corkscrewed deeper into the ship and burst apart in a cloud of gremlins. They fell shrieking, dissolving as if they had never been. The others withdrew to study from a distance, rushing in her wake.

"Good to know," she said.

She banked around the next curve and saw the exit she had been seeking; daylight burned bright path down this corridor, the blinding warmth allowing Dorothy to breathe easier. How much time would have passed? What of her family and the camps? Her throat tightened.

At her side, Ruth gave her the thumbs up and Dorothy echoed it. They were good to go, and she let Ruth loose her bombs first, following quick on her tail. The shadow of the Mustang swept over the Corsair as they flew toward the portal, and then, a rushing tide of gremlins.

Dorothy could not tell if they were trying to push the plane out or pull her back in; she felt a final ghostly coldness cross her skull and drain down her neck as she dropped every bomb she carried into the metal maw behind her. As the bombs began to blossom in the belly of the beast, the coldness departed as if swallowed.

The Corsair burst from the vessel into blue skies and Dorothy spied Ruth's Mustang already a fair distance ahead. Dorothy moved toward her, and they turned in tandem, wanting eyes on the massive storm. Dorothy expected the entire thing to erupt in a violent tornado of fire, but the explosions were more contained than that, rocking the entire thing loose rather than destroying it outright. Every bomb they set off ignited another inside the vessel, each explosion vaporizing the clouds that cloaked it.

The clouds disintegrated to reveal what looked more like an untethered and floating city than a singular ship. Dorothy had never seen its like – it was larger than four air carriers – dozens upon dozens of structures crafted from space-worn metal rising from a ragged platform of roaring engines. The dark walls were occasionally pierced by what appeared to be windows, some glowing with light, while smoke vented from spires and other rooftop structures. The base of the city vessel exhaled a massive cloud of black smoke as a fighter squadron screamed its approach. The radio crackled back to life.

Dorothy was jolted from the strange poetry of the whole thing by the idea that it might be shot down in the wake of its uncloaking. She reached for her headset, struggled to get it on, to tell them to stop, but even as she did, she saw the upward motion of the ship city. It churned more smoke and debris as it went, clawing a wide path of black smoke across the summer-blue sky, and before the fighters could intercept, it was gone. The entire world shuddered as the vessel burst through the atmosphere, dead planes trailing in its wake.

Without the city ship's influence, the planes plummeted to Earth. Dorothy could only watch from a safe distance as they did, guiding her own plane back to Mines Field. In her headset as she neared, she heard the now-familiar rumble of Minsky's voice.

"—everything going to take you eight months, Sakata?"

She closed her eyes for a long moment, only breathing as the plane rumbled around her. She knew landing would change everything and she didn't want everything to change. She wanted, very much, to keep flying until she ran out of sky, and then go a little further.

"I'm usually . . . much quicker," she eventually said, his laughter like thunder in her ears.

When she landed, everything was much as she had left it; the war was not over and her people were not free, even if she had rattled the gremlins loose. London, Tokyo and Berlin had all reported clear skies ever since Dorothy's "recon" mission; sometimes, Dorothy told Minsky and Avery over a beer one night, recon took a little longer than normal. Sometimes.

Dorothy wanted to ask Minsky about the camps, but their administration was out of his hands. She saw how this weighed on him, his eyes saying things he often could not; she saw how it bowed his shoulders and set his jaw every time their paths crossed. She supposed it should have been enough that her own family was free, that for her effort they had been allotted a small house with a beautiful garden, a soft lawn, and a view of the ocean. Her parents were safe and so too her aunt, but it wasn't enough.

Despite all she had done, they took her license and considered her an enemy alien, ineligible for flight. And she knew they watched her. Whether through Minsky or other means, they watched, just as she always watched the skies.

Ruth was given much the same; Ruth, who couldn't wrap her mind around the time variance between Earth and the gremlin vessel. She felt as though the world had moved on, so stayed in the skies as much as they let her. Even among the WASPs, she was a strange creature, often found talking to herself. Voices in her head, she might have said, if they wouldn't have yanked her planes for the honesty. When she and Dorothy drank, it was in a shared silence that neither found uncomfortable or in need of breaking.

It was no surprise then, that it was Ruth and Minsky who found her after she'd stolen her way into a Mines Field hangar, planning to take a Black Widow on a little night flight.

She was admiring the lines, so like the experimental XD-2 she and Ruth and Ina had taken up, but sleeker, darker, more ready for war.

She looked at them and they at her, and if they ever contemplated telling her no, if they ever contemplated tackling her to the ground and turning her over to the MPs, they didn't say a word. Ruth slid under the plane's belly, cracked the hatch, and stepped inside. Dorothy looked at Minsky, eyebrows raised. Some of the horror was gone from his eyes, even if she felt it still lingering about his edges; he needed this as much as she did. To fly, to be free for a little while.

"Pretty certain we haven't got all night," he said. He opened the hatch to the front compartment and climbed inside, taking the gunner's seat.

Dorothy cranked the propellers, then followed Minsky inside, stowing the ladder and securing the hatch before buckling herself in. There was a low tremor in her hands, that old excitement she'd always known after climbing into a cockpit. She pulled the shoulder harness tight and exhaled.

"There's clouds on the horizon," Dorothy told them, and hoping the clouds were the gremlin disturbance she longed for. To fly again. To get in the sky and *do* something. She failed to keep the excitement out of her voice. "All things being unequal between here and there, I'd say we have as long as we like."

Instead of a Loving Heart

Jeremiah Tolbert

I hate it here. It is too cold for my motors, and it never stops snowing, but Dr Octavio says that the weather is conducive to his experiments. I'm still not certain that what he is working on isn't meant to replace me. He tells me impatiently that it isn't, but I live in constant fear of it. I have nightmares that he will withhold the fuel that is my sustenance, that my parts will run down slowly until they can no longer nourish my brain while the rest of me turns to red dust. No oil can would bring me back.

It is a terrible sort of death; one that I could sit back and watch unfold in gruesome detail. I want to go quickly, when the time comes.

We are somewhere among the tallest mountains of the world. When we arrived, I was locked away in a cargo hold, so I don't know exactly where. Our home is a small, drafty castle and a separate laboratory. Dr Octavio had the locals construct the lab before he tested the new death ray on their village. There's very little left there. In my little bit of spare time, I try to bury the bodies and collect anything useful to the doctor's experiment.

My primary duties consist of keeping the castle's furnace running and clearing the never-ending snow from the path between the two buildings. Sometimes, it falls too fast for my slow treads and shovel-attachment to keep up with and I find myself half-buried in the snow. It is horrible on my gears when this happens, but I use heavy-weight oil now and it helps.

It is one of the few benefits of my metal frame that I appreciate. Life in this contraption is like being wrapped in swaddling clothes. I wonder if I would feel anything if my casing caught on fire? I need to ask the doctor when he isn't in one of his moods.

I am plowing fresh snow from the path when the wind begins to blow harder than usual. I swivel my cameras and spot Lucinda's flying machine landing on the rocky field behind the castle. Dr Octavio calls it a helio-copter. It is the perfect transportation for a jewel thief of her skill; painted black, with stylized diamonds on the sides. She calls it the *Kingfisher* because it can hover above her prey. It is faster and more agile than a zeppelin, her previous method of transportation.

I feel a twinge of happiness that she has caught up with us, even though it will send the doctor into a fit of anger. Before the Protectorate destroyed our previous laboratory, they argued and she left without telling me goodbye. Dr Octavio grumbled the next day about money. Often, Lucinda became stingy and demanded "unreasonable results", so said the doctor.

Dr Octavio assembled this new fortress on a very tight budget. We have no automated machine-gun turrets, or shock troops. We do not even have rabid yetis to protect the compound. There is only me and my flamethrower attachment against whatever is out there. The death ray broke down due to the cold.

I roll up the path as fast as my treads let me. Lucinda climbs out of the *Kingfisher* wrapped in a scarlet cloak, her trademark color. Her raven hair is braided into ponytail that flails in the wind like a dangerous snake. When she sees me, she smiles. I examine myself for a reaction. I cannot find one.

I have no heart, like the tin woodsman from the Baum books I read as a child. Only he was lucky enough to lose his body a piece at a time.

"Zed! What are you doing out in the cold?" she says. She uses the name Octavio gave me, Z-03. I try not to imagine what it was like for my predecessors.

"I must keep the path clear of snow for the doctor," I answer in my monotone, mechanical voice. I hate it nearly as much as the loss of my hands; I once prided myself on my ability to tell jokes. Now even the funniest punch line falls flat. "I saw you land. Come into the castle where it is warm."

She shakes her head. "I need to see Father immediately."

"He left me with orders that he is not to be disturbed."

Her smile fades. I cannot disobey Dr Octavio's orders, she knows this. My body inflicts unbearable pain when I do.

"Fine then. Lead the way."

I plow a path around the castle to the servant's entrance into the kitchen and allow Lucinda inside while I swap my shovel attachment for my manipulators. They have pressure sensors.

Inside the kitchen, I put a kettle on the stove while Lucinda warms herself beside the radiator. "The tea will be ready in a few minutes," I say.

She doesn't answer, and I turn to see what has captured her attention. She has uncovered my easel and is looking at the latest of my failures. "Hmm? That'll be fine, Zed." She takes a seat at the small table in the corner. I recover the painting and roll to be opposite her. She reaches out and holds one of my manipulators in her hand. Six PSI. Six PSI.

"What's his mind like these days?" she asks. She looks at me when she speaks, unlike the doctor.

"It's fine," Dr Octavio says, voice full of irritation, from the doorway. I hadn't noticed the gust of cold air. How could I? "What are you doing in here?" He points at me. "You're *my* servant, not hers. Get out there. I nearly broke my back on the ice, you useless heap of scrap!"

When I see the doctor, I see him in his youthful prime. He has designed me that way. Where his aged voice comes from, I see a stretched-out man with fidgeting hands and fevered blue eyes. I know that he must be decrepit by now. I do not know exactly how old he is, but he rants about the American Civil War as if he were there.

Lucinda gives me an apologetic look, and I roll outside, but stop on the opposite side of the door. I extend my microphone and maximize the gain.

"I saw the village, or what was left of it anyway. So you're a mass murderer now?" Lucinda shouts. "What did those people ever do to you?"

"They knew too much," Dr Octavio says, raising his voice to match hers. "The Protectorate found me too easily last time.

No one must know we are here. But you needn't worry. The death ray failed to function afterwards," he grumbled, sounding like a child with a broken toy.

"Thank God for small miracles," she says. "I want to inspect the weapon, to be sure that you're not lying again, *Father*." It is quiet for a moment, and I fear that I might have made a sound. No one comes to the door. Finally, Lucinda continues. "What are you working on now?"

"I don't have to tell you that!" Dr Octavio nearly shrieks. "It's not a weapon, if that's what you want to know."

"It had better not. The Germans are looking for weapons, and if I find out you have been dealing with them, you will learn the true meaning of poverty." If I could shudder, I would at the tone of Lucinda's voice. She can become as cold as this mountaintop when dealing with the subject of money.

They argue about money for an hour, and then the subject turns to Lucinda's latest heists, so I hurry away to the path.

I still sleep, much to the doctor's dismay. Sleep is a requirement of the mind as well as the body. Mostly I have nightmares, but sometimes I have a real dream. I dream that I still have hands that can paint, that can sculpt, that can play the piano. In the dream I have six arms, and I do all at once. When I drift awake, there are only the manipulators, reporting pressure. Zero PSI. Zero PSI.

Lucinda left in the evening, and Dr Octavio retired to his chambers. My internal clock tells me that it is six a.m. and I must wake the doctor. I take the crude elevator that he has rigged to allow me access to all the floors. His bedroom chamber is dark and baroque, full of intricately carved furniture. The set was a gift from Lucinda last Christmas, and somehow he managed to retrieve it from our previous fortress in the South Pacific.

"Dr Octavio, it is a new day," I say tonelessly. He groans and rolls out of the bed, apparently a well-muscled man in his mid-twenties. Well-endowed. He shuffles into the bathroom and waves me away. "Go clean or something, Zed."

I obey.

★   ★   ★

Once, Lucinda asked Dr Octavio why he chose me, an unknown painter, to be the brain of his servant-machine. His reply is burned into my mind.

"Because he is an artist. Art serves no purpose but to distract. How does it improve the lives of men? Science is ultimately the true path of all men, even artists like him. Unfortunately, he is stubborn."

Dr Octavio kidnapped me from my Paris studio, removed the brain from my body, and implanted it in a machine, to prove a philosophical point to no one in particular.

That is how the man's mind works.

"Zed, I need your assistance in the laboratory," he says to me from the doorway. His words hang in the air amid the fog of his breath. How long has it been since he last asked me to assist him?

I turn from my shoveling and join him inside the laboratory. I wait for my lenses to clear. When they do, I see his latest experiment.

Rows and rows of vacuum tubes connected with haphazard wiring line the walls, connected to more arcane machinery that I have no words to describe. Some of the machinery resembles parts of me, especially a manipulating arm that resembles mine, but significantly more advanced. I feel a deep pang of greed at the sight of it. The emotion surprises me, and I relish the sensation.

"What is your bidding, Dr Octavio?" I ask.

He motions toward the arm. "I need you to interface with this. Come over here."

Dr Octavio attaches me to the arm, and I flex it, checking the wiring. It seems good. It relays seven decimal pressures to my brain, far more sensitive than my own manipulators. "What would you like me to do with it?"

He shrugs, his attention already returning to a workbench crisscrossed with wiring. "I don't care. Give it a through testing for range of motion and dexterity."

"Can I retrieve a few things?" I ask.

"Fine, but don't be long. I have other tasks to attend to," he barks.

I collect my easel and paints from the kitchen and bring them to the laboratory. Dr Octavio impatiently hooks me to the arm again, and I take up my brush.

An hour later, I want to weep. I haven't been able to achieve this level of technique since Paris. I call for the doctor to inspect my work.

He picks up the canvas and examines it passionlessly. He walks to the furnace and throws it inside the burner. "The quality of the arm is sufficient. You may go."

It is spring when Lucinda returns. The snow has turned into freezing rain, and I've been using my flamethrower to clear ice from the path for a week. Clean the path before sunrise because I cannot sleep. After the Doctor caught me using the arm late one night, he has kept the lab padlocked. He shattered the sculpture with a sledgehammer.

Lucinda's helio-copter lands quietly and I watch as she leads several gray-uniformed men to the laboratory. They make short work of the lock, and I hear them breaking things inside the laboratory. Several minutes later, they leave with armfuls of equipment. Lucinda walks down the path to me.

"I'm sorry to do this to you, Zed," she says, and I can see that her face is bruised. "I owe money to some people." She stares at the castle for a moment, and then curses. "I'm sorry I'm leaving you here with him. One day I'll come back for you."

"Will you be all right?" I ask.

She forces a smile, and I almost believe her when she says yes. "There's a war breaking out in Europe. The Germans have taken Poland. It will be a good time for someone in my profession." The men come out of the helio-copter and shout down at us in German. They have guns. Lucinda walks back to the helio-copter, slipping only a little. She waves at me from the cockpit when the *Kingfisher* takes off.

"Failed projects," Dr Octavio says when he inspects the damage. "All junk. They damaged my masterpiece, but it will only take a week to get back up to speed." He grins and rubs his hands together. He enjoys a good setback. They give him an opportunity to refine work that his manic brain would not otherwise allow.

"What is this project?" I ask.

"Why should I tell you?" He says and squints at me. "I'm not going to let you use the arm again. You'll waste its potential on worthless doodles."

"Will it replace me?" I ask.

The doctor muses for a moment. "I think that in the end, it will replace all of us."

"What is it?"

He grins again. "It is my greatest invention. A machine that will be smarter than me. A thinking machine, capable of creating machines more intelligent than itself."

"How can you create a machine that is smarter than yourself? Isn't that a . . . paradox?" I ask.

Dr Octavio laughs. "No, it is not, but it is a good question. To create a mind smarter than my own, I only have to improve upon my design and give it a desire to further improve upon itself. By eliminating the flaws in my own mind, it will be superior. Then from its heightened perspective, it will analyze itself and continue to improve, all much faster at thinking than even the Human Adding Machine." He taps his head. "It will be the Supreme Intellect, my ultimate achievement, and the ultimate achievement of science!"

"So the arm is for creating?" I ask, fear growing in me. I can sense my brain sending signals to a non-existent body. Run. Do something. The body does not obey these primitive signals.

"It will create others in its own image. I suspect humanity will become extinct in a century at the most," he says. "I have more vacuum tubes being air-dropped this afternoon. Go wait for them, and bring them straight to me when they arrive."

I obey.

There is no doubt in my mind that these machines will have no use for me. They will create themselves to be capable of serving all their needs. They won't need assistants. Nor will they need artists.

I roll down the unused road to the old village, keeping an eye on the sky for the airdrop. I maximize the gain on my microphone, listening for the hiss of radio static.

I awake from my nightmares to the sound of explosions. The castle shudders beneath me. Outside, it is raining in the darkness. There are voices inside the castle, speaking in British accents. I can hear Dr Octavio calling for me above it all – he is using the radio commander. "Come quickly! Kill all who stand in your way!"

I attach my flamethrower as quickly as my manipulators allow and then I roll out into the hallway. British commandos spill through a break in the wall. They ignite like cheap wax candles and flail around uselessly. I press past them toward the elevator.

Dr Octavio has fallen silent, and I suspect he has been captured. When I arrive at the highest floor of the castle, a commando opens fire with a machine gun. Bullets ricochet from my armor-plating and kill him.

Allen Stone, leader of the Protectorate, has Dr Octavio handcuffed to a chair. "Tell us where the super-weapon is, Octavio!"

"What super-weapon?" the doctor asks. His eyes search around him wildly. Blood trickles from a cut in his upper lip. He sees me. "Zed, tell them I am not making a weapon!"

I roll from the shadows. Stone and his men train their weapons on me. I can barely make the words. "It is in the laboratoryyy . . ." My mechanical voice shuts down.

As my body shuts itself down, piece by piece, the world seems to speed up.

Dr Octavio lurches forward in his chair roaring. One of the commandos spins and pulls the trigger. The gunshot deafens me, overriding all sound from my microphone. "Destroy everything down there," Stone says on his radio. My microphone shuts down.

Then the cameras. I am in darkness.

It starts as a buzzing sound. Someone is speaking to me. My cameras come back on line and focus sluggishly.

"He can hear me now?" Stone asks the balding technician in a white parka. The technician nods and backs away.

"Stone," I say.

"Good. It's time to leave," Stone says, cigar clenched between his teeth. We stand on the open field beneath his zeppelin. The laboratory billows smoke below us. Nothing will have escaped the fire.

"I am waiting for someone," I say.

He looks away uncomfortably. "That wouldn't be Octavio's daughter, would it? Infamous jewel thief Lucinda Octavio, aka 'The Ghost?'"

"Yes," I say. I feel something familiar rising from the depths of my reptilian brain. Fear – I have almost missed you.

"I guess you have no way of knowing, living out here . . ." His voice trails off. I stare at him. If he doesn't say something soon, I will set ablaze with the remaining fuel in my thrower.

"She's been captured by the Nazis." He pauses, considering his words. He stares at me with a perplexed expression, one I recognize as the result of searching me for outward signs of emotion. I feel sorry for him. "Seems she tried to steal from Hitler's private stash. They've been trumpeting it in their papers and on the radio. Truth is, we've been afraid she would lead them to Octavio. That's why we moved so quickly when you radioed us."

I try to pretend that I don't feel anything. I don't have a heart.

"Look, mate," Stone says, "come with us and you can make a difference in this topsy-turvy world. I can't promise you anything, but maybe you can rescue her. British Intelligence has a lot of questions for her. What do you say, Zed?"

"My name is not Zed," I say. "But yes. I will come with you."

"What is your name then?"

"Call me Tin Man."

Stone shrugs and walks up the ramp into the gondola hanging a few feet above the ground. I turn my cameras to watch the smoke from the laboratory for a few more minutes, until I can be sure that I will never doubt that every last bit of Octavio's last experiment is gone.

Steel Dragons of a Luminous Sky

Brian Trent

Li Yan, brigade commander of the National Revolutionary Army and secret lieutenant of the Luminous Sky, spat into his goggles, wiped the lenses, and refitted them over his eyes to watch the *qilin* galloping up from the beach toward Qiantang River Bridge. Its red eyes burned holes in the choking smoke, and more red lay behind it: the crackling sampan villages and embers of Hangzhou Bay were like fireflies in the air.

The American pilot, Eva Eagels, tracked the galloping shape with her pistol. "I see it," she muttered. "That one of ours, Li?"

Li winced as another Japanese shell exploded overhead. "It's Chinese," he answered evasively.

"Well I hope it swallowed something useful," Eva said, lowering her weapon. "Otherwise we're in shit creek without a paddle."

He regarded the chestnut-haired aviatrix beside him, her face streaked in soot, her knuckles white around her trusty M1911, and her alert gaze studying the hellfire rolling up from the beach. "That passes for proverbs in the West?" he asked.

She opened her mouth to reply when another explosion rocked the darkness, showering them with sand. Against the red fires, the giant robots were descending like old gods returned. They resembled samurai. Blue-hot plumes of flame fanned from their boots, controlling their terrible descent toward the beach. Li supposed their construction had as much to do with Japanese tradition as with psychological warfare. Even as murky silhouettes they cut a nightmarish sight – twenty-foot-tall machines in the shape of men, overlapping steel scales cladding their frames, and the decorative *kabuto* they had for heads displaying curling horns like prehistoric monsters. Their appearance conjured not-quite-vestigial memories, too, of wood-block paintings Li had seen showing past invasions of China . . . the ruthless hordes of Genghis pouring through the Great Wall.

In the predawn gloom the Japanese navy had arrived and quickly reduced the defenders' junks to smoldering flotsam on the bay. Next the turrets had turned their attention on the beach defenses themselves. Only then had the actual invasion begun, not as troops from the sea or battalions from the land, but as machines dropping down from the sky . . .

Li craned his neck to the heavens. Stars and moon were lost behind the pall of diesel fires and gunpowder, but he wasn't interested in such lofty things. His eyes scanned for the ominous shadow of Tengu Castle, floating high and terrible above Shanghai.

"Li!" Eva tugged at him. "Here it comes!"

He glanced back to the beach. The *qilin* was nearly at Qiantang River Bridge, weaving around what remained of the barbed wire and Cointets. Its movements were gyroscopic, hips snapping fast adjustments as it avoided debris, bodies and descending robots. Those flaring eyes spotted him where he crouched on the hilltop, and then the *qilin* leapt full onto the ancient bridge.

One of the hovering robots shot a spotlight onto the fleeing creature.

"Run, boy!" the American cried.

The stuttering muzzle flash of Gatling guns illuminated the miasma.

Qiantang River Bridge had spanned the river for a hundred years; now it shredded into sawdust around the weaving, galloping qilin.

For an instant, Li thought the machine had been obliterated. Then his heart lifted as it darted out of the sawdust-haze and scrambled up the hill toward him. The hilltop was thumped by shrieking 50-caliber rounds, forcing Li and Eva to duck. The qilin leaped the hillcrest, soaring over Li's head; he had a view of its smooth steel chassis, the actuators and steel coils throbbing wildly. Then it landed nimbly in the reedy wetland below them, turning its vaguely lion-like head to regard Li expectantly.

Li tugged at the American. "We can leave now!"

She scrambled up and ran toward her Fiat CR.32, which waited where she'd landed hours ago like a patient bird on the high banks opposite them.

"Eva, no! Not that way!"

The pilot had taken two steps toward the embankment when suddenly a shell screamed past them and struck the plane. The detonation of fuel tanks blew her, Li, and the *qilin* backward, and all went dark.

When Li came to, he was being dragged by the boot through the muddy banks of the bay. Flies swarmed around him, attracted by his sweat. The *qilin*, dutifully pulling him out of harm's way, left him by the water's edge and then eagerly sprinted back to fetch Eva; a moment later she came jogging alongside it, a dark expression on her face. The *qilin*'s leonine countenance remained fixed in a serrated grin, its scarlet eyes swiveling in their rubber sockets to regard the Japanese navy filling the bay.

"Eva, you're alive!" Li said stupidly, and for a moment his eyes moistened. He thought he'd spent all tears at the loss of Shanghai's beach perimeter. The surge of emotion made him appreciate that the war wasn't over yet, even if Shanghai had fallen.

Don't let the war deaden you.

The words from his eldest brother Qimei came back to him. Growing up in a small household, Li had always idolized his brother, seeing in Qimei everything he wanted to be: Handsome, confident, courageous. It was hero worship as well as brotherly adoration, and Li's enlistment had as much to do with his brother's short-lived military career as with the need to defend China herself.

The night Li was to ship out to Shanghai, his brother embraced him on their bamboo porch and whispered the hard-earned advice: *I've seen how war can deaden a person, little brother. I've seen men transformed into shambling husks, as if the horrors of battle had killed their spirit. Promise me that*

*won't happen to you, Li. Don't lose your smile, even if you must
hide it at times.*

"You're alive," Li told Eva again, and he nodded. "I
thought . . ."

If Eva noticed his tears, she was pretending not to so he
could save face. Against the clouds and fiery bay, she was as
wild-eyed as the demon empress herself, black hair a tangled
mass about her face. Another woodblock flashed into Li's
mind: a female hungry ghost, escaped from one of the Eight
Hells to feast on the living of *zhonguo*.

"They blew up my *Damsel*!" the American raged. "Just get
me some replacement wings, Li, and I'll take back the skies,
gun chattering like the doomed brothers in *Hell's Angels*." She
glared and jabbed a finger toward the qilin. "I hope this *thing*
was worth it, goddamn it all!"

Li squatted in the mud. "*Qilin*, what did you find?"

The machine sat back on its haunches with a wheezing squeal
like rusted door hinges. It bowed its head, jaws swiveling open,
like a dog bringing back a bone. It disgorged something from its
throat and then looked at them expectantly.

The *qilin* were designed for battlefield reconnaissance and
delivery of supplies. While not combatants, they were designed
to do whatever was necessary to obtain things their sensors
deemed worthwhile.

Li blinked.

The thing the machine had disgorged was a young Chinese
woman.

For perhaps half a minute, Li stared, trying to accept what
he was seeing on its own terms. He wondered if the *qilin* had
gone berserk, abducting some poor peasant from the rice
paddies.

Eva peered over his shoulder. "Who the hell is she?"

The woman was unconscious. She looked young, slender,
almost frail, with delicate bone structure suggesting noble
stock. She also wore a peculiar amulet tightly around her neck.

"Assist me, please," Li said, taking the sleeping woman by
the arms.

"Why?"

"If we leave her here, she'll be taken as a comfort woman for the Japanese."

Together, they bore the mystery woman toward the water. "But why did the *qilin* grab *her?*"

It was a good question. Li mulled over the last orders he'd been given from his superiors: Find the *qilin* and recover its catch. It has something from the Luminous Sky for the war effort.

At the water's edge, Li fidgeted with his ring.

Something from the Luminous Sky for the war effort . . .

He checked his ring, made sure the jade dragon sigil was facing east. Then he held it over the girl's face and squeezed the ring.

Pale, fuzzy light sprang from the dragon and rippled over her face.

"It's a girl, Li," Eva chided. "You really need a flashlight to tell?"

Ignoring this, he directed the light to the unconscious woman's forehead. Golden calligraphy materialized under the beam, and Li gasped.

Luminous Sky!

She was Luminous Sky, just as he was!

For a moment he forgot about the invading robots and the loss of Shanghai's defenses along beach and bay. The Luminous Sky was *not* destroyed! There were others! Others besides *him* . . .

A top-secret agency formed after the First Sino–Japanese War, the Luminous Sky was tasked with defending the Middle Kingdom. Even in a country torn apart by tribal loyalties – local warlords tangling with Nationalists, Communists, dieselmages and Manchus – the Luminous Sky represented something all could agree on: the nation must be defended against the rising specter of the Rising Sun. Its top agents were known as "steel dragons".

Li scooped the girl back into his arms and waded out into the bay, keeping her head safely above the debris-strewn water. Eva splashed in behind him.

"Where the hell are we going, Li? Gonna walk to Sidney?"

He halted at an unsightly pile of flotsam. Tangled beams,

netting, and planks of ruined sampans floated unceremoniously on the water.

With his free hand, Li reached under one of the lacquered beams and found the secret knob. He twisted it.

Unseen pneumatic levers hissed. The water began to froth. The wreckage lifted up, like a weary animal, exposing a deep, dry gullet.

"Inside!" he said. "Quickly, Eva!"

Once within the secret, water-tight compartment, Li flicked the propeller switch, and the flotsam began drifting through the sizzling, fiery bay.

Leaving China in flames behind us, he thought.

Pushing out into the Sea of Japan.

"I've heard of junks before," Eva said, hunkered down in the depths of the secret watercraft. "But this is ridiculous, Li."

The interior of the vessel was little better than a cramped, damp closet. Li hunched over the mystery woman, emptying some his canteen onto a cloth and rubbing it over her lips. She came awake slowly. Li helped her drink, squeezing the cloth into her mouth. She sat up, wary of the low ceiling, and blinked dazedly in the gloom of the single wall-lantern.

"*You are safe for now*," he told her, speaking in Mandarin.

She nodded dreamily.

"*I am LiYan, Brigade Commander of the National Revolutionary Army*," he said, and then, quieter even though the American couldn't speak a word of Chinese, he said, "*I am also a Steel Dragon lieutenant of the Luminous Sky.*"

There. Her eyes glimmered in reaction to this. She glanced to the *qilin* which sat obediently beside them, its red eyes attentive.

"*My name is Xin*," she said at last.

She had a soft accent, vaguely Northern. Her skin, too, was ruddy, red-tinged; product of that cold country where even rice refused to grow and life was hard.

"Say," Eva interrupted, "You got a drink in this tub, Li? Hell, I'll even settle for some of that cheap local beer."

Ignoring this, Li helped Xin drink more from the canteen. The woman was fully awake now, and she drew herself into one cramped corner beside the *qilin*.

"*I was sent to recover you,*" Li explained, hoping she could shed some light on the next stage of the mission. "*The Luminous Sky also provided this craft . . .*"

The woman seemed to be studying Li's face. She turned next to Eva. Now that she was awake, there was something almost harsh about her gaze – something dangerous and bright, like tempered steel in the gloom.

Finally, she said, "*The steel dragons were being sent to the front. Our cars were converging well out of range of the Japanese naval guns . . .*" Her eyes narrowed. "*Or so we thought. As the last car came around the bend there was an explosion. We had been fired on from above – those robots were already coming down from Tengu Castle. I pulled myself out of the flaming wreck, and the next thing I remember was the screeching whine of their .50-caliber bullets all around me, and then . . .*" She patted the *qilin*'s metallic paw appreciatively.

"Glad to see we're all friends," Eva observed, pulling off her leather flying cap. She shook free her chestnut curls. "Li, you know I don't speak a lick of Chinese. Care to fill me in on what's going on?"

"She is Luminous Sky."

"Great! Except that *you're* Luminous Sky, too, and you didn't exactly save the day out there, you know?"

In perfect English, Xin added her voice to the conversation. "The Japanese invasion is being controlled by Tengu Castle," she said.

Eva sighed. "Not exactly news, sister."

"The Luminous Sky was sending its steel dragons – its highest agents – to infiltrate the castle and end the invasion."

"*What?*"

But Li felt a smile twitch at his lips, a smile born of desperate hope. The mysterious Luminous Sky, always inventive, always operating in the shadows. He believed in them. While the in-fighting of China's political factions had left the land vulnerable to attack, the Luminous Sky always operated in the service of the Mandate of Heaven.

After all, what was the mantra of the Luminous Sky?

All Under Heaven.

It was the ancient dream of a unified world. A world in

which peace was not a dream of poets but a daily, irrevocable reality. A world without borders. A world of one government, one law, one purpose.

Eva scoffed. "Tengu Castle is thousands of feet above us! Li, what's going on here? People say the Luminous Sky is crazy, and I'm starting to believe—"

Xin stood so swiftly, so suddenly that Eva reached for her Colt. The Luminous Sky agent strode to a section of the wall and pried open a hatch Li hadn't known was there.

"The Luminous Sky wishes to reach Tengu Castle," Xin said. She reached into the hatch and suddenly the junk began to rumble, exactly as if hidden engines were whirring to life. "Therefore, we shall reach Tengu Castle."

Li felt the junk lift up from the water. He and Eva exchanged an astonished look.

Outside, a black balloon had snapped open from hidden compartments. The core of the junk was listing into the air like a newborn cicada crawling out of its terrestrial shell and climbing into the night sky.

Xin smiled, and switching back to her vaguely accented Mandarin, said, "*All Under Heaven, Li.*"

It was called the *Lantern*, Xin told them.

Eva grumbled. She drew open the junk's door, revealing a sea of clouds around them and the fires of China glowing far, far below. The wind immediately leapt in through the opening, biting them all with icy fangs.

They had ascended above the fog of war into the clouds themselves, until it seemed they were skating along on a wispy sea. The starry firmament turned this dreamlike horizon into quicksilver, and the *Lantern* – born aloft by its ebony-colored balloon – glistened like a sea creature peeking up from the depths to consider the wonder of the firmament.

Eva pointed across the sea of clouds to a distant black shape floating perhaps ten thousand yards off. It looked like the tip of an island jutting up from a misty sea.

"Is that the castle?" she asked.

Xin nodded.

Eva gave a savage grin. "Know what a balloon buster is,

sister? Every flying ace worth her salt knows how to look for observation balloons and shoot them out of the sky. Its standard protocol: knock out the enemy's eyes. You think the Japs are any different? If we don't reach the castle before the sun comes up, we'll be a big black target hanging against the dawn sky."

"We will reach the castle," Xin said simply.

"By being at the mercy of the wind?"

"Are we?"

Li closed his eyes in the silence that followed and listened. Then he smiled for the second time that day. The *Lantern* was *not* beholden to the wind. He could hear the whir of propellers beneath them, pushing them straight toward the flying castle of their enemy.

But Eva slammed the hatch door shut and said, "Li, get that idiotic grin off your face! Have you ever met this dame before? How do you know she's not a spy for the enemy? Maybe this is their plan: scoop up the last Luminous Sky – *you* – and bring him to the castle on a silver platter?"

His smile slipped a little. "She has the Luminous Sky mark . . ."

"I have a skull tattoo on my arm. That doesn't make me a bone doctor. You're betting our lives on blind faith!"

The blind faith of his brother, Li thought. Qimei had spoken with unflinching worship of the Luminous Sky. He was a true believer, and therefore Li had been one too . . . enough of a believer to seek the group out and pledge himself to their cause.

Still, some of what the American was saying snuck through Li's certainty, and he gazed at Xin with a sudden flash of paranoia.

Come to think of it, she didn't look especially Chinese. Not a Han, at any rate . . .

"You are from the American regiment," Xin said to Eva.

"That's right," the aviatrix replied, not appreciating the subject change. "The Flying Tigers. We're not here in an official capacity, but our President knows it's only a matter of time before we get drawn into the war. Besides, can't have our Chinese brothers and sisters falling before the Jap war machine. So we get a paycheck and open license to fight."

"So you're mercenaries?"

Eva stiffened. "We get paid, sure, but that don't mean we don't believe in this. And no salad would make me work for the enemy."

Li sighed and, switching to Chinese, said to Xin, "*Salad, an American euphemism for—*"

"Greenbacks," Xin answered swiftly in English. "I spent a year studying in Chicago."

He was startled. "The Luminous Sky sent you to America?"

"And to Paris the year before. And Berlin in 'thirty-four."

"You speak all those languages?"

Xin smiled politely. "My mother called me 'Bird of a Thousand Songs'."

Eva said scornfully, "That's terrific, sister. But let's keep on target here: How does reaching Tengu Castle end the invasion? Is your intention to somehow take control of the robots by using the Jap transmission tower? That's crap. You'd need the security codes!"

"The Luminous Sky has figured out a way to bypass the codes." Before the aviatrix could retort, Xin continued, "Control radiates out from the castle's tower, yes. Your America uses the same technique to control its Minutemen robots, broadcasting control signals from the Statue of Liberty. Paris utilizes the Eiffel Tower to control her *soldats en acier*. Switzerland, Britain, Spain, they all follow this model. Even Mussolini has control towers jutting like needles from the Pantheon's dome." She went silent for a moment, losing herself in a faraway land of contemplation. "And of course, Japan prefers its own method of *hakkō ichiu* to be mobile and aerial: Tengu Castle. If we can wrest control of the tower, we control its robots. We end the war."

Eva made a disgusted sound. "American technicians have tried inventing an override signal for years. You're saying that your secret little band has done something no Western nation could manage?"

"Well we did invent paper before you," Xin replied softly.

Li had to choke back a laugh.

Eva didn't smile, but she began to clean her pistol, rubbing a rag across the brown grip and iron sights in loving strokes.

"Look, if you think you can override the robots, that's swell. Just tell me what you need me to do."

"We may encounter resistance once we're at the castle," Xin said. "I shall need you to watch my back."

By way of answering, Eva cocked the Colt's hammer and grinned.

The *Lantern* crossed the airy gulf to Tengu Castle and now, only a hundred meters away, Li saw what distance had hidden before: sleek black shapes moving around the castle like sharks he had once seen while pearl-diving; ominous shapes hanging above him in the murky water. These shapes were black, nearly invisible and betrayed only by the winking of starlight around them as they made their lofty patrols.

"It's a dragonboat fleet," he breathed, and he looked to Xin for signs that the Luminous Sky had anticipated this.

Or for signs of treachery in her face, he thought. The American's doubts were growing like a toxic seed in his own mind. What if this was all a trap?

"I see now why you told me to ground my plane," Eva admitted. She had donned her flying cap and scarf again, out of habit, perhaps, or a pilot's superstition that they had talismanic powers of protection beyond simply protecting her from the chilling wind. "If we'd *flown* up here . . ."

"Even the best flying ace would have attracted the Japanese dragonboats' attention," Li finished for her. "It looks like the entire invasion force, aside from what they sent to soften the beach and bay."

Soften, he thought bitterly. *Now I know I'm a military man. Thousands of my countrymen have been "softened", and in the summer heat their dead bodies will grow soft indeed.*

The *Lantern* tilted backward slightly, like a rickshaw drawn by an over-eager driver. They were bearing down on Tengu Castle now, slipping silently past the dragonboats in the predawn darkness. Snow glittered on the curving tenchu-style castle roof.

Sure enough, a transmission tower stood out from the uppermost roof like a mighty acupuncture needle. Xin lifted a hatch and pulled out a length of black rope ladder, which she dropped over the Lantern's side and let unroll below them. "I'll go first, with Li behind me. Eva, I'm switching the *Lantern* over to manual control. While we're down there, you steady her until I can plant the override device and get back."

"I'm a Flying Tiger," Eva snapped, "Not a glorified balloon mistress!"

"Since we're fresh out of glorified balloon mistresses," Xin said crisply, "you'll have to do."

Li helped her clamber down the rope ladder while the American went to the manual wall-controls. The shingled rooftop was only meters below them. He was relieved to see the absence of guards; the thin, cold air precluded them from being stationed outside.

He followed Xin down the twisting ladder. The *Lantern's* propeller chassis fought against the wind; Eva fought to steady them.

When Xin reached the rooftop, she slipped on the icy surface; Li caught and steadied her. Snow like confectioner's sugar spilled off the shingles and fell, in dream-like slowness, to the roiling ocean of clouds.

"All Under Heaven," he said with a smile.

He expected she might grin at the small joke. Instead, she peered into his face, as if trying to read lines on an oracle bone.

"Do you believe in it?" she asked pointedly.

"Of course," he said defensively.

"I wonder how many do? China has returned to the Warring States period; it is all chaos. The foreign devils merely compound an underlying fracture." She fingered her amulet and craned her neck to regard the transmission tower, the blinking lights reflected in her eyes.

She took a step toward the tower. Li watched her go.

It seemed that someone punched him from behind, a sharp blow to his kidney. The snow in front of him splashed red, resembling the Imperial Japanese flag with its streaks of crimson lines.

"Xin!" he screamed – tried to scream – but a second bullet slammed into him. He pitched forward, lost his footing on the ice, and rolled to the edge of the shingles. He stopped just short of tumbling off the rooftop altogether.

From this angle, he could see Xin climbing the tower like a cautious spider ascending a weathervane.

Then he heard snow crunching under boots. His body was suddenly sluggish, and he could feel numbness spreading along his limbs. He managed to lift his head, staring up into the eyes . . .

. . . of Eva.

For a moment, all he could do was stare uncomprehendingly. Above her, the *Lantern* spun in a neat circle, like a balloon caught in a strange combination of drafts so that it rotated around and around, listing dangerously but going nowhere.

"You . . ." he began. "You were . . . my friend!"

Eva clucked her tongue. "We've known each other a goddam week. You set a low bar for friendship. Now . . ." She turned and aimed her Colt at Xin on the tower.

"No!" Li pleaded. "Please don't!"

"Don't what, Li?" Eva cooed. "Don't conclude my deal with Hirohito and be made a rich lady with a fleet of planes under my command and my own palace in the Orient?"

Xin was a tiny figure now, a delicate creature, only two-thirds of the way up now.

So close . . .

"You're not with the Americans?" Li asked Eva, trying to stall her.

"Remember what Odysseus told the Cyclops? 'I am Noman.' Same with Captain Nemo, whose very name means 'no man', beholden to no country, no people. Well, that's me!" The woman flashed a smile that was so warm, so brilliant and full of charm, that for an instant Li was half-convinced this was all some sort of joke: the blood on his back, the pain he felt, the spreading numbness, this was some silly prank, and all would be well, Xin *would* reach the top of the tower . . . the girl was only *six meters* from the zenith now!

"But no one can be that selfish!" Li whispered. "Why would you betray all of us?"

"Salad," Eva replied, laughing. She had removed her leather flying cap while in the *Lantern*, and now her chestnut curls flailed wildly around her head. "You're a Nationalist, Li. But there are other factions in China who were willing to parley with the Japanese, just to see your side defeated. They struck a deal with the emperor and prime minister. The best part? I get paid in triplicate. China, America, and Japan."

Li began to mount another stalling effort, but Eva shushed him.

"Want to see me slay a Steel Dragon?" the aviatrix purred, and she inched the pistol's sights higher, turned the barrel slightly into the wind, and fired at Xin.

She missed! he thought, hoped, prayed.

But she hadn't missed.

Xin was only two meters from the top of the needle, now, but something was wrong. She was no longer climbing. She was clutching the steel rungs as if she had fallen asleep there. A dark stain began to spread from the center of her back.

"What was that thing she kept saying?" Eva asked, aiming the muzzle a fraction of an inch higher. "What was it, Li?"

Li squinted at the Lantern spinning above them. "All . . ."

"All Under Heaven!" Eva laughed. "Watch me send your Luminous Sky friend straight to hell."

She closed one eye and steadied her aim. For a moment, it seemed to Li that she actually *was* summoning hell itself, for the aviatrix was suddenly aglow in fierce, crimson light from no discernible source. Then Li saw that something was leaping out of the *Lantern*'s hatch, dropping down upon them. Something with burning red eyes . . .

The *qilin* landed against Eva and knocked her sprawling. Whatever else she was – traitor, villain, spy – she was also as agile as a cat; she rolled over backward, avoided a lunge from the best's steel jaws, and fired point-blank into one of its eyes.

Sparks exploded, wires hissed like a nest of vipers. The *qilin* lunged again, head-butting her and driving the wind from her lungs. Despite only one eye functioning, it succeeded in clamping its jaws down on her pistol-hand. Eva's eyes bulged and her mouth stretched into a howling scream as she squeezed off more rounds into the creature's metal throat.

Then the qilin wrenched its head sideways. Eva's hand came away.

Li pulled himself to his feet. He looked toward Xin. She was barely hanging onto the tower's rungs. Her tunic was sodden with blood, yet he watched her pull herself up another rung.

One meter from the top now.

The *qilin* lunged again. Even wounded, Eva proved her agility; she nimbly sidestepped the beast, drew a smaller, concealed pistol from her jacket with her left hand, and aimed. The beast slid on the icy roof, turned to face her.

She fired into its other eye.

The *qilin* shook its head, wires dangling, smoke gushing from its ruined sockets. Still, it lunged for her, striking out at the last place it had seen her.

"To the right!" Li cried – but his voice wouldn't come. He collapsed, the strength leeching out of his limbs. He fell to his knees in the snow.

Eva tossed her last pistol to the roof's edge. The *qilin* leaped at the sound, lost its footing, and slid to within an inch of the last row of shingles. The aviatrix hurled herself into it, giving the needed push to send it rolling off into the endless sky. She laughed as it fell out of view.

Summoning his very last vestige of strength, Li held up his hand, palm out, to Eva. The hand with the ring from the Luminous Sky. The dragon sigil was still facing east.

He rotated it so it was gazing north.

In that same moment, Eva turned to face him.

Li squeezed the ring.

Light sprang from the sigil, only it wasn't the soft revealing beam he'd used to identify Xin. This was a golden lance that shot forward, hitting Eva squarely in her face. She shrieked wildly, and suddenly the air stank of burning flesh.

When the light went out, Eva was a half-melted, blinded thing. She flailed in a tight dance of agony, arms lashing out for him. Her boots slipped on the ice. She tumbled away, cursing wordlessly, and vanished after the *qilin*.

Li let out a satisfied sigh. His arm fell to his side. He tried to turn his head to see how Xin was progressing, but now his sight was failing, graying at the edges and, finally, turning dark.

In that private darkness, he heard his eldest brother's voice: *Don't lose your smile, Li, even if you must hide it at times.*

Li smiled, and with that smile, he died.

★   ★   ★

Xin pulled the medallion off her neck and, with the last of her strength, she slapped it against the tower antenna. The wind bit and shook her. Her hands were numb.

Below her, the rooftop door flung open, and the first of seemingly endless Japanese troops scrambled onto the snow like ants emerging for war. They fanned out, found Li's body. One soldier spotted her, and every rifle swung in her direction.

In the howling gale, she never heard the bullets.

Bloodied, entwined into the antenna like a wet flag, she grinned as much as Li's corpse was grinning below her.

All Under Heaven, she thought.

It was a Chinese concept that world peace was only possible when the divided countries of the world were united under a single banner. But China had failed miserably. War-torn Europe had failed. The Middle East, the Americas . . . all were squabbling barbarian states. None of them were deserving of the mandate. None of *them* could bring about a unified world.

Only one empire had come close, *so close*, to achieving global conquest. To achieving peace.

Xin fell from the tower, hitting the rooftop with a sickening collapse of bones. Her body slid along the shingles; a soldier reached for her but missed, and a moment later she was tumbling down from the sky and into the clouds.

The tower began broadcasting its secret signal, freezing the Japanese robots on the shore, yes, but also rippling out, nabbing every other communication tower from the Eiffel to the Statue of Liberty, bringing all under one control, one command . . .

Xin tumbled down to the ocean, weeping in joy.

One world, united, *under the Yassa of a resurrected Mongolian Empire.*

Long live the Great Khan, she thought, and even as she died, robotic feet all across the world marched to a new pulse.

Tunnel Vision

Rachel Nussbaum

Folks around here used to think the sky was freedom. Of course, that was before two things: air traffic control and prohibition. Now the sky's a mess with airships full of ritzy snobs flying round the globe, trying to find a place to wet their beaks. I don't like looking up at the sky at night these days. All those constant blinking lights give me a headache, and you can't see the stars or moon anymore. This isn't freedom.

I'll tell you what freedom is.

It's right beneath your feet.

Today, I got a spring in my step. As I walk down the street to the oddity shop, not even the darting shadows of the airships above can sour my mood. I've just made bank, got a list of several new clients begging me to give them top picks at my excavations, even got myself a new haircut. But I know that ain't the only reason I'm feeling so chipper.

I'm going to see Alma.

Around the World Curios is the poor man's sky tour. Despite the heavy traffic up in the clouds, not everyone can afford their own airship. Some can't even afford a pay-by-the-hour tour. Because of that, this little oddity shop has managed to carve out quite a niche for itself, selling wonders from half the world over and displaying odd old antiques and contraptions. I open the door and saunter in, past the Chinese jade sculptures and the mounted rhino heads on the walls. But I'm not looking at all that. I'm looking at the counter in the back.

And there she is. Alma.

Like everything else in her parent's shop, Alma's a bit odd.

Her full length dresses and bodices are at least twenty years out of fashion, I've always figured she wore them to attract business to the shop. For some reason, they've never made her look like an old maid. They make her look like she's from a different time. Mysterious. She's as pale as I am dark, and she's got these wild brown eyes. Her copper hair is as bright and shiny as a new penny, and she wears it long, although today it's twisted out of view under a large feathered hat, only a handful of locks spilling out from the sides. As I walk over to the counter, she looks up at me with those big, brown eyes, and lowers her book, shooting me a crooked smile.

I swear, that smile could make a dead man's heart start up again.

"Well, well," Alma says, looking me up and down. "If it isn't The Prospector."

"Is that what they're calling me now?" I ask.

"It wouldn't be the worst thing you've been called. What can I do for you, Lloyd?" she asks.

"Your father asked me to bring in anything interesting, got some iron pyrite and some pretty nifty quartz formations," I say, pulling the pouch out of my satchel and putting it down on the counter.

Alma puts her book down and starts thumbing through it, humming as she pulls out the pieces that interest her and casting aside the ones that don't.

Alma's brothers and I were friends back when we were youngsters in school together. They were supposed to help her run the shop, but being experts of antiquity around the world, they both ended up captaining a fleet of trade airships, networking and finding more business partners for their parent's shop along the way. Alma, though, while she accompanies them plenty, she never got a ship of her own. She stays here, managing the store, which was probably wise on everyone in the family's part – she's not exactly diplomatic. A real bearcat, and not afraid to hiss at anyone.

That's one of my favorite things about her.

"So Prospector," she says, picking up a chunk of fools gold and pulling it up to her eye to examine. "How's the dirt these days?"

"It's keen. I heard your brothers just came back from Egypt. Any chance they brought a mummy back? I always wanted to unravel one of those and see what they looked like in the center."

"They did get back from Egypt, but no mummy," she says. "Speaking of their airships, you never took us up on our offer. My father really wanted you to go up on the last trip with him."

"No thanks," I say, waving my hands. "Not a fan of heights."

"Not a fan of heights, but not afraid to drill down into the ground and be buried alive," she says.

I smile and shrug, and Alma shakes her head.

"You know, Father came across a drill once, a really old one. It was too big to display in the shop, though."

"All drills are really old. Mine was made at least fifty years ago, and that's being generous," I say.

"Really? How does it manage to stay running?" Alma asks.

"Those old beasts could last three hundred years. You should have seen what kind of condition old Jules was in when I refurbished her. Now you'd hardly recognize her," I say, feeling prideful just thinking about it.

"You named your drill Jewels?" Alma asks, looking amused. "Bit presumptuous on your part."

"Not Jewels, Jules. Like Jules Verne." I say.

Alma raises her eyebrows.

". . . The author of *Journey to the Centre of the Earth*?"

"The one and the same. Pretty clever, right?" I say.

"Imagine that! A well-read prospector," she says.

I beam at Alma and she shakes her head and chuckles.

"Well, just remember, the offer still stands. Father has a business proposition for you. He thought you'd enjoy the scenery during the meeting."

"That's swell. But he can talk to me about it on the ground, where I like to be," I say.

"Well, if you ever think about upgrading, you know where to find us," she says.

". . . Upgrading?" I ask, and I can feel my face turning up into a grin as I do.

Alma furrows her brows in confusion.

"Remind me," I say. "I remember this one fella, Erwin? The one you were sweet on?"

"His name was Ervin. And I was not sweet on him. His parents are good friends with mine. I thought he was a bimbo." Alma says, rolling her eyes.

"Right. Now, remember how he'd always show off that airship his pop bought him? Regular drugstore cowboy; he'd ask any girl who passed him on the street if they wanted to take a ride to Paris with him—".

"He did not ask *every* girl," Alma laughs.

"Right, right," I say, waving my hand. "So correct me if I'm wrong, but I've been hearing he got into some trouble with air traffic control recently. I heard – again, correct me if I'm wrong – that when he stopped through customs on his way back from Singapore, they found him with a case of herbal liqueur under a stack of silk."

Alma looks down and scratches her wrist.

"It's true," she says.

"Now I ask, what do you think good old Ervin was up to yesterday?" I ask.

"He's still in jail. His parents are so ashamed of him they won't post his bail," Alma says, trying to suppress her smile.

"That's a damn shame. Know where I was yesterday?" I ask.

"Why don't you tell me?"

"I drilled twenty-two miles out from the quarry and struck a gold bearing quartz vein. Surfaced and sold enough gold to Avery Jewelers to pay for the next three trips to the grocers. Got back in my drill, drilled down to the speakeasy in Twin Pike, and you know what I did there?"

"You had yourself a Scotch," Alma says, smirking.

I grin.

"I had myself a Scotch," I nod.

"Fair point. Now let me make mine . . ."

Alma pushes me the pouch of rejected stones, opens the cash register, and slides a few coins into my hands. I glance down at them for a moment before nodding and pocketing them.

"Good deal," I say.

"The price is always right down at Around the World

Curios," she says in a singsong voice. "Now are you going to beat it, or am I going to have to give you the bum's rush?"

She winks, and it makes me feel weak in the knees.

"One more thing," I say.

I reach into my satchel and pull out the small black spiral I'd been saving, and set it on the counter top.

"A fossil?" she asks, picking it up to examine.

"An ammonite," I nod.

"Hmm. It's in pretty good condition. How much you asking for?" she asks.

I can feel my cheeks flush and I clear my throat.

". . . It's um, not for sale. I'm giving it to you," I say.

Alma looks up at me then, and for the first time in a long time, she looks like she doesn't know exactly what to say. I use her rare moment of stunned silence to regain my composure.

"Well, since it's yours now, you *could* sell it. But you'd be breaking a poor old prospector's heart," I say, tracing a tear down my cheek.

Alma looks up at me with those beautiful brown eyes, and raises an eyebrow.

"So level with me. You got a never-ending supply of gold, crystals and gems at your fingertips, and out of all that, you decide the best present to give a girl is an old dead animal?" she asks.

"Well, yeah. This was more interesting," I say. "Thought it suited you."

Alma stares at me for a moment before her lips curl up into a smile.

"I love it, Lloyd. It's nifty."

I give her a nod and turn to walk away before I melt.

"Hey!" she calls after me. "Don't be afraid to come back soon. If you got any more iron pyrite you want to get rid of, I mean."

"I'll be back in soon, then." I nod. "With some iron pyrite, of course."

"Berries. Don't take any wooden nickels."

Alma winks at me again, and I can feel my heart singing. Walking out of the shop, I look up into the sky, at all those little specks darting across the clouds, and I almost feel bad for all of them.

They don't know what it really feels like to fly.

I may be goofy over Alma, but that doesn't mean I'll ever forget about the other lady in my life.

The hike down the quarry always goes by quick. I step off the trail and head out to my shed, pulling my key out of my pocket. I stick it in the padlock and swing the doors open.

And there she is. Faded and half a century out of style, and still one of the most beautiful things I've ever laid my eyes on.

"Morning Jules," I whisper.

Roughly the size and shape of an automobile with the treads of a tank, Jules is a dull bronze with gold-tinted studs and panels. Her drill is about half as long and twice as tall as the rest of her. She's got a few dents and I've had to repair her glass windows several times after surfacing in the past few months, but she's as resilient as they come. And someday when I'm dead in the ground, she'll still be running, providing for my children and their children alike.

There's no stopping a bird like Jules.

Mobile drills were invented back in the tail end of the eighteen hundreds, fueled by the California gold rush. They never really caught on too well – wildly expensive and intricate, not many gold miners were keen on making such an investment. On top of that, drills are complex and require not just an understanding of how to operate and maintain them, but of the geologic surroundings you're boring into. After several fatal accidents, the bad publicity was enough to dampen what little interest there was for drills, and they stopped being produced entirely soon after.

Drills made a comeback in a different way a few years later, when the Central Pacific Railroad thought that an underground railway would be a worthy investment. They refurbished old mining drills and commissioned a handful of special drills for the job, big ones that could collect mineral deposits and pave the way for a steam engine at the same time. I remember being a kid; sitting on my grandad's lap as he showed me the old newspapers he kept from that time. I remember that big leading drill, the Star Garnet, and how massive she looked in that faded old picture, surfacing out of a crater in all her gold and black glory. It was something spectacular.

And then, airships were conceived, making all forms of extended travel across the ground obsolete. The Central Pacific Railroad shut down not a year later, and their drills were either stripped of their metal or lost to time. It took me many months and a lot of dough to track down all the missing parts for old Jules.

But the old girl has paid for herself five times over these past few years.

I climb up her footholds and twist open the hatch, dropping my satchel, canteen, and lantern down into the passenger's seat. I lower myself down in and pull the hatch closed behind me, pulling my key out of my pocket and turning it into the ignition. Jules's dashboard lights up, and I make sure to double-check her oxygen levels and air tank before I back her out of the shed.

"What do you think, Jules?" I ask her. "Feeling lucky today?"

I don't have to take her far out into the quarry before I find a good spot to start drilling. I yank my pen out of my satchel and quickly mark on my map where I'm going down, and make a quick estimate of where I'll go. I want to keep close to yesterday's route, just in case that vein went on farther than I thought.

And more importantly, to see if I left behind any iron pyrite.

Smiling at the thought of getting to see Alma again so soon, I prep for descent. With everything in place, I turn the lever and grip onto the wheel. With a quick buck, Jules swivels on her sides and her drill roars to life, dipping into the ground. Dirt and gravel sprays out of the way, and after a few minutes, I push on the pedal and let her sink into the hole.

There's always a brief moment of darkness, when I'm engulfed in dirt and earth and all I can hear is the roar of my drill.

And it's exhilarating.

After that moment though, Jules's automatic lights flicker on, and I can see the gravel and rocks smearing across my window as we tunnel downward. I measure our decline, and when I'm sure we're about a half mile down, I turn her horizontal and set her on a straight course.

It's smooth sailing from here on out, no real need to do much of anything except check the filters every few minutes. Normally I pick up a newspaper at Marla's Diner to bring down with me, but I was so set on going to Around the World Curios I didn't stop by this morning. I reach to my satchel to pull out the book I've been reading, but I stop, remembering I finished it yesterday down in Twin Pike.

With a sigh, I sink back in my seat and let my mind wander back to Alma. I should invite her to come down with me during one of my digs sometime. Someone like her would be able to appreciate this – burrowing through stone and dirt as slow or fast as you please, no traffic control to tell us to stop or go or pull us over for inspection. A world of treasure at your ready and the means to go wherever you want.

Real freedom.

As I trek along, I decide now would be a good time to check the filter. I turn around and pull out the drawer along the panel behind me, catching a small sample of the contents of the containment tank. A flurry of pebbles and rocks. I pick one up, and immediately see the streak of shimmering yellow stained into its sides. Not iron pyrite. Real gold.

"Attagirl Jules!" I yell.

I yank the lever into reverse and stomp on the pedal, backing her up before I let her swivel down and bore into the sides of the tunnel. Drilling down and back up from a gold-bearing tunnel is always a good way to tell how deep a vein runs. I wonder if this is left over from yesterday's vein, or if I've come across a new one. Two gold loads in as many days, boy that would be swell. I wait a few minutes before I let Jules descend.

And suddenly, there's no sound. No roar, no cracking rocks splintering apart, no pebbles hitting my window. For a moment, I think I see light.

Jules bucks hard, and I go lurching forward. My satchel and the filter both go flying against the window.

We're falling.

I don't have much time to think about what could be happening. I fly out of my seat and hit the window, and I quickly wrap my hands over my head to shield myself.

Jules hits the ground of whatever we've fallen into with enough force to crack the windows. We go rolling, and I claw forward, trying to get my grip on something, anything. After getting tossed around for what has to be a few yards, we land upright, and I fall smack-dab on my ass, back into the seat.

I sit still for a few moments, my heart pounding in my chest. I feel pretty banged up and sore, and my cheek is stinging something fierce, but for the most part, I think I'm okay. I snap out of it quick when I realize Jules's drill is still roaring away. I quickly lean forward and grab the lever for the drill and turn it off. As the rumble of the drill dies down, I lean forward to observe the damage.

The crack could have been worse. Old Jules's windows are thick so the whole pane didn't shatter to pieces, but a few shards seem to have broken loose. *My cheek*. I reach up and sure enough, I feel a piece of glass imbedded in my skin. I grit my teeth and yank it out, my eyes watering as I do. I glance out of the windows, trying to make heads or tails of my surroundings. Did I fall into an underground cave? I can't really see much of anything through the web of cracks. I suck in a deep breath and stand up to twist the hatch open. I just hope the damage Jules took isn't too bad.

I swing the hatch open and immediately, I notice a dim light pouring down above me. How on earth is there a light source down here? I pull myself up and I jump down onto the ground.

And there's a gun being pushed into my face.

A man dressed in working slacks and suspenders points a gun at me, his eyes narrowed.

"On your knees," a gruff voice barks from behind me.

On reflex I swivel on my heels to turn around. Another man stands behind me pointing a gun, this one wearing a dark suit and a fedora.

"I said on your knees, palooka!" the man in the suit yells.

I cough as I feel a foot stomp onto my back. I put my hands up and go limp, slamming down to the ground, utterly confused and scared shitless. The foot is removed, and I look up, trying to get my bearings.

There's a series of lights on the ceiling illuminating the cavern I've fallen into. I follow the cables with my eyes before I realize I've fallen into a tunnel. A massive tunnel. I redirect my gaze to the men that have me at gunpoint, about half a dozen, all of them in work clothes, and all with holsters. I bite my tongue, forced to stay quiet as several of them climb up to inspect Jules. As I look over to the man with the suit, he catches my eye and immediately advances upon me.

"You a cop? Huh!?" he barks, walking up to me.

"W-what? No! I'm just a miner!" I yell.

"Bullshit!" he snarls.

"Hey, Robbie. Come check this out!" one of the other men calls from inside Jules.

Robbie glances down at me and sneers, kicking up dirt into my face as he stalks over to Jules. I have to fight the urge to yell at them to stay away from her, but I catch myself. They have every advantage here – I'm lucky I ain't dead right now. I keep my head low and decide to button up and listen.

"He says he's a miner. You fucking believe this guy?" I hear Robbie scoff.

"I think he's telling the truth," I hear someone else say from inside Jules. "Look at this stuff. What kind of copper would come down here with no gun?"

"So what is this thing then?"

"It's a drill, you know. From when they were making these tunnels all them years ago."

". . . Well I'll be a monkey's uncle."

"So what do we do with him? Should we . . . ?"

"Hmmm. No. Not yet. We should take him to the boss. Jackie is gonna want to see this."

Robbie walks back over to me, pocketing his gun and looking down at me in amusement.

"Okay, miner. Why don't you take a little walk with us?"

A pair of arms pull me to my feet, and I weigh my options. There's no way I can fight these men off, and even if I did, they'd shoot me down before I got five feet away from them. I glower at Robbie, but stagger along in time with them.

"Hey, what about his drill?" One of the workers yells.

"George, Louis, you two stay here with it. I'll send some more of the fellas up to help you figure it out."

And with that, a gun digs into my back and we go marching off. I should be thinking about how to get out of this mess. I should be thinking about what horrible thing could be waiting for me, and what best way I can meet it.

But all I can think about is Jules, and if I'll ever see her again. I turn around and try to steal one last glance at her, but in the dim light of the tunnel she's already faded away.

I sit on the floor of the closet Robbie and the workmen locked me in, chucking pebbles from my pocket against the wall. They had marched me through half a mile of tunnel until we came to a manmade cavern filled with more workers, just like them. Pushing wheelbarrows, dragging carts, glaring at me. They shoved me to a small shack built right in the middle of it all. Despite its shoddy appearance, there was a relatively nice office on the inside. Not that I got a good look at it before they shoved me in here. I don't even know how long it's been.

It's a good thing I ain't afraid of dark, enclosed spaces.

My pebble bounces off the door and rattles across the ground. I reach forward, pick it up and throw it again.

I wonder if anyone will come looking for me. It's not too far-fetched. Sooner or later the boys down at Marla's will notice I'm missing. And Alma, I told her I'd been mining down in the quarry when I saw her, she'd be able to tell them where I am.

And then I remember that up on the surface there are a dozen holes and tunnels branching off in every direction for miles. I sigh and sink back.

So much for that.

I hear footsteps against the floor outside, and I stop tossing my pebbles. The door opens and Robbie scowls down at me before snapping his fingers.

"On your feet," he growls.

"Ain't gonna give me a hand?" I mumble, pulling myself up.

"Stuff it," he says.

I follow him out into the office, and he pulls out a chair for me by the desk.

"What a gentleman," I say, sitting down.

Robbie reaches into his pocket and whips out a handkerchief, and throws it right into my face.

"Clean yourself off, you're covered in blood and dirt and shit," he barks.

I glare at him, but I take the handkerchief and run it over my face. The cut on my cheek must be bad, because it's still bleeding.

"You going to tell me what the hell's going on?" I ask.

Robbie gives me the crooked eye and cracks his knuckles. I sigh and look away, and just focus on wiping the blood off my face.

"Here's how it's gonna play out," Robbie says. "My boss wants to come in here and have words with you. You're gonna be goddamn respectful and you're not going to act like a jackass. If it weren't for Jackie, I'd have shucked and chucked you back in the tunnel where I found you. Remember that, and remember I have no problem disposing of you if you try anything or mouth off. There are an awful lot of places to bury a body when you're this deep under. You hearing me?"

". . . Fine," I sigh.

"Good. Sit up straight and don't touch a damn thing."

And with that, he turns and walks out of the office, slamming the door behind him.

Immediately, I start looking around for anything that could help me out. The desk is fairly empty – a lamp, an ashtray, an ornate paperweight sat over some gold leaf stationery. I glance around the room. Filing cabinets, a liquor cabinet, a potted orchid, nothing. I peak around the desk, wondering if I have enough time to search through the drawers, and something on the floor catches my eye. Caught between the stout legs of the desk and the shag of the area rug, there's a tortoiseshell fountain pen.

I can hear footsteps approaching again, so I act fast. I slide out of my seat, snatch up the pen, and yank myself back up. The doorknob turns just as I slide it up into my sleeve.

I turn around to look at the door and a woman walks in. She's wearing a short, form-fitting black dress, and a long string of pearls cascades down to her waist from her slender neck. A mink stole is draped around her shoulders, and she wears a dark cloche hat with white silk roses embroidered on the sides. Her face is pale and striking – red lips and emerald eyes – and her short black bob frames it perfectly.

She slowly walks across the office, her heels clicking against the floor as she does. I keep my eyes pinned on her as she walks past me and behind the desk, settling daintily into the seat. She leans up and adjusts her hat.

"Lloyd Williams," she nods over to me in a smooth, elegant voice.

". . . How did you know my name?" I ask warily.

"The boys found your license in your satchel," she says. "They said you made quite an entrance. Would you mind explaining to me how it was you came across my tunnel?"

". . . *Your* tunnel?" I ask.

She stares at me and blinks.

"It is now," she says.

She doesn't say it curtly or with an edge. She says it like she's just stating a fact. Like the sky is blue or the grass is green. It catches me off guard. Her calm demeanor, her appearance, all of it. I sigh and slump back in my seat.

"Look," I say. "I have no idea what's going on here. I'm drilling for gold one minute and the next I'm falling through an underground cave and Al Capone out there is waving a gun in my face."

The woman blinks again.

"And you're not working with anyone? No cops?" she asks. I snort.

"You think if I was lookin' for some underground tunnel I'd come at it at a steep angle and risk falling in like I did? I enjoy my neck in its current trajectory, not for lack of trying," I say.

The woman glances off to the side for a moment, as if weighing what I've said.

"All right. I believe you," she says with a nod. "I do apologize for the misunderstanding and the brutality on Robbie's part, but this is a very delicate operation we're running here, easy to get jostled. Let me introduce myself – Jacqueline Watts."

She sticks a hand out and with a moment of hesitation, I reach forward and shake it. She has a strong grip.

"Can I get you anything? Smoke? Martini?" Jacqueline offers.

". . . I'm fine, thank you," I say.

"If you change your mind, offer still stands," she says with a nod. "Moving on, you must be wondering what's going on here. Do you have any idea what this all is?"

I'm wary to speak up, but I find myself shaking my head.

"You seem to be an intelligent man, Mr Williams. We're deep underground, in a massive tunnel only accessible by drilling through the earth. Use your deduction skills," she says.

I sigh and rub my temples before it clicks.

Only accessible by drilling.

"This is an abandoned tunnel from the Pacific Railway," I realize out loud.

Jacqueline snaps her fingers.

"Now you're on the trolley," she says.

"I didn't know they made it to Illinois before they shut down. Shoot, I didn't think they even made it past Colorado."

"Not many people do," Jacqueline nods. "That's our main advantage."

"So . . . what is it you all are doing down here?" I ask.

Jacqueline raises an eyebrow at me, and I can tell she wants me to use my deduction skills once again. I look around the office, trying to find some clues. My eyes trace across the room, around the desk, the filing cabinets, and finally, on the liquor cabinet.

Holy shit.

"You're rumrunners," I say.

"Well done," she says. "Though personally I don't care for the word. It has so many negative implications attached to it. I run a world-class operation here. This isn't a bunch of rubes carting panther piss they made in their garages. You ever get a drink down in Twin Pike?"

"Um . . . yeah. I was down there yesterday." I nod.

"That's our supply you're tasting, and we get it imported from all over the world. Finding my way into these old tunnels wasn't even the most difficult part. Before we could begin, we had to find a covert way to get the alcohol off the airships before docking, without being seen by air traffic control. It took a great deal of time and money to orchestrate, but I'm not the kind of person who gives up easily. Once we found our blind spot, everything slipped into place. It's been a large success. And I make quite a lot of money off of it."

She stops talking and waits, staring at me with unreadable eyes. Finally, I do the only thing I can.

I whistle.

"That's pretty brilliant," I say.

"Thank you," Jacqueline nods. "But I'm not telling you all of this to impress you."

The sobriety of her tone gives me goosebumps at this point. Jacqueline breaks eye contact with me to fish in her desk, and she pulls out a cigarette case and a box of matches. She removes a cigarette and brings it to her lips, the pulls out a match and strikes it.

"Sure you don't want a smoke?" she asks.

". . . I'm fine, thank you," I mumble.

"Just let me know if you change your mind," she says as she lights up.

I look down at the desk and tap my fingers. I've got this terrible, sinking feeling that things are about to go from bad to worse.

"So . . . why is it you're telling me all this?" I ask.

I look up and Jacqueline meets my eyes again before removing the cigarette from her red lips and exhaling a cloud of smoke.

"That drill you have. Where did you get it?" she asks.

". . . It was in disrepair. I fixed it up myself." I say slowly.

"Hmmm. That must have taken a while. The boys said they found some gold in it. That what you mine?" she asks.

"Not very often . . ." I say.

"I'm not interested in your gold, don't worry about that. But I am curious, how fast does she go?"

I don't like what she's getting at. Not one bit. I keep quiet, and Jacqueline takes another drag of her cigarette.

"The boys said the speedometer went up to a hundred and ten miles per hour. That true?" Jacqueline asks.

". . . I've never driven her that fast. I keep her at ten an hour," I say.

"Ah that's right. You're looking for gold, after all." She nods.

". . . Right," I murmur.

"You know, I've considered looking for a mobile drill," Jacqueline says. "This tunnel runs halfway across the country and throughout most of the state, but there are only certain access points. Now, I've been quite complacent the way things are. I make a substantial amount of money doing what I do, but not so much that I was willing to gamble it away trying to track down a piece of lost history. Imagine my surprise when Robbie comes and tells me a drill's fallen right into my lap?"

I've got this sinking feeling building up inside of me. I open my mouth, but I can't say a word. Jacqueline regards my state for a moment before continuing.

"With a drill, I could expand my empire exponentially. I could triple my clientele in a matter of weeks. It would be worth a great deal to me," she says.

"Mmhmmm," I nod.

I'm not a stupid man. I can see exactly where this is going.

But that doesn't make it any less torturous.

"So. If I asked you how much your drill was worth to you, what would you say?" she asks.

"I wouldn't. It's priceless," I say firmly.

"And I can understand why," Jacqueline says, taking a puff of her cigarette. "Now, when it comes to my business dealings I can be exceptionally fair and generous. But in order to get to where I am today, I had to break a lot of laws, and twist a lot of arms. So I'm going to level with you. You have something I want, and I am not a good person. What do you think's going to happen next?"

I look down at the table and try not to shake with rage. I'm suddenly very aware of the fountain pen in my sleeve. It may be pathetic, but it is sharp.

I wonder if it's sharp enough to defend me against a tunnel full of armed gangsters.

"So what are you going to do with me after you steal my drill?" I ask, trying hard to keep my voice from sounding spiteful. I don't want to make this any worse for myself.

"You insult me. I may be a criminal, but I wouldn't steal from you," Jacqueline says.

"Then why don't you explain to me exactly what is going on," I say through gritted teeth.

"Certainly," she nods. "You're going to show us how to operate your drill. You're going to give us a series of demonstrations of its capabilities until we're certain we can run it on our own. Then I am going to have you sign a contract transferring ownership to us, and I'll cut you a more than reasonable check."

I have to wrestle every fiber of my being to stay calm. I can see how Jacqueline operates. She wants to pay me so I'll be less likely to go to the cops afterwards, and if I do, she'll have proof we did business together and drag me down with her. She's clearly cunning. I tell myself to tread carefully around her. To keep my wits about me and not do anything rash.

But for the love of god, they're trying to take Jules from me. I clench my fists.

"Hypothetically speaking. What would happen if I told you to go fuck yourself?" I ask.

Jacqueline raises an eyebrow before leaning forward. I find myself flinching and drawing back, but she flicks the ash of her cigarette into the ashtray.

"I'd say that's extremely unfortunate, and I'd be forced to let Robbie step in. I'd warn you though; he can be very cutthroat when it comes to negotiations. He's developed a bit of an obsession with his cigar cutter lately," she says.

I swallow, and gently retract my hands from the desk.

"Anyway, I'll let you think about it overnight, we need to replace your cracked window before we start anyway. I hope you can forgive your impromptu accommodations, we don't usually hold people in this facility. I'll have the boys bring in a cot for you and something to eat. Any requests?" Jacqueline asks.

". . . No," I mumble, looking down.

She leans forward again, this time, putting her cigarette out on the tray.

"All right then, I'll have them surprise you."

And with that, she reaches up, readjusts her mink stole and stands.

"It was a pleasure speaking with you Lloyd. I look forward to doing business with you tomorrow," she says.

She walks around the desk, over to the door and steps out. The door closes, and weight of the entire world comes crumbling down around me.

When I was a kid, I used to use my mother's hairpins to try to pick locks on doors. Just to see if I could. On a few occasions, it actually worked.

Trying to pick a lock with a fountain pen is much harder.

After Jacqueline had left, a few of her workers came in with a cot like she said they would. They cleared out a bit more space in the closet before sticking it in and jamming me in there with it. I won't lie, it took me a while to calm down. Even longer to try to figure out a plan. But by the time Robbie opened the door to chuck a lunch bag with a sandwich into my face, I had a rough idea.

If I could wait long enough, night would fall, and there will have to be less activity, or at least a shift change – either less people to observe me, or people who haven't seen my face yet. This closet is full of work clothes. Maybe, just maybe, I can get out there without being noticed. They'll be guarding Jules, no doubt about it. But I can get out of this tunnel. I hate the idea of leaving Jules behind with these people. I hate it so much it makes me feel sick. But there's nothing I can do from here. I'll get out of this tunnel. Go to the authorities. Tell them everything, show them where to go, conduct the search with them, hell, I can take them down to the speakeasy in Twin Pike and they can watch me beat answers out of the barkeeps. I'll get Jules back, no matter what it takes. It will all turn out okay in the end.

If I could only find a way to pick this damn lock.

Suddenly from outside the door, I hear footsteps approaching.

Damn. Damn, damn, damn.

I quickly pocket my pen and throw myself back into the cot, facing the wall. The door opens soon after.

"Get up," Robbie barks at me.

"Aw gee Mom, Can't I get another five minutes?" I whine, turning over to glare at him.

"I've had just about enough of your attitude, miner. Get out of the closet now or I'll go outside, get a rock and bash all your teeth out of your skull."

I sigh and pull myself out of the cot.

"I don't have time for any shit. Just follow me."

He leads me out of the office, out into the cavern. There are fewer workers here now than there were before, but they're all hard at work, carting crates I now know must be filled with liquor.

"How long did you lock me in there?" I ask, glancing around.

"Not long enough. Keep moving," he says.

"Jacqueline told me we weren't starting until tomorrow. It can't have been a full day yet," I say.

"Maybe she did, but I had the windows repaired, and she doesn't want to waste time. I don't either, so keep moving."

We walk out into the tunnel, and I take the time to glance around. There really aren't that many workers, and none of them are looking at me.

"Don't try anything," Robbie growls at me. "I'm keeping my gun holstered because Jackie told me to show you some courtesy. So let me indulge you in some privileged information – out of common courtesy – I'm the quickest draw in the state. You take off, and I'll fill you full of lead before you get two yards away."

"Thanks for the warning. Awful decent of you to tell me how good you'll be at killing me," I say.

"Who said I'd kill you? Jackie wants you alive. I'm sure you can operate your drill with one good leg – especially if getting to keep your other one is your incentive."

I open my mouth, but I decide not to say anything. There's no point to it. I keep my trap shut for the rest of the walk through the tunnel, and before long, I can see Jules's silhouette in the dim light. There's a fleeting moment where just seeing her intact is enough to make my heart flutter – seeing that she wasn't damaged in the fall, that her window is no longer broken. Jacqueline and several workers come into view as we walk over to them, and that feeling dies almost instantly.

I'll never have that feeling again.

"Thank you, Robbie," she says as we walk up. I see that she's changed her clothing. The dress has been exchanged for an embroidered blouse and a pair of sports pants tucked into boots, no doubt in preparation for our journey through the tunnel. Her mink stole has been pinned in place around her shoulders with a broach, and I can see she's wearing a holster beneath it, two guns at the ready. I focus in on the blank glass eyes of one of the minks on her stole, its little terrified face, frozen in the fear of its last moments alive. It makes me feel uneasy.

"Lloyd," Jacqueline says, turning to face me. "It's good to see you again. I hope you got some rest. I apologize that this meeting had to be moved forward, but we're running on a tight schedule here. Were you able to come to a decision?"

I stare daggers at her. Decision. Oh yes, the big decision. Either I do what they want or they'll torture me until I do.

This is it. I have no other choice.

"I'll do it," I whisper, my heart breaking as I do.

"Attaboy," Jacqueline says, and turns to the two workers by her side. "Louis, George, go inform the others we'll be taking the drill out for a test run. I trust you two will be more than capable of overseeing operations in my absence."

The two men nod and walk off down the tunnel, and Robbie prods at me with his elbow.

"Okay miner, get in."

With heavy feet, I trudge over to Jules, trying to detach myself as much as I can. I climb up and twist open her hatch, lower myself down and settle into her seat. Robbie comes in after me and as he sits down, he reaches into his pocket and pulls out his gun.

"That's not necessary." Jacqueline says, sliding inside and taking her place next to him.

"Jackie, what if he—"

"What if he what? Tries something funny? Then you can pull your gun out then. But he's been cooperative so far, so let's not reward his compliance by making him drive with a gun to his temple. He needs to be calm and level headed so he can drive."

Robbie sighs and then turns and glowers at me.

"Well?! What are you waiting for?" he snaps.

I stand up, close the hatch, and slump back down. Jacqueline passes over a map.

"For the first demonstration, I want to see how fast this drill can go. Take us north-east," she nods.

I barely glance at the map. I don't care where we go. It doesn't matter. Nothing matters. Instead I just focus on prepping Jules. The key is already in the ignition. I turn it, pull her lever and she lurches forward, and with a quick glance at the compass built into her dashboard, I turn her east and drive her over to the walls of the tunnels.

I turn the lever and grip onto the wheel. Jules bucks as her drill roars to life, grinding against the stone and dirt of the tunnel wall. Dirt and gravel sprays out of the way, and after a few minutes, I push on the pedal and let her drive ahead.

There's a moment of darkness, where I'm engulfed in dirt and earth. I can hear Robbie swearing, barking orders, and I can hear Jacqueline telling him to let me do my job. But they both sound miles away. Right now, all I can hear is the roar of Jules's drill breaking through rocks millions of years older than her and I both, splitting apart the earth like an angry goddess.

She's just as magnificent as the first time Grandad ever showed her to me. And here I am, about to hand her over to a couple of thugs without even putting up a fight?

I can't go down this easy. I won't.

I won't let them take her from me.

Jules's lights flicker on and I tighten my grip on the wheel. Strange, in the thunderous roar of the drilling I find myself able to think clearer than ever. Neither Jacqueline nor Robbie know how this machine works. I may not be able to try anything in this enclosed space, but I'm still the pilot. And we go where I say we go.

I glance back down at the map. I'm too far out of town by now to go circling back, but if I tilt upward her just a little, eventually, we'll surface. I glance over at Robbie, who's looking fairly uncomfortable and queasy, and at Jacqueline, whose eyes are pinned on my speedometer.

Well, she wanted to go fast, let's go fast.

I twist the lever, bringing us up at the slightest of inclines, and then I stomp on the pedal, letting Jules plow through the earth like it was tissue paper. I wasn't lying when I told Jacqueline I've never seen how fast Jules could go – but now's as good a time ever to find out. Twenty miles. Thirty miles. Forty. Fifty.

"I'm gonna upchuck," Robbie mumbles, pulling out a handkerchief and bringing it to his face.

Sixty miles. Eighty. A hundred.

"This is good for now. Keep this pace for an hour. I want to see how she fares," Jacqueline says.

I nod, and quietly calculate to myself, shifting the lever gently for her to tilt upward just a little bit more. I incline her only slightly – I can barely even feel it, and I've got the advantage of years of operating her. My two companions are oblivious to the shift. We barrel through the dirt, and the minutes tick by like hours. But they creep along slowly. Eventually Robbie stops complaining about feeling sick, though he still looks green. He and Jacqueline begin conversing, oblivious to the changing sediment as we get closer to the surface. I begin to notice the window creaking slightly, probably a shoddy patch job. Morons.

"If it can handle this speed, not only will we be able to make more tunnels for steady clientele, but we could make special deliveries all over the states in this drill," Jacqueline says to Robbie.

"That's a whole lot of clams," Robbie whistles.

"It opens up a great deal of opportunities," she nods.

"We'd probably have to pay off more airships to meet demand—"

Suddenly, with a great crack and a blinding stream of light, Jules breaks through the surface of the earth. With such speed propelling her we go up in the air for a few moments before crashing to the ground with a thud, speeding forward over a rocky path. Robbie yelps and instinctively puts his arms in front of Jacqueline, and I stomp my foot on the breaks. We lurch to a loud stop, and I lean forward and kill the power to the drill.

"What are you trying to pull?!" Robbie yells, reaching into his pocket for his gun.

"I don't know," I lie. "I've never gone this fast before. I guess in theory, if we were going up at the slightest of angles, we were bound to breach eventually."

"Cool it, Robbie. He said before he's never gone this fast before when I talked to him earlier. No harm done. Open the hatch. I want to see where we are."

Robbie stands up and opens the hatch, helping Jacqueline out first before turning to me.

"Shake a leg," he says.

I stand up and pull myself out with him right on my heels. I hit the loose dirt and look around. We're in a grassy plain, rich and green and full of trees. Robbie leads me forward as we follow after Jacqueline, who pushes through grass and foliage. After walking for a few minutes, the grass fans out into sand, and we're staring down rolling dunes and into crystal blue lake.

"Holy smokes," Robbie says. "That's Lake Michigan."

"That it is. I was keeping track of our trajectory on the map. We're in Indiana now," Jacqueline says.

I realize that while they're both slightly behind me, neither one is particularly focused on me. I look out at the dunes and weigh my options. No way I could run. I don't doubt Robbie was lying about how good a shot he is. Maybe I could turn and try to overpower Robbie? But Jacqueline has a holster too. I dig my hands in my pockets, trying to think of a better plan.

And my fingers graze the tortoiseshell pen I found in the office.

I don't even have time to think about it. The pen is in my hand, I've spun around, and I grab for whoever's closest. Everything passes in a flash. There's a yell, an elbow hits me in the face, but I don't let it shake me.

And in the next instant, I've got my arms wrapped around Robbie and I'm pressing the sharp tip of the pen into his throat.

"You slimy fucker! You think you can pull a shiv on me?! I'll break your goddamn neck!" he barks, struggling against my grip.

I stick the pen deeper into his skin, drawing blood. He stiffens and I hear a click. I turn around and face Jacqueline, who's pointing her gun at me.

"That was a quick draw, Lloyd. Didn't think you had it in you," she says.

I pull Robbie up in front of me.

"Put the gun down," I say. "Or I'll slit his throat."

"Don't do it, Jackie. He doesn't have the stones," Robbie yells.

"Hmm. What do you think's going to happen here?" Jacqueline asks.

"You're going to put your gun down, and kick it away," I say.

"Like hell she is!" Robbie spits, kicking his legs. "I'm gonna tear you apart, miner. You're dead. You hear me?! You're fucking dead!"

I glance over at Jacqueline, who's staring at both of us with her unreadable eyes. In that moment, I realize something. Her expression is as unchanged, as emotionless as it was during our first meeting.

"Robbie?" she says.

He stops struggling and he looks over to her.

"I'm sorry."

The shot from the gun echoes out over the dunes, almost immediately followed by Robbie's gurgled cry. In shock I let go of him and step back, and he falls to the ground. I stare over at Jacqueline in horror as she steps over to me.

"Hope I didn't startle you. You all right?" she asks, pointing the gun at me.

I glance down at Robbie, at the puddle of blood pouring out of his head.

She shot him.

She killed him.

"W . . . why did you do that?" I stammer.

"Because either two things were going to happen. You were going to slit his throat, or he was going to break free and shoot you, and of the two, the latter seemed a lot more likely. Right now, you're worth a lot more to me than he was. So I chose. It's fairly simple." Jacqueline says.

"But . . . he was your . . ."

I swallow. I can hardly form words.

"He was," she nods. "But he had a temper problem, and he didn't know how to drive a drill. Shall we get going? I'd like to make it back to base sooner rather than later."

Jacqueline leads me back to the drill wordlessly, and she points her gun at me as I climb inside. She jumps in after me and closes the hatch, and silently I turn Jules on and we descend into the ground a few yards.

"Apart from that unpleasantness, it was a successful demonstration," she says once we're back underground.

I say nothing. I listen to the roaring thunder of Jules's drill.

"You seem disturbed Lloyd," she notes. "I thought you'd appreciate the fact that I just saved your life."

". . . You just . . . you didn't even consider letting me go. You could have done what I asked and I'd have let go of Robbie. But you just killed him. Like he was nothing," I mumble.

"Letting you go was not a choice, Lloyd," she says. "And neither was giving Robbie the chance to break free and shoot you. I need your drill, and for now I need you. It's a shame what I had to do. Robbie was a model employee, a close friend, and back at base I've got ten men who will be wrestling each other to the ground for the chance to replace him."

She says it like she says everything. Just stating the facts. I glance over at her, her blank emerald eyes, and she looks over and meets my stare. There's nothing behind that stare. No guilt. No remorse. No anything.

And she's the most terrifying person I've ever seen.

"I told you when we met I wasn't a good person," Jacqueline says.

". . . Do you care about anything?" I ask.

"Just one thing," she says. "And it's the only thing in this world worth caring about."

I open my mouth, but suddenly, there's a loud crunch from outside, and Jules bucks hard. We lurch forward.

"What was that?" Jacqueline asks.

Her gun hovers close to my face, and I swallow, leaning forward and pulling a lever.

"I don't know . . ."

Jules lurches forward again and suddenly she comes to a stop, her drill whiring away out of control in front of us. I suddenly become aware of the groaning glass of the windows. I look up and see the sediment pushed up against the window.

That shouldn't be happening. Jules clears a tunnel ahead of her. Aside from small pebbles and clumps of dirt and debris, there shouldn't be anything pressed up against the windows. I squint at the pale sediment pressed up against the creaking glass.

Sand.

The sand dunes. I drove her into the sand dunes.

"Lloyd. What is going on?" Jacqueline asks again.

Back during the gold rush, there were so many ways people died in their mobile drills. Drilled down too deep and got swallowed up by the magma in the earth. Drilled into lakes, into tar. Drilled into dirt too loose to work through. I've always been careful, never went down too far, but always drilled deep enough under loose ground and kept my eye on the map.

Until this very instant.

I gently ease Jules into reverse and start to back her up. The treads roar beneath us, but we hardly move an inch. There's not enough friction. I stomp on the brake, trying to get some torque.

And the glass cracks.

There's a flash of white as the sand pours in around us. Jacqueline lifts her arm to protect herself from the wave of sand and broken glass, and I get a big mouthful of it. I sputter as the glass splinters apart and more sand rushes in around us. Jacqueline is standing, trying to twist the hatch open, but the weight of the sand pushing down around Jules is too much. She's sinking.

This is the only chance I'll get.

I swing my legs out of the sand collecting around my waist and I take a deep breath. I throw myself forward into the torrent of sand, closing my eyes and pulling with all my might. I'm blind to everything around me, and I can hardly move, but the jostling from the drill is at least making the sand looser, and I propel myself forward. I can feel a hand wrap around my ankle, but I kick it off quickly and pull myself forward. Somehow, I'm able to get my footing on the tilting window frame, and I frantically push myself forward, trying to swing my arms, grabbing for something, anything.

And my fingers wrap around a wad of roots.

I grasp the knotted roots and yank on them, and although whatever plant is above comes sinking down, it provides me with enough momentum to pull myself up, and break through the sandy surface.

I gasp in air as I yank myself into a bed of dried grass. I gulp in air, coughing as bits of sand make their way into my lungs, and thank every deity there is that roots can grow so deep in ground with little water. When I've finally caught my breath, I open my eyes.

A few feet away from me, there's a large dip in the sand, and it pulsates, no doubt propelled by Jules's drill only a few yards below. I watch the sand throb and die down as Jules sinks away beneath my feet.

I don't know how long I sat there, waiting. At some point, I pulled myself up off the ground, and walked off down the dune. I don't know what propelled me to keep going. I walked by the lake, following its shoreline until I found a small cluster of buildings. A restaurant. For a while, I just stood there, staring over at it. I felt so empty. So numb.

I still feel numb.

Finally, I dig myself out of my stupor and walk over to it. I reach into my pocket, pull out some change, and stuff it into the payphone slot before pushing the numbers. The phone rings and I stare back out at the lake, at the dunes. At the blue, unforgiving water, the miles of rolling sand, the darting shadows of the airships up in the sky, the final resting place for my drill. My Jules. The love of my life.

She's gone.

A voice clips on to the other end of the phone.

"Around the World Curios. You've reached the front desk."

"Hey Alma," I say, my throat sore and hoarse from all the sand I swallowed. "Do you think one of your brothers could give me a lift?"

It's been a week since I lost her. It didn't get any easier.

I made two trips to two police stations in two different states. They collected Robbie's body and after a few days they dug Jacqueline out of the sand. They called me in to identify her at the morgue. Some vile, vindictive part of me wished it hurt her when I first heard. That she died screaming, gasping for air, and that her face would be contorted in pain and fear like those on her mink stole. But her expression in death was the same in life. Blank. Unreadable. Uncompromising. It didn't feel like a victory, or justice, knowing I made it and she didn't. It felt like nothing.

They dug as deep as they could, but they couldn't find Jules. She sank too deep, and her drill was still on full blast. She could have drilled right through the crust of the earth by now. The heat would have warped her beyond function or recognition.

Back in Illinois, the cops were able to find the tunnel through the speakeasy down in Twin Pike. They raided the rumrunner's base, and it made the headlines statewide. That didn't feel like a victory either – one less place for me to find a drink.

And I've been doing a lot of drinking these days. Luckily some of the boys down at Marla's were kind enough to supply me with plenty of moonshine and hooch. It's damn horrible, but it's better than being still with my thoughts.

I wake up to a pounding at my door, and immediately I moan when I open my eyes. I feel sick and nauseous and my head feels like it got run over by a freight train. I battle my way out of bed, trying to pull on my slacks as I make my way to the door.

"Hold your horses, I'm coming," I mumble, slamming the door open.

She stands at the doorway with a parasol in one hand and a basket in the other. She's wearing a long peach-colored dress, mother of pearl buttons dotting the bodice. Her sleeves hang off her shoulders, exposing her pale skin, and her shinny penny hair is done in a braid, cascading down her side. She smiles up at me with warm, brown eyes, and I can't help but melt.

"Alma," I whisper.

"Hey there Prospector," she says.

"Heh. Well, not so much anymore," I say, feeling a ping of sadness. "Looks like I'm out of a job."

Her face falls, and she reaches out and touches my hand.

"Sorry. I didn't mean to . . . how have you been?" she asks.

I know it must be pretty obvious how I am. I haven't shaved in days, and I must stink of bootlegged alcohol. But still, she's trying to be nice.

"I'm Jake," I say, forcing myself to smile.

"You're a bad liar. Here, I brought you some soup," she says, passing me her basket.

"Thanks Alma, that's really swell of you," I say.

"That's me," she says grinning. "So, if I were to ask you when the last time you went outside was, what would you say?"

". . . I don't exactly remember," I shrug.

"Why don't you save the soup to heat up for later and take a little walk with me?" Alma says. "Some fresh air will do you good."

I open my mouth to protest, but Alma's shoving the basket inside my door, grabbing me by my hand, and pulling me out into the street.

"Come on. Let's ankle!" she says.

I sigh, and trudge along in time with her, blinking in the sunlight and the airships darting across the sky. Alma moves her parasol over me.

"Sun a little too bright for you?" she asks, chuckling. "That's what happens when you're blotto twenty-four seven."

"I'm not blotto. I just was last night," I sigh.

"You are aware it's late afternoon?" she asks.

". . . I am now," I mumble.

"My brothers said you threw up on the ship when they brought you home. Was that your first time in one of them?" she asks.

"It was," I say. "It . . . wasn't as bad as I thought it would be, though. I just . . . wasn't feeling well."

"I can't imagine you would be. They told me all the details that got left out of the papers. I'd have come down sooner but I needed to man the shop. I just . . . I'm so sorry, Lloyd. I know how much you loved that drill."

I nod. For a while, we walk forward quietly.

"It was my grandfather's," I say gently.

"Huh?" Alma asks.

"My grandad," I say. "He bought it back during the gold rush, used it to mine for gold in Sacramento. He was good with it. When the gold got picked clean, he was hired by the Central Pacific Railway to help clear the tunnels. They tried to just buy the drill off of him, but he refused. And once they saw how good he was with it, well, they begged him to come on board. He was as resilient as they come."

I chuckle to myself, thinking of Grandad.

I miss him so much.

"He's the one who named her Jules. Not me. I remember being just a kid, sitting on his lap while he read me *Journey to the Centre of the Earth*. It's still my favorite book," I say, smiling.

I glance over at Alma, and she's staring over at me with sad eyes.

"What happened?" she asks.

"You know what happened," I shrug. "Airships were invented, and the railway shut down. You think I don't like airships, you should have heard Grandad go off on them. Ever see an old man swearing up at the sky? It was like he was telling the almighty himself to go dry up."

Alma chuckles. We walk across the street, and she gestures for me to follow her down the road.

"I've got a big family," I say. "A lot of cousins, aunts, uncles. An older brother and sister. Both my parents. But when it was time to read out Grandad's will . . . he left Jules to me. The entire time I knew him he was telling me stories of the railways and the mines, it left me star struck. And then he just . . . out of all of his children and grandchildren, he gave her to *me*. She hadn't been used in decades – she was in such a state of disrepair my parents said the most I'd get from her would be selling her for scrap metal. But I swore I'd get her running again. Restore her to her glory. Make sure she could do what she was made to do. Make my grandad proud."

I look down at the ground and kick a pebble, watching it roll across a road stained with shadows from above.

"And I lost her," I sigh.

"It's not your fault, Lloyd," Alma says. "You gotta know that."

"I do. It's just . . . it's just . . . I'm all balled up. I don't know what to do now. What comes next? I feel lost," I say.

Alma nods, and quietly, she takes a hand off the handle of her parasol and points to a large warehouse.

"We're here," she says.

"We were going somewhere?" I ask. "What is this?"

"Never been here before? It's the warehouse for the shop. I figured my brothers would have taken you here when we were kids, although it didn't fill out like this until after they got their ships. I need to pick up some new inventory for the showroom. Come on," Alma says.

She pulls a key out of her pocket and starts to walk over to the large doors.

"Get a wiggle on! I don't have all day!" she shouts at me.

I follow her up and step inside the warehouse with her. It's huge inside – large Conestoga wagons left over from the great migration West, giant boulders of petrified wood, a small cluster of life-size soldier statues from some far off land.

"I didn't know you had so much stuff," I whistled.

"You're telling me. Father's trading has gotten out of hand as of late. One more shipload and we'll have to get a second warehouse," Alma says.

She motions for me to follow her before she disappears behind a row of shelves. I roll my eyes and take off after her, twisting through the shelving units.

"Back here!" she yells.

I sigh and duck around another shelf, and come out next to Alma, who's grinning at me like a mad woman.

". . . What?" I ask.

Alma pushes me out from behind the shelf, into the middle of the warehouse.

And I swear I feel my heart stop beating.

Standing in the middle of the room, in titanic, faded glory, is a drill.

She's the size of a cable car – one of the few special drills commissioned for the Pacific Railway. Her hull is golden, and she's got black, stylized paneling that twists up and down her sides, overlapping across her hood. I float over to her hull and walk along her side, mesmerized by the interlacing golden stars that splash across her.

I know that pattern.

"This is the Star Garnet," I say in awe. "This is the leading drill from the Railways."

"Now that's a Prospector who knows his drills. You can see how she'd be a bit too big to display in the shop?" Alma says slyly, walking up behind me.

I open and close my mouth. I can't believe this.

This can't be happening.

"You look like a goldfish," Alma chuckles.

"How?" I ask, turning to her. "How did you get this?"

"One of Father's business associates found it abandoned in a landfill out in Utah, Father was visiting her and he saw it on display in her garden, gathering weeds. Took some big trading to get it – and moving it out here was no picnic either. But I think it was worth it. What do you think?"

I look down the length of her. She's faded and stained, covered in dents and rust, but I can see through all that, down to the foundation. Down to who she used to be in those old pictures my grandad would show me, in all her magnificence. And she's something spectacular.

"I think she's the most beautiful thing I've ever seen in my entire life," I say.

Alma laughs and smacks me on the back.

"Good! I know Jules was a different kind of drill, so it stands to reason it might take longer to fix this one up. Father will be available to meet with you this Saturday to talk about what parts you'll be needing . . ."

". . . What?"

I turn around and look at Alma.

"The parts you'll need. You know. To fix it," she says.

"Fix it?" I stutter. "You mean . . . you're . . . you're giving this to me?"

Alma laughs again, and gestures for me to follow her over to a cabinet.

"Think of it more as a . . . partnership. You help us fix it up, you run it, you keep half of the payoff. Now I know half doesn't have as good ring to it as owning your own drill . . . but she is a big drill, she should pick up a lot more and at a faster rate too," Alma says, clearly pleased.

I stare at her, and back at the drill. The Star Garnet.

"I . . . I can't believe this Alma. I think I may be dreaming," I say.

"I could pinch you if you want."

"This is too good of you. Of your family. Why?" I ask. "Why are you doing this for me? You're all sitting pretty with Around the World Curios and your brothers' ships, why spend money on something like this? You don't need it."

Alma looks at me amused and shakes her head. She reaches into the cabinet, pulls out a bottle, and blows some dust off of it.

Scotch.

"What's your favorite thing about drilling, Lloyd?" Alma asks. "I know it isn't about the gold or the dough. I've seen the look in your eyes. There's something else down there in the dirt for you. But what?"

She looks into my eyes, and I feel naked. I feel like she's penetrating my soul, staring deep down inside me with those wild brown eyes.

And I hope she never looks away.

"It's the freedom," I say. "Being able to go anywhere, no air traffic control, no random searches, no being told you can't drink or being forced to dock whenever you're told. Just . . . going wherever you want, whatever direction you want, miles away from anyone who wants to control you."

"That's respectable," Alma nods. "For me, it's about the adventure. The thrill of the unexpected. Sometimes there are restrictions for it, rules you gotta follow, but I don't mind standing in a line to get to the main attraction. See, I've got this thirst for the unknown, and I'm willing to do whatever I can to find it. Fly. Dig. Sail. Drive. Walk. Sit around in a store full of treasures from all corners of the globe all day long and see who walks through my door."

She winks at me, and I can feel my cheeks flushing.

"So those are my terms, Prospector. Fix this drill for me, and take me on an adventure. Think you can do that?" she asks.

I look at her, her mischievous crooked grin, her wild brown eyes, and unyielding spirit. That look. It could make a dead man's heart start up again.

"Alma, baby, for this, I'll mine out every diamond in the

United States for you. I'll pull out every last inch of gold and buy you a coat made of clouds, hell, I'll break all the stars out of the sky and make you a pearl necklace out of them," I say.

"Mighty swell of you," she laughs. "But I'd rather go mining for fossils. I think that's more interesting."

She holds up her glass, and I raise mine in return.

"To freedom and adventure," she says.

". . . To expanding our horizons," I say. "And to wherever the future takes us."

Thief of Hearts

Trent Hergenrader

The man called Hieronymus Dismas, Grandmaster Thief of People's Granada, stood alongside his compatriots inside the rundown Taberna Fin del Mundo, all staring mutely into the depths of their beer mugs as they listened to the radio announcer writhing in orgiastic delight as the bastards from Madrid stroked in yet another goal.

"Five-two! In the eighty-third minute, Jesus Alonso!" The announcer's voice crackled through the speaker, the words echoing off the tile walls. "The power, the precision, the grace. They make it look so easy. Even Generalísimo Franco is on his feet, applauding in the royal box. Real Madrid five, Granada two!"

Someone to his left muttered to the barkeep to switch the damn thing off but Hieronymus and the others quickly shouted him down. Six years ago to the day he and his Republican brothers had gathered in this very bar to listen and mourn as the fascists trumpeted the news of their final victory in the nation's civil war. He and his comrades had withstood the ignominy of defeat in stony silence that day, so surely they could handle their team getting stuffed in a stupid sporting contest. *Football is not life*, Hieronymus told himself.

And yet he could not deny football had given life back to them in the aftermath of the war. The season after league play resumed, tiny Granada CF won promotion to the first division where they enjoyed rubbing elbows with their moneybags neighbors from Valencia, Sevilla and Barcelona. For four proud seasons, Granada CF had avoided relegation, refusing to budge from their spot at the aristocrats' table. More importantly, in that time they had not once but *twice* beaten the dictator's golden boys of Real Madrid. On those drunken nights, the streets were awash with wine and celebration, as working-class folks allowed themselves – even if only just for a moment – to forget the wounds of the recent past, to soak in the pleasures of the present, and to muster enough courage to believe in the future again. Hieronymus knew it was the football team's fighting spirit that had helped restore the dignity to the city's downtrodden.

But Granada CF's run in the top flight looked to be ending after tonight's humbling loss in the capital. From the start, the season had seemed like a battle against inevitability. To Hieronymus it felt altogether too much like the beginning of 1938, the year that saw the end of the war. While the French and Soviets presented the Republicans with outmoded guns and an arsenal of empty promises, the Germans and Italians conferred their Nationalist friends infinitely more valuable gifts. Combat dirigibles firebombed the Basques around the clock and automaton soldiers that needed no food, shelter, or rest, laid siege to Barcelona, while clockwork gendarmeries suppressed any revolutionary rabble in provincial backwaters like Córdoba and Granada. When Catalonia finally folded, the rest of the world turned its back on Spain to focus on the next European war that, unbeknownst to them, would soon over-run the globe.

Of course, the man called Hieronymus had been living a civil war from birth. As a child of the streets and of uncertain parentage, he changed names more often than his clothes during the thin years of his youth, foraging the gutters for food, sleeping in alleys, begging with gypsies beneath the noses of the sneering bourgeoisie. As a student of the streets he became one with the city. The twisting maze of alleyways in the Moorish quarter was etched in his memory, and he knew the names of each family in the working class sections of town. When the civil war broke out, he found work as a runner between Republican outposts. His good looks, sharp mind and wry wit won him many friends, and before long they placed a gun in his hands. Unlike other young fighters who either deserted or fell asleep at their posts, he fought with distinction, executing any order – even those of the most brutal nature – without hesitation or question. The Republicans meant to exact retribution for every Nationalist crime, which led to an escalating contest of atrocities. He became a monster more than once on those grim nights, shedding whatever name he bore after he committed the deeds, as if abandoning the name would grant him absolution. And he did it all unflinchingly in the name of his comrades and their noble cause. For an all-devouring war that pitted brother against brother, it had given him a family who rewarded his sanguinary devotion with unconditional love.

Sadly for them, the resistance in Granada did not last long. Isolated from their comrades in arms in Madrid and Barcelona, the Republican revolution in Granada was soon quelled and the city came under Nationalist control, allowing Franco to turn his attention north. The will drained from the movement as fighter after fighter traded resistance for acquiescence, though they would buy little safety with that cold coin. All looked lost in those dark days. But it was against that backdrop of blackest night that his star had risen.

For it was then that the revolutionaries discovered his talent for stealing.

He enjoyed flaunting the skills he had perfected in his youth. He ran night-time raids through the Nationalist encampments, where loose cash and sensitive military documents were drawn to his fleet fingers as if by magnetic attraction. His comrades dubbed him Hieronymus Dismas to commemorate his artistry in robbery, and granted him the honorific Grandmaster Thief of People's Granada. They even held a ceremony bestowing on him a key to the city, all done in mockery of the ridiculous system of titles and offices used by the country's nobility. Hieronymus dedicated his life to being a gadfly, an irritant, an agitator who tasked himself with reminding those in power that while the war had been settled in Granada, the Republican spirit would never die. It was a dangerous game, teasing the Black Squads into chasing shadows, but the last remaining revolutionaries in the city loved him dearly for it. He sold the stolen goods and information to the highest bidders and purchased guns, bombs and ammunition to fuel their guerilla warfare. In retaliation, the Guardia Civil swept through the old town tracking down most of the rebels who were too proud or too stupid to realize they were beaten. They abducted most of his comrades, riddled them with bullets and dumped the bodies in the choked ravines outside the city limits, like so much trash.

Yet Hieronymus continued stealing. He turned his attention from the military to the aristocracy, breaking into their homes after dismantling their expensive Swiss security systems, with their polished brass gears and long golden chains. After looting as much as he could carry, he would paint the names of his fallen brothers on the bedroom ceiling in goat's blood, letting the thick red ink drip down onto the pillows. With no further use for weapons in Granada, he then directed funds to the last Republican holdouts in Spain; and after they too had fallen, he sent guns and bullets to any outpost on the continent who could put them to good use. He again began to use many names in a never-ending shell game to throw off the authorities, but the name Hieronymus – the only name he had not taken but had been given – he kept close to his chest. Now only a handful of his most trusted brothers knew him by that secret name; the others were all long dead.

The speakers in the Fin del Mundo squelched, bringing him back to the present as the football announcer's voice rose in excitement as he described the action. "Huete to Berrida, Berrida to Rafa and back to Berrida. Madrid on the attack with space on the wing. Out to Ipina, who centers . . . GOAL MADRID! The cross to Jesus Alonso at the back post, who nods in his third goal on the night, the sixth for the Madrid. Astounding! Goals in the first, eighty-third and eighty-fifth minutes for Jesus Alonso."

The mood in the bar soured further and the curses turned angry. A drunkard smashed his mug in the fireplace. "Jesus, Jesus, Jesus," Hieronymus cried above the din. "That guy's *always* on the end of a cross."

The blasphemous joke won him a round of grudging laughter before he raised his mug and declared a toast to their brave comrades who had fought bravely but fell in Madrid. He drained his drink and made his way to the toilet on wobbling legs. As he relieved himself, he rested his forehead against the cool wall to keep the room from spinning. As he buttoned up his trousers, he felt a sudden sting of intuition and his fingers froze. The tavern had gone impossibly quiet. No clinking of glasses, no chatter of conversation. The crowd wouldn't have filed out into the streets yet; they'd stay late into the night recounting their grim stories of football and war, drinking to their shared sorrows.

"The players take a victory lap, applauding the crowd," the football announcer's voice echoed from the barroom, distant as if in a dream. Hieronymus swallowed. The closet in which he stood had no other door, no window, no air shaft. Nowhere to escape. Nowhere to hide.

The bathroom door hinges shrieked as Hieronymus emerged. Those in the bar stood as a forest of frozen men, their arms stiff, their pinched faces drained of color. The cheers from Madrid crackled over the speakers before the radio snapped off. Hieronymus crouched, took a long sidestep, and spied a half-dozen black clad figures, their beaten copper faces gleaming beneath their military berets. Each pointed a short-barreled shotgun.

"Hieronymus Dismas," a strident mechanical voice blared.

He straightened and raised his hands without a word. Not a second later he heard the swish of a truncheon end with an audible crack as it landed behind his ear, and the bar disappeared.

When Hieronymus opened his eyes, the rush of pain was immediate and overwhelming. Through the waves of agony, he mentally congratulated his captor on the ingenious nature of the torture. Hieronymus hung nude in the center of a spotlight in a darkened room, suspended horizontally by millions of threads, each of which was attached to an individual hair on his body, tugging his flesh into jagged peaks. The length of his legs, under his arms, on his toe knuckles, the nape of his neck, his eyebrows, between his legs. A chill breeze wafted over him and he twitched, initiating an ecstasy of pain as the millions of threads tightened and retracted to keep maximal tension on every hair without tearing a single follicle from his skin.

Once he mastered his spasming limbs, Hieronymus couldn't help but laugh at his acute state of misery. "I must say," he spluttered, addressing the darkness, "the pain is exquisite. Makes me glad I shaved my chin whiskers this morning."

"Pain? What would you know of pain?" boomed a voice in reply, deep and haughty.

The room exploded into light and Hieronymus flinched, cueing another round of excruciating convulsions. As he flailed, he heard the plinking of steel gears and the ragged hum of a mechanical contrivance as the threads pulled his body into a vertical position. Hieronymus blinked away stars of pain to discover that he hung a few feet above a stone floor in a floodlit cavernous room. A giant of a man stood before him, adorned in rich velvet robes with gold piping that flowed around him. His prominent Roman nose and lidless, hawkish eyes – obviously the handiwork of one of the city's top physiognomers – suggested he belonged to the city's aristocracy. His mouth twisted in derision.

"At present, I know quite a bit about pain, thank you," Hieronymus said.

The man smiled and gestured behind him to a hulking construct of gears, belts and pulleys. At the top was a flared brass cylinder where the milky white threads emerged and curved upward to the ceiling. The contraption clicked and clacked as it made minute adjustments in tension.

"I'm glad you appreciate quality craftsmanship. The spirit of the Inquisition married to German ingenuity."

"Diabolical," Hieronymus admitted, fighting to remain conscious.

The room echoed with his laughter, but when he spoke it was with pure scorn. "Hieronymus Dismas, Grandmaster Thief of People's Granada. I'd heard that you were clever. It took a small fortune to sniff you out but, happily for me, I have a *large* fortune. Fail me though and you shall regret it."

"Fail you?" Hieronymus asked, perplexed as he struggled to remain focused. Someone had betrayed him. Who? It must have been a brother whom he had trusted with his life as no one else knew him by that name. It was a black thought. He since the moment of his capture he had expected a lengthy torture and execution as payback for one of the many crimes he'd committed as a foot soldier. Yet now it seemed as though this aristocrat was to lay some task before him? His mind raced. Perhaps he had burgled some priceless family heirloom.

"Do you need my help recovering an item you might have – misplaced?"

The aristocrat snorted. "Property? If it were that easy I could employ any common thief. I need a man who has the guile to steal the horns from a bull, a burglar who can infiltrate the most ironclad fortress. I need a thief of legendary status for this work."

Despite a sudden surge of pride, Hieronymus's will hardened. Through his teeth he muttered, "You mistake me, sir. For your kind, I am not for sale."

The man smirked. "Fine. If you don't agree to help me, I'll firebomb the Fin del Mundo. During the midnight hour, of course, when the rabble packs in shoulder to shoulder to stuff their sweating faces with cheap food. And then I'll bomb the next door down, and the next. I will raze every sleazy hideout in the old town until you bend your will to mine. You shall not refuse me, for I am Don Rodrigo Álvarez de Montefrio."

Neither the name nor title fazed Hieronymus, as he recognized neither. After the war the city had spawned minor lords like a kitchens did cockroaches, far too many to keep track of, though the tabloids tried their best.

"Surely you're joking, Don Rodrigo. The city's wounds are still raw and weeping. Such an attack would cause a riot. Whole neighborhoods would burn."

Hieronymus let the thought trail off. His comrades had surrendered because they were exhausted, outnumbered, and outgunned. Six years on and none of that had changed. Any uprising would be utterly crushed beneath a steel-shod heel.

Don Rodrigo shrugged. "Not *my* neighborhood. Remember thief, your betters dwell in towers high above the city. Whatever stink your kind dredges up blows away on the wind before it reaches our thresholds. When the unrest ends, things will return to what they were before, but with fewer of you rabble roaming about. And you, with all that blood on your hands."

His captor chuckled as he watched Hieronymus's expression change.

"Ah, so the stories are true then. You love the common man. A terrible affliction, love, isn't it? The way it holds one captive? The way it raises your hopes, only to dash them on the ground. And there is no greater pain than being forsaken by one you love."

Hieronymus remained silent.

However when Don Rodrigo spoke again, it was *his* cheeks that were wet, and all traces of his arrogance trickled away with his tears. He presented an altogether smaller man. He spoke in a voice quiet and measured.

"My lover has severed ties with me. Her parents wish to improve their family's station by marrying her away to a duke, not some provincial lordling like me. My Dolores prays that I will drop my courtship if she rejects my correspondence, but I am made of sterner stuff. I shall pursue her until the end of my days if needs be. Our kind of love only occurs once in a lifetime. She will be mine, whatever the cost."

Don Rodrigo dried his face with his sleeve and retreated to the machine. A high-pitched whine filled the room and Hieronymus felt the threads suspending him go slack and he was falling. His feet stung and pain shot through his limbs as he clattered to the cold stone floor, covered by the fine threads. He struggled to a kneeling position, tearing handfuls of threads from his body. His skin was aflame. Don Rodrigo stood before him, brandishing a yellow envelope below his nose.

"Dolores has instructed her people to refuse my correspondence. You must see that she receives this letter. Secrecy is of the utmost importance. People talk, and the aristocracy cannot be seen consorting with the lower classes," he said, looking the naked man up and down.

The thief did not reach for the envelope.

"Come now, Hieronymus. Think of the cretins."

Grudgingly, he opened his hands.

Hieronymus was seized, clothed, hooded, frog-marched, bundled into a vehicle and strapped to a seat. Tires squealed, the stink of burning rubber filled his nose, and his head rapped smartly against glass after a wicked left turn, and then another. Time stood still beneath the suffocating hood as the vehicle executed a bewildering series of turns. Then there was a long, fishtailing stop. The vehicle doors opened and he felt hands under his raw armpits. Then he was weightless until he felt the bite of concrete on his knees and the kiss of brick on his cheek. Dazed, he peeled off his black silk hood in time to see brake lights disappearing around the corner of an alley.

Don Rodrigo's goons had dropped him in an alley on the south-eastern side of the crowded Albaicín, the ancient Moorish quarter packed with shops, restaurants and tavernas. He heard the gurgle of the River Darro beside the Sacromonte, the steeply sloped hill of caves where the city's gypsies had made their homes for hundreds of years. In the distance, dozens of newly built towers punctuated Granada's skyline, standing like paranoid sentries against the Andalusian night.

From across the river, he could hear the faint caterwauling and stamping feet of flamenco. Despite his aching body, Hieronymus managed a smile as he recognized a few voices of his good gypsy friends. Deep in the old town where the aristocrats would never deign to go, they sang with an unnerving sorrow that soaked into the stone walkways, was absorbed by the river and carried out to the sea. For a moment, Hieronymus felt his heartstrings pulled in the direction of the voices. Perhaps he could simply forget about the humiliation he'd endured and enjoy a night of drink and dance.

Then he remembered Don Rodrigo's threat. Too easily he imagined orange fire exploding from the windows, the cries of the wounded mingled with the screaming of horses running in circles as their guts leaked out, shadows dancing to the staccato rhythm of gunfire, and weeping children clutching at the sacks of meat and bone that had once been their parents. And he shuddered. These same neighborhoods had been bombed mercilessly at the start of the war and he could not bear to see it happen again. Yet somewhere in the night's bustling sea of so-called friends was a traitor, the one who has sold his exact whereabouts to the Don. Sobered by the thought, Hieronymus withdrew the envelope he'd been given. Written in a looping pen was:

Doña Dolores Josefa y Téllez-Girón de la Soledad
47th floor, Torre de Castidad

Hieronymus looked into the night sky, the ghostly shapes of zeppelins sliding between clouds, their searchlights glowing in the misty gloom rolling down from the mountains. He did not know offhand which was Torre de Castidad, but he knew the manicured neighborhoods of the wealthy almost as well as the mazy back alleys of the Albaicín, and it would not take him long to locate the duchess's tower.

With a wistful glance at the music, Hieronymus turned and slipped into the folds of the night.

Torre de Castidad was an octagonal tower over sixty floors high, an affront to the eye and lacking any aesthetic quality whatsoever. Hieronymus found it was also slick with rain and devoid of good handholds as he ascended. He counted floors by the balconies he passed, keeping a steady pace and pausing only to blot the sweat from his forehead. Evading the airships lazily trolling spotlights was simple enough, but on the lower levels he faced cascading tripwires strung from every balcony. Springing one would mean certain death. He pushed the thought away and concentrated on finding grooves for his seeking fingers.

After an eternity of climbing, Hieronymus reached the forty-seventh floor. He wrapped his fingers around the balcony supports and, mustering strength in his exhausted arms, he pulled himself over the safety rail as noiselessly as a cat. In the moonlight, the snowcapped Sierra Madres appeared to float on the sea of fog that had settled over the valley. Granada lay beneath the white blanket, its billowy smoothness perforated by dozens of towers, the sounds of the city's nightlife lost to his ears.

Hieronymus dipped his hand into one of his coat's myriad pockets and withdrew his lock pick set. The beveled glass patio door featured an imposing brass deadbolt of German design. Hieronymus drew a deep breath and knew picking such a lock would take patience; no doubt it would have small gaps to exploit, and the pins would set so delicately they could easily escape his notice. Then there was the question of an irregular tumbler shape . . .

He hadn't yet touched the lock with the tool when he heard a click and the whirring of gears as the glass door glided open.

Heavy purple curtains framing the door billowed inward with the breeze.

"Señor Dismas, I presume," an icy female voice said from inside the apartment. "You're late. We've been expecting you."

Stout hands lurched at him through the curtains. Hieronymus leapt for the railing but not fast enough. He felt a fist close on his hood, and his head jerked back as a purple mountain fell on top of him. Blows rained down like bombs.

Hieronymus swam upward into light, the ether of his unconsciousness thick and sour. He had a pounding headache and his mouth tasted of copper and cotton. A medicinal tang stung his nose and the dull ache he felt in his chest was offset by the pain in his arms, which were pinned behind his back by two brass gendarmes, stiff and lifeless as statues. The cold mosaic floor on his bare feet was the least of his discomfort. He shivered from a terrible chill at the core of his body. It was as though he'd been packed in ice and left in the rain.

His eyes focused on a hand-carved four-poster bed with a ruby red comforter and carefully arranged gold-tasseled pillows. Staring back at him with sparkling jade eyes was a clockwork ocelot, its inner workings an audible buzz as its orange and brown spotted tail thumped listlessly against the pillows. Against one wall stood a drab armoire and on the other a vanity table with enough mirrors and accoutrements that it would have dwarfed the counters of most fashion salons. Two miniature golden trees stood on the vanity, jewels hanging from their fine limbs like exquisite ornaments, each tree topped with a diamond the size of an acorn. Nightstands flanked the bed. On one stood an ornate cage with a gilded thrush inside that preened in unnerving jerks, stopping every few seconds to raise its head and reset. On the other table rested a second birdcage covered by a crimson cloth.

Hieronymus's visual reconnaissance was cut short by the clap of heels on the stone floor. A tall, slender woman in a sweeping crimson nightgown entered the room, planting her hands on her hips; her glittering golden fingernails looked as sharp as talons. Bleached white hair stood stacked atop her head, tightly woven like intestines. Her thin features were strikingly beautiful.

"Doña Dolores, I presume," Hieronymus croaked.

She offered a demeaning smile. With false cordiality she said, "Welcome to my home, Señor Dismas. And to whatever do I owe your intrusion? Not a robbery I hope?"

When the thief said nothing, Dolores sashayed to her vanity, opened a drawer, and withdrew two envelopes.

"You're probably wondering how I captured you so easily. Don't fret, your pathetic skills aren't in question. I bribed the servants in Rodrigo's employ to keep me apprised of his plans, so I knew exactly when you would be coming. I've already relieved you of your message and read Rodrigo's romantic twaddle. He should have thought about that before he treated me like a serving girl before his friends." As she said this, she touched the yellow envelope to the candle and watched it catch fire, then brandished the second. "And you shall return my response."

"With all respect, Doña Dolores, I came here as a one-time favor to Don Rodrigo. I must politely decline your request." A sudden chill racked his body. His arms and legs felt leaden and it took an effort to hold his head up. Again, he wondered about the identity of the spineless, traitorous scum who had brought him to this misery. Hieronymus vowed to make him suffer, should he himself survive this ordeal.

"You may wish to rethink your answer – and your tone."

With a flourish, Dolores whisked the crimson cover from the birdcage on the nightstand. It was no birdcage but rather a large glass vat filled with bright bluish liquid. Suspended at the center, shot through with wires, was a beating human heart.

She rushed forward and tore open his shirt. He didn't need to see the six-inch zipper embedded in his chest to know what had happened. Dolores's silvery laughter echoed through the bedroom, piercing his ears like ice. She grinned and moistened her lips and, in that moment, with her face so close to his, she looked radiant. Hieronymus fully understood Rodrigo's attraction.

Her lips touched his ear, sending a thrill down his spine. "You're mine now, little thief," she whispered.

Hieronymus felt his chest seize and he gasped for breath. He belched a mouthful of thick, black smoke, stinking of a thousand cigarettes. Through his open mouth he could hear the wheezing of a tiny working engine, and he could feel the vibrations in his sternum up through his throat. Dolores's expression soiled as she waved away the stench.

"Uncouth creature," she muttered.

"My heart," he managed to say, his voice hollow.

"I collect them. Didn't Rodrigo tell you?" She gestured to the guards, who instantly sprang to life and wheeled Hieronymus around, forcing him through the open patio doors. While he had been unconscious the fog had lifted, revealing a glittering golden city beneath a sea of stars. The coming dawn was a pink line tracing the horizon. A bracing breeze roused him to his senses as the twin gendarmes lifted him off his feet.

"What a grand morning," Dolores said, beaming as she stepped onto the patio and breathed the crisp air. She tapped the second envelope on her palm. "I hope when Rodrigo finds you it will put an end to this foolishness."

An acrid burst of smoke jetted from Hieronymus's nostrils and he spluttered. "You don't need to do this, Doña Dolores," he said weakly, struggling against the vicelike grip of the guards as they hefted his feet onto the railing. This will end nothing. Rodrigo promised to pursue you until you are his. He swore this to me. He vowed to continue for the rest of his days."

Beneath this feet, eternity spread out before him.

His statement was met with silence, and when Hieronymus craned his head back he thought that Dolores was laughing. Only a moment later realized she was weeping behind her fist. She stood silently contemplating the city and the gently glowing traces of its labyrinthine streets, full of secrets, her eyes shining. The moon still hung low and full over the mountains.

"Oh Ruy," she said so full of sorrow that it struck Hieronymus like a blow.

Then Dolores jammed the envelope down the front of his pants and waved him away as if he were a fly. The next thing he knew he was airborne, the night air freezing his face as he plummeted toward the streets of Granada.

*   *   *

Broken bodies.

Mounds of broken bodies piled in the streets, heaped in communal graves, quicklime coating heads and limbs like snow on the peaks of the sierras, most eyes were closed but some were open, staring in silent accusation. They visited Hieronymus in his darkest dreams, these insatiable dead, never speaking. Their memory came to him unbidden as he rushed down to meet them in the black hole they called their forever home.

"Brothers and sisters," Hieronymus whispered, eyes shut tight as he hurtled downwards, and his breath was smoke.

He heard a pop and felt a jerk on his shoulders, righting him in midair as his headlong descent transformed into a glide. Stunned, he looked up to see a rectangle of silk spread out above him, connected by taut lines tethered to his back. No sooner had he realized that his hands were free when a tower loomed before him, growing larger by the second. Panicked, Hieronymus jerked on the cords and the parachute veered him to the right and he passed the tower unscathed. Flagpoles and radio antennas on rooftops snatched at his feet as he sped past. Hieronymus heard the engine in his chest whirring as the blood thrummed in his ears, and he prayed that its tiny pistons held out.

Hieronymus glided over the empty streets of the Albaicín, a ghost town in the predawn darkness. He gathered the lines in his fists and jerked, arresting his flight. He drifted in a lazy spiral into the abandoned Plaza del Triunfo, perfectly silent except for the whine emerging through the metal teeth of his chest zipper. Hieronymus's feet touched down and he collapsed, buckling under the weight of memory and despair, his cheek resting on the stones that had tasted so much Andalusian blood.

The parachute fell over him, covering him like a shroud.

The sound of squealing tires interrupted his respite. Soon he felt the silk being torn away and rough hands dragged him to his knees. He squinted into blinding headlights at the hulking silhouettes over him, the pitiful sound in his chest mercifully drowned out by the vehicle's growling engine.

His capacity for terror and pain exceeded for one night, Hieronymus felt only relief that now it might end. How many better men than him had been bundled into cars and never heard from again? And how many times had it been his hand on the steering wheel on those late night drives? His finger on the trigger once they arrived at the destination? By disposing of the names he had worn had been an attempt to keep such memories at bay, but when whenever dark thoughts claimed him, their cold phantom fingers stretched from the grave to settle on his neck, their whispers crossing time to caress his ears.

"Hieronymus Dismas?" one silhouette asked, its recorded voice shrill.

"Am I? I do not know. I only know that I am both a robber and the robbed."

A moment of awkward silence followed as they processed that information, but then the automatons executed their commands.

"Hieronymus?" Rodrigo's voice swam through the murk.

He remained perfectly still.

"I know you're awake. You were talking in your sleep. Now open your eyes."

Resigned, he did as he was told, but he did not elsewise move. He was lying flat on his back on a cold steel table, covered by a sheer muslin sheet. His tongue probed the corner of his swollen mouth where the metal fists had struck him. He tasted blood.

"I know you've seen her. What did she say? Tell me man, what she did say?"

Without a word, he reached into his pants and produced the envelope. Rodrigo snatched it and ripped it open, reading the contents twice, running his finger vertically down the page. Rodrigo glanced past the page and parted his captive's shirt, revealing the purple angry scar. He spoke in a hush.

"I can't believe she actually did that to you. During an argument once, she threatened to have her surgeon cut out my heart. I didn't think she meant literally."

Then he added in an even quieter voice, "She's capable of great malice when incensed."

"Who isn't, Don Rodrigo?" His voice was spent.

After a moment of silence, Rodrigo crumpled the paper in his fist and said, "The game is up. Her parents have arranged a marriage to the Duke of Segovia with an engagement celebration to be held in two days' time. She has programmed her guards to shoot either of us on sight should we be seen on the festival grounds. There is no hope. Forgive me all of this nonsense. A quick death would have been a kinder fate than the trouble I've put you through."

Hieronymus stared at Rodrigo and, after a lengthy pause, spoke. "Last night you said I possessed the skill to break into any fortress. You must trust that the walls your lady has built around her are not impenetrable."

"Do you believe that?" Rodrigo sounded surprised.

He fingered the metal teeth embedded in his chest and then shrugged without enthusiasm. "I have to believe that a stolen heart can be reclaimed. Or else, Don Rodrigo, I fear we are both lost."

The gypsies' wagons rattled on the cobblestones as they wheeled cart after cart brimming with gourmet courses of suckling pig, delectable whole legs of jamón serrano, stews of calf, rabbit, and partridge, bushels of olives, and Valencian paella, each dish more decadent than the last. Others trucked along casks of ciders, beers, and the finest wines from every corner of the country. Led by an unusually tall man garbed in bright purple robes and a smaller figure in a humbler cloak of dark gray and an enormous round hat, they brought it all to the rear gates of the festival grounds. The chef and planner on site seemed more relieved than suspicious at these unexpected reinforcements and instantly began barking orders at their newfound charges.

"That was almost too easy. What do we do now, Hieronymus?" whispered the man in purple, sweating under a generous layer of white face paint.

The other man gritted his teeth. They had been over this countless times on the long walk from the caves of the Sacromonte and all through the market as they bought their provisions.

"First of all, *my* name is Federico. *Yours* is Don Horacio. Best remember that. Secondly, we wait for our opening, just as we planned. Wait for my signal."

They had spent the past forty-eight hours rehearsing and Don Horacio had done better than Federico could have hoped, though his timing still needed refinement. They would need to be perfect for the plan to work, for failure meant death for the both of them. They watched as their band of gypsies, disguised in white serving coats, assumed their positions as they blended into the ranks of the bustling wait staff.

"Stop fidgeting, Don Horacio. You'll draw attention," Federico commanded.

"I can't help it," his opposite said, chewing his lip.

"Act naturally. Let us converse. Answer me this, Don Horacio, for this question has been weighing on my mind and I should like to know the answer before I might die: how did your guards know that I would be at the Fin del Mundo? Who sold me out?"

He had spent every free moment daydreaming, rehearsing the unspeakable things he would do with the traitor once he had ferreted him out. He had bided him time and was salivating for the answer.

Until Don Horacio provided it.

"A child, in fact."

Federico blinked. "A child? Who?"

His ruse of starting a conversation had worked to steady Don Horacio's nerves, and the other now let his gaze drift over the festival grounds full of bored faces, settling on the stage where Dolores sat between her parents, her expression creased in annoyance. Her face was powdered white and her hair stood tall on her head, a finely sculpted pillar. Her beauty trumped her scowl. A few seats to her left sat a prune of a man Federico guessed could only be her betrothed, the lucky duke.

Distractedly, Don Horacio answered. "Some starving urchin orphaned in the war. She said her father knew you, once pointed you out to her and whispered your name in adulation. Finding someone to give you up was the most expensive part. She sold the secret quite cheaply. All it took was a few changes of clothes and all the food she could carry. However, fair warning: if you desire revenge, good luck finding her. She's one of a thousand unwashed miscreants scrounging in the alleys. I don't think she even had a name."

"Everyone has a name, Don Horacio," Federico said quietly.

A sudden wave of shame washed over him. He knew such children well and counted them among his family. He had always been quick to share with them a smile or a jape to bolster their spirits. He imagined he was preparing them to be ready foot soldiers in the next revolution, with their empty stomachs driving their devotion to the cause. Yet he had overlooked a more pressing need: perhaps they were hungry. He thought of the sheer amounts of money that had passed through his hands over the years as he liquidated stolen goods to foster bloodshed. Not once had he thought to spend a cent on a crust of bread for those he claimed so much to love.

Federico cleared his throat and attempted to change the subject. "Where did you first meet Doña Dolores? Despite her temperament, she is a fine creature."

Don Horacio grinned and his eyes had a faraway look.

"Some cotillion. I can't even remember whose. Why the nobility insist upon inflicting each other with such painful social obligations I cannot say, but at least some good came from that one. If you call such a reckless, blinding love a 'good' I suppose. It turned out our fathers were business associates. I goaded mine into making an introduction. Dolores and I wandered the garden grounds talking until sunbreak. Her father was wroth when I returned her. I cowered in my apartment for a week fearing retribution. He's an important comandante in the army you know."

Federico hadn't known. "And your family? How did you come to money?"

"Munitions. My grandfather invested in a factory at the turn of the century. Quite shrewd business, as it turns out. The world never runs out of need for bullets," he said smugly.

Federico suddenly felt ill. The hole in his chest widened into a chasm as he processed what he had learned, turning over in his mind his role in this violent web of rich man's games. He had always fancied himself a spider, yet it turned out he was merely a fly. He stared dumbly at the painted face of the man before him, who was oblivious to his partner's sudden change in demeanor until he glanced over. His face creased in worry. "Are you unwell, friend? You've turned white."

Federico clutched the other man's wrist and whispered, "Steel your nerves. The time has come to reveal ourselves."

Without waiting for a response, Federico hooked his false beard over his clammy cheeks and fetched the guitar he'd had stashed beneath a shrub. He ignored Horacio's tug on his shoulder as he climbed atop a table, clapping his hands and shouting, "Doña Dolores Josefa y Téllez-Girón de la Soledad, we are honored to perform in celebration of this most glorious day!"

The crowd stiffened and went silent. Dolores's father balked and the jawline of her mother's plastic face ticked in alarm. A dozen truncheon-bearing automatons appeared from nowhere, advancing with programmed determination. The valve in his chest whined so loudly in his ears he feared it would give them away.

Dolores, however, appeared bemused. She put her chin in her hand and sat forward. "Let him be," she called to the guards. "For now."

Hieronymus clapped his hands thrice above his head. Hearing their cue, the gypsies cast off their serving coats and lifted their voices in sudden song. They flooded forward and formed a ring of clapping and stomping that slipped into a steady, driving rhythm. One gypsy tossed Hieronymus a chair and he sat, thrumming the strings of his guitar. The crowd of onlookers ebbed away, hands on their mouths as they watched the spectacle unfold. A beautiful young gypsy woman in a black dress with red accents seemingly blossomed from the sand, climbed the opposite end of the table, and began her dance. The flowing dress swam through the air tracing her fluid motions, her high-heeled shoes stamping in time with the clapping and shouting of her brothers. Beneath the brim of his hat, Hieronymus concentrated on his playing. This combination of music and dance was provocative, dangerously combustible. Everyone in the courtyard was transfixed by the moment, none more so than Dolores.

Rodrigo rose and took his place beside Hieronymus. The crowd heard a voice emerge, faint at first as an echo coming from the far off mountains. The tremulous voice grew in strength and merged with the music of the guitar and the rhythm of stamping feet on dust. The voice was one of sorrow, one that at once seemed on the verge of tears yet as stout and resolute, indomitable. It was a voice of passion and anguish, love and despair. It resonated off the stone and drenched the bricks of the courtyard. Then words began to form.

Of course, Rodrigo was only lip-synching.

Had anyone not been entranced by the display, they might have noticed that his lips did not perfectly match the lyrics, and that in fact the voice emanated from beneath the guitarist's broad-brimmed hat. Hieronymus knew hundreds of flamenco songs and, a student who had learned his lessons well, he chose to improvise, blending the traditional with the tragic. The song he sang was original, born before them all in that very moment.

The song started in his belly and then rose, reverberating in the chasm that once housed his heart. He began with the history of the wandering people searching for a home, of a parentless boy born to a city divided, of brother murdering brother, and the suffering of a true love found and lost, never to be regained. Words fluttered from his mouth like a wounded bird, a meandering river of a tale telling of shattered souls struggling to piece together their lives in an uncertain future, where their meager hope for redemption lay in a forgiveness borne of love.

The song ended with a thunderclap. The crowd was so stunned by the performance that no one noticed Rodrigo had missed his final cue. Hieronymus nudged him with his foot and Rodrigo, as if roused from a dream, stepped forward, brandished a cloth, and wiped away his face paint.

"Sweet Dolores, it is I, Rodrigo Álvarez de Montefrio, and I have come to pledge my love before the finest people in the city," he said, his voice shaking now as he approached the stage.

"Your parents say I am unworthy, but love transcends petty politics. You know that our hearts are united. May we not join our houses and begin a family anew?"

Hieronymus nodded in satisfaction at the recitation of the lines he had scripted but the others seemed unsure. The only sound to be heard was the twittering of birds on the breeze. Dolores's father's face looked waxy and rigid as his eyes darted back and forth in his skull. As for herself, she said nothing.

Rodrigo's voice broke as he whispered, "Lola, I beg you. Let us forgive each other's wrongs. Take me back. Make us whole."

For a moment she gazed at him, stoic. Then her glacial veneer cracked and slid away, revealing a face Hieronymus could almost describe as warm. She pushed her way past her father and rushed down to embrace her lover. Their lips met, and the gathered crowd sighed in unison. Then came the applause, the cheers and a thousand flashes of light bulbs as the local reporters snapped pictures for their gossip columns.

Rodrigo wiped away the caked makeup from Dolores's tear-streaked face and shook every hand offered before looking to thank his companions, but he found only a wide-brimmed hat, a false beard, and an empty gray cape alone in the dirt. Hieronymus and his gypsy contingent had long since disappeared, as though borne away by the wind.

Much later that night, under the cover of darkness, Hieronymus made not a sound as he slipped over the railing, his arms exhausted from climbing forty-seven floors. It took but a second to disarm the balcony's alarm and neutralize the security systems installed on the sliding patio door. Behind him, the lights of Granada shimmered beautifully but he did not dwell on the view. He was at work.

In the moonlight streaming through the window, Hieronymus could make out the shapes of two nude figures intertwined on the sheets, their bodies fused into one. The room's musky blend of sweat and sex contrasted with the crisp night air wafting in behind him. Hieronymus took a moment to gaze at Rodrigo and Dolores as they slept, and he smiled. It was a genuine smile of one who has learned to recognize love in many forms, and respects it as the fragile, wondrous, dangerous thing that it is.

Then he went about burgling the entire apartment.

He stole their cash, their pricey perfumes, and carefully packed their rare artwork in towels and linens. He took rings, bracelets, brooches and watches. He smothered the mewling ocelot with tasseled pillows and twisted the thrush's head until he heard its delicate springs snap and stuffed them both in a sack. He stripped the golden trees on the vanity of every diamond and jewel that hung from their branches, and then stole the trees as well, piling bag after bag against the balcony railing. With the apartment looted, he threw their keys over the ledge, cut their clothing into strips, jammed all the locks with broken picks and plugged their toilets.

He drew out his camera and took dozens of pictures of the nude couple from the most indelicate angles and left the empty film canisters on the nightstand atop a stack of gossip papers, knowing his message would be clear. On the ceiling above the bed, with a tube of blood-red lipstick, he wrote *SINCEREST OF THANKS FROM YOUR ONE-TIME FRIEND*.

Then, sensing that dawn was near, Hieronymus went to the vat on the bedside table and stole back his heart. The money from the stolen goods would be more than enough to bribe the best surgeon to fasten it back in place. As for the sizable remainder, he planned to round up every last homeless child in the city and provide them with as many clothes and as much food as possible. With patience and perseverance, he was convinced he could find the girl who had sold his name for a scrap of bread and beg her forgiveness for his vanity, lust and greed. And perhaps, with time, he could even convince her that he was a man worthy of her dead father's memory.

At last, Hieronymus flung his bags of plunder over the rail, watching the glorious procession of billowing parachutes drifting toward the waiting hands of his friends below in the Albaicín. Then he fastened a chute securely onto his own back and stood on railing, pausing to drink in the majestic view. Then he dove headfirst over the ledge and Hieronymus Dismas, Grandmaster Thief of People's Granada, was aloft over the city he so dearly loved.

In Lieu of a Thank You

Gwynne Garfinkle

The man you killed taught me a lot about Lepidoptera. Butterflies have two sets of wings, the forewings and the hind-wings, all of them covered in minute scales – but you don't want to hear about that.

Of course I was afraid at first, Charles. I never said I wasn't. Rocco cut quite a menacing figure with his hatchet profile and black hood. The party at Bertie's had become tedious, so I'd left on my own when it was still twilight. Yes, I know you would have preferred that I not walk home unattended! Jimmy had offered to run me home in his Rolls, but it was such a lovely summer evening, the air caressing my skin. I suppose I was a bit tight – there'd been rather a lot of champagne at the party. I strolled aimlessly for a while, and I was loitering in front of a shop window, contemplating whether a midnight blue satin cloche with feathers might be rather nice for our honeymoon, when Rocco came up behind me and grasped my shoulder. I gave a jump, turned and let out a pathetic squeak at the sight of him. Then he jammed the cloth soaked in chloroform over my nose and mouth.

I came to on a pallet on the stone floor, and Ernest was peering down at me. I took in his piercing gray eyes beneath wire-rimmed spectacles, his fine and lofty brow, his short pale hair that looked as if it had been touched by electricity. I became aware of a mechanical sound in the room, a purring and a whirring, and saw from the corner of my eye flashes of light in the already harshly lit room.

"Is she awake, Master?"

Behind the slender, fair man in the lab coat loomed Rocco's black-clad bulk. He had lowered his hood to reveal his bald, egg-shaped head and cruel blue eyes. You'll be glad to hear that I cowered.

"Don't be frightened, Miss . . ." Ernest said.

I struggled to a seated position. I was briefly dizzy and nauseated, but I mastered myself. "I am Miss Grand. Vanessa Grand. And I demand to know who you are and where you have taken me, and for what purpose."

"I'm pleased to make your acquaintance, Miss Grand. I am Dr Ernest Clive." He seemed timid, even eager to please me. Unlike you, Ernest was ill-versed in the ways of love, hearts, and flowers and everything designed to trap a woman. I *was* trapped by Ernest, of course, but there was something honest about the arrangement. "I hope my assistant Rocco hasn't mistreated you."

"Aside from drugging and abducting me, Rocco has been a perfect gentleman. However, I'm certain my fiancé and my father are looking for me. Is it money you're after? I'm sure that can be arranged to everyone's satisfaction." A bit shakily, I scrambled to my feet and dusted off my green silk frock. "But really it would be best for all concerned if you allowed me simply to walk out of here . . ."

And then I saw.

The high ceiling with the skylight. The hospital bed equipped with straps and wires. The beakers bubbling with ruby and emerald liquids. The machinery softly chugging up and down. The flashes of electricity crackling in their circuits. The aquarium in which swam . . .

I let out a gasp. Did you see them, Charles? The canaries that swam in the aquarium? The cage full of tropical fish that flew, their scales flashing blue and green and purple? Or were you too busy rescuing me to notice such wonders?

"You needn't be afraid, Miss Grand," Ernest said.

"Won't do you any good, anyway," Rocco remarked. "Dr Clive will do as he likes with you!"

"Be quiet, you fool," Ernest said.

I was transfixed by the fish that seemed for all the world to breathe the air through their gills as they floated in their cage. "Dr Clive, how is this possible?"

"You wouldn't understand," he muttered impatiently.

I bridled. "Because I'm a woman?"

"No, Miss Grand. Because no one does. I'm a genius, you see." He lifted his chin and would not meet my gaze, as if to convey that genius was a proud and lonely lot.

"All this is your handiwork? Dr Clive, it's magnificent!" My heart pounded, but there was exhilaration mixed with the fright. In that moment, at least, I knew I was alive.

"Ain't you going to scream?" Rocco asked dejectedly. "Usually they scream. Even Miss Georgina screamed."

"Be silent!" Ernest said.

"Who is Miss Georgina?" I asked. I wondered how many women they had brought to the laboratory, and for what purpose.

"My fiancée," Ernest murmured.

"I see. Have I mentioned that I have one as well? He'll be searching for me, you know," I repeated.

"Dr Clive don't have no fiancée no more," Rocco informed me.

"Why? Did you . . . harm her?" I began to shiver.

"Of course not," Ernest said. "We were to be married until she saw – all this. I thought she'd be proud of her future husband's work. Instead she was horrified. She called me mad. Then she married my rival."

All about us Ernest Clive's work sparkled and flashed. "What a little idiot Miss Georgina must be," I said.

Ernest's glasses had slipped down his nose. He pushed them back up and stared at me. "Miss Grand, do you truly think so?"

Rocco shambled toward me, his big arms swinging. "Don't listen to her, Master. She's trying to talk her way 'round you."

I backed away from Rocco until the cold stone wall stopped me. "What do you mean to do to me?"

When Ernest didn't reply, Rocco volunteered. "Half woman, half butterfly. Well, wings on a woman, at any rate."

My eye fell on the bed with the straps, the electrodes. On a little table next to it glinted scalpels and other instruments. I hugged myself and felt the gooseflesh on my arms. "The women who screamed – was it because you tried this

procedure on them?" Then I stopped shivering. I turned to
Ernest. "I say, would I be able to fly?"

Ernest gave a start. Clearly he wasn't expecting such a
response. Screams, yes, but not this.

"Shall I prepare the electrodes, Master?" Rocco asked.

Ernest appeared not to hear him. He kept staring at me as if
I'd only just appeared in the room. Rocco repeated his question, and the doctor seemed to shake himself awake. "Prepare
a room for Miss Grand, Rocco. She's going to be our guest."

"But Master—"

"Do as you're told. The room nearest the front staircase on
the second floor will be the most comfortable, I think."

Grumbling, Rocco trudged away.

I placed my hand on Ernest's arm. "You didn't answer my
question, Doctor," I said. "*Will I be able to fly?*"

Don't look at me like that, Charles! When I was a little girl,
I wanted to be a doctor like my favorite uncle Anthony, but
that, of course, was impossible. I was pretty and clever and
would make a good match someday. By the time I met you,
I was already laughing the empty laugh of the dead. Oh, it
was all amusing – the foxtrots and surreptitious kisses, and
knowing that my blonde waves and trim figure gave me
power over a handsome man – but with Ernest, I regained
the ability to be surprised. Did you really think I wanted to
be a society wife pouring out endless tea and listening to
endless chatter about frocks and parties and engagements?
Did you think I wanted my belly distended by a squirming
creature growing within? Talk of being experimented upon!
I tell you I wanted to fly.

I was given a room in Ernest's ancestral estate, full of secret
passageways and crumbling staircases. I could have spent
years exploring its recesses. At first he had to chase me 'round
the laboratory, I was so eager to explore. "What does this one
do?" I asked, my hand poised above a lever.

He rushed to my side. "Don't touch that lever! You'll blow
us all to kingdom come!"

How I laughed! He gazed at me as if I were the one astonishing thing left in all creation. Then he caught me about the waist
and kissed me.

It's true he had tried the experiment on a couple of the village girls, grafting wings on their backs and then removing them when he saw where he'd gone wrong. But there was minimal scarring, and Ernest erased the entire episode from the girls' minds before he released them. (No, Charles, I do not believe he would have done the same to me.) He hadn't dared take another girl from the village, lest suspicion fall on him and Rocco – hence Rocco's trip to London in Ernest's battered automobile, and my abduction.

Once he got to know me, Ernest no longer wanted to go ahead with the experiment as planned. "I don't want to cause you pain, my darling," he said. "We'll find another girl. You may assist in the procedure, if you like."

"I can endure the pain," I told him. "Don't you dare give another woman this privilege. I believe with all my heart that you can give me the gift of flight."

His eyes filled with tears, and he clasped my hand and told me he would prove himself worthy of my trust.

How his long, deft fingers traced where the wings would be on my bare shoulder blades, making me shiver deliciously. The original wings had been gray and functional, but Ernest insisted on redesigning them to make them both beautiful and capable of sustaining longer, swifter flights. They were irides-cent blue and orange, and they would have been my flesh and bone. Tucked beneath my clothes when I didn't use them – rather like a penis, don't you think? – but ready for me to unfurl, to fly bare-breasted and free. I even designed a chemise with slots in the back from which the wings could protrude, in case I wished to fly more modestly attired.

I loved that Ernest wanted to improve upon the wings for me, but it delayed the experiment. If only we had not delayed! It's hard to believe I was with him for less than a month, we made so many plans. There's an island – I won't tell you where. We were going to live there and fill the place with such marvels. It would have been a second Eden, one in which the quest for knowledge went unpunished.

The morning of the experiment, Ernest and I were elated, though our joy was tinged with fear. Even Rocco seemed touched by the magnitude of what we were about to attempt.

He was quiet and solemn, respectfully averting his eyes from my partial nudity. Ernest had removed my wings from the refrigeration unit and placed them – I assume you didn't notice them – on the long table beside the hospital bed on which I sat, the sheet draped around me. All seemed hushed and still, in spite of the crackling volts of power and the chugging of the machinery.

Ernest and I exchanged a last, long look. Then he prepared the syringe, and I held out my arm. He bent to administer the injection, and I held my breath, waiting for the needle's prick.

When the shot rang out, at first I didn't understand what had happened. Almost I thought it was part of the procedure, until I saw the shocked confusion in Ernest's eyes. The syringe clattered to the floor, and Ernest fell.

Then I saw you – my hero.

When Rocco made for you with a snarl, I hoped he would wrest the weapon from your hand and exact vengeance. But alas, you are an excellent shot.

I know you thought it womanly hysteria that made me struggle as you secured the sheet around me. You cared more for my modesty than for Ernest lying in his swiftly spreading blood, his face chalk white, eyes staring behind crooked spectacles, much less for Rocco dragging himself along the floor whimpering in pain. Hysteria, you thought, made me scream and kick and fight you as you slung me in your arms and carried me down the spiral staircase and outdoors. I would have run back to Ernest as soon as you set me on my feet, the mob of villagers with their rifles and scythes be damned – if not for the explosion.

"It's all over now," you gloated, pulling me into an entirely unwanted embrace.

You think I'm crazy, don't you – that he was mad and infected me with his madness. Papa and Mama and my sisters and brothers understand me as little as you do. Mama begs me to be grateful for your "rescue", to thank you for your pistol shot that laid waste to one of the greatest minds this world has known. I am lucky, she says, to be safely back in London, away from that dreadful place. She says that soon I will have forgotten everything that happened there, like a bad dream, and then you and I will marry! But I will never forgive you for dragging me away as he died on the laboratory floor, without me to hold his hand, to help him into the next world – a world, I trust, full of enough wonders to keep the most brilliant scientist happy. Here I remain, without even his creations to remember him by. Rocco must have pulled that lever, preferring death by his own hand to whatever fate others meant for him. I can't say I blame him.

Have no fear, I shan't take my life. Ernest's work was devoured by the conflagration – gone, the birds that swam and the fish that flew, all gone, my beautiful blue and orange wings – and I have not his genius, but I do have his daring. I shall learn to pilot an aeroplane. Laugh all you want, Charles, but there are women pilots in this world, and I mean to fly. Perhaps I will fly to our island, and then I will be free of the lot of you.

This Evening's Performance

Genevieve Valentine

I. Cast off Your Raincoat, Put on Your Dancing Shoes

"Shit," Emily said, as they pulled in to port. "They've lined up Dramatons to greet us."

Roger looked up. "They wouldn't."

"Photographers everywhere," she said, tugging at her coat. "An Ingénue, a Hero, a Femme Fatale, a Lothario, two Gentlemen – a thin model and a big one, I suppose they didn't know your size, Roger. One Dame, of course. And she's wearing my coat."

She pulled the curtain. "If they're trying to discourage us, they're making quite the argument."

Across the cabin, Peter checked his tie in the mirror and wrinkled his nose. "They want to compare? Let them. Roger, wear your gray coat. Emily, can you find something that doesn't look like you're trying so hard?"

She looked down. "The point of this coat is that you look like you're not trying."

"Or as though you're about to molt," Roger said, pocketing his libris and smoothing his shirt. "Which is preferable to making nice with Dramatons."

"It will pass," said Peter. "There are always little phases." He grinned over his shoulder on his way out, like a romance poster. "They won us the war; let them have their little triumph while people still love them. Come on."

After Peter was gone, Roger said, "Well, I'm not waiting. I'm throwing myself off the gangplank."

"Stop stealing the scene," she said. She fastened the last button on his black morning jacket and turned to him. "How does it look?"

It was big at her shoulders, small at her hips, and she wore it the way she carried off anything absurd. She was a good comedienne; during their first production of *This Bright Affair*, when Peter got sick and she'd had to play the randy near-sighted grandfather, Roger had broken at least once a night.

"Like you're not trying," he said.

Peter was waiting, brushing imaginary dust off his lapel.

He took Emily's arm with, "Break a leg, darling," and Roger followed them down the plank to face the Dramatons.

The worst thing about Dramatons, Roger thought as the press closed in, was how hard it was to hate them. He still managed, but it meant that he felt like a heel on top of everything else.

Their deployment in the Great War saved thousands of lives. Peter and Roger got draft papers just before the first automaton regiment shipped out, but as it happened, they were clever; the draft was postponed, and postponed, and within six months the war was over.

(When the automatons marched down Piccadilly, victorious, the whole troupe threw confetti and cheered until their throats were hoarse. Emily cried, denied it.)

The automatons were decommissioned (treaties demanded), but the government knew better than to dismantle such toys. Now they were riveters and train conductors and porters. They had endurance to thresh fields, and dexterity to assemble car engines. (Watchmakers were safe; they weren't as nimble as the hand of an artist.)

An industry for the displaced sprung up overnight: automaton maintenance and modification.

With the proper aesthetic mods, automatons were even decent on stage. It was only a dumb show with recordings piped through, but audiences had embraced worse performances.

Every city in the Empire had a set, a gift from a beneficent government.

They put actors out of business. Actors had put up a fight, but against changing tastes, there was only so much a troupe could do. One by one they caved; the Understudies were now creaking along, the last troupe that had existed before Dramatons.

Not their fault, though, he thought; they were programmed to act and pose, and knew nothing else.

Roger stood beside the thinner Gentleman, whose face was now a mask of dignified age. It turned to each camera as it flashed (it always knew which one was going to go off, of course; the mechanoid hearing).

Emily was looking at the Femme Fatale as if it was about to sprout a second head.

The Dramatons looked into the flashbulbs without blinking, smiling at the pivot points in their mouths. The Dame was more stoic than the rest, but her handler stood by in case she got *too* cool and needed adjusting.

Peter winked and waggled his brows and did all the elastic-face things Dramatons couldn't. The cameras went wild for him. They always had; thirty years running, Peter had upstaged anything that got in his way.

"Three weeks," he told a reporter. "No two performances alike! It'll be magic! Wait until you see these two on the stage! Humanity at its best."

Beside Roger, Emily shook hands with the Ingénue, allowed the Lothario to kiss her wrist.

"Cheeky gentlemen in your line of work," she told the Dame.

After a pause, the Dame repeated, "A gentleman is merely a rascal, better-dressed."

It was from *Vacationing in the Summer Palace*, from the dullest scene in that whole dull play.

Roger told Emily, "They're no good for conversation, that's their problem."

"Oh, my!" trilled the Ingénue, resting one hand on Peter's chest. She went up on tiptoes to drop a kiss on his cheek, the clicks of her joints barely audible under the sound of the cameras.

"Yes," said Emily, "that's their problem."

"Smile!" someone called, and a flashbulb went off.

*   *   *

The flat was shabbier than the last one had been, which had been shabbier than the last.

Peter said too firmly, "This is close to the theater. Perfect for rehearsals."

Roger knew better than to answer.

"We should talk about the run," said Emily, closing the door after the porter. "I saw the newsstand. They've set up a romance with an Ingénue and Hero. Thirteen magazine covers."

Roger had wondered how long it would take for them to catch on to that facet of the business. "Is the romance just in London, or everywhere?"

"I'm scared to look."

"You sound like Phil and Rose," Peter muttered. "Why don't you retire if you're going to jump at every shadow?"

It wasn't jumping at shadows, it was common sense, but Peter had never understood the difference.

Roger wondered how Emily had stayed married to him for so long; she was usually so ruthless about facing facts.

Emily had married in a brown velvet suit. She pulled back her hair with a silver comb from Rose, and walked the aisle with nothing but a little brass orchid.

(The papers gasped. 'Turn in Bridal Trends Expected!' claimed the *Tribune*. *Blushing Bride* panicked: 'Have We Seen the Last of White?' Some botanical magazine ran a feature on why natural orchids were better than brass, and asked for a letter-of-complaint campaign.

Greaselight Weekly cut to the chase: 'WHEN STARS COLLIDE'.)

In the receiving line, Rose shook Emily. "The comb was for the veil, you mad thing, I can't believe you went bareheaded! Peter, come here, darling, kiss me."

"That veil was like frosting myself," Emily said to Roger, next in line. "Horrible stuff."

She moved to kiss his cheek, but he froze, and they stood, her lips ghosting his skin, a moment too long.

"Horrible stuff," Roger agreed, moved down the line to shake Peter's hand.

The guests flooded the dance floor. Roger had never been much of a dancer. He considered signing the guest book. Didn't. She'd ordered a plain cake with chocolate icing, and it sat forgotten on a side table away from the band and the lights.

After he got home he hailed her libris.

"Sorry I didn't get a chance to see you. I thought I had, but turns out you dressed to match the cake. When they cut you up I was beside myself."

He didn't say, *I can't believe you did it*. He didn't say, *Peter wants to be famous and you want to be good and those are very different things, Emily. Emily.*

"Hope the honeymoon is lovely," he said, hung up.

Three days later he had a message, a screenful of tidy capitals.

BORED TO TEARS IN PARIS. NEED TO BE ACTING. WROTE PLAY OVER WEEKEND. GOT LETTER ABOUT HOW I HATE ORCHIDS; PEOPLE ARE MAD. HUSH ABOUT DRESS – ALL WAS LOVELY – YOUR LOSS.

They sat down at the table with a bottle of Scotch to work out the run.

Peter pulled out his libris, scrolled furiously through their catalog. The case was a scrap of poster from back when venues begged for charity shows. (It still had a sliver of the 'SOLD OUT' sign.) Sometimes Roger caught Peter smiling at it when he thought he was alone.

"We've got to start with a comedy," Peter said.

"Agreed," said Roger. Dramatons had never mastered timing; automaton-comedies relied on sight gags.

Peter frowned. "*The Last March of Colonel Preson*? It's still our best."

He was right (he was often right). Roger slid it to the front page.

"Then a romance," Emily said, and Roger said, "And end on a drama."

They didn't bother discussing which romance; it was time for *Mira*.

"The drama's got to be stunning," Peter said. "None of the old stuff. They're too good with that."

Emily skimmed her libris (still in the factory case); the light cast shadows along her face.

"It seems unfair they can do Shakespeare," she murmured.

Peter said (because it would have to be Peter who said it), "What about a War play?"

It was the one thing no one wanted from Dramatons; automatons had jobs to fill because English sons had died. Dramatons never touched on the War.

"I think we'd do better with *The Condemned Woman*," Roger suggested, not looking at Emily.

Peter dropped a hand to the table. "And have another Cardiff on our hands? No."

"Stop acting like we killed someone," Emily muttered, but she didn't look up. A moment later she said, "We could try *Pale Ghost*."

"And what am I supposed to do while you two are making cow-eyes at each other?" Peter asked, but then he stood, so it was settled.

The room seemed dimmer with Peter gone (rooms always did), but Roger preferred it. He was getting to an age where dimming the lights a little did a world of good.

"I miss Phil and Rose," she said.

He glanced down at his hands, which he'd folded over his libris (ebony inlaid with a little tin star).

She tapped a rhythm with her fingers.

"I'm going out," she said at last.

No surprise. Emily haunted theatres to watch the enemy in action.

She'd be going to the Theatre Dramaturgica. He'd seen posters on the way to the flat; they were staging *Regina Gloriana*. (Emily was too old for the part, now.)

What surprised him was the question, "Come along?"

He looked at her for a moment.

Then he stood. "By all means," he said. "After two weeks on choppy seas I've really been glutted on rest; I'm just aching to stumble around a strange city at all hours."

"You could just say no, you ham," she said, which was the first time he'd even thought about it.

★　　★　　★

The Dramaturgica was a temple of geometry. The seats were arranged in a trapezoid; the curtain was pulled straight across like a Japanese screen; the proscenium inlay was a mass of acute angles.

"Clever," said Emily as they took their seats.

As the lights went down, Roger saw why.

The Dramatons were sculpted and padded and dressed and painted until they were almost human, but the effect was . . . not quite. The sharp points of the proscenium helped soften the rough edges of the players.

The audience seemed unaware, but Roger could see it. It wasn't much. Maybe one beat in twenty stuttered. They moved like player pianos: the right notes on time every time, with no grace or life.

But they had flawless faces, sharp and perfect bodies. Even the aging King was handsome. All of them had a flashy beauty, a mask of quality. No one in the audience cared to know that anything was missing.

It felt like the balcony was tilting, like Roger was going to crash to the ground.

It always did, when he saw them act.

This, Roger hated most. In every city, Dramatons were doing their job. Standardized. No mistakes. No changes. Thirty years from now, an audience not yet born would be watching this scene exactly this way.

When the Queen embraced her consort it was a moment late, and her face was flat and unworried; but in filmy robes against a throne of eight-point stars, who else would think to see it?

At the interval he said, "Not comforting, is it?"

"No," she said, sounding far away.

"Maybe Peter's right," Roger went on. "The novelty is something, but after a while it will grate, won't it, all this ratcheting about? People will want human actors back. These will be old hat in a few years."

"It had better be a very few years, or we won't live to see it."

She was right more often than Peter was.

He stood up. "We should go home."

"You go if you like," she said. "I've forgotten how this one ends. I'm going to stick it out."

On his way out he glanced behind him; her hands were clenched in her lap, her eyes fixed on the stage.

She came home late. He heard her moving through the flat, walking quietly so as not to wake Peter, and Roger wondered if she had stood at the stage door.

(The stars went back to the dressing rooms only after stage-door photographs, to be calibrated by their handlers. Roger hadn't waited since the first time, ages ago – once was more than enough for that. But Emily – well, they all had bad habits.)

The Metropolitan was bright-scrubbed and shabby, and Mr Christie greeted them with the same forced cheer that was Peter's signature.

"Mr Elliott, Mrs El – Ms Howard, apologies, Mr Cavanaugh, a pleasure. Your journey was uneventful, I trust?"

"Do you know who set up the Dramatons at the dock?" from Emily.

Christie coughed. "The Metropolitan and the Dramaturgica are at the start of a relationship, and thought it would – we like to draw a little attention when we can."

"Of course," said Peter, hopping onstage and looking around. "Happy to be here."

"You'll find the dressing rooms sufficient, I hope. And the flat's suitable?" Mr Christie frowned, as if just remembering his stars might not like bunking up together like bit players. "Rents, you understand—"

"Nonsense," Peter cut in, grinning. "We're piled on each other backstage, seems right to bring it home. We're just excited to get to work. The dressing rooms?"

He and Emily walked with Mr Christie past the curtain. Roger looked out across the audience. The seats were uphol-stered in dull gold, fraying at the edges. Seat 5L was missing, an empty socket stage left.

He was too old to be here. This was a battleground for soldiers young enough to have a fight left in them.

When he caught up, Peter was glad-handing the secondar-ies, and Emily was in discussion with Mr Christie.

"The result's worth the extra rehearsals, you understand."

The last was mimicry, too subtle for Mr Christie, who only heard someone he liked, and nodded. Emily was quieter than Peter, but she was a deft hand at business.

("It's like an auto, isn't it?" she'd said to Roger ages ago. "You watch the engine for a while, the rest is common sense. Pass the salt.")

"I hope you can get by without the stage for a while," Christie said to Roger as if he'd asked. "The secondary players are bit out of practice, and we'll need the space to block them all."

"He doesn't need to rehearse," Emily said. "He's the best actor in the world."

Mr Christie took a proud breath, patted his pocket square like he was wired for sound. "Yes. Of course. Only the best for the Metropolitan, we've always said."

"Except seat 5L," she said quietly, after Mr Christie was gone, and Roger looked over at her a moment too late to catch her eye.

Peter was giddy; he turned up the radio and skipped Emily around the maze of the living room; then he stopped, spread his arms.

"We'll throw a party," he said. "Thespians aren't a dying breed! Alive and well in London, this autumn! I should call Christie."

Roger and Emily looked at each other.

Roger said, "We might want to rehearse first, Peter."

He smiled and danced into the kitchen. "Nonsense! This is going to be the story of the year on the newsreels, you watch me. Most of them are hopeless, but no one's going to notice, and there was some David and some Penelope who have a chance at it if they work. She'd be lovely in *Pale Ghost* as your sister, Emily."

"She would," Emily agreed smoothly, the way she always did when Peter mentioned a girl he was going to sleep with.

"Better get started," said Roger, and stood.

He closed his bedroom door tightly and studied his script until the words ran into each other, a maze of letters he didn't understand.

II. Little Tin Stars

Emily got Peter to see reason, and they rehearsed for a month before Peter announced the party.

Christie wasn't happy. "Mr Grant, of course that's a generous idea, but the terms of your lease forbid—"

"Oh, we'll have it here!" Peter said, as if that had been the plan all along, and Emily looked with sympathy at poor Mr Christie, who was out of his league with Peter when it came to finding loopholes.

Roger was gnawing on his bottom lip to keep his countenance. (Born gentleman.)

But as Christie moved past her, Emily winked at Roger, and of course then he smiled.

Twenty years ago, whenever they'd gone on tour, Emily and Rose had four trunks, not counting Rose's jewelry. Emily hated the stuff (once during *The Duchess* the fake pearls had broken and they'd spent the interval frantically sweeping so they wouldn't break their necks), but Rose slung bangles over her wrists like armor.

Every night the five of them had walked out together into blinding flashbulbs, a knot of long jackets and long gowns, a cluster of stars.

Their shows were staged in opera houses, and they'd gathered in the wings at the start of each performance to listen to two thousand people applauding as the curtain rose. The whole stage trembled under their feet.

Emily opened her suitcase and shook off her good gown. If she hung it in the bathroom while she bathed, most of the wrinkles would fall out in the steam. The rest of the wrinkles didn't matter; they'd match her face.

"Oh, we've got just LOADS of people interested," Penelope said. "Nearly three hundred people came to our last one, it was smashing!"

Emily looked out at the sparse collection of guests. The three photographers who'd bothered to show were drinking the good gin and not taking any pictures.

"God," Penelope went on, like it was a conversation, "I can't WAIT till the run. We've been gnawing since we knew you were coming – I mean, THE Peter Elliott, THE Emily Howard! I've loved you for AGES, ever since I was little! I won't let you down, I promise."

Emily glanced over at Penelope and her dress, made of beaded netting and optimism.

"We should try the bar," Emily said. It would give the photographers something to shoot, and she needed a drink.

Roger was talking with two young men; they were his sons in *Pale Ghost*, and the suitors in *Colonel Preson*, and something in *Mira* she didn't remember. They were hanging on his every word, nodding solemnly in tandem, and she would have laughed, except it was Roger and he generally deserved someone's attention.

"Darling," said Peter from beside her, "things are picking up! What do you think?"

He pointed to the bar, where Penelope was posing for two cameras. She moistened her lips and glanced at Peter.

Emily had never looked at Peter that way, not once.

(He had a soft spot for the exception to the rule.)

"Well, go on," Emily said at last.

Peter kissed her cheek. "Sweet old thing," he said, and then he was beside Penelope.

The flash washed away his crow's feet, the bastard.

"Christ," Roger said beside her, "help me, it's like the lectures of Socrates over there."

This close, she could feel his warmth right through her sleeve.

"It's respectful to learn from your elders."

He snorted. "I was going to ask if you wanted a drink," he said, and moved ahead.

He walked between Peter and Penelope, so they had to step back from one another, and for a moment Emily's dress was too tight, like she'd taken too big a breath.

A flash went off, catching everyone at the bar: Penelope frowning at Roger, Peter frowning at the cameras, Roger with a glass in his hand, looking around without a care in the world.

*   *   *

Peter folded his arms under his head.

"Do you think we'll be all right?" he asked, his voice nervous in the dark.

His voice always gave him away even if his face was composed; it was why he was a mediocre actor, and why he was so fond of photographs.

Sometimes she thought he'd married her just so she'd figure that out about him. Sometimes she thought she'd married him just to find him out.

Sometimes she thought she was a fool.

"No," she said finally. "We won't be all right. They're shit, and we're old."

"Oh, what are you like? You'll jinx us if you keep talking like that." He thumped his pillow. "I'm going to start sleeping with Roger."

"Don't, please," she said. "There's got to be someone left on the planet you're not sleeping with."

After a long silence, Peter kissed her hair. "You'll see. We'll come out in front."

He'd said the same in Dublin, and in Cardiff, and the Isle of Skye, where the wind beat so loud against the ramshackle theatre that the fifty people who came couldn't hear. The Dramatons staged the same play a week later, in the concert hall, to an audience of a thousand.

"Here's hoping," she said.

Her good dress was hanging from the back of the door, and when Roger turned on the light in the living room it bled through a little hole in the left sleeve.

Better mend it, she thought after a moment, as long as someone else was awake.

Roger was sitting at the kitchen table studying his libris. The screen hummed like it was a holy text and not a comedy about a drunk Colonel who misplaces his soldiers on the way home from war.

He didn't look up as she sat across from him, and she was well into her work before he spoke.

"Painting the town red this evening?"

"We might have another party," she said, moving the needle through the fabric (she'd gotten good at mending). "I can't have a hole in my frock. It doesn't do to be threadbare in front of fine people."

Roger glanced up, held her gaze. The seconds ticked by on the kitchen clock.

"Except you," she said, half-smiled around the tightness in her throat. "You're fine people."

Sometimes she thought that Roger knew about it all. "You always look lovely," he said, dropped his gaze. "I'll go back to my room. Don't want to wake Peter."

Sometimes she thought Roger was a fool.

"Of course I came back," Roger said. His face filled her vision. "Would I let death stop me now?"

Emily took a shuddering breath, on the verge of tears. "But at dawn . . ."

"Dawn is not upon us yet," he said, lowered his face to hers. She rested her hand on his elbow. They hesitated.

"Good," said Peter. "Fine. Penelope, wait for them to break the kiss, and then come out and cross downstage. Penelope? Good morning, Penelope, are you with us?"

"Sorry," Penelope said like she had been woken from a dream, "I was just – caught up."

"Well, if you would actually catch up, I'd appreciate it," said Peter.

Penelope scurried to her mark, her shoes clomping on the cheap wood.

"Good. I like that composition. Roger, please remember, when you step back you have to stay in reach of the spot. Right, then I need the sons. Sons, could you perhaps stir yourselves on cue?"

Peter only had eyes for the stage when he was directing. Even if he looked over, he wouldn't see how Roger had turned his face so his mouth wasn't so close to her mouth; he wouldn't see her fingers wrapped around Roger's arm to hold them steady.

Peter was an indifferent actor; to him it was all artifice of some kind or another. Didn't much matter why, so long as it ended with applause.

She was never lonelier than during these minutes, when Peter was lost in the play, and Roger was just lost.

"Roger, then you step back – Roger?"

Roger's arm slid through her fingers; he vanished out of the spot, and he was behind the shield of the rotting curtain, and Emily was standing alone, looking after him.

"Lovely," Peter said, "just the thing. Now, older son, I forgot your name, cross to your mother and take her by the shoulder; you want to see what the matter is."

During Emily's first week at university, Peter and Phil had put on a vaudeville act.

The writing was so awful that no one noticed the act amid the booing, but she was captivated despite the rough; they were like rubber men, painted eyes gleaming above infectious grins.

She could tell that Phil had more sense and Peter had more spark. (It would amaze her later how easy it was to see how people really were, and how you tried so hard not to see, but back then she had been clever.)

The next day she caught up with Phil on the green outside St Catharine's.

"You're one of those lads looking for a writer."

He'd frowned. "We're not."

"You should be."

Phil glared at her from his impossible height (she wasn't short, but Lord, he loomed). She met his eye until he laughed.

"We might, yeah. Come meet Peter."

Peter shook her hand with the same false welcome he gave everyone, and had nodded along with her ideas, smiling and winking and telling her they were going to have a hell of a time.

"And with your lovely face we'll do a bit better for ourselves," he said, half to Phil, grinning.

"It's not a face you need," she'd said, "it's a script that doesn't put the audience to sleep."

Phil laughed and shook hands, and after a moment Peter gave her a sixpence grin and shook, too.

A week later they were banging out something for the New Year.

In October she found out that Peter hadn't wanted to share credit, and it had taken Phil two weeks to force him to agree.

She confronted Peter. He'd frowned like he wasn't sure how to frame a real answer, and said finally, "No one likes someone to say they're better at his craft than he is. Takes the wind out of you."

"What, you'd have kept that awful act for years? You're so afraid of hearing no?"

He'd looked at her and said, "No, you're right," as if it was the first time in his life he'd realized it was possible for a girl to be right.

The flirting stopped. He started taking her advice.

And he ended up having plenty of practice sharing credit; Phil was always taking in strays.

Rose had been refused a part in *Twelfth Night* amid rumors her Olivia would have been a bit too fond of Viola. Just as well; they were getting desperate for a romantic lead. (Even Phil could play a more alluring ingénue than Emily could.)

"It's a pleasure," Peter said, shook Rose's hand with a wink, and as soon as Rose was gone Peter grinned and said, "I'm in there."

Emily had cut off Phil's protest, and she and Phil and Rose enjoyed three months of Peter tripping over himself running after her, until Rose brought her bosom friend Agnes to rehearsal.

"You're all a bunch of bastards," Peter said when he saw them holding hands, and they'd laughed until they cried, even, eventually, Peter.

That first year, the Understudies staged plays with as few characters as possible, Emily and Phil rending costumes backstage to play housemaid and dowager, best friend and priest, while Peter and Rose pitched passionate woo.

The second year, Carol and Fitzpatrick joined.

Peter's choice, those two; he would pick two charming lookers without asking for so much as a line reading.

As it turned out, Carol and Fitz had no talent, but they had chemistry. Their *Romeo and Juliet* could draw tears before intermission. They couldn't handle much else, but they pushed through play after play on nothing but frenzied stage kisses and longing looks, and the Understudies began to draw a crowd.

Mid-season, Carol and Fitz slept together.

They announced their engagement, and Rose and Phil and Emily had wished them joy, but Peter was quiet.

"It's over," he said afterwards, in Emily's room. He sat back on the bed and frowned at his knees. "Now they've slept together, it's gone."

"We've slept together," Emily pointed out.

"We didn't have any chemistry to start with," he said. "We've always been the old woman and the man wooing her daughter."

After a moment, Emily said, "Well, they have nothing but chemistry. They'll hang on to it. They have to."

Peter shook his head.

Their first performance after the holidays was *Twelfth Night*; a scout came from London to see it.

Fitz and Carol's chemistry was gone. It was a massacre.

Rose, wide-eyed, gripped Emily's wrists and hissed, "Do something!"

The scout left without speaking to one of them.

Carol and Fitz left at the end of the season. Noises were made, but roles for youthful mannequins with no chemistry were thin on the ground, and no one regretted their going.

(They were all, Emily found out later, thinking of going themselves.)

That spring, Phil found Roger.

Roger wasn't even trained; he was just in Phil's student house, and Phil only found out he could act when Roger ran lines with him as a favor.

"You won't believe it," Phil had told Emily.

Roger's pants were threadbare at the knees, his collar askew, his face too angular, but as soon as the first words were out, it was all over.

His monologue was from *The Condemned Woman*. When Peter said, "Well, you'll do," she knew Peter hated him. (That had been Peter's pet role; Peter couldn't touch it now.)

"Good to meet you," said Emily, "we need someone dour," and Roger had made a noncommittal face, then smiled at her when no one else could see.

When the curtain first went up on *The Condemned Woman*, Emily was wearing a deep blue cloak spangled with little tin stars, and from the wings Roger crossed to her and held her hard enough that the points cut her.

The audience went stone silent until they broke apart.

The next night, an audience of twice as many went twice as quiet.

Every night of the run, playing to a fuller and a fuller house, Emily and Roger stood tangled in the cloak of tin stars, listening to an audience enthralled.

The last night, as Roger embraced her, there was such desperation in it that someone in the audience gasped.

The scout came back; spoke to them all.

They packed their bags for London.

At first, Peter courted whatever press bureau was willing to send a man to photograph a bunch of upstarts. Soon, clusters of them waited outside their hotels. They all took to dressing sharp, just in case.

They started getting offers from the Continent.

Rose developed a voracious appetite for jewelry. Peter developed a voracious appetite for anything. Roger took every spare hour to sneak out and watch other plays.

"Sizing up the competition," Phil said. "Very clever."

"No," said Roger, quietly, and Phil said, "Don't be embarrassed, it's good business," and ordered another round.

Roger looked at Emily and said, "I just . . . love it all," and she felt for a moment like the others and the pub and the cameramen outside had fallen away, and he had seen right through her.

"I know," she said, quietly.

Roger was searching her face, and his eyes were gray, and his lips thinned out when he really smiled.

Then Peter was bringing her a beer, and the world came rushing back, and a flashbulb went off in the window.

★   ★   ★

Phil and Peter got them better and better contracts, but Emily put her foot down in Prague.

"The non-compete clause is so shoddy they'll never be able to hold us," Phil said.

"One great gig in every city isn't much unless they want us back," she'd said. "Bad form. Better to take less money and have a place to come home to."

Peter had said, "She's right."

(It was the first time he'd stood up for anyone but himself.)

"You owe me an auto for the money I'm giving up," said Phil, tearing up the papers with a sigh.

In Prague, Peter found real English tea, and brewed it all night for Emily when she was memorizing lines.

In Prague she began to love him.

For months they clacked around in trains, threading through vineyards and snowy forests. They stalked around stages four times as large as their hotel suites, avoiding scrim-riggers and carpenters as they tried to work out the kink in this scene or that one.

By then, some things were understood.

When Emily and Roger were in a scene together, carpenters tended to stop what they were doing. Peter sometimes made them practice *The Condemned Woman* just to get some quiet if they couldn't hear themselves over the hammering.

(It was nice, Emily thought; Roger was so quiet otherwise, it was nice to share something.)

If they went on too long, Phil would clear his throat.

"Just making sure he's paying attention," she'd say at once, and Roger would look around and say, "Wait, isn't this Vienna?" and the carpenters always laughed.

At night they all cinched themselves into gowns and tuxedos and went to supper clubs, a crowd of glittering talent blinking into the flashbulbs, signing *cartes de visites* for awestruck girls.

Emily hated the gowns. She started wearing trousers on the trains and in rehearsal.

It was a small scandal, but by the time they made it back to Paris, the wife of the theatre owner was wearing a pair of tweed trousers when she came to greet them.

"Now see what you've done," Roger told her, when they were out of hearing, and she made a caught-out face at him and grinned.

"If you keep on this way you'll be more photographed than Rose," he called over that night, as they unpacked in their connecting suites.

It didn't seem likely – the cameras liked glitter – but she sighed.

"Then I'll wear shoes on my hands. That should help; that doesn't look very sharp."

"I happen to look very distinguished when I do it," said Roger.

Peter came in.

"You have to come downstairs," he said. His eyes glittered, and he was coiled with nerves, and as soon as she took his hand she knew what was coming.

He proposed on the bank of the Seine, on one knee, and she laughed for a full minute before his expression registered.

"Emily, I mean it."

His eyes were bright; without trying to be charming he still was, the bastard.

"The first time you look at another woman, it's over," she said.

He grinned and kissed her, and then they went upstairs to tell the others.

"You're mad," said Rose, and Phil said, "He's a prat."

Roger said, "I wish you well."

It wasn't the answer she'd expected, and she didn't know why.

But they forgave her, and after photographers snapped pictures of Emily's plain gold band for a week they got bored and went back to Rose's fabulous jewelry.

It would be all right, Emily knew – they were all young and flush and happy, and she and Peter could make a go of it if they wanted, and night after night she could walk onto a stage.

Peter stayed late after rehearsal at the Metropolitan.

"To whip these secondaries into shape," he said, and kissed Emily on the cheek.

"Wonderful," she said. She almost said, *Roger and I will go to bed, then*, but it didn't do to sound jealous, and she wouldn't dare pull Roger into this.

"See you," she said instead, and Peter gave her a genuine smile and didn't say, "I'll be home later." The omission was as close as he could be to honesty.

"You take it well," Roger said when they were outside.

She shrugged and slid her hands into her pockets. "I've had practice."

He shook his head and fell silent; beyond this point they never went. Instead, they got fish and chips from a kiosk and went home to read lines.

At midnight, halfway through the double-entendre scene in *Mira*, Roger sat back and clicked his libris shut.

"God, I'm too old for this. It's about first love. We'll be laughed off the stage."

"Who's asking if you've been in love before or not?" She pulled a cigarette from the packet on the table, lit it from Roger's lighter. "You think the robots are out there convincing people they fall in love? Give the audience something different."

He frowned at the libris like it was feeding him the wrong lines. "If I were a better actor, maybe."

"I don't know why you play at this," she said. "You're really something."

"Something aged," he muttered, went in the kitchen.

For such a quick study, Roger was dense as a brick. She didn't understand how he couldn't see that whenever he took the stage he filled it, his voice moving over the audience like a living thing.

For three weeks it went that way.

Roger almost kissed her as the Pale Ghost. She boxed Roger's ears for leaving his regiment behind in *The Last March of Colonel Preson.* They stood side by side and mocked the world in *Mira*, which felt like the rest of their lives, except that in *Mira* he kissed her at regular intervals.

Peter came home later and later.

One morning she saw he hadn't come to bed at all, which gave her a pang. It was one thing for him to find a woman younger, less likely to have a go at him; it was another when he found a woman more worthy of his time.

(He should be faithful some way. It was the least he could do.)

Peter was sitting at the kitchen table, drinking tea and staring at the kitchen cupboards.

"Just get home?"

He gave a guilty start, nodded.

"You need to come home at night," she said, sitting opposite him. "It looks—" She stopped.

He flinched into his tea. "Do you think I'm hurting you, Em?"

"Just come home," she said, which wasn't a real answer, but he took it. The real answer wasn't something to examine. No point, after all this time.

He rubbed his forehead with his thumb. "I've always cared for you, Em, you know that."

"I do." You couldn't go thirty years on nothing.

He leaned in. "And you?"

She never remembered Peter onstage; he was charismatic, but it was all for the audience and not for the actors, and she forgot.

What she remembered was Peter taking the piss with Phil or Rose, brainstorming their next break. And it worked, right up until the War.

Even after, with the Dramatons, they'd put up a better fight than most. Peter was married to the troupe, even if he forgot he was married to Emily.

"Let me get tea," she said, standing up.

In the early light he looked his age at last, the wrinkles that had gouged the rest of them finally showing up under his eyes, bracketing his mouth.

He didn't look at her, like her answer had upset him, but when she handed him the cup he drank, and when she sat down across from him he rested his hand on her hand, and that was how Roger found them.

"Peter's staying late," she said when she met Roger outside the Metropolitan. "We should go out."

"But we've seen that one already."

She grinned. "Get your coat."

It wasn't the same play. ("That's what I get for whinging," Roger said, "wind out of my sails.") It was a preview, *The Rendezvous*. They had to queue to get in.

At the door, one reporter stuck out a microphone. "Mrs Elliott – sorry, Miss Howard? The Understudies?"

"Yes."

"Last of a dynasty! Sporting of you to be here!"

Emily managed not to make a face, but when she shot a look at Roger the reporter followed the gaze and piped up, "And who are you with?"

"I'm the carpenter," Roger said.

"Oh, the stage is *gorgeous*, congratulations!"

"Thank you," he said. "We worked very hard."

After that it wasn't worth trying to sit through the play, since Emily couldn't even keep a straight face in the lobby, so they cut out and went home.

Her bedroom door was closed.

"Pretend we're alone," she said.

"If only," he said, but closer than that they never got, and he banged around the kitchen making tea as she tuned the radio.

They listened to the news, and the local society-page gossipeuse blew a lot of smoke about the beauty of the Dramatons in the new production, and how they were without doubt the best artistic invention since the violin.

"Even human actors can't deny the appeal of Dramatons," said the broadcaster, "as Emily Howard of the Understudies made an appearance in the company of one of the set designers."

Emily laughed herself into a coughing fit.

"... at her best, even as her smile masked heartache. Ex-husband Peter Elliott was announced as the new Artistic

Director before the curtain rose, and received with thunderous applause. The premiere Saturday should be a smashing success, and well deserved. Best of luck to Elliott and company!"

The broadcast continued in the silent room. There were five minutes of compliment-clips from the audience. Two minutes of pre-recorded audio from the play.

Roger got up and switched off the set.

"First you've heard," he guessed, looking at her.

She cleared her throat.

That's what Peter had been talking about in the kitchen. You couldn't make new coats from old cloth. The moment he'd met the secondary cast he must have known.

He'd been a clever boy. Selfish, clever boy.

The Understudies were down to two.

She washed her face, and ate a bit off a chocolate bar, and at last she sat down beside Roger with a bottle of Scotch and got to work a glass at a time.

The couch seemed smaller.

"A prince among men," he said, like he'd been waiting to get it off his chest, and after he'd finished that little speech he took the glass from her hand and drank.

"It's not a tragedy," she told him a little later.

They were sitting at the table, with tea and some pastries he'd conjured out of nowhere. It felt strange to be really alone with him.

"That's just how it is," she said. Her voice was worn, like she'd screamed. "It lights like a candle, and it just burns out."

"I see," he said.

Steam slipped past the cheap seal on the kettle, dissolving into the dry air, and she felt like something had cracked that could never be repaired.

He didn't ask her any questions; closer than that they never got.

III. Everyone Take Your Places

As Roger expected, Mr Christie was not pleased.

"It's unconscionable!"

Emily folded her arms and said, "As unconscionable as making your leads rehearse for a month without wages?"

That threw him, and before he could go on Emily said, "Roger and I have both directed. The shows are blocked. There's no reason the run can't go on, if you're willing to back us."

"Mr Elliott was in all three plays. Where will you find an actor to fulfill the terms of the contract?"

Phil, Roger thought at once.

He looked at Emily, and she said to Mr Christie, "Give us a day."

Phil owned a hotel in Kensington that had a dress code just for the lobby.

Roger put on his gray suit in the cramped bedroom. The reflection in the mirror looked more dignified than the first time he'd put it on; he'd looked solemn and foolish then, like a boy in an old photograph. Now he had the wrinkles and the bearing that suited him; now, when it was too late to put them to any good use. He was too obsolete to act, and too tired for love affairs.

"Emily?" his reflection called. "Are you ready?"

From inside the other bedroom Emily said, "One moment. Trying to look as though we're worth throwing in with."

"Too late for that," he said. "Just mend up your shabby and come out."

"This dress makes me look like a coffin."

"It does not," Roger said, and when she opened the door he amended, "Only slightly."

"I'll just wear a suit," she said with a sigh, closed the door again.

"Whose?" Roger asked, though he knew.

She even wore Roger's top hat, so when they walked side by side they looked like a vaudeville team. The black trousers were too long on her, and only her heels kept the hems out of the dust.

The host stepped in front of them before they had set foot on the soft carpet.

"Madam—"

"Miss."

". . . I'm very sorry, but the Maitland maintains a very strict dress code."

"And I'm *wearing* the full suit," she said, and Roger tried not to laugh in the poor man's face.

"Yes, thank you, but I'm afraid I can't allow it."

"Let the poor woman through, she's only gone senile in her old age," said Phil from behind them, and then Emily was laughing and embracing him, one hand pressed against the crown of her hat to keep it from falling.

Phil was still tall and thin and elegant. The white at his temples was the same they painted in when he was Colonel Preson. Frozen in time; that's what a life of honest business did for you.

The hotel restaurant was discreet to the point of being underlit, and Roger fumbled his way through the four courses guessing what he was eating.

Emily hardly ate; she and Phil traded horror stories and laughed and made small talk like he didn't know why Roger and Emily had come by his posh hotel.

Phil was lovely about these things, though; always had been. Back when they all might as well have been shooting at each other, Phil was the one who smoothed over quarrels, who stayed friendly with flings in every city.

When Phil left, Roger had acted from Phil's example; some-one had to smooth things over.

Roger had forgotten how he'd missed Phil until they were sitting in the club after dinner, in a comfortable silence, and Phil sat forward and said, "Children, children, what a bloody mess you're in."

Roger laughed, and even as Emily nudged Phil she was smiling.

Emily should have married Phil – better to have been stuck with Phil all these years, Roger thought, stopped himself.

"How are you holding up?" asked Phil.

Roger looked at Emily.

She shrugged. "Don't know, really. It's like my parents are divorcing, not me. I feel old, is the pity. You shut your face," she said, and pointed, and Roger closed his mouth with exaggerated care.

Phil laughed. "And Roger?"

"Unemployed," Roger said, "now that Peter's fucked off and left us."

Phil sucked in air through his teeth. "God, I hadn't thought of that. That's awful."

Emily gave Phil the full force of her concentration. "Don't suppose you're dying to play one last London run?"

Phil sat back and looked at the cigarette in his fingers. On the dance floor behind him, couples were swaying to the music of a human orchestra.

Roger held his breath, prayed there was something he hadn't thought of that would convince Phil to come home.

"Don't suppose I would be," Phil said after a long time. "That was ages ago. Different time. I've got a reputation, you know; can't go about at my age trying to relive an old dream."

Phil had bowed out right on the cusp of the trouble, the first of them to go. He kept his eye on sales, and after two seasons of Dramatons outselling them he was gone, quietly investing in the hotel, quietly wishing them well, quietly stepping back.

Roger looked up at the crowd swanning in and out across the marbled lobby outside the club; and Phil, across from him, master of it all and not aged a day.

Phil had been very wise.

Beside Roger, Emily tapped on the brim of her hat. "We could really use you, Phil."

"I'm sorry." He sat back. "After all this time, I couldn't."

Before Roger could think better of it, he asked, "And should we quit, do you think?"

Emily looked at him, back at Phil.

Phil, to his credit, met their eyes.

"No shame in it," Phil said. "Better that than a dead run. Leave them wanting more."

Roger could see in Emily's profile that the gears were already turning; she was calculating odds, weighing her chances, looking ahead with those hard eyes.

"Phil, let's have a dance," she said. "It's been ages since I heard a human orchestra."

Phil grinned and took her hand as he stood. "It's one of my amenities," he said. "No automatons. Unless you count some of the concierges, they're dull as planks, but what can you do?"

"You can stop with the hiring practices and dance with me," Emily said.

She left her hat at the table. Roger rested his fingertips on it. It was smooth; too smooth in some places. Soon the brim would fray.

Her hair was bobbed, and with both of them in suits she and Phil looked like the beginning of a burlesque. They danced with half-closed eyes and happy smiles, Emily chatting and grinning like she was content.

You'd never guess anything was wrong, if you didn't know how she looked when her heart was broken.

Roger tapped the beat with two fingers on the crown of the top hat and gathered his nerve.

The next song was slow, and before he could second-guess himself Roger was standing, taking her hand, leading her onto the floor.

They'd danced together onstage. For three years in London they'd done society plays where half the dialogue took place on the dance floor.

(He'd always felt sorry for Rose, who was a foot shorter than any of the men and got trod on six nights a week for three years.)

Roger wasn't sharp at it, but he could trudge back and forth to a sad song as well as anyone.

He took the stage embrace, but she stepped closer into his arms, like the beginning of *The Condemned Woman*. Conspiratorial. End-of-the-line.

After a moment, he lowered his head until his chin was beside her temple.

"Rose is here," Emily said to Roger's lapel. "She and her lady friend live on the sixth floor. And the Theatre Dramaturgica just checked someone into one of the suites."

Peter.

Roger frowned. "What a reunion."

"We should decide what we're going to do," she said. She tightened her grip on his shoulder, turned to look at him. Her nose brushed his cheek. They were nearly kissing.

"Tomorrow," he said.

They were going to fall to pieces later, but they hadn't danced in ten years, and it was a beautiful song.

After a beat, she said against his jaw, "You're a bit crap at all this."

"I know," he said, kept dancing.

It was raining on the way out, and he nudged her into a taxi over her protests about the expense. They were penniless, but he'd be damned if they were going to run into Peter sopping wet like a couple of refugees.

"I was thinking of writing," she said to the window. "People may want things performed the same way, but they always need new things to perform. People are odd."

Her face reflected off the glass; against the cityscape he could see narrowed eyes, a drawn-thin mouth.

"Peter could use the help," he said.

"Don't."

He watched the streets sliding past the window. It felt like something pressing on his throat.

"I could voice," he said. "They're always looking for people to do interpretation. Poor sods can't do it themselves, can they?"

"Oh. I hadn't thought of that."

He frowned. "You disapprove?"

"For you? Nonsense, you're wonderful. Brilliant idea."

His chest tightened. "And you?"

She shook her head.

"God, I need a smoke."

"You do," he said, watched her tap out a pattern on the glass.

*   *   *

Mr Christie was a man of discretion; their contracts and canceled lease were delivered, so they wouldn't waste a trip to the theatre to be sacked in front of the secondaries.

Roger poured them each a drink. They finished in single swallows.

"Right," he said. "Let's pack up, and we'll go flat-hunting this afternoon."

"If you want anything of Peter's, now's the time to claim it."

He had no interest in anything of Peter's, but he said, "Would you like a hand?"

"No," she said, closed the door.

Emily packed Peter's things neatly in his case and sent them to the Maitland Hotel.

"No big scene?" Roger wasn't sure what to expect, but after a quarter-century of marriage she might feel like setting his good shirts ablaze.

"I kept all his braces. He'll have to buy belts."

"Petty theft is the best revenge."

"Hush," she said, and handed him a paper bag. "Enjoy your braces. I have to bring these downstairs."

He started to offer, but she shook her head and went down alone.

The bedroom bore no sign of Peter, as if he'd only been an overnight guest; as if a single suitcase had carried away anything he'd ever done.

When Emily came back he had her drink ready.

"I always said you were a gentleman," she said, toasted him silently.

"To whom?"

She shrugged. "There must have been someone I talked to besides you."

It was the last of the Scotch, and as Emily cleaned out of the bathroom and her bedroom, Roger found things in the kitchen, and they ate the last bits of cheese and fruit from the icebox so they wouldn't go to waste.

Emily moved slowly, seemingly unconcerned that the landlord was coming for the keys at five. She rolled her perfume bottles into her socks, folded her good dress in newspaper.

"Keeps the wrinkles off," she said when she saw him looking.

As they were putting on their hats and coats, the porter returned from the Maitland with an invitation for Mr Roger Cavanaugh and Ms Emily Howard to avail themselves of his hotel, free of charge, until such time as they should find suitable employment.

"About time," Emily said, and then Roger realized why she'd made the good-faith gesture of sending over the luggage; a guaranteed guilt response from Phil, who did so love settling quarrels.

The relief stung him.

"God, I could kiss you," he said.

She looked at him for a long time before she said, "Let's get a taxi."

At the Maitland the concierge nodded when they gave their names. "And would you like adjoining suites?"

"Just the one," said Emily.

Roger frowned, but Emily only touched his back and said, "We shouldn't take more space than we need."

Long after they were in the suite and she'd gone into the bedroom to hang her things, he could feel where the warmth of her hand had seeped through his jacket.

There was no mention of parting.

After a debate about whether or not to dine downstairs ("Should we?" "No." "Right."), they got bread and cheese and pears from a grocer. Roger insisted they get *something* from the hotel, so they ordered tea from room service and paid the tab promptly. It made Roger feel less in Phil's debt, though he knew one night in this suite was probably worth Roger's salary for the entire run.

They listened to the news on her bedroom radio. The Dramaturgica got another interview.

"The range of material is stunning," Peter said, his voice tinny. "These are some of the most knowledgeable actors I've had the pleasure to work with in all my years in theatre. Opening night is going to be groundbreaking."

"We can hope," said Roger.

She frowned. "Don't."

Emily had never vilified Dramatons the way other actors had, back when it was a battle. She joined the Actors' Rights Union but never campaigned, and declined the "Live Theatre is Really Living" radio spots. She and Roger had rows over it, loud and mean enough that Phil had to intervene.

Roger didn't understand why Emily seemed so devoid of disgust for them. He wasn't given to it, but he hated their fame, and he hated audiences who couldn't see the difference between real and manufactured.

"I'm going to talk to United Entertainment tomorrow," she said. "They're always looking for writers."

"Fine," he said around the ache in his chest. "Best get some sleep, then. Lots of groveling in the morning."

"Go to your room and shut your face, I'll be brilliant," she said, and got up to brush her teeth.

United kept her for three hours.

He'd gone with her, and it only made sense to apply as a voiceover artist while he was waiting. They sent him home with a table-top recorder and a stack of scripts.

"Whatever you think suits," the lady said, in a tone that made it clear this was his first test of employment.

So they set up on his bed, and Emily flipped through the scripts and sorted them into piles.

"Crap," she said, dropped one onto the larger stack beside the bed. "Crap. Crap. Very good," she said, tucked one under her knee. "Crap. Crap. You should give these people a talking-to, they sent you home with awful stuff."

"I'll have to take your word for it, I have yet to see anything."

She shoved something into his hands. "Read this first, then we'll do the other one."

It was a good monologue, that gray space between hero and villain that he most liked to occupy. Inflections, intonations, pushed forward from the page. All he'd have to do was open his mouth.

"What's the other?" he asked.

"The one where I'm your wife," she said, dropped another

on the pile. "Watch out with these people. They're trying to turn you into a Lothario. At your age it will kill you."

When he woke it was full night. The darkness pressed on him through the window, as if the streetlights had turned away. Music poured from the club downstairs; some foxtrot he didn't know.

Emily was asleep, turned away from him. The libris was still on, resting in the space between them, the Condemned Woman's speech flickering faintly in the dark.

(Two years ago, in Cardiff, she'd missed a line and thrown them three minutes past the pivotal reconciliation. There was no way to go back from where she'd put them, and they'd had to go on without it. The audience didn't know the play enough to complain, but they knew something was missing; it read in the limpid applause.

Peter was furious with her; Emily was more furious at herself than Peter was.

"It's just not what it was," she'd said, shaken, after Peter had stormed out of the dressing room. "I mean, you're rubbish in the farewell scene anyway, aren't you?"

"Terrible," Roger agreed.)

After a minute he realized; in a pinch, you could cut out crowd scenes and the magistrate and perform the play with two actors.

He held out his hand to her, hesitated. When she breathed in her shoulder almost touched his palm; when she breathed out it sank away from him, out of reach.

Downstairs they struck up the first bars of "Forgetting You". The bandleader murmured something into the microphone, and the singer began.

Roger brought his hand back to his chest, stared at the ceiling, tried to breathe.

IV. When All Else Fails, Drop the Curtain

For six weeks Emily wrote afternoon radio dramas – half an hour minus the time it took to advertise ipecac and baking soda – and clocked them quickly enough to make an income.

It was great fun; it was every overwrought scenario from vaudeville without a sense of humor, and she and Roger sat up nights running lines and trying not to break.

"'Oh, Charles, my dearest love, shot, shot down in the street! The Black Masques must be behind this! Oh, Detective Allan, you must believe me! You must help me!'"

"'By all heaven's gold, I will do neither!' God, Em, really?"

"Keep going. I need to fill two minutes before the butter advert."

Eventually, British Broadcast Radio 4 began to send back notes suggesting that her characters make good use of baking soda, or butter, or men's suits.

"They're not serious," said Roger.

"Oh, I've taken care of it." She handed him a paper.

"'Damn you, Brewster, the police will be on us any second! We have to get this blood off our clothes! Quick, grab me Lincoln's Own baking soda!'"

"Too much?" she asked.

He grinned.

The BBR chose not to record that scene.

Instead, Autumn the socialite insisted that the cake for her dinner party be made only with Lincoln's Own, "since anything else is simply déclassé."

"They're censoring art, you know," she said.

"Dictators," said Roger from his half of the bed.

Six weeks they'd slept in the suite, and neither of them had put a hand out of line.

Rose (when Rose finally showed, in the lobby bar, two weeks after they arrived) was mortified nonetheless. Rose loved being mortified.

"WHAT are you doing sleeping in one bedroom with Roger?" she said between kisses on the cheek. "We've all heard, it's a scandal, you've gone mad, are you trying to give Peter a heart attack?"

"Oh, I could never top what he did," Emily said, reassuring.

Rose rolled her eyes and twisted her long braid. "Can you imagine? I nearly fainted when I heard, I turned right to Phil and said, 'Well, that's the end of it, innit,' and it was just terrible, terrible to hear, I could hardly work all the next day I was so distracted, I felt so awful."

"You poor thing," said Emily, and then Rose had the grace to look abashed and laugh.

"Well, at least you and Roger are finally left to yourselves."

"Rose."

"Oh, come off! Your stage tricks are no better than anyone's." She leaned forward, planted her elbows on the bar. "How long did he wait before he kissed you? Phil said Roger seemed likely to wait until you were here, but I guessed it was right off."

Emily smiled. "Rose, we're too old to go mooning around. We're only sharing a suite so that when one of us kicks the bucket the other can call the concierge."

Rose changed the subject.

She was a designer for one of the London houses – car coats. (She'd always been flash. Emily approved.) She lived in the hotel because Phil kept rent low and because she fancied having someone else change the sheets.

Abigail was a fit model when they met, "Oh, ages ago"; Abigail had grown tired of standing around getting stuck with pins, so now she was a comptroller, cataloging Rose's expensive fabrics.

"I love her to pieces," Rose said when Emily asked. "Just to pieces. We've been three years now. She's always taking the piss, it's brilliant, it's just like the Understudies again, only not so difficult." Rose flushed. "I mean, not that it was difficult, it was never difficult, it's just that now. Well, now."

Rose gently spun her glass between her fingers as if she was turning back the clock.

"You'll realize soon," Rose went on, sounding happier now that the worst was out. "No more stage fright, no more living out of bags, no more worrying if you have enough money for a cup of tea. No more stage managers. No more smearing up your face and acting a fool every night. It's lovely."

Rose was lying. Smearing up her face and acting a fool had been Rose's favorite thing in the world, and she pounced on any play that had the ingénue in disguise. Rose loved a pantomime more than anyone.

Maybe the fashion business wasn't such a fine idea.

"Do you go to the theatre much?"

Rose blinked hard several times, shook her head, stared into her glass. "Oh no, no. Not often. Abigail doesn't care for automatons, and I'm so busy these days. And it's so different – sort of sad sometimes, too, to see all those plays we used to do. You understand."

"Of course." Emily signaled for drinks.

They laughed through the second one, peeled away the years until it was as it had been when they slept in rickety train bunks, shuddering to a stop and falling to the floor before the sun was out.

"Do you remember," said Emily, "the night in Venice for Carnival, and we got masks and kitted up like birds? Roger looked an idiot, but you were lovely, remember?"

"I think the machines are beautiful," Rose said.

Emily fell quiet.

Rose looked mortified, but after a moment she went on, too far in to turn back. "I mean, all of them, even the old men and women – even their wrinkles are smooth somehow, have you seen them up close? I went backstage once. Someone recognized me and wanted to show me around."

Rose dropped her gaze back to the bar. "Their eyelids are all painted over with different colors, you know – from far away it looks like it's just shadows, but the Ingénues have purple and the Lotharios have dark green. Their eyes aren't colored, it's just little lumps of celluloid in the sockets, so they color the lids instead. It's a real stage trick. It frightened me the first time I saw; it's one thing to think they're all just lovely robots, but to paint up their faces to fool the audience, that's human. I can't even be afraid of them, though, they're so beautiful."

Rose looked up from her drink. "But you never hated them like the rest did, anyway, did you?"

"No," Emily said after a minute.

"So you've seen them, too."

Emily shook her head. "Three of them went to war instead of Phil and Peter and Roger. When I look at the Dramatons all I think is, *Was it you?*"

Rose had no answer.

"Don't tell Phil or anyone," Emily said after a while. "They'd think I'd gone daft."

Rose shook her head. Emily believed it. Rose had her own secrets about Dramatons.

"God," said Rose after a moment, trying to revive, "it's just like the old days, innit?"

Emily's new drink was cold; the bartender had put ice in it. She set the cubes on the bar, watched them melt.

Roger ended up playing a three-off villain in one of her radio dramas.

"You wrote that for me on purpose," he accused when he came back from his first day at the recording studio. "You knew they'd call me in."

"Nonsense. If I'd written it for you he would be taking Doctor-Make ipecac for his rheumatism. Have you brought anything?"

"Thought we'd eat in the lobby," he said. "Phil's invited us to eat, with Rose."

"Do we have to?"

"We're staying in his hotel for free. The least we could do is provide some company."

"I know that profession."

"It would be a gesture. And I've wanted to see Rose."

"Don't ask her about the Dramatons," Emily warned him, gathering her notes. "She's gone sentimental."

The divorce papers were delivered by a bellboy, on behalf of Peter's attorney.

She didn't know he had an attorney. She wondered if the Dramaturgica had given him one so he could squirrel out of it all above board.

She showed Roger. "Pretend you're an attorney."

He looked them over, frowning now and then. "Am I pretending to be a good one?"

"You're not *that* good."

But it was clean-cut – she kept the rights to the Understudies name, and her accounts were untouched. It was the most generous exit Peter had ever made.

It was, for Peter, as close to an apology as he was capable of. She signed them without any changes.

When he wasn't in his hotel room to receive them, she walked all the way to the Dramaturgica.

Peter looked ten years younger, having cast off the troupe that had weighed on him. His shirt (new, crisp white, just right for photographs should a cameraman happen to stop by) was rolled at the cuffs and open at the topmost button, as if he was too busy creating wondrous art to bother fastening his shirt properly.

"I want the queen to pause before she gives the order," he was saying, "make the audience think she might not. Ramp up the drama."

The handler wrote some notes.

"Yes," the automaton said, blinked. She had no lashes, just dark-painted lids, and her celluloid eyes gleamed under the lights.

"I think five seconds," Peter said after a moment.

The queen-Dramaton nodded. "Five seconds. Yes."

"Again," said Peter.

The automatons walked back to their places and waited with hands held at ease, in arcs like lobster claws.

"Your Majesty," said an automaton dressed as a page, "the King demands his answer." The page swung his arm wide.

(Emily thought, *Was it you?*)

The queen walked to the edge of the stage; her arms were aloft to make the most of her sleeves, and if it made her look like a pageant winner, she was a lovely one.

Emily counted: one, two, three, four, five.

"Tell the king he shall have his wedding."

The next went flawlessly (of course); the King made his entrance, was revealed as the man the Queen had fallen in love with when he was disguised as the shepherd, and they were wed with much fanfare amid a parade of faces, all lovely, all smooth, all somehow exactly the same.

The queen's cloak was blue velvet, spangled with stars. Emily hoped it was coincidence.

(The King's voice was Allan McGannon. The Understudies had invited him one season to play the husband in *The*

Bright Affair. Greaselight Weekly had a picture of McGannon with Rose at the premiere, both grinning under the headline 'SHINING ROMANCE BETWEEN THEATRE'S BRIGHT-EST STARS'.

Rose's particular friend was visible just at the edge of the flash, holding Rose's coat and laughing with Phil.

They'd played the romance out all season – Peter's idea. They'd made a mint.)

"Wonderful," Peter called. "So the curtain falls, the end. I'll have some notes for tomorrow; I'd like to see the handlers at four? Is that all right?"

There were murmurs of assent.

"Lovely. Dramatons, thank you. That is all."

Like he'd spoken a command, the automatons slumped, hands slack, two dozen iron jaws snapping shut.

"Finally," Emily said, "actors who listen to you. You must be elated."

Peter turned.

Behind him, the dozen handlers moved onstage and slid keys into their charges. They shuffled into the wings in pairs. At last the stage was empty.

Peter said, "Emily."

"Well, at least you came up with a stunning rejoinder in the interim." She held out the envelope. "I've brought your papers."

Peter frowned. "Can I buy you dinner?"

"Yes."

He buttoned the topmost button on his shirt.

The restaurant was nicer than they'd been to in years, the sort where the menu was determined for you.

Pete spent the first four courses saying how lovely the Dramaturgica was, and the next two courses apologizing.

"Really, Emily, I never meant to hurt you."

"And the divorce?"

"Well, I thought I might as well get out of your way."

"Nicely done."

"Well, I only thought." He frowned, trying to work through something, but apparently his bravery came in bursts and he'd run out for the moment; he shook his head, prodded at his beef medallions with his fork. "Would you have stayed with me, after I did this?"

She laughed. "No, of course not."

He leaned forward, nearly getting his cuffs in the gravy. "There's no honor, you know, in being the last of a line. If we had come back from it with something – I couldn't let some shabby theatre be my legacy, Em, you know I couldn't."

"Don't apologize to me."

"Who, then? Roger? What do I have that he doesn't have, now?"

An income, she thought, but Peter was looking at her like he still loved her, and instead she said, "You should be ashamed of yourself."

"I am. I'm so sorry."

She took pity on him, and changed the subject.

Over dessert he said, "Of course you and Roger will come to the premiere?"

Emily watched the streetlight bleeding through the drapes.

What do I have that he doesn't have, now?

"What happened?"

Roger was in the bedroom doorway; his voice was rich and even. You'd never know he'd been asleep.

She wanted to tell him she'd been to see Peter, to tell him what Peter said, ask Roger what it meant.

But she knew what it meant; it was why she hadn't told him she'd been to see Peter.

She said, "I should write plays."

Roger picked up the phone and ordered breakfast.

"You should," he said after they'd eaten enough to wake up. He put the glass back on the butter dish. "You write very well."

"Don't expect a part from me," she said with a mouthful of toast. "Human geriatrics are right out."

He smiled, and the room around them lit up.

She dropped off the scripts with United, pocketed a check, and picked up a typewriter they'd set aside for her because her penmanship was so awful.

"Are there any companies that might want plays?" she asked, as if it had only occurred to her.

He looked through his ledger. "You can submit something on speculation. A historical. Georgian. Not your usual; something light and clever, please."

"Deadline?"

"End of the week."

"Oh, *lovely*."

"Prize money's three hundred."

"You'll have it by Thursday," she said with a smile.

The place was a warren, and though she could hear Roger there was no chance of finding him, so she sat in the lobby thinking up a clever Georgian history.

When he came out he had one script in his hands.

"Rumbly villains thin on the ground?"

"It's a script for an American play," he said, not looking at her. "Traveling company."

"Oh," she said, felt the floor crumbling under her feet.

When they got back to the suite he put the script in a drawer and she worked for hours on the typewriter, keys clacking, while he read the pages she'd written.

Finally he said, "Go to bed, Em," and she realized it was night.

"The radio drama wants another villain," she said as she stood. "Can I bring you back from the dead to kidnap an ingénue? You'll owe me a pint."

When she glanced up into the bedroom, he was looking at her over the top of his script. He had already been looking at her. He looked at her too much.

"Emily," he said quietly, "there won't be more parts. I'm getting old. There's nothing left."

"You bloody coward," she said tartly, because the idea of him being gone left a cavern in her chest.

He snorted. "A coward and a wise man sleep on the same pillow."

From *The Condemned Woman*.

"Don't you dare spit lines at me," she snapped, and launched herself away from the desk into the bedroom. She was furious, suddenly, had to be away from him, as far as she could get without losing sight of him.

After a moment he appeared in the doorway, looking more composed than she felt.

"Emily, really." He'd put his robe on over his pajamas, and it made him look like the boudoir scene in a comedy. "You can't be surprised I'm getting old."

"May I be surprised you're giving up?"

He folded his arms. "It's one thing to write. It's another to try to fool people into hiring you when we're up to our ears in beautiful machines. You can't keep the past going. It's over."

She shook her head, wondered if they were still talking about acting. "I'm still here."

He spread his arms. "I don't see you setting foot on stage! Even if I was the best actor who'd ever lived, I can't fight this alone!"

"But you ARE! You're just a coward! I've been telling you for thirty bloody years and you've never listened, because you're too much of a coward to hear me! Why do you think you've never—"

She stopped, but they both knew what she hadn't said. The damage was done.

He took a slow step backward.

(She recognized the breath he took onstage when he was about to deliver an insult that rang.)

"Yes," he said, "that's one mistake I never made."

Thirty years, and this close they had never come.

His voice was like a living thing.

When she could breathe she said, "Then I won't trouble you. Good night."

Her coat was where she'd thrown it, and if the concierge noticed she had pajamas underneath when she asked for a separate room, he had the good training not to say.

"And did you leave anything in your room we could bring you, Miss?"

There was a long pause before she said, "No."

V. This Bright Affair

Roger's room was horribly quiet, but it took him a day and a half to find a reason to leave.

When he did, he wondered what he had been afraid of. Emily wasn't in the lobby; she wasn't on the street; she wasn't at the club when he stopped in for a drink.

He felt foolish. It wasn't as though he was going to see her, no matter where he looked. He shouldn't have worried.

The American play was about a man whose business partner betrayed him to the Mob. The man's wife was murdered. The second act had three gun standoffs.

When Roger reached the line, "I'll have my revenge, you rat, no matter what it takes!" he got up from the table and turned on the radio.

He never finished the third act.

When the company called, he said sea voyages made him ill, and agreed to do a radio commercial for men's suits.

Roger looked up at the marquee of the Theatre Dramaturgica with its knife-sharp silver edges, and knew he was old.

Rose, who'd given him her left arm (Phil had her right), whistled as the flashbulbs went off. "Peter knows how to premiere, I'll give him that."

Ahead of them, Peter was dressed to the nines and flirting with the cameras. They'd brought an Ingénue for him; she stood beside Peter, grinning vacantly and winking at intervals. Her face was pulled tight and gleaming, but when the cameras went off she looked human enough.

"Well, at least she's more fun than Rose," said Phil.

"Ta," said Rose, and dropped his arm.

Roger smiled and walked Rose through the photographers.

Rose could flash a coquette's smile as well as any Ingénue, and flashbulbs skittered around them. She'd even cut her hair for fashion, and her Marcel gleamed.

Just before they passed under the marquee Roger looked back for Phil and saw he was escorting Emily, several crowds behind.

Emily was wearing her good black frock and smiling at the cameras like she knew something they didn't, and they took her picture and then shrugged to one another.

Roger took Rose inside, didn't look back again.

Turned out Peter, in a blaze of consideration, had seated Emily apart; her box was stage right, as far from them as the theatre allowed. She was perched on her chair, looking down at the stage.

Roger got interested in his playbill.

Phil took his seat. "Apparently the other seats are taken, or I would have stayed there. Bit of a bastard, Peter, really."

"I've half a mind to go over there," said Rose.

"I've half a mind to find Peter," said Phil.

But the lights went down and the curtain came up, and it was time for the play.

It was an old story, acted in an old way; the audience clapped at the end of all the right speeches. However, Roger could see Peter's mark on the way they moved, on the differences in their pauses and their use of the stage.

Peter had given them the illusion of trying. Peter had at last stumbled onto his genius.

Emily would be heartbroken.

When the screen slid shut after Act One, Roger turned to comfort her, but it was only Rose, who was quietly mutilating the playbill.

Phil frowned. "Are you all right?"

"A bit under the weather, is all," Rose said, tearing another corner. "Lots of excitement these past few weeks. More than I'm used to; Abigail's so steady, and Phil's a bore, of course."

"Ta," said Phil.

But Roger wasn't surprised when he looked over a few moments later and saw Phil watching Rose with an expression of fondness and chagrin.

(He *was* surprised the look lingered; Phil was studying her with the fondness of a long acquaintance, the fondness that goes unspoken between people who know one another enough to keep company in the face of all good sense.)

Phil glanced up and flushed at being caught out, but shrugged without shame, and gave Roger the same look.

Roger had thought Phil offered them space for old times' sake, that because he couldn't persevere he had instead provided.

But Phil loved them. He loved them enough to want them all to live with him, close at hand and never really changing, sparing Phil a world of strangers and doubts.

Roger thought of Emily, who had never looked at him like that in thirty years. When Emily looked at Roger it was to size him up and see him as he was, and if she ever found him lacking she said as much, and if she ever found him excelling she told him that, too.

And when she had looked at him with love (fleeting, joyful, terrifying moments), it had never been for the sake of something that was gone.

He stood up so quickly he had to clap a hand to his hat to keep it from falling. "Rose," he said, "if you're ill I'm happy to take you home."

"Please."

By the time applause started for Act Two they were in the lobby, free from the silhouette in the box across the way, the sight of the beautiful machines.

The idea that Phil was paying for *two* charity suites drove Roger into the world; if he was going to stay in London he'd have to start paying his way.

(It wasn't quite true – he'd heard three episodes of the radio soap that could only have been hers, and the Georgian play stood a good chance – but it didn't do to think too long about Emily.)

He walked through Covent Garden catching signs in the windows: Shop girls Wanted; Hiring Barkeep; Automaton Handler Positions Available. A bookshop off Mercer was seeking a seller; a tailor was looking for a decent drafter. The sign said, NO ARCHITECTS.

When he noticed he was at the door of the Olympia Theatre, he was almost surprised.

I've been telling you for thirty bloody years and you never listen.

He stepped up to the will-call window. "Excuse me. I'd like to audition for the company."

The ticket-taker (a boy no more than twenty) frowned and looked around for help. None came.

"Have you brought credentials?" he asked, looking proud of himself for asking.

Roger said, "I'm the last human actor."

"Right," said the boy after a moment, "let me just, erm . . . hm."

"I've a monologue prepared," said Roger, "if that helps you."

The boy smiled thinly and disappeared, and Roger was just beginning to wonder if he should give up when the theatre doors opened and a gentleman strode through. He was wearing a vested suit and still had gloves on. Roger recognized a director.

"I'm Michael Brinn. I understand you're auditioning to be a handler."

"An actor."

Mr. Brinn frowned. "Beg pardon?"

Roger took a breath for courage. "I'm the last working actor," he said. "I've been doing this for thirty years. I'm a commodity."

Brinn snorted. "You'd go up against a Dramaton?"

Roger just looked at him.

In less time that Roger expected, Brinn spread his arms, a picture of patience, and led the way inside.

"You're joking."

"I'm not."

"Roger, that's – are you sure?"

He raised an eyebrow. "Yes, Phil."

Phil sat back, crossed his arms. "So, what did – Well. Congratulations. Couldn't have happened to a better man."

Phil called Rose; Phil called for champagne.

Then Rose was there in a flurry of robes, kissing them and congratulating them both like Phil had done something, too. She had one forgotten bobby pin sticking out of her Marcel and a spot of masque on her temple; her accolades couldn't wait for fashion.

★   ★   ★

Roger had hated Dramatons, on and off, since the beginning.

(On, whenever he thought what would happen to all the actors he'd watched in all those cities, the breathless dark of the theatre.

Off, when Emily told him to be kinder.)

When there were Dramatons in the papers – Ingénues in baggy dresses that hid their hip joints standing next to grinning Heroes, a smooth-skinned Femme Fatale standing alone (the only women Dramatons who stood alone in photographs) – he'd looked at their blank celluloid eyes and thought, *Naught as queer as folk.*

The plays began promptly and were always perfect. It didn't matter to the audience that Dramatons weren't real. It was no concern of theirs that the shells were empty.

Let them settle, he'd thought, back then.

Now Roger was older, and had to pick his battles. Acting alongside Dramatons seemed as hopeless a battle as any. It would make a fitting end.

He spent the first night memorizing *The Condemned Woman*; he was surrounded by walking libraries, and he'd have to be note-perfect.

Four times he turned to ask Emily for help.

At last he gave up and called Phil. "I have to memorize this," he said.

Rose and Phil were at his door ten minutes later, bearing breakfast.

"My lord," said Rose around a grape, "if you ever loved me, do not force me to beg for mercy. Let me die as I have chosen to."

"But you are not guilty! Must you take another's crimes on your shoulders for that long walk to the grave? Must I mourn you twice – tomorrow, and now tonight?"

"So soon," Phil piped up. "And now, so soon, tonight."

"Bugger." Roger cleared his throat. "Must I mourn you twice – tomorrow, and now, so soon, tonight?"

"I hoped you would not love me enough to mourn," said Rose, and made a sympathetic face at her libris.

"Don't you cry," warned Phil.

She threw a grape.

*   *   *

His co-star was a Dame; they gave her salt-and-pepper hair and a thinner build than necessary.

"She answers to the character name," said her handler, an obscenely young man. "And the other major titles – my wife, my love."

Roger felt a bit ill. "And it changes every show?"

"Of course. How else would we call them?" The boy shoved his spectacles up and closed the panel on her forehead. "She's set for the blocking, Mr Brinn."

From the orchestra seats, Mr Brinn's assistant opened the script for him.

"We'll open with you in the wings, my lady, if you please."

"Yes please," the Dramaton said, and walked behind the curtain.

"Mr Cavanaugh, enter stage left and embrace her."

"Yes please," said Roger pleasantly, and went to mark before anyone could reprimand him.

When he wrapped his arms around the Dame she was unyielding, her body warm from all the little motors.

"I told you not to," the Dame said.

He said, "How could I help it?"

They went scene by scene, and as they traded lines and waited for cues ("Pause before the next line." "Yes please."), Roger could hear her blinking just under the sound of her voice.

If it made Roger a little sad, he was careful not to show it. He'd asked for a place in the future, and this was it; lovely automatons without one comment that wasn't programmed in. If it was lonely work, at least it was something to do; better to be lonely here.

Roger left Emily a note with the concierge.

> *Congratulations on the Georgian – Rose told me. It's a lovely piece. Hope they treat it as it deserves.*
>
> *Changed my mind about fighting alone –* The Condemned Woman *goes up at the Olympia in a month. Doing what I can.*
>
> *Take care.*

After two weeks Roger understood why Dramatons had stayed away from naturalism; the Dame overheated three times trying to accommodate both Mr Brinn's stage directions and Roger's speech patterns.

"You could be more uniform, Cavanaugh," Mr Brinn suggested.

"You're paying me to *not* be uniform," Roger pointed out, and that was the last time that came up.

After three weeks there was talk of a newer model.

They put an ad in the paper: "SEEKING DAME-MODEL AND HANDLER FOR HIRE. HISTORICAL DRAMA A MUST. HUMAN-LEVEL CALIBRATION STANDARDS. SIX-WEEK RUN."

"We'll use the old one until then," said Brinn.

No one answered, and Roger began to feel a flicker of hope that maybe someday human-level calibration might turn into actual humans again. Not that he'd live to see it, but still, dare to dream.

When he took the stage, the Dame model walked out to meet him in her star-spangled cloak, her face calibrated to be noble in suffering. The expression never altered; even when she simulated weeping, serenity remained.

Emily had made it ugly; her Condemned Woman was noble when she could manage it, but was angry and terrified and jealous by turns, and at the end of the play, just before she schooled her features to go out and meet the hangman with decorum, she'd gripped his hand like she wanted to drag him down with her.

He stepped up to the Dame model, embraced her.

"I told you not to," she said.

He said, "How could I help it?"

("Too mournful," said Brinn.)

If there was an ache in his chest from beginning to end of every run, he didn't worry about it. You got all kinds of aches and pains at his age.

"Are you excited?" Rose asked him as soon as the waltz was over. "Just think, in a week you'll be back at the Olympia! God, it's been ages since we were there, a life ago, it's mad that you're back there, Abigail thinks it's the maddest thing when I tell her.

"And with the old Dame's having all the mechanical trouble! What if she breaks in the middle, you'll really be in it then, Emily talks about it sometimes, about what would happen if they just broke and there was nothing you could do – I can't imagine how you're feeling."

"Like a foxtrot," he said.

She took the hint, and they finished the dance in silence.

Roger wasn't surprised to see Peter at their table, waiting for him like the evil Duke in a melodrama.

Phil and Rose vanished onto the dance floor.

But Peter had never been good at playing villain, and when Roger said, "You look well, Peter," the worst Peter could summon was, "Better than some."

"How's the play going?"

"Well, it was going well until I found out there was a novelty act down the street."

"It's only a novelty the first time. Soon it will be so commonplace you won't even have to worry about it."

Peter sighed. "I didn't mean it like that, Roger, it's just – Christ, this is important to me! How could you do it? You couldn't find some other way to act?"

Roger finished his drink rather than answer.

"Right, sorry," said Peter. "But it's still a bit of a blow. Not that you care, now that you've made your point. I'll hand it to you, though, I didn't think you had that kind of showmanship in you. You should have seen Emily's face when she told me."

Roger's lungs contracted for a moment. "Oh?"

"Said it served me right, and you'd show everyone what they'd been missing. You know how she gets when she's excited about something."

Roger smiled. Poor Peter, upstaged for the first time in his life.

"I hope to see you both opening night."

"I'm busy," Peter said, but when Roger said, "A seat in the boxes?" Peter said, "Well, I might do."

*　　*　　*

The papers went wild.

What had been a pathetic last stand when there were three of them was now one man's *cause célèbre*.

The *Examiner*: "MAN VS MACHINE: HAPPY ENDING OR END OF ALL WE HOLD DEAR?"

The *Nation*: "Cavanaugh to get into gears"

The *Evening Standard*: "WAS THIS WHY WE FOUGHT THE WAR?", which Roger thought was unfair all around.

The only one Roger bothered with was *Greaselight Weekly*. He set it on the night table so he'd have something to look at in the mornings before rehearsal.

"LAST LIVING ACTOR TO GO DOWN SWINGING."

The house was packed, and for a moment Roger wasn't sure he'd be able to go on in front of that big an audience. Then he remembered he'd done it in this same theatre a quarter-century ago.

"Damn fool," he muttered, and stepped onstage to a hail of applause and a smattering of jeers.

The condemned woman stepped out into the lights, her blue velvet coat spangled with little tin stars.

It was Emily.

Emily, who was clutching the edges of the cloak in her fists, terrified and exhilarated and amazed as she'd always been at the beginning of the play all those years ago; just the same.

When they embraced, he crushed her in his arms, and she took in a shuddering breath, buried her face in his shoulder.

The audience was rapt.

It would never be like this again; it could not have been this without thirty years together, without their fight, without this fierce surprise pressing against his chest.

Roger wrapped his arms tighter.

He stepped back, letting the edges of her cloak slide slowly through his fingers.

"I told you not to look for me," she said.

He breathed, "How could I help it?"

She shook her head; her eyes were bright.

He took her hand and led her to the wooden bench that marked her prison cell, where the condemned woman would spend her final hours.

Everything else would wait until after the performance.

Into the Sky

Joseph Ng

From a hundred feet up in the air, the Great Wall didn't look so great.

It was a miserable, cold night when I observed this, curled up in my gondola as the balloon was tossed by violent winds. The air outside was an impenetrable darkness and the soggy snow came in from every direction. The frost bit through the fur on my winter uniform, nipping at my ears. Even the flame from the burner, so vigilantly fighting the cold, could not reach me with its warmth.

I could, of course, blame a great many people for my predicament. I could blame Hou, for falling sick and, indirectly, forcing me to replace him up here. I could blame Zhihe, who swapped schedules with me (Saturdays are my off days). I could blame General Zhou for conceiving the idea of hot air balloons in place of watchtowers to save costs; or even Emperor Qing (may He live ten thousand years) for agreeing to the proposal, for putting the Lüyingbing, particularly our division, in charge of watching the northern border.

But what was the use? I was already up here, and there was nothing that could change that.

As I peered up into the endlessly swirling snow, past the acrid black smoke from the burner, I thought I could see a faint twinkle in the darkness. The light of a star.

Amid the howling wind, I heard a distant sound, like a burst of firecrackers. It stopped. Then the sound came again, nearer this time. Finally, it ended up some half a kilometer away to the left of my station. Begrudgingly, I got to my feet and released the safety on the railgun, then gave the trigger a light squeeze.

The sound was like punctures. Like car tires bursting open. After a series of six shots into the dark unknown that laid beyond the wall, I released the trigger and engaged the safety again. Then to my right, the watcher in the next station started his routine check. We had to do this, especially in the snowy weather, so the gun parts did not freeze when we needed to use them.

I curled up again in the relative comfort of my gondola. The icy storm gave no indication that it was going to let up soon.

With my arms tucked inside my armpits and my body curled up as tightly as possible, I fell asleep until the next fire check came. By that time, daylight had already come.

If you asked me, I couldn't have told you what it was that I felt, or when was the exact moment that I felt it. All I can say for certain is that when I spoke to Xiaoyan, I felt connected to her somehow, in a way that was deeper than all the relationships I have had before. I suppose you could call it Yuanfen: a binding force between people that transcends conventional knowledge and lifetimes.

When I first met her, we were on a march through the northern villages. A show more than anything else, to inspire confidence in the people that we were there to protect them.

We had marched up the narrow roads through Yinchuan and out the other end, where we made camp. Usually, no one paid attention to us foot soldiers. The six Terracotta Warriors, arranged in two lines of three out in front, just behind the banner, took up most of their attention. It was better that way – no one to distract us from our duties. It also made a good show of China's might.

The Terracotta Warriors were, strangely, not made of terracotta. It was an artifact name, revived by the Emperor with reference to the army Qin Shi Huang took with him to storm the afterlife. The records told us that no less than eight thousand men and one thousand horses were buried alive, so that they may continue to serve the First Emperor, even in death.

The modern Terracotta Warriors were different in two key ways: firstly, they were made of iron and stood about nine feet tall, towering above the common man. Secondly, the men encased inside were alive. They were more useful that way. The Warriors were also beastly heavy things, quaking the ground as they walked. One simple swing of its arm, I suspected, would have been enough to take a man's head off his shoulders. Only veterans were allowed to pilot the Terracotta Warriors. The rest of us had to earn our stripes, prove our loyalty and wait for the death of a veteran so the spot would be free for us to fill.

In the middle of Yinchuan, as we did at every town, we halted as Commander Long saluted and gave the word of the Emperor to the elder of the village. We were disciplined to keep our eyes dead ahead, our backs straight, and our chins up as long as we were marching; but from the corner of my eye, I could see her there.

Xiaoyan carried herself with a certain elegance that was captivating. I remember, even studying her in the blurry edges of my vision, she stood with grace and dignity. I felt her smile upon me. And then, without a word, she took a delicate step forward and tucked a single flower into my belt.

Later, when we made camp and I loosened my belt, I looked and saw that it was an orchid, glowing white and purple in the bloom of the evening sun. I crushed it between the pages of my journal so I would smell it whenever I opened the book.

The second time I saw her, I did not recognize her. It was a midsummer's day, and our section of the Great Wall was pleasantly shaded in the shadow of a passing cloud. She came in a six-wheel transport that came rolling in, stepping out behind nine boys who, awed by our show in their village, wanted to put their lives behind them and join the Lüyingbing.

It was a Saturday. I was near the gates having a cigarette with Hou. Greeting guests were none of our business – we were soldiers, nothing more, nothing less. But then she saw me, smiled and came walking toward me.

"Hey, Mako, you never told me you had a girlfriend," Hou jested.

I ignored him. "My lady," I said, standing up. "What brings you here?"

"I'm just here to see the wall," she said. "Hong, our driver, will be taking a little while. I thought that it was a good opportunity to come and see the Great Wall with my own eyes."

I was going to tell her that she may look around, but not wander up onto the wall itself, as that was against regulations. Then Hou appeared from behind and wrapped an elbow around my neck. "Our boy Mako will be glad to show you around!" he said. "Would you like to climb up and see what lies beyond the border? Or take a ride in one of the watchstations? Mako will be glad to do it for you!"

"Hey," I said, "If you're so eager to show her around, you should do it yourself."

"But alas!" Hou let go of me. "I cannot claim the privilege, because I suddenly remember that I am on kitchen duty today."

"You're not," I snapped. "Even if you were, kitchen duty doesn't start until five o'clock."

"See you!" Hou yelled over my words, taking off toward the barracks, which was nowhere near the kitchen. I was left alone with this strange woman whom I had only just met.

"Your name is Mako?" she said. "That's a nice name. Very masculine."

"I apologize on behalf of my friend," I said. "His mouth is faster than his thoughts. What is your name?"

"Xiaoyan," she said, and that was how we met.

Despite Hou's promises, I could not take her up the wall. The stairs leading up were all guarded so that only those on patrol may pass. Xiaoyan told me that she didn't mind, so I showed her what I was permitted to.

I showed her the eating hall, where we were fed some variety of gruel for every meal. It tasted like mud, but it was easy to make in large volumes, and it seldom caused episodes of stomach upset, due to how easily digestible it was. I took her as near as I could to the training grounds, where we had marching drills every weekday morning and physical training every weekday evening. Since it was a Saturday, a group of about twenty men were using the space to play ball. Then between the barracks and the motor pool, I decided to show her the latter. I couldn't imagine there was anything of interest for a lady to find in the men's barracks. The same cannot be said the other way around.

Usually, we rode the four-wheeled buggies in groups of eight from the training grounds to the motor pools. But since there was only two of us, we walked instead.

I told Xiaoyan a great deal about how we lived and how, in my three years with the Lüyingbing, the most intense conflict I had ever found myself in was when a group of wild boars attacked us in the middle of training. No one came out of it seriously injured, but there was a great deal of commotion, ending only when a couple of quick-thinking fellows took their training sticks and subdued the beasts. Zhihe, for one, received a nasty gash on his left leg; but on the bright side, there was pork enough for everyone during dinner that night.

She laughed loudly at every turn of this story. When I asked her questions about her life, however, she evaded the topic and asked me another question instead.

The motor pool was being cleaned that day, and all the vehicles were on their monthly maintenance runs, so Xiaoyan was one of the lucky few members of the public to see them in action. The maintenance crew also seemed to be in a more jovial mood than usual, laughing as they pushed the limits of the vehicles' engines, speeding up and down the tarmac and leaving thick black smoke in their wake. They started with the lighter, more agile vehicles first: the standard personnel carrier and the light gunner; and then progressively they tested the heavier vehicles: the armored trucks and then the battle tanks.

At the end of it, like the climax of an opera, came the Terracotta Warriors, taking lumbering steps out of the garage. In reality, they walked faster than the average man; but due to their size, their large steps appeared slow and clumsy. I recognized Commander Long's weathered face in one of the cockpits.

There came a revving sound from Commander Zhou's Terracotta Warrior. To my surprise, the Warrior leaned forward and eased into a full throttle down the tarmac, going as fast as a twelve-wheel truck. At the end of the tarmac, it slowed, and within three steps it came to a standstill. Black smoke spilled out the exhaust hatch behind the Warrior's shoulders.

Xiaoyan clapped her hands at the display. "Spectacular!" she said.

The trouble with mechas, I told Xiaoyan as I led her back, was that like humans, they were easy to trip. All it would take to incapacitate a Warrior was a high-tension cable wrapped around its ankles. Stuck in the mud, all that's left is for an enemy battle tank to roll right over it.

"Unless it learns to fly," she said.

When we got back, we found, to Xiaoyan's distress, that Hong had driven back with the transport, leaving her stranded. I found Captain Lee and told him about Xiaoyan's situation. Captain Lee brought it up to Lieutenant Wong, and then Lieutenant Wong relayed the words to Commander Long. Finally, the word came back down to me through Captain Lee. He tossed me a set of keys.

"You know how to drive a light transport, right?" he asked. I told him I did, and he nodded. "Make sure that truck comes back in one piece," he growled. "If the diesel is low, have the tank filled somewhere. There's money in the dashboard. Be back before the gates close."

Xiaoyan and I talked and laughed some more on the one-hour drive back to Yinchuan. She had me stop in the middle of town, halfway down a nondescript row of shops.

"Tell me, Mako, before I leave," she said. "Did you keep the flower I gave you?"

The memory then swam back to me. "Yes, I did," I said. "I keep it in my journal."

"That's good," she smiled. "It needed a new home."

I looked outside the window. These shops had living quarters on the second floor. "Do you live here?" I asked.

Instead of answering my question, she asked me, "If you could leave your past behind and go wherever you wanted to, where would you go?"

The question caught me by surprise. "If I could leave the past behind?" I repeated. "But that's impossible, isn't it? Your past follows you everywhere you go."

"But let's say that you can," she said with a serious look. "You can go anywhere you want and start a new life. Where would you go? What would you do?"

I took long seconds to think the question over. Finally, I said, "I would be a wanderer, without any place to call home.

I would go from town to town, city to city, country to country, until my life is over. And then I would do the same in the next life."

"Why?"

"Because everyone has a past they are running from," I said. "And if you don't continue moving, the past will eventually catch up with you."

There was a beat in which Xiaoyan just looked at me. And then, without any warning or buildup, she held my face and pressed her lips against mine. It was a quick, sweet kiss; and before I even knew it was happening, it was already over.

"Don't ever change," she said. Then she got off the transport and disappeared into the night.

How can one resist change? Change is all there is in the world. The second hand on the clock ticks by whether one likes it or not. People grow old and weary against their wishes. With enough time, even mountains erode and seas dry up.

Between the second and third time I saw Xiaoyan, summer changed into fall.

Political tensions were brewing all around the world outside China's borders. There were rumors that Mongolian forces were gathering in the south, amassing their strength. At the same time, there were talks of a revolt about to erupt in the central provinces.

With Hou's transistor radio, we could occasionally get snippets of the international news broadcast. A very important man in Austria had been killed at the end of June, and the whole Western world was thrown into crisis. A war was inevitable, the announcer said.

"But never fear," Hou leapt up and proclaimed, "If the war comes to us, we shall welcome it gladly! When the white men come to the wall, we will show them the might of China and smite them all!"

Someone told him to shut up and sit down. I think it was Zhihe.

One evening at the end of July, as we were having dinner, there came an urgent call to gather outside. We dropped our spoons and left our food on the table. Within the minute, all two thousand of us were gathered in the training area. Commander Long made the announcement with a hailer.

The extremist political group Kuomintang has sparked an insurgency in the central and southern regions of China, headed by the traitor Sun Yat-sen. Various divisions of the Lüyingbing was being called back to aid in the quelling of the insurgency. Our division wasn't one of the ones required to go, but we were to be on standby, ready to leave in a moment's notice.

I stole a glance at Hou. For all his talk about fighting the white men, I think the last thing he anticipated was for the conflict to start from our own people.

"It's hopeless," Zhihe declared that night in our dormitory. "The Emperor is waging a pointless conflict. Before a battle is won, it is first won in the mind," he tapped a finger against his temple for emphasis, "and if you follow the news, you will see that the Kuomintang has already won over the people's minds."

"Ridiculous!" Hou replied. "Without the Emperor – may He live ten thousand years – we will be just like these Western nations, always squabbling and killing each other over some small thing! How can a nation stay together under a ruler without the Mandate of Heaven?"

I was paying them no mind as I scribbled into my journal, at the same time taking in the fragrance of the crushed orchid. It was growing fainter with each passing day.

"Hey, Mako, what do you think?" Hou suddenly asked. I slapped my journal shut.

"Sorry?"

"What are you doing there, anyway?" Hou said, peering at me suspiciously. "For the past few weeks, you've been doing nothing but scribbling into that notebook of yours. Are you writing an opera?"

I laughed sheepishly. "An opera?" I said. "Of course not! Why would you think that?"

"Then what is it?"

"It's nothing," I said quickly, but perhaps a little bit too quickly. I saw the suspicion grow in Hou's eyes, and the mischievous grin that came creeping across his face. I tried to put my journal away as nonchalantly as possible, but it was already too late.

"Hey, Zhihe," Hou said, getting up to his feet. "I'll hold him down; you get that journal and see what he's been writing."

Heart palpitating, I glance at Zhihe. Even the ever-serious guy had a little twinkle in his eye as he said, "Let's do it."

I put up a mighty struggle. I punched, kicked, grappled, and flailed, offending the other fellows in the dormitory as I tried to keep Hou and Zhihe away from the journal; but in the end, to paraphrase the idiom, even two idiots can outsmart a genius. Before long, I was pinned to the hard floor as Zhihe flipped through the pages.

"Teeth, like stars twinkling in the night!" Zhihe began reading out loud. I begged him to stop, but he kept going. "Lips, like a rose blooming in the spring!"

He managed to get a couple more lines out before I viciously smacked Hou in the face with my elbow and pried the journal from his hands. By that time, I was already blushing all the way to my ears. All around, I could hear the other guys laughing.

"Poetry?" Hou laughed. "You're writing poetry, Mako?"

"What is it to you?"

"It's that girl, isn't it? That one that you had to drive back?" he asked. Then noting my expression, he began hopping up and down. "Mako's in love! Everybody, the day has come at last! Mako's in love with a girl!"

"Shut up," I said weakly. Even Zhihe was grinning amid the commotion.

"Honestly, I had my doubts about you, Mako," he said. "For a while, I thought you were queer."

"You're such a romantic guy, Mako!" Hou said. "If I were a girl, I would fall in love with you straight away! Oh, hold me, Mako! Hold me in your big, strong arms!"

Hou puckered his lips and came toward me with his arms spread wide for an embrace. I drew my fist, ready to punch him. Then the door burst open and Captain Lee stepped in.

"What's all this noise about?" he barked.

The dormitory became very silent. Then someone from the other end shouted that Hou, Zhihe, and I were the cause of it all. The three of us then spent the night holding water-filled buckets outside the dormitory instead of sleeping.

"Thanks for nothing, you two," I muttered as my arms shook from the exertion.

"Teeth, like stars twinkling in the night," Zhihe recited, and then the two of them started snorting with laughter all over again while I blushed furiously.

When Xiaoyan came to camp one Saturday in the middle of August, there was silence wherever we went, though I could feel eyes on us everywhere. Occasionally, there came a snort or a giggle.

"What's going on?" Xiaoyan asked me.

"Ignore them," I said. "They're just being stupid."

Thankfully, none of them decided to do an impromptu performance of my butchered words they identified as poetry. This time, there weren't many places for me to show her; but we were happy to just walk around and talk about everything under the sun. She expressed genuine concern about the rising conflicts in the Western world as well as the insurgency spreading like fire in the heart of China.

"But what will happen if we don't have an Emperor?" she asked.

"Then we will live under the rule of men," I said. "Subjected to the laws and whims of men who would crown themselves above us."

She flashed a smile at this. "You know," she said, "You really have a way with words."

"Do I?"

She made no reply and skipped ahead.

Later, as we sat outside the motor pool beneath a yellowing sky, she suddenly said, "Time goes in a circle."

"What do you mean?" I asked. She smiled mysteriously.

"We have been here before," she said. "I have been at the front gates of this camp before, and you talked to me. Then you took me here, to this very same place. Even though things and other events have filled the time in between, we still find ourselves in the same place, just like spring again at the end of winter."

"But this time it's different," I said. "I know you now, and you know me. Before this, we were strangers."

"Just like how two summers are never alike," she said, "And how two lifetimes are never the same. They are different, and sometimes one is better than the other." She wrapped her arm around mine. "I think I like this one better," she said, resting her head on my shoulder.

Just then, there came a crash from within the garage. We both leapt up and raced inside to find one of the Terracotta Warriors bent and broken on the concrete floor. There was a cloud of smoke, like a disappearing specter, in the air. A technician I did not recognize crawled out from the broken cockpit of the Warrior. Other technicians and engineers rushed to his aid, but he appeared to be unharmed.

"What happened?" I asked. No one answered me.

Then Xiaoyan tugged at my arm and pointed to the back of the Warrior. Attached to the Warrior's spine was something that resembled a backpack, from which extended four arms. The top two arms held symmetrical turbines, each as wide as the Warrior itself, and the lower two arms ended in what appeared to be machine guns with grips suitable for the Warrior's hands. The exhaust vents that were once mounted into the shoulders had been united and relocated to the bottom of the backpack-like attachment.

I looked up and surveyed the other Terracotta Warriors, still secure in their wall mounts. They all had identical attachments. There was no question what the turbines were supposed to do, or what was the cause of this Warrior's crash.

"They taught them to fly," Xiaoyan said with wonderment in her voice.

On the way back, Xiaoyan told me to stop the vehicle right on the edge of town, before we became visible under the burning sodium lights. I gladly obliged. From out of nowhere, she pulled out what looked like two folded paper bags with wire frames in the middle. I stared at them in confusion.

"What are these things?"

"Kongming lanterns," she said, opening the door of the transport. "Come outside, I'll show you how it's done."

She gave me a pen. "You write your wish on the outside, you see," she explained. "Then you unfold the whole thing and

light the burner at the bottom – careful not to burn yourself –
then when the air inside is heated up enough, you let go of it,
and it floats into the sky."

I did as she said. I ran into some trouble trying to set the
burner alight, but soon enough the fire was burning with a
bright yellow flame. It took two of us to hold the lantern properly so it wouldn't topple and catch fire.

After my lantern had taken off into the sky, we prepared
hers next. I tried to see what she wished for, but she hid that
surface away from me.

"No peeking," she said playfully.

When we released her lantern into the air, it turned around,
and I could see her simple wish written in plain characters:
"To run away," the words read.

Xiaoyan hugged my arm and rested her head against my
shoulder as we watched the two lanterns drift off into the night,
becoming little specks of orange in the distance, and then
finally disappearing into the darkness.

I did not see Xiaoyan for a long time after that. Every Saturday,
I would sit near the entrance, having cigarettes with Hou, waiting to see if she would appear, but she never showed up.

Meanwhile, the news that came to us got darker and darker
with each passing day. The conflict that had started out as
scattered embers in the Western world had, as the radio
announcer predicted, escalated into an all-out war. Meanwhile,
south of the Great Wall, the insurgency had bloomed into the
people's revolution, with pockets of resistance rising even from
territories previously assumed to be free from Kuomintang
influence.

Near the end of September, the word of the Emperor came
to us, and our entire division was split in two. One half was to
continue watching the northern border, and the other half was
to march south to help quell the fires of revolution. Our
company was part of the half that was to stay behind.

Zhihe all but said, "I told you so."

Even Hou, who had been so gung-ho about being a part of
the fighting, became solemn and, if I read him correctly, a
little bit scared. He no longer talked about the glories of war

and the trampling of foes beneath our feet, only listening in pained silence as the conflict beyond and within our borders grew in intensity.

Like that, fall passed and changed into winter.

I thought about Xiaoyan often, about where she was and what she was up to. I realized that in all the times we'd spent together, I had never found out anything about her: whether she supported the dynasty or the revolution; if she liked music or sports; or if she read books or watched the occasional opera. All our interactions had always been about me, my life, what I was doing, what were the things I liked. I resolved to devote the next time we met to find out everything I could about her life.

One morning in October, as the winter chill was just beginning to set in and we were still getting used to our winter uniforms, the alarm sounded. The sound was so unfamiliar that none of us recognized it at first. We exchanged glances: *are you hearing what I'm hearing?* Then, as a collective realization settled upon all of us, we pulled our boots on and sprinted out into the training area.

The space seemed larger now, with half of our numbers gone. Commander Long gave us a hurried briefing: Mongolian forces had crossed the northern border not too far in the east. So far, there hadn't been any action yet, and General Zhou was being transported over with the fastest airship we had available; but in any case, it seemed like a conflict was imminent, and we were all to be on the standby.

That afternoon, the whole camp came alive like I'd never seen it before. We all had to be in full gear at all times, and all over the camp, the reserve firearms were being tested and vehicles being refueled. Over the next few days, as negotiations were carried out between the generals, we were drilled on battle formations and open combat situations. Out in the open plains, none of the quick-response, close-quarter techniques we were taught had any value. Shoot first, shoot accurately, don't get shot. It was as simple as that.

Our weekends were taken away from us. Hou grumbled especially loud. I took this in stride – it wasn't as though our enemies would cease fire just because it's a Saturday. We had to be prepared.

For days, and then for weeks, nothing happened. Which, if anything, only served to put us all further on edge. In this period, we saw how each other reacted to pressure. Hou was still making stupid jokes and treating everything lightly, but you could tell that there was something profoundly disturbed beneath that façade of aloofness. Myself, I thought that I acted no different than usual, only a little bit twitchier than I was before.

Zhihe, on the other hand, seemed to have gained some kind of transcendental clarity. Like he was suddenly enlightened, and was on his way to Nirvana.

"Personal gain, selfish ambition," he said as he drew lines in the sand with one hand and held a cigarette with the other, "All extensions of self is what perpetuates the cycle of *samsara*. Realize that the self, in itself, is suffering; and when you eliminate the self, you will also eliminate suffering. Only then there is freedom from the endless cycle. *Amitabha*."

All I could offer in response to his divine insight was a thoughtful "Hmm" before I drew another long puff.

"It's okay, you know," he said, coming back to earth. "If you want to be a poet."

I gave a laugh. "I never said I wanted to be one," I said. "Even if I did, I don't need you to tell me that it's okay to be one."

"That's exactly it," he said. "You don't need to care what I think. You don't need to care what anyone thinks. The only person who needs to be in agreement is yourself."

I wondered if this contradicted with what he just said about the elimination of self and all, but the matter proved to be too much mental work, and I shoved it aside. "I don't want to be a poet," I said.

"Really? Then what do you want to be?"

"No one." The cigarette was down to the filter now. I crushed it into the hard soil with my boot.

"Very good. If that is all you aspire to be, then you're already there. You're already living the dream."

But that wasn't true. No one was no one. Even the most mundane person on earth was significant, in the way that he is the absolutely most boring person on earth. That in itself was something. As long as there was someone who knew you, recognized you, you were someone to that person; and being someone to somebody carried with it expectations and unwritten contracts and unspoken agreements. The only way you could be absolutely no one was to be a ghost, always traveling to new places and leaving before anyone got to know you.

"War," Zhihe said suddenly, lapsing into another one of his philosophical episodes, "It's all so pointless.

I thought again about what I said to Xiaoyan, about wandering the earth endlessly, and wondered if it wasn't what I really wanted after all.

I tried writing letters. In the minutes – sometimes five, sometimes thirty – between one activity and the next, while the others gathered in groups to discuss what was really happening to the negotiations between General Zhou and the Mongolian general, I sat with my journal and attempted to write letters to Xiaoyan.

It was cathartic, if nothing else. Even if I did write a letter that I was happy with, it wasn't as though I had the guts to mail it. Not that it stopped me from trying.

I miss you, I'd write. You should come and visit again. I want to know more about you, and your life. All I know is your name. But even if you don't want to talk about yourself, I'm also fine with just spending time with you. I hope to see you again soon. I miss you.

And then I would tear the whole thing up and flush the pieces down the toilet.

Putting one's feelings into words is a tedious task. When it came to writing poems, even shitty ones, one could hide behind all sorts of fancy words and euphemisms. But when it came to articulating my feelings in plain terms, I found myself at a complete loss.

"Hey, Hou," I asked one night, as we were washing up before going to bed, "How do you be honest about your feelings?"

He looked at me, water still clinging to his face in droplets. Then as he wiped his face, he said, "What do you mean? You just be honest. There's no trick to it."

I realized then that I had asked the wrong person and left it there. But once you got Hou's curiosity, you were in for the long run. "What's this about?" he pressed. "Are you still seeing that girl? I haven't seen her around lately."

"No," I said as simply as I could, "But I want to see her again."

"That's just it then," he said. "Just tell her that. When it comes to being honest, the fewer words you use, the better."

That night, before the lights went out in the dormitory, I finally wrote a letter that I was happy with. It simply read, "Let's run away." Then despite my fragile courage, I sent it off that Saturday.

The war began on the first day of November, and even more of us left. In the future, when students reach the chapter about the war that began at the Great Wall, they will be happy to find that it began on such an easy date to remember, I thought.

At the same time, an unexpected stormy weather hit the Great Wall, giving us the coldest winter we ever had. All day and all night the blinding snow fell from the sky, forming dirty piles of slush everywhere. We took to wearing our winter uniforms to sleep, and even then the cold bit. Some of us went to sleep with our boots on.

Many fell sick then, especially those who were on the night watch. Hou, Zhihe, and I were called upon to replace the men who were now burning with fever in the infirmary.

From the ground level, the idea of watching the border from a hot air balloon sounded simple, if a little bit silly. I thought I was doing so well, too, when I first stepped onto the gondola and successfully balanced myself. But that was when it was floating barely two feet off the ground.

At a hundred feet in the air, the winds were wicked. The balloon and gondola both swayed and shook so violently that, at several points, I was convinced that the balloon was going to snap free of the wall and get carried off into the dark unknown. But the tethers were secure; and somehow I managed to make it through the night. Over time, I managed to overcome the vertigo, but there was no helping the cold winds.

The radio signal grew strangely weak in those cold, cold days. The only way we could receive news on the outside world was through the words of people who came delivering supplies and the weekly newspapers. The Kuomintang was rapidly gaining traction, and with the imminent threat coming from the north, the dynasty was at Morton's Fork: give in to the revolution and be dismantled, or focus so much on quelling the revolution that it left itself wide open to an invasion.

The war in Europe, as far as I could tell, hadn't made any progress in the past few months. It was just battle after battle, skirmish after skirmish, endless rounds of suffering and bloodshed all across the battlegrounds.

Round and round we go. Where does it end?

I sent in my resignation form to Captain Lee. He took one look at the document and then laid it face-down on his desk.

"Have you thought this through?" he asked.

"Not really," I admitted.

"Once you opt out, there is no returning," he said. "No matter how hard you try or who you know. You also won't be able to get a job with the government anymore, and you'll be surrendering your pension."

"I know that."

He stared at me for a good few seconds, saying nothing. His gaze pierced into my eyes, as though searching my soul, making sense of my motivations. Then he said, "I'm not going to ask you to stay. If you want to leave, that's your choice to make. But you need to know what you're sacrificing when you give up your uniform and walk out of these gates: security, a future, friends . . ."

"It's a price I'm willing to pay."

He nodded. "Very well, then," he said. He turned my form face-up again, pounded his rubber stamp into an inkpad, and then stamped his office at the bottom of the document before signing it. "You will leave on December twenty-four," he said. "Until then, you will assume all your roles and responsibilities as usual. I will tell you when your official statement of release is ready. It shouldn't take more than two weeks."

When I saw Xiaoyan again, she was positively beaming. In front of everyone, she held my face and gave me a good, long kiss.

"I got your letter," she said.

Hou was distraught, to say the least, when he found out about my decision.

"What?" he all but shrieked when I told him over breakfast, drawing the attention of several people around us. He didn't bother with their looks. "You're just going to leave me here? Alone?"

"You won't be alone," I pointed out. "There's Zhihe. Not to mention at least one thousand and nine hundred other people in camp."

"You know that's not what I mean, idiot! What . . . What happened to our pact? What about our brotherhood?" he looked to Zhihe beside him, who had been silently eating his breakfast this whole time. "You tell him, Zhihe – you tell him that he's wrong! He's making a big mistake!"

Zhihe said nothing. Neither did I. What was the use of words when there was nothing left to say?

"You're not even going to say anything?" Hou shook. For a moment, I was afraid that he was going to cry. But then he just threw his half-eaten toasted bread at me and stormed off. I spent the better part of that morning picking out breadcrumbs from my hair.

"You should have said something," Xiaoyan said when we were together again. "You could have at least dulled the pain. Make it easier on him."

"Is there any easy way to say goodbye?" I asked.

She thought about this for a long while. "No," she said at last. "I suppose not."

Captain Lee shot me an incredulous look when I made my request known.

"Are you serious?" he asked. I told him I was. He gave a bemused expression and said, "This is most unusual. Why can't you just take the damn transport like everyone else?"

"I've grown attached to it," I said. "It seems like a good way to go. I'll pay for it, if that's the main concern."

"Are you stupid?" Captain Lee growled. "We have no short-age of money. But we don't make a habit of giving souvenirs to people, least of all military equipment. If you need a memento that badly, take a dead bullet, or something. You want to spend the rest of your life explaining to officials how you came into possession of a watchstation?"

But I wouldn't let go of it. Finally he sighed and said that he would bring my request up.

"But don't get your hopes up," he said. "Be prepared to be disappointed. I can almost imagine the look on the command-er's face." He shook his head. "What has gotten into you, boy? Are you caught in some identity crisis?"

"Quite the opposite," I said. I thanked him and went on my way.

When the dawn came to end the miserable, cold night I spent curled up in the gondola, I was jolted from my uneasy slumber when a burst of fire, like the sound of firecrackers, went off in the distance. The endlessly swirling snow was gone, and the plains were bathed in cold morning sunlight. The watchstation to my left completed its fire check, and it was my turn.

I turned the safety off and fired six rounds into the north. The gondola shook with each shot. When General Zhou thought this up, he obviously wasn't thinking much about its practical applications in combat, I thought.

To my surprise, there was a celebration of sorts in the eating area when I went there for breakfast. Adding to it, it was a celebration for me, for my last day at camp. Someone had went through the trouble of getting a small fruitcake and lit a candle on top of it for me. Zhihe flashed me a thumbs-up from the fringe of the small crowd.

"Here's a little bit of poetry I wrote for Mako, who is the dumbest person I know," Hou said as he stood on a chair. There was laughter all around. Hou cleared his throat and read from a piece of paper. "Mako is a friend of mine, I know him very well," he read. "He has rocks for ears and shit for brains, as far as I can tell . . ."

The poem went on more or less like that for about four stan-zas. It was a terrible poem from start to end, but it wasn't for me to criticize it. When it was done, I laughed and applauded him along with everyone else.

Hou stepped off his chair and gave me a hug. "I'll never forgive you," he said. "Be sure I don't see you after this, or I promise you, I will shoot you."

Xiaoyan was waiting for me when I emerged from the eating area. I was free to go anytime, as long as I left before the gates closed at eleven o'clock that night. I could have gotten my bags and left through the gates, never looking back. But sentimentality got the better of me, and I suggested that we take one last walk around the premises.

We walked by the training grounds, where an early group of guys had already gathered in full uniform, ready for marching exercises. We took the long walk out to the motor pool, where they were replacing old parts on broken down vehicles. Through the open door, we could see the six Terracotta Warriors, as good as new in their mounts.

I managed to get Xiaoyan to talk about herself this time. Like me, she was an orphan, except her parents were not deceased. She just did not know who they were. Her mother was a prostitute in Xingan and her father was likely one of her mother's clients. She did not even know what they looked like – her earliest memories already had her out on the streets begging for food with whatever words she learned from the other street orphans.

"Maybe she was an orphan too," she said wistfully, concerning her mother. "Maybe it's the curse of my lineage, to go through the same cycles over and over again."

I told her about my grandfather and great-grandfather, both of whom had fought and died in the Opium Wars that plagued the better part of the last hundred years, and my father, who was involved in the quelling of the Dungan Revolt and Miao Rebellion before I was born. They were soldiers before me, and we never had to worry about food or shelter for that reason. At least not until the second Dungan Revolt came and took civilian lives along with theirs in its wake.

"I wonder if we're doing the right thing," Xiaoyan mused as we sat watching the cold winter sun descending toward the horizon. "Maybe our fates are as sure as gravity pulling the water downstream. Or maybe we are already living the best lives we could possibly live, and breaking out of the cycle can only make things worse."

Moments like these, I wished that I was like Zhihe, ever able to provide the profound question an equally profound answer. All I could say was, "We'll just have to see."

It was almost sundown when we arrived back at camp. Captain Lee was surprised to see me.

"And here I thought you had left just before you got what you fought so hard for," he said. "Such a waste. It would have been a funny story to tell. Anyway, the general has approved your request. But we'll have to strip the gun from it, for obvious reasons."

I found the hot air balloon waiting for me atop the wall, still tethered to the stone anchor. There was only an iron mount where the railgun used to be, but everything else was in place. Even the propane tank was still full of gas. On the balloon, they had sewn on canvas flaps attached to ropes, so I could steer it when the wind came.

"I hope you know how to fly this thing," Captain Lee said. "If you die, there's no one who's going to come to retrieve your dead body, or attend your funeral. You're on your own now."

I smiled and saluted him for the last time. He did a little raise of his eyebrows, and then did an about-turn and left without a word. Xiaoyan joined me as I fired up the burner, taking comfort in the heat.

"That's a big fire," she said. "Won't the balloon get burned?"

"It hasn't burned before," I offered.

"There's always a first time for everything."

I laughed. "We'll just have to see."

By the time the air was heated up enough and the balloon was just beginning to tug against its anchor, the sky had already turned a deep ebony with tiny pinpricks of twinkling white. There wasn't a cloud in sight. The gondola took Xiaoyan's weight without any problem. When I stepped aboard, the gondola swayed a little, but did not touch the ground.

There was a crowd gathered by the foot of the wall. I recognized some of their faces. The rest, I figured, were just here for the show. I gave them a wave.

"I hope you crash and die!" Hou's voice came shrill and clear from the crowd. "Do you hear me, Mako? I hope you do!"

Someone told him to shut up. It sounded like Zhihe.

"Who is that?" Xiaoyan frowned.

"The man who introduced me to you," I said.

"Oh."

I undid the first tether. The whole balloon jerked forward and upward, as though it was impatient to leave, only to be held back by the safety. When my hands closed over the safety – the second and final tether – I hesitated for just the slightest of moments.

And then I undid it too. We sailed upward effortlessly. Within seconds, we were already fifty, sixty feet into the air and still rising.

Behind me, Xiaoyan sighed. "Too late to turn back now."

A slight breeze was carrying us southwards. I stuck my head out beyond the edge of the gondola and continued looking at the wall. I heard that if you went up into space, you could still see the Great Wall, if the clouds weren't in the way. I continued looking until the lights on the wall became little specks of orange in the distance, and then finally disappearing into the darkness. Only then I exhaled heavily and turned my gaze back to the inside of the gondola.

"Well," I said, "it's time to go."

I took hold of the ropes connected to the sails and steered us off into the sky.

The Double Blind

A. C. Wise

Ronnie looked up at the blinking lights of the theater marquee. People swirled around her, snatches of conversation and laughter washed up against her and barely registered. In broad daylight, it was all so innocuous. There should be a scar, something to mark the violence.

She pictured it at night, the sidewalk empty, Sarah pausing under the marquee's glow to steal one last sip from her silver flask before heading home. Ronnie tried to remember what her sister had been wearing that night, fix an image in her head of the moment before Pruitt's men grabbed her, dragged her into the shadowed alley beside the theater, and beat her nearly to death.

Ronnie blinked against the ache building behind her eyes. If she'd been with her sister, like she was supposed to be, would they have grabbed her instead? Or could she and Sarah have fought them off, together? Ronnie crossed the street, setting her pace to leave the what-ifs behind. Once the theater was out of sight, she stopped to light a cigarette with shaking hands.

It brought a measure of calm, but not enough. Tension remained, knotted in her belly. Perhaps she shouldn't have come, but she'd felt the need to remind herself why she was doing this. By the time she finished the cigarette, her hands were no longer shaking. Ronnie ground the stub beneath her heel and dug the newsy cap from the leather satchel slung over her shoulder. She pulled the cap low, tucking any stray hairs beneath it before moving on.

The padded motorcycle leathers were too warm for the day; sweat already stuck her shirt to her skin under the jacket. But they would offer at least some protection if things went wrong, and more importantly, they hid the shape of her body, making her anonymous. She wasn't Sarah Dutton's sister, J. T. Dutton's daughter. She could be anyone inside them, and it was liberating.

The streets quickly lost their grid structure, tangling into a warren of tenement buildings. Ronnie took the motorcycle goggles from her satchel and pulled them on, obscuring half her face. Now she was truly invisible.

She ducked into the narrow alley beside the building, the place where Pruitt's men were supposedly laying low after he'd bought them out of ever having to stand trial. Nerves fluttered in her stomach as she scanned the zigzagging fire escape bolted to the bricks. There was an open window halfway up.

Reaching the landing, Ronnie crouched, peering inside. As her eyes adjusted to the dim interior, she spotted a boy who looked about five playing with a wooden toy. Before she could change her mind, she let out a low and sharp whistle. She tensed as the boy looked up, but gestured him closer.

The boy glanced over his shoulder. Ronnie braced for a shout that would bring his mother running, but he rose, taking in her outfit with wide-eyed silence. Ronnie drew a coin from her pocket. His eyes widened further. He hesitated only a moment before snatching it, turning it over in wonder.

Her hands trembling, Ronnie drew the worn newspaper from her satchel. The faces of the two men under the blaring headline "Dutton Heiress's Assailants Captured!" were burned into her mind, but hadn't stopped her from unfolding the page almost every day since Sarah's attack.

"Do you know these men? Have you seen them around here?"

The child chewed his lower lip. It took all of Ronnie's strength not to climb through the window, grab the boy, and shake him. After a moment, the boy nodded. Ronnie's pulse beat in the roof of her mouth. The child glanced over his shoulder again, then beckoned furtively.

As quietly as she could, Ronnie eased through the open window, hoping the floor wouldn't creak, hoping the boy's mother wouldn't choose this moment to check on her son. The boy reached for her hand, and Ronnie flinched before taking it. He tugged her toward the door.

Ronnie followed him down the stairs. Sounds filtered from other apartments, raised voices from one, Gershwin playing on a radio in another. On the first floor, the boy pointed to the end of the hall where a door had been propped open with a brick. A slight breeze came through the gap, along with more voices. Before Ronnie could question the boy, he slipped his hand from hers and scampered back up the stairs.

An announcer's voice crackled over a radio, excitedly narrating a horse race. Invisible. Even if she was spotted, no one would recognize her. Ronnie breathed out and peeked around the door. A group of men clustered around the radio in a small interior courtyard, smoking and passing a bottle in a paper bag between them. One rose to pace as the announcer's voice grew louder, and Ronnie jerked back.

She pressed her back against the wall, counted to ten, then pulled the Leica from her satchel. With shaking fingers, she extended the camera's lens and locked it in place, setting the infinity focus as well. She glanced through the door again. The men were absorbed in the race, not paying the slightest attention. The one closest to her, he looked like the same man from the newspaper, now folded carefully back into her satchel. But she had to be sure.

Ronnie clicked, advanced the film, and clicked again. She ran out the film before slipping the camera into her bag, and fleeing down the hall and back outside.

Ronnie smoothed her dress as she climbed the steps over the garage and knocked on the Double Blind's door. She schooled her expression, trying to keep her excitement in check until she could talk to Emielle alone.

"Password?" The door opened a crack, showing Vincent's mock-serious expression.

"Hmm." Ronnie pursed her lips. "Is it Bit-O-Honey today? No, wait, Baby Ruth?"

The corner of Vincent's lips twitched, and he stepped back.

"Kidder." He swatted at her arm.

"You know me." She blew a kiss over her shoulder, making her way deeper into the smoky club.

To the left of the bar, a trio played soft jazz on a small, spot-light-washed stage. The clack of billiard balls came from the right. In-between, a scatter of low tables circled the cleared area serving as a makeshift dance floor, and Emielle held court at one of these.

The girl perched on Emielle's lap was done up in Mary Pickford curls and a white peignoir tonight. Last time, it had been a Louise Brooks bob and long ropes of pearls. As Ronnie approached, she fluttered her eyelashes, affecting a coquettish giggle. The pearls had done a better job of hiding her Adam's apple, but the blonde hair suited her more.

"You look darling, Tommy." Ronnie air-kissed as the girl slid from Emielle's lap, careful not to smudge either of their make-up jobs.

Tommy tossed a wave over her shoulder, wiggling her fingers as she made her way toward the bar.

"How's my best doll?" Emielle leaned back, grinning, but didn't pull Ronnie into her lap to take Tommy's place.

Once upon a time, that had upset Ronnie, until, in a quiet moment, Emielle had whispered in her ear, "Because you're not for show," answering Ronnie's unspoken question.

"Your best girl needs a drink. But come find me later? I have something to show you."

Emielle's expression flickered, showing strain, and guilt kicked in Ronnie's gut. Was she that easy to read? Emielle's lips pressed into a thin line, then her smile returned. Emielle – with her pinstripe three piece, slicked back hair, spats polished to a high shine, and the white carnation in her lapel – was part of the Double Blind's image, its unflappable owner, always dressed to the nines. If she guessed at Ronnie's news, knew where she'd been, and was upset, she wouldn't let it show. Not yet.

Ronnie put on a smile of her own and blew a kiss as she moved past Emielle to the bar. She let her hips sway, hoping to distract Emielle from her disapproval. Of course she'd tell her everything, later, when they were alone. Ronnie was gratified at the appreciative gaze following her.

"What can I get you, sweetheart?" Phillip asked.

Ronnie leaned against the oak bar, once gleaming and now

scarred with the memory of drinks and cigarette burns. Emielle had gotten it second hand, salvage, and despite its battered condition it was still the pride and joy of the Double Blind. Ronnie scanned the bottles behind Phillip, each with a carefully hand-written label.

"Sidecar, please." The bar was well-stocked tonight. Either the boys who legged booze were getting bolder, or Emielle had turned up the charm requesting this week's shipment. Ronnie suspected a little of both.

Her drink arrived. Ronnie turned, bracing an elbow against the bar, and surveyed the room. Emielle had joined the billiards game, handily beating two of the men who worked for her in the garage below the Double Blind. She was just one of the boys, whether she was in her three-piece, or in a grimy, oil-stained jumpsuit tearing down motorcycles and putting them back together again.

Ronnie drew a cigarette from her satchel, trying not to think of the photographs tucked beneath them. Tommy was being led onto the dance floor by a man Ronnie didn't recognize, and she let that take her focus. The man gripped Tommy's upper arm, both steering her and trying to keep his balance. His drink sloshed as he spun Tommy, making her Mary Pickford curls fly. The man swayed counter to the music's rhythm, then pulled Tommy close, his free hand sliding to cup and squeeze her behind. Tommy jerked away. Flustered, the man grabbed her upper arm again, digging his fingers in hard.

She shoved at the man and he staggered, off-balance for a moment before lunging at her. Tommy hurled her drink in the man's face, stopping him cold. The music died as the man spluttered, face reddening, swiping ineffectually at his suit.

"What's the idea, sweetheart? A man buys you a drink, and you throw it back in his face when he wants a little gratitude?"

He reached for Tommy again, but Emielle was there, blocking him, jaw set below a tight smile.

"I believe the lady wants to be left alone."

"This is none of your business." The man tried to step around Emielle, but she planted her hand in the center of his chest, immovable.

"When a lady tells you to stop, you stop."

"Lady?" The man snorted. "Lookit the way the little sissy is dressed. He was asking for it."

"It's time for you to leave." Emielle's voice dropped, her expression hardening to match.

"Yeah? Who's going to make me? You?" The man pushed Emielle's hand away with a sneer.

Emielle caught him in a wrist lock. As he tried to twist free, she used his weight against him, dropping him and pulling his arm up behind his back.

Emielle addressed Tommy. "You okay?"

Tommy nodded, stunned.

"Get yourself a drink on the house." Emielle hauled the man to his feet, keeping a firm grip as she steered him to the door. "This is last call." Emielle spoke over her shoulder as she ushered the man out.

A gust of cold air came with the door banging closed in the man's wake. Ronnie rubbed at the gooseflesh rising on her arms as Emielle returned, straightening her suit.

"Are you okay?" Ronnie asked as the tentative murmur of conversation returned.

The quick change in mood already had some people drifting to the door, not even bothering with one last drink. Behind Ronnie, the band had started to pack up. Strain showed in the line of Emielle's shoulders, but she touched Ronnie's waist, brushing a distracted kiss across her cheek.

"I'm fine. What did you want to show me?"

"Can we talk downstairs?"

Weariness rode her voice and the line of her shoulders, but Emielle nodded. "I think they can make do without me."

Ronnie followed Emielle down the spiraling metal stairs. The garage smelled of oil and a scent she always associated with dust and rain no matter how many times Emielle tried to explain the actual components of the motorcycles and the various parts and concoctions that kept them running. It was comforting. It was Emielle's smell, and it released some of the tension coiled beneath Ronnie's skin.

Emielle paused beside a BMW R32, fingers resting lightly against its paint. Ronnie smiled, thinking of Emielle enthusiastically trying to explain the recirculating wet sump oil system, and why it was so innovative. She'd finally had to kiss her to get her to shut up.

Ronnie's smile faded, knowing the moment couldn't last. She tilted her head to indicate the worktable in the far corner, and Emielle withdrew her hand from the bike, regret in the motion. Ronnie turned on a small lamp hanging over the table, drawing the photographs from her satchel and spreading them like a hand of cards.

"I found them. These two are the men who hurt Sarah. I compared these shots to the newspaper clipping and it's definitely them. Now I know where to find them." Ronnie tapped the photographs.

Emielle frowned, then let out a breath.

"Okay." She turned, arms crossed, leaning against the worktable. "You found them. So what happens next?"

Ronnie ignored the tightness in Emielle's jaw, the look in her eyes.

"I brought something else. Here."

Ronnie smoothed a sketch out on top of the photographs.

"I thought maybe you could build something for me. They're like bracers, see? They'd strap right over the jacket's sleeves, and there are spring-loaded blades here . . ."

"Ronnie. Stop."

Emielle straightened, dropping her arms to her side. Her expression caught Ronnie off guard, not angry, but pained.

"Do you hear yourself? What do you think you're going to do with spring-loaded blades? Walk up to these men in broad daylight? Sneak back in the dark of night and murder them in their beds?"

Ronnie's cheeks flushed. She opened her mouth to protest, but Emielle's words left no space for her own.

"I'm tired, Ronnie. Let me take you home." Emielle shook her head.

The lingering pain in Emielle's eyes deflated Ronnie. Silently, she gathered the photographs and the sketch, slipping them back into her satchel. Emielle hefted a duffle bag from beside the worktable, snapped off the light, and slipped her other arm around Ronnie's waist.

Ronnie stiffened at the touch. If Emielle noticed, she ignored it, and Ronnie forced herself to relax. Emielle wasn't her enemy. She leaned into the touch, allowing herself at least for the moment to enjoy the warmth where their bodies fit together.

Ronnie lifted her head from the pillow to find Emielle propped up on one elbow, watching her.

"I didn't realize I'd fallen asleep. What time is it?" Ronnie squinted at the window, the light indeterminate.

"Before dawn."

Ronnie flopped back, covering her eyes with her arm. Emielle continued to watch her, and Ronnie lifted her arm, rolling over.

"What is it?"

The weight of the conversation they hadn't finished hung between them, but Ronnie sensed there was something more. Behind the deep green of Emielle's eyes was a thought she'd been worrying over. Had she slept at all?

"You spent so much time tracking down the men who hurt Sarah, and now you've found them. Don't take this the wrong way, but you're not . . ."

Emielle looked away. Ronnie sat up, leaning against the headboard.

"You're saying I've led a sheltered life." An edge of bitterness crept into her tone.

"It's not that." Emielle brought her gaze back to Ronnie's. "I think you're just underestimating the marks violence leaves on a person."

Ronnie flinched. Emielle sat up, lacing their fingers together and running a work-calloused thumb lightly over Ronnie's knuckles. The garage had kept the muscles in Emielle's arms hard. The rest of her body had softened a bit, but not enough to hide her fighter's shape. In the pre-dawn light, her scars were visible – the stitches that had left pale lines like comets streaking across the sky, welts and burns that had never quite faded, the marks she'd chosen, and the ones she hadn't.

Guilt tightened Ronnie's stomach. She'd only seen Emielle fight once, but the lights, the smoke and sweat of the place remained steeped into her skin. The tiered seats around her had been filled, but the crowd's roar wasn't enough to drown the impact of flesh against flesh. After, Emielle had limped from the ring, left eye swollen shut, blood crusting her nostrils, breath whistling painfully.

What Ronnie had seen then and what she saw now were the same thing. The marks of violence were in Emielle's eyes as well as her skin, ghosts.

"I just want you to understand what you're getting into." Emielle's words pulled Ronnie back.

"And," Emielle continued, her gaze now fixed on the motion of her thumb, tracing patterns on the back of Ronnie's hand, "I want you to understand that whatever you choose, it doesn't just affect you."

Emielle looked up again, her expression keeping Ronnie from interrupting. This was it, the sliver behind Emielle's eyes that she'd been working over as Ronnie slept. The weight of it tugged at Emielle's shoulder, and Ronnie bit her lip, forcing herself to stay quiet and listen.

"I used to fight because I had to, to keep my father from killing me and to stay alive once I ran. When I got off the streets, I kept fighting because it was the only thing I knew how to do, until I realized I could make money in the underground clubs. From that point on, I fought so I could make things better for other people, and I stopped as soon as I could."

Emielle ran her free hand through her hair. Ronnie kept her silence, but the words pressed against her skin. Emielle didn't have any siblings, she couldn't know what it was like to lose someone, not physically, but to pain. The Sarah who'd returned from the hospital wasn't the sister Ronnie knew – her wounds had healed to a hard scab of anger, and Sarah was lost somewhere inside. And it was Ronnie's fault.

"I worked hard to make the Double Blind a safe place for people like us," Emielle continued. "That meant cutting out everything I did to earn the money to buy the club. Violence doesn't protect people, it makes them vulnerable."

Emielle sighed, looked away again.

"Last night, when that man attacked Tommy, I could have hurt him, badly. It's not just that I don't want to be that person anymore, I can't. I can't give the world an excuse, anything they can point to justify the names they call us, the laws they make against us. I have to be better. We can't go to the cops. We can't count on anyone else to keep us safe. We have to do that ourselves."

Emielle let go of Ronnie's hand. Ronnie gripped the sheet instead. Didn't Emielle see that's exactly what Ronnie was trying to do, protect Sarah and make things better? Emielle leaned over the side of the bed, pulling the duffle bag onto her lap.

"I was going to give this to you before . . . everything." She shrugged, unzipping the bag.

Emielle drew out what looked like a rifle, its body painted matte black, a gleaming copper tube in place of a muzzle. Ronnie caught her breath. There was a canister welded onto the top where a scope might be on a normal gun, and short lengths of rubber tubing leading back to the rifle's body.

"What is it?"

"A grappling hook gun." The corner of Emielle's mouth lifted in a regret-touched smile. She ran her fingers over the gun's body, not looking at Ronnie. "I built it from spare parts around the shop. I wanted you to have the right tools, for whatever you decide."

Emielle handed over the gun. Despite the relative lightness of the build, it felt heavy as Ronnie accepted it.

"The hook and rope are in the bag." Emielle slid out of bed, bending to gather her clothes.

Ronnie wanted to say something to reassure her, but what could she say? Her fingers tightened around the gun, trying to anchor herself, but she couldn't shake the feeling of the world sliding out from under her, everything slipping beyond her control.

Ronnie stared at the ornate frieze-work on the elevator's outer doors as she waited for the car to descend. The pattern matched the stonework on the face of the building – a nautical scene of tall ships, stylized waves, and the curling tentacles of sea monsters – celebrating the shipping trade that had made her father his first fortune. This building was just one of many her father had designed throughout the city, all full of the same hard, angular lines and grandiose details.

The doors slid open and the operator in his pressed uniform opened the cage door before touching his cap.

"Good afternoon, Miss Dutton. Top floor?"

"Please."

Ronnie's heels clicked across the lobby's polished marble, the sound swallowed as she stepped into the elevator's cage. She fought the urge to fidget, smooth her blouse, or most of all, light a cigarette. She kept her hands firmly on the bakery box she carried instead, her peace offering.

They rode up in silence. Exiting the elevator, Ronnie let herself into the penthouse and found Sarah sitting facing the window. Ronnie paused, trying to shake the guilt at how long it had been since she last visited.

She took a steadying breath, studying the back of her sister's head, framed by the city view. There was more amber than honey in Sarah's hair, more like their father than what Ronnie remembered of their mother. She wore it in the same style as Ronnie's, long and softly curled, falling to her shoulders. But that was where the similarity ended. What Sarah had from their father, Ronnie had from their mother, and vice versa. And now, Sarah' body listed slightly to the left, as if the shattered bones on that side, even healed, weighed her down.

"I brought you something." Ronnie crossed the room and knelt by Sarah's chair, placing the string-wrapped bakery box in her sister's lap.

"You smell like cigarettes." It was a moment before Sarah turned from the window. "And don't do that."

"Do what?"

Sarah's mouth, set in a frown, puckered upward on the left hand side where a scar traced its way from her eye to her chin.

"Kneel down so our faces are level."

"Sorry." Ronnie straightened.

Tension crawled beneath her skin. No longer holding the box, Ronnie knotted her fingers together.

"You could say thank you." Ronnie regretted the words the moment they were out. The last thing she wanted was to start a fight.

"I'm not hungry." Sarah set the box on the table beside her.

Ronnie pushed down annoyance. She wouldn't let Sarah goad her. As she searched for safe ground, Sarah's chair finally registered. It wasn't the plain one from the hospital. The back was printed to match the frieze on the elevator doors and the outside of the building. The wheels and handles given the same bronze flourish as the window guards and railings.

"Your chair . . ."

"Do you like it?" Sarah spun abruptly, the left wheel knocking into the table and tumbling the bakery box to the floor. "A gift from Daddy."

The scar only accentuated her sneer. Ronnie bent to retrieve the fallen box. She picked at the string, fingers trembling. When she opened her mouth, the words that came out surprised her.

"I tracked them down, the men who did this to you. I know where they're hiding now."

She watched her sister carefully. Would the information finally shock Sarah out of her sullen anger? It took a moment for Ronnie to recognize the ugly sound her sister made as laughter.

"So now what? You're going to avenge me? Ronnie the vigilante. That's rich."

"I'm trying to help you."

"Please." Sarah's laughter died, but roughness stained her voice from the exertion, a legacy of hands around her throat nearly crushing her windpipe. "You're just as bad as Daddy."

"I'm not . . ." Ronnie bristled, but the twist of Sarah's mouth stopped her.

"No? When Pruitt bought his men out of jail before they went to trial, don't you think Daddy could have hit back? He could have had those men killed. Instead, he let them live and made sure Pruitt knew about his 'act of mercy'. And he made sure the world saw him hold up his lily white hands, a simple, honest businessman grieving for the wrong done to his family."

"Sarah."

Her sister continued as if Ronnie hadn't spoken.

"Those men could have killed me, but they left me alive to send a message to our father." Sarah's right hand tightened, the left trembling slightly as her fingers failed to grip the chair's arm. "And it couldn't have worked out better for

Daddy. Now he can hold me up as his martyred angel, his pretty songbird cut down in her prime. Oh, the career I could have had. The man I would have married. All the beautiful children I'll never have."

"I'm not . . ." Ronnie said again, but Sarah cut her off.

"It isn't about me. Not for Daddy, not for Pruitt. I'm just a pawn in their war. But you, at least, I thought . . ."

Sarah shook her head, her bitter smirk deepening.

"You're not taking revenge for my sake, you're just trying to clear your guilty conscience and prove you're more than just a spoiled little rich girl."

Ronnie's hand snapped out before she could stop herself. The crack of flesh on flesh rocked Sarah's head back. Ronnie's hand flew to her mouth, her eyes stinging.

"Oh, Sarah. I'm so sorry, I didn't mean . . ."

Sarah touched her cheek, rubbing the red imprint of Ronnie's hand covering her scar. When she lowered her hand, she was still smirking.

"That's the first time you've treated me like a human being since I got out of the hospital."

"What?" Ronnie stared at her sister.

"The way you've been swallowing your arguments, tiptoeing around me. Christ, I'm so fucking sick of it." Sarah snapped the fingers of her good hand. "Hey, give me one of your cigarettes."

"You don't smoke." Ronnie reached into her bag, handing over the cigarette automatically.

"Yeah, but Daddy'll hate coming back to find the place smelling like smoke, and I can blame it on you."

Sarah's eyes glittered with wicked light. Ronnie lit the cigarette for her sister and lit one of her own, her mind still whirling to catch up. Sarah coughed and made a face.

"I don't know what you see in these things." Her second drag was smoother; she blew a stream of smoke deliberately toward one of the richly upholstered chairs.

"You know, in a way, it's actually a relief." Sarah's tone was casual, conversational; Ronnie marveled at it. "I outgrew the idea of being Daddy's little princess when I turned sixteen, but he'd already pinned all his hopes on me after the way you turned out."

Ronnie opened her mouth, but Sarah ignored her.

"Now, he doesn't expect anything of me at all, other than to be a prop he can push around. Most of the time, when he doesn't need me to make him look good for some gala, or some stockholder's meeting, he just ignores me. I finally have the space to figure out what I want to do with my life."

"What do you want to do?" Ronnie voice was surprisingly even for all that she was still trying to catch up. The woman before her was a stranger, not the sister she'd known before the accident, but not the one she'd known since, either.

Sarah gave a lopsided shrug, her mischievous grin returning. "I'm thinking maybe politics. Now that women can vote, maybe it's time we started making some of the laws, too."

She pointed her cigarette at Ronnie, ash drifting to carpet. Ronnie automatically ground the ashes with her toe.

"And," Sarah said, "I don't need you ruining it for me by getting arrested for murder. If you're really nice to me, maybe I'll even make it legal for you and all your bulldagger friends to get married one day."

"I . . ." Ronnie couldn't think of a single thing to say.

Sarah finally reached for the bakery box, balancing it in her lap and untying the string. Ronnie watched her eat three cookies in a row before leaning back, powdered sugar dusting her fingers, her blouse, and her self-satisfied smile.

On the Double Blind's stage, a tall, colored man – hair done in smooth finger waves, wearing a shimmery silvery dress – sang Bessie Smith low and sweet. A few couples swayed together, heads pressed close to suit the melancholy song. Ronnie's head was still swimming, trying to process everything that had happened with Sarah. She needed to find Emielle and apologize. She needed to lean against her, hear herself forgiven, and ask her how to make everything okay again.

The need was childish, but she'd been a child this whole time – a spoiled little rich girl, making Sarah's injury about herself until she couldn't even see her sister anymore. Emielle had tried to tell her as much, and she'd refused to listen.

She scanned the room, spotting Emielle by the bar. Tommy, her look inspired by Norma Shearer tonight, stood with her, their heads bowed close, speaking low. At the expressions on their faces, all thoughts of Sarah fled from Ronnie's mind.

"What's wrong?"

"A couple of places got raided last night." Emielle looked up, weary expression matched to the rawness of her voice. "The Flamingo and the Diamond Room."

"The cops were pretty rough." Tommy sounded like she'd been crying, her eyes behind the smoky make-up confirming it. "A couple of my friends got beat pretty bad. Some of them were held overnight."

Tommy's shoulders hitched. Ronnie stepped close, slipping her arm around the girl and pulling her head against her own shoulder, stroking her hair.

"You don't think . . ." Ronnie's gaze swept around the room. "I mean, we've been so careful. We'll be safe, right?"

Emielle's gaze flicked to Tommy who straightened, smoothing her fingers nervously down the front of her dress. The quality of her fear shifted, incorporating an element of guilt.

"The man who grabbed me, before he was bragging about the clubs he goes to, where they hire girls like me to . . . entertain . . . gentlemen. He bragged about how he got one of them closed down."

Tommy looked down, fresh tears gathering on her lashes.

"I should have kept my mouth shut. Not made a scene. I should have let him . . ."

"No." Emielle took Tommy's shoulder firmly, shaking her once. "It's not your fault. Don't you dare apologize."

"You don't think he could do that to us?" Ronnie said. "Wouldn't he implicate himself?"

"He could leave an anonymous tip." Emielle let go of Tommy, but her tone remained distracted. After a moment, she squeezed Ronnie's fingers, already turning away. "Don't worry, we'll figure something out."

Ronnie stared after her. The ache she'd felt earlier became a hollowness where anger and fear warred, buzzing between her bones. That a man like that could hurt Tommy, make her guilty and scared, then turn it around and hurt everyone in the Double Blind . . .

The unfairness of it crashed against her. It wasn't just big acts of violence, like the one against her sister. There was small, petty violence in the world, too, and it was just as damaging. One phone call, one word to the right people, and everything Emielle had built would come crashing down.

Her fingers curled, digging into her palms. She forced herself to let go, to breathe. The first hint of a smile crept across Ronnie's lips. Maybe she was just a spoiled rich girl, but that didn't mean there wasn't still a way for her to make things right.

Ronnie lowered the goggles over her eyes, making sure no stray hairs trailed from beneath her cap. She slung the satchel with the Leica over one shoulder, hefting the duffle with the grappling gun over the other. Discrete questioning and money across the right palms had brought her the name of the man who'd assaulted Tommy – Gordon Wexler. From there, it had been surprisingly easy to track down his regular haunts. Ronnie stood outside his favorite now, a Gothic mansion that had once been a private residence, the lower two floors a conventional gentlemen's club with a dining hall, library, billiards room, bars, and the top floor catering to more particular tastes.

Light spilled from windows on all three floors, but the grounds were shadowed with massive oak trees. Trusting to the darkness and her leathers to keep her hidden, Ronnie aimed for one of the largest of the trees growing close to the house. She set the duffle down at its base and drew out Emielle's grappling hook gun.

Her father had taught both his daughters to shoot when they were young. The lessons served her well now. She braced the stock against her shoulder, took a calming breath, and squeezed on the exhale. The hook caught in a fork between two high branches. Ronnie tugged the line to make sure it was secure, then climbed.

Her arms shook by the time she reached the lowest branch that would hold her. She refused to give in to the temptation to look down, and kept climbing until she was even with the third floor. The tree was big enough that even this high up, the branches could easily hold her. She crawled as far out as she could, getting close enough to the house that she could practically touch the window.

Ronnie had a clear view into a brightly-lit room holding a baby grand piano, a bar, and a scatter of wing-backed chairs and small tables. She prepped the camera as she scanned the faces in the room. Her pulse skipped as she spotted Gordon Wexler, a boy in a spangled silver dress and feathered headband at his side.

Unlike Tommy, this boy proudly let his chest hair show, dark curls visible above the dress' plunging neckline. Perhaps that's what Wexler had requested. He squeezed the boy's behind and guided him to a chair. Ronnie brought up the Leica, scarcely daring to breathe. She snapped Wexler nuzzling the boy's throat, the boy sitting in Wexler's lap, Wexler's hand on the boy's thigh, hiking his skirt higher – clicking until she ran out of film.

Adrenaline shook Ronnie's body as she climbed from the tree. She wanted to whoop aloud, but held the sound inside. She coiled the grappling gun, packed it back into the duffle. Things could still go wrong, the pictures might not turn out. She knew it rationally, but in this moment, her heart refused to acknowledge anything but victory.

Ronnie couldn't keep the grin from her face as she entered the garage. She breathed deep of the dust-and-oil smell, nodding to the men as she made her way toward where Emielle crouched beside the R32. Emielle looked up in surprise, wiping her hands on an oily rag as she straightened.

"What are you doing here?"

Even the strain in Emielle's expression wasn't enough to dampen Ronnie's mood. She pulled the envelope, thick with photographs, from her satchel and handed it over. A duplicate envelope sat on the bed in Ronnie's apartment, waiting to be anonymously mailed to Gordon Wexler.

"What's this?" Emielle lifted the envelope's flap, but didn't remove the contents, doubt clear in her eyes.

"Insurance." Ronnie's grin deepened. "I've decided what kind of vigilante I want to be."

Black Sunday

Kim Lakin-Smith

Friday April 12, 1935

Wesley Sanders edged the drink onto the table.

"There ya'rl, Miss Nightingale. Iced lemonade, or as Momma's prone to call it, sunlight in a glass."

The eight-year-old grinned. His teeth were large and very white, as if slicked with whitewash like the exterior of the Grace Presbyterian Church. His cheeks were nut-brown apples.

Carrie-Anne leant forward in her rocker and put her toes to the floor. She smiled back. "Thank you, Wesley. Tell your momma, she sure does know how to soothe the spirit."

Wesley bobbed his cap. He waltzed off down the porch, humming one of those slow sad Negro church songs he was prone to. Even after he'd swung through the inner gauze and disappeared inside the house, Carrie-Anne could hear the tune. It seemed to nestle down inside the dry Oklahoma heat and stay there, whispering at her.

She picked up the lemonade, rested the sole of a bare foot against the table and rocked. Julie Sander's eldest, Abraham, had painted the porch a light gray color before he'd abandoned Bromide for Oklahoma City last fall. That afternoon, the paint shade complimented the troubled sky where blue and lavender clouds roiled.

A storm was coming. What kind, Carrie-Anne wasn't sure. This time of year, it could be hail, could be lightning, could be a twister. But she welcomed it. The weather was unseasonably close. It licked at the nape of her neck where her shoulder-length hair clung, and at each underarm, leaving sweat stains on her new cotton dress. Everything induced slumber. Except the cold lemonade.

Carrie-Anne put the glass to her lips and sipped. She wanted to stay mindful. The back gate needed fixing; she'd set the new yardman on it with instructions to go about replacing the struts. One of her stockings had a run that wouldn't darn itself. Plus the whole house needed airing.

She'd noticed as much that morning. Rising from her blankets at the tail end of night, she'd descended the stairs and glimpsed the place as with an outsider's eye. Everything was layered with dust. She'd got a rag to it. But as she beat the motes, she'd felt a familiar, inexplicable crackling along her bare arms. Lips parted, she'd held up a hand to the window. In the first rays of dawn, the dust had appeared to dance near but never touch her skin, as if magnetically repelled . . . Seconds later, she'd heard footsteps on the stairs and Julie Sanders saying in her quiet way, "Sure is dusty, Miss Nightingale. I'll light a flame under the coffee pot then get to helping ya."

Carrie-Anne braced her foot against the table and stayed tipped back on the rockers. Having filled the role of nursery nurse ever since Carrie-Anne first arrived at Boar House, aged eight and orphaned, Julie was like family, as were her boys. Which was how the woman knew to fill the house with the clarifying aroma of coffee and just join in shaking out the dust that morning. Also how she knew to dispatch Wesley with cool lemonade when the gate was still broken, the stocking still torn, the house still dust-riddled.

All the same, Julie's best efforts had failed. With the heat cooking in around her, Carrie-Anne found it impossible to rouse herself to any thought but one.

Where the hell were they?

Even wearing ear mufflers, he couldn't escape the terrible clanking as fragments of rock in the sand ricocheted off the drill. The cockpit shuddered with each impact. His jaw ached from clenching his teeth to stop them jarring. The four-point Sutton harness rubbed the same sore spots it did every run; Virgil imagined Carrie-Anne slavering the blisters with peppered grease. Lust alleviated his discomfort. The excavations were pivotal to his work, but, Christ, he missed that gal. Her baby scent when she soaped the sweat offa her. Those frank blue eyes and wide mouth. He liked her off-beat beauty.

"Stop tugging your little john back there, Virgil, and crank the boiler. That last sheet of bedrock took the best of old Bessie's heat." Straining at the front harness, Josephine Splitz attempted to glare back over her shoulder.

Virgil knew he'd just be a blur at her peripheral vision. He crossed his arms over his crotch all the same.

"Sorry, Jos. It's hot's all. Got me sweating like a hog ripe for slaughter."

Grabbing a battered iron scoop off a hook overhead, he drove it through the coke trough that ran alongside his chair and used the other hand to open the iron flap in the Burrower's wall. A tremendous gush of heat spilt into the cabin. He shook the coke down the shoot and shut the hatch.

"Another couple."

If the old coot'd had eyes in the back of her head, Virgil guessed they'd have been lit up and smiling. Twice more he drove the scoop into the coke and threw the fodder down the boiler's throat.

Reaching overhead, he took hold of a leather loop and tugged several times, feeling the papery air off the bellows feed the cabin and boiler simultaneously. Glancing past Josephine's shoulder, Virgil saw the needles creep up in the rack of brass and glass gauges. The steering wheel juddered under the old girl's hands, and he thought he heard her wince despite the wads of muslin she'd taped around the triangulated steel bar. Any other octogenarian shoehorned into the cramped quarters of the Burrower would've screamed for death's release long ago. But Josephine was a wizened fruit, long past the point of any residual softness. She reminded Virgil of a small hunched Asian man in her navy-blue mandarin jacket, loose pants and soft cloth hat, except her fierce single-mindedness was peculiar to the matriarch.

"Got your mind up top too soon, Virgil Roberts. Long as we're still beneath, we're just one mistake away from being buried alive." Jos's voice got that molasses quality it always did when she wanted to aggravate him for kicks. "Nothing certain in love or geological exploration, I promise you. By the time we break surface, chances are Carrie-Anne will've hooked up with Preacher Richards' son. Great strapping lad, all thighs and neck and buttocks like quartz boulders. Or Jeffrey's boy. Part store keeper, part donkey."

"In place of a lab rat that spends his time parked behind the arse of some old dame," Virgil shot back. His mouth twisted. Jos sure liked to tease, but part of him guessed she might be right. Why was Carrie-Anne laying down with a freak like him? He'd spent so much time underground this past year. His eyes had a skim on them like spoilt milk. Likewise, his skin was colorless through lack of sunlight. Danger was, sooner or later, he'd fade right out.

Even without seeing his face, Jos was astute enough to know what he was thinking. "You're okay, Virgil Roberts. Wouldn't choose you for my bedfellow but Carrie-Anne's got the right to."

"It bother you if I said I wouldn't choose you for a bedfellow either?"

The old gal snorted. Any retort was cut short by a tremendous scraping noise. The steel undercarriage bucked beneath their feet, the motion immediately offset by the concertinaing of the Burrower's riveted steel roof plates. It was a filthy, stinking, terrifying ride, thought Virgil, but Jos's design was immaculate. The torpedo-shaped main carriage had a dual layer of modular pneumatic tiles, or 'scutes' as Jos called them in homage to her greatest muse as a bioengineer, the horn-coated dermal bones of the Armadillo. As a geo-engineer, she'd applied similar tessellation logic to the rotating bit of the twelve-foot Tungsten-Carbide-plated nose cone, likewise the corrugated neck frill that funneled the spoil out behind as they pressed forward on sharpened steel tracks. The unstable nature of the terrace deposits was counteracted by gills in the outer walls that released a fine mist to solidify the sand. Hot, thin, rust-scented air was siphoned into the cabin from the tunnels. Water bladders were grouped at the back end of the machine like egg sacks.

The turbulence abated.

"Five minutes more. Just time enough to make yourself look pretty for my niece." Jos adjusted in her seat. She handed a metal pot over her shoulder. "And to empty the piss pan."

Carrie-Anne plunged forward in the rocking chair and stood up. She rested her hands against the corner strut of the porch then leant her whole body into it to better feel the vibrations. The keen of ruptured earth was just audible. Dust misted the field beyond the garden.

"Wesley!"

The boy was already at the swing door.

"Momma knows, Miss Valentine. Says she's drawing Miss Splitz's bath and fixing Mister Robert's Gin Sour."

"Good." Carrie-Anne stared at the dry field, littered with entrance and exit wounds inflicted by the Burrower. "That's good," she repeated softly.

The ground shook. There came a sudden explosion of brilliance in the center of the field as sunlight touched the tip of the emerging nose cone. A geyser of dark sand erupted. The cacophonic whirring of the engine ripped through the air. The Burrower wormed up from below like a giant silver maggot castor.

I shall not run to his side, not this time, thought Carrie-Anne. *I will be the lady of the house, patiently waiting on the porch, lemonade glass in hand.*

Though it was hard to stand still as the terrific machine sledged up into the air, slammed back down and coasted forward, its twin steel tracks sending up two great tides of dust. The engine sound changed to a discordant chug. Steam spurted from the side valves.

"Want me to run down to them, Miss Valentine?" Wesley stared up at her in round-eyed innocence.

"No, Wesley." She stuck out a hand as though to brace his chest. "You know better than to get near Miss Splitz's excavating machine so soon after surfacing. It's a big old unpredictable cottonmouth till it cools some. Look!" She felt a rush of longing as jets of steam escaped the rivets of the roof hatch. "Even those inside take their time when exiting," she murmured.

The roof hatch cranked up. Aunt Josephine was first to emerge, un-crumpling herself as she went with all the decorum of a farm hand. She dropped heavily onto the ground, agitating the dust. For a brief moment, she applied her thumbs to her spine and arched backward. Then she made for the front of the vehicle, kicking out stiff legs as she walked.

Carrie-Anne's gaze returned to the roof hatch. He was visible now as a coil of flesh that stretched out to become a tall, thin figure. Her heart got hot at the sight of him. He raised a hand to wave.

There wasn't chance to respond. Her aunt was shouting and gesticulating toward the huge steaming drill. Virgil answered her and threw an arm toward the house.

He's waving her away, thought Carrie-Anne admiringly.

Sure enough, the old maid turned heel and began to stomp toward the house.

Carrie-Anne watched Virgil slide down off the Burrower's roof. With his shirt sleeves rolled and one suspender dangling loose from his waist, he strode up to the drill and dipped under it, one arm raised as a shield against the heat. Virgil's in-depth mechanical knowledge made Carrie-Anne aware of her own internal workings; he seemed to grasp them too. And while she wanted to keep her eyes on him, her aunt was already at the garden gate.

". . . peach of a ride till we hit that friggin' boulder. Now the damn drill's breached. Virgil best check the depth of those gorges good and proper else I'll be roastin' his sweet cherry ass on old Bessie . . ." Aunt Josephine plonked down on the porch steps, untied her boots and kicked them off. She didn't falter in her monologue, ". . . not like we weren't prepared. Hit wet sand and Virgil was gonna switch from steam to soot mix, gloop the walls to stop them caving in. But we didn't find one patch of moisture. 'Course it's bone dry up here on the surface. Just the same, no water bodies, not even fifty foot below? It's strange. Not strange, it's unnatural."

The old woman stopped prattling suddenly. Her hooded gaze fell on Wesley.

"Help your momma black the stove?"

Wesley sucked his lip and nodded.

"Kept the dirt from growin' between them fat little toes?"

The kid caught a foot up in a hand and used his fingers to scoop between the toes.

"Am all clean, Miss Splitz."

The old woman gurned at him and he giggled.

"Here." She held out a fist.

Wesley dropped his foot. He ran over, offering up cupped hands, and Aunt Josephine opened her fist over them.

"Thank you, Miss Splitz." The boy eyed his prize then pocketed it.

Carrie-Anne smiled; she knew the ritual. The treasure was a mundane stone recovered from several miles below ground. Wesley would add it to his collection.

Hand on the stair rail, Aunt Josephine levered herself up. Stalking over to the front door, she paused to cut her eye at Carrie-Anne.

"Told lover boy you'd've shacked up with a new fella by now." She slung her gaze over to the field where Virgil had shifted his attention to the cooling engine.

Carrie-Anne felt panic worm between her eyes.

Her aunt must've noticed.

"He missed you," she relented, and shouldered the fly-screen door and disappeared inside. Wesley followed after like a child bound to a witch by invisible silken thread.

Carrie-Anne rested her forehead against the corner strut. Eyelids lulling, she watched the ghost of a man at work out in the field. Minutes passed. He became less and less solid. Late afternoon ebbed and swelled around her. A cicada soloed ahead of the insect symphony at sundown. Through the open bathroom window, she could hear Aunt Josephine's prattle and the slow pour from a water jug as Julie endeavored to clean up her mistress. Wood creaked; to Carrie-Anne, it was the sound of the house groaning under the weight of memories impregnating its walls. She listened past the familiar sounds of her environment, out to the dusting plateau of farmland and the drone of nothingness.

Her flesh crackled. Her eyes shot wide.

Virgil stood on the porch a couple of paces away.

Carrie-Anne's first reaction was indignation at his material-izing like that when she expected to watch him approach from the distance of the field, to get used to him closing in. Her anger was blunted by the sight of him, hands and forearms etched in coke dust, shirt savaged at the neck. Lifting her eyes, she saw a death mask of skin so terribly white and dried to the bone. He went against what common decency said a man should look like. Yet his was a salt-preserved masculinity which made her drip away from herself.

Carrie-Anne let go of the strut and wrapped her arms around her waist. Virgil kept on staring. She felt transparent.

"Lose your tongue as well as your mind this trip, Virgil Roberts?"

He smiled and the death aspect was replaced by tangible sensuality. Now she saw a slender man with well-worked shoulders, high cheekbones and generous lips in need of moisture. Only his eyes remained strange with their misted irises and pupils gone over from black to lead gray.

"I was drinking you in, Carrie-Anne Valentine," he said quietly.

The gauze door yawned on its hinges and Wesley emerged from the house.

"Yu Gin Sour, Mister Roberts."

The glass was offered up. Virgil gulped from it, his gaze on Carrie-Anne. She felt his stare graze her flesh like a steam burn.

Bromide had been parched for months now, in spite of its draw as a spa town not fifteen years past, when the railroad carved through the district and millionaire, Robert Galbreath, found a hole into which to sink his oil money. Back then the town supported three general stores, two drugstores, a bank, a meat market, two hardware stores, two restaurants, a blacksmith's, and a dry goods. Four grand hotels wined, dined, and bed-timed. A public bath house doused and rinsed. Meanwhile, Bromide's unique geology gave rise to a cotton gin and yard, a rock crusher and quarry, a wagon maker, a sawmill, a gristmill, and even a bottler who shipped out the medicinal waters.

But fame is nothing if not fickle. Come 1930, folk moved further afield. As quickly as it was raised, the town was brought to the ground. The excursion trains were canceled, the bank closed, the hotels emptied. Five years more and Bromide looked set to simply blow away like a handful of dust.

Knees in the dirt, Reg Wilhoit wondered which piece of his town's history he worked up beneath his fingernails. Not much left to see of old Bromide now. Just slim pickings like the Baptist Church, a double-doored cattle barn of a place built of the usual dreary stone whose pews were regularly buffed, as if that would be enough to wipe the grime offa the place. There was the shack of the post office, which stank of old maid and kerosene, given Mrs Johnson's partiality to warm her knees by a stove. And there were another forty or so dwellings still bothered by human breath. Mostly though, ruins scattered a three mile radius, like markers to a ghost town.

"Ya need a hand there, Mister Wilhoit?"

The old man shone his eyes up. Preacher Richards' boy blocked out the sun.

Reg could guess how he looked to the kid. Seat of his pants patched. White cotton candy hair around a craggy face. Bent over like that. A marionette cut from its strings.

"Them calipers giving you gyp? Come on." Ben stuck out a hand the size of a rib steak. "Let's be havin' you."

"I'm fine, I tell ya."

Reg tossed out a fistful of dirt; luckily for Ben, no wind meant it sifted back down to the ground rather than flick up into his eyes. Not that the kid noticed.

But he wouldn't, mused Reg. Nice boy like that would've been raised with Preacher Richards' good grace. Yet sometimes manners got in the way. He wished to hell the kid'd kept on walking and not had to go and play Samaritan.

"Move it along, kiddo. Got a cramp in this knee's all." Sidewaysing onto his ass, Reg rapped one of the steel side bars of his left leg brace.

The preacher's son offered him a big dumb smile. But there was a wary glint to the eye.

"All right then, Mister Wilhoit. I'll just be at the store gettin' Momma her sewing notions. Hollerin' distance if you need me." Ben pointed to the far end of Main. Reg squinted over at the rubble shack of the general store, one of a handful of buildings to survive fire or abandonment and keep on serving what was left of the community. Same way it always had.

The old man said nothing, just stayed still as a tombstone, ass in the dirt.

"All right then," repeated the lad. He tipped his cap and set off, letting the sunlight back in like a holy blaze.

Reg watched him go. Then he bent forward and dug his fingers into the dry dirt again.

Virgil drove his knife through the pork. Eying the mashed potatoes, gravy, black-eyed peas, and collard greens, he pressed a little of everything onto his fork.

"Fine pork shoulder, Julie," he announced as the maid re-entered the room carrying a jug of iced water. "You get it from Bobby Buford's farm?"

Julie flashed her generous smile. "Bobby Buford's, Mister Roberts. Quality hogs he's got penned. Decent price he charges too, 'cept we always exchange goods of course. Mister Bulford, he's all gone on my cornbread and fresh picked tomatoes. It's so warm, see. I got to planting unseasonably early."

"Sure is a helluva dry spell. Not that visitors to Boar House would notice with a garden this lush." Virgil leant in on his elbows, knife and fork laid over one another like a silver cross. "How'd you do it, Julie? How'd you grow vegetables and herbs like you do when the field opposite is shredding its epidermis quicker than a rattlesnake?"

"'Cause I designed the best irrigation system in the state. And 'cause Julie gets a big ole milk churn and hauls ass to the well night and day to keep the system's water butts topped up." Jos jammed her own elbows onto the table. "Sissy boy like you'd struggle to lift that churn five yards."

"Better a sissy boy than a bad-tempered gasbag," shot Virgil from the opposite end of the table.

Jos got a sour twist to her mouth. "Better a bad-tempered gasbag than an incompetent navigator."

"Oh, come on now!" Virgil was peppered on the inside. His skin got some color to it. "Much as I'd love to look into a crystal ball and know what's gonna hit before we get there, you know as well as me we can hit waterlogged sand or a boulder anytime underground. Because of water pockets, we got the soot mix, and as backup, the tar tap. Because of boulders, we got a Tungsten Carbide drill bit." He raised an eyebrow. "Maybe you need an early night, Jos? All this hard work and staying up late is bound to make an old crone cranky."

Jos stabbed at her greens. She ladled in a mouthful and chewed it up into one cheek. "It's your job to survey the route. Establish the orientation of bedding planes and steer us clear of joints in the rock," she insisted, adding aside, "Julie, you go get your supper now." Her gaze cut back to Virgil. She swallowed the mouthful. "We hit that last stretch of gravel hard and we hit it clumsy. Now we gotta pray there ain't a hairline fracture in the bit."

Virgil dug in fingers at his hairline. "And if there is, it'll blow itself and us to kingdom come." He dragged his hands back over his scalp. "I got my nose into every inch of the Burrower this afternoon. Like the one who built her, she's a tough old bird."

He allowed himself a smile. Sure, he was smarting that Jos felt the need to pin the blame on him – and maybe if he'd surveyed the field's surface for the thousandth time, he'd have guessed at that curl of gravel a few hundred yards below. But, no . . . Virgil kept his smile in place. Deep down, he knew there was no magic way to see exactly what lay in the Burrower's path, only estimations based on months' worth of surveys of the rock formations up top. He also knew that while Jos'd take a bullet before she'd admit it, they were both dog tired – which was why their usual banter had a caustic edge.

Luckily, there was Carrie-Anne to agitate the atmosphere.

"You know, Aunt Josephine, there hasn't been a scrap of wind these past four days you and Virgil have been down under. Not a scrap. Still the dust creeps in under the doors and windows. I was up before cockcrow this morning. When I saw a fresh layer over this place, my first thought was how come there's any ground left for the Burrower to dig through?" Carrie-Anne threw out her hands to indicate the paneled dining room, and, presumably, the whole house. "Julie and I spend our days sweeping it up."

Glancing at Virgil, she rubbed one side of her nose with her knuckles as if to rub away a soot smear. He recognized the gesture as slight embarrassment and he understood. Carrie-Anne wasn't really one for words. Not that she couldn't hold a conversation if she wanted. Just she was a girl who spoke with her eyes, or a wisp of laughter, or the sorcery of her tongue at his navel.

Jos was talking now. Thanks to Carrie-Anne, the old gal had been lulled into a softer frame of mind. Conducting a symphony of science with her cutlery, she appeared intent on using her niece as a sounding board for the plethora of geological theories Virgil had helped her construct.

". . . over-intensive arable farming methods. I told Bobby Buford so two years ago when he still had land worth plowing and hadn't pigs shitting over every inch of it. Drain the land of mineral, strip it of ground cover, and you're gonna get a wind tunnel. All's needed was a turn up in temperature and lack of rain, and, hell, I told them!" Jos screwed up her face, itself parched of moisture.

"But as I said, Aunt Josephine, there's been no wind. Just this thick baking in."

Carrie-Anne's gaze shifted toward him as she spoke. Virgil felt the same mix of emotion he'd felt when he'd stood on the porch a couple of hours earlier and soaked her in. Everything had misted into the background except Carrie-Anne. The only thing worth seeing. After so many hours spent in twilight underground, he'd fed on the colors offa her. Then Wesley had stepped out onto the porch, and the mist and colors evaporated like a broken spell. Only Carrie-Anne's tangibility had remained. He'd longed to mold her with his hands like wet sand.

"The wind will come," he said softly. He carved at the lump of roast pig on his plate again.

"And when it does, we'll all be blown away like stupid shitting pigs in straw houses," cut in Jos. She scraped back her chair. "Now I've a mind to get Julie to cut me a slice of that pie I smelt baking earlier."

Passing Virgil, she put a hand to his shoulder. "You want?"

It was as close to an apology as he'd get from Josephine Splitz.

Virgil glanced sideways, his mouth softened. "No. No thank you, Jos."

He dared believe she might disappear into the kitchen and stay there, stuffing her face with pie, while he and Carrie-Anne got to sit together and talk some. But then Jos paused in the doorway.

"Go to the workshop and get all maps sketched in the last two months, Virgil. We musta missed that seam of gravel somewhere. And no . . ." She raised a hand to block his objection. "Tomorrow won't do. We ain't seeing the warmth of our beds till I'm satisfied we're not gonna drill a goddamn minefield in two days' time."

"Two days? But that's a Sunday?"

Virgil could see Carrie-Anne turning her mind inside out in search of arguments against.

"I promised we'd all be at chapel Palm Sunday. Our attendance – or lack of it – has been noted, and not just by Preacher Richards. Folk talk, Aunt Josephine, and talk leads to trouble."

"That it does, Carrie-Anne, and it's gonna lead you into a great deal of it right now if you don't stop gassing and get yourself to bed." Jos's eyes shone out like coal chips.

Virgil watched Carrie-Anne intently. His gal would never show that dry old coot what she felt on the inside. Oh no, she'd keep it stitched into the flesh lining over her heart and ribs.

He, on the other hand, knew no such restraint. But just as he would've happily strangled Jos on the spot, the old woman let her shoulders stoop. She looked incredibly tired all of a sudden.

"Please, Carrie-Anne. We're out to save lives here. And that includes protecting our own."

Saturday April 13, 1935

Saturday. Town Day. Once upon a time, Main Street would've thrummed with the footfall of folk who'd journeyed to Bromide to trade, swap and stockpile. The ice man would have busied his pick. The blacksmith would have chipped at his anvil. The pharmacist would have returned a whisper across the counter and deposited some bottle or canister of powder into a bag which he'd carefully fold over. The girl at the dry goods store would have dragged the fabric bundle off the shelf and measured, snipped, and ripped. In every store and business premises, proprietors and staff would have busied themselves to satisfy Saturday's rush. Meanwhile, townsfolk and families from surroundings farmsteads would have gathered to speculate, commiserate, and nose into one another's business. Once upon a time.

But Bromide had gone from riches to rags. All that remained of Town Day were a series of "*How'd you do*"s, "*See you around*"s, and all the idle talk in-between. Womenfolk oohed and aahed in the shade of the porch belonging to the solitary general store. Children chased each other like hot-footed hens or formed puddles of lilting conversation. The menfolk, meanwhile, kicked up dust out on the road, swigged Coca-Cola or root beer, and smoked and talked in the hazy, drawn-out way men are prone to.

"Johnson said his cattle went on and ate the grass despite the dust. Lost half the herd to mud balls in their stomachs," said George West, a pharmacist who'd stayed on after the drug store closed to farm his own patch of land before the drought hit.

Ben nodded. "Franklin Herby had the same, 'cept he bailed a month ago. Packed Rita and the boys up in that old cart that was his daddy's, hitched a nag to it, and moseyed on out. Rumor is he got a great aunt owns a fruit farm in California. So I'm guessin' he's all made up now."

"Don't you be so sure, Ben. I'm inclined to believe the news on the radio and as far as folk makin' their fortunes out West, yeah, they get work on the fruit farms but they don't make enough offa it to keep a bag-a-bones donkey in feed." Quarry worker, Samuel O'Ryan, eyed the preacher's son. *It hadda be nice to still have the shine of youth on you,* he thought to himself. *All that belief life's gonna come good in the end. All that gullibility.*

"Yeah, I guess." Ben bowed his head. But something must have itched at him and he added, "Ask me, folk should have more faith."

"Easy for you to say when your daddy's the preacher. Come judgment day, you and your daddy'll be sitting pretty on the right hand of the lord. Rest of us, well, we'll starve to death and find ourselves looking up at ya from the pit of hell," hollered Dixon Goodwin, tinker and sometime yard's man, who had the devil's gift for saying exactly what would stir a man.

"Pit of hell? Ain't we there already?" Samuel beat his hands. His laughter had a sour note, but was echoed by the harrumphs of the others.

Drawing on his cigarette, eyes pinched against the smoke, Dixon kept on staring at the preacher's son.

"Can't but wonder though, Ben. While the rest of us are working the scrap of land we got left, or raising swine on soap weed, or fixin' to leave the only home we've ever known, how'd you and your daddy manage to keep your shoes so nicely shined and sweet potatoes on the table? No, no, now . . ." Dixon raised his hands against an undercurrent of complaint. "I ain't criticizing Preacher Richards. He's a man of the lord. I'm just interested to know if the preacher's boy thinks he suffers like the rest of us."

Ben eased back ox shoulders. "Me and my daddy seen suffering aplenty, Dixon. We take relief supplies to farmsteads as far out as the abandoned Indian academy. We're the ones that dig a hole for them that have died of the dust pneumonia, who say a prayer o'er them. As for our shoes being shined, I was raised to mind what my neighbor thinks of me. As for sweet potato . . ."

"Why're you picking on Ben here? Flea biting your ass?" shot Samuel, who apparently saw no good reason why Ben should explain what food ended up on his father's table. The quarry man added, "You know darn well if there's any fresh vegetables to be had around here, they're from Miss Splitz's homestead."

George and a couple of others nodded.

Dixon hacked and spat into the dust. "Just 'cause I got a spot as the new yard man out at old woman's Splitz's place, you think I'm in the know?"

"Aren't ya?" shot one of six quarry lads sat in the road.

"Aren't I what?"

"Aren't you the one to fill us in on the place?"

"Whadaya wanna know?" Dixon kept a smile behind his

teeth. No harm in splashing out a little gold dust about Boar House and its residents. He plumped out his chest. "The old gal's machines? They're helluva big, I tell ya. Steam-breathing hogs the lot. She's got 'em holed up in a workshop out back. As I heard it from their last yardman, place is lined with tools plus a whole host of thingamajigs Miss Splitz engineered alongside the hired help – guy called Virgil Roberts?" Dixon weighted his voice just right. Outsiders were the worst sort of intrusion when folk were down on their luck.

"This . . . Virgil. He a relation?" piped up another quarry lad.

Dixon ground his smoke under a boot heel. He breathed in slow and took his time. Wasn't often folk listened without him having to shove his opinion up under their noses.

"No relation," he confided.

The men hushed. Dixon could hear the womenfolk over at the store, their soft laughter alongside the chirruping of children.

"Josephine Splitz hired him in from some big college outta state," he said to the men surrounding him. "Place called Stanford."

The quarry boys kept on chewing their tobacco like calves on the cud. Only Ben got a knowing look. Dixon paid him no mind.

"Anyways. Pair of 'em have butchered the field in front of Boar House good and proper with a great big drilling machine. The Burrower they call it. This Virgil and Miss Splitz, they climb inside and drive it underground for days, leaving Miss Nightingale to keep house."

One mention of Miss Nightingale and he'd really got their attention now, these men with unsatisfied needs and empty pockets.

Not everyone was seduced though. Dixon dragged the back of his hand across his nose and got a whiff of disproval off Ben, Samuel and George.

Samuel beat his big hands again. This time the gesture was threatening. "I ain't interested. Folks's business is their own."

"Unless it has a bearin' on others!"

Reg Wilhoit made his way into the group with that stiff-legged, foot-scrapping motion of his. He halted, one hip at an awkward angle. "Jos should be forced to stop with the crazy machines. Liable to get someone killed."

The quarry boys had sense enough to hunch their shoulders and look away. Samuel swallowed the last of his soda, eyes scrunched shut against the sun's glare, then peered on over at the newcomer.

"It ain't up to us to tell grown folk what to do in their own time on their own land, Reg," he said quietly. "Just as no one had the right to warn you off working them machines before they decided to take a piece of you?"

"Thought I was helping Jos mine for new branches off Bromide Spring," Reg embarked, deaf or bloody-minded. "Ten years ago, folk thought we could breathe new life into this town's dry and weary bones and tempt the visitors back. Least that's the way I saw it. 'Course it wasn't me that got to go underground in a giant metal worm."

"That the problem, Reg?" Samuel's tone stayed gentle. His words were more caustic. "You jealous some outta towner gotta ride in the big machines?"

"And lose my life, not just a pair of useful legs? No thanks, Sammy. I got crushed enough under that iron hoisting crane ten years ago. Just as well too. I've learnt to stand back and see Jos Splitz for what she really is."

Dixon wore a sly look. "Miss Splitz, hey? Well, what'd ya know? Seems even old folk gotta get their kicks." He let his mouth hang open.

"Mind outa the gutter, Dixon Goodwin. I'll tell ya what Jos Splitz is. She's a conjuress! A leech!" A fleck of spit escaped Reg's sunken mouth. Shifting his balance awkwardly, he cast wild eyes about the group. "Not one of ya's got the first clue what that dame's doing over at Boar House."

"I know plenty," cut in Dixon with a grimace that suggested it was his time to talk and weren't no cripple gonna shake him off his perch. "I know Miss Splitz is spitting mad at Virgil 'cause he might've broke something on her burrowing machine. Heard her riding him for it when I went to the kitchen last night to get a glass of lemonade offa their house Negro. I know Miss Spitz calls us farming folk a bunch of shitting pigs, blames us for killing off the land and leaving ourselves with nothing but dust."

Dixon wove his words well. There wasn't a man present who didn't tuck a frown into their face or sheesh through their teeth or curse a dry old coot who'd got no right to judge.

Reg rounded on the group, dragged feet drawing snake-coils in the dirt. "There was nothing natural about the way that big old crane unpinned from its earth footings to come crashing down on me . . ."

"We gotta go there again, Reg?" It was the turn of George, ex-pharmacist, failed farmer, to roll his eyes.

Reg rolled his own back. "I know, it's the word of a mad old cripple against those respectable whores at Boar House."

"Shut your mouth, Reg. There's an awful bad smell coming out of it." Samuel threw out his arms. "Wasn't a soul near you when the accident happened. Said so yourself all them years ago." His stance was reinforced by mutterings from the quarry boys. Miss Splitz could go hang, but no one badmouthed a doll like Carrie-Anne. Not when there were so few young and single women left in Bromide for a fella to set his hat at.

"Yup, I sure did say as much." Reg drawled his words. He seemed to burrow into himself. "But there is change afoot and Miss Splitz and her apprentice are at the heart of it. I feel them breaking through the earth beneath our feet more often these days. Vibrations offa those great tunneling machines work their way up through the flesh and the metal and make my legs cramp."

"What they burrowing for anyways?" said a quarry boy.

"My daddy says they are investigating why the land's gotten so barren in these parts. And, yeah, you're right about hunting out more branches of the Bromide Spring, Reg, but way I heard it, Miss Splitz's thinking is to siphon water from deep below ground and find a way to feed it in beneath the crops since surface spray'd evaporate too quick." Ben realized the entire group was fixated on what he had to say. He faltered. "Well, it goes something like that."

Reg scrubbed at his cotton hair with two hands. "Except maybe it's Miss Splitz's mining activities which drained the land in the first place. Ever think of that?"

Over by the store, the women were creating their very own storybook, layering it with soft tones and sudden laughter. The children had sticks and were offering up war cries. Reg's inconstant eyes flicked about the now-hushed menfolk.

"Nah, you didn't think of that, hey?" He nodded sagely. "As I said, a conjuress and a leech."

The garden at Boar House was as sweet-smelling and fertile as any botanical institute. Either side the lawn was a great spread of Indian blanket, hundreds of small pink suns tipped with gold. The leafy vines of morning glory tendriled the wooden fence, flowers peeping out like midnight-colored eyes. Potato ferns filled eight large beds. Peppers and egg plant gave off their grassy, sap-like scent.

While the rest of the panhandle was barren, Boar House garden flourished for two reasons, the first of which was Josephine Splitz's patented sprinkler tripod and underground irrigation system of interlocking copper tubes fed from giant water butts, and the second being that, when it came to dirt and what grew in it, Julie Sanders had the Midas touch.

"Tastes like the blood of summer." Carrie-Anne manipulated what was left of the tomato with her tongue.

"Here." Julie dug a hand through the vines and snapped off another. She offered it. "A fresh sacrifice?"

Carrie-Anne put the fruit to her nose. It smelt of the rich, red dirt of her childhood, when the plains of wheat and prairie grass were flowing.

"They're going under again. Virgil and Aunt Josephine, I mean." She kept the tomato under her nose like smelling salts. "I asked them not to since it's Palm Sunday tomorrow. Their absence from church'll be even more marked than usual. Folk are already noticing."

"Then folk should learn to mind their own!" Julie snapped. She stared over at Carrie-Anne and added blankly, "Yeah, I see the glint of disapproval in your eye. A housemaid shouldn't talk so about good white folk as fix their hair and attend the preacher's sermon every Sunday."

Carrie-Anne frowned. "I didn't mean that, Julie." She cupped the tomato in a palm. "You surprised me was all. Most days, you're a ball of hot roast sunshine. It's odd to see you in shadow."

Julie raised her large bovine eyes to the endless blue overhead. "I apologize, Carrie-Anne. Something's hunkered down in the air these last few days, niggling at me. Might just be a woman's flush? Might be the dry heat?" She lowered her gaze to Carrie-Anne, who felt its touch like a mother's hand. "What I do know, chile, is we can't take much more. A storm's needed. Even hail'd be better than this devil's blanket we're under!"

Carrie-Anne popped the tomato into her mouth and chewed. Following Julie to the nearest vegetable bed, she knelt alongside to help shovel dark composted manure around the bean poles and fledgling sunflowers.

"Remember those great rocks of ice that came slamming down in March? The tale of Nancy West's little girl run ragged trying to keep the chicks from being crushed out in the yard. They lost half the poor mites in one storm." She indicated the plants with her trowel. "Don't reckon this crop'd survive either."

Julie sat back on her heels stiffly and used the corner of her apron to dab at her temples. "This crop, no. But we'd start again. Trade what we did have for what we didn't."

Perhaps noticing Carrie-Anne's muddled look, she chuckled all of a sudden. "Chile, I'm playing with you. I don't take one inch of this land for granted, nor the good Lord blessing me with the knowhow to raise crops on it." Julie got a fresh trowelful of manure and leant in to the plants.

"You know all about the way dirt beds in around Boar House," Carrie-Anne said softly.

"Well, I ain't alone there." Julie kept on working. Sunlight rained over her skin like a downpour of black diamonds.

Carrie-Anne pinched up her eyes. She didn't want to dig inside herself, was afraid to, and instead rocked back on her heels and moved to the neighboring bed, umbrellaed with the pinnate leaves of the Mississippi peanut. Bending down, she trailed a finger along a leaf coated with blown-in dust. The particles expelled to either side of the leaf at her touch.

"Watch you don't step in grasshopper poison." Julie stood up, supporting her lower spine with her hands as she unfolded. "Mix of molasses, bran and lemons I scattered at nightfall couple of evenings back."

Gazing at the ground, Carrie-Anne noticed wads of vegetable matter distributed between the rows of peanuts. "Say a spell too?" she teased.

Julie tucked a smile into a corner of her mouth. "Carrie-Anne Nightingale. I worry about your soul."

"Well, there is some sort of magic at work in this garden, Julie. Beyond the boundary of this fence, I've seen field peas and tomatoes blighted by the wind, potatoes like coyote dung half-cooked in dry dirt. But here, all is plump and ripe and perfumed. You're a weaver of dreams, Julie." She gestured to the nearest clump of grasshopper poison. "A potions mistress."

Julie snorted. "Gotta keep Miss Splitz in fried okra and cornbread's all. Then there's the extras we trade for canned goods at the store. You know how partial Miss Splitz is to pineapple chunks. She always saves the juice for Wesley. Soft old thing."

Carrie-Anne didn't contradict. Aunt Josephine was as much of a dragon as any giant machine birthed from her workshop. But she did occasionally expose a chink of humanity, such as the stones she brought back for Wesley from below the surface, or her reserving pineapple juice for the boy, eyeing him as he supped as if she was a kid herself feeding treats to a puppy.

The wizened old prune also had an acid way with words which Virgil thankfully seemed to relish where his predecessors had been burnt.

"My aunt's certainly got her own brand of kindness. I wonder if she always appreciates Virgil's worth though. He's one of the state's top geological surveyors, you know." Carrie-Anne got a shine to her. "He's got the papers to prove it."

"Don't need to persuade me Virgil's worth something, Carrie-Anne. He wrote the letter of recommendation that got Abraham a teaching post at Douglass High in Bricktown, Oklahoma City." Julie picked up the wicker basket she used for cut flowers and fresh vegetables, and deposited her trowel in it. She started back toward the house; Carrie-Anne watched the peculiar twist to her hips as she walked. Julie was arthritic. She was also a polio survivor.

Carrie-Anne followed after.

"I love him, you know!" She blurted out the words, afraid they'd drive tiny hooks into her tongue and stick there.

Julie swung around. In place of shock or elation, she simply jutted her chin as if to say "that so". Then she turned heel and started again with that jarring gait.

"Is that it?" Carrie-Anne flushed. She'd built up to the revelation, weighing her options in terms of who to confide in before settling on her old nursemaid who was sure to have grace enough to understand. Why was Julie acting so?

"I don't get it." She ran alongside. "It's not like we're hurting you, or Wesley, or even Aunt Josephine." Julie didn't stop marching and Carrie-Anne was forced into a sideways polka as she spoke. "He's a good man and he's got my heart taped up. No escape for me from this one, Julie. But what's so terrible about me and Virgil Roberts anyway? You know his worth. Said so just now."

Reaching the foot of the porch steps, Julie stopped suddenly, mouth parted as she tugged air into her lungs. "I gotta spell it out for you, chile? Well okay. You mix your environment according to your mood. Move one speck o' dust from this spot to that. Shake it all up any which way you feel."

"I have absolutely no idea what you're talking about!" spat Carrie-Anne. Her chest ached.

A flame was struck in each of Julie's beautiful bovine eyes. "You could cause real damage, chile. I'm just not sure how the dust'll settle on this one."

"Think I'm playing with Virgil, don't you?" Carrie-Anne felt the insinuation bite at her on the inside as if she'd swallowed live termites. "Good Lord, Julie. You raised me!"

"That's not what I meant . . ."

"Whatever else could you mean except to suggest I'd go all blue-eyed and brainless on Virgil, get him hooked then look for something, for *someone* better? How dare you, Julie! After the kindness my aunt has shown you and your boys. After her treating you like a family member and not the slave that you really are."

Her words were as violent as if she'd lashed Julie round the jaw. Carrie-Anne knew it, felt the poison seeping in as the housemaid she loved like her own flesh and blood got cold in the eyes.

"Yes, mam," said Julie evenly. She turned away and climbed the steps to the porch, where she pulled open the inner gauze on complaining hinges and disappeared inside the house.

Carrie-Anne stood alone in the garden. A light breeze brought in dust from the field which danced about her ankles.

Cicadas droned in the long grass outside the workshop. A moth performed its tortured tarantella around a kerosene lamp hooked on a nail to one side of double doors. The sun had left its heat on the place like a layer of hot grease.

Inside the workshop, nothing moved except the dust motes. Chisels, mallets, pliers, hammers, and wrenches lined the walls like a field surgeon's medical kit. A large scarred workbench held a mechanical arsenal: grimy gears, chamois-leathers like stomach linings, chipped china cups full of nails and nuts and bolts, bushels of wire, wire wool, chain-link, hose, valves, and fuses. The floorboards were strewn with the lost limbs of iron smoke stacks, greased levers, punctured flotation balloons, sled tracks, even a pair of outsized bellows like an ogre's shoehorn.

Grease and metal filings perfumed the air. All was still but for dust fall.

Virgil had his hand at her throat. Time drew out like a strand of spun sugar. His eyeballs flickered. Blood drove inside his ears.

Slowly, he eased his hips against hers. A welt of heat spread through his groin as she rose up onto tiptoes. Her flesh glistened. He leant in, bruised his lips against her fragile jaw and found the soft wet sacramental hollow of her mouth. It wasn't enough. He wanted to get past the physical, the hindrance of blood and cartilage, skeleton and skin. Raking his hands through her hair, nails digging in at the baby softness of her skull, he meshed his lips against hers until she gasped.

It was her tongue's touch which quietened him, its curl of motion at the sliver of skin connecting his upper lip and gum. He felt tethered, and a new depth of need as she worked his shirt free of his pants and imprinted his spine with her fingertips. His own hands were awkward extractions of flesh; he fumbled with the buttons of her dress as she molded his shoulder blades under her palms. Sweat soaked in at his shirt collar. Her dress fell away.

He stepped back to gaze at her every niche and curve. Her breasts were white fruit burred with damson-colored seed heads. The pour of flesh to her hips was slight. A half-moon of tiny brown freckles arched above her belly button. Soft brown down spread out from the cleft between her legs.

Dragging his shirt up and over his head, Virgil bundled it into the hollow of her lower back as she drew him back against her. The sour tang of sweat worked up between them; she dragged her tongue along the underside of his chin like a saltlick.

He drove his head down and she curved her spine, offering each breast to the ebb and flow of his mouth. At the same time, her hands cupped his ears so that he was back in the dark with the iron drone of the Burrower. With one difference. Here above ground, the heat was breaking out of him as much as it was tunneling in.

She moved her hands away and his lips found her throat again. It was a small bewitchment, a brush of mouth against skin which always made her fold herself into him. He flung his shirt aside. His fingers skimmed the rough warm wood of the workbench and spooned her buttocks which tensed at his touch. She carved at his hipbones, digging her fingernails in ever so slightly at the underside of his belt before dragging them diagonally down in a tingling swipe. His gasp was a thin dry reed of air.

Dixon Goodwin stared down at the patch of ground and clucked his tongue. The pipework he'd exposed was the color of rust in the moonlight; he guessed it was copper. Nice choice of metal for water transportation, even if it was an expensive material to sink below ground. Of course, the old gal, Jos Splitz, belonged to one of Oklahoma's oldest, richest bloodlines. A few lengths of copper boring wasn't about to see her bare-handed, even when her fellow Okies were sell-their-mother desperate.

So, the secret to Boar House's fertile ground was an irrigation system? Dixon kept hold of the trowel he'd found in a basket outside the kitchen, twirling the handle between two palms. There hadda be, what, a couple of acres of garden tucked around the house, every bit of it fed by those underground pipes? It was a helluva thing, and not just to afford the raw materials but to engineer and physically locate them. He shook his head like a fly-bothered mare. Jos Splitz was a withered old gourd, but she'd the wherewithal to keep herself afloat while all around were going under.

But who'd got the muscle to install that rig? There was this Virgil character, this brain from outta town. Vampire morelike by the look of him, Dixon snorted to himself. And Boar House had its slaves, though rumor was Jos Splitz behaved like an old witch in her professional capacity, but she was a pussycat in terms of how she ran her household.

Dixon twisted his mouth aside and spat. What good was kindness to the sow or the rooster? Didn't fatten them beasts any faster. Sameways with the black man; kindness only made a slave waste time on smiling. His daddy had taught him that much. Few folk wielded a lash as neatly and as effectively as Dixon Goodwin, Senior.

But whether them soft-handled Negroes installed it or the ghost face Virgil, all that was of interest was that Jos Splitz had gotten herself a means to pump water into dirt. Except, where'd the water come from?

The night had stitched itself in around him but there was a weak glow coming off a kerosene lamp over by the workshop. Dixon narrowed his eyes, noticing a ridge of earth running parallel to the brick path. He dragged a forearm over his forehead. He mightn't be worth much to folk in Bromide, but he'd a tendency to work things out.

Walking slowly along the path, his footfall soft, he traced the ridge to the far side of the workshop, where it broke ground to emerge as a series of the rust-colored pipes. These plumbed into two vast water butts located side by side and interlinked by a vertical winch system hooked up to five large buckets.

Dixon stroked his throat. One thing was for sure: Jos Splitz wasn't feeling the effect of no drought. In fact, she was sucking up the juices of the land while the rest of the state died of thirst.

The question now was what to do with that knowledge.

He walked back around to the front of the workshop. The

kerosene lamp gave out jaundiced twilight, and it occurred to him what a curious thing it was to find outside the workshop at that hour. The old gal was hee-hawing in her bed like a sunbaked mule; he'd heard the housemaid remark on it. So, some fool musta lit the thing for the ghosts, or more likely, as a deterrent against starving hobos, of which there were plenty.

One side of the double door's latch wasn't quite caught in its slot. *Careless keepers make for loser-weepers,* Dixon thought acidly.

He was about to secure the door when it occurred to him that a late night check of the grounds, along with the investigation of any mysterious circumstances, might well fall within the duties of a yardman. He gave the door a gentle push and stepped inside.

Great black rafters overhung a room divided into two separate work areas by a mottled, semi-opaque glass sliding screen. Since this "wall" was at most eight foot, he was able to see the upper section of the vast machine referred to as the Burrower at the far end of the workshop. Moonlight filtered in at high narrow windows, reflecting off the tip of a colossal metal bore like an exploding star.

Dixon tucked his arms in tight to his body. Either side of him were shelves laden with cartons, jars, bottles filled with some milky substance, balls of string, small plump sacks lined up like Humpty Dumpties, and boxes containing preserved weed, bark strips, tubers, cotton bolts, and all manner of weird in-between.

"I'll be damned," he whispered, leaning in to study a jar. He wasn't much for learning but his daddy had insisted on him getting his alphabet licked. "U . . . S . . . E. Use. A.T. At . . ." He spelt out the words phonetically. "M.I.D.N.I.G.H.T . . . Use at midnight?" Puzzlement wormed up at his brow. The contents looked like something scraped outta pig sty.

Dixon peered closer at the racks of jars. Seeds, burs, dried flower heads . . . it hadda be a gardener's store. Carrie-Anne liked to mix dirt, he thought, remembering how her cotton dress had scooped tight across her buttocks as she'd worked her trowel into a flower bed that afternoon. But no, that didn't sit right somehow. Carrie-Anne was too refined to stock that queer larder. What he did suspect was that this corner of the workshop had been given over to the house Negress who used it for potions and witchdoctoring.

Coloreds know no betta than to side with the devil. Their womenfolk'll entice ya and ride ya with all kinda words and intoxications. Sap the spirit from your manhood and leave ya outta dry.

His daddy's words played over and over in his head. Dixon felt parched even as sweat glistened at his brow. Placing one foot carefully behind the other, he started to back off from that devil's altar.

It was the small catch of breath which made him pause mid-step. He listened intently. There. A whisper of sound, girlish and sensual. Momentarily he was afraid that the housemaid's brews had attracted some intoxicating spirit come to steer him to sin and feast on his soul. Then he heard a second murmur, a man's baritone that was distinctly human and coming from the other side of the glass screen.

The baking heat crested and broke over him as, through the thick, lichened glass of the sliding screen, he made out the outline of their rutting bodies. His nostrils flared. It hadda be the sorceress, squeezing the life from some poor soul between her flanks.

An old parlor chair rested on two legs against the screen. Dixon eased it back down, placed one boot on the seat and tried out his partial weight on it. Reassured the chair would hold him, he stepped up level with the top of the screen and tentatively peered over.

The air was torn from his lungs. In place of black flesh, he saw the bow of a pale breast, the crush and rise of white thighs, and unsoiled nails that cut in at a man's spine, causing him to buckle and thrust harder. As moonshine spilt out into every corner of the workshop, revealing an ocean of dust motes, he saw Virgil Roberts with his pants down and Carrie-Anne Valentine's angelic face twist in grotesque ecstasy.

Sunday April 14, 1935

There'd been many occasions in the past when Carrie-Anne and Julie had exchanged words. When she'd pulled the rags from her hair and worried out the ringlets an hour before Great Aunt Rita's annual visit. Or when she'd cut down a bed of sweet potato fern to use as a posy for her "marriage" to a five-year-old Ben Richards. Or when, more recently, she'd scolded Wesley for beating a carpet near the spot of lawn where she was resting. Listening in from the porch, Julie had puffed up like a prize-fighter and stomped on over. "Carrie-Anne Valentine!" she'd embarked with a shake in her voice. But even though Carrie-Anne demanded then cajoled then begged her to continue, Julie seemed to think better of her anger and just take herself back off inside the house. It was a different story yesterday afternoon. Then Julie had decided to stick around and say her piece . . . although, as it turned out, it was Carrie-Anne who dug up sentiments that should never have been voiced.

Arranging her gloves on her lap and leaning back against the hard pew, Carrie-Anne was haunted by Julie's blank expression when told to remember her place. And it occurred to her that she had seen that look before, on the faces of the field Negroes who toiled and starved and hated their master.

The thought festered. Boxed in on either side by Mrs Lisa Goodwin's plump respectability and old Mrs Johnson's hoary bones, Carrie-Anne felt jostled into a slot that didn't fit. Somewhere at the back of that dull stone coffin of a chapel, Julie and Wesley were amongst the other colored's standing because the lord's house didn't see fit to offer them a chair.

"Your aunt is not with you," shot Lisa Goodwin suddenly. Her tone sat the wrong side of polite.

Carrie-Anne watched Preacher Richards lean in to discuss the sheet music with his wife, the organist, and willed him to start his sermon.

Old Mrs Johnson peered over her. "Josephine Splitz? Ain't she dead?"

Lisa Goodwin bundled her arms beneath wasteful breasts. Her eyes betrayed a mind full of nasty. "Word is she's alive but no one's seen hide nor hair of her at chapel for three months. What do you say, Carrie-Anne? Is your aunt still with us?"

Carrie-Anne sensed the weight of her respectable gloves on her lap. Humming lightly, she rocked forward onto her toes and back.

"Is she dumb?" Mrs Johnson squirted sideways, sucking her bottom lip like a teat. "You dumb, girl?"

"Dumb, no. Ignorant maybe." Lisa Goodwin's hot fat fingers branded Carrie-Anne's arm. "Your coltish act don't work with me, girl. Just like your aunt, think you're better than the rest of us. In her case, because she got brains and money. In yours, because you've got beauty and you know how to *spread* it."

A mind full of nasty, thought Carrie-Anne. She kept humming, imagining the tune dispersing through her like sunlight.

There was an undercurrent in the chapel that morning, half-whispers that left a shadow on the glorious day outside. Young men, who usually snatched off their caps and shuffled whenever she walked by, had watched her with a new, hawkish intensity. One even spat on the floor. Everywhere she'd looked, she'd seen the folk of Bromide grouped about the chapel walls like a swarm; they'd stung her a hundred times with their barely disguised distaste.

Let them judge, she decided, stilling herself as the preacher took to his pulpit. They'd find fresh meat inside the month. What's more, she couldn't help agreeing with them in part. Aunt Jos should've honored Palm Sunday, should've cared enough about events on the surface to let alone what lay below. But instead, at six a.m. that morning, the Burrower had lowered its nose and descended with a tremendous roar of grit and steam. And she'd been left to drape herself in fresh cotton, put a tea rose behind her ear, meet Julie's stone-faced silence, and come alone into the lion's den.

It's a dark spell, Carrie-Anne thought to herself. Virgil's fresh absence so soon after the last, Julie's cold-shouldering, the hungry, bored minds of the townsfolk. *A dark spell. But soon the clouds will pass.*

She fixated on a shaft of sunlight streaming in at the nearest chapel window. Dust whirled in its soft golden element. She could hear the preacher's voice as from a distance, and for a moment she imagined that she was back on the porch again, head resting against the corner strut, listening to the stillness of the plains. Virgil had come to her then . . . just as he came to her now as a memory of tenderly bruising lips and franticness. She smiled secretly.

"Smears up her mouth even now," hollered a male voice, piercing the illusion so that she refocused to find a sea of eyes turned toward her.

"What's that?" Her voice sounded set adrift.

"Dixon, please." Preacher Richards gripped the lectern, his face lined with irritation. "This sermon is about aiding your fellow man not abusing him. If there is tension in our community, let us resolve it at an appropriate time and without resorting to verbal attacks." After a brief pause, the preacher held his arms out from his sides. "My words are a lesson in scripture. They illustrate that . . ."

"'Their god is their stomach . . . their mind is on earthly things.' Ain't that what you read out just now, Preacher Richards?" Dixon Goodwin rose up out of his seat on the far side of his mother and stared over at Carrie-Anne, an angry crease between his eyes. "Some folk fatten themselves like hogs while the rest don't have a bean."

"Need I remind you this is a house of God, Dixon, not a two buck brawl pit?" said Preacher Richards in the deep voice he reserved for children who couldn't sit still in the pews. There was a waver in his tone though. Anger at the interruption or something else? Something like fear he could not control his flock?

Carrie-Anne wanted to start humming her song again. She wiped her gloves between her palms. Heat pawed at her.

"You better sit your backside down, son," said Lisa Goodwin quietly. Carrie-Anne detected a trace of indifference, pride even. *Yes, I have raised my son well. He takes a stand when no other will. He is the rock all others hide behind.*

"Sure, Momma. Just as soon as I get the measure of what preacher's teaching. 'Their God is their stomach?' Well, I'm here to tell ya there's one home near Bromide where that sure does apply. Boar House. Seen it with my own eyes. I work there as a yard man . . ."

Not anymore. Carrie-Anne dabbed the moist hollow of her throat with the gloves. Not content to pore his eyes over her – oh yes, she'd felt their weight, familiar, uncomfortable, and a sensation she'd labored under before several years ago – it appeared that Dixon wanted to invent some hocus-pocus about those she held dear.

Go on then, she urged. Expose the darkness in the hearts of Boar House's occupants. Tell these good folk all the horrors you have witnessed.

"Take a seat or leave, Dixon." Preacher Richards was flushed. His son, Ben, got to his feet at the fore of the congregation – Carrie-Anne marveled at the height of him and thought again of the potato fern posy she'd picked as a child. Had time ebbed so quickly that Ben Richards was now built like a quarterback while a squirt of a kid could evolve into a creep like Dixon Goodwin?

"All I'm saying is there's a reason why they're growing crops while the rest of us are struggling to harvest soap weed. More than that, ain't we preaching abstinence from earthy things?" Dixon jabbed two fingers at his eyes. "Out there, I seen filth. I seen fornication. I seen witchcraft."

A few folk gasped audibly. Carrie-Anne felt a squeezing tight up inside. She resisted twisting about in her seat and staring at the back of the chapel; best thing she could do in that moment was sit soldier-straight and offer no emotion.

"Witchcraft?" Preacher Richards's eyes appeared to supplicate his wife from her seat in the organ pew. Whatever he saw there must have reassured his indignation because he rose up out of the girdle of his hips and asserted, "A vicious accusation, Dixon, and not one that we abide inside the lord's house. I repeat, I must ask you to leave. Mr and Mrs Goodwin . . ."

The preacher would not win over Lisa and Dixon, Senior. They rose to stand alongside their son, oozing superiority and righteousness.

"Preacher, my son's got news about Josephine Splitz and her kin which is of interest to this congregation," said Dixon Goodwin, Senior, a barrel-bellied man with a circlet of white hair and the same bristled baby face as his son. He planted his hands on his hips and revolved at the waist. "So I ask ya, folks. If my boy says what he's got to tell ya is in keeping with the preacher's sermon, shouldn't the rest of us rightly hear it?"

"This is not the time or place to discuss disputes between

individuals," embarked Preacher Richards. He was immediately shot down.

"Ain't no matter between individuals. This is town talk." Dixon, Senior thrust a finger toward the back of the chapel. "This is about one of 'em Negresses and her pantry of potions in Jos Splitz's workshop!"

There was a second expulsion of air from listeners' lips. Ugly words were spoken under breath.

Dixon, Senior rubbed a hand around his bald spot. "You seen it, ain't you, son? And that ain't all he seen? Tell 'em about the giant maggot, a burrowing machine that sucks up all the water."

Was she laboring under a brain-fever or were folk speaking in tongues? Carrie-Anne glanced back at Julie; the woman had the look of a startled jack rabbit and was working hard to push Wesley away. Carrie-Anne recognized why; when colored folk were accused of something, only way to protect those they loved was by disassociation. Wesley didn't get a bit of it though and kept wriggling his head up under his mother's arm, all the while nervously flashing that broad smile of his as if he'd found it got him fuss before and he figured it might work now.

Carrie-Anne stood, her upper body bathed in the rich sunlight so that she was forced to squint against its brilliance. She tried to speak. Her throat clamped around her vocal cords.

"I am in no way a scientist, Mr and Mrs Goodwin, Dixon." She nodded at each. "But it is my understanding that my aunt and her assistant, Mister Virgil Roberts, have been excavating below ground in a bid to find water and to understand what it is about the land beneath our feet which has left us in such dire straits."

"Except, you ain't in dire straits, are you, Miss Valentine? Not only have you water to feed the soil where you wanna, but a sorceress to raise them crops up with spilt rooster blood, devil's weeds, and every other kinda wickedness. 'Use at midnight.' That's what I read, Miss Valentine. Written stark clear on a label it was. Use at the devil's hour!"

Dixon's expression was seven ways of wrong. And he wasn't alone. More voices were cutting in.

"What a slave doin' with her own store while we're left to scrape around for seed and other provisions?"

"Always said Jos Splitz was lead-lined."

"Heart of stone, that one."

"Except when it comes to coloreds. Then she's soft as marshmallow."

"Coloreds with the know-how to mix magic? That's a straight up sin. Ain't no defending that."

The eyes moved from Carrie-Anne to Julie. There was fragility in the air. One audible breath and the line between peace and pandemonium would be muddied.

"Exodus 22:18. 'Thou shall not suffer a witch to live'," said Lisa Goodwin, soft as the wind.

Carrie-Anne felt as if she was suffocating. So much white flesh crushed in around her like pulped pages from a Bible.

"Enough with your accusations!" she spat. Her heart pulsed violently. Forcing her way past old Mrs Johnson, who shrunk into her desiccated bones, Carrie-Anne strode to the back of the chapel. Twice, a figure stepped into her way. Twice a voice told them to let her be. Through the smear of angry human shapes, she made out Samuel O'Ryan and George West. Good, honest men in a town awash with hokum.

She found Julie, fear and unshakeable knowledge etched into the lines of her face. Wesley was a phantom limb at his mother's hip, arms encircling her.

Carrie-Anne reached out. The air inside the chapel turned shroud gray; she parted it with her hands like scissors slipping through silk. When her fingertips made contact with Julie's wrist, she felt the housemaid shiver in spite of the tumbling waves of heat.

"Let's go home, Julie."

Out the corner of an eye, she saw a figure lurch from the back pew in a jilting motion. Cold dread poured down the inside of her ribs. She would not meet that vile stare. She would gather up Julie and Wesley to her side and she would walk with them out of chapel that day and deliver them safely home.

"Know what else I saw?" continued Dixon, a serpent at her back. "Last night, I was checking the grounds as is my employ-ment when I find the workshop unlocked. Lotta fancy engine gear in that shack. This day and age, lotta folk in need of stealing such. So I slip inside. And I hear this ruckus. Any idea what I'm talking about, Miss Valentine?"

Eyes swirled toward her from every angle. The sun went in.

As Dixon went on with his sordid description, Carrie-Anne sensed the young men of Bromide wipe her from their palms like chaff. In a barren town, she had been the one sweet-smelling flower they could admire and dream of owning. Except now she was gone over. Another clean thing corrupted.

Their agitation was immediate. No insult was spared inside those hallowed walls. She was Jezebel, Salome, the Babylonian whore, and every other breed of temptress. But their anger was good. Anything to deflect attention from Julie.

Carrie-Anne made her way to the chapel door, Julie's blistering handhold in hers, Wesley bundled into Julie's folds . . . Only to find the exit was guarded by its own gargoyle of hunched flesh and mangled bone.

"About time the witches of Boar House paid their dues," said Reg Wilhoit. His voice was a tar scrape, thickened over time. Hands that used to twist up inside her blouse and maul at her unformed breasts were pressing into and over one another, molding the situation into his preferred shape.

"Move aside, Reg." She concentrated her revulsion, taking strength from it.

"Time to pay, little lady." A foul whisper. A forward shuffle on crumpled limbs.

"Stand away from the door." Her eyesight blurred as a great hollow wind seemed to drag itself up beneath the underside of the chapel door and shriek past her ears. *The sky is darkening,* she thought, *where I dreamt only of light.* Far below the surface, her aunt and Virgil were crushing through the sand and rock in an effort to find fresh reserves of water, in an effort to save the lives of these nasty, vicious souls who would dig them out like louse and burn them for trying. *Keep them below,* she implored the subterranean world under their feet.

Reg teetered. He kept his sneer stitched in place.

Beneath her fingertips, in the creases of her palms, at the tender flesh of her lips, the baking air reverberated. Dust drifted out the corners and alcoves where it slept, leaving a soft gray charge in the atmosphere. Heat surged in at every chink in the chapel walls, gushing and churning and soaring all around her. Sweat bled from Carrie-Anne's temples, and the dust, so much dust, roared like the battle cry of an archangel.

The latch snapped up on the chapel door suddenly. Someone pushed it open and Reg was elbowed aside in a rush of zigzagging steps.

A young man's face appeared, cherry-toned by the midday heat.

"Preacher Richards!"

Carrie-Anne heard the preacher's somber acknowledgment, and through her black rage, the man's hesitant explanation.

"Preacher, I hate to interrupt service but my daddy says I gotta tell ya there's a dust cloud growing out to north and it's a fierce 'un. Bigger than anything my daddy ever seen. Folk might need to get off home now, tie down what they need, forget what they don't. There's a helluva storm coming."

"Drag on that soot mixer, Virgil Roberts!" came the shout from up front of the Burrower. "You feel it, you Mary-Anne? We've gone and hit wet sand."

Scooping his fingers around a small leather loop that hung alongside the larger one linked to the air duct, Virgil hauled down on it. As he did so, he tucked his head into his right shoulder and tried to peer past Jos's front seat. The view was limited, but he got an idea that the soot mix was piping through the gills either side of the main hub thanks to the black spray coating the viewing pane.

"Lights . . . Hit the lights! Christ, man, if you ain't gonna cease daydreaming over Carrie-Anne, I'm gonna pack her off to Michigan. She's got a bitch of an Aunt Rita out there. Nibbling little ferret who'd have Carrie-Anne married off to some rich bilious bastard quick smart, I can tell ya."

Virgil paid Jos no mind. He felt to the left of his chair for a triangular brass panel containing one squat flip-switch. It was an awkward location for a seemingly essential mechanism, except, as Jos has instilled in him a thousand times over when he had first started working for her, what real need was there for light when the bore that went before them was as blind as a mole. Best to feel their way through the earth's materials, acclimatize themselves to the rat-tat-tat of sand, the plug and crack of rock, the lumber through shale-sounding gravel. But, on occasion, even Jos's curiosity could not be contained, and that's when she called for him to fumble for the switch and flood their murky world with light.

A blaze of illumination accompanied his tug on the switch. Virgil blinked wildly against its burn.

Jos, on the other hand, seemed insusceptible to alterations in light and dark. Yet clearly she benefitted from the refreshed view.

"There. Sand, and wet sand too. How's the tunnel bearing up?"

Virgil revolved a polished wooden handle to crank the drive shaft that ran up the back of Jos's seat. The whir of clockwork was just audible over the grind and sluice of the Burrower in motion. Lanterns affixed to the roof of the cabin as well as a number of spots integrated into the corrugated iron floor flickered then strengthened. Virgil stared at a rack of dials above his head. Indigo and ruby glass shields protected fine spindles which twitched or held firm.

"Whiskers say we're okay for now," he stated in the loud clear voice Jos had beaten out of him. "A little fallout to the right of that rock gorge few moments back."

"Then we're gonna haul anchor and get ourselves a sample of that pretty wet stuff, my boy." Jos half-leant back, her vinegar features squeezed up in an attempt to express happiness.

It was Jos's job to steer the Burrower, as it was to dig the twin steel sleds at the undercarriage into whatever matter lay beneath in an effort to slow then cease their motion. Virgil watched her leathered hands punch, skip, and tug their way around switches, wheels, plungers, knobs, gears, and levers, and the rest of the coke-dusted motorization bank.

"Keep an eye on those whiskers."

Jos eased off on the steam release and drew the Burrower to a juddering halt.

The engine wheezed noisily then idled. A faint sensation of crushing in threatened to overwhelm Virgil. He pushed that to the back of his mind. It was just his imagination . . . or an innate knowledge of how preternatural the circumstances were that had brought him below ground. Somehow it was more eerie to be at a standstill in that freshly-cut tunnel, the illumination from the floodlights spilling either side of the colossal bore. All that lay ahead and behind was tight-aired darkness, hence the detection of any faults in the tunnel walls being left to a backend full of softly sprung copper spines, or "whiskers" as Jos was prone to call them. If matter sifted down too heavily, the weight of it would trigger a kick-back action in the spine, and, with it, a clockwise shift of the farthermost dial in the rack above his head.

All was still for now.

"Dig your little horn into the belly of this beast, Jos," he said softly, doing a mental check of the fill level of the coke channel to his right.

Jos worked a small fly wheel in the ceiling forty-five degrees right. There was the slightest rocking motion as the sample needle took its two foot worth of rock sample then withdrew. Jos rewound the lever in the opposite direction.

"Wet sand . . . No time to shake hands on it now, Virgil Roberts," she tossed over a shoulder, and in a tone which implied he had attempted to. "We're only a couple of lengths below the surface. Best get you back to that strawberry of a niece of mine. You sure do seem to like the taste of her." The old gal snorted, like a smaller version of her vast grunting machines. "Let's shake free of this sand and haul on up."

It was difficult not to wipe his glad, tired eyes, not to pat the whorled dragon on her shoulder and say, "Well done, Jos. Well done you wise old dear," not to dream of ice chips pressed to Carrie-Anne's lips, her jugular, her glistening sternum, not to just sit and sigh and sleep.

Instead, Virgil dove the scoop hard through the coke, ripped open the iron flap in the wall and shook off the fuel, feeling his skin flush and hurt with the heat. The engine bubbled under, then roared in its gullet as Jos maneuvered the twin steel tracks free of their footings and the tremendous hammer of a machine thrust forward and up.

"Tell you one thing, Virgil. That water gotta come from someplace. Don't know if you been over the way of the old Indian academy recently?" Jos made a sound like spit had caught up in her throat and spun there. "Now there's some suffering. I've been hiking up there with a back seat of beet and sweet potato and the rest whenever I get a minute. 'Cept what do you do? Help the few or try to fix the root problem? That's what we're aiming at, ain't we, Virgil, boy? Let's hope we gotta a break through, hey?"

Jos Splitz. A devil of a woman on her dried up exterior. A polished silver heart on the inside. Virgil broke out a smile.

It was such a small, simple instance of happiness – snatched away the very next second. A noise, like the scream of a great wind buffeting a hide of metal scales. The Burrower shuddered and the whole cabin seemed to tear forward on inch then sling back several feet. Virgil heard the wind cut from Jos's throat; the old gal caught it badly, sucking and choking to guzzle down air.

"You all right, Jos. You all right, girl?"

What the hell had they hit? A sheet of bedrock? Wasn't possible at that angle. He'd surveyed that stretch of land like a mother knowing every inch of her baby's skin. Wouldn't do to risk that nose cone on a more difficult stretch. Something was hard up against them though.

"Jos? You gonna answer me there?"

Unclipping his harness, Virgil manhandled himself up to lean a short way over the front seat. Jos's head lolled toward him as he dug a hand into the metal boning of her chair, eyes closed so that she looked like a husk of a woman whose clockwork had just run out.

No chance to move her. Never was. The notion of a stalemate underground was something they'd both signed up to. He had no choice then but to attempt to work the motorization bank by stretching his limbs at grotesque angles. The pain cut at his mind like a lash, but he succeeded in engaging the gears and driving the Burrower hard forward. At impact, his ribs jolted against the driveshaft that fed the lights, plunging the cabin into darkness.

Virgil gulped down the baking air and tried to calm himself. He'd promised Carrie-Anne they'd surface by midday, that she would have her afternoon of shared breath underneath a ripe gold sun. If Jos would just wake up. If the Burrower could just work its way home.

His stomach crunched around a sickening mess of feelings. The pitch black thrummed.

I ain't never seen a glimpse of hell on Earth like it. Rolling in it was, from the direction of the old Indian academy out north, a great black cloud, thick as flies swarming. How far it stretched I ain't sure, but miles it was. A mouth that yawned back on its jaw and scooped in everything in sight. And the scream, like demons loose upon the land.

"We've got to get back," Miss Carrie-Anne said. "Let's go now, while they've no time to intervene." And she steered me outta the chapel and into Mister Roberts's automobile. Plopping Wesley on my knee, she got that engine whipped up and we were back out on the road in no time, the darkness snapping at our heels.

"It's a good thing Miss Josephine and Mister Roberts planned a short trip. They'll be back up top now. Sat on the porch worrying themselves sick I shouldn't wonder, and who can blame them. Dust cloud like that on the horizon . . ."

I kept on yapping like a screech owl because Carrie-Anne, she got that soulless look like I'd seen whenever her strangeness came over her, alongside which, the talking helped trample down the fear that burned inside 'a me like a brand. Wasn't the way of things for a colored woman to be accused of devilling and not end up as some sorta strange fruit hanging offa tree. Not that that stopped a man from attacking a person any way he found how if he got a mind to.

My thoughts were softened by the sense that Wesley'd got a fever to him. I felt his shakes above the jitterbug of the engine and turned my chatter to a lullaby. That soothed them both, Wesley going soft as a raggedy-Anne and aslumber while Carrie-Anne took up her own hum of a song.

She stopped though. Her face turned to mine.

"I'm sorry, Julie. Seems I don't get far into a day anymore with stirring up pain in one person or another."

I saw tears fall like longed-for rain, and I noticed the way the silvered dust in the air danced about her head like a halo.

"Hush, chile. Ain't no bother."

"I made the dirt keep the Burrower below," she exclaimed,

wild about the eye. "I wanted to keep them safe." She glanced deliberately at the rear-view mirror, and I went the way of her eyes to see for myself the great stain on the summer sky.

"What if I can't get it to let them go?" she sobbed.

There'd always been peculiar ways to the girl. Ever since she was a child, I'd seen how the light would get supped up then spill out from her with one glance. How the lay of dust would alter when she tried to sink her duster in among it. How the dirt would mix its own swirls when she skipped by. But what of it? I'd got nothin' to teach the girl about the Lord's good brown earth in that way. Raising crops, I knew a good fix or two, since taking care of Boar House garden was kinda like it was my own bit of freedom. Might never be more than a maid in the kitchen, but when I grew them crops, it seemed as if I was master at last.

But Carrie-Anne, perhaps them folks weren't broad of it. She had a way for rearranging the flow of things. I'd witnessed as much the day I saw Reg Wilhoit lay his hands on her ten-year-old bones, all up over her he was, and I wanted to make some commotion but didn't know the best way how. It was then that the earth shifted, and that great iron crane swooped down on Reg and crushed the juice from his limbs.

Yes indeed, Carrie-Anne Valentine had a gift. But no matter what folk'd said in chapel, there weren't no spells or hocus-pocus. If there hadda been, I might'a known how to ease her now and bring back the sun.

Somehow the girl managed to steer us home. As the motor cut, I scooped Wesley up into my arms and put a shoulder to the door. The wind was awful strong now and battering at the long-dead prairie. Birds tried to fly ahead of it; the pull of that great black mouth was too strong. I hadn't got the wings to take flight, but Boar House would do for me and mine like a wall of stone.

"Gotta get inside now, Miss Carrie-Anne."

The girl, though, was rooted, hand on the open driver door, her stare taking in the empty porch.

"Why haven't they surfaced by now? The danger's passed. They should be surfaced."

The words seemed to bite into her flesh, and she was gone suddenly, striding out toward the field.

"Miss Carrie-Anne! Miss Carrie-Anne!"

The dust was too thick to see past my own hand. A mighty cold swept in. Wesley was a tugging piglet at my neck and shivering so. With backward glances, I fought my way up the steps to the porch, burst in past the gauze, got a grip on the front door and shut the howling out.

It was the blinding mercury where the sun's glow hit the nose cone which drew Ben Richards to gather up a few of Bromide's best men and take them out into the field. For the breadth of an afternoon, the men toiled against the welts of the dust dunes. Long into the amber eye of the evening, they worked to expose the Burrower's cockpit. It took the quarry worker, Samuel O'Ryan, twenty minutes more to put a crack in the toughened glass hub.

When they'd laid the bodies of Virgil Roberts and Jos Splitz on the ground, those men found space in their lives to stand and stare a moment, and wonder who else among them would have traveled far below the ground in that steaming dragon. Some wondered if the two dead had indeed tunneled in search of life-giving water. A few feared a modicum of truth in Dixon's tale of draining the land. One wondered if the field of bore holes had contributed to the death of Oklahoma's farming land, its seas of dust. Ben Richard, whose face was etched with the rawness of the storm like a charcoal map. Across the field and the churned garden, he saw Miss Splitz's housemaid and her boy stood still as waxworks at the carnival and just watching.

He strode on over.

Shreds of Indian blanket flowers carpeted the porch steps, which creaked a little as he climbed as if weary.

"Julie Sanders?"

Keeping her hand on her boy's shoulder, the Negress turned her face toward him. She was a living well of emotion. Fear and loss flowed and ebbed across her face.

She struggled to keep the boy back but he broke away.

"Yu need take these back, sir?" The kid held out a palm with five small pebbles in it. "Miss Splitz. She found them underground."

Ben squinted down. "Nah, boy. Keep 'em."

He dipped his head and peered over at the housemaid.

"Ain't no sign of Carrie-Anne, but we'll keep on looking."

"I reckon she's gone, Mister Richards. Back to the dirt from which she came."

"Well, we can hope she didn't suffer." Ben tucked back the bob of pain in his throat. "Meantime, my daddy says how's about you and Wesley settle yourselves with us for a while. You can always come right on back at the first sign of Carrie-Anne."

The housemaid tucked her son back in under her arm. "Yes, sir. We'll pack a few things and say our farewell to Boar House. But first, if it's okay with you, I'll just watch a while longer."

"'Course, Julie. Take your time."

The preacher's boy strode off down the porch steps and through the tangled remains of the garden. Dust lay over everything as if the garden and house had been asleep for a thousand years. There was no bird song, no evening insect chorus. Only the distant voices of the men and the emptiness of the clean-swept plains.

We Never Sleep

Nick Mamatas

The pulp writer always started stories the same way: Once upon a time. And then, the pulp writer always struck right through those words: Once upon a time. It was habit, and a useful one, though on a pure keystroke basis striking four words was like taking a nickel, balancing it carefully on a thumbnail, and then flicking it right down the sewer grate to be washed out to sea. Four words, plus enough keystrokes to knock 'em out. Probably, the pulp writer was chucking eight cents down the sewer, but that was too much money to think about.

Here's how the pulp writer's latest story began.

> ~~Once upon a time t~~ *The mighty engines had ground to a halt, and when the laboratory fell into silence, only then did the old man look up from the equations over which he had been poring.*

It was all wrong; past perfect tense, the old scientist's name couldn't be introduced without the sentence reading even more clumsily, and by introducing equations in the first graf the pulp writer was practically inviting some reader to send in a letter demanding that the equations be printed in the next issue, so that he could check them with his slide rule. *Oy vey.*

The pulp writer had to admit that writing advertising copy came much more easily than fiction. And the old man with his unusual ideas paid quite a bit for copy based on a few slogans and vague ideas. The pulp writer was never quite sure what the old man was even trying to sell, but money was money.

Industrivism deals with the fundamental problem of modern experience. Both the Communist and the Christian agree – the workaday world of the shop-floor and the noisome machine rob us of our essential humanity. Even during our leisure hours, our limbs ache from eight hours of travail, our ears ring with the echoes of the assembly line. Industrivism resolves the contradiction by embracing it. Become the machine, perfected! You're no longer just a cog, you're the blueprint, the design, the firing piston of a great diesel—

It was possible to write this junk all right, but the pulp writer couldn't imagine that anyone would believe it. But the old man liked wordy paragraphs that were half religious tract, half boosterism, all nonsense. He was a foreigner, obviously, and had little idea what Americans wanted: not just crazy promises, but crazy promises that could be fulfilled without effort and with plenty of riches, revival meeting hooey, and a Sandow physique to boot.

Nobody wanted to *be* a factory. Heck, nobody wanted to work in a factory. People just did. Even pulp fiction was a factory of sorts. The pulp writer's fingers were as mangled as any pieceworker's thanks to the Underwood's sticky keys, and there was no International Brotherhood of Fictioneers Local Thirty-Four to help a body when the cramps got bad or the brain seized up.

Speaking of brain seizures, it was time for a drink. The pulp writer figured that a paragraph's worth of beers would be fine for the night, and that included the possibility of fronting another patron a round. And down the block at Schmitty's, the pulp writer's friend Jake was always ready to drink F&M beer on somebody else's dime.

"Oh my, could I use a catnap right about now," said Jake to the pulp writer with a yawn. "But, up here, it just never stops." He pointed to his temple. Jake was everything the pulp writer wasn't. Big, with a huge right hand that wrapped around the beer stein like a towel. And quick too. The pulp writer was small and slow and a woman. Her specialty was scientifiction, but she also did romance pulps, and Jake was heavily involved in the scheme – he delivered the manuscripts to the office downtown, throwing them over the transoms of the editors of *Incredible Science Tales* and *Thrilling-Awe Stories* so she wouldn't be spotted. For the romance pulps, Jake was the model for the dark hero, reformed and repaired over and over again by the power of a woman's love, twice or three times a month for *Love Stanza*, *True Stories of Love*, and *Heart Tales*. The pulp writer was Lenny Lick, Lurlene St Lovelace, Leonard Carlson – and whomever else it took to get a sale.

"You could," the pulp writer said. "You don't have to think about work at all the second you step through the factory gates and rejoin the rest of us unemployed chumps down here at the bar. What is the old Wobbly demand again? Eight hours of work, eight hours of sleep, eight hours for what we will?" The pulp writer liked to tease Jake sometimes.

"No, I can't," Jake said. He took a long sip of his beer, and didn't bother to wipe the suds from his lip. "The Reds don't sleep. The saboteurs don't sleep. We're doing important work, all classified. There will be another war starting soon, in Europe. You'll see."

"It's been twenty years! You'd think they—"

"Button your lip," Jake said.

"But you were just ta—"

Jake looked at her. "My mistake." He burped lightly then muttered, "Wobblies. I can't believe you're still talking about the wobblies."

They finished their beers in silence. The pulp writer thought about a story she had in her trunk; an unpublished one about a terrible world in which Prohibition had actually been declared and the criminal fraternity had begun working overtime to corner the market on illicit booze. Machine guns and mini-dirigibles and pocket-stills, and . . . nobody wanted it. Who would believe that criminals would employ scientists and engineers, the rejection slips said, and besides the story made it seem like crime paid.

"Pays better than pulp fiction anyway," the pulp writer said, and Jake responded, "What?" and she said "Never mind."

The pulp writer licked her lips. "Will you be coming up?"

Jake shook his head. "Nah, I'll just take the manuscript and go."

"Fine," she said. Nothing was fine. She slid him the envelope that had been resting under her left elbow. "Next Tuesday then?"

"If not sooner," Jake said, but the pulp writer didn't respond, so he took the envelope and left.

Jake didn't know if he was strictly allowed to read the commissioned work, but he always helped himself to the first few pages when delivering the manuscripts to the publishing companies, and saw no reason why tonight should be any different. After all, it was Jake who recommended her to the old man in the first place. So he took a look as he walked along St Mark's Street and into the West Village and read:

Have You Heard Of
INDUSTRIVISM??

– the document was entitled. Industrivism was the idea of "intrapersonal industrial development", of using "psychological and philosophical methods to improve the self" and become a superior being. In the same way that factories made superior products by assembling them one step at a time, so too could a human being be improved by embracing "psycho-industrial processes" that would refine and eventually perfect both mind and body.

The very first step was the hardest – admitting that you were a know-it-all, or a wallflower, or a bohemian, or a workaday drudge, a second-hander, or a thug. The list went on at length. Once you had determined your own Essential Flaw, there were a number of exercises one could do to become a True Industrivist, a superior being able to control one's own fate. The pamphlet only hinted at what these exercises might be, but Jake was intrigued, even as he diagnosed himself as an also-ran.

He had no idea what the old man was planning, but what else was new? *It had been twenty years*, Jake thought. Twenty years ago, when Jake was just fifteen, and working on a sewing machine alongside his parents in a ten-story factory. Then when they came for their shift one morning, all the sewing machines were gone. The foreman sent everyone home, and he had plenty of Pinkerton muscle backing him up. They had truncheons, stood in a line like soldiers, and one burly Irishman hefted a repeating rifle. His parents and all their friends could do nothing but mutter in Yiddish and go home and further dilute their cabbage soup. At least the morning papers would have some other job postings, and it would be back to the twelve-hour grind.

Except for Jake. He got up the next morning, went to the offices of the Pinkerton Detective Agency and offered his services – he was bilingual, knew the neighborhood and all the families, had a quick jab, and hated Reds, and thought the *rebbe* was a fool. And he found the Pinkerton slogan compelling.

We Never Sleep.

They signed him up and a few months later sent him back to the factory, right on the banks of the Hudson, a few blocks south of the Chelsea Piers where all the rich people sail off to England and back. He retrieved the old man from his ship with a four-horse team, and then helped install him in the factory.

It had taken six days. Jake broke *Shabbos* for the first time. After that, he practically had to live in the factory as his parents cast him out. Twenty years later, and here he was, still at the same factory he'd be sent home from at gunpoint, but at least he wasn't bent over a machine, half-blind with bleeding fingers.

Jake went down to the basement, taking the special pneumatic elevator that looked, from the shop floor, like a broom closet. Jake had the run of the place, you might say. He went where he was needed; his job was to keep the old man happy, if it meant pitching in on the line or dealing with troublemakers and agitators out by the gates.

Jake knew the factory very well. He could talk to it. And it talked back, in reverberations and slammed doors and clanking pipes and hideous grinding. And sometimes it spoke through the mouth of the old man in the basement.

The old man slept, mostly. He needed his rest. Actually, he wasn't even that old, but he was very sick, and his skin was shriveled and dry like jerky. He lived in a giant iron lung, though the lung was like nothing Jake had ever seen, not in newsreels and not in the pages of *Life*. More like a giant under-water suit ten feet high, and vertical, up against the wall, limbs spread like in the middle of a jumping jack. And the old man's head was behind a plate of thick glass. Tubes and piping came in and out of the lung, making it look like the contraption had a dozen smaller limbs in addition to the main four. Jake figured that all the old man's business was somehow dealt with via the plumbing. He had seen a canteen cook shovel perfectly fine mashed potato and gravy down a drain hole once. Who knew what was coming in, or going out, through the other pipes?

"Sir," called Jake as he entered the room. "We have the latest carbons from the writer." Jake couldn't help but shout as the basement room was largest room in which he'd ever been. His childhood *shul* could have fit down there.

The room growled. Under the basement, there was another factory, with a whole other set of workers pulling the swing shift, manufacturing . . . well, Jake didn't know. He didn't even truly *know* that the old man had them on a staggered shift to keep them segregated from the other workers – it just seemed obvious. The sub-basement line had fired up and was hammer-ing away at something. It felt like the old man was angry, like his heart had started beating like a drum.

The factory often talked to Jake. The old man rarely did so. But now, he did. There was a click, a crackle, and a tinny voice came from the two great loudspeakers.

"READ IT. SLOW. ALOUD."

Jake wasn't much for elocution, but he did his best. It was hard not to snicker, but surely the old man wouldn't be able to hear the laughter catching in Jake's throat.

"WHAT DO YOU THINK?"

Jake stood for a long moment, stunned. The old man had never asked for an opinion before. He'd only ever given orders, and in a precise Germanic tone, via his phonograph contrap-tion. Jake didn't know what to think. He never really had been in a situation where he had to be politic before. *What would the pulp writer want him to say . . .*

"Well, uh, sir," he said, "I think that Industrivism could be the wave of the future."

"THE FUTURE."

"Yes. They'll be talking about it all over the nation, like Populism or Prohibition," Jake said. "Even if everyone doesn't agree, it'll be a topic in the newspaper editorial pages. I can see people handing these out like they do copies of the *Daily Worker*, just to strike up conversations with passers-by." What Jake kept to himself was that the populists and temperance people were horrid anti-Semites he'd as soon spit on as say "How do you do?" to, and that the Commies were even worse.

"PUT THE MANUSCRIPT IN THE TUBE."

Jake rolled up the carbons, stuck them in a capsule and inserted it into a pneumatic tube. In the morning, who knew what would happen. This was the fifth text Jake had brought over from the pulp writer, and they'd all been sent upstairs, where as far as Jake knew they were being used to wrap fish.

The pulp writer imagined a lot of things: monsters from the depths, clever young men welding de Laval nozzles to locomotive tank cars and transforming them into high-powered bullet-fast tanks, a former silent picture star discovered begging for change with her career-ruining froggy voice, only to find true love with a film producer turned Pinkerton guard . . . but she never imagined seeing her work in the slicks.

And yet, in the current *Henderson's Lady Weekly*, there it was: Industrivism. A whole article on the cockamamy scheme, breathlessly and enthusiastically written by one Doctor R. D. E. Watts. *An obvious pseudonym*, was the pulp writer's first thought. Her second was to wonder how she could get in on such business, given that the slicks sometimes paid one thousand dollars for feature essays. A thousand dollars could get her out of her current accommodations and into an apartment where the bath tub was in the washroom instead of in the middle of the kitchen. An elevator building with a doorman. A zeppelin trip to Frankfurt, or even to Rio de Janeiro.

The pulp writer caught her mind wandering, and with it her fingers twitching. A zeppelin would be a great setting for a romance tale, or even a spy yarn. Perhaps a zeppelin-shaped starship that generated anti-gravity in its lattice frame, or due to some static charge generated by aircraft dope rubbing against the frame. It wasn't quite kosher science, but it was close enough for the pulps . . .

"And that's why I'm not in the slicks," she said aloud to herself.

The Industrivism article was clever, in that to the pulp writer's trained eye it was obviously an advertisement in the shape of a feature, and had been purposefully placed in the feature well to further obscure its pedigree. The old man Jake worked for must have paid a pretty penny for such placement.

At Schmitty's that night, where the pulp writer drank alone and safe from molestation thanks to the protection of the bartender, the word "Industrivism" floated by twice. Perhaps one of the men's adventure pulps, or even a general interest slick, had been paid to run an article much like the one in *Henderson's*.

It was nearly last call when Jake finally walked in, looking like a wet sheet that had been wrung out but never spread to dry. He took his seat on the stool right next to the pulp writer's, careful not to kiss her on the cheek.

"Gosh," the pulp writer said. "Please let me buy you a round for once. I haven't seen you in two weeks."

"We've been busy down at the plant," Jake said.

"Wobblies smashing the conveyor belts?"

"Interviews. We've got three full shifts and are still hiring."

"There's a depression on, haven't you heard?" the pulp writer said.

"I'll drink to that," Jake said. "We have a line of workers stretching around the block starting every morning at five a.m. Grown men climbing over the fences – I even had to fire a couple of warning shots at a trio coming in on a row boat."

"Cheaper than the Hudson Tubes," the pulp writer said.

"What is Industrivism?"

"How did you know," the pulp writer asked.

"I can't make heads or tails of this Industriv—" Jake started. "Wait, how did I know what?"

The pulp writer held up her arms and set type on an invisible headline in the air before her. "'What. Is. Industrivism.'

"That's the title of my next piece for your boss. I got a

telegram this morning. He's hot for copy. Wants a new Industrivism piece every week."

"I bet," Jake said. "So what is Industrivism?"

"Doggoned if I know," the pulp writer said. "I would have thought you could tell me. The first proposal was vague. The second had a bit more meat to it, but I was just winging it. The third was just the telegram I told you about – no details at all. I suppose it doesn't really matter what Industrivism is, so long as people hear about it."

Jake frowned at that. "How does that even work?"

The pulp writer shrugged. "It's like the American Dream. What does that even mean anymore? Or 'use a little wine for thy stomach's sake' – recall that the Dry League claimed that the Bible was recommending that we spill booze all over our bellies rather than drink it. Anything can mean anything.

"Really – the less clear an idea is, the more likely it is to be popular."

The pulp writer peered down at her drink. She didn't even ask Jake if he were coming up this time, and Jake didn't hover like a fly, waiting to be asked, as he used to. She had no manuscripts for him to deliver to either his employer or the various pulp publishers about town, and it sounded like he had no time to do any errands anyway.

Upstairs, the pulp writer pored over a slim volume, *The March of Diesel*, published and distributed by the Hemphill Diesel Schools of Long Island City, Boston, Chicago, Memphis, Los Angeles, Seattle, and Vancouver. It covered the basics of the technology, and made some breathless predictions for the future-sort of a low-rent version of what she was doing, and oriented toward getting some down-on-their-luck pigeons to pay for a course on diesel mechanics. Then inspiration struck. Her fingers flew over the keys.

What Is Industrivism?

Industrivism is the engine of life in America itself during this, the Era of Diesel.

Like the mighty diesel engines that power our factories and automobiles, Industrivism is a Four-Stroke Process.

> *Intake Stroke: The nation itself, home to all the peoples of the world, and every race and creed. E pluribus unum!*
>
> *Compression Stroke: The communities – the great cities and towns where we live, work, play, and love.*
>
> *Combustion Stroke: The workplace, where we come together with furious energy to build a nation that shall lead the world.*
>
> *Exhaust Stroke:*

Well, "exhaust stroke" was a tricky one, the pulp writer had to admit. Exhaust carried connotations of both the polluted and the bone-weary, which she had decided were the very opposite of Industrivism. The deadline was tight and no pulp writer got anywhere by wasting time, and ribbon, in revision. Sometimes thinking was the wrong thing to do. Let the fingers handle it.

> *Exhaust Stroke: Rejuvenated and refreshed by a gentle breeze from the oceans that protect this great nation from its jealous enemies, we redouble our efforts.*

The pulp writer's only remit was to somehow make the diesel engine a metaphor for America itself. The pulp writer was creating a Bible of sorts for other writers to interpret and embellish. She imagined them bent over their own typewriters – Remingtons and Olympias, some portables and others iron monsters from the war era – a thousand literary pianos playing together, or one large and radically redistributed factory, all creating Industrivism for the slicks, for pulps, for religious publications, for the community pages of daily papers in English and Yiddish and Greek and German and Italian. All based on her notes. And like an assembly line, they'd all fall idle without new material. The pulp writer caught a second wind – an exhaust stroke of her own – and wrote till dawn.

While the pulp writer toiled, Jake wondered. There was something special about being foreman and factotum, specifically he didn't need to know very much about what was actually happening at any given moment. When he was confused, he'd point to a worker and ask what he was doing, and what this process was for, and how it contributed to the final product, and he could then pretend to be satisfied or discomfited with the answers.

Jake could never bring himself to ask what the final product of all this production was, and not because he was embarrassed not to know, but because he was comforted by the idea that at least the workers on the line knew, and he couldn't bear to have that illusion shattered.

But still he wondered, so he took the steps to the first floor where the electroplating vats bubbled away, as the 'platers had time to chat.

"Fellas," Jake said, and the three men straightened out and muttered nervous hellos. "What is Industrivism?"

The three men looked at one another, glancing back and forth as if deciding who would speak. Finally, one of them who Jake had pegged as a snickering wisenheimer type, said, "Sounds like a new radio show."

"It's a kind of foot powder," said a tall, heavyset man.

The third fellow kept his eyes on the bubbling vat, as if electrodeposition would cease if he ever stopped staring.

"You fellows are pretty funny. Tell me even one more joke, and I'll make sure you have plenty of time to take your act on the road," Jake said.

"It's the heart of a diesel engine," the staring man said without looking up. "It's the heart in all of us."

"Sounds good to me," the heavyset man said. The first wisenheimer just looked confused.

Jake went off without another word. He could always ask the old man, but what would the old man know? He wasn't even American, which is probably why he depended on the pulp writer for his political ideas.

The heart of a diesel engine . . . the heart would be where the fuel goes, like blood.

He tried someone else, just a random fellow leaning over a compressor. "What are you making?"

"Compressors," the man said. "Wiring."

"For what?"

The man shrugged. "Frigidaires?"

"You think . . . we're manufacturing refrigerators?"

The man shrugged. "Look son, I just got this job this

morning, and I don't mean to lose it this evening by falling behind."

Jake couldn't fault the man's attitude. He pursed his lips and tried again. "Sir, in a few words, how would you describe the American Dream?"

The man looked up, and Jake saw that he was very old. Old enough that he probably wouldn't have been hired at all under normal circumstances. "I say I'd describe it as getting a job in the morning and starting work some minutes later, and not being laid off by the end of the first shift."

It was a taciturn bunch, but of course Jake couldn't expect men hard at work to wax philosophical. Intellectuals liked writing romantic stories about the proletariat and its struggles, but all in all Jake preferred to read *Six-Gun Stories* and *Mad Detective*. Even that put him ahead of the shift workers, who couldn't be bothered to read the labels on their beer bottles half the time.

"What's the heart of a diesel engine?"

"The cylinder," the man said.

"How do you figure?"

The man just laughed. "It was a guess. Why don't you just go away?"

Jake fired him on the spot. Let the compressors pile up for a few minutes; it hardly mattered if nobody even knew what they were manufacturing.

That night was like every night – Jake slept fitfully, dreaming of a factory. Not the factory for which he worked, but another one, darker and larger, in Europe. Jews marched in when the bell rang and out the back end the factory spit out exhaust and shoes. Jake's rational core, the bit of himself that woke him up, knew what was going on. He grew up on hair-raising stories of pogroms and riots from his parents and uncles and cousins and family friends, and he felt guilty for throwing it all over for the Pinkerton job. So the back of his brain gnawed away at his spine every night, poisoning his system with visions of an industrial pogrom, a diesel-powered völkisch movement.

But his parents were fools. Europe was a happy, prosperous place, and even the Germans were doing well thanks to all the imported beer Americans liked to drink. There would never be a pogrom of any sort again. How did the President put it when he stared down the Kaiser at the end of the war? "Send us your tankards, or we'll send you our tanks to fetch them." It was a fair and free trade, and everybody was happy now.

Jake took a slug from his own emergency Thermos-stein and tried to sleep. It worked for once. He even slept through the morning alarm.

The pulp writer was extremely nervous. The old man had sent another telegram, again circumventing Jake. He wanted to meet, in person, that afternoon, and Jake's name was absent from the telegram as well. It would likely be a one-on-one luncheon. The old man had no idea the pulp writer was a woman . . . or worse, perhaps Jake had let it slip and that was why she had received such a sudden invite. Romance, crime, horror, all of them were possibilities. Would it be love at first sight, or would some greater intrigue about Industrivism be revealed, or would the old man chase the pulp writer around his great mahogany desk his lips pursed and his hands clenching and unclenching like pincers?

The pulp writer decided to bring her hatpin, and a brick for her purse as well. But she also applied some rouge, chose a superior hat, and decided to walk rather than take a crosstown bus to both save a dime and keep her clothes from being wrinkled by the crowded carriages.

Industrivism was in the air – literally. A skywriter had been to work, and the letters "RIOLOGY" had yet to dissolve in the sky. It was a waste anyway, given that in New York only yokels and bumpkins pointing out the skyscrapers and dirigibles to one another ever looked up at all.

Why did the pulp writer, who was born in Canarsie and had a diploma from Hunter College High School, look up? She had taken a moment to pray. It was a prayer for protection that, when she saw those letters in the sky, transformed into one of gratitude.

The city was limned with Industrivism, though the pulp writer had to wonder if she was just especially sensitive to the presence of her own ideas and phrases on posted bills, on the back pages of newspapers hawked by children on the street corner, flitting by in overheard conversations. When she crossed Broadway, the pulp writer decided that she would studiously ignore all things Industrivism and instead concentrate on some symbol sure to be ubiquitous: the American flag.

There were . . . some. A lunch counter offering All-American Pie and Beer. A single legless veteran of the war with a flag draped over her shoulders as she puttered past in a hot-bulb engine wheelchair, begging for change and showing off her stumps. The West Village's local post office flew one, as did the Jefferson Library.

And there was one close call – a great flag two stories tall was draped over the side of warehouse just two blocks from the old man's factory, but where the stars should have been on the blue field instead were crudely stitched white cut-out gears.

The pulp writer stopped to gape. The passers-by, and in New York the streets were always choked with pedestrians, workers loading and unloading diesel trucks, and tourists, ignored the flag. She blinked hard and rubbed her eyes, and then someone grabbed her wrist.

She jerked away, but the hand held strong. A man in a cloth hat and a shapeless worker's jumpsuit tugged to him and he asked with quivering lips, "Lady . . . what is Industrivism?"

The pulp writer pursed her lips and yanked her wrist away. And then she told him, "Oh, hell if I know, fellah! It's just some gibberish somebody made up to get you to work longer and sell you soap . . . and you could use some soap!" She brought her hand up to her hat and withdrew the pin, but the worker scuttled backward, palms up. "Sorry, ma'am, sorry!" he muttered as he retreated.

The pulp writer realized that if she ever became a famous writer, she was going to have to come up with a more politic answer to that question. Her meeting with the old man was certainly going to be longer than he likely anticipated, and she hoped that he had cleared his afternoon schedule. She already had a piece of her mind apportioned out and ready to give him.

In the factory, Jake stalked the shop floor, looking for someone else to talk to. Maybe it was true that every workaday Joe Lunch Pail-type was just dim. The old man's factory was

unique – no management, just Jake, and occasional instructions from the basement. All decisions were built into the
construction and layout of the assembly lines, including redun-
dancies and contingencies. The place was packed with
machines and crowded with people, but nobody had more
than a couple of words for Jake. Then he had a brainwave and
rushed to the loading dock where the hogsheads were delivered daily. He opened a barrel with a crowbar and scooped out
some peanuts, then filled his pockets with great handfuls.

"Hello!" said the pulp writer, waving from the asphalt.

"What are you doing here?"

"What are you doing here?" the pulp writer said, squinting.
"Lunch break?"

"You can make diesel fuel with peanuts . . ." Jake started.

"One of the many miracles of the diesel era, yes I know," the
pulp writer said. "You can make diesel fuel with pretty much
anything. But what are *you* doing?"

"What would you say the heart of the diesel engine is?" Jake
asked.

"Why . . . the combustion chamber," I suppose, the pulp
writer asked. "It's where the fuel goes, and fuel is like blood.
But the peanuts—"

"But wouldn't it be the crankshaft," Jake said, his voice rising
querulously. "That's what transmits power to—"

"Metaphors are never perfect, Jacob. Now why are you
stealing peanuts?" the pulp writer said.

Jake pulled one from his pocket and held it out to her,
wiggling it with his thumb and forefinger. "Want one?" She
just glared at him.

"I just want someone to talk to me for more than ten seconds
in here," he said. "I was going to scatter these across the floor,
and maybe someone would stoop to pick one up, or even trip
and fall. Then I could talk to him, and . . ." Jake realized that he
sounded insane. Too many all-nighters. When was the last time
he had even been home, in his own bed?

"You're a Wobblie after all," the pulp writer said. She stood
up on her toes and wobbled a bit. "Get it?" Jake snorted.
"Anyway," she continued, "it is almost impossible to find one's
way in between shifts, and I have an appointment with your

employer. We can talk about your, uh, 'shenanigans' later." She waved the telegram like a tiny flag.

Jake ate the peanut and led the pulp writer across the shop floor under a cloud of embarrassed silence. The factory was too loud for them to talk much anyway, but Jake was full of questions, for her, and for himself. What had he been thinking, with his little stunt? Why did the old man want to see her in person, and why hadn't he been informed? Maybe he had been informed, and had forgotten, but what would that mean for his mental health?

What is Industrivism?

In the small, secret, lift, he spoke. "I should tell you something about the old man. He lives in an iron lung of sorts."

"In the basement of a factory?"

"Don't believe me?" Jake said. "You can see for yourself." And the doors parted and they walked into the huge basement room.

"That, sir," the pulp writer said, "is not an iron lung."

"Well, it's *at least* an iron lung," Jake said.

They approached quietly. The pulp writer was reminded of any number of cover paintings – the old man's head was visible behind a windowed helmet, just as a spaceman or deep-sea adventurers might be on this month's *Captain X's Space Patrol* and others. But he was wrinkled and brown like a pealed apple left out too long in the sun, not an astronaut with a right-angled chin.

The pulp writer heard something like the arm of a phonograph dropping onto a record, and then the old man spoke.

"THANK YOU. WHAT IS YOUR NAME?"

Jake stepped forward to introduce her. "This is Lurle—"

"Doris," the pulp writer said. "You can call me Doris." She turned to Jake. "Can he even hear us?"

It occurred to Jake that he had never had a lengthy conversation with the old man. That is, he obeyed orders, made suggestions, and once or twice tried to engage the old man, but now he realized that nothing that old man had said was really informed by Jake's actions. It was all "DO THIS" and "DO THAT".

"I am not quite clear on that, all of a sudden," Jake said.

"MY NAME IS RUDOLPH DIESEL."

Rudolph Diesel, the inventor of the diesel engine, who had famously committed suicide twenty years prior. The pulp writer, whose name was not Doris either, knew that much. Fortune had turned to failure, idealism to despair, and the man had left his wife the sum of two hundred marks in an attaché case, booked passage to England, and then had thrown himself from his steamship. His waterlogged corpse had been found ten days later by a fishing boat, which had retrieved his effects and thrown the body back into the ocean according to the Code of the Sea.

Occasionally, the true crime pulps raked over the details and suggested instead that Diesel had been murdered. He'd been going to England to sell the patents to the Queen and thus save his family and thwart the Kaiser, and a Hun assassin had first thwarted him. Not a bad theory, except that British rolling dreadnoughts and American Diesel-Jeeps and Diesel-Leaps and had won the war in six months, so who had actually been thwarted? Another common story played up the Red angle: Diesel was a naïve Utopian who was going to meet with Irish radical James Connolly and break the Dublin Lock-Out by creating a new factory where diesel engines the size of a fist would be manufactured, and the capitalist overlords overthrown.

The pulp writer had never cared for such speculation in the true crime rags, but her mind was already running like sixty to . . .

"This is Industrivism, isn't it!" she suddenly shouted.

"PLEASE WRITE ABOUT ME."

"You hear that, Lur . . . uh, Doris? He doesn't respond. Not really. He just has a stack of records in there somewhere and when he wants to say something he plays one. But he only has a handful of phrases recorded," Jake said.

"I want to know if you somehow survived your suicide attempt, or if it was a murder attempt, or are you the murderer who dumped someone else into the sea to start a new life . . . if you can call this life!"

"NO."

"Don't ask multiple choice questions," Jake said.

"Yes, I know that now!" the pulp writer snapped. Then, loudly, to Diesel. "Were you the victim of some crime?"

"YES."

She was silent for a moment then said, disappointed, "Well, that's that. Jake, why did you never tell me, or anyone, about this?"

"Not my job. My job is keeping this place running, no matter what. Anyway, I got a question – What is Industrivism?"

"THIS IS."

Jake often thought he could hear the factory talk to him. This time he felt the whole place take a deep breath. Not in anticipation, but in preparation for release. The pipes gave way with groans and a hiss of steam, and the long limblike projections separated from them and began to swing. Herky-jerky, like a bus-sized toy automaton, Diesel began to move. After three steps, he stopped, and black smoke belched from the exhaust pipes projecting from the contraption's "shoulders", as Jake thought of them.

"WRITE ABOUT ME."

"What do you want me to write?"

"I WISH TO WALK AMONG YOU ALL."

"Is that supposed to be what Industrivism is? Just getting people used to the idea of you walking down the street in this, uh . . . tank-suit, tipping a steel hat at the ladies?" Jake said. There was something happening to Jake. He didn't know whether to be angry or awestruck, or just to take himself out back and punch himself silly out by the loading docks for being such a fool. He had spent too much time just being a cog in the big machine that he hadn't taken notice, *real notice*, of anything until the past few days. Past twenty years, maybe.

"It sneaks up on you, doesn't it," he said to the pulp writer. "All these changes."

"Snuck up on me, and I was the one who came up with the word 'Industrivism.' I wanted 'industraturgy' at first, but I was worried that people wouldn't know what the suffix – turgy meant."

"INDUSTRIVISM"

Now it was time for Jake and the pulp writer to both inhale sharply.

"INDUSTRIVISM IS"

The pipe on the left shoulder of Diesel's tank suit blew and the sound reverberated throughout the basement almost as if had been designed with that acoustic effect in mind.

No, not almost, Jake realized. Exactly.

Where the tank-suit had once stood there was a door, and now that door opened. It was the swing-shift, the noon till eight crowd. All men, as was typical, and . . . *not* all men.

The first was armless, but his limbs had been replaced with a remarkable set of prostheses. He actually had eight hook like fingers at the end of each arm-rod, and then opened and closed like a rose whose petals could snap shut in the blink of an eye. Behind him was a legless man, his waist a corkscrew, legs thin and pointed, but perfectly balanced in their way like a drafter's compass in expert hands.

The entire shift, and there weren't many of them, had some replacement. Jake had never seen any of these men before, not in the factory. Maybe on the streets, one or two begging, or just idling listlessly. The last man seemed to Jake to be whole, and he Jake recognized. It was the man from the electroplating vats upstairs, the utterly normal-appearing man with no defect at all. He walked up to Jake and the pulp writer and undid several buttons of his work jumpsuit, to show off the chest still fresh with a huge incision.

"I have a combustion chamber for a heart," he said, fingering the surgical line. Thick staples held his flesh together. "You know what's interesting about Industrivism, what we all just found uncanny about it? Every other ideology they're selling out there – Communism, Americanism, Kaiserism, you name it, they all promise that you're going to die. Spill blood for your country, or your class, or the Glorious White Race, or something. The only difference is that they all promise that the other fellow will kill you worse.

"But Industrivism, when I started reading about it, I noticed that nothing about death or blood or glorious combat was ever mentioned. It sounded sweet, so I came here and went looking for it. We all came here, just over the last month or so, for the same reason."

Jake glanced at the pulp writer, who was smiling.

"I don't think we're ever going to die," the man with the combustion chamber heart said. "We're making tank-suits." He hiked a thumb at Diesel. "They work fine. He doesn't even need to dream anymore."

"THIS IS MY DREAM."

Jake said to the pulp writer, "Good thing it was you, eh? I bet most fellows would have to throw in a little of the old blood and guts."

The pulp writer shrugged. "Women know a lot about blood and guts. I was just tired of writing about it.

"Mr Diesel, I'll be pleased to write about you."

"What about me? What am I supposed to do with all this!" Jake said, suddenly red in the face. It was fine when the pulp writer was just as confused as he was, but now she had signed on for something he still didn't understand at all. "How come you didn't tell me, 'old man'? I did everything for you!" He pointed to the pulp writer, and seemed nearly ready to shove her in Diesel's direction. "I found her for you!"

The pulp writer tensed, and deep within Diesel's tank-suit something whirred and whirred. Finally, from the horn came the words.

"I APOLOGIZE.

"I NEEDED YOU AS YOU ARE."

"But why?"

"CONTROL GROUP. IN THE FACTORY, BUT NOT OF THE FACTORY."

"We've been working on something for you," said the man with the combustion chamber heart. "We're building all sorts of devices and implements, all diesel-designed if not diesel-powered. Tank-suits for men on the edge of death, limbs for vets and even spines. We haven't gotten your thing quite perfected yet, but maybe . . . how would you like to never need to sleep again?"

Jake shivered and started to cry. The pulp writer reached into her purse for a handkerchief, and laughed when the tips of her fingers caressed the brick. She recovered the hanky from under it and handed it to Jake, who took it without a word and blew his nose into it.

Finally, Jake said, "I have to get back to work."

"Spoken like a True Industrivist," said the pulp writer.

~~Once upon a time~~ *There was a knock on the door of the second-class stateroom, but Herr Diesel's embarrassment was not due only to his reduced circumstances but to the fact that he had been on his hands and knees, ear pressed to the ground, to listen to the reverberations of Dresden's steam engines. An article Herr Diesel had read promised that her steam engines outputted twenty boiler horsepower at five hundred revolutions per minute, but Herr Diesel suspected Dresden's capabilities had been overstated by its proud engineers.*

The door opened, and the mate who opened it jingled the keys on the wide ring he carried. He was English, but Diesel was a polyglot and so understood the man perfectly.

"You're to come up to the poop now, sir. There is an unfortunate issue with your accommodation."

Diesel rose to his feet and dusted off the knees of his trousers, which was not strictly necessary as the rooms were kept clean, even in second class.

"What would the problem be, sir?"

"Well, there's an issue with the water," the mate said. "The water supply, I mean to say. The WCs are all overflowing, the urinals as well, so we need everyone to clear out. All the other passengers are already in the dining hall, sir, but you had not answered any previous knocks." With that, the mate made a fist that flouted several large white walnut-knuckles, and knocked on the open door slowly, three times. Then he crooked a finger and said, "Come along then, sir."

Herr Diesel followed the large mate out of the second-class area. Something was very wrong, Diesel knew it. He asked, "Pardon me, boy, but what is the problem with the water supply?"

"It's the piston in the pump, sir. It got all stuck like a you-know-what in an underserviced you know where, eh?" The mate winked at his own crudeness, reveling perhaps in the reputation of sailors and the absence of any of the fairer sex as he led Herr Diesel to the poop deck.

"Why, sir, have you led me astern if the rest of the complement is in the dining hall, presumably at least enjoying some English tea, if not a glass of complimentary beer?" Herr Diesel enquired.

"Well sir, it's a bit embarassin' to say, but we know your reputation. You're the famous Rudolf Diesel, inventor of the eponymous engine. We have a lot of toffs in first class, sir, and you see they caught wind of your name on the manifest, but also that you were sequestered in, erm, humble accommodation. We told them that in addition to our own capable mechanics, we'd have you take a look."

"I see, and you've told me that the problem is the water pump's piston."

"Yes sir."

"And this was explained to you by the German hands, or by a fellow Englishman?"

"Sir, we are all bilingual round here. Sea life, eh?" The mate winked again, crudely, and nudges Herr Diesel with his elbow.

"Then, sir, I am now convinced that you are not simply mistaken, and I have diagnosed the mechanical difficulty. It can be repaired instantly."

"It can?" the mate said.

"Yes. You see, you mountebank, Dresden is outfitted with a pulsometer pump, a clever and economical design which takes advantage of the principle of suction. A ball valve separates two chambers, one filled with water, and the other with steam. A pulsometer pump requires no piston, and has no piston, as it depends solely on suction!"

"Suction, eh? Yes, something like that!" The fraudulent mate, in actuality a paid assassin in the employ of certain Germanic interests determined to keep the patent on Herr Diesel's inventions the exclusive property of the sons of Goethe, launched himself at the man. But Diesel, forewarned by the inaccuracies in the thug's narrative, had already plotted a stratagem. He ran to the right, evading the killer's apelike arms, and secured for himself an emergency flare from the poop deck's box.

"Stay back," Herr Diesel cried, holding the flare before him. "Or I shall ignite it!"

The assassin paid no heed, having taken the measure of the inventor and finding the man's courage wanting, but he had again misapprehended Herr Diesel. Diesel yanked the cap

*from the end of the flare, igniting it, just as he was tackled by
the assassin. Flaming and tumbling, limbs coiled about one
another like a pair of enraged octopodes, they rolled the length
of the poop deck and fell into the churning white sea below,
dangerously close to Dresden's rudder head, where surely both
lives would be lost.*

Jake slipped the carbons back into the envelope, reared back
like a major league pitcher, and flung the manuscript over the
open transom and into the office of *Espionage!* a pulp dedicated to spy stories and non-fiction features about a new
philosophy dedicated to anti-Communism, technological-
organic unity, and physical immortality. It was catching on.

Cosmobotica

Costi Gurgu and Tony Pi

Earth gleamed like a jewel against black satin on the other side of the porthole, mesmerizing Henri Coanda by way of H-bot's iconoscopic eyes. If it weren't for the shadow of nightside and the whorls of white below he might even see where his mind presenced from, the peaks of the Carpathians. Romania, his home. Awe and pride overwhelmed him. This was the opposite of his catastrophic failure almost three decades ago at the International Aeronautic Salon in Paris, when he had flown his *Coanda-1910* – the first jet airplane in history – for a brief, glorious minute before crashing and burning.

Tomorrow, on June first, 1939, he would land a cosmobot on the Moon in the name of Romania. *This* was triumph.

Henri felt a tear roll down his face, the real face under his connect-helmet Earthside. His chrome-and-steel cosmobot had been built to copy many things his body could do, but not that.

"Dialing a course correction. Firing engines three and seven," Tiberiu Avician radioed via his cosmobot unit, designation T-bot. The robot twisted a Bakelite knob on the bronze-and-glass flight board, a grand plaque whose perimeter was etched with stars and comets. The cosmoship *Luceafarul* eased into the new course correction. Tibi took T-bot's metallic hands off the board, while Henri maneuvered H-bot back into the pilot-pod beside him. "Estimated arrival in Moon orbit: nineteen hours and fifty-six seconds. Just imagine, Henri. In a few short years SoloCorp could have mines on the Moon, perhaps even Mars!"

Henri grinned. If T-bot had real muscles under those steel cheeks, he'd see Tiberiu's warm smile. Although two decades younger, Tibi was his best friend.

He hovered over the flight board, monitoring the glass gauges crowded around a *bassorilievo* of two angels trumpeting above a sun-disk display. The central glass was lit with emerald stars marking the latest flight-path between the Earth and the Moon. "Oversees says we have exactly two hours till we fall over the horizon. We need to perform a last inspection." Henri turned H-bot's head to the front porthole. There it was: the Moon, its scarred surface almost all that Henri could see. "Look at its splendor, Tibi. No man or bot has ever come so close to the Moon, nor seen it as we see it now."

Henri sensed a sudden movement and turned. T-bot's cable-snake arms were flailing uncontrollably, its bell-shaped head shuddering and twisting as though from a war of impulses inside. Henri tried to catch T-bot before he crashed into the flight board, and the two-second radio delay between command and movement was barely enough. Henri constrained T-bot and pushed it backward, as far as possible from the flight board.

"Oversees, Tibi's in trouble. I'm coming down!" Henri sent through the frequencies. He tethered T-bot behind the pilot-pods using its safety cable, then checked the flight board one more time to ensure they were still on course. Then Henri plugged H-bot back into the pod and presenced down planet-side to the Launching Center.

He awakened disoriented inside the Navibot Sphere, dangling in the sealed chamber in his rubber harness. Once the dizzy spell passed, he pulled off his cosmobot helmet and looked to his left. Tiberiu spun and flailed uncontrollably in the harness next to him. His friend was having a seizure.

Henri unbuckled himself from his harness and dropped gently down onto the cushioned surface below. He tried to grab Tiberiu to steady him, but it was hard to approach without getting kicked or hit by Tibi's flailing.

The door to the Sphere opened and the cosmo-jockeys, clad in padded uniforms and cushioned hats, rushed in alongside Dr Ana Aslan's medical team. The jockeys stepped in on his behalf, their gear giving them adequate protection. Sometimes their charges would twist their bodies in the same way as their piloted cosmobots in space, and end up tangled dangerously in their harnesses. Experts in their job, the team brought down the distressed cosmonaut without injury to him or themselves.

"What happened to my son-in-law up there, Henri?" an authoritative voice asked from the door. It was Grigore Cuza, the de-facto owner of Solomonar Corporation, the mother company behind Cosmos Exploration Enterprises. Grigore was as usual a statement of power and controlled image, stalwart in his signature dark brown wool suit.

"One moment we were looking at the Moon, the next T-bot became erratic. It doesn't make sense." Henri said, looking desperately to Ana. "How is he?"

"I gave him a tranquilizer, and he's stable for now," she replied. "We'll need to run some tests to find out what caused the seizure."

The medics struggled to carry Tiberiu, a bull of a man, on a stretcher out of the Sphere. Henri, Ana, and Grigore followed them into Bay 1 where wires and pipes clung like webs against the vaulted ceiling.

"None of this makes sense," Henri said with a trembling voice. "Tibi's young, strong, and has survived far worse trauma when he was a test pilot. Is he having a reaction to the cerebralizing serum?"

"We can't rule it out," said Ana. "You shouldn't have presenced back to Earth, Henri. I warned you about breaking the trances. There's a limit to how much serum your brain can handle."

Grigore offered Henri a glass of water, and Henri drank deeply from it. He didn't realize how tired and thirsty eight hours of presencing had made him.

Grigore was the same age as Henri, but years of political struggle had left its mark on him. Henri admired him for being able to stand up against a multitude of opponents: the board of directors at Solomonar; the ministries; the Royal Court; the politicians of the Romanian Parliament; and, especially, all the foreign agents who tried to infiltrate, steal, and extort their way into their research secrets.

"Don't worry, my friend, we will take good care of Tiberiu," Grigore said. "You, on the other hand, need to finish the mission. The nations are on the brink of another war, but we can give the world a better ambition: *travel to the stars*."

This had been Grigore's crusade from the start. Who else but the Great Grigore Cuza could have assembled the brightest minds in Romania to change the world? Odobleja, father of psychocybernetics. Vasilescu-Karpen, inventor of the limitless Karpen Pile battery. Botezatu, mathematical genius. Oberth, maker of the first rockets. Ana Aslan here, whose research in brain aging led to the cerebralizing serum that made presencing possible. Even he, creator of the jet plane. The technological advances developed by the Solomonar Corporation had brought new prosperity to Europe. The latest advances in cosmobotics meant that space explorers didn't need to worry about life support or a return trip, allowing Mankind to aim for the Moon earlier than anyone imagined, even if it was by robot proxy.

"Grigore, this dream of yours . . ."

"It can work, I know it. We've invested decades in this. If we lose this cosmoship, if we lose *Luceafarul* . . ."

Grigore's conviction in this plan made Henri believe it, too. He had seen this beautiful dream from up there, this blue and brilliant planet. It could still be saved.

"I simply cannot recommend this," Ana protested. "Two injections a day's already dangerous for a man your age, and we're not even factoring in you breaking your trance!"

"I tested each and every one of my planes myself, Ana, back when people thought heavier-than-air flight was madness," answered Henri. "I'll take the risk. Grigore, you take good care of my boy."

"He's my boy too, Henri."

Henri's team of cosmo-jockeys strapped him back, fit his helmet on, and prepped him for the cerebralizing injection.

"Oversees, tell your team I need them to recalculate the path as soon as possible. I'm alone now on the ship and we have little time before falling over the horizon. "

"Understood," came Marcela Avician's quivering voice over the intercom. After what happened to her husband, Henri wouldn't fault Marcela if she asked to be by Tibi's side instead of doing her job, yet she soldiered on, with only her voice betraying her anxiety. "Our team is verifying the calculations as we speak. I'm sure that by the time you presence back into H-bot we'll have everything we need for the next twelve hours."

"Thank you, Marcela." For her sake, Henri pretended that everything was all right, but the truth was, he wasn't sure of anything anymore.

"Good luck, Henri."

Henri presenced back inside H-bot and synchronized with its vision. It was still looking out the front porthole. He tried to move to check the flight board but couldn't. Something was wrong with *him* now! Could a seizure be next? What could trigger that?

No, he was *restrained*. H-bot's arms and legs were bolted to the pilot-pod. He turned his head. Tiberiu's robot, T-bot, was back in its pod and was *piloting* the cosmoship.

What's going on?

T-bot was doing every gesture twice, as if to make sure things were done right. It also looked intently to the very place it was operating for a couple of seconds before doing the gesture, then another couple of seconds afterward. This was definitely not Tiberiu controlling the bot, but someone not trained for the two-second lag between the bot-pilot's mental command to the moment the bot executed the instructions, and the two-second lag before the bot-pilot received visual confirmation that the bot performed the action.

The ship was being turned away from the Moon.

Henri looked around for a way to free H-bot, but the cabin was small and almost bare, safe for the flight board and their pods.

"Oversees, Oversees, this is an emergency! T-bot's reprogramming the *Luceafarul*'s path. I don't know how or why!"

Static.

Henri repeated the emergency call. Again, just static. Sabotage? It was likely a matter of time before the saboteur would scramble the bot-pilot channel too and then Henri wouldn't be able to presence to the ship again.

T-bot abandoned its navigation adjustments and turned toward H-bot.

"Who are you? What do you want?" Henri asked T-bot over the interbot channel.

He heard a click, then over a clear frequency, the voice of Razvan Ilie, his machinist. "We didn't expect you back, Coanda."

"Ilie? What are you doing?"

"Delivering the cosmoship to those who have paid well for it. I truly am sorry, but you are just in the way."

Ilie, inside T-bot, stood and tried to grab H-bot's head. But again, Ilie's lack of training showed as it pushed its legs to stand, an action that propelled it upward from its pod. It bumped into the ceiling and floated there for a couple seconds of time lag. By the time Ilie realized what he'd done wrong in zero-gravity environment, it took another two seconds for him to correct the bot's movement. Henri could do nothing to fight back, not with its arms and legs locked into the pod—

Only, a pilot-pod was more than just a chair.

"Whoever thought of mounting a chair on this ship?" Tiberiu asked on their first boarding of the Luceafarul. "Why would robots need to sit? They never get tired."

"It's not for the bots, but for us. We're used to piloting in a seat and this will give us the right frame of mind to operate the ship through the bots. And if we happen upon a solar flare, the pod will reset the bot-units and recharge them. The pod also has a back-up communication system in case something happens."

T-bot finally floated close enough to the floor to magnetize its feet and stick to it. Then he grabbed H-bot's head and began to pull with all its mechanical strength.

Henri shifted his awareness into the pod. If he could presence into his backup bot in the storage hold under the navigation cabin, he'd be free of this incapacitated unit. Why couldn't he remember the frequency? He'd trained for fast transfer, but those times he did, no one was trying to rip H-bot's head from its socket.

Henri could see through H-bot's eyes as its head came loose, with only a fragile cable still tethering the floating cranial unit to its body. The rogue bot needed two seconds to see the results of his efforts. It had to be now. Henri focused and coded in the frequency, praying that it was right.

Henri surged through the connection and two seconds later, he stirred in the darkness of the storage hold, and flexed the mechanized fingers of his backup robot. He slid the battery button to full function, tapping into Bot-2's Karpen Pile. Henri gave a sigh of relief. He still had a working bot on *Luceafarul*. He hadn't lost the ship yet, and if he were to keep it that way, there were things that needed to be done planetside first.

Returning to the Navibot Sphere, Henri opened his eyes. His helmet was dripping with sweat and his eyes felt like they were covered with spider webs. He gulped for air and felt the cosmo-jockeys helping him out of the straps. Once safely on the ground, he grabbed the first jockey's arm. "I need Cuza here, now!"

Henri struggled to his feet, pulled off his drenched shirt and threw it out of the Sphere. Then he pressed the connect button on the intercom: "Oversees, we have a problem."

"Henri, you shouldn't have presenced back. Ana said—" Marcela was still in charge of flight control oversight. Her voice was now firm and professional. Could that mean Tibi was out of danger? Or did it mean she played the iron lady she needed to be to hold the mission together, for the sake of her husband and her father?

"*Luceafarul* is under enemy control. I repeat, *Luceafarul* has been compromised."

Grigore stepped in, his face darkened and confused. "What did you say?"

"Ilie, our machinist, presenced into T-bot while Tibi was still in it. That's why Tibi had the seizure." Henri inhaled and leaned against the Sphere's soft wall. "Ilie's destroyed H-bot, but I managed to transfer into my backup. For now, our enemy doesn't know I still have a way onboard the *Luceafarul*."

Grigore sputtered. "Ilie betrayed us? Who's he working for?"

"No time to debate that. I need everybody to listen carefully. Oversees, what's the time left on the clock?" Henri put on the new shirt that a cosmo-jockey brought him, and allowed the man to button it up for him.

"One hour thirty-seven minutes to fall over the horizon."

"Good. Enough time if we move fast and precise."

"What's to be done?" asked Grigore.

"Ilie's experienced, but not as practiced as Tiberiu or me. Nobody else should be able to ride T-bot but Tibi. The robotic brain's mirrored after his mind. Anybody else trying to presence in should be rejected."

"But Ilie managed to presence into T-bot nonetheless?" said Grigore in disbelief.

"Each bot-unit has a sub-brain that allows maintenance access. I suspect Ilie had tampered with T-bot's. The sub-brain shouldn't be able to control the bot a hundred percent, but it can still be used to issue simple commands like moving and pressing buttons. Enough to navigate the ship."

Grigore was fuming. "Unbelievable!"

"Ilie couldn't do this without outside help. He needs someone who can calculate new flight paths, and someone who can back him up here."

Marcela cut in over the intercom. "To be able to pirate the radio signal, Ilie could only be using the Radio Tower or had a secondary transmitter built on a very high point nearby. The closest summit to us is twenty kilometers south in the Bucegi Mountains, which is too far. We need to send teams to check the facility."

"Do it," Grigore said.

Henri stood. "Grigore, I bet his accomplice had destroyed our backup electrical generator and he's waiting for the right moment to cut off the power. They hijacked T-bot exactly two hours before our control window closes, when Romania's position will not allow us to stay in contact with the ship. That means they don't want to destroy the ship, but to bring it back into orbit where the foreign power can keep it out of our reach."

Marcela interrupted again. "They need at least ninety minutes to turn the ship onto a path where we can't re-link. After that they can cut the power and leave us in the darkness while they can retreat with everything they got from us."

Grigore swore and punched the cushioned wall.

Henri lay a hand gently on Grigore's back. "We don't have time for anger, Grigore. I need you."

"I'm here, Henri. I'm here."

"Good. Send men to every point where a spy could cut off the power. Not only in our base but outside too, on the entire mountain and especially in Brasov. Tell them to take the spies by surprise, so they can't alert anyone."

Grigore hurried out of the Sphere.

"Oversees," Henri continued, "get in contact with Dr Odobleja and ask him if there's a way to stop Ilie's control over T-bot."

"But Dr Odobleja is at the psychocybernetics conference in Vienna!"

"Our success depends on it, Marcela."

Henri turned to one of the jockeys. "My training bot, in Bay Two. Prepare it."

Henri presenced into the training robot, the serum from his previous injection still effective for a short-distance connection such as this. He stepped outside of the Spheres Facility inside O-bot, adjusting to the lack of lag planetside. As a reflex he paused to breathe in the mountain air, but of course O-bot could neither transmit back a scent-signal or fill Henri's lungs. The Launching Center perched atop Mount Timpa, above the city of Brasov. In the gloaming, the city was a sea of flickering lights landlocked by the black woolly mountainscape, and the road down the forested slopes was a slither of electric lamps. No motion in the Center's yard. Everybody here was either inside the Spheres Facility, or inside the Oversees Building.

Henri steered O-bot around the Spheres Facility, a huge concrete cupola without windows. The Facility was back to back with the Oversees Building, a magnificence combining the graceful vertical Art Deco lines and the honeycomb pyramidal style inspired by Henri's latest invention, the *beton-bois*. This type of prefabricated structures was meant to make house construction affordable to a wider array of social classes.

He stopped in front of the Radio Tower. O-bot's eyes zoomed in to the top of the structure, and caught sight of something close to the pinnacle. Ingenious – Ilie had actually built a camouflaged nest there right under their noses, a small-scale replica of the Navibot Sphere, practically a tin ball fixed in a wooden frame and tied with wires inside the Tower's structure. The saboteurs were more resourceful than he imagined.

O-bot began climbing the steel tower, not a difficult prospect for a robot that could magnetize its feet. Although initially the saboteurs' hideout sounded clever, it now seemed dumb to Henri. It was too easy. They needed two hours to make their plan work. How could they stay uninterrupted when they were so easy to spot—

Henri heard a click under O-bot's right hand and stopped abruptly. A wire ran up and up to the middle of the tower. O-bot's eyes saw clearly that wires had been attached to the entire metal frame, connected to firing mechanisms for smaller charges meant to set off the larger payload: the bomb clamped to the girders. If O-bot were to let go of its right hand, the first charge would detonate, and in a matter of seconds, the entire tower would topple, possibly crushing the buildings beneath.

If the Radio Tower fell, the mission to the Moon would fail. If Ilie couldn't steal the *Luceafărul*, he was willing to sacrifice himself to prevent anyone from saving the cosmoship. Henri wondered what kind of debt or pressure had driven Ilie to such madness. He never took the time to get to know Ilie, he realized. And now his neglect could cost them everything.

Henri clamped O-bot's hand to the frame so it wouldn't release and detonate the charge. Likewise he locked the robot in place on the girders so that it wouldn't move, even when Henri presenced out. Then he decerebralized from O-bot's brain and woke up back in the Navibot Sphere.

"Damn!" He ripped the helmet off his head and dropped out of his harness. The two cosmo-jockeys ran to his side, but he pushed them away.

"Henri, you were right. The backup generator's destroyed beyond repair," said Grigore, re-entering the chamber. Despite everything, Grigore still looked impeccable: not a wrinkle in his suit or dust on his spectator shoes. But his face fell upon seeing Henri. "What happened?"

"I found them. They're in the Radio Tower. Unfortunately they rigged the tower to blow. We can't risk climbing the damn thing."

"We'll find another way, Henri." Grigore sighed. "Even if it means I have to grow wings and fly up there."

Henri grinned. "Smart man."

"What?"

"We need a hot-air balloon. If we can't scale that tower, we can certainly float up to that bastard's nest and pluck him out of there."

Grigore went from enthusiasm to panic between blinks. "Where am I supposed to find a hot-air balloon?"

"Steal a dirigible from the city, if you have to." Henri switched on the intercom. "Oversees, what do we have left on the clock?"

"One hour and twenty-two minutes," came Marcela's reply. "Dr Odobleja said to tell you, *Mirror, mirror, on the wall, who are you, once and for all?* What does that mean?"

Silence. Everyone looked expectantly at Henri. Henri sighed. "Odobleja, you bastard. Couldn't you be more cryptic?" No time to ask for clarification. He donned the helmet, offering his neck for the next injection. "Strap me in again, boys. I'm going back to *Luceafarul*."

As he drifted into his trance, Henri thought he heard Ana's voice protesting over the intercom. *Heart attack. Seizure. Phantom trauma.* She was right: any of those might kill him. But the world needed Grigore's dream of space, and of peace.

He presenced forth, ready to retake his ship.

Back inside Bot-2, Henri floated through the cargo hold slowly. The ship was airless and would carry no sound, but vibration remained a cue that might alert his foe. He still had the element of surprise, and he might as well use it. If only he could find something, anything, that could help him. No ideas yet, but if he kept searching, something might inspire him.

Mirror, mirror, on the wall, who are you, once and for all? What did Odobleja mean by that? Was it something to do with the psychocybernetic brains that might give him an advantage?

Henri stopped and stared at Bot-2's faint reflection in the chrome pane of the Lunar cart. He switched on the forehead lamp, and the metal brightened. He could see Bot-2's reflection in the mirror-like surface, in great detail. He knew what Odobleja wanted to tell him.

Scientific knowledge wasn't adequate enough to build an autonomous intelligence inside a robot, but Odobleja invented the next best thing – bots that could be piloted through a displaced awareness via radio signals. Ana Aslan's serum had made the cerebralization process, or presencing, possible. The bots' brains worked more or less the same as human brains, in that a robotic brain could control the robot only because there was a personal image that matched its many parts. The moment that self-image changes, the brain starts transmitting distorted and misfired signals. Henri had an idea of what Odobleja wanted him to do, but would it work?

Henri unlocked the hatch that led out of the storage hold and into the navigation room. He reviewed the details he needed to incapacitate T-bot. The distance to the pods from the hatch; where the reset switch was on the base of T-bot's head. The reset only worked on the bot's primary brain, not the maintenance sub-brain. However, it would at least take the sub-brain off-line for ten seconds. Enough for Henri to accomplish his true goal – wake up T-bot's main and true identity.

The moment he sprung the hatch, Henri had only two seconds before any visual cues would be sent back to Earth, and two seconds for the saboteur to do something about it through T-bot. Four seconds to get to the bot and flip its reset switch. He could do it in two, given how small the navigation room was. No way in hell could he miss this chance.

Bot-2 opened the hatch and burst through the opening, magnetizing his feet and locking onto the metal floor. One second. He made the two steps to the pods in another second-and-a-half, and stretched out his hand to flip the switch.

Nothing happened.

Three seconds had passed, and T-bot was still running its activities without reacting to Bot-2's ruckus. But at the same time, the reset switch wasn't . . . there anymore? It was, but it was covered up with tape! Ilie had actually thought about the reset switch and had taken measures to make it inaccessible.

Next second – T-bot turned in Bot-2's direction. Henri was out of time.

Bot-2 reached in front of T-bot, who tried to stop him but four seconds too late. Henri reached above the porthole and grabbed the photo of Tiberiu, Marcela, and their daughter. Tibi's personal touch, his real presence aboard the *Luceafarul*. Henri taped it on the flight board in front of T-bot. He was just in time. T-bot smashed into Bot-2 and threw him through the hatch, back into the cargo hold. Pain flared in Henri's chest. Was this the phantom pain the doctor warned him about?

Before Henri could re-orient Bot-2, the hatch closed and locked from the navigation side. Ilie had initiated the emergency protocol for dumping the cargo hold. Henri's photo-identity ploy had failed.

Damn.

The cargo container shook violently as the first set of clamps released. Henri looked wildly around for an escape. The second set of clamps disengaged and the module separated from the ship.

No, no, no. Henri raced to open the hatch to the outside, and clambered out. He hooked the carabiner of his safety line into one of the handles embedded in the main hull just before the hold was jettisoned away from the *Luceafarul*.

His bot now floated a few meters behind the *Luceafarul*, towed at the end of its safety line. Henri could cry right now – this had been Tibi's idea for the bots' safety while working outside the ship, if the need arose. Sweet, thoughtful Tibi.

Henri's thoughts faltered. *All is not lost.*

The view was incredible – on one side of him was the Earth, perfect and glowing like nobody could ever have guessed, not the ancient Greeks, not Galileo, not even the modern astronomers. It was simply breathtaking. Then there was the graceful shape of the cosmoship *Luceafarul*, a sleek silver angel seemingly motion-less in its flight away from the dark and beautiful Moon.

Henri knew he was almost out of time. This was a fight for young people like Tibi, not dinosaurs like him. He made Bot-2 pull itself back to the *Luceafarul,* engage its electromagnetic feet, and cling to the hull. He mulled his options. The pilot-pod might be his last chance.

Bot-2 clambered atop the ship, slowly, grasp after step after grab, until it stopped next to the emergency control panel for the grand Karpen Pile that powered the *Luceafarul,* the undying heart that could sustain the cosmocraft to the end of time. Henri had helped Vasilescu-Karpen mount this model in the ship. He hoped he remembered his way around it well enough to execute his plan.

He unbolted the protective panel with a spanner-extension hidden in Bot-2's wrist tool kit and took a look inside. It wasn't very complicated, yet extremely fragile if exposed. There was a two-second lag, Henri reminded himself, counting his steps again. He removed Bot-2's secondary battery and disconnected the wires, and attached it to the Pile's control panel. Wiring the first cable to one of the connectors to the ship, Henri then wrested a red wire from the cosmoship's Karpen Pile, the one that he'd been warned to always keep completely isolated from the others. He pulled another wire free from his backup battery. Henri prayed that this would trigger an overcurrent that might supercharge the pods and take T-bot offline.

He brought the two bare ends into contact.

Sparks flared in the darkness of space.

Did it work?

The only way to check was to get back inside. If T-bot had been reset, it would take five minutes for it to gain full functionality. But if it hadn't, then it would be Henri versus Ilie, cosmonaut versus saboteur, in a final showdown.

Henri opened the external hatch and slid inside, closing the opening behind him. He waited a few seconds, then spun open the hatch to the navigation room, ready to fight.

T-bot was still in its pod. No noise, no movement. A trap?

He floated quietly to the pods and grabbed T-bot by the arms, hoping to immobilize them. T-bot didn't react. It was dead. Henri sighed, magnetized Bot-2's feet and re-taped the photo onto the window right in front of T-bot's eyes.

He unbolted H-bot's dismembered hulk from its pod, tethered it out of the way, and inspected the flight board. T-bot had been in the middle of introducing the last adjustment calculations received from Earth.

Henri canceled the previous path. The clock had been set to countdown the time until the *fall over horizon* event, when Romania would be on the other side of the globe and the ship and its bots would be out of contact with the human pilots. Twelve minutes left. Henri re-established radio contact with Oversees.

"Oversees, this is Coanda, now back in command of the cosmoship *Luceafarul*. I sent the exact coordinates of my position. Please recalculate my flight-path. I have twelve minutes to dial in the new calculations."

He heard the cry of relief from Marcela. Then as she spread the news, Henri could tell Marcela was crying.

Henri fed the new calculations into the flight board as he received them.

T-bot's arm shot up and struck Bot-2 in the head, sending Henri reeling. The phantom pain was so intense that Henri was sure something had broken inside Bot-2's neck. But T-bot, instead of attacking again, hesitated and looked at the photo.

Henri raised Bot-2's arm to parry. "Oversees, send a reset signal to T-bot and switch it to its primary brain, now!"

T-bot scored another agonizing strike against Henri, then it was half-standing, magnetizing and trying to grab Bot-2's head, but it couldn't quite manage to synchronize the movement of its hands with Henri's dodge. The time lag saved Henri again.

Henri shoved T-bot back into its pod, keeping its head toward the front window, eyes aligned with Tiberiu's photo.

"Look at yourself. You are Tibi. Tibi is you," he sent through the channel, hoping the self-image of the real T-bot was still in there somewhere, fighting Ilie's presence.

T-bot remained unmoving in the pod. Henri released his grip and checked the flight board. Five minutes left. He continued his litany while he dialed in the new course corrections. "You're Tibi, Tibi is you."

He felt something ram into him, forcing him from the flight board.

Henri fought to breathe against the crescendo of pain in his chest. He had to stay conscious.

"Come on, T-bot!" Henri shouted through the channel. "It's time we showed the world this beautiful dream. It's time we make this world a better one."

T-bot faltered, its impulses likely at war: Ilie in its sub-brain versus the core persona in the primary.

Henri fought the urge to weep. He'd failed them all. Again. So close and he still couldn't make it to the finish line, just like in Paris when his jet plane had crashed and his investors had abandoned him. "I'm sorry, Tibi. I'm destined to fail. I haven't been a very good mentor."

T-bot's hands froze.

Henri didn't lose a second. He pushed the inert T-bot away, returned to his pod, and started punching buttons and spinning dials to execute the final course corrections.

The last digit, the last click of the dial.

Blackness cut his vision. That was it – the fall over the horizon. Exhaustion pulled him under and he lost consciousness.

Henri squinted from the sunlight filling the room. He kicked away his blanket. Why was he in his bedroom in the Brasov Orbit Launching Center? Wasn't he supposed to be on a mission? He jumped out of bed.

"Easy now, Henri." Tiberiu entered the room.

"Tibi!" Henri hugged his friend. "You're fine?"

"I'm good. I was waiting for you to wake up."

"How long have I been asleep?"

"Almost eighteen hours."

"Oh, my God, the *Luceafarul*! I lost it, didn't I?"

Tiberiu laughed and hugged him again. "You saved it, old man. You saved it. Come on, get dressed and come down. We've got one last thing to do before you retire."

"Eighteen hours, but that means . . ." murmured Henri with a shiver.

"Yes, we've reached the Moon's orbit. We're there." Tiberiu smiled. "I've been waiting for you to do us the honor of landing the first bot on the Moon."

Everybody, from fawning politicians to anxious investors, gathered in front of the Navibot Sphere. And, for the first time,

Grigore had allowed journalists with their cameras and super-iconoscopes within the facility. They were all eagerly awaiting Henri and Tiberiu to presence into their bots on the *Luceafarul* and land them on the Moon.

"Did you get Ilie?" Henri said under his breath to Grigore.

"Ilie and two English spies. We got everything under control and into the morning papers," Grigore whispered in his ear. He then spoke aloud for the journalists. "Ladies and gentlemen, we're here today to witness the most extraordinary event yet in human history, the first landing on the Moon. Do us all a favor, Mr Coanda and Mr Avician – land the damn thing on the Moon and make history." He shook their hands.

Henri nodded. "It is time for us all to forget greed. To forge peace. To fly to the stars."

Applause erupted as he and Tiberiu entered inside the Sphere. The team strapped them into their harnesses and prepared their helmets and injections.

Bulbs ignited like drumming strikes of lightning, leaving a fleeting flash blindness in Henri's eyes before a cosmo-jockey lowered the connect-helmet over his head. He felt a slight pain in his neck as the syringe injected the cerebralizing serum into his bloodstream, but he welcomed it.

Henri awakened inside Bot-2, back inside the *Luceafarul's* navigation room. Tiberiu had reclaimed T-bot, now freed from enemy control.

The Moon's surface was just beneath them, a stone's throw away.

Act of Extermination

Cirilo S. Lemos
(Translated by Christopher Kastensmidt)

The Killer and His Boy

Jeronimo Trovao rolled up the *Adventure Magazine* like a straw and smashed a fly which slogged through the cake on the table. After an entire night of studying escape routes, blueprints, and the complex assembly scheme of an Enfield, he was too tired to do anything beyond collapsing into the armchair. He wasn't going to spend more energy trying to understand what the hell a time warp was.

Outside, the city was in motion, a cacophony that mixed factory whistles; the roar of automobiles; the light hum of the dirigibles crossing the clouds of smoke on their way to Estação Centro do Brasil; the crude, unintelligible murmur of port workers on the other side of the street. Familiar noises, authentic background music to which anyone who wished to live in a metropolis like Rio de Janeiro had to get used to. Many couldn't. When his eyelids closed, he was thinking of the story of the miner who, coming with his family from a tiny, rural community, couldn't stand the endless clamor and bustle of the big city. He shot himself through the heart and left a note asking to be buried in his hometown. That was a long time ago. Six or seven years. But it stayed in Jeronimo's memory as an example of how a man could be devoured by that jungle of reinforced concrete and lakes of gasoline. He thought to himself that even those who got used to that type of life had their own share of insanity.

Like himself. Every once in a while, Jeronimo Trovao was visited by a Saint.

He had been too shocked to do anything besides breathe and feel his heart tighten – although he'd never confess that, not even to the Saint – when she arrived limping over the arid ground, her head covered by a very blue veil and parts of her belly shamefully bare, coming, as she herself would say, from hyperspace, where the Saints live. He didn't know that that meant, but he had no alternative except to accept her sanctity. The smell of the Lord emanated from her through a thorn-filled heart, a strong and ferrous perfume which cleaned the motor smoke from the air. Not even to her, who was a Saint and, therefore, possessed a soul, would he confess the terror which took hold of him upon seeing her in that land filled with people, just as he would never say how much he adored seeing her appear from the distance like a mirage.

She appeared shortly after the *Adventure Magazine* was tossed in a random corner. She carried her halo beneath one arm, her sacred heart dripping blood. She had no smile when she stopped in front of the armchair, her skin slightly grayed by the dying light which entered through the window. She extended a hand to him, gazing at him with Nancy Carroll-painted eyes. He kissed the hand respectfully, but without ceremony.

You are but a dream of Anthony of the Desert, she said. The voice was a hoarse swish. *He sleeps now to have the strength to resist the demons for one more day.*

"I'm not a dream. I'm a man." Jeronimo's replay lacked conviction.

He is out there at this moment, sleeping. Sheltered in this dream to rest before the battle against the next hoard. You can't let the Desert arrive.

"I'm not a dream," he repeated. He felt the tiny hand rise to his face and he felt himself flooded by her golden eyes.

You're a killer, Dream-Man.

He shivered. The words sounded like a judgment, the confirmation of a fate carved in stone, unalterable. He heard dry explosions coming from somewhere. At the same instant, he perceived he was no longer sleeping.

Someone was beating on the bedroom window.

Jeronimo went to the dresser. Below yesterday's edition of

The Integralist Monitor lay a loaded 96 Mauser. He grabbed it and moved slowly toward the window. Back to the wall, he tried to make out anything through the gaps in the Persian blinds. He saw nothing. He turned to the window on the other side. He saw nothing there beyond the faded sun that had begun to draw stripes over the room's dirty rug.

He was certain he'd heard something. Maybe his head was mixing pieces of dreams with reality. He raised the pistol barrel almost to his chin. With a quick movement, he opened the blinds. The gray day took half the room by storm; a pigeon, dirty with oil, fled. He stooped over the parapet to observe the alley three floors below. The only thing there were the grimy longshoremen taking a shortcut to Rodrigues Alves Avenue, and a web of lines drying clothes in the hot steam which rose from the storm drains. Above, in the gap between the buildings where it was possible to see the sky, a dirigible penetrated a column of clouds. He was about to return to the armchair when the bathroom door opened noisily. The squat figure which stepped out came face to face with the 96 Mauser.

"Why didn't you use the door?" Jeronimo recognized his son the moment he crossed the threshold. Even so, the gun remained leveled. "I'm having a very strange day. I could have blown your brains onto the wall behind you."

Deuteronomio Trovao (shorted to Nomio, by his own choosing) was barely fourteen years old. He wore a soot-stained shirt, pants made from a thick fabric, and soldering glasses raised up on his head. He wanted to look like one of the air raiders from one or two decades past, but that was the best he could do with the change he earned from his father.

"I thought I was being followed," he stuttered, undecided whether to lower his arms or keep them raised like a fool.

"Did you do like we agreed?"

"Yes, sir. Two taxis in different directions, then the streetcar."

Jeronimo lowered the pistol.

"Next time, use the door."

Killer. Carved in stone. Unalterable fate.

He lay the gun on the chair's arm. He gestured vaguely to the boy.

"Have you eaten anything?"

"No."

"There's coffee and cake on the table. The coffee is burned and the cake fallen."

Nomio filled a cup, took a sip, and made a face.

"It's terrible."

"I warned you."

The kid ate three big pieces of the corn cake while trying not to look at his father. He knew the gravity of those lines forming on his forehead. Something was bothering him, and it wasn't the fact he'd come in through the bathroom window. The best thing to do on these occasions was to leave him in peace and pretend not to have noticed anything. Maybe his father was becoming sluggish. He knew too well what happened to sluggards in that field. They ended up in a swamp with a bullet between the eyes, rotting among the crabs. He wiped the crumbs from the corner of his mouth and ripped the paper which covered the crumpled tailcoat.

"I need to return it by Friday. There's a brown stain on the trousers, but it was the only one I could find in my size. I got a nice discount."

"It'll do."

"And the car?"

"Outside," was all Jeronimo Trovao said before turning away.

Nomio's smile couldn't be bigger.

License to Groan

General Protasio Vargas always knew that his place was among great men. Surrounded by busts and canvases which portrayed the lineage of the Portuguese kings, he felt at home. Not just at home, in fact: he felt greater. A strong man, with the will and vigor to save a nation from the centrifugal forces which had begun to undermine the Empire's rule.

That was more than could be said about the human ruin which carried the crown on his head. The old man dozed in one of the chairs, a thread of saliva running from the edge of his mouth. Even in the heat, he wore velvet-lined pajamas and covered his head with some kind of knit cap. Every once in a while, his head would dip until his chin touched his chest. He would jump, snort, and right himself, only to start all over again. A man seated in front of him enjoyed the scene, sipping at a glass of liquor.

His Majesty, Dom Pedro Augusto of Saxe-Coburg, third sovereign of the Brazilian Empire, and his principal minister and lawyer, Artur Bernardes, Baron of Viçosa.

To Protasio Vargas, the scene illustrated the national political panorama: a debilitated old man who drooled in his own beard and flattering dandies fearlessly snapping up new titles wherever they could find them.

The Emperor's rooms in Petropolis were more austere than those of the palace at Quinta da Boa Vista. There was a huge mahogany bed, a small desk, some chairs near the window which looked out over the garden and a fireplace that the recent, excessive heat – even there, at the top of the sierra – had turned into nothing more than part of the decoration. On top of a console table, a radio played a melody from the Gray Noble orchestra, right beside one of the mechanical maids which had become fashionable among rich people. A crib completed the room's furnishings, which caused the General a type of surprise that was difficult to disguise.

"Just the man we wanted to see," said Artur Bernardes, getting up.

Vargas bent before the Emperor and kissed his hand. The monarch awoke with surprise, mumbled something and cleaned the back of his hands on the pajamas.

"It's the medicine." Bernardes smiled at Vargas's embarrassment. "His Majesty had another one of his fits."

"I understand," replied Vargas, shaking his hand.

Fits, he thought. A great euphemism for the schizophrenic outbreaks which afflicted Dom Pedro III with increasing frequency. The Emperor had been caught having heated discussions with the Empress, deceased more than fifteen years, or on occasion discussing with invisible interlocutors the advances in Nazi astronautics. Most of the time, the cases were covered up, but murmurs had begun to spread beyond the Court. Opposition papers unleashed ironic notes among the theatrical articles which propagated the idea that there

would be no fourth reign. Vargas heard some of the stories told
in the Military Club, like the one that the Monarch's constant
trips to Europe in his youth were actually for treatments by a
certain doctor named Freud. But seeing with his own eyes his
fragile state was, in a certain way, a deception.

"I have an important subject to treat with His Majesty."

With effort, the Emperor raised his dim eyes. He wanted to
say something, but Bernardes anticipated him: "It's good that
you've come, General. We also have an important subject to
treat with you. You spared us the trouble of sending a messenger to your house."

"The messenger would have been a National Guard recruit,
of course."

The minister motioned Vargas to make himself comfortable
in one of the chairs.

"You military men are incapable of rising above these institutional jests? It's not polite to speak to the Emperor and his
principal minister looking down at them, General. Sit with us.
We're admiring a fine, genipapo liquor." He filled only two
glassed, one for himself and the other for Vargas. "To your
health, Majesty."

"In the Army we aren't in the habit of forgetting 'institutional
jests', Mr Minister-President. Not while we have the National
Guard and its farmer-colonels receiving money for their gaudy
projects while we barely have enough to feed our soldiers."

"Those farmer-colonels, as you insist on calling them, are
what have kept the Empire united since 1870, General. It was
the strength and support of these men that permitted a tran-
quil turn of the century for the institutions of this country."

"Without a doubt. We who died on the Paraguayan Gran
Chaco and were poisoned by toxic gases in the Great War had
nothing to do with that. The legitimate guardians of this country are the heroic landowners interested in protecting their
unending source of income."

"Your family was one of the first to benefit from those
advantages, don't forget," jabbed Bernardes, watching Dom
Pedro III from the corner of his eye. "The Vargas family were
quite satisfied upon receiving from the Court all that heavy
machinery for their farms."

"My grandparents just upheld the law. The British forced the old regents to take our slaves in exchange for machines imported from Manchester to perform the heavy field work. The skies of the land where I was born became a big oil spot, the industrial English became even richer, and the Empire gained an absurd quantity of Negroes walking around loose.

"You're talking like a Communist."

"No, I'm talking like a history enthusiast. I'm a soldier, and my preoccupation is for my country."

The Emperor had a coughing fit so violent that it took both Vargas and Bernardes to support him.

"Not even here does one escape this insufferable smell of smoke," said the minister. "Should I call Dr Pena?"

The Emperor didn't respond. He asked to see the boy. Bernardes rang a bell. A black woman entered holding a baby.

"Come see, Vargas," whispered the Emperor, his chest rasping. "Your future sovereign."

To the General's surprise, the child was absolutely normal. No trace of the genetic deformities of which his informants at the Balisario Pena Laboratory had informed him. He looked at Dom Pedro's face, then again at the baby. The old man's features were easily recognizable in the boy. As improbable as it seemed, the Emperor had fathered the prince of which he had been incapable of producing for the last fifty years.

"Where is the mother?" stammered Vargas, notably perturbed. He had seen the pregnant woman a few times in the newspapers. Then she had disappeared completely.

Dom Pedro caressed the baby.

"A good woman," responded the old man. "Faithful to her country. She's in Europe, now."

"You insult the Emperor with this type of question," admonished Bernardes. He wiped his glasses with a handkerchief. "Which, by the way, is becoming common among your equals."

Vargas perceived some kind of tension forming there. He had expected it.

"So we're back to institutional jests?"

"This is more than a mere jest, General. I'll go direct to the point. We will no longer tolerate the Army's insubordinations. Your boys need a muzzle."

"What are you talking about?"

"I'm talking about that half-penny lieutenant publishing paid articles in the newspaper. What we least need at this moment is officials of our own Armed Forces criticizing the Cabinet and disrespecting His Majesty in public. It is not an opportune time for that, General."

"And when will be the moment, Mr Minister-President? When we're victims of an armed uprising by the revolutionary groups? Because that's exactly what I came to discuss. There are indications that the AIB is receiving German weaponry by way of the Plata. And of the Anarchist-Luddites and Socialists articulating themselves around the ALN. They're preparing something big, and soon. When that happens, I'm certain that you won't like having an Army in rags begging around for ammunition."

Bernardes began to fidget. He did that when nervous.

"The National Guard is prepared to defend us, in case the Army proves incapable."

"This revolt could assume catastrophic proportions," insisted Vargas, trying to ignore the provocation. He shot a discreet look at Dom Pedro, who snored once again in the chair. "Brazil could end up in the hands of an enterprising fascist. Or worse, opportunistic communists."

"Yet to me, the Army has revealed itself much more problematic than the communists, General. Know that the article by this lieutenant, or whoever is behind it, won't go unpunished."

"Don't threaten an armed man, Mr President," Vargas riposted in an icy tone. His thumb grazed the leather holster.

Bernardes followed the gesture.

"I also know how to use a revolver, General," he said. He tossed his jacket back, revealing a nickel-plated .38 at his belt. The two stood there, motionless, each one conscious that it was nothing more than a game of will that would never come to pass.

Another coughing fit from the Emperor put an end to the embarrassing scene.

"The natural order will return when the Heir Apparent is officially presented to Brazil, as the Law of Succession requires."

Dom Pedro III squinted at the General. "Don't worry, Vargas. No conspiracy will overthrow the Empire."

A Pawn in the Tower

Nomio straightened the tailcoat's collar. He detested that kind of clothing: too tight, too uncomfortable. For twenty minutes he had circulated through the elevator hall among a sea of people, trying to pass as a messenger, waiter, anything of the type. He found the integralists ill-humored; when they laughed their teeth showed and their eyebrows arched like the evildoers that Democrata, his favorite superhero, confronted. They seemed to be scheming something.

He kept an eye on the door. He concluded that it wouldn't be difficult to block it when the time came. Passing a chain and padlock in a loop through the handles would be enough, and nobody would get out of there until his father finished the job.

He pulled up the tailcoat's collar when, arm in arm with a man with huge bags under his eyes, the most beautiful woman he'd ever seen passed him by. She wore a gray dress and a white hat, which revealed only bits of red hair. She reminded him of his mother. She had never used makeup like this woman, not that he knew, but that didn't diminish the intensity of the sensation. He stood there, immobile, watching the woman and feeling an immense longing.

"What is it, boy?" asked the baggy-eyed man. "What to ask the lady in marriage?"

Nomio turned red.

"That was mean, Cassiano," laughed the woman, playfully slapping her companion's forearm. "And you, boy, you think I'm pretty?"

"You look like my mother, ma'am." Nomio struggled to force the words from his mouth.

"How sweet. And where is she?"

"She died."

The woman blushed, not knowing what to say. She ended up allowing the baggy-eyed man to lead her away to the ballroom. Nomio shrugged and concealed himself among the plant vases nearby, where the backpack with the radio was hidden. He turned on the device.

"When he enters, I'm going to lock the doors," he said, not forgetting the face, a spitting image of his mother.

True and False Futilities

Trains originating from the four corners of the Empire converged in the subterranean terminals of Estação Central do Brasil. Its hexagon-shaped top received cruise dirigibles from the entire world. Joana Bras had already been on top of the largest station in South America on other occasions, but this was the first time she allowed herself to enjoy the view.

She didn't like what she saw. Rio de Janeiro was ugly from above. Old chimneys of exposed brick vomited columns of dense smoke that went, almost motionless to those who watched, to mix with the huge, perpetual gray cloud that covered the city like a velvet blanket. Tubing of every form and fashion passed through the streets from top to bottom, transporting gas, oil, and every kind of chemical fluid necessary to grease the good performance of the hundreds of ovens, bellows, cauldrons, exhausts, gears, valves, stacking machines, drills, belts, forges, presses, pulleys, spotlights, printers, dynamos, vaporizers, band saws, hydraulic jacks, conveyors, assembly lines, treatment stations, workshops. The pipes pierced the asphalt, stretching above and below the earth, coupled with buildings and monuments. Shanties pockmarked the city's many hills, which, from time to time, enormous tractors would knock down. But it was impossible to remove the hundreds of habitations which arose every day. Immense slums grew and spread out in waves around the neighborhoods, the shacks made from whatever could be found: cardboard, tiles, wood, zinc sheets.

Joana surprised herself with the thought that progress charged a high price to the poorest, and knew that the time she had passed with the communists had infiltrated that kind of idea in her head. But it was difficult to think differently. At five in the morning, sirens rang in the manufacturing plant habitation complexes, strident and tremulous whistles that added up until becoming a single sound, which advised all the workers of the start of a new work shift. One by one, the houses – identical, cublical, crammed together – lit up. The workers, repeating movements made automatic by routine, got up, made their beds, drank coffee. Those that lived far away crammed the buses, the trains, the streets. They passed their perforated cards in the punch clocks, put on their overalls, performed their functions. At noon, they ate lunch, had a shot of coffee, smoked a cigarette, and started everything again. Modern times.

Tall constructions were not permitted around the Estação Central do Brasil due to the dirigible traffic. From the panoramic window of the convention center, high above the clock, Joana could see from far away the immense skyscrapers of steel and glass, symbols of the modernist architecture that intruded into the tastes of their proprietors, in general, foreign companies. Inside of them, she thought: magnates, financial operators, executive secretaries, and directors observed the Empire's capital with greedy eyes, managing every detail of the production worksheet, overseeing by way of a hierarchy bound to the work progress from all sectors. When things went as planned, the smiles were whiter than anything else in the city managed to be. When they didn't, they berated subordinates shrunken with fear. To compensate all this was a blurred sea of orange from the sunset. That was something that could still make her smile.

In the glass's reflection she saw behind her a man break away from the circle of intellectuals, grab two glasses of champagne from a waiter's tray, and slide toward her. Joana breathed deeply and prepared to be frivolous.

"A million reis to know the motive for that sweet smile," said Cassiano Ricardo.

"I was thinking that Marx might have had a point."

Cassiano Ricardo seemed mildly disturbed by the unexpected answer, but composed himself when Joana giggled.

"It's dangerous to say that kind of thing at an integralist meeting, my dear."

Joana accepted the champagne glass he offered.

"Artists shouldn't be afraid to express themselves, Cassiano. A poet like yourself should know that better than anyone."

"Political preoccupations almost make me forget the Arts."

"Yet they shouldn't." Joana offered him an arm. "Come on, I want to hear Menotti and Lucia's funny stories."

Joana found the AIB meetings tedious, full of ultranationalist bravado, shows of authority, and dubious art. To be fair, Cassiano Ricardo's poetry wasn't all that bad. *Songs of My Tenderness* even proved to be an agreeable read. But watching Plinio Salgado recite sterile verse while being applauded by men in green shirts in no way matched her idea of a good time.

She wasn't there to have fun, however. The ring on her finger, slightly tight, didn't let her forget that. She performed an important role, infiltrated in the increasingly radical group captained by Salgado. But she was a woman of action, and there was nothing worse for someone like her than being among those people, pretending to worry about fashionable dresses or the hairdos of movie stars. To reduce the tediousness of the inflammatory speeches – repetitive with every comma – and the dead conversations, she sought out the company of the Green and Yellow group, composed of painters, futurists, Dadaist writers, and modernist poets (or any of those combinations). Men and women like Menotti del Picchia, secret admirer of the literary trash of an American editor called Gernsback; Lucia Amado, with her paintings which, according to herself, were a scream against the emptiness of the modern feminist mind; and Cassiano Ricardo himself, who predicted he would one day have a seat in the Brazilian Academy of Letters. They were artists. A bit bridled by the integralist ideas, but artists nevertheless.

When she met with them, Joana only pretended to drink. When the alcohol began to elevate heads and loosen tongues, she inserted apparently innocent questions to try and uproot some relevant information. She had been hearing rumors that needed to be confirmed, like the one that LATI was being used by the Italian fascists to send German money and weapons to the AIB; or that an upcoming insurrection was being planned, now that the Emperor had one foot in the grave and no one to succeed him directly, according to an 1893 constitutional amendment. The Green and Yellow group, however, didn't know much of those things. Probably because of their frequent bouts of drinking. Plinio Salgado, although a mediocre poet, was intelligent enough to know that not everyone who shouted "*anauê*" was worthy of confidence.

While she laughed with the others at Menotti's jokes, Joana discretely studied the conversation groups which spread through the convention room. The very space chosen for the meeting, a ballroom with panoramic windows above the Estação Central clock, was a clear indication that the AIB now disposed of a great deal of money. The place's rent was exorbitant, as must have been the buffet with formal waiters and an immense flag – a black sigma inside a white circle – which took up the entire wall, floor to ceiling, behind the pulpit. A lot of money seemed to be flowing into the integralist coffers. If it were true, then there was a good chance the rest of it was as well. But the Green and Yellow group didn't know that. She needed to approach the right people.

Plinio Salgado arrived in the convention room and was greeted with a thunderous *anauê* by those present. He waved to them all, shook hands with a few, drank water from a crystal jar. Joana always thought his figure a contradiction. A thin man, his bony face decorated by a square moustache, his hair meticulously parted to the side, stuffed into an excessively starched integralist uniform. Not impressive to look at, but with tremendous charisma when he spoke to his partisans. Joana was still studying his movements when his eyes fell upon her for a few seconds, before declaring open the extraordinary meeting of the AIB, and giving the projectionist the signal to roll the film.

Black curtains covered the sigma. The lights went out. A beam of light projected "3, 2, 1". Joana wasn't familiar enough with the cinema to know if Leni Riefenstahl was an expressionist or not, but understood the motive for the civic ecstasy that the movie caused among the integralists in attendance. It was basically composed of close-ups of perfect Aryan faces, colossal battalion marches, and images of an imposing Führer, filmed from below looking up, to salute the brave German people, the eagle standard waving in the background. Wagner's music lent an almost Biblical tone to the film, and each time the swastika appeared there were those who responded with a proud *anauê*.

When the lights came on, a round of applause exploded in the ballroom. Plinio Salgado ascended the pulpit and began to speak. He laughed playfully at being informed that the microphone was turned off. A brief, shrill sound from the microphone, and the problem was resolved. He drank another glass of water and opened his mouth to let loose what would be his most fearsome speech.

The microphone amplified a high-pitched squeal followed by a wet pop. One second later, Plinio Salgado's brains spread out over the flag's sigma.

To Remove the Hell from Yourself

The big advantage of working for important clients is avoiding the complicated details of the business. How, for example, to get to the top of a building carrying a big suitcase full of heavy equipment. The doorman asked no questions when Jeronimo Trovao crossed the lobby of the Solemar building and climbed twenty floors by elevator with a three-barrel Enfield machine gun, a 96 Mauser, and sufficient ammunition to declare another war on Bolivia.

The building wasn't tall, principally when compared to the skyscrapers on more distant blocks, but it was one of the only ones to reach the maximum permitted height within the traffic zone of the cruise dirigibles that headed to the station. That meant a much lower possibility of curious spectators. It left only the dirigibles themselves and Estação Central do Brasil as higher observation points. He wouldn't need to worry about the first, generally filled with wealthy tourists so interested in each other as to prefer traveling days in a superballoon instead of hours in a CD-13; neither the second, on the other side of Avenida Dom Pedro II, a good fifty meters distant, more than enough for the nosey to be incapable of making him out as anything more than a dark point.

Just in case, he mounted the equipment underneath the rust-eaten iron structure which supported an antenna. It took a little more than twenty minutes to prepare all the parts of the machine-gun rifle, oil the triple barrel, line up the sight. He'd brought five-thousand six-hundred ammunition cartridges in four noise-suppressing cylinders. The Contractor wanted to cause a lot of damage. He lay down beneath the antenna, placed his eye in the gun's sight. He saw the Estação Central clock. He rotated a series of dials to adjust the focus, raised the sight a little. The panoramic window of the convention center ballroom appeared. There were a lot of people in front of what Jeronimo thought was a big E on the wall. The pulpit was there, just like they'd told him. He inserted a punch card in a little box linked to the sight by cables. He pulled a tiny lever. The Enfield vibrated slowly as the box began to automatically adjust the distance and covert the American gauges to Brazilian measures. He coupled the ammunition cylinders to the gas tubes, freed the trigger, and waited.

Half an hour later, the lights went out in the hall. A movie was projected, as expected. Also as was expected, Jeronimo heard Deuteronomio's voice on the radio: "When he enters, I'm going to lock the doors."

"Leave the building as soon as you're done and meet me at the rendezvous."

The shadows were already beginning to stretch across the city. Night would fall in two hours or less. He didn't need to worry much, however: in forty minutes, the curtains opened and the lights came on. The chaotic noise of traffic on Avenida Dom Pedro II didn't allow him to hear the round of applause that arose among the integralists.

On the radio, Deuteronomio: "He's going in, Dad."

Jeronimo saw Plinio Salgado's lanky figure cross the ballroom like Caesar himself and ascend the pulpit. The intersection of vertical and horizontal lines in the sight was on the insignificant space between his upper lip and nose.

Jeronimo's finger was already on the trigger.

You're a killer, Dream-Man, said the Saint.

He squinted. She was sitting above him, in the antenna's hardware.

"Not now."

You're going to kill a man.

"A bad man."

Take a life.

"Things aren't that simple."

You're going to turn yourself into a nightmare for Anthony, weaken him in his fight against the demons.

"Be quiet."

Killer.

"Please."

If you kill that man, you will unite your destructive path with that of the Boy.

"Please."

The three souls will be condemned.

"Shut up!"

He pressed the trigger.

Plinio Salgado's head exploded.

He looked up. The Saint was no longer there. The sweat began to fall into his eyes. He switched the Enfield to automatic. The triple barrel began to spin, the capsules flew like bees. And thus, Jeronimo Trovao sent the integralists to hell. Just to remove it from himself.

Hell in the Tower

The ten seconds after Plinio Salgado's head disappeared in a red stain were eternal. Joana Bras saw people screaming, but didn't hear their voices. She heard nothing.

On the eleventh second, the sounds returned. The extraordinary meeting of the AIB transformed into pandemonium. The panoramic window exploded in a cloud of sharp fragments. A rain of bullets swept the ballroom, shattered wine glasses, destroyed the buffet, filled the curtains and flag with holes, perforated the walls, burst light bulbs, broke the projector, an unending racket, people falling, screaming, crying, not believing, dying.

Cassiano Ricardo's blood squirted onto Joana's white hat. She felt the poet's arm go limp and slide away. Before her friend's body touched the ground, her vain, frivolous disguise had already evaporated and her survival instinct emerged. She jumped on top of a table and, from there, behind a pillar. The shots passed whizzing by her head, then ceased.

Once she allowed herself to breathe, she looked around. All that was left were dead or dying people lying on top of each other, ripped-off arms, punctured chests, eyes rolling outside their sockets, legs thrown far from their owners. A ruby pool formed on the checkered floor full of glass shards, food, and bits of plaster. Joana waited another minute before standing up, back against the pillar, hands trembling at knowing she was the only one in that place still alive. The double doors were locked, as had been painfully discovered by the men and women piled there. Joana tried to control her panic. The Estação Central do Brasil ballroom had been turned into a slaughterhouse.

Those people woke up today, got dressed, and went to die, said the Saint.

Jeronimo Trovao pretended not to hear. The ammunition cylinders were empty. He waited for the Enfield to cool and began to quickly disassemble it. He stuffed the parts into the big suitcase. He went toward the terrace door.

The Saint followed after.

Someone survived, Dream-Man.

He descended two flights of stairs, entered the first corridor that he saw. He threw the bag in a trash compartment there and listened to it fall through the zinc duct. That was that. Just like the Contractor wanted. One of his busybodies was in charge of making it disappear.

A woman.

"I know." He could no longer ignore her, although lately, he had been trying hard. "I'm going after her now."

No, don't go.

"I'm going."

You mustn't do that now, Dream-Man.

"Why?"

Because she'll kill you if you go there.

Jeronimo Trovao had his reasons to believe it when she said those kinds of things.

His name was Antonio Gomes. He was one of the principal reporters from Associated Dailies, considered by many the largest newspaper conglomerate in Latin America. From time to time he would steal a glance at the bottle of vermouth on the table and feel his mouth water. "That's not a story," said Ronaldo Aroeira. "It's a rumor, my friend. It's a cock-and-bull tale."

The man before him seemed smaller than the suit he wore.

"There could be some truth behind it."

"We saw the woman that the old man was screwing, didn't we?"

"We did, but . . ."

"If you're telling me that the son isn't his, I'd at least understand. But this story about the Emperor producing a son inside a test tube, like he was Dr Frankenstein . . . Not even Pedro Augusto can play God.

"This doesn't have anything to do with God," retorted Gomes. "It's science. It's creating a brave new world."

"Not so new, nor so brave."

Aroeira filled the cup with vermouth and offered it to Gomes, who squinted and waved it away with both hands. Aroeira shrugged, impatient.

"How else do you explain that the Emperor, an octogenarian at death's door, suddenly had a son? He, no less, who couldn't impregnate anyone his entire life."

To Aroeira, the answer was obvious: "An ample-breasted courtesan, if she has the talent, can do miracles. Or the son isn't even his. No matter what, there's no heir while he hasn't been officially presented to the country. When that happens, and only then, will we talk about this."

Gomes shook his head, displeased.

"So we don't have any story that hasn't been reheated and . . ."

The telephone rang, interrupting him. Aroeira attended the call. Gomes saw the man's jaw drop in surprise from what he heard. One minute later, he hung up.

"That was Mr Chateaubriand. You have your headline. Write it down: alliance members foment slaughter at integralist convention.

Destructive Rumors

The country was flooded by dozens of newspapers whose capitalized headlines insinuated – when not outright declaring – that Moscow-supported communists sponsored an attack that was, in truth, the first step in an uprising. The relationship between the ANL and AIB, which was already hot enough without the extra fuel, became a powder barrel with a short fuse. Before sunrise, students and bohemian intellectuals of socialist inclination were already being accosted in the streets. The word *anauê* appeared painted on walls and monuments. A mob threw stones at the tiny Soviet embassy building, where Luis Carlos Prestes supposedly met with the Russians to orchestrate a series of attacks that would initiate the Red Revolution. The wave of rumors transformed the Empire's capital into a city even more scared, which waited for the worst to happen at any moment.

At noon, a law student recited his "Ode to Lenin's Spirit" and ended up lynched by integralists who had left a nearby meeting. He was gravely wounded. By way of a radio program, the ANL rallied its members to defend themselves against their aggressors, not all of which were integralists: "We regret yesterday's barbarous crime, but we do not accept responsibility for it. We will not tolerate further aggression for no more than our loyalty to our ideals," said Prestes, in a recorded message.

The Emperor was advised by Bernardes to travel down from Petropolis to Rio de Janeiro and speed up the official presentation of the heir. Dom Pedro III barely had the strength to stand, but agreed. The cabinet ministers, the true government, released a statement lamenting the occurrence and assuring that every measure was being taken to find the culprits, but it was not the time to act impulsively and start a witch hunt.

It made no difference. A group of more than one hundred integralists, reinforced by members of the Nazi Party, initiated a disturbance in São Paulo. In the following hours, the same thing happened in distant places like Porto Alegre and Recife. There were no fatalities: all the fury concentrated itself on the commercial establishments belonging to socialist or anarchist sympathizers. The police took to the streets, but the Court managed to cool things down by asking for some time to investigate the facts. The integralist leadership conceded, coming away stronger. A story began to spread that they were taking advantage of the truce to plan more disturbances, probably armed.

A police gyroplane took Joana Bras to the Solemar Building. One quick look was enough to discover the location from which the shots had been fired. She held an empty shell that the shooter had forgotten to collect. She rolled it between her fingers, stored it in her purse. It was 7.62 ammunition, military use. That was when she understood that things were going to get much worse before they got better.

Meeting with the Contractor

Extraordinary mental activities were verified in at least 0.9% of the test group. The psychobiophysics relate, in their majority, cases of extra-sensorial perception (ESP) in Levels 6, 5, and 4, considered the lowest; and 3 and 2, considered elevated and of uncommon frequency. Level 1, considered Clairvoyance, is even rarer, being observed in only one specimen since the beginning of the project. Vasili Kharitonov was born in Siberia, with nothing that differentiates him from a common man. However, he was capable of discovering the location of seven submarines, pointing them out on a map. In later tests, it is recorded that he was capable of anticipating attacks against his physical integrity and foreseeing results in situations controlled by the laboratory. Profoundly religious, Kharitonov insisted on the idea that the Archangel Michael told him what to do. The project's psychobiophysics are working under the hypothesis that the mind projects a personage who makes the bridge between the part of the mind which remains awake and the profound zones of the subconscious, where the process that permits Clairvoyance likely occurs. This personage would probably be the representation of an influence marked by strong religious devotion.
Passage from the Bazaev Protocol

The Contractor drank tea. Despite the dry heat, a hot drink – with the exception of coffee, he hated coffee – always improved his mood. It was no surprise to find the Cabral Bakery open on that uncertain morning. Not far from Rua Gonçalves Dias, the establishment's location, lay Avenida Dom Pedro II, where a multitude of integralists and sympathizers was growing. Many businesses resolved not to risk becoming targets of depredation and locked themselves down. Apparently, the Cabral Bakery wasn't one of those. Its reputation had been built upon delicious dainties, but to that could be added some degree of constancy in times of political turbulence. The Contractor had no doubt that, even with Rio de Janeiro under attack from Wells's Martians, he would find the place open for business. That was the reason he had chosen that place for the meeting. Although he had to admit, the guava and cheese cookies also had a hand in that decision.

Not far from his table, a television set transmitted the morning program of Guarani Broadcasting. The image wasn't the best, principally when compared to the movies. But television had its advantages, like not needing to leave home to watch adventure series or the news. He still hadn't gotten used to it, but they said it was the future and if there was something he didn't fear, it was the future. Even the electronic brains would have one of those, to replace once and for all the paper they consumed by the spindle. Like it or not, television had been the method chosen by his civil partners to diffuse the definitive proof against the ANL. If images were worth more than words, twenty seconds of ably manipulated footage was worth a ton of newspapers. Once people saw with their own eyes, no one could snatch that truth away from them.

The Contractor saw the man he waited for enter the bakery. He wore a suit and hat, one that almost accentuated his rude demeanor. Almost, because the spiky beard and sideburns insisted on making him look like a bandit. He seemed lost for a few moments, as if he wasn't sure he was in the right place, until the Contractor signaled to him.

"I thought you wouldn't come," he said, when the man sat down.

"Why wouldn't I come?"

"The Empire awoke less secure today. There's a storm brewing."

"I'm not afraid of rain." The man's voice seemed coarser than normal.

"Principally with a name like yours. By chance would you be related to the deceased Lopes Trovao?"

"Not that I know of. Can we get straight to business?"

The Contractor pointed with his chin to the teacups and tray of cookies.

"We're civilized men. We should act like them."

The Saint was standing right beside Jeronimo Trovao.

Don't drink the tea. It's full of poison.

"Don't you agree?" asked the Contractor.

Jeronimo shifted in the chair.

"Yes."

"Are you well? Your eyes just fluttered."

"No, I . . . I'm fine."

"Drink a little tea. That always helps me."

Don't drink it. This man wants to see you dead.

"There were survivors."

"What?"

"Survivors," repeated Jeronimo. "One, actually. Pretty, red hair. Judging by the vaults she made to escape the bullets, she must work in a circus."

"You left someone alive?"

"I didn't leave her. She did it by her own merits."

The Contractor slapped the table. When he realized he was drawing unwanted attention, he breathed deeply and composed himself. He pulled some photos from his pocket. He chose one.

"Would this by any chance be her?"

Jeronimo examined it.

"Yes. Who is she?"

The Contractor took back the photograph.

"Joana Bras. She belongs to the Aviz Ring. The Emperor's secret agents. If she was there, we have a problem."

"No. You have a problem. My part in this is over. Where's the money?"

All the kindness present in the Contractor's face evaporated, substituted by a dark expression. He slid an envelope over the table.

"Do me the favor of not counting that here."

Jeronimo opened the envelope and glanced quickly at the thick wad of bills. Everything seemed to be in order. He stored it in the jacket's inner pocket and moved to stand.

"I hope you remember to maintain discretion as agreed," advised the Contractor.

"Oh, but I'm discreet. If I weren't, I would have already spread your name around. Don't you agree, Mr Protasio Vargas?"

"Go to hell."

"That might be where I'm going," said Jeronimo, getting up and closing the meeting.

Vargas observed him walk away toward the men's bathroom. He signaled to a man at a table on the other side of the bakery.

Jeronimo entered the door and the Saint followed after. The window, through which entered a slice of day, was little larger than the cookie tray. A great inconvenience: he'd planned to leave through there to throw off Vargas.

"I don't believe there was poison in that tea," he grumbled, displeased.

Yet there was, said the Saint.

He thought about going back, but she stopped him.

A man is going to come in, Dream-Man. He has a revolver and he's going to use it against you.

A soft footstep came from outside. Jeronimo positioned himself beside the door so he could surprise from behind whoever entered without needing to kill anyone. A man appeared, holding a pistol with a silencer. Jeronimo threw himself against him. The two rolled on the tile, wrestling like street dogs. The man got on top, was struck by a head butt, and ended up pushed to one side. Jeronimo tried to force his forearm against the man's trachea, but had to give way when he felt the gun barrel touch his ribs. With a punch, he sent it flying to the urinals. The man got up and, quick as a cat, reached the pistol and turned to shoot. Before he had time to squeeze the trigger, he felt a sudden pain in the neck. The last thing he saw was a thread of smoke rising from the barrel of Jeronimo Trovao's 96 Mauser.

Protasio Vargas choked on his cookie when he saw the individual he judged to be dead leave hurriedly from the bathroom and exit the bakery. He rose in a hurry and ran to the sidewalk, just to see him enter a metallic Supersuiza and tear off toward Avenida Dom Pedro II.

He threw his hat to the sidewalk and cursed. He needed to advise Chateaubriand if he wanted to get his hands on the cretin before he disappeared.

The Incredible Supersuiza against the Flying Men

Nomio threw his *Adventure Magazine* to one side and started the car's engine the moment he saw his father leave the Cabral Bakery, as they had planned. His father got in and slammed the door.

"Floor it, boy."

The Supersuiza burned rubber on the Rua Gonçalves Dias cobblestones. In the rearview mirror, father and son saw Vargas have a fit of rage and run back into the store.

"I think we've escaped," laughed Nomio.

Jeronimo shook his head.

"He shouldn't have seen the car."

"Why?"

"The military have their resources . . . Look out!"

Two women appeared suddenly, crossing the street. Nomio spun the wheel left. The Supersuiza made a tight turn, jumped the curb, and flattened a fruit stand. Oranges, tomatoes, and cabbages scattered on the ground while the fruit vendor raised a fist.

"Sorry," said the boy, his cheeks red with embarrassment.

"The car's not ours, really."

The Supersuiza entered Avenida Dom Pedro II at full speed, zigzagging through the traffic. Drivers honked and cursed with every dangerous passing. Nomio smiled roguishly from the corner of his mouth. He even took both hands off the wheel to lower the soldering goggles over his eyes, which made the car jerk to the right. Jeronimo held on to the seat.

"Pay attention, kid."

Outside the window, the city passed by like a whirlwind. The Estação Central building, six dirigibles moored on top, grew in his field of vision.

Jeronimo lit a cigarette. In the rear view mirror, he saw the Saint's translucent figure in the back seat. He blew smoke, waiting for her to speak.

Look back and up.

He obeyed. He put his head outside the window and saw, among the buildings, a gyroplane closing in quickly. Two men equipped with jetpacks and gauntlet guns, one on each side of the tiny cabin.

"A gyroplane and two armed flyers. They're going to dive at any moment."

"We can't go any faster than this," advised Nomio.

"I have a surprise here for them."

Jeronimo stretched his body into the back seat. There was an N12 rifle there, hidden by a blanket. He looked sideways at the Saint, but she said nothing. He grabbed the gun, cocked it, and positioned himself once again in the window.

The gyroplane roared less than fifteen meters behind the Supersuiza, projecting the shadow of its helices over it. The shot from the N12 exploded the cabin's glass, catching the pilot by surprise. He lost control for a moment and had to turn onto a cross street to avoid an encounter with the buildings.

"Let's get off this avenue," shouted Jeronimo. "We're too exposed here."

There's no time, said the Saint. *A flyer-man is going to appear by your side and blow up your son's head.*

In the rear view mirror, Nomio saw two trails of flame emerge from between the buildings and close the distance at absurd speed.

"Dad, the flyers!"

"I see them. Take the next exit." Jeronimo checked the quantity of ammunition in the glove box. The next exit came and went, without the boy managing an opening to get off.

"Sorry," he said, apprehensive.

"Forget it. The flyers are going to try and line up with us. When that happens, I want you to broadside."

"Huh?"

"Swerve the car at him when he's beside us."

"How do you know he's going to do that?"

"I know."

The world outside the Supersuiza was a sonorous chaos formed by wind, motors, horns, and by the roar of the jetpacks, already near the point of appearing in the mirrors on the Flyer's faces. Nomio saw one of them appear on the passenger side. The gauntlet gun pointed straight at his father. He didn't falter; he swerved the car into the man, who whirled over his own axis and, in a risky maneuver, dodged over the roof, only to meet up with a motorcycle coming in the opposite direction. Motorcyclist and flyer transformed into a pile of hardware, fuel, and blood on the road.

The Saint was right again, thought Jeronimo, seeing his son look at him oddly. He was going to say something funny to alleviate the situation, but a hail of bullets came from above and transformed the hood of the Supersuiza into a sieve. The next moment, the second flyer passed them and curved upward until becoming a miniature against the Estação Central clock.

"Are you hurt?"

"N-no . . ." muttered Nomio, frightened.

"He'll be back," said Jeronimo, quickly putting more ammunition into the N12 and positioning himself once again in the window.

But of course he will, he heard the Saint say, with the softest, most enchanting, bitchiest voice in the world.

The flyer made another curve and descended upon the car. He raised the gauntlet gun and unloaded against the Supersuiza. A line of bullets passed sparking near Jeronimo's head, but he had cold enough blood to keep the man in the center of the rifle's sight. In the next instant, he pulled the trigger. The shot disintegrated the flyer's shoulder. He lost control and tried to charge them. His jetpack drew a flaming arc in the air and he crashed against a building.

"I thought that thing would blow up," commented Jeronimo, apparently disappointed.

They left Avenida Dom Pedro II to avoid the patrol cars that attempted to control the multitude around Estação Central. They took a street that followed beneath an oil pipeline to the edge of the Providência slums. They abandoned the Supersuiza there, where the gyroplane couldn't see them, and disappeared among the street vendors' tents.

First Effects

Although the assassin contracted by General Vargas had proven more difficult to sweep under than rug than expected, the pursuit he led through downtown wasn't a complete disaster to the Army's plans. Actually, it was the opposite. All of the destruction along Avenida Dom Pedro II– conveniently close to Estação Central – ended up being blamed on the ANL or AIB, depending on the ideological orientation of whoever told the story. Two lives had been sacrificed in the process, but in chess and politics some sacrifices were necessary. Chateaubriand would succor the widows.

In the eyes of the people, communists were hydras ready to step over families with their bread, land, and liberty; seed anarchy; burn good customs; and destroy honorable jobs. In compensation, the integralists and their allies might even have a point, but didn't hesitate in trying to achieve their objectives with a scary dose of force. The Army saw both types as dogs that barked a lot – which always generated a nice effect – ready to be incited against the weak and necrotic Empire. The ingredients were already in the pot, as they said in the South. Once the boiling began, the country would realize that Dom Pedro III was just a schizophrenic old man on the throne of an anachronism that had lasted too long.

But there were a few rounds left until checkmate. The next move should be occurring that instant on Guarani Broadcasting. Chateaubriand guaranteed that it would go on the air before the imperial censure had time to act. So it didn't matter whether or not the participation of the communists in the massacre was true: an environment of civil disorder would have already been established.

The integralists took to the streets. The convergence began at the foot of Estação Central. They were no longer satisfied with just marching, calling words of order, and threatening. Now they carried clubs, rocks, knives. Firearms. Explosives. Many used kerchiefs to cover parts of their faces. A woman with a megaphone fired up the crowd, speaking of martyrs for the national cause, of the necessity for a strong leader and, above

all, integralism, to take the reins of the country and uproot
from it the putridity of the socialists. Shouts against the Empire
bubbled up from a sea of people more agitated every moment.
And, just like the sea, the multitude crossed Avenida Dom
Pedro II as if the police were nothing: paralyzing traffic,
assaulting passers-by, depredating stores, cars, monuments.
Buses were burned in Catete and Urca, a streetcar was
destroyed in Santa Teresa. They set fire to the ANL headquar-
ters. No one was killed, but the blaze lit the mettle of the
socialist, communist, and anarchist groups that organized
themselves around the Alliance. Neo-Luddites destroyed oil
ducts and mechanical arms in a construction site on Rua do
Ouvidor. Stalinists and Trotskyists held hands before the
symbolic (and, soon after, literal) ashes of their refuge.
The alliance column met an integralist legion in the middle of
the city. The police were in the middle of the disturbance, but
much more than that was needed to stabilize the situation.

The Empire Tries to Strike Back

The President of the Ministers' Council, Baron Artur
Bernardes, had never been so tired. The day had been long,
every minister and representative calling at the same time. He
couldn't think straight, his thoughts had gone blank as soon as
he realized what the images he had just seen on the television
meant. He looked to Lima Carvalho, his assistant, then to the
Emperor lying in his bed, his head drooping from side to side,
an oxygen tank vibrating on a nearby support. Bernardes knew
that the solution wouldn't come from there. The salvation of
the Empire and the maintenance of his own status would come
from the other Pedro, whose diapers were being changed that
moment by his wet nurse. But he needed more time.

"Summon the National Guard," he said to Lima Carvalho.
His head seemed ready to explode. He didn't want to invoke
that alternative. If things got out of control, they could slide
into civil war. Those São Paulo republicans would like that,
liberal sons of bitches that they were. However, he had no
other option. He was felt like a punching bag and didn't like it.

"Colonel Teles Filho doesn't have the resources to mobilize

and equip a force greater than two hundred men in the next hours, sir," informed Lima Carvalho.

Bernardes punched the Emperor's desk. He needed at least two thousand men on the streets, to reinforce the police.

"They chose now to cry about money?"

"Exports have fallen considerably, sir. The money that the colonels used to invest in the National Guard is now being used to keep the plantation accounts paid. They're functioning at a minimum. My suggestion is to let Teles Filho test his toy on the streets today, sir. He's invested a lot of time and money in it. The name is Cylindroid, I believe. It might work."

"Order him to bring what he can."

"If he had permission to permanently incapacitate some ten or fifteen . . ."

"Kill, you mean."

"Yes, sir. So that the others see that the Empire isn't playing around and has the resources at its disposal to quell any attempt at insurrection."

Bernardes knew that the gravity of the situation demanded a lot more than mere dispersion. The Empire's Third Reign had marked an accentuated decline in imperial power. The provinces had revindicated – and won – an increasing autonomy without Dom Pedro or the Cabinet able to slow down the decentralization. The financial crisis had weakened the economy but strengthened groups that preached new forms of government. Killing rioters wouldn't resolve much more than broken windows.

"But it will give us some time," he concluded, thinking aloud.

"What, sir?"

"Summon Colonel Teles Filho. Tell him to bring his weapon. And he can permanently incapacitate your ten or fifteen."

"Of course, sir."

Lima Carvalho left to make the call. He returned shortly after, his face livid.

"Sir, Teles Filho's militia is no longer responding."

Bernardes leapt from his chair.

"What happened?"

Cylindroid vs Thirteen

Two hundred men of the Jacarepaguá detachment had been assembled, with extraordinary speed, in a mansion constructed on a round hill. The place was the property of Colonel Fonseca Teles Filho, Baron of Taquara. Standing before the militia in formation, he gave an inflamed speech about honor, duty, and love for one's country. Shortly before, he had been unraveling all the financial difficulties through which the country was passing, and how those reflected a substantial cut in the budget allocated to the nation's true guardians. Luckily, every soldier, captain, and colonel had not allowed these times of crises to bring them down. Through their own means, these men had pledged the quantity necessary to complete the first one hundred percent Brazilian mechanized combat unit, designed, modesty aside, by himself.

Matias Figueiras, the sergeant chosen to pilot the machine, was sufficiently nervous that the colonel's entire speech sounded to his ears like a big, senseless verbosity. He didn't like to be the center of attention. There were at least two hundred guards there whose eyes seemed fixed on him. This number was capable of making him confuse his own legs, not to mention the levers and buttons of a four-meter tall, five-ton machine.

The applause severed his thoughts. Some officials shook the colonel's hand. The speech had ended; it was time for a demonstration. At a gesture from Teles Filho, he turned right and marched to the hangar the baron had ordered built in the old slave house. He entered through a lateral door, sweating buckets inside the black coveralls.

The inside of the hanger was like a big workshop smelling of diesel oil and gunpowder. Tools, gallons of fuel, motor parts, and metal plates spread across the walls, workbenches, and even the ground. But what caught the eye of whoever entered there was the enormous cylinder equipped with machine guns, grenade launchers, and big pincers on the ends of two mechanical arms. It stood on two small, articulated legs, connected to an axel that allowed three-hundred-and-sixty-degree turns. Brazilian technology, designed to the slightest detail by Colonel

Teles Filho. His dream was to see the Cylindroid, as it had come to be known, being mass produced and becoming the Empire's principal weapon. To Figueiras, that contraption looked much more like a barrel with arms and legs than an armored vehicle, and was far from perfect. The armament was efficient, as they had shown the ten cows turned into ground beef by the machine guns and the cars scrapped by the grenades, but there were problems: a) it was too heavy, which forced the reduction of armor at several points; b) the legs were fragile, making them an easy target for any .23; c) it was slow, and would never reach the target without costly aerial or terrestrial transport.

There was a hatch at the end of a short ladder behind the Cylindroid. Figueiras stuffed himself through it. The cabin was tight, barely large enough for the chair. He made himself as comfortable as he could, put on the helmet, and turned on the engine. Lights lit up on the panel, gauge pointers began to move, a tiny vent began to blow. Something warm dripped on this arm.

"Oil leak," he grumbled.

He buckled the seatbelt. Through the periscope, he watched the hanger door open.

He set the Cylindroid to walk.

Figueiras breathed deeply. Stupefied looks fell on him like arrows.

Teles Filho was beside himself with pride: "I present to you the country's savior."

A round of applause, amplified by the external microphone, almost exploded Figueiras's eardrums. He pointed the microphone up. He heard a long, shrill whistle. Figueiras turned the periscope skyward.

"My God."

Something that looked like a rocket came in his direction. He tried to scream, but the impact was almost instantaneous.

Three thousand meters above, on board the American bomber *Total Care*, the crew celebrated upon seeing on a screen the taxi-missile transform Jacarepaguá mansion and Colonel Teles Filho's militia into a pile of rubble.

The shock wave threw the Cylindroid against the hangar like it was made of paper. The electronic brain that managed the gauges announced failure of the principal transistor. Through the periscope, Figueiras saw a wall crumble over him. It trapped him to the ground. He tried to move the appendages of that crummy barrel, in vain. Red lights lit up in the cabin. Without options, he armed the machine guns, hoping that the .50 caliber rounds would destroy the bricks without affecting the Cylindroid's armor.

Inside the crater that formed on the patio of the Baron of Taquara's mansion, the taxi-missile opened. It had been designed to unload, intact, cargos over enemy territory from vast heights. A man appeared. The hat and number thirteen engraved on a star on his chest gave him the air of a cowboy. He wore a dark camouflage uniform that looked more like armor, full of plastic parts, metal, recesses, protuberances, tubes connected to the helmet. There was a rifle secured to a box on his back by cables. He leapt from inside the taxi-missile and pulled two rough pistols from his belt. He crept through the smoking columns and piles of debris, mindful of National Guard militiamen that had survived his arrival. He saw the metallic armored vehicle trying to move underneath a sheet of bricks. He walked over slowly, cocking the pistols.

Fifty caliber machine guns roared. Dust and debris flew, pulverized by luminous projectiles that flashed in the night. The Cylindroid stood, its metallic joints grating. Inside, still dizzy, Figueiras tried to adjust the periscope.

"Damn," he said.

Bullets ricocheted from his armor. He pulled the lever to raise the machine gun. Once he did, Thirteen was no longer there.

The periscope quickly traversed the ruins. A blur appeared suddenly and shattered the lenses. Visual contact disappeared completely. The Cylindroid had barely entered into action and was already operating blind and at half strength. Figueiras had no idea what was happening. He pulled levers, turned dials, and checked gauges in hope of keeping the thing working.

He felt the impact of more shots reverberating on the lower part of the Cylindroid. Whoever that guy was, he had already noticed the weak legs and was trying to destroy them. A sudden jerk to the left, more shots, a drop to the right, and many, many curses. The armor lost its support and fell heavily to the ground. Figueiras checked the ammunition in his revolver and prepared to abandon the pile of tin.

"That thing's not gonna bother anybody," said the Controller, hundreds of meters above, watching the scene through the cameras installed in Thirteen's eyes. He sent a series of commands to him with one hand, while the other ably dunked doughnuts into a mug of coffee. "Let's get this over with. The Brazilians are waiting to give us a lift to the king's house."

With effort, Figueiras managed to push open the hatch. He had just unlatched the seatbelt when two grenades entered through the opening. One fell on his chest, the other under the seat. The last thing he thought was how much he hated that barrel.

Conversation in the Club

The officials spoke in whispers when Protasio Vargas entered, slamming the door. Flesh and blood officials divided the table with conference screens where the austere faces of generals based in other provinces could be seen. Expensive equipment, donated by their communication magnate allies, interested in the opportunities of the coming new order.

"I've learned that disturbances are occurring in other capitals, General," shot out Colonel Gois Monteiro, folding a newspaper. "Will we be able to control them?"

Vargas took a chair.

"Good evening to you too, Monteiro. As a matter of fact, a good night for the Brazilian Army. To answer your question: yes, we're going to control the disturbances. We destroy one side and financially strangle the other. And if that doesn't work, the *USS Rogers* isn't far from here. The American marines are prepared to guarantee our revolution. But it won't come to that. We'll accomplish our agenda with a minimum of external interference. For now, I'd like you all to approve this draft of the note we're going to divulge in the next few hours.

A young lieutenant came forward with a document in hand. Vargas gave the signal for him to begin reading.

> *The High Command of the Brazilian Army declares that, start-*
> *ing at midnight, the Monarchy is abolished as a form of*
> *government in Brazil. Pedro Augusto Bragança of Saxe-Coburg*
> *is considered deposed and exiled, as are any and all of his rela-*
> *tives to the third degree. A military junta is provisionally*
> *assuming command, to ensure the liberty of the democratic insti-*
> *tutions. At this same time, the National Guard, assemblies, and*
> *Cabinet of Ministers are dissolved, and these shall be detained*
> *until it is certified that they present no threat to the new Republic.*
> *God save Brazil.*

A murmur ran through the room. The officials were darkened silhouettes, whose medals and insignia occasionally reflected the light of the image tubes.

"That is the message that will circulate through the media and official departments. It must be short, succinct. To speak to the people we must adopt a different rhetoric. We have to sound like zealous parents. I'm already drafting an appropriate speech, don't worry. After our pronouncement, the President of the United States will recognize the new regime. Most Western governments will follow the same path. It will be a domino effect. With that, we can deflate the Empire's only play to achieve any support from the population, which would be to announce the crown prince and appeal to the sentimental-ism of tradition."

"That thing isn't human," said one of the military on screen, the voice full of static. "It was produced by the Emperor's eugenicists. It's an insult to any Christian who values God's law."

"And that is what the vast majority of parents will think," laughed Vargas. "The people fear Science. The Empire is finished."

You Can Hear the End Approaching in the Motor Noise

Watching the moon above the trees from the main window of his library, old Miguel Ventura finally accepted the fact that the Aviz Ring had reached its end. There was no longer reason for the organization once Dom Pedro III died. Very soon, as he had verified the last time he saw him. He wasn't sure exactly what his role would be, as an agent of the highest hierarchy, in relation to the little clone that Belisario Pena had managed to produce. Times were much more complex than they used to be. For the second time that day, he had the sensation that he really was a nineteenth-century man. The first was when he cleaned his favorite gun and noticed it was a mother-of-pearl-handled Colt.

The door opened. The wet nurse's head appeared.

"Mr Ventura? The lady is here."

"Ask her to come in, please."

Joana Bras had never been pretty, in his opinion, but the natural haughtiness of her poise became the center of gravity in any setting. When she entered, however, that seemed to have disappeared in a mixture of weariness and badly removed makeup.

"Miguel," she sighed.

"Joana. You look terrible. Like you came here on foot."

"I did."

Miguel didn't doubt she was truly capable of walking the ten kilometers which separated their houses.

"They're following me. I couldn't think of anything," she added, embarrassed.

"Miguel glanced down the corridor to be sure they were free from curious ears. He locked the door, turned back to Joana.

"Who is following you, my dear?"

"I'm not sure, but I suspect it's someone tied to the military. I was there, Miguel. I witnessed the massacre of the integralists. The shooters were outside the building, not inside, like everyone is saying. That's pure fiction. Someone is playing the communists against the integralists to create a crisis."

"General Protasio Vargas," said Miguel.

"How do you know?" asked Joana.

She saw him look discreetly at the revolver. With a brusque movement, she tried to snatch it, but despite his age, Miguel still possessed an astonishing agility. Before her hand even came close to the table, he grabbed the gun and pointed it at her face.

"I need you to think clearly, girl. The Aviz Ring is heading for an inglorious end, but don't panic." He opened a drawer and placed the revolver there.

Joana studied his eyes. There was sadness and some resignation there, but no vestige of a traitor's shame or remorse.

"I'm sorry, I . . ." She allowed her shoulders to droop. "I don't know whom to trust anymore."

"A few days ago Cicero brought me evidence that military men of high rank might be involved in some conspiracy. His source in the American embassy sent him a copy of a cablegram destined for Washington. We're fighting big dogs, Joana. We can't stand up to the Americans, weakened as we are. Maybe . . ." His voice failed him at that point, as if the words cost dearly. ". . . it's time for us to withdraw and review our options."

"I can't believe I'm hearing this."

Miguel sighed. He drew six silver rings from the pocket of his robe.

"There is no more Aviz Ring. We're the only two left. An old man and a confused woman."

Joana felt her knees weaken.

"And Antonio? Cicero?"

"Cicero was assassinated this morning. The others came to the conclusion that there is no point in dying for a condemned Crown. They deserted. Antonio just left. He was the last to bring his ring. I thought you'd come to do the same thing."

"Never."

"You make me proud. But it's over, Joana."

A whirlwind of thoughts crossed her mind. Things to say, things to ask.

Outside the night brought a rumble of motors.

"They're coming," advised Miguel.

"We don't need to confront the military and the Americans." She spoke at first to herself, then, more confident, to him. "Our job is to protect the Emperor and the heir."

"No."

"What do you mean, no?"

"We don't even know if that . . . child . . . is really human. It was made in a laboratory. Our obligation dies with the old Emperor."

Joana bit her lower lip.

"It least give me a decent gun."

"You'll die if you go to the palace."

"Are you going to give me a gun or not?"

He sighed. He pointed to a painting between two bookcases, which portrayed a bunch of heads with smokestacks in the background. There was a niche hidden behind the canvas, full of guns. Joana chose a Tokarev submachine gun, little larger than a pistol, and hid it under her clothing. They looked at each other, not knowing what to say, until someone knocked truculently on the door.

"Open this door, Mr Ventura," ordered a gruff voice.

"Hide under the desk," said Miguel.

Joana obeyed.

He unlocked the door, unhurried. Uniformed men entered, armed with assault rifles. The leader identified himself as a captain and raised a document in Miguel's face.

"Sign it."

"What is this?"

"Your resignation from the public functions that you exert, official or not, and a declaration of support to the military junta which is deposing the Emperor."

"I'm not signing anything."

Joana heard the muffled blow and moan of pain. She repressed the urge to leave her hiding place, shoot those traitors, help Miguel. That would gain nothing. She would end up a prisoner, or dead, and that would be the end of the Emperor and the child. That's why she stayed there, hearing the man who taught her everything being beaten until he could stand no more. With sadness, she felt the silent shame when he, unable to take any more, signed the document.

"The Emperor will return," he grunted, just before being dragged away.

Joana understood it as a last sparkle of valor, a way of supporting her. Miguel didn't deserve to end up that way. The Avis Ring didn't, either.

. . . And That is Why You are an Assassin

Two heavy Army trucks entered Avenida Dom Pedro II, which was crowded with people. On top of the trucks, turrets equipped with machine guns, spotlights, and soldiers wearing gas masks. The soldiers called for the people to obey the order and return to their homes.

A spotlight passed over Jeronimo Trovao and his son. The two continued on, trying not to call attention. The plan was to arrive at the Plaza Maua pier and rent a boat with enough fuel to cross the bay to Magé. From there, they would climb the Iguaçu river and hide in the mostly abandoned city of the same name, until the dust settled.

Jeronimo shouldered a path through the sidewalk. One hand in the big pants pocket, where he held the Mauser. The other carried the rifle wrapped up in a blanket and sheets of newspaper. He hadn't seen the Saint for hours. He couldn't say that bothered him. Each day it became harder to conceal. The boy already suspected that something wasn't right. He didn't want to worry him. Living with a father who committed crimes to earn a living was already complicated enough.

Nomio came close behind, his head shrunk between his shoulders, heedful of every laugh, yell, or curse word around them. He was starving. Sleepy. But he didn't want to say that to his father. His father's life was already complicated enough without worrying about a crybaby.

They arrived at the pier. The slats croaked under their feet. A dense layer of clouds padded the nighttime sky.

"It's dark here," said Nomio.

"Better that way."

The boy shrugged.

A small boat appeared. It was guided by an old man with a threadbare shirt, long pants, and flip-flops. Close to the pier, he turned off the motor. He stood, hand conched over his forehead.

"That's not going to make you see in the dark," said Jeronimo. "Is this the beauty of a boat you mentioned?"

"That depends. Do you have the money?" The old man spoke with a north-eastern accent: lazy, singsong.

Jeronimo took two bills and waved them like a fan in his face. The old man jumped to the pier and grabbed the money, reckless.

"If you want, I can take you."

"No," responded Jeronimo, stepping into the boat together with the boy. "We're going alone. We'll leave this old tin can with Sister Celia, as we agreed."

"Right, right. And where are you going?"

"That's none of your business," said Nomio. He sat at the prow, while his father, laughing at the rude response, made himself comfortable near the motor.

The boat was slowly swallowed by the night.

They went in silence for nearly half an hour, father and son. They heard only the waves tearing themselves below the hull. They were a good distance from shore, enough for the city of Rio de Janeiro to transform into a jumble of luminous points blinking against the darkness of the night.

Nomio felt cold. He wrapped his arms around his knees and lowered his head, blowing hot air inside his shirt. Every once in a while, he spied his father out of the corner of his eye. He seemed like a statue, hands on the gunwale, staring fixedly forward. He felt a stab of shame for having thought bad things of him. His father was still in the game. He still had fuel to burn. He thought of asking forgiveness, but didn't have the courage. The closest he could come to that was asking where they were heading, after all.

"I told you. Iguaçu village. A ghost town," responded Jeronimo.

Nomio insisted: "You mean it's deserted?"

"Practically. It's a complex of ruined constructions on the edge of the river. It was once an important point on the gold trail from Minas Gerais to the capital's port. But things happened."

"What things?"

"The river became too shallow for large boats. Then came the epidemics of cholera, smallpox. There were no doctors. Those who survived, left. To top it off, the Baron of Maua built the railroad a long way off. Everyone ended up leaving to live beside the railroad and abandoned the town."

"Seems like God doesn't like the place much."

Nomio saw his father smile. For some reason, that didn't seem like a good thing.

"Well, that's where we're going. Then, when it's safe to travel by land, we'll go to Guararema, in São Paulo province."

The boy hid his face back between his legs and didn't say anything else.

Rays scratched the sky around the sierra.

Your destiny isn't Guararema, Dream-Man.

Jeronimo gulped. The Saint sat in the same place as him. The sensation was strange, but he didn't risk asking how that was possible. He wasn't expecting her presence so soon.

Saint Anthony will soon wake from his dream. Everything will disappear. You. Your son. The sky. Everything, everything, everything. To be recreated on the following night.

"What do you want from me now?" he whispered. He didn't want his son to hear him conversing with an invisible saint from outer space and take him – rightly so – as a madman.

You mustn't flee.

"If we stay here, my son and I will end up dead."

If you turn your back on my message, death will reach you anywhere. That's the way you must go. The Saint stood and pointed at a distant bank, her blue veil dancing noisily against the wind.

Jeronimo feared that the sound would awake the boy's attention, but he only raised an uninterested gaze and rolled back into a ball, sleepily. He'd seen nothing but his father, heard nothing beyond the boat sailing the waves.

Jeronimo Trovao, for his part, had all his senses aroused by her presence. The divine scent, the hoarse voice, the marble skin that contrasted with his – the color of coffee with cream. She turned to the open sea. A bit of night broke off and formed, before Jeronimo's eyes, the gigantic figure of a battleship. He knew it wasn't truly there, it was another vision, but, like the Desert, it was real. The long cannon tubes; the anti-aircraft batteries; the supersonics; the more than two thousand shadowy marines with high-technology weaponry; the stars; the red and white stripes. Everything was real. At some spot not far from the bay there was an American aircraft carrier just waiting for an excuse.

He also saw – or felt, or imagined, he never knew for sure – all the links of a chain of events that would transform saviors into exploiters. Exploiters into opponents. Opponents into enemies. A friendly smile and figures flaunting the swastika. A terrible war devastating the entire globe; immense flashes vaporizing Brazilian cities. The Desert, at last.

"I'll be far away when that happens."

Of course you will. And that is why, Dream-Man, that you are an assassin.

He noticed, with terror, that *you are an assassin* left his own mouth.

"What is it?" yawned Nomio. His father steered the boat toward the bank.

"We have to go somewhere."

Nomio knew he wouldn't say more than that. The best thing to do was wait. See with his own eyes. Avoid annoying his father. He was every day more taciturn: whispering to the walls, making him pretend he couldn't tell what was happening. But he could tell. And it hurt like hell.

After a time that seemed longer than it actually was, his father broke the silence, speaking to himself again. Nomio followed his gaze: a recess in the shore a few dozen meters away. A mangrove swamp, thick with trees and roots, spread out into the waves, a rotten smell coming with the wind. Shortly after, a gyroplane coming from the hillside road flew over the beach, maneuvered above the waves, and hovered over the swamp, searchlights lit.

Jeronimo was already standing, removing the blanket and newspaper sheets which swathed the N12. The rifle shone in the moonlight.

"You stay here," he said to Nomio. He handed him the 96 Mauser.

"But . . ."

"If I'm not back in ten minutes, leave."

"What's going on?"

His father had already jumped into the water and was swimming toward the marsh, his right arm holding the rifle just over his head. When he penetrated the vegetation, Nomio let out a breath and draped himself over the stern. He felt the weight of the pistol in his hand. He pointed it at the gyroplane, felt his finger graze the trigger.

A shot echoed from the swamp like a small explosion.

"Dad!" yelled the boy. Without thinking twice, he threw himself into the sea.

No Matter How, It Ends Tonight

The throne room was situated on the second floor of the São Cristóvão Palace. Every time Joana Bras entered there, normally accompanied by Miguel Ventura, she admired the sumptuousness of the place, its majestic chandelier, the columns like an ancient palace. Above all, what most impressed her were the walls: painted to create the impression of high relief, they seemed to jump out at her. But this time, she didn't have time to be impressed.

Passing by the guards outside hadn't been a problem. The Aviz Ring gave her free access to the Palace, guaranteed by the Emperor himself. Joana found him sitting in a padded armchair, between two doors that led to the balcony. A blanket covered his legs up to the waist. He seemed even feebler, breathing with the help of a complex gas mask. A nurse stood at his side, ready to wipe away the saliva that ran from his mouth from time to time. In the wet nurse's lap, the Heir. Pacing from one side to the other, the Minister-President Artur Bernardes; and a National Guard official, harbinger of bad news.

Joana knelt before Dom Pedro. He motioned for her to rise with a vague movement of his head. He tried to say something, but there wasn't enough oxygen in his lungs to form the words. After calming him, she turned to Bernardes.

"He and the baby aren't safe here. We have to take them somewhere secure."

"How? The entire cabinet has been arrested, His Majesty can barely stand. The government disappeared from one moment to the next."

"And the National Guard?"

The Minister-President and the Guard official looked at each other.

The official spoke without the courage to look beyond his own boots. "The closest militia was in Jacarepaguá. All the equipment was destroyed. We're neutralized at least until the first hours of morning, when troops from other municipalities and provinces can arrive."

Joana knew what that meant: she was alone. There would be no help for several hours, if there would be any. Suddenly, she felt deeply tired.

A voice broke the silence that had taken over the room. The Emperor was trying to speak. The nurse slowly removed the oxygen mask and bent over him.

"The Emperor wants to know where his ministers and agents are," she said.

Bernardes started stuttering an explanation, but Joana interrupted him.

"Majesty, everyone left is in this room right now. The Palace is the heart of the Empire. The conspirators won't delay in coming here to stab it."

While she spoke, the official was called to the door by one of his subordinates. He returned shortly after, his face contracted in a grave expression.

"I've just been informed that Army vehicles are approaching the Palace. My men want to know what to do. I must remind you that they have families and are far outnumbered, sirs."

The Emperor mumbled again in the nurse's ear.

"His Majesty doesn't want to see the place where the memory of his parents and grandparents resides stained by the blood of his subjects. Everyone here, servants and guards, should surrender when the soldiers come in.

They heard a whirring sound.

A gyroplane descended suddenly before the windows, casting a blinding spotlight into the throne room. A megaphone thundered: "This is the Army of the Brazilian Republic. The São Cristóvão Palace is surrounded. Put down whatever weapons you have, turn over Mr Pedro Augusto Bragança of Saxe-Coburg and the child.

The baby bawled, frightened. Joana dragged herself to the Emperor and squeezed his bony hand.

"The succession . . . The prince . . ." he said, his voice so low that Joana could hardly hear. The old monarch handed her a tiny golden key. His pulse was weaker by the second. Sadly, she recognized his end was near.

Outside, the soldiers had already burst open the gate and climbed the path to the palace. They found dozens of servants leaving through the main door, hands on their heads.

Joana said goodbye to Dom Pedro III. With her heart pounding, she took the baby from the wet nurse's lap. The child was crying. She pulled the tiny copy of the old Emperor against her chest and walked to the throne.

"What are you doing?" asked Bernardes, his arms held up like a pedestrian surprised by a thief.

"I'm taking the Prince away from here. But I need help." She fit the key in a discreet elevation on the throne's backrest. With a crack, the imperial chair slid to one side, revealing a passage.

A warning shot hit the wall above her head.

"Get away from there," growled the megaphone. Joana shrunk back.

The guard looked at her, then at the baby. He drew his pistol.

"Go," he said. He turned and unloaded the weapon against the gyroplane. The aircraft retreated some meters, a spotlight blown.

"Thanks," responded Joana, diving into the passageway. She still had time to see the door close down before the throne slid back. She descended a ladder as fast as she could with only one free hand. She tried not to think about shots and death.

The descent was longer than she imagined.

She reached a dark chamber, probably contiguous with the generator that fed the Palace, judging by the electric buzz she heard. There was a corridor there. She followed it, her back bent to not hit her head on the low roof. Small lamps lit up when she passed.

The corridor was also longer than she expected.

She calculated walking for fifteen or twenty minutes before reaching a wall of wet bricks with a cross hanging on it. Apparently, the exit was a hatch just above her head. With some difficulty, she opened the rusty iron and climbed into a miniscule room. The only door was locked by a device composed of three bolts and a cylinder. The ring was the key. She put it in the cylinder, turned it. The door opened.

The moon's yellowish halo had begun to overpower the clouds. She tried to figure out where she was. She had just left a hut, concrete on the inside and slats on the outside, embedded in a hillside, after crossing almost two thousand meters underground. Ahead, a deck rose above the rocks to the sea. Anyone looking down from the road railing behind her would see nothing more than a fisherman's shed.

Joana walked to the edge of the deck. Where there should have been a motorboat waiting for the Emperor, only waves licking the rocks. She descended to the narrow strip of sand that ringed the beach up to a mangrove swamp. She didn't know what to do, nor where to go, the baby's sharp sobbing boring into her ears. She was scared. She didn't have much time to think on it, however: an HS-4 gyroplane passed, flying low, toward the water.

Joana ran as fast as she could. She plunged into the swamp. Her feet sank in the mud. She held the baby with one hand, while she released the safety on the Tokarev with the other. The gyroplane flew over the mazelike vegetation, forcing her to crawl through a tangle of roots. Flightlight beams passed nearby.

The baby began bawling again. She pulled him close to her face, softly begging him not to cry, please, or they would both die. By a miracle, he went quiet, watching her with big, blue eyes. Joana was going to smile, but a sudden glare descended on her, forcing her to flee. The sea appeared among the jumbled branches.

There was nowhere to go.

Resigned, she stopped running.

Just before the gyroplane backed off and disappeared behind the road, she saw a figure leap from it to the mud, then lift itself heavily. There was a star on its chest. Sheriff's star, cowboy hat. Rubber gloves reached almost to his elbows, and served as insulation from the electric rifle he pointed in her direction.

Joana raised the Tokarev, but wasn't fast enough. A ray traversed her chest, knocking her backward into the mud. The blood spread quickly. Everything became cold, except the baby, suddenly irradiating heat like the sun.

Poor baby.

The star grew in her field of vision. She remembered a character from an adventure supplement, what was his name? He used a white shirt, red tights, blue underpants, a mask over his eyes. Mysterious and handsome.

Democrata, that was his name.

The rifle in her face wasn't as scary as the growing sound of accumulating electricity. She hated getting shocked.

Jeronimo Trovao hit the star dead center with his N12. The American reeled back, but didn't fall. Part of the uniform's cloth disappeared, revealing reinforced ceramic plating. *Killer*, Jeronimo said to himself. He knew that man would raise the weapon and explode his head in the next second if he didn't take advantage of this chance. He raised the sight a little and shot again. A mixture of sparks and something like blood exploded from the American's neck. He fell to his knees, then to one side.

Easier than Jeronimo had expected. He needed to get out of there before the gyroplane's occupants realized what had happened. He bent down near the woman. A river of blood sprouted from her chest and mouth. He recognized her. Jeronimo could hear a low whistle when she tried to breathe. Even in agony, she didn't release the child which sobbed in her arm. She grabbed Jeronimo's shirt and tried to say something. All that came out was a gurgle.

Take the Emperor, Dream-Man, said the Saint, her blue veil whipping like it were alive.

"I can't do that," said Jeronimo.

He'll die if you leave him here. One more death on your long list. A death that will never stop tormenting you. A death that will bring other deaths. Save him, he will show you the way. Don't kill the boy, Dream-Man.

Don't kill the boy. The sentence deadened his thoughts. She had harassed him for so long, brought him to this place. Don't kill the boy.

Joana no longer breathed. Her eyes were glassy. Jeronimo took the baby from her hands. The poor kid was soaked, his little lips purple. He trembled with cold.

Dream-man, screamed the Saint.

Jeronimo hardly had time to lift his head. Thirteen's boot met his nose and threw him three meters, where the mud disappeared below the sea water. His vision blurred, the swamp whirled. The baby was no longer in his arms. He could hear its cries nearby, mixed with the Saint's hysterical chatter warning him of something. I know, he wanted to say, but the American was already on top of him, holding him by the collar.

"I'll kill you with my own hands, monkey," he said, a voice speaking in English and sounding like a badly tuned radio. He was so close that Jeronimo could feel the warm liquid which ran from its open neck drip on his skin. It wasn't blood. It was oil. The American wasn't all meat, after all. He thought of spitting in the foreigner's face, like the heroes did in those magazines his son adored. But there was no hero there, and all he could do was close his eyes and try to endure the blows that battered his face. One, two, three, seven, ten of them in sequence, overpowering like a sledgehammer.

Then the slow drowning began.

Iron hands forced his head under.

The air painfully leaving his chest. The lungs becoming like bricks. The Saint's voice filtered by the water.

Time to die, he thought.

Not yet.

Later, all that Deuteronomio Trovao remembered was closing his eyes and pulling the trigger until his fingers hurt and the ammunition ran out. And he also remembered someone saying: *I'll guide your hand.*

There were nine shots and a lot of luck.

Thirteen staggered, disoriented, the remote receptor destroyed by the bullets. Unable to receive commands from his Controller, he tumbled into the mud.

Nomio searched for the voice's owner. Standing near a crying baby, a tall man faced him. White shirt with a big star on the chest, red tights, blue underwear, a mask over his eyes. That was Democrata, his favorite hero. In the middle of the mud, speaking with him. His favorite hero. He rubbed his eyes. He was still there.

You need to get your father and the kid before those men arrive, Democrata said, pointing to the far away road. *Or things are going to get complicated.*

Nomio took the baby into his arms.

"Help me take them to the boat."

You can't go back to the boat. The helicopter would be on you before you made it thirty meters. You'd be turned into a sifter.

"So, what do I do?"

Calm down. I'll lead you down a completely new path.

"Who are you talking to?" grunted Jeronimo. He looked like a drunk trying not to fall.

"To Mr Democrata."

"Who's Mr Democrata?"

"He's right here, Dad. By my side. He's going to show us the way to escape."

Jeronimo supported himself on the roots. He looked around, then at his son. Nomio held the baby in his arms, the pistol stuffed into his belt, just above the water. There was no one beside him.

When he finally understood, Jeronimo Trovao burst out laughing. It was his form of panic.

Epilogue

General Vargas listened to opera.

It was as if his music spread around the world.

He closed his eyes to appreciate the violins.

Then came the oboes, the bassoons, the machine guns downing integralists and alliance members by the dozens.

A chorus of angelic voices.

Upriver, a boat motor. The baby had finally calmed down, rolled up in the blanket that had once covered the rifle. Jeronimo Trovao and his son sat in silence for a long time, on their way to oblivion in a lost town in rural wherever. The killer and his boys.

Cymbals, drums, trombones. The night was dying.

The first orange spots began to appear in the lower part of the sky, spilling over the aircraft carrier which maneuvered in the bay. The admiral had received congratulations from his president, satisfied with the results obtained in the field tests. Despite the damage suffered by the Thirteen prototype, luckily recovered in time, remote-controlled soldiers had proven themselves viable. Far from there, however, sitting on their skull and bone thrones in an obscure Yale University building, the true rulers of the United States of America wanted much more.

In some place of time, space, or memory, Saint Anthony awoke to confront the demons of the Desert.

Blood and Gold

Erin M. Hartshorn

The dragon, Rashall, clung to the skeleton that would be the Chrysler Building and gazed toward the port, his eyesight bringing everything into sharp focus as though it were mere wingspans away. Stevedores and dockhands labored, offloading the casks and crates full of contraband alcohol under the watchful gaze of the well-paid policeman, there solely to ensure no one took the bootlegged items except those who had actually paid for them.

A voice raised in a panicked scream from a nearby street, and Rashall swung his head. His eyes took a moment to refocus. By the time he saw the woman, her body lay on the street, blood across her chest. His feet released from the girders, and he dove at the body, his wings folded back against his trunk, an arrow fired without a bow.

Closer, he unfurled his wings to brake his momentum. He alit softly to the street, sheltering the woman beneath his chest. Her hat had fallen from her head, and blood speckled the pearls on her neck. Her perfume mixed with the grime of the streets and the tang of her spilled blood. He raised a claw and touched it to her chest, letting the red liquid wick up into his reservoir. If he were human, he might feel guilt at hastening her death, but he had no room for such an emotion.

He could do nothing for her, but she could help him, for just a short while.

A whistle sounded close by, its shriek rising over jazz notes from a hidden club, and one of his ears twitched in response. It was time to go. He gathered his legs beneath him and bounded up the side of the buildings. No flight, not yet, but soon – he'd need more blood to fuel that. The police would not look up, however; he was safe.

Another night, another bit of life snatched from oblivion. He'd been living on borrowed time since February, when he left Chicago. The other dragons had come too close that time. Three months now of being on the run, with no safe house on the horizon, no one to turn to. Even Lillie was dead now – not in Chicago, but out of the country, dead of old age. His one pet who had never failed him, and now he had no time to take another such. Just as well. He'd always outlived his pets, but she – she had been special.

He rippled his black scales. What was wrong with him? This was no time to indulge in nostalgia, not if he wanted to survive. He spared a glance for the scene below. The flatfoot whose arrival had necessitated Rashall's departure now blew his whistle again, summoning aid from the dark streets. Other footsteps rushed toward him, and a Black Mariah, not that there was anyone to lock up. Whoever the woman had been, the police cared. All the more reason for him not to be on the scene.

Slithering to the top of the building, he slipped onto the warm rooftop, grateful that the night was not yet hot enough for the building's residents to come up in an attempt to escape the heat in their apartments. He would wait here until the excitement died below, and then he would seek shelter before dawn. Somewhere to hide without fear of machine guns and alcohol.

Blood – he needed more. Gold would be better, and since the end of the Great War, it had been easier than ever to obtain here in the States. Still it was rarer to come across than blood, which there was in plenty, and both the police and the bootleggers only too willing to spill more. That, indeed, had been why he had fled; if anything, there had been too much blood in Chicago, enough to make the other dragons look for him there. They had seen his hand in the mobs.

That was what he truly feared, not discovery by humans. But if humans found him, word would reach dragons soon enough. Thus, he hid from all sight.

He still needed a plan. Snatching what he could kept him alive, barely, but what he needed was sustainable life, somewhere to live – and enough gold to live on. That was why he was in New York. With High Society and the Jazz Age, people living high, there were riches to be had. Maybe, just maybe, the warmth and pulse of the dead woman's blood would stir his mind and enable him to think more than an hour into the future, past finding somewhere to hide from the daylight gaze of humans once more.

A quiet thought nudged him, telling him he should find the woman's murderer. Not even her pearls had been taken – there was money and blood behind this death, a warning to someone for stepping on another operation's toes. A severe warning – the one she was close to had to have ignored more subtle menace. The one who had ordered this death had money, could get Rashall gold.

Or perhaps he should find out who she was, who was being warned off. He wouldn't be getting this warning if he weren't a threat, and the next step was obviously the man's own death. He might pay well, in bullion and coins, to avoid that fate.

Who would pay him more? Again, he missed having a pet, someone to look at this incident and tell him about the people involved, tell him who had more to give him. He would sleep on the question, let the sun warm his body, stir him, and when night came once more, listen near to the great jazz clubs or to laughter and gossip coming from the Upper East Side high-rises, the places where the rich looked down on the rest of the world.

Satisfied that he knew what he was doing, the dragon sought a familiar resting place, the roof patch between a stairwell and an abandoned rooftop pigeon coop. Very few places looked down on this roof, and those that did – well, the workers on Chrysler's new building were too busy riveting steel to pay attention to a lump of rubbish somewhere else. He jumped up and over, moving swiftly and surely to his accustomed spot.

On the edge of the rooftop, he paused. The faint scent of blood tickled at him, mixed with the woman's perfume. She was not here, could not be, but her killer – ah, yes, he might be, and with the bloody knife still on him, as strong as it smelled. Rashall needed to learn more. He slid forward, a sinuous shadow surrounding the pigeon coop.

The man inside the coop did not smell of beer or whiskey, and the only tobacco smoke on him clung to his clothes, not his breath. In fact, other than the smell of blood and perfume, the man was clean. That much the dragon could tell before he even saw the man.

But cleanliness implied a home, somewhere to go, and a hand behind him who wasn't just after deniability. Why come here, then?

Even huddled in the far corner of the coop, with the shadow of the roof over him, the man was clear to the dragon's sight. His clothes were more informal than his victim's – suspenders, no jacket, not even a tie. However, he clearly had access to some money, as his fedora and wristwatch were new. As to why he'd hidden here, that, too, was clear to the dragon's sight: four scratches across his left cheek, no doubt left by the dead woman. If any beat cop saw that, the man would be taken in right away, at least now that the woman had been found. If she hadn't screamed, if he could have hid her body away in an alley, he could've walked down the street without a care, knowing that the only comments he'd get were on the appropriate punishment of the dame who'd done that to him.

"Why did you do it?"

The man startled, banging his head against the wall, then leaned forward, peering intently to see who was speaking. He said nothing.

Rashall moved closer, out of the shadow of the stairwell, where the moonlight would glint off his scales. He repeated his question. "Why did you kill her?"

If a disembodied voice had spooked the man, seeing the dragon terrified him. He paled and shrank back into the corner as if he could disappear. Still he said nothing.

For a brief moment, Rashall considered draining the man of blood. It would be enough to power flight for a short distance. The woman's blood came to his rescue, reminding him that was short-term thinking. He could use this man, this puppet, to get him more, to let him be free of pursuit.

The man, however, didn't need to know the dragon wouldn't kill him.

Surging forward, Rashall laid one claw on the side of the man's neck. "Why?"

The man's voice quavered. "It wasn't personal or nothing. It was just a job. I didn't know you wanted her safe."

"You didn't even know I existed."

"That's true enough." His Adam's apple bobbed nervously. "How could I? But honest, I wouldn't have killed her if I had."

His voice ended as a squeak, and the dragon let the silence settle around them. If there was one thing he was good at, it was waiting.

Finally, the man broke the silence again. "Sparky Jones paid me. I was just supposed to kill her, leave her where she could be found, and vanish."

"Who was she to Sparky Jones? An inconvenience? A loose end?"

"I don't know. I don't. I've been trying to get the attention of one of the big shots higher up, move up in the world, you know? This was my chance, and I didn't ask no questions."

If the man was going to be this useless, Rashall might as well kill him. First, though, he needed whatever information he could get.

"So who was she? He had to give you a name, a way to find her."

"Hazel. Hazel McIntyre. Said she'd be at the Brass Ring most nights."

The Brass Ring being the night club on the street below. "Sparky own the Brass Ring?"

The man barked a laugh. "Sparky and Dutch don't get along no how. And if he did own the Brass Ring, he'd just have someone slip her a bad drink, you know? Easy way to off her with no one the wiser."

"So Sparky had Hazel killed to send a message to Dutch, then?"

The man frowned as he thought that over. "That could be. It's not as obvious as a hit on the club, but if Sparky did that, he'd have to buy off the coppers that Dutch is paying, and he wouldn't want to do that."

Of course not. The dragon understood men like Sparky and Dutch, with their urge to gather money and gain territory.

These men were dragons at heart, even if gold didn't actually prolong their lives. The cardinal rule of such men was to never spend money you didn't have to.

"Why Hazel? Why not a random hit on whoever was leaving the club?"

The man's eyes shifted sideways, looking away from the dragon. "Sparky didn't tell me."

Rashall's claw scratched the man's throat – not over the jugular or the carotid, barely enough to draw blood, but enough to scare the man in front of him, who yelped in response. "You're holding something back from me. Tell me about tonight."

"All right, all right. I got there early, hanging out on the street, looking like I was trying to decide whether I had enough money to go in. Flatfoot ran me off, but not before I saw the doll going in on Dutch's arm. She was no It Girl, but I figured they'd be a while, so I ankled it and came back just a bit ago to catch her coming out."

"And no one around to see?"

"A couple other birds, but they'd had way too much of the giggle water and headed the other way down the street. So I cozied up to Hazel, told her she looked a real biscuit and asked if she wanted to go to a petting party I knew of. That's when she scratched me. I just bumped her off right there in the street and lammed it. What else was I going to do?"

The dragon puzzled through this narrative. "Where was this party you were going to take her to?"

"There weren't no party, see? I just wanted her to follow me where I wasn't going to get caught by the shamos."

This man was worthless. Rashall could ask him to go bring gold, to use information or ideas the dragon gave him to play the stock market, but Rashall could never trust him. Sparky probably didn't even trust him, merely gave him the job to see if it would get done.

Twitching his nail against the man's neck, the dragon growled. "Where can I find Sparky Jones?"

"He's at the warehouse tonight, checking on the shipment that's coming in. He won't be alone – lots of guys around, including a handful of cops, ready to swear they were playing poker when the dame bought it. Hell, for all I know, that's exactly what they're doing while guys like me break our backs moving the booze. Does he know you wanted her alive?"

The dragon considered before answering. Twice now, the man had assumed Rashall cared about keeping the woman alive, as though she were his latest pet, instead of a bare meal he'd had, something to tide him over. But that would work for the dragon.

"I doubt it. He knows of my existence no more than you did. He will before the night is over, however."

"How you going to catch him by hisself?" The man was entirely too curious. Time to quash that.

"Perhaps I won't. I rather think anyone babbling about seeing me is going to wind up either arrested as drunk or shipped off to – what's the name of the local facility? Pilgrim?"

Judging by the man's shudder, that was the place. Not that it mattered. Rashall had no intention of being seen by anyone who would or could talk about it later. Humans might not believe, but other dragons would.

The first loose end to tie up was the man before him. Quickly, Rashall placed his nail against the scratch he'd already made and let the blood wick upward. The man beat at the claw and tried to pull away, but he had nowhere to go. Soon, he collapsed, faint from blood loss. Killing him outright, however, wasn't the plan.

The man's tongue took a couple tries to pull out, and more blood was spilled. He would not be speaking of what he'd seen. Would he try his hand at writing it down? Not the way he'd blanched at the mention of the mental institution. Rashall would be safe.

The dragon scooped the man up with one foreleg and skittered down the side of the building on his remaining legs, pausing above the level where the people below would be looking. Yes, there were still police all over the area. Dutch must really care about the dead woman; there would be a bloodbath coming, one way or another.

More slowly, sticking to the shadows, Rashall slipped lower, angling for the nearest alley. There, he deposited the man in the shadows, then banged deliberately against the cans and refuse scattered about before scarpering up the side of the building once more.

Whistles sounded, and feet pounded as men converged on the alley. Above, Rashall listened to accusations of sloppiness and excuses for missing the man on the first try. What would they make of the man's missing tongue? Not that it mattered; the scratches on the man's face and the bloody knife in his pocket painted his guilt clear for all to see.

Now Rashall had business elsewhere. Between Hazel and this man, he had blood enough to keep him for a while, but that just meant clearer thinking, planning even further ahead instead of scraping out survival by the day or week.

The dragon could use his information to gain concessions from Sparky, but would Sparky be a source of what the dragon really needed? He wasn't likely to have bullion, and might not even have much specie on hand, unless he was stockpiling that rather than drawing attention to himself by banking the money. Some of the mob bosses were going to get themselves in trouble that way eventually, but maybe Sparky was brighter than that.

He'd have to be if Rashall was going to work with him.

Rashall had to wait to catch Sparky alone, first until the shipment had moved from the docks to the warehouse, then for the police dancing around each other with Dutch's paid men unable to say the others were dirty liars and Sparky's asking whether the others wanted to sit in on the next hand of poker, and finally for Sparky to send his men out of his office, leaving fewer witnesses.

The gunsels weren't the brightest of guards. They didn't have to be; they only had to shoot anything they saw moving. Sadly for their boss, they never saw Rashall move.

He slid into Sparky's office, high over the warehouse floor. Sparky had some trinkets lying around – a pile or two of bills, a jade vase, and an oil painting leaning against the wall were readily seen. There was gold, too, though Rashall couldn't see it. He could smell it, and that was enough. He knew it was there.

"Why did you have her killed?"

Sparky didn't look up from his books. "I don't know what you're talking about."

It was the same response he'd given Dutch's cops earlier.

The dragon threw the hired man's tongue onto Sparky's desk. "That's not what I heard."

Sparky pushed his chair back violently. "What the hell is this?"

"The killer's tongue. I don't like being lied to."

"Who – what – are you?"

Fear. Yes, he could work with that. Especially with such a clearly intelligent man.

"Your new boss."

"I don't work for no one," Sparky said, getting to his feet and reaching for a gun that lay next to his blotter.

Rashall moved before Sparky had time to blink, knocking over his chair and pinning him against the wall. "You do if you want to live." He eased up his pressure so Sparky could put his feet back down on the ground. "It's not like anyone but you and I will ever know."

"You think you can just waltz in here and take over?"

"You think you can spend any of your money if I kill you now?"

Sparky paused, and he stared upward as if doing calculations in his head. Debating whether he could get away? Or trying to decide how little a cut he could get away with? "So say you do come on board as some sort of silent partner – what's in it for me? Or you just planning on taking all the money without taking any of the risks?"

Sensible questions, assuming Sparky got anything besides his life out of it. But Rashall knew the man would be less likely to rat out the dragon if he had an investment to protect. Rashall released Sparky. "I'll give you investment advice, help you build your empire into a legitimate business that'll keep going even if Prohibition doesn't. Together, we'll own this town."

"Yeah? And what do you want in return?"

"Blood and gold. Blood and gold."

Floodgate

Dan Rabarts

September 1922 (Year eight of the Great War of Empire)
Northern Sahara Desert, Tunisia

Rubber screeched and wind roared as Flight Lieutenant Flinder hoisted the airbrakes to full. The Sopwith Wildebeest's Vickers engine howled, a squealing descant of gasoline and hot metal, momentum battling the will of the pilot as she choked back the throttle and fought to keep the biplane in a straight line. The aircraft hurtled down the impromptu desert runway, bouncing as the wheels shredded dust and loose stones. Flinder grappled with the jerking stick, swallowing her rising panic. At any moment a chance collision with a stone could tip her crippled craft, a wingtip grabbing the earth and sending the whole plane cartwheeling in a bright blossom of fire, torn metal and splintered timber. Then the tailwheel touched dirt, inertia and gravity asserted control, and the plane slowed.

Flinder breathed deep as the Wildebeest decelerated to taxiing pace, the engine coughing and missing. She nudged the biplane around in a half circle, until she was facing back the way she'd come, looking through the blur of the propeller at the trail of smoke that marked her descent. Small dark shapes looped and arced against the clear sky amid crisscrossing streaks of black. Cannon-fire flashed bright like summer lightning. Flinder breathed the smell of motor oil, hot metal and woodsmoke. Her eyes settled briefly on the blood spattering the glass, before she realized that one of those black dots was coming around, bearing this way. Probably the Hun blighter that had peppered her plane and co-pilot full of lead. She twisted to look over her shoulder, confirming what she already knew: Croft hung slumped in his straps, his leathers soaked in blood. Maybe, if she could haul his dead weight from the cockpit and get to the cannon controls in time, she could shoot down the incoming *Fliegertruppe*. But she would be open to the enemy's machine guns, and the same burst of fire that had ripped through the plane might've shredded the wire controls that swiveled and fired the rear cannon armament.

Either way, she'd be a sitting duck. She and the photographs that Croft had died for; photographs that filled her with dread every time she thought of what she had seen in the lake at Tunis. More urgently, the smoke was growing thicker, and she could smell fuel. It might only be minutes before fuel met flames and fire engulfed the Wildebeest.

"Sorry, mate," Flinder said, tugging her tinted goggles over her eyes and wishing there were more words. Her skill as a pilot had served her well, up until now. This time, it hadn't served Croft a damn.

Like her hands in the rising waters, hadn't been enough to save Matthew.

The dot swelled against the cloudless sky, taking on the silhouette of a biplane. Flinder unclasped her belts, hooked the survival pack from under her seat onto her back and jerked the Enfield rifle from its restraints before sliding out of the plane, into the desert heat. Buffeted by the reek of fuel, oil and smoke, she released the bolts latching the hatch on the fuselage's underside. The camera folded down on slick oiled hinges, miraculously unharmed by the Fokker's deadly burst. Disconnecting armatures and releasing the straps that held the cumbersome camera on its spring mountings, she lowered it into her arms and set off at a run. From the distinctive thrum of its engine, Flinder guessed the approaching plane was a Hannover CL.IV, sent to destroy the grounded aircraft and its precious cargo. Pilot and tailgunner both would be looking for survivors, fingers ready on triggers. The Wildebeest was a goner, Croft was going to be cremated and, if she didn't get to cover, she'd be shredded by German lead and left for dead in the desert. The photos taken over Tunis, lost.

Flinder kept running.

Sound in the desert was treacherous, bouncing off hardpan and the surrounding foothills, so when she heard the rumble of an engine up ahead she thought it was merely an echo of the approaching attack plane. Up until the moment the halftrack crested a rise in front of her. The clatter of its crawlers filled her with dread, memories of tanks appearing across the trenches of France.

Just a few hundred yards away. Scrambling to get airborne, shellfire erupting around her . . .

Flinder darted toward a tumble of rocks as the armor-plated quad-barreled cannon turret rotated, then fired. Once. Twice. Three times. Flinder slid into cover, tucking the camera to her chest and ducking her head. The Hannover's roar changed to a fiery metallic shriek punctured by the detonation of airborne shells. Behind her, the fireball plummeted to the desert floor.

Ears ringing, heart racing, Flinder picked herself up and started forward. Presuming this was indeed an ally and not just a misguided German patrol vehicle, she could hopefully find transport, maybe even commandeer another plane, and get the film to Tripoli where Command was amassing to strike against Tunis. They would go into the battle forewarned; that was, if anyone could make sense of the formless shapes half-sunken in the waters of the lake behind the seawall.

The halftrack's passenger door opened and a soldier stepped out, dressed in New Zealand khakis, his skin a rich brown.

Flinder recoiled before she could stop herself. Recovering, she bit her lip and threw the officer an abrupt salute. "Captain."

Through tinted goggles, the captain looked her over, returning the salute. "Nice landing, Lieutenant." He scanned the desert and the smoldering wreck of her biplane. "What about your co-pilot?"

Flinder shook her head. "He didn't make it."

"Well, we can't leave the poor bugger there, eh?" The captain signaled at the truck. With a yell, a door clattered open and half a dozen soldiers appeared, hurrying to the captain. Flinder stiffened, but said nothing.

"Sergeant Rapu, check the plane, and if it's safe, retrieve the body inside."

Flinder drew back, startled, as the squad of burly *Māori* troopers set off at a run toward the smoking Wildebeest. "Captain," she read the name on his khakis, struggling to pronounce it, "Hara-wear-a? The plane's on fire and leaking fuel. It could go up any moment."

"That's why my *toa* are running, Lieutenant. And it's *Harawera*. Looks like we got here just in time, for you *and* your friend."

No, she thought, *it's too late for Croft*. But she said, "How did you know?"

Harawera shrugged. "We saw a plane coming down, figured if it was one of ours, we could pick up any survivors. If it was one of theirs? We'd make sure there weren't any. Did you save your radio?"

Flinder ground her teeth. "No." And she'd thought she had a chance of surviving in the desert? Idiot!

"No worries. If you've got any messages for Command, I can get our operator to pass them on. Transmission's terrible through here anyway."

Flinder nodded. "I got reconnaissance photos over Tunis. I need to get this film to Tripoli."

"But you've seen what's there? In Tunis?"

She nodded. "Yes, sir."

"Then you know why we can't turn back. You're part of Company E now."

"But Command—"

He waved a hand vaguely. "Command tasked us with handling what's happening at Tunis. Did you know it's built on the site of the ancient city of Carthage?" He grinned, his dark features spreading in an easy manner Flinder didn't find reassuring. Abruptly, he changed the subject. "You're Aussie, eh?"

"Yessir. Seconded to the British Royal Flying Corps."

Harawera nodded. "New Zealand *Māori* Battalion, but you probably guessed that, eh."

Flinder frowned. "I thought the *Māori* Battalion were pioneers? You look more like a combat squad than engineers."

Infuriatingly, Harawera ignored her question, and pointed at the blood on her face.

"Any of that yours?"

Flinder touched a gloved hand to the stickiness on her cheek. "Um, no, I don't think so . . ."

"Corporal Patua," Harawera yelled. "Bring your gear!"

"Captain, I'm . . ."

Harawera held up a hand, as another *Māori* soldier wearing a white armband emblazoned with a red cross emerged from the halftrack and came their way, bearing a heavy medical supply pack. He set his bag down and began looking her over.

"Lot of blood, eh? Get your flight cap off for me, Lieutenant."

Reluctantly, Flinder removed her cap and goggles, peeling the leather away from her skin where blood was congealing in the heat. Patua doused a white bandage in water from a canteen and reached for her.

Flinder flinched away.

Patua cocked his head. "Haven't even touched you yet. Where's it hurt?"

Flinder stepped away from him, her pulse pounding, her throat tight. "No, don't touch . . . I'm not hurt, it's all Croft's blood, I . . ." She clenched her teeth, her grief undercut with revulsion. "Honestly, I'm fine. Can I, maybe, just get out of the sun?"

Camera clutched to her chest, she walked toward the halftrack, giving Patua and Harawera both a wide berth. The sun pounded her into the ground, yet just for a moment she was cold, right to her core.

She eased herself down against the halftrack's front wheel, thankful for the meagre shade. Laying the rifle on the dirt and resting the camera on her knees, she uncapped her canteen and swigged water that tasted like sand and oil, bitterness and blood. The taste wasn't in the water, but in her mouth.

"Lieutenant?" Patua crouched beside her, his voice warm as the earth. "You survived being shot down. I gotta check to see if you're hurt. Don't want anything going septic, eh?"

"Don't touch me," she growled, low in her throat. The last thing she wanted right now was a *Māori* man putting his filthy hands all over her. She could feel the rage, building up like floodwater against riverbanks, her horizon black with rain. She wrung her hands, haunted by the memory of fingers slipping from hers; a memory she had crossed the world to escape.

Patua offered her the cloth. "Here you go. You do it then."

She snatched the cloth. Through the heat haze, a clutch of soldiers were moving their way, carrying a limp figure between them, while a pillar of fire clawed the sky behind them. She bit her lip and began to wipe away the blood and the dirt, the water cool as death on her skin.

Harawera found Flinder pouring tea from a billy. The rest of the column was spread out behind the halftrack; two more anti-aircraft halftracks, six troop trucks, a supply truck, a fuel tanker, a water tanker, and two Holt tractors hauling eighteen-pounder cannons. The captain handed his cup toward her to be filled. Her spine stiffened. White-knuckled, she tipped the pot for him.

"I'd heard there were women flying missions in Europe. Never met one before now," he said, tipping his cap to her.

Flinder fussed with the billy, avoiding his gaze. "Safer than being on the ground."

"How long've you been flying?"

She sipped her tea. "I trained back home in 'sixteen, got shipped out to Europe and began flying recon missions over France."

"So you've lasted six years? Reckon that must be some kind of record."

Flinder paled, remembering the many she had known, now gone. "For combat pilots, maybe. Six *weeks* is a long run for fighters. Recon's a bit different."

"Still, you're a target up there. That takes guts. Makes you wonder if the war's just not done with you yet." Harawera blew over his mug. "Lucky for us we found you, then. When we get to Tunis, I could use your skills. You know what we're up against."

Flinder shook her head. "No, I don't really." She never wanted to get that close to those gently bobbing shapes in the water again. The mere memory of them chilled her blood. "I'm not sure if I can be of any help, Captain."

"You mean you can't, or you won't?" Harawera's tone didn't change despite the accusation in his words. "We're all fighting for the same thing." There was more he didn't say, Flinder knew, which twisted her up on the inside, but she refused to bite. "If you've got a problem with me or my company, you leave it back there in the desert. We've all got each other's backs. Yours too. Understood?"

Flinder glared, hating so many things about him she'd never voice. It was bad enough that she was a lone woman surrounded by men, indebted to them for her life, and that she felt as much a target here as she ever had in the sky. But of all the people to pull her out of the teeth of certain death, why did it have to be the *Māori* Battalion . . . ? "With all due respect," she grated, "why have they sent you? Honestly? Tunis is a fortified city. It'll take bombing raids and divisions of infantry and artillery and naval bombardment to push the Germans out. You've got what, a hundred men?" Even if High Command felt the same about the South Pacific natives as she did, they weren't inclined to throw soldiers away for no good reason. "It's suicide."

Harawera shrugged. "You go to war. You follow orders, right?"

"Of course."

Harawera nodded. The sound of a guitar and voices drifted across the dark, filling the void between them with song.

"You know what they're doing out there?" He gestured toward the sound of singing, rising into the night in a language Flinder guessed was *Māori*. "They're digging your boy a grave. Wishing him safe to the other side." He handed her a shovel. "Why don't you go show your appreciation?"

She took the shovel, tipped the dregs of her tea in the dirt, and stalked toward the low glimmer of gas lamps at the edge of the camp. Only when it was completely dark did she let a tear escape, and even then only one.

North of the Sahara, the foothills of the Atlas Mountains surrounding Tunis were largely wooded in stunted, dry trees that reminded Flinder of her Darwin home. They muffled much of the rumble of engines and the clatter of treads that would've otherwise signaled the company's advance. Perhaps because the *Fliegertruppen* were looking east, to the Mediterranean and the Libyan desert, *Māori* Battalion Company E were able to bring their two eighteen-pounders, three anti-aircraft cannons, a few machine guns and roughly eighty rifles within range of the city, under cover of the paper-thin scrub canopy. Either that, or the German garrison never anticipated anyone would have the audacity to drive into range of the city and set up their guns.

Flinder lay on her belly a short distance from the infantry. The city and airfield spread out beneath them, the ancient Carthaginian walls dim moonlit silhouettes in the pre-dawn gloom. The wide black expanse of the two saltwater lakes that lay between city and sea; in one of those lurked the outline of a German dreadnought, bristling with cannons. In the other the hulk of a scuttled French tanker ship and, though Flinder couldn't see them, a string of orbs like massive pearls, just below the surface. Each a dreadful promise.

"Lieutenant?"

Flinder flinched at the whispered voice at her shoulder.

"Sergeant."

"Sorry Miss, didn't mean to startle you." Uninvited, Sergeant Rapu wriggled down beside her. "You're not scared, are you? The Captain's got it all worked out."

"I'm not," she lied. "But I've seen what happens when too few men try to take fortified positions. They end up in the ground."

Rapu's teeth gleamed in the darkness. "That's not why we're here."

Flinder felt suddenly sick. Harawera had made sure she didn't have her radio. She didn't know if he'd actually transmitted her messages to Command, in the days it had taken them to advance on Tunis. He'd said he would, but had he? "Please don't tell me this isn't a sanctioned mission."

"OK," Rapu said, looking away. "I won't."

Flinder curbed a sudden nausea, a chill like the waters of the Blackmore River, rising around her while she screamed. "It's them, isn't it? The things in the lake."

"*Taniwha*, Miss."

"What?"

"Monsters, if you like."

She half coughed, half laughed, and shook her head.

"When did you stop believing in magic, Lieutenant? Was it before or after you first flew in the sky?"

Flinder was about to say something about how only ignorant savages believed in magic but, instead, she bit her tongue. Whatever their color, she owed Company E her life. She could at least show them some good manners. "That's not magic. That's mechanical."

"Maybe it's just magic with a different name," Harawera said, behind her, as if he'd been there all along, corpse silent.

"But you've decided to commandeer Empire soldiers and equipment and carry out an illegal combat mission, because you people still believe in magic?"

"We people? *We people* are here to do something that has to be done. The *Māori* are an ancient race. We haven't lost our warrior ways, or forgotten our legends. You've seen the shadow on the lake. Stirs the blood, doesn't it?" Harawera crouched and lifted a set of binoculars. "Even when memory fails, blood doesn't. We haven't forgotten our *taniwha*. We can *feel* them. I felt them when we landed in Tripoli.

"The British located this one and its eggs in a loch. Evidently the Kaiser learned about them when he was there, years ago. Mad old bastard's been plotting this for a long time. Because it's a sea creature, its eggs wouldn't hatch. But it's not a mortal creature either; it survived in the cold fresh water of the loch even if it didn't thrive. It just waited for the world to turn, for its time to come again."

Flinder shivered. "Pretending you're right, and this isn't some sunstroke delusion come from being too long in the desert, how did they move them, and why bring them here? Why Tunisia?"

"See, that's the wrong question," Harawera said.

"How about," Rapu offered, "Why *Carthage*?"

Flinder gritted her teeth, irritation heavy in her voice. "OK, I'll play along. Let's say the Germans have gone to all the effort of surreptitiously kidnapping a sea monster and its eggs from a Scottish lake while they're trying to hold Europe and fight a war in the Middle East and now Africa. How'd they move them anyway?"

"Blimps, apparently, and then a stolen French tanker ship. That one, down there." He pointed to the scuttled hulk that blocked the seaward entrance to the southern lake.

"Then why dump them in Tunisia?"

"It's all here," Harawera said, his voice suddenly weary, like he'd only made it this far by feeding on his own fear and desperation. "The lake is warm, salty, but it's more than that. The Romans sowed the land with salt after they destroyed Carthage, so nothing would ever grow here. But they sowed more than just salt. They sowed their hatred into the earth as well."

Flinder could feel the weight of that hatred, crushing up against her, like the waters of the Blackmore breaking free, rushing over the gurgling earth, sweeping everything away beneath the raging black sky.

Matthew, riding out under those howling skies, because of the girl. The girl their father had said he wasn't to see, because she was a filthy Abo, riddled with sin and disease. Because he'd catch the black off her, and no son of his was going to have mongrel kids, thank you very much. Black girl like that would only get a good white boy into trouble.

Elizabeth is only a minute behind him, riding through the thrashing rain, the trees screeching and bending in the gale, and he won't turn back, not even with his sister screaming at him as best she can over the cyclone howl.

Flinder blinked away the memory. "So you're here to destroy the eggs? And the monster? That's all?"

Harawera frowned. "There's a monster down there filled with hate, so that means we have to destroy it? That's what you think, Lieutenant? Because that's what this war is about, right? Bringing an end to the hatred?"

"Something like that."

"Has it brought an end to yours?"

Matthew, running across the muddy plain to the low huts where the Abo families lived, dragging his horse behind him, calling Kirra's name. Her small dark hand gripped tight in his as he tries to get her up on the horse. Lightning, right overhead, and his horse rears and is gone, running riderless into the flood. Matthew, seeing Elizabeth.

How she slows the horse. How she hesitates, seeing her brother and the girl, so imperfect, so tainted. How Daddy will thrash her if she helps him save the girl Daddy hates. Yet she's riding on, closer, and they're running toward her, smiling, the rain plastering their hair to their faces, even as the floodwaters rise, fast, so fast, the river spilling over the land and swallowing the world beneath it.

"How do we destroy them?"

"We're not here to destroy the *taniwha*. We're here to free them."

Matthew, waist deep in water, grabbing the girl around the waist and passing her up to Elizabeth, his face full of furious hope. Sliding her over the horse's shoulder to sit in front of her. Not a girl at all, a young woman, so much terror in her voice, not for herself, but for Matthew, still in the water, at the mercy of the torrent. Elizabeth, reaching for him, fighting for balance on the rain-slick saddle.

"Free them? You just said they're monsters!"

"Given a choice, would you rather have hate, or freedom?"

Flinder took the binoculars and studied the dark waters. Moonlight rippled silver where something moved beneath the surface. She felt sick to her core. "What do you want me to do?"

Harawera nodded toward the airfield. "Anything down there you can fly? Something with guns?"

The Fokker D.VIII – known as the Flying Razor when it first started slicing up biplanes and pilots in the skies over Europe in 1918 – might have been practically a vintage by wartime standards, but it was still a deadly piece of hardware in the right hands. At Sergeant Rapu's hissed command, Flinder and the rest of the squad broke cover and ran, crouching low, toward the lines of silent aircraft. Ground crew worked on the far side of the field, checking over a spotter plane just returned from patrol. A fuel truck idled nearby, while one technician rolled out a black rubber hose. None of them were looking toward the Razor, and the squad reached the shadow of the monoplane's large rounded tailplane unseen.

Giving Rapu a nod, Flinder slipped along the fuselage and scrambled up the small ladder behind the cockpit. In a moment she was hoisting the camera over the lip and lowering herself into the pilot's seat, sliding her arms through the parachute straps out of habit. She'd once had the chance to study the layout of a D.VIII, captured outside of Marseilles when its engine had failed and the pilot had landed in a paddock before being taken prisoner by the French. Not an auspicious or thorough introduction, but Flinder wouldn't let that bother her. She took a moment to familiarize herself with the gauges and dials, and gave the stick an experimental tug to judge the tension in the aileron wires. The flaps and rudder shifted easily under her guidance. Taking a deep breath, she fastened her flight cap, tugged down her goggles and, hunkering in case anyone looked her way, waved over the side. Moments later, she heard the chocks being pulled from the wheels. While she waited for Rapu to signal the artillery, she tried to ignore the memories that refused to leave her alone.

Matthew, struggling to get a grip on the saddle, to haul himself up. A branch torpedoing out of the water, knocking him off balance. Elizabeth, lunging forward to grab him, her hands snatching at his. But the rain, so slick, so wet, his fingers slipping through hers. The floodwaters surging around them. The girl's voice a ragged cry. Matthew, going under, surfacing, reaching, shouting, gasping. The tree, barreling through the deluge like a fist, a juggernaut crushing the soft, weak things in its path.

The first boom of artillery fire snapped her back to herself, and the real danger at hand. Smoke and dust burst from the seaward fringe of the darkened city. Flinder flicked the battery switch as someone ran alongside the plane and, with a heave, set the propeller to spinning. She gunned the throttle and the motor caught, roared. Immediately, the Razor rolled forward. Flinder nudged the stick over, easing onto the runway. As soon as she had the plane pointed down the runway, she pushed the throttle open, leaping forward with a thundering shriek. The silhouettes of Gothas, Fokkers and Hannovers whipped by. Even over the growling motor, she heard rifles firing, bullets ricocheting. The tailplane lifted and she pulled back on the stick, the earth dropping away, her stomach falling with it and her spirits rising, as they always did. She banked up, up, praying the German anti-aircraft gunners wouldn't immediately realize one of their own planes ought to be a target. That wouldn't last long.

Company E's cannons fired, reloaded, fired again. Bright plumes of smoke and flame swelled along the breakwall, where the lake had been cut off from the sea by piles of rubble and the hulk of the French tanker. For a moment she glimpsed movement below the water.

Something moving in the water. The girl yelling. Elizabeth torn with the knowledge she has to get off the floodplain, that she won't be able to find Matthew, can't save him without being swept away herself. The dirty black girl, black as sin, whose fault this all is, shouting that she has to save Matthew, while the horse bucks and whinnies under them.

Elizabeth, tugging on the reins, trying to bring the horse under control, to get it moving to higher ground, to safety. The girl, fighting her for the reins.

The girl, screaming for Matthew.

Flinder pushed the stick over, easing the throttle back, coming around in a clean arc toward the besieged city and the rising clouds of smoke. She found the sweet spot where the plane would hold itself steady, freeing her throttle hand to grip the trigger of the twin motor-synchronized machine guns on either side of the propeller shaft. She lined up the airfield through the rotor blur. German soldiers were materializing on the city side of the runway, rifle-fire flashing in the gloom, while the ground crew hurried to evacuate the fuel truck.

This was the moment.

She could pull back, gain altitude, soar over the Atlas range and make for a friendly landing zone somewhere on the coast. She might even reach Algiers from here. She could abandon Harawera and his insane, treasonous mission. Report him to High Command. Let the dirty *Māori* boys get everything they deserved.

The Abo girl, a young woman, a mere slip of a thing. Elizabeth, a farmer's daughter, raised hard by the north Australian desert. It made her sick, thinking what Matthew must have felt, putting his hands on her like he did. Tainting himself with her spittle, her sweat. Daddy would be so mad. But not as mad as he would be with Elizabeth, for taking the horses and riding out into the storm, and coming back not with Matthew, but with the girl. Barely more than a girl.

Flinder choked back a sob, her hands poised between the control stick and the trigger. So easily, they could both slip through her fingers.

The thunder of artillery jolted her to action. A plume of smoke spooled from the dreadnought in the harbor. A bright flash and a cloud of debris erupted from the hillside.

Betray those who had rescued her and chosen to trust her, despite her antipathy toward them? Or fly on, and return to the Empire which had led so many thousands to their bloody ends?

She'd run out of time to choose.

Flinder squeezed the trigger. The hammering report rose above the noise of the engine, the flare dazzling. Below her, the stationary aircraft shuddered under the rain of strafing lead, until the deadly line of fire hit the fuel truck. In a blinding eruption, the truck became a fireball, consuming the planes and men arrayed to either side of it. Flinder held her line until she had peppered the last plane on the right-hand side with shot, then banked away, hard. The cold morning sky swam in her vision, her goggles misted by tears she hadn't known she was crying.

A shockwave rocked the Razor as incendiary shells exploded around her. Flinder hauled back, gaining altitude, yawing side-on to the city to give the gunners a smaller target, and rolled the stick sideways to throw the plane into an arc. More explosions shattered the sky, and she cut the throttle. For a few seconds she hung, momentum and gravity bleeding together. Then the plane dropped, nose-first, howling.

More shells erupted above her, but she was falling fast. Gunning the prop again, she pulled back and drew the plane into a low, tight arc over the scrubland outside the city. With any luck, with the sun still below the horizon, she would be invisible to the anti-aircraft crews as she raced along, rushing like water over the ground.

More flashes from the warship, more bursts of burning dust from the hillside. Flinder arced about, lining up for a second sweep over the airfield, to cripple the planes on the other side. For a moment the Mediterranean stretched underneath her, and then she was over the lake.

Pale, round shapes beneath the water.

Like fingertips, reaching for her.

Something pushing through those shapes, black and sharp.

Like fingernails, scraping her skin.

Flinder closed her eyes and gripped the trigger tight, losing herself in the clamor, no longer wanting to hear the voices she had left behind that day on the Blackmore River.

Matthew.

The girl . . . Kirra.

Her machine guns shredded wings and wheels and fuel lines. As she pulled up, choking back bile, smoke and flames boiled into the sky.

And still, explosions tore through the seawall.

A shape moved down there, a serpentine hump, a half-seen fluke dripping seawater as it rolled up and over, the beast moving toward the smoking hole in the seawall where the rising tide rushed in, like floodwaters.

Flinder could barely draw her eyes from the sight, until an anti-aircraft shell exploded yards off her port side, raining the monoplane with shrapnel and shredding that wing, sending her into a sudden spin. Pain. A warm slick of blood. The Razor twisted and dipped, the engine belching smoke. She hauled on the stick, knowing she wouldn't be lucky enough to survive two crash landings. The plane rolled and bucked, fighting her.

Like a horse in a raging flood.

In her periphery, five dark fingers slipped between the rubble, the tide drawing them away.

It's easier than Elizabeth had imagined.

So light, this slip of a girl, her bones delicate thin, like a bird's.

Flinder yanked the stick back, hammered the throttle, forcing the Razor to climb, the weight of the sky pressing against her as the lake fell away. More explosions, more machine-gun chatter. Everything becoming faint, a blur. She levelled off and brought the plane around, finally looping the camera over her neck and juggling it to point back at the city.

Overhead, the rain thrashes down, and the clouds crash as if in adulation.

Through the barrage of shellfire, Flinder had eyes only for what she saw down the camera lens; the shape surging through the seaway and into the northern lake, massive and gleaming with scales, teeth. The sea boiling around it as it slammed into the side of the German warship.

The dreadnought rocked, and Flinder snapped the shutter.

Harawera had only asked two things of her. To do what she could to disable the *Fliegertruppe* before they could get airborne, and to get photographs of the *taniwha*. Not for him, because Flinder was fairly certain Harawera had little hope of making it away from Carthage alive, but for the wider world. She had to prove why *Māori* Battalion Company E had deserted their Command, and crossed the Sahara to converge on Tunis. She didn't want to think of it as his dying wish, more as his reason for throwing himself and his men into the teeth of the German war machine, with no hope of return.

The girl's dark fingers graze Elizabeth's as the rage takes over, and she tumbles from the horse into the flood.

Another shell erupted several yards from the Razor, hot shrapnel ripping through metal, wood, and flesh. Flinder cried out. The motor shuddered and died.

Gripping the camera tighter, she snapped the shutter again as the creature rose up, wrapping around the warship, and plunged back into the lake. Mooring lines snapped free and several thousand tons of German steel rolled like a child's plaything, its spine broken, its guns silenced.

She snapped the shutter again as the *taniwha* snaked clear of the smashed ship and slid under the water.

Smoke poured from the Razor. Wind whistled over tattered wings, audible in the silent void left by the dead engine. Below, the barrage from the hill continued.

Flinder snapped the shutter a final time, capturing the great dark shape making for the sea where the other, smaller creatures looped and dived, awaiting their mother. Then they were gone, disappearing into the cobalt waves like they had never been.

A hand lifts above the water, for a second, dark fingers grasping for the sky, and then gone.

Hands trembling, dripping blood, Flinder unclipped her restraints. Clutching the camera, she pulled herself from the seat, tottering on the edge of the cockpit above the Tunisian coast before dropping free, letting everything else fall away as she tugged on the parachute ripcord.

Dragonfire is Brighter than the Ten Thousand Stars

Mark Robert Philps

NEWSREEL (i)
SPY-RING SENTENCED
Today, in an Eikstown courtroom, the Commissariat showed how the people of the Commonwealth meet threats to their freedom: with the cold machinery of Justice! In the gallery, members of the accused watched with the hooded and reptilian eyes of a Draco as their sentence was meted out. The tribunal deliberated, and swiftly their verdict came down: It was to be Death. Let the jackals of the Mandate be warned: the Commissariat stands ready, the sword of the party! But the sword must have its shield – the watchful citizen! Report any Suspicious Activity to your local Commissariat for State Security office. Be Aware! Be Vigilant!

1

City of Whitebottom, one mile south of Green Banner Electrical Station No. 45. A cold evening in winter.

I ducked beneath the fire-cracked lintel of a gutted patrician mansion, reached into the mended-and-remended pocket of my woolen overcoat and once again pulled out her letter. The thick paper card was sooted by the same coal dust that coated my aching hands. The words on it I had already committed to memory.

Kaffa Brewcourt. 22:00 tonight. res mutatae non sunt. The note wasn't signed, but that last phrase was written in blotted black ink, and it was all the signature I needed.

Attia.

Years ago, amid the bright-eyed passion and the party slogans and the thinly veiled tension of the university annex in Ravenna, we had together composed those words, a political slogan as true of revolution as it was of love and war. But in the twenty years since the bloodshed at Aelia Capitolina, since I'd last seen her, I'd barely thought of it. I'd been too busy running, keeping low and quiet in backwater cities, stewing on old betrayals. Hiding from the Commissariat. That was until today. Until this yellowed slip of paper had appeared in my pigeon-hole at the electrical station. Attia. Twenty years since that night in a rundown kaffahouse, stinking of sweat and sulfur, waiting for a woman who had never arrived. Twenty years since she'd broken my heart. So why now, after so much time?

I stuffed the letter back into my coat and stepped onto the rain-slicked streets of city I still thought of as *Vindobona.* The air tasted wet, bitter, as thick as the heavy fog. She was out there. Somewhere in that gray atmosphere. I moved from beneath the shadow of the abandoned mansion. On the stone-work above me dragons and dragonriders were trapped in time on a blackened frieze.

"*Cacō,*" a shrill voice exclaimed. "*Dulcis cacō!*" agreed another. Kids, running ahead through the white haze like wraiths, cackling to each other in high voices. Latin was still outlawed, so naturally the child-gangs that overran the New Commonwealth had adopted it as their native tongue. I hesitated, waiting until their voices receded further into the fog. Then I folded my shoulders and splashed hurriedly down the street. I slipped past an idling diesel truck, turned a sharp corner plastered on both sides with Party recruitment posters, and stopped at the glass door of a soot-stained kaffahouse.

Kaffa Brewcourt. I stepped up to the glass and peered inside, my heart thudding. The inside was lit with low hanging lights; the high ceilings and peeling plaster walls fell away into shadow. Marble tables stood in a ragged line and a piano with keys like yellowed teeth squatted in one corner. A pale, ox-boned proprietor slouched behind the dimly lit bar, polishing chipped porcelain cups with a discolored rag. No sign of Attia. I glanced at my timepiece. Still early.

The door squealed as I pushed it open. Hot air and the smell of roasting beans and stale cigarettes buffeted me as I stepped cautiously up to the bar. The proprietor did not look up as I sat, just thudded over to a brass machine that groaned and spat steaming kaffa into a small white cup. I spared a glance around the room. Empty but for a large man in the back corner, sweeping again and again the same bit of floor. The proprietor turned back to me, rattled a cup and saucer onto the bar.

"Thank you," I muttered. 22:01. No Attia. I fought off a shiver. I thought of the last time I was supposed to have met her in a kaffahouse. She hadn't arrived then either.

I took a shaking sip of kaffa and spun a ring-stained newspaper that had been left on the counter toward me, attempting vainly to seem casual. Bold black headlines proclaimed heightened tensions along the New Commonwealth's continent-spanning border with the People's Mandate, the state of arms purchases from the long broken away colonies across the ocean in Nova Roma, and the newest ever increasing production quotas. It didn't take much subtlety to read the subtext: yet another war with the Mandate was looming.

Someone stepped into my field of vision. "More kaffa?"

A shadow fell over me: a thickset man with deep-set eyes. The one from the back corner. I hadn't heard him move. I flicked my gaze down to my cup of thick kaffa, which was still more than half full; along the bar, where the proprietor was now nowhere to be seen.

It all slotted into place with brilliant and icy clarity: the typed letter, the too-empty public house, the proprietor's strange attitude, the truck idling outside . . . That letter wasn't from Attia. She wasn't coming.

After all these years hiding, the Commissariat had found me.

"No," I managed. I snaked a hand across the table toward the small porcelain cup – the closest thing I could see to a weapon.

"I insist," he said.

My hand found the saucer. I didn't plan my next move. I lurched back on my stool and with a flick flung the cup of steaming kaffa at his face. The thickset man swore and

stumbled back, steaming black kaffa running down his cheeks.
The cup bounced off his head and then exploded on the tiled
floor. Still holding the saucer I smashed it against the counter
and grabbed hold of the largest piece: a jagged half-crescent
which I swung at him like a blade.

His meaty palm caught my wrist with a wet slap.

And then from behind, unseen hands snatching me roughly
by the shoulders.

"Easy," said a high quiet voice behind. "We just want to
tal—"

Gloved hands were holding my shoulders. I twisted my wrist
half-free and then cranked my neck. I bit down.

"Shit!" said a not-so-quiet voice behind me.

"Put him out," the thickset man growled.

Barely a moment to cry out before being shoved to the
ground. In the gap between that first push and the moment
when my face hit the ground, my mind raced through the
twenty-some years that I'd spent on the run – the failed relationships, the arms-length friendships (my landlord Viktor,
with whom I shared a single nod once every day, as close a
friend as anybody) and the days and days spent with my head
down at the electrical station, trying hard to not to be noticed,
shoveling coal into a high pressure boiler that roared hot and
burned nearly as bright as dragonfire.

A wet boot pinning my cheek to the sticky, sweet-smelling
floor; a black burlap hood that reeked of stale sweat. And then
a needle lancing my arm, pain more bludgeon than prick, and
lightness spreading through my body, blooming behind my
nose and eyes and mouth.

"Time to go, Artur."

EXCERPT FROM "ON DRACI AND REVOLUTION"
(CENSOR'S COPY, REDACTED)
*Self-satisfied Imperial historians called the two millennia of
uneasy peace that existed between Roma and Cháng'ān the Pax
Draci. We accept now that these two words are a lie, do nothing
to convey the suffering that the two imperial powers wrought
upon their own people. And yet in the bloody lie there is some
gleaming black bone of truth.*

2

Attia. So much of my life had revolved about her. Since those days when we'd first met, young students at the university with not much in common but a hatred for the Commonwealth, and the Party, and every apparatus that had risen up to replace the Emperor, and the patricians, and their dragons. Not uncommon sentiments in universities during those days, which was how we'd found ourselves at a protest that became a riot that now stood like a firewall between the two halves of my life.

Even now, all these years later, I found myself trapped in her gravity. Even now I dreamed of her. Of course I did. We were at a party I was hosting with my roommate Sina, and she was perched on a wing-backed chair. In this dream she seemed luminescent against the shadowed walls of my squalid walkup. She was scrawling left-handed notes in a ubiquitous copy of Wagner's *Green Book*, the book that held the living word of the Party. But the notes she crammed into the margins of revolution were not words but tightly packed equations – numbers I recognized dancing with strange ideograms I didn't.

Was this even sleep? Or did I lurch through some soporific induced hallucination? It was a dream and it was a memory. Or it was the liminal area between. When I looked up the weeping walls of the garret seemed to fall away vertiginously, though the other students who crammed the party and chattered in some lost Vandalic dialect that I couldn't quite decode didn't seem to notice. This was still the early days of the revolution, some part of me realized, long before the chaos in Aelia Capitolina, those first years after the Emperor had been shot in the crypts beneath the Palatium Magnum and the last dragons had been sieved with hot bullets by squads of Revolutionary Guard. This was the first night I'd met her. Or some version of it.

And then I was looking her in the eyes, mismatched eyes, one a murky sort of green, the other dark and completely dilated (she was nearly blind on that side, I would learn later). She appeared in my dream as I remembered first seeing her: small and fairly bony, her body disappearing into the over-large tunic suit that hung about her shoulders. I realized with a start that I looked as I do now, and laughed.

Hot wind on my back. I turned. The wall behind me had fallen away completely, and thrusting a feathered, prehistoric head from the fog that grew beyond was a dragon. It opened its mouth, revealing triple-rows of jagged teeth. A smell like kerosene and spider webs and old book glue. Its plumage glimmered red and gold and green. All the party guests continued their discussions, ignoring the massive, autocar-sized head that heaved into the cramped garret. They had all, I noticed suddenly, been burnt black, charred meat sticks oozing blood and pus from their seared flesh. Their eyelids had been scorched away, so they looked at each other with bulbous eyes and expressions of constant surprise.

"They dragons are dead, Gaius," Attia said. "We killed them all."

The dragon pushed its head through the living room until it was so close I could feel heat radiating from emerald and sapphire down that covered its snout and glinted in the bronzed light. This was a Nile Dragon, and it looked nothing like the creatures of string and wire that jerked across the screen in those Committee sanctioned historicals that featured Otto Marx as the heroic Octavian, making his doomed stand against the black powers of Antonius and his mount Apophis. This felt real, as real as the dragons who had been shot to death in the air above the Bautai plateau, in pens beneath patrician mansions. Who died roaring at the chattering of machine guns, the buzzing of warplanes, the winking lights of tracer fire.

The jaw of the beast yawned wide and hot fire spewed forth, so bright that everything became white light and heat

Then Attia was gone and I spoke words I couldn't fathom into a black room. I couldn't even hear what I was saying. My mouth was dry and my words sounded like drunken mumblings in my own ears. I stopped speaking abruptly, aware suddenly of how much my entire body hurt. My arm throbbed. I turned my head, and realized that it wasn't the room that was black, but rather the hood draped over my head.

It all flooded back. I cried out involuntarily.

I sat in a hard wood chair, hands bound tight behind my back. I could hear an electrical hum and the occasional soft thud of heeled boots. Light spots danced in the hooded darkness. But beyond the dull pain lancing through my head, all I felt was numb surprise.

I thought back to Attia's letter that for all I knew was still in my coat pocket. How could I have been so stupid, to think it was her? She had left me more than twenty years ago.

"Gaius Plebius," said a nasal voice.

Gaius was dead, killed during the riots in Aelia Capitolina. I was Artur now. The hood came off in a rush and I blinked into a bank of high-powered lights.

"My name is Artur." My words sounded slurred. I might as well hold onto that, though I had no idea how much I had said already, mumbling away in a drug-induced lunacy.

Faint movement on the far side of the room. A mechanical lever clanked down and two of the lights popped off, leaving behind only the ghostly orange of cooling filament wire.

Two figures resolved from the lessened glare, both staring at me from across a low table made of polished wood.

I blinked and looked around. I had expected to find myself in a concrete interrogation room with discolored walls and a rusted iron door. Instead I seemed to be in some kind of living room – an apartment or hotel I couldn't quite be sure. Light walls and gray carpets; beach wood accented furniture and coarse gray upholstery; thick white curtains filtering bronze streetlight.

What was I doing here? I turned to the two figures on the sofa across from me. A man who was seated and above him a tall woman with her arms clasped behind her back. The pair of them wore gray. A floodlight stood on a tripod behind them, its cable snaking to an outlet on the wall beneath a white radiator.

"Awake now, I see." The man was looking intently in my eyes. For signs of awareness, I realized belatedly.

"Where am I?"

"You are in the Grand Whitebottom Hotel," he said. "I'm sorry that the room is not so grand as it once was. Such are the times, Gaius."

"That's not my name." This had to be some trick. Some kind of interrogation technique. The Commissariat's Internal Security Directorate was shrouded in mystery and rumor, but everyone agreed they were subtle. And deadly. I wasn't going to admit to anything. I was, after all, still tied to the chair.

The man sighed, looked up at the woman standing beside him. She showed no reaction. The man was pale and had dressed in the drab uniform of a Commissariat major (brass buttons, red piping, bright green New Commonwealth flag on the collar) and the woman – Han, apparently, which made her a strange sight standing beside this particular man – wore a party tunic-suit with a pointed collar that was cinched tightly to her throat. They were a contrast in shapes: him short and formed something like a tortoise, with a tiny shriveled head and a body that ballooned out at the waist, her tall with broad shoulders and a broad face, long black hair tied into a tight tail. She had large calloused hands, and kept her eyes turned down toward them, never looking at me directly.

The man slid two fotos out of a hemp folder and placed them on the table before me. "Gaius Plebius," the major said for a third time. "A carded member of the Ravenna Student Continuance Council. Wanted for counter-revolutionary activities. A known instigator during the Aelia Capitolina riots."

I had a brief image of Attia, there, on a street filled with blood and screaming, smoking rifling clenched in too-tiny hands.

I found myself leaning forward. The foto was black and white, grainy, but still intelligible: a young man sitting alone in a kaffahouse. I felt my heart lurch. The figure in the image looked twenty years younger and much thinner than the reflection I saw every morning in the cracked mirror of my one-room flat. I recognized the kaffahouse too, the same one in Aelia Capitolina where I'd laid low for three days, hiding, waiting for Attia.

I'd lost her there amid the blood and smoke and screaming. I'd run through those mad streets to a backwater kaffahouse where we'd agreed to meet in case we became separated. I'd waited in that kaffahouse three days, looking up each time the door opened, hoping vainly to see her walk back into my life, hoping vainly that she hadn't been arrested or killed. But of course she never had. In the end I'd fled, taken a new name, and gone into hiding. In my heart I'd thought of her as dead.

Shock still thrummed through my body, reverberated down every nerve. They had known I was there, in Aelia Capitolina, in that kaffahouse, waiting for her. Why hadn't they arrested me? "Where did you get that?" I whispered.

He started pulling more fotos from his folder. With each new print I saw that same man, the same reflection, but ageing as the prints and the years went by – the last twenty years of my life spread out there on the table

I almost couldn't breathe. I'd been hiding from the Commissariat for twenty years. Certain that they would arrest me if they ever found me. That I would be sent to the northern labor camps and worked to death like so many friends I'd had. But they'd known. They'd always known. They'd followed me from afar for years. *Why?*

"Song, would you untie Gaius please?"

The woman – Song, apparently – frowned at the major and then with a blurred movement whipped a sling blade out from some hidden sheath. She paced around and sliced the ropes that bound my hands. When she leaned close I caught the scent of stale tobacco. Why were they untying me?

"I'll be honest," the major said, "we aren't much interested in what you did or did not do twenty years ago. This all would have been much easier if you hadn't tried to kill poor Charlez with a saucer." The major's smile revealed a glittering nest of amalgam fillings that wove through his teeth. "We can assure you that if we were from the Political Directorate you wouldn't have even had the chance to defend yourself."

I struggled to follow what he was saying. The Commissariat Political Directorate protected the state from sedition and counter-revolutionary activities – the crimes I was guilty of. So if these two weren't members of the Political Directorate . . . "Who are you?"

"We're with the Primary Directorate."

The second true shock since I'd woken. Primary Directorate. Foreign Intelligence. Spies. What would spies want with me?

"We brought you here," the major said, as if in answer to my question, "because we need your help."

The room, my life, my understanding of the word, all of it wobbled. What was happening here? A widening gulf between expectation and result. "Why – I mean . . . For what?"

Song stared at her strong hands. Flexed them. She still hadn't looked up at me. The major kept on smiling.

"When was the last time you saw Attia Vitellia?"

I felt my gut twist. The telegram. They had sent it.

"We know you were both at the riots," the major said. "We know that you were lovers."

Lovers. Once. Old betrayals die hard. "The last time I saw her," I said, "she on the front page of *The Truth*."

That had been the final knife. Years after the riots, years after thinking her dead, I'd woken one morning to see her smiling face with its mismatched eyes splashed across the front page of the Party newspaper. There she was, the woman I'd loved, who I'd thought hated the Party as much as she loved me, shaking hands with some minor functionary. A desperate scan of the article revealed that she had become a magistra at one of the state universities and was being awarded a medal for some breakthrough she'd managed in physics. The fact that she was still alive was enough of a shock. But there she was: working *for* the Central Committee. She hadn't died or been captured. She'd betrayed me, our friends, everything we believed in, for the sake of her fucking work. If any vestige of Gaius had remained, that had killed him.

The major leaned back and smiled a little bit. "When did you last *speak* to her?"

"The riot," I knew that was an admission. At this point I didn't care. I'd followed her from a distance, as she published her papers and became one of the most famous physicists of her age. But I couldn't bring myself to do more than that. I couldn't bring myself to confront her.

Too afraid . . .

"What does any of this have to do with her?" My anger thrummed through me, vibrating along every nerve.

The major flitted his gaze up to Song and she responded by finally meeting my eyes. "There's no reason for you to know this," she said, "but five years ago theoretical metallurgist Attia Vitellia defected to the Mandate government."

A thought and a pang, one that I recognized as both familiar and irrational. And yet there it was: *how could she have left without me?* We'd often spoken of leaving the New Commonwealth altogether, to forge a new life in Nova Roma, or even maybe the Mandate. I gritted my teeth. *But that was twenty years ago. She left because she doesn't give a shit about you.*

The major adjusted the round spectacles on his nose. "At least that's what everyone but Song, myself, and now you believes." The major straightened in the sofa. "Vitellia has, for each of those last five years, been working with us. Spying for us. She's been deep cover on the inside of a top-secret Mandate military project in the Taqlar Makan desert."

Slowly I came back out of the past, out of the bitterness that waited there. I came back into the cold white hotel room. For the first time I noticed that the major seemed worried. "What?" I said.

The major sighed. "She's a double agent. Attia is our best scientist, and the Mandate were all too willing to believe that she wanted to defect. She's been feeding us military secrets for years."

Song pursed her lips unhappily. "About a month ago Vitellia came to me."

"Song," the major interjected, "is Attia's courier and control officer. Her local contact inside the Mandate."

Song continued, "Attia said that she was ready to come in from the cold. Back home to the Commonwealth. She said that she was going to bring . . ." The tall Han woman paused there for a moment, as if searching for a word. "Bring a high value asset with her."

The major nodded and drummed his fingers on the table. "The extraction was supposed to have happened two weeks ago."

I was still trying to process everything they were saying. Why were they telling me all this? Why would they reveal state secrets to some one-time counter revolutionary who had been hiding like a coward for the last twenty years? Was it part of some elaborate ruse? It didn't make sense . . .

Unless they need me. Instantly I knew it to be true. Why else would they bring me here, why else tell me this? I licked my cracked lips and leaned forward. "What happened to her?"

Song shook her head. "She didn't show. She disappeared from her apartment, her labs. Vanished without a trace. Our initial assumption was that she'd been burned. Caught by counter-intelligence agents."

"She makes a habit of missing appointments," I muttered.

"But then," the major continued, "last week we received a coded message from her at a secondary dead drop. Vitellia wants to meet again."

Curiosity warred with anger. "So what? What does this have to do with me? What do you want?"

"The message indicated that she would only meet with one man. One Gaius Plebius, known currently by the alias Artur Liefson."

Song pointed to my pocket. "She gave us that letter."

Something shifted inside me. A small gap opened and all my fear drained away. All that remained was anger. *She left me sitting alone in that fucking kaffahouse for three days. For twenty years. Until now, when she wants something.* Another betrayal, in a long line of them "What," I nearly growled, "what does she want?"

"We don't know." The major folded his face until it manifested as something miserably unhappy. "We need you to find out." He entwined his fingers and leaned forward. "You and Song will travel to Korla in the Eastern Mandate, and there make contact with Vitellia. We need you to talk to her. Find out what happened."

"You are going to help me extract Attia and the asset."

I wanted so badly to laugh. It was just too ridiculous. Travel with spies into the heart of the Mandate? "And why," I said instead, "should I help you?"

The major flashed his row of capped teeth. "Curiosity?"

All mirth was gone now. I glared at him.

His own false smile fell. He pulled a gun from his pocket and placed it on the polished wood table. "You're going into the Eastern Mandate, or you're being pulled out of here by your feet. Your choice."

I stared down that cold barrel. I wasn't afraid, I realized. A Commissariat bullet was how I'd always thought I'd die, though I'd always pictured it happening with me blindfolded and lined up again a brick wall rather sitting in a well-appointed hotel room.

I couldn't help but feel that I had nothing to lose. I ignored the gun and locked gazes with him. "You wouldn't have brought me here unless you thought you needed me," I told him. "Sounds like if you kill me then you'll never be able to get her out."

The major narrowed his eyes. "Maybe so. But getting her out is merely our preferred option."

Song stepped forward. "We need your help," she said. "If you help us then you will get your life back."

"I don't want my life back," I said, thinking of the moldering apartment that was my home, the rusted gas element and sink full of pots that was my kitchen, the ceiling with flecked spots of black mold, the bookshelf with a handful of dusty volumes, the bowed mattress with stained sheets. The walls without picture frames, paintings or art.

"Your old life then," she said.

Smoke and blood and screaming students in Aelia Capitolina. I wasn't sure I wanted that back either. I flicked my gaze from Song's pleading eyes to the major's expressionless ones, to the cold barrel of the gun. "You said that she was bringing out a high value asset. What is it?"

I could see him hesitating, weighing.

"Tell him," Song said.

Finally, he just shrugged. "Dragon's eggs," he said.

This time I really did laugh. The major blinked in surprise, which just made me laugh harder. The last dragons had died out nearly forty years ago, along with the Empire and their patrician masters. And now the New Commonwealth, a state founded to destroy them, worked to bring them back. And somehow Attia was in the middle of all of it.

Res mutatae mutatae non sunt ... The words – her words, our words – came back to me then. All humor drained away. Was this why she'd written them. Had she been trying to tell me something?

I looked to the Song, and the major, still waiting, breath baited, for my decision.

I realized then that I'd already made it.

EXCERPT FROM "ON WINGS OF VICTORY"
(TRANSLATED FROM THE ORIGINAL MANDARIN)
The first mechanical flight – conducted in what is now the Commonwealth, on the Dis Pater Collis by the brothers Antropov – was actually witnessed by members of no less than five patrician families, a cartel of dragonriders who had funded the endeavor on a whim. Upon seeing the brothers' rickety wooden contraption skim a bare two hundred feet down the side of the hill, the riders are said to have only laughed. The thought that one of these flying machines might ever pose a threat to the great draci of their houses was beyond anything they could imagine. They couldn't see a future for that ridiculous contrivance of wood, string, and wire. In the Mandate, however, officials would take the brothers, and their invention, a little more seriously.

3

I sat with Song in the back of a military plane, a noisome Ruz-54 that glinted silver in the sunlight and juddered from the power of its twin props. We were to go south and east to Eikstown, and then on to Marakanda on the Mandate border. We would cross the border by train, as air travel between the two nations had been once again severed.

It was the first time I had ever flown, and I realized quickly that I hated it. The rumbling engines roared so loud I could barely think, and the brief moments of free-fall that accompanied every patch of turbulence were terrifying. At my feet was a disintegrating leather bag stuffed with spare clothes. In my hands I clutched a copy of the Party Green Book. I'd grabbed both from my apartment before we'd left, inspired by the words that had been written on that letter.

I flipped the book open. On the inside cover: *res mutatae mutatae non sunt*, scrawled in her handwriting. I flipped it open to a random page where the margins were filled with more of her cramped writing.

It was the same book she'd been writing in the night I'd met her, at a party for disaffected students Sina and I had hosted

in our walkup. Even in those days she'd had been something of
a prodigy, assisting the university's most senior magisters with
experiments at the cutting edge of chymistry and physics. She
hadn't been political when we'd met, it was only after the
struggle sessions and university closures of the Cultural
Adjustment had threatened her work that she'd fallen in with
radicals like Sina and I. It had taken some time to get started,
but our affair had burned hot and bright.

She'd given me the book the night we'd snuck into the great
hall of the university library, after it had been locked and shut-
tered, to make love beneath the suspended ebony bones of a
dead dragon. We'd been lying, sweaty and tangled in a scratchy
woolen blanked that we'd thrown hastily over the marble floor,
when she had pressed the book against my chest. I remember
feeling the weight of it, the heat of her beside me as she lay
curled against my body, watching the dragon above us sway
slightly on its hanging wires. "When I'm a famous magistra
and find my new element," she said, "I'm going to name it
after you."

It was the night I'd known that she loved me. Now the
memory of that set my teeth on edge.

"What a good little Party member you are," Song said, raising her voice to carry over the droning engines. She was sat
across from me in the long, bare metal fuselage of the transport plane.

I blinked and looked down at the book still in my hands. I
shoved it into the leather bag. "A different kind of memento."

She stood and stepped surely across the deck toward me, a
thick folio clutched in her strong hands. She had changed
outfits, eschewing her gray Party tunic-suit for a dark pleated
jacket and thigh-length skirt, fashions, I gathered, that were
popular now with women in the Mandate. She had unbound
her hair and it fell loose about her shoulders. She sat down. "I
don't like having to yell."

We hadn't spoken much since leaving the interrogation
room. She and several broad, featureless men with meaty
hands had escorted me from my apartment to the aerodrome,
but the men had stayed behind when we boarded the plane,
which was now empty except for the unseen flight crew.

Song nodded at the book I had stuffed away. "A present from your lover?"

There had been a time when I'd looked at that book and thought only of how much she had once loved me. "A reminder that not everything stays the same."

I could feel Song's gaze boring into me. "She might not be how you remember her," the agent said. "It's been a long time." She brushed invisible lint from her skirt. "You really haven't seen her since the riots?"

I shot a glare over at the agent. "No," I said. "And what does it matter anyway?"

Song was shaking her head. "I got to know Attia over the last few years. We worked together a lot. She – I think of her as a friend." She dropped her gaze. "I don't understand why she didn't show up to the meeting. It's not like her."

"Doesn't surprise me," I muttered, thinking again of the empty kaffahouse.

"I don't understand why she wouldn't meet me. I don't understand why she sent for you."

"That makes two of us."

Song sighed. "It's possible that she *has* been burned," she said. "It's possible that Mandate intelligence is pulling the strings here."

I shrugged. "So I stay here and get killed by the Commissariat or go there and get killed by the Mandate. Does it matter? I'm dead either way." I smiled a bit. "It's only you that has to worry."

She looked at me. "And what about Attia? What about your former lover? Are you worried about her?"

"No," I said, but even as I did I knew it was a lie. *If she's dead then I'll never know why she left me,* I told myself, but knew that wasn't quite the truth either. I cared for the same reason I'd brought that copy of the little book. "She's always managed to take care of herself," I said.

"She saved your life," Song said. "That has to be worth something."

I didn't say anything. What could I say to that? It was true, even if I tried not to think of it. I saw her there again, in the smoke and the haze of Aelia Capitolina, rifle clutched firmly in hand. Saving my life, only hours before she would leave me forever. *Why, Attia?*

Song reached down and pulled a hemp envelope out of the folio that rested now at her feet. She passed it over. "Take a look," she said.

I unwound the red string that sealed it and looked inside.

It contained: a handful of creased Mandate bank notes pressed into a soft leather billfold, a cheap nickel-plated watch, a passport with a foto and another name, and several type-script pages detailing my new identity.

Yet another new identity. What fork had my life taken to lead me to this?

"You'll need to memorize that if we have any hope of getting through the border," Song said.

I nodded. The border between People's Mandate and the New Commonwealth stretched across the center of the conti-nent, through deserts and steppes and heaving mountain ranges. Countless wars had been fought over that massive frontier, but the unforgiving terrain and sprawling distances reduced battlefields to charnelhouses where hundreds of thousands of men were minced for the gain of a few spare miles. Every decade or so since the revolution another war would spark, and millions would be bundled onto trains for the front line, to be cut down by machine-gun fire, or pressed into the earth by an artillery shell. Economies would teeter, food would become sparse, and then an armistice would be signed, giving each state enough time to recover before the cycle would repeat.

It had been nearly a decade since the last war had ended, but by all signs another would start soon. Maybe within weeks.

"You'll probably pass."

I looked up from the folio open on my lap. Song was eyeing me.

"For what?"

"You look like a mongrel," she said seriously. "You can pass for a local in any number of cities. How much Türkik do you remember?"

I had taken several classes at the university. When I wasn't writing slogans and hosting counter-revolutionary meetings, I had actually been studying linguistics. *Of course* the Commissariat knew that. "A little."

Song nodded. "Try to stick to what you know. It will be slightly less obvious than Gothic." She twisted her mouth a little. "Or Latin."

We refueled at the old capital in Eikstown (once *Byzantium*) where the Plaza of Heroes could be seen easily from the air, a long concrete slab that had been built over the ruins of the Hippodrome and now seemed to blend with the lead sky and gray seas.

"We're operational now," Song said as we lifted off once again. "From now until we're back, you are Unal." It was the name on the passport that I now held in my hand. He was a man who had been born in Kyiv, lived now in Persia – a client state of the Mandate – and sold petroleum drill bits. "The Mandate have spies everywhere, so don't feel safe because we're still in the Commonwealth. The hardest part will be getting through the border without raising any eyes."

"What do I call you," I asked. "What's your alias?"

She cocked her head quizzically and then laughed. "Song," she said.

We flew east again, closer and closer to the Mandate border. Out the window, the mountains crawled by. I pictured a dragon soaring somewhere below, its feathered wings stretched out in full flight, the small figure of a man strapped to its arched back with ropes and leather harnesses. Ptolomey had flown this way, I remembered suddenly, while mapping the East for his *Geographica*. I thought of Attia, who must have also traveled this way before defecting. What had she been thinking?

"Why is this egg so important?"

Song's eyes were closed and her thin long fingers were clasped lightly in her lap. "Because the dragons are all dead. You know that." She didn't open her eyes.

"A dragon isn't going to win any battles. Not anymore."

She opened her eyes. "The shooting with the Mandate has stopped for now, but the war still continues underground. A living dragon would be a rallying-point. An important victory in the psychological struggle."

"I thought the Central Committee said that dragons were a tool of oppression?"

"Anything can be politically rehabilitated, Unal. Even you."

I ignored that. "And so what about Attia," I pressed. "What does a metallurgist have to do with dragon's eggs?"

Song shrugged. "I'm no magistra."

I stared out the small porthole in the transport, at the desolation crawling by beneath. "Attia hated dragons. Her grandmother had served in a patrician household, had watched her sons and husbands fed alive to the family *draco* because they'd offended their master. She was as opposed to their existence as anyone I've known in my life." I shook my head. "As much as anything has changed, I can't imagine her working to bring them back. I can't understand why she would help you do that. It doesn't make any sense."

When I looked back to Song she seemed pensive. Then with a bare shrug she closed her eyes again and leaned back. "You'd be surprised, Unal. Not everyone who works for the Central Committee is as sinister as you'd believe. Some people end up in places they'd never expect, for reasons they never dreamed of. Anyways, like I said. There's no more true power in dragons. They're symbols. Nothing more."

Who was this woman, this Han, a native of the People's Mandate who now worked for her nation's enemy? Lies and mysteries, layers and layers that I couldn't even begin to penetrate.

EXCERPT FROM ON "DRACI AND REVOLUTION" (CENSOR'S COPY, REDACTED)

The causes of the First Mandate War (as we call it here in the West) were varied and complex. Treaties, alliances, wars between client states: all these things contributed. But the most widely believed cause is this: some strange ailment was afflicting the Himalayan Draci within the Mandate of Heaven, and for decades they had been dying. The Mandate was, the patricians of the Empire thought, defenseless. A fruit ripe for plucking. And yet why did they strike when they did? The truth was, they were afraid. Afraid of the growing strength and wealth of the Mandate, the political reforms that had ended the monarchy there and transferred power to the proletariat (though in truth it was the burgeoning merchant class who held the true power, then as now). And so it was fear that led the children of the Great Patrician Families to gather their ancient draci and strike in a writhing, flame-wreathed fist at the Mandate capital.

4

The Mandate border crossing was crammed into a narrow point between weathered granite cliffs, and everywhere I could see barbed wire and concrete. Bundled soldiers squinted down from metal watchtowers, their faces wrapped tight against the cold.

We had landed in Marakanda and then taken a train up into the mountains, traveling through the night in a freezing sleeper car with windows that rattled like loose change. Song had made me go over border procedure again and again, memorizing each typescript that had been inside the hemp folder. After hours wending up into Tiān Shān Mountains we had finally pulled to a stop at a depot several hundred feet from the border. The Mandate used a different gauge of rail, and so we would transfer to another train once through the border.

If we got through the border.

It was nearly evening when we poured off the train, and gray clouds had drawn in around us like a heavy wool blanket, threatening snow. The wind was cold and ferocious, pushing through the pass like air through the lips of a dying man. It even *smelled* cold up here. Commonwealth guards peered closely into our faces and escorted us from the train to a concrete building where they would process our exit papers.

I shivered, from nerves or cold I wasn't sure.

We were ushered through the document check and then out of the cold concrete building where found ourselves outside once more, on a flat band of freshly plowed cement that stretched for three hundred feet between the New Commonwealth and the Mandate, an empty kill zone over-watched by searchlights, guard-towers, and machine-gun nests. On the far side sat another barbed wire fence and a brick building to counterpart the one we'd just exited. Above the brick building the red-and-blue flag of the People's Mandate snapped in the wind. We walked out and into the kill zone.

It was the longest three hundred foot walk of my life. With every step I expected to hear alarms or sirens, the chatter of machine guns, or the bright flare of a searchlight. But the only sound was the wind and the clapping of our boots against cement ground. The low brick building across from us gradually grew larger.

"Are you ready?" Song asked.

"No."

"Remember, they're going to separate us to be processed, so stick to the prepared notes in case they cross-reference our stories." She smiled at me then, and I was so shocked that for a moment I forgot all about Attia and defection. "Don't worry," she said. "Everything will go fine."

I could only nod.

The inside of the Mandate Custom House was heated and lined in eggshell-painted plaster. Soldiers separated us into lines that wove through cordoned pathways toward a row of polished wood kiosks.

Even through the freezing cold I could feel sweat in my arm pits and on my palms.

A Mandate Border Officer waved me forward. He did not look up when I approached. Instead, he held out his hand expectantly. I froze. What was I supposed to do?

The man raised his head and frowned at me. "Papers?" he said in a slightly pitched and strange sounding Germanic dialect.

I hastily handed over the passport clutched in my sweaty hand. Gods! I could almost feel the fear seeping from my pores.

"I see those Commissariat officers really scared you," the guard said with a smile.

I opened my mouth to respond, and then snapped it close with a click.

I could defect.

I could tell him that I was being forced against my will to engage in espionage and that the woman now in line with the pleated dark coat was a New Commonwealth spy. I could start another new life for myself, somewhere near the coast. Shàng hǎi or Guǎngzhōu, maybe. I'd heard they were nice cities.

I shot a glance over at Song, who was talking to another guard not twenty paces away. A word and I could be free. A word and she was most likely dead.

The guard seemed amused as he flipped through the pages of my passport. "Don't worry, I won't make you say anything you're not supposed to. What is your destination in the People's Mandate?"

"Korla," I croaked.

The guard nodded. "Purpose?"

Espionage. "Petroleum drill bits." If I was going to say something I should say it now. This was the moment where I got to choose. Until now I'd been pulled along by a rope, tugged by the whims of Song and the Commissariat and Attia. If I wanted to take my own route, this was my chance.

But what would happen to Attia? By necessity defecting meant revealing who and where she was. One way or another, it meant her death.

"Born in Kyiv, were you? I visited there once after the war. Those bridges over the Danapris!" The guard shook his head as though they were the most wondrous thing he'd ever seen. "What is the name of that tower bridge again? With the big red cables?" The guard looked up at me, mouth smiling but eyes dead behind big round glasses.

A test. The names of the bridges hadn't been in the typescript.

The guard's smile was frozen. His eyes bored into me. Gods! I should tell him everything now!

And then I felt Attia's fingers walking up my back and I wasn't Artur, or Unal, but Gaius again, lying in bed with her, sweaty and happy after having made love. "When I was young we lived in Kyiv," she whispered in my memory, "my grandmother used to take me down to the river and tell me stories of Kyi and his sister Lybid, who founded a city to keep their people safe from dragons."

I had turned over and smiled. "Was that true love, then?"

She shook her head. "True love is something else. Brighter even that dragonfire."

"The Lybid," I whispered now to the guard. *Damn you, Attia.* I thought.

"What?"

"The Lybid. They call that bridge the Lybid." I said again, louder. Even now I couldn't betray her.

I wondered if she'd known that.

EXCERPT FROM "ON WINGS OF VICTORY"
(TRANSLATED FROM THE ORIGINAL MANDARIN)
The Battle of the Bautai plateau is considered to have been the death knell of the Roman Empire. It had been so many centuries since the Imperial Air Command had used the dragons in battle that they made no attempt to adapt their strategy to fit the changing reality of war. The Mandate, on the other hand, had been desperately devising a way to meet the dragons that they knew were coming. Their draci had been dying slowly for decades, and unlike the Patricians, they had few qualms about developing new technologies. And so four hundred Mandate warplanes intercepted the Imperial flight on its way to strike Cháng'ān, and with carbines roaring brought down an entire generation of riders in a fusillade of tracer fire. Two hundred and thirty dead draci. In all the years since Actium, the Empire had never been defeated in battle. It is perhaps unsurprising that the Revolution followed so soon after.

5

The Korla safehouse was squared into the second floor of a three-story tenement that sat on the outskirts of town. Out the window I could see a brightly lit filling station with a name written on it in characters that I couldn't read. It must have been the tenth such station I'd seen already. As far as I could tell, everybody in the Mandate had their own damn autocar.

Everything in the safehouse felt like it had been produced in a factory somewhere. The paintings were all prints that felt vaguely familiar, and the plastic-and-stainless-steel kitchen furniture looked utterly alien. The walls were papered in deep mustard yellow (printed with geometric designs that didn't line up along the rolled sheet's prominent seams) and plastic, lotus flower curtains covered the windows. Everything smelled like the chemical mothballs that were stuffed into the cabinets and between sofa cushions. A transistor radio sat on a side-board in the living room, along with a pack of cigarettes. They tasted weaker than Great Northern Canal, and had little foam filters built into the butts. I sat at the plastic table in the kitchen and smoked them, trying to wrap my head around the strange world I now found myself in. After turning over the entire flat to make sure it hadn't been bugged, Song had gone out into the city, to speak with her local contacts and leave a message at the hidden dead-drop for Attia.

The Mandate felt like an entirely different world. I'd noticed the difference as soon as we boarded the new train on the other side of the border. The seats were woven fabric and leather, and the private compartment even had a tiny little desk lamp bolted into the tinier side table. The glass on the window did not rattle.

"I think I was flagged at the border," Song had said as soon as we were settled into our sleeper car.

"So what happens now?" I had asked.

"We stay alert."

We had descended from the mountains at night and passed into the desert. I had quickly fallen asleep.

That first night my dreams were fractured and nonlinear. Perhaps a residual effect of the drugs they had given me. I would be at work, shoveling coal, and then falling through foggy skies, sinuous dragons winging around me as I fell, breathing fire in bright flashes that lit up the white fog like signal flares. They would emerge briefly from the thick atmosphere and snap at my ankles with rows of jagged teeth. I would kick at them and then try to fly away but my legs transformed into fused blocks of granite. Legs that dragged me down to the surface, into murky dark, that weighed me down, down, down.

I had woken sweaty and restless to find we had stopped. Outside it was still night, the sky stretching endlessly over cold empty desert. Canopied trucks were parked alongside the train, and shadowed figures moved between them. Army men in olive coats and polished jackboots were on the train, check-ing passports and shining heavy electric torches in the faces of passengers. I felt my throat closing.

Song must have seen my face. "Don't panic," she had said. "This is routine."

So I showed my passport to a bowed reed of a boy with thin dark whiskers sprouting from his lip and chin who barely glanced at it before moving on down the carriage. Then were moving again.

Night, day, and night again. More checkpoints. I slept and dreamed of Attia and of dragons.

I woke one morning to find we had arrived in Korla. One more check of documents and then out into the winter desert city.

It was an ancient city, a desert town in the Eastern Mandate that had at various times been part of other kingdoms and a key stop along the spice trading routes. It had been swallowed by the Han Empire centuries ago, and had stayed part of that state when the Mandate had moved from Heaven and to the People. The massive damming and hydrology projects of the previous decades had allowed Korla to boom into some kind of desert metropolis, with people fleeing the overcrowded cities of the East to settle on cheap land opened by networks of culverts and aquifers. Beyond the city limits sprouted new residential areas that had row-upon-row of symmetrical wooden dwellings with south-facing doors and hipped roofs tiled in baked clay.

The military loomed everywhere. Soldiers stood at every cross-street and it seemed that every other vehicle was a diesel-belching truck laden with strange equipment being ferried out into the freezing desert. If anything the troops here felt more edgy than those in Marakanda: so tense as to be almost fragile.

The research station where Attia had worked was out in the desert and restricted to military personnel. I didn't want to think of how many more troops might be out there.

I lit another smoke. I was struggling to comprehend this place. Such an arid landscape, transformed now into something that teemed with life. Everything felt so deeply exotic to me.

I heard footsteps outside the door. Song, probably, returning from her reconnaissance. The door squealed open, and slammed shut with a thud. Song entered the laminated kitchen. "I think we're clear," she said.

"Any word from Attia?" I asked.

The spy shook her head. "No. There was no message from her at the dead drop. I'm not surprised. I think she must be laying low. The whole city is on edge. They know the military is looking for somebody. But they don't know who. Or why. I'm going to leave a message for her tomorrow." Song shrugged. "We have to hope that she responds."

I raised my eyebrows. "That's it? We wait for her to get in touch? That's the Commissariat's master plan?"

"Attia is hiding somewhere in this city, with half the Mandate army looking for her." Song walked over to a kitchen cabinet and took a tin off the shelf. "Roadblocks, dogs, door-to-door searches, the whole thing." She wrested the tin open and measured a few heaping spoons of dried *chá* into a glass pot. "They want her back, no doubt, but more especially they want the dragon's egg she took with her."

I frowned. "If they want her back so badly why haven't they plastered her face on every lamppost from here to the border?"

She set a kettle onto the stove and lit the gas burner. Blue fire flickered beneath the chromed steel. "When she defected it was on the front page of every newspaper here. The most prominent Commonwealth scientist, defecting – one more proof of the superiority of the Mandate way of life. If they admit that she's a fugitive then they have to admit that they let a double agent into the most secret of their military research projects."

I thought of Attia hiding in some tenement or basement here in this dusty, cold, desert city. Now it was her turn to sulk in the shadows, afraid that at any moment a heavy-booted kick would splinter a door and end her life. I wondered if she had any friends here, anyone she could trust.

Did she have a lover? Still, now, after *so much* time that thought made my heart ache.

"Do you want a drink?" The kettle barely had time to whistle before she whisked it off the element.

"Not any of that. You have kaffa?"

Song indicated a cupboard. "There's some up there. I never drink it so you'll have to brew it yourself." She smiled apologetically. "I don't know how. I always make my guests brew their own."

"You get many guests here?" I asked as I walked over and opened the cabinet beside her. She indicated a tin painted with peonies and I slid it off the shelf.

"Song has many friends." She brushed her shoulder against mine as she poured steaming water into the large glass *chá* pot. "She works selling petroleum. She hosts dinner parties once a month. Her friends think it queer that she never married."

I put the kaffa tin on the counter, didn't open it. "Why do you work for them?"

"What?"

"The Commissariat. Why do you work for them?"

Song smiled, regarded the *chá* leaves that unfurled inside the clear glass pot. "How could I betray my country, you mean?"

"No. That doesn't offend me. I would betray the Commissariat in an instant."

She laughed. "I suppose you would." She stirred the tea and then placed a lid on the glass pot. "So what *does* offend you?"

"Why would anyone work for them unless they had to?" I said, thinking of Attia.

"Would you think less of me if I told you it was for the money?"

"I don't believe it. Maybe if you were some minor functionary passing secrets in the mail for the occasional wad of cash. No. You're in too deep, you know too much. You're too good at what you do. You actually *believe* in them."

Song was quiet for a long time. For a moment I wasn't sure if she was at a loss for words or simply didn't know where to start. "I did, once," she said. "I'm well past a belief in anything now."

She turned to me and our eyes met in a rush I was aware of how close she was, the heat of her body . . . in one moment there had been nothing between us, and in the next I felt some spark of tension or energy. I realized suddenly how long it had been. Her hand rested on the counter by the brewing *chá*. I placed mine on top of it. Without making a conscious decision, without considering, I leaned in.

My lips met a single finger she had raised between us. My eyes, which I didn't remember closing, shot open. She took a half step back, opening a space between us that felt like a gulf, that snapped whatever energy I might have imagined between us. That finger could have been a wall, a thousand feet high. I felt my face going red. *You've known her for less than a day.* "I'm sorry," I muttered.

Song just shrugged, picked up the pot and poured *chá* into an earthenware mug. "Tomorrow we will hear from Vitellia," she said casually, as if nothing had just happened. "Hopefully we will get a better idea of what she wants. Why she wanted you brought out here."

I nodded lamely, shuffled back. "What . . ." I cleared my throat too loudly. I was only half-considering her words, still mostly thinking of how much of a fool I was. ". . . how do we get her out?"

"We've made plans. Here," Song reached into the same tin she'd pulled the dried *chá* leaves from. This time she removed a snub-nosed revolver. She placed it on the counter between us. "In case things get out of hand."

And like that, the moment between Song and I was forgotten. I reached forward cautiously and picked up the gun. It felt cool and heavy, nickel plated with a handle inlaid in polished black dragonbone. I hadn't touched one in decades, had never been trained to use one properly. I swung the chamber open and saw eight brass slugs inside.

Song's face became contemplative. "I have no idea what Vitellia was thinking when she insisted that we drag you out here to meet her. Why would she want you, a man she hasn't seen in twenty years?" She sipped from the steaming mug. "I keep coming back to that. Why you?"

A question that I asked often enough myself. "She saved my life once," I said, thinking again of Aelia Capitolina. *Smoke and fire and blood. So much blood.* "Maybe she thinks I owe her."

Song reached out and touched my cheek, the rough brush of her calloused hand reminding me of that attempted kiss. My face went hot again. "Get some sleep tonight. We have a lot to do tomorrow."

Then she turned and left me standing in the kitchen, revolver still cradled in my beat-up hands.

NEWSREEL (ii)
YOUTH RISE TO THE CALL OF THE CENTRAL COMMITTEE
In Ravenna, and Eikstown. Aelia Capitolina and Roma itself, loyal youth fed up with the counter-revolutionary excesses of the intellectual-class are rising to the committee's call! The universities, those festering wens of patrician thought, are being occupied by the young guards! The intellectuals are denounced! In town squares, in view of all they seek to oppress, these patricians confess their crimes! But the Party is benevolent! It's seeks not to punish, but to re-educate! To the fields and the mines they send those who have not labored a day in their lives, to learn inner peace through honest hard work. The young guards look on in approval, knowing that today, the Commonwealth is stronger.

6

The next morning saw Song drive her autocar through the bustling center of Korla to the Tiānlóng War Museum. Low mountains dusted with snow rose to the north of the city, and as we drove along the straight paved roads we passed ancient sandstone stupas and temples that sat beside low brick office buildings with brightly colored awnings. The sidewalks were crammed with people: men in pressed suits with large open cuffs, women in long high-cut dresses with satin or silk shawls, an underclass dressed in gray coveralls covered in grease or coal, and hawkers with carts piled high with the fragrant dried pears that grew in orchards that surrounded the city. On the streets were hulking autocars with big round headlights and engines that growled like starving animals. When we finally pulled into the large gravel parking lot by the museum, I leapt from the stuffy cab and into the cold desert air. Chrome-sided buses were parked in a neat row, and groups of tourists thronged everywhere, some chattering in Mandarin, others in Türkik dialects I couldn't quite understand, most wielding hefty foldout maps and taking grinning family fotograms. *They all seem so rich.*

"We've been using war museum as a deaddrop for the last year," Song had told me as we drove up. "There's a potted plant in a Tiānlóng exhibit – when either of us need to communicate we mark the pottery with chalk and sink a deaddrop spike into the earth."

I felt a knot in my chest. Just knowing that Attia came here regularly was almost too much to handle. What if she was here now? Twenty years separated us. Would I recognize the woman she'd become?

The museum had once been some kind of temple or palace: its façade was several stories tall and built of smooth stone the color of desert sand. Pointed niches and intricate scrollwork ran along the second story, above large brass-bounded doors that stood open in an arched portal. Around the entrance leafless polar trees clustered along wending paths dotted with benches, their empty-fingered hands clutching at a gray winter sky. Song gestured, and then followed the surging mass of tourists as they flowed into the building. "The deaddrop is in the third exhibit hall," she whispered, as we squeezed with the rest of the tourists through the tall open portal. "Anybody could be watching. Stay back from me."

I suddenly wondered why she'd even brought me here. I felt the weight of the revolver in my pocket, pressing against my thigh. I shot surreptitious glances at the tourists who milled about, doing my best not to seem scared. I felt keenly an outsider here, no matter what Song said about looking like a mongrel. In Korla there seemed to be more Urghyrs than there were Hans, and many other races as besides: in theory an easy city in which to blend in. In theory.

We stepped into the large domed entrance and found ourselves beneath the outstretched wings of a dragon. Its skeletal frame was suspended from wires and lit by spotlights that reflected as small pools of bronze against polished black bones. Hanging opposite the dragon was a decommissioned Mandate warplane, nose-mounted prop still, under slung machine guns quiet. The creature above us was a Nile Dragon, the breed cultivated and brought to Roma, distinguished by its longer tail and lack of crest horns. Plane and dragon had been positioned by some drama-loving curators so that they were locked in frozen combat.

As we shuffled toward the wooden kiosk to buy museum tickets I was reminded that this wasn't a culture that hated dragons, at least not the ones that had belonged to their own people. The Mountain Dragons – Heavenly Dragons, as they were still called here – were regarded with something verging on nostalgia.

We purchased tickets and entered into the first exhibit hall. "Wait here," Song whispered. She disappeared into the crowd.

I stood alone in the middle of a long, dimly lit rectangular room dominated by a ceremonial stone arch, crenelated and covered with glazed brick. The arch was topped by an archery tower with a bowed roof that nearly brushed the ceiling of the exhibit hall. Along the black-painted walls there liteboxes with fotos of the original ruin standing in a mountain pass – "Iron Gate" was written in Türkik below the characters I couldn't read; "Re-creation" scrawled beside the tall arch. Tourists milled about, passed beneath the arch, peeked down from the archery tower above.

My head felt light and my hands jittery. Fear crept into me, seemed to pool in my gut. What if this was a trap? Song had said she thought she might have been flagged at the border.

I ran my gaze over the arch that rose in the middle of the tall-ceilinged room, trying to appear as if I was taking in the architecture. Instead I watched the people milling about it. Which of them might be spies, here to catch us.

Then, in the corner of my eye I saw her.

A woman, dark shawl wrapped about her head, dark glasses covering her eyes. I sucked in an audible gasp. She moved through the crowd, appearing and disappearing like a drowning swimmer being carried out to sea.

Attia. It was her. I knew it. Was so sure.

Just a glimpse in a crowd, a woman turning a corner into another exhibit hall, away from the gate. Away from me. I stood numbly. I wanted to call out to her. My heart thudded against my ribs.

Had it been her? I'd barely even glimpsed her face . . .

I was moving.

I pushed through the crowd and into the other hall. Dragons hung above me. I ran my gaze desperately through the crowd, searching for that dark shawl and dark sunglasses. Faces of grimacing tourists and laughing children swam through my vision. I shoved past them. Where had she gone? I had just seen her!

I was running. People cried curses as I elbowed past them. Through one exhibit and into another. Hanging planes. Machine guns and gas masks and shells as big as autos. Dragons, horned and not.

But no Attia. I was back in the domed entrance.

Am I hallucinating? The people milling around eyed me strangely. I didn't care. I opened my mouth to call her name . . .

. . . and then Song was there, gripping my shoulder in a powerful hand, her broad forehead creased in anger. "What are you doing?" she hissed. I let her drag me across the tiled floor to the side of the room.

"I saw her," I gasped. "Attia is here."

That seemed to startle her for a moment. But then she shook her head and started hauling me toward the entrance of the museum. "It's too late now," she said. "I've been marked. There was a man watching the deaddrop. He's following us."

"What?" I craned my neck to look behind us.

"No," she barked, and gripped my arm tighter. "Don't look back." She pulled me tighter as we passed the bronze doors and into the flat winter light. "I'll deal with him, you hope he's alone." She pushed me away, toward the parking lot. "There's a bus leaving in exactly one minute. Get on it. It will be safer if we split up. It will stop by the filling station. I'll try to meet you at the safehouse tonight. Don't trust anybody. If Attia is here I'll find her."

For a moment Song was another woman standing before me, saying much the same thing. *Split up, it will be safer. I'll meet you tonight.*

But before I could say anything Song turned and hurried in the opposite direction along a path that wove through the leafless poplars. "Wait!" I called after her, questions only now bubbling into my stunned mind, but she did not stop or turn. She ducked, weaved, and then was lost in the crowd.

I turned to the parking lot. A bus was being loaded: a wobbling old man dressed head to toe in khakis was being helped up steep stairs his equally wobbling wife.

My gaze skittered through the crowd that milled in front of the museum, searching desperately for Song or Attia. Only blank and unknown faces looked back. They all seemed to be watching me. *I've been marked.* I felt a shiver. Suddenly every man in the crowd was a Mandate officer. Every pocketed hand was reaching for a gun.

In the parking lot the bus door rattled shut. The engine growled. Air brakes hissed.

And I was running. Out into the lot, away from the museum and the dragons. From Song and Attia, and whatever men hunted them. I ran into the path of the bus as it started to turn out of the lot, beat my open palms against the aluminum grill. The driver swore as he slammed the breaks. I ran to the side door and hammered on the glass-and-metal until it folded in. I managed a mangled apology in Türkik and pulled some creased banknotes from my pocket. I didn't bother to count them as I shoved them at the driver. He and everybody on the bus stared at me as I made my way to an empty seat at the back.

My breaths came in short gaps. Had I been seen? If Song was marked then there was no way I hadn't been. I ignored the disapproving looks of my fellow passengers and stared out the window, waiting for olive garbed soldiers to come running toward the bus, brandishing lights and guns. But nobody approached, and after a pregnant moment the driver yelled something at me I didn't understand and then pulled out of the lot and onto the road. We turned a corner and the museum disappeared behind us.

On my chest I could feel the weight of my terror and in my pocket I could feel the weight of the gun, pulling me, down, down, down . . .

EXCERPT FROM, "ON DRACI AND REVOLUTION"
(CENSOR'S COPY, REDACTED)
The First Mandate War ended shortly after the Glorious
Revolution, with the New Commonwealth Committee suing for
peace after being unable to organize anything resembling a
defense. Many of the former Empire's Northern and Eastern
territories were ceded to the Mandate, a sore wound that would
fester in the heart of the Old Empire. Some hoped that a new

government would mean an end to all war between the two powers. They were wrong. The Second Mandate War began some ten years after the end of the first, with the New Commonwealth government demanding the return of ceded territories. The conflict has raged since, fought mostly in the mountains and steppes of the central continent, with intermittent ceasefires that last sometimes years, sometimes only months.

In the current estimate some ninety-eight million men have died over a border that has shifted imperceptibly in the last forty years.

7

I was a piece in some game being played and I didn't understand the rules.

I took a drag of a cigarette and watched the darkened outline of the safehouse. I had been out here for hours, smoking cigarette after cigarette, waiting for any sign that the safehouse had been compromised. Waiting for Song. Waiting for some sign from Attia.

Had that truly been her?

I lit another cigarette.

Don't trust anybody.

That wasn't new to me. I'd known that since those bloody days in Aelia Capitolina, the massive student rally that was supposed to have been the beginning of our own revolution. The Commissariat had known all about the rally, of course. They had infiltrated our local organizing councils with spies and agents.

People like my roommate Sina.

And at the height of the riots, as the students gathered at the foot of the Great Hill and the army brigades had closed in around them, Sina and those like him had pulled out their guns. They didn't even try to arrest anybody: they had just started shooting. We were unarmed. Many of my friends, the last true friends I could remember having, had died in those desperate moments.

In that bloody chaos Attia and I had become separated. We'd made desperate plans to meet in a rundown kaffahouse and gone our separate ways. It was safer to split up, we'd thought. But of course she had never shown up.

And now I stood in another city in front of another safehouse, waiting for another woman to come meet me.

Res mutatae mutatae non sunt . . .

The cigarette butts built up about my feet.

It was well past midnight when I slunk through darkened hallways up to the second floor and entered the safehouse. The inside was black. I stumbled around the dark room, trying to remember where the light switch was, cracking my toe against a wood footstool and banging my shin against a low glass table.

I stumbled into the kitchen. Through moonlight filtering in the window I could see the outline of the peony-painted kaffa tin still sitting on the counter. Quiet. Empty.

I flicked on the kitchen light and picked up the tin. In that moment there was nothing else in world I needed more. I filled a pot with water spat from groaning pipes and cranked the gas burner. I prized the lid off the coffee tin and scooped down inside.

Something beneath the powdered grounds. I reached into the tin with my hand. My fingerers found something. A thick piece of card. I pulled it free.

Words and numbers, written in a blotted black script that I knew so well.

Don't Trust Her. Come Alone. Res mutatae
279.0557 φ, 274.552 λ

Attia. I knew that writing anywhere. She had been here. But when? A woman in a shawl, moving away through a crowd.

Heart hammering, I stepped backward and slumped into the kitchen chair. *Don't trust her.* Who, Song? The woman who had brought me here, who had probably just been arrested? Had the note been left for me? It must have been. But how would she know . . . the kaffa tin. Song never uses it.

Come Alone. But where? How to find her? My head swirled. The numbers . . . an address? Map coordinates?

I heaved out of the chair and back into the living room, to a tall red-mahogany bookcase with an oversized atlas. I dropped it onto the table and flipped it open to a massive map of the world. There was the zero degree line, running through Sháng hǎi. I ran my finger along it. *274.552 λ*. I frowned. There were only 180 degrees in each direction. 274.552 didn't even exist as a position. More from habit, I ran my finger along the equator, and then counted lines to the north, were the pole was marked 90. Neither coordinate was even on the map.

It doesn't make sense . . .

Why the riddles? Why all the games? I was furious. I ground my teeth so hard I thought they might explode into talcum.

Focus. Obviously it was a code. One I could decipher and Song couldn't. *Res mutatae* . . . Those words we'd thought were so clever. That she'd inscribed in that copy of the Little Green Book.

Suddenly inspired, I reached into the worn leather bag that still sat by the door where I'd left it. I pulled out the copy of her book. *279.0557 φ*. I flipped open to page 279. Her scrawl filled the margins: symbols and numbers raised to the power of crazy. Nothing stood out. Frustrated, I flipped to 274. The same. I thumbed through the book, looking for either of those old Greek letters.

"*Cāco*," I swore. What the hell was Attia playing at? Why the hidden messages? Why all the secrecy? Why had she not left a message for Song at the deaddrop and have done with it? Why had she brought me all the way here . . .

I was staring at the last page of the book, with the airbrushed image of Wagner smiling benevolently. Attia had defaced his image with her pen, making him look like some kind of demon or evil spirit. She had hated the Party, the Central Committee. What had happened to her? Why had she changed so suddenly and so much? That was the real question.

On the blank page opposite the Chairman she had scrawled our slogan.

And a number. No equation this time, just a single long string of digits: 239.0521634, followed by a 'u'.

I looked back at the thick card I'd pulled from the kaffa tin. *Res mutatae*

Things change . . .

Pen, paper, some hastily scrawled equations. If I took each number on the note, subtracted it from the value in the book . . . I ran my finger along the map. West and then north. My finger ran along the map, drawn to the new coordinates like a lodestone. It stopped in the desert to the south and east of Korla. I felt triumph, and then a cold chill. There. Attia was there.

I'd need a more detailed map to find out where, exactly, but she was there.

People talk of butterflies in their stomach – I felt more like mine was being gnawed at by a nest of rats. I took a calming breath. Think clearly. Things weren't always what the seemed. How had she known I'd take the book? How had—

Footsteps outside the door. I slammed the atlas closed and shoved the green book into my bag just as the door swung open.

Song stood in the doorway. I found that I was holding my breath. *Don't trust her.* She looked me over, ran her gaze through the room, over the atlas on the table, the leather bag on the couch beside me. Her thin lips pursed into a line. After a moment she stepped inside, bolting the door behind her. "Going somewhere?" she asked.

I tried to keep my breathing calm, my voice steady. "I thought you might have been arrested."

"I managed to slip him." She took the plush chair beside me. "Were you followed?"

"I-I don't think so. I waited outside to make sure."

She nodded. Her eyes searched my face, and I couldn't meet that gaze. I studied the closed atlas before me. "Did she get in touch with you, Artur?"

Should I tell her? Did I have any reason not to trust her? "No," I said, though I knew that I'd hesitated longer than I should have.

Song reached over and put her hand on my leg. Firm pressure moving up my thigh. I was hard almost immediately. All those years alone, hiding, nobody to trust or to talk to . . . My eyes met hers. That arcing energy I'd felt the night before and thought imagined sparked in her eyes.

Don't trust her . . .

I sucked in a ragged breath. No. This wasn't right. I stood up suddenly.

"What's wrong?"

"I need the bathroom," I managed. I grabbed my leather case from the seat beside me.

Song stood up, but I was already moving. Into the hallway and toward the bathroom. I did not stop or think. I slid through the doorway and slammed it shut behind me. I yanked the light-chain and rattled the lock across.

My breath was coming in ragged gasps. What has happening?

I shoved my hand into my pocket and pulled the gun out. The gun Song had given me. If she meant to betray me why would she had given me a gun? I snapped open the chamber. Inside: eight brass slugs, arranged in a tight ring.

Song padded to the threshold. She tried the door, which rattled against the lock. "Artur," she said. "What's going on? Let me in."

I pulled one of the rounds out of the gun. Turned it over in my hand. My stomach was doing somersaults. The casing was empty. There was no bullet loaded inside.

Don't trust her . . .

The door rattled again. "I didn't mean to scare you."

I didn't think much about what I did next. I shoved the gun in my pocket, threw open the bathroom window, and climbed outside and into the cold.

NEWSREEL (iii)
LOYAL DOG LEADS FLIGHT CREW HOME
There goes the air-siren, and the Commonwealth's furriest air-man is ready to meet the threat! Wheel-blocks away and up into the sky! But what's this? Mandate Sabotage! From the wreckage Dieter pulls his unconscious crew to safety! And now, stranded in the vast and empty plateau, they must survive. But don't worry boys, Dieter knows the way! Home to a warm bed and a few extra bones, right Dieter? Air-Marshall Yakupov awards Dieter the distinguished air-medal! Courage, Bravery, Loyalty! And love for the Party!

8

I had spent too much time worrying, thinking about things that were lost and could never be replaced. I needed to act.

I needed: an auto, petrol, food and supplies, a map that would show me exactly where the coordinates I'd scrawled onto that wrinkled slip of paper would take me.

I started with the auto.

The night streets of Korla were cold and dimly lit. Streetlights like paper lanterns glowed softly: rows of firebugs perched on a wire. The only movement on the streets were the lines of military trucks that hissed by now and again in the gloom, and the occasional vagrant who would stumble drunkenly into my path.

I slunk through the night streets, sweating despite the cold, looking back over my shoulder, sure that Song or a Mandate Army man would be behind me, gun leveled at my face. But each time I looked back there were only empty streets. I found a line of parked autos on a side street and settled on a heavy sedan. It was all rounded curves and chrome finish, and the long front-end stretched out like the barrel of a gun. I could see a pair of keys glittering in the passenger-side footwell. I took the butt-end of the revolver and smashed it into the side-window. The shattering of glass made me jump and close my eyes. A dog barked wildly.

Lights flickered on in the gated row houses. I keyed the ignition and pressed the gas pedal all the way to the floor. The engine roared to life. I swung the auto onto the road and drove off.

I looked furtively back in the rearview mirror as I peeled away. No Song. No sign of chase. I wanted to vomit.

Cold desert air pressed through the shattered window. A massive sign perched atop of a warehouse across the river and bled red light into the dark. I couldn't read the ideograms, but recognized the ubiquitous double-happiness *shuāngxǐ*. Reciprocal joy, like that shared between lovers.

Attia . . . had she changed so much? Was she even the woman I remembered from all those years ago? She was a magister of the first order, one of the most respected metallurgists in the world. What did that have to do with dragon's eggs?

Did I even really care anymore? Or was it about Attia. At one time our love had burned hot. Brighter than dragonfire. And now what? I was hurtling down night streets of a city I didn't know, drawn into the orbit of a woman whose motives I didn't understand, who had left me for dead and then drawn me back into her mad world.

I needed the map and supplies now.

Dawn was breaking and I drove through the chaotic morning traffic (blowing through intersections, driving at turns too fast and too slow, and all the time feeling my heart hammer at my ribcage as the wheel slipped though sweaty palms) until I found a filling station by a ramp that led onto an expressway. The store seemed to have a random collection of items: packaged foods, a gun-rack, maps and traveling equipment. The man running the station was Han, tall and thin but with jowly cheeks that drooped like empty bags. He had eyes always on the verge of laughter and spoke Türkik well enough for us to communicate.

I opened the billfold that had accompanied my passport and laid several wide bills on the counter. "I need a grid map, four petrol cans, and several jugs of water." I then pulled a last item from my pocket and placed it on the counter. "And I need more of these."

The merchant considered the bills laid out on the counter, and then my face.

I had no idea how much money I'd lain down. I had no idea of the value of the goods I'd requested. I was in no mood to bargain.

After a moment of silence, the merchant muttered something to himself in his native tongue and gave a quick, curt nod.

As he filled out the order, I spread a grid-map open on the hood of the autocar. I unfolded the yellow slip of paper and traced my finger along coordinate lines. It moved across desert, stopping finally off the shore of a large body of water marked in characters that I couldn't read.

I waved the owner of the filling station over. "Where is this," I asked the man, indicating the spot on the map.

The merchant squinted and leaned in to inspect the place

that I'd indicated. "Lop Lake," he said. Then he frowned. "Why are you wanting to go there?"

I said nothing.

The man watched my face for too long a moment, and then shrugged. "Not much to see. The lake's all dried up now. The dams." He gestured broadly as if that explained everything. "It's all desert. Not much but sand and salt."

"There's not anything there?"

"Just ruins." He chewed a bit and then spat. "Lots of army out there. Trucks been driving things out into the desert day and night. Rumor says that this is about where they are going." He surveyed the stolen auto. "That part of the desert . . . Death Sea, they call it."

"Sounds friendly," I muttered, and when the merchant stared at me dumbly I realized that I'd spoken Germanic. Not a very good spy.

"You're not planning on taking this?" The merchant rapped the hood of the large sedan.

"Why?"

"That autocar is for towns. The roads out in the desert are not for town autos."

"I'll take my chances."

The merchant shook his head and then pointed to a two-seat truck hidden behind the petroleum pumps. "I'll trade you for my truck."

The truck's paint was chipping and it was covered in gray dust. "How much is it worth?" I asked.

"Same as the sedan."

I shook my head. "I think this sedan is worth four of those trucks."

The man considered my stolen auto. "The window is broken," he said. And then he looked me in the eyes and any sense of mirth was gone.

I swallowed. That truck looked like it would fall apart at any moment. I glanced at my watch. Time was moving fast. "Get the keys," I said.

EXCERPT FROM, "THE DRAGONRIDERS"
REVISED EDITION, RAVENNA UNIVERSITY PRESS

Dragons imprint. It is how the first riders tamed them. Some part of their avian, prehistoric brains will attach to one rider and bond to him for life. This process seems to have no relation to filial instinct. A wild dragon will imprint not upon its parent as a child, but rather upon its mate as an adolescent. So in some real sense the dragons viewed their masters not as parents or guardians, but rather as lovers. The lengths to which they would go to defend the body of a fallen rider are legendary.

9

I drove all day and into the next night. The landscape stretched endlessly in all directions, hard clay and loose gravel, colored like a cigarette stain. I couldn't shake the feeling that I was being followed. The first part of the journey had been over paved, arrow-straight road. There had been two army checkpoints, but I'd been waved through without incident. As night fell I had turned off onto a smaller road of hardened earth and had bounded slowly over a rugged dirt track that faded beneath me with the light. I was actually glad for the truck. The engine made noises I didn't like or recognize, but the thing seemed to do well on the ripped up road and I made better time than I would have in the autocar. The desert was featureless but for wind-carved yardangs. I felt almost like a dragon rider, setting off into the air above the wide ocean to discover the New World. Into uncharted territory.

What was Song doing now? Searching for me, most likely. I charged on. The need to sleep pressed down on me like a massive weight.

I had nearly nodded off at the wheel when a flare of headlights moving toward me snapped me back. I geared down and pulled to the side of the road. The lights were so bright that I had to squint, and they jerked like bad dancers as a vehicle bounced over the hardpan. As it neared the vehicle swung into the middle of the track and stopped.

I chewed my lip. Army? Magistrates? Some lost farmer?

I skidded the truck to a stop and plumes of dust spiraled up and away from the big wheels. I was very suddenly and very definitely awake. With the glare of headlights in my eyes I couldn't see anything. My hand found the revolver on the seat in beside me. I rolled down my window.

"Need help, friend?" I called in Türkik. The engine of the auto before me shuddered and stopped. The lights remained on. I heard a door swing open. Heeled boots crunched against the desert. A figure crossed over the lights, a silhouette that marched toward me. Tall enough to be Song. What if she'd found me?

The silhouette called out something in Mandarin, his voice hard and sharp as a razor. That settled it. Army. I picked my passport off the seat and held it out the driver-side window.

"I'm here on business." I called out in Türkik.

"This is a restricted area." This man spoke it naturally. He sounded hard. Not some half-trained boy like those who ran most checkpoints. "Turn off your headlights."

I did. And then pulled back the hammer of the revolver. I could see from his silhouette that he didn't have a weapon drawn. But who knew how many more men might be in that truck. I licked my lips. Pulling out the gun might be a death sentence. But then maybe I was already dead.

He started walking toward the truck. A mistake. It would make this easier. I held the revolver against my belly, low enough that he wouldn't see it until it was too late. He reached down to his belt. I tensed, waiting for him to take out his firearm. But instead he unlooped an electric torch from his belt and clicked it on.

"What are you doing out here this late?"

"I'm on my way to the base," I said, squinting against the lights that beamed into my face. "They're importing machine parts for the tests." The dragon-bone handle was slick with sweat. I just needed him to get a bit closer . . .

"The base is three hundred miles to the south. What's your clearance? What—"

The desert scuffed beneath his boots as he stopped before the drivers' window. His eyes locked on the gun that was pointed up at his head.

"How many more in your truck?" I whispered.

"Three." He said it without hesitation. This close I could finally see his broad pock-marked face, his shaved head with long angry scars webbing their way across the scalp. Patches of shadow hid his eyes, but I knew they were narrowed about my face. "Drop the gun and everything will be okay."

"Step back," I said, calmly as I could manage.

He didn't move for a moment, and then took a half pace away from the truck. I dropped my documents and then opened the truck door, gun aimed at his face. I swung out into the desert. I waited for a sound or cry from the still-idling truck. Nothing. I didn't know what I was going to do. I had no plan here. "Drop the torch."

He glared at me, and then let the long chrome tube slip from his hands. The glass cracked against a rock and the light flared out. "Turn around," I said.

"No."

The word hung in the air. I was shaking. Could I pull the trigger? Could I kill this man in cold blood? "There's nobody else in that truck," I said. "We both know it."

"Put down the gun," he said. "I'll let you get in the truck and drive away."

Sweat ran down my brow and froze against my skin. "Just turn around," I whispered. I could hear the desperation in my own voice.

He stared at me a moment, and then turned his back to me. I sucked it a breath. Without taking the gun from his back I knelt down and picked up the torch in my spare hand.

"I don't know what your plan is," he said, "but you can—"

I swung the butt end of the torch with all my strength. It cracked against the base of his skull, splitting the skin open. He staggered forward, blood flowing over the collar of his uniform. He cried out in pain. I hit him again. He staggered to his knees. A third hit and he was face down in the desert, not moving. Blood pooled beside him.

I was panting. In the light of his truck's headlights I could see dark red glinting on the end of the torch. Had I killed him? Cautiously I paced over to his prone body. As I neared I could see his chest rising and falling with shallow breaths.

Relief flooded into me. I took calming breaths. Now what to do? I looked up at his truck, then mine. I looked up at the horizon, where the faintest glow of dawn was beginning to spark in the distance. I needed to make a decision.

The petrol cans and water I moved over to his truck, which was actually a canvass-topped reconnaissance car. I stuffed them into the flatbed which already held several boxes of spare uniforms. I tore the sleeve off one and tied it about the unconscious man's wound, and then dragged him over to the back of my own truck. I punctured the fuel tank and let all the petrol run out into the desert sand. Even if he did wake up he would be miles and miles from anything or anyone, unable to alert the Mandate army before it was too late. By time he walked back to the road and flagged down a passing truck I would have Attia and be out. Or so I told myself.

I jumped into his military car, turned a tight bouncing circle, and then drove off into the desert, glancing back only once at the silhouette of the rusted truck I left behind. I hurtled forward toward Attia and whatever else waited for me.

It was dawn when I arrived. The sun had just lifted over the horizon when I saw a massive dark form come into view at the end of the track. There, its enormous skeleton half-buried, black rib bones arcing into the sky like scythes, was a dragon.

I rammed the transmission into a lower gear and rolled down toward the body. The road seemed to end here. Beside the dragon loomed a rock tower that at first I'd thought was a massive yardang, but on closer inspection seemed to be ruins of a building. Nothing moved as I neared. I rolled the vehicle to a stop and carefully climbed out.

I closed my hand tightly about the curved handle of the gun. "Attia?" I called. My voice seemed to boom over the desert and salt flats.

No response. I crunched over the gravel toward the crumbling stone tower.

"Attia!"

Silence. Just a ruined tower and a long-dead dragon. I was alone. Just like in that kaffahouse, all those years ago. She wasn't here.

She wasn't coming.

I felt something inside of me break. Some fragile lockbox where for years I'd held all my hope. I yelled at the dead things in front of me. Screamed. I could feel tears welling in the corner of my eyes. I spun back to the auto. I didn't know what I was going to do. Where I was going to go. She had left me again.

But then, as I spun back around, blinked through tears that still welled in my eyes, I saw a plume of dust rising up on the horizon.

My heart wedged itself in my throat. Somebody was coming. Was it Attia returning? Or had somebody found that army officer already.

Blood thundered in my veins. My head felt light and dizzy. What was I going to do? *Hide.* The tower, looming above. I ran to the base of the rock hill that it stood on and scrambled up the loose slope. I ducked through the low doorway and into the dark tower.

The inside was pitch black and colder even than the desert. I pressed myself against the wall by the door. I could not see far into the ruin, and had no interest in exploring. Anyone or anything could be in that darkness, watching me.

I heard the tires of an autocar rattle over the gravel. A door opened and then slammed. Boots crunched on the loose rock.

"Artur," Song called. "I know you are here."

My mouth was completely devoid of moisture. How had she found me? I remembered her eyes in that hotel where I'd first met her, in the safehouse as she'd studied me. I pulled the gun from my pocket.

What could I do? Hide until she made her way up here? Shoot her when she stepped into the building? What if Attia was wrong? Or was playing me for a fool? What if Song was who she said she was and was only trying to help me? I had been so sure Attia would be here to explain it all! *What a fool you were.* I felt the gun in my hand. The weight of it. Something inside of me resolved.

I stepped out of the tower and into bright sunlight.

Song stood between the two trucks. She had eschewed the business outfit that she'd worn through the border and now sported desert khakis.

She spun toward me as I emerged from the tower, the gun in her hand trained on my head. I raised my hands into the air and paced down the rock slope toward her.

"She's not here," I said. "If you were hoping I would lead

you to her, then I'm sorry. Looks like neither of our plans worked out."

She lowered the gun. "Why did you run off like that? You scared me."

"Don't pretend, Song, or whatever your real name is. You've been in control the whole time, moving me like a piece on a bloody game board." I dropped my arms to my sides. "You, Attia, everybody has been acting *on* me. Acting *through* me." No more. I'd been pulled around by my nose for too long. I wanted answers. I raised the gun, aimed it at her.

Song looked neither surprised nor afraid. "What are you doing, Artur?"

"There never was anybody else at the museum, was there? You've been lying to me the whole time."

"Artur, listen to me. If I meant to betray you, why would I have given you that gun?"

"Because you loaded it with empty shell casings." I cocked the hammer back. "I sorted that out though." The shopkeep had helped me with that.

Her face became a stone mask. "Has she been in contact? What did she tell you? Tell me what she said to you."

"You wanted me to be alone after the museum. Why?"

"I thought if I left you alone Attia would make contact. I didn't realize she had until I came back to the safehouse. How did she get a message to you?"

"The kaffa tin."

Song closed her eyes and shook her head. "Of course." She looked at me then. "Whatever she told you, you can't trust her. She has used you for your entire life. How do you not know that by now?"

"And so what? I should trust you?" I said the words, but at the same time couldn't shake her words. Why *was* I putting my life on the line for a woman that had betrayed me and everybody I loved? Who had pulled me halfway across the world for reasons that I couldn't understand. Why?

Song said, "I can't tell you that you should trust me but—"

And then, mid-sentence, she threw herself to one side, raised her gun.

I squeezed the trigger.

Two gun-blasts exploded through the desert. I squeezed my eyes shut and when I opened them again I was on my back, looking up at the big blue sky. Pain radiated from my shoulder.

Oh . . .

And then desert became the streets of Aelia Capitolina and I was on my back again, surrounded by screaming students and hammering feet, the diesel belching of trucks and the *rat-tat-tat* of machine guns. Feet crunching toward me through the cold and wind of the desert; in the muggy heat of the city, Sina pacing, gun in hand. Two skies, both blue and yawning.

Sina-now-Song leaned down over me. Their faces were one face, separated by twenty years. Agents of the Commissariat, cold, calculating.

They aimed their gun at my face. I was, had been, certain I was going to die. I squeezed my eyes shut. I had cheated death the first time, all those years ago, and now it had come to find me again. Full circle. What choices, what path had led me out here to this patch of desert to die?

I had come here because I loved her still, I realized now.

Another gunshot. A final one.

My eyes fluttered open. Blue sky. No Song, no Sina. I turned my throbbing head and saw her.

Attia. She looked the same, just older. A few more lines. But those eyes, those beautiful mismatched eyes. She stood like a figure from memory, in the entrance of that stone tower, a Mandate rifle smoking in her hand. Attia stood just like she had stood in Aelia Capitolina all those years ago with a gun in hand and a look of shock on her face. This time there was no shock.

"Attia," I croaked. She looked at me. All at once those years were swallowed up.

She scrambled down the loose rock that led from the tower and came to kneel beside me.

"*Cacō*, Gaius," she said. "I'm sorry. I'm so sorry." There were tears in her eyes.

What is happening?

She felt at my arm, pulled my shirt open. I turned my head and saw Song's body beside me in the desert. Her face, slack now in death, looked no longer like an immovable stone.

462   *Mark Robert Philps*

"You saved me," I whispered.

"No," she replied. She sniffed through the tears. "Not yet."

She untied a kerchief knotted about her neck and pressed it into my shoulder wound. I growled in agony. "*Res mutatae mutatae non sunt*," she intoned. "The more things change, the more they stay the same." She laughed bitterly through the tears. "Probably not quite what we meant."

What does this all mean, I tried to ask. Why weren't you there? Why did you leave me? Why are you here now . . .

But the pain was bright light and it was shooting through my vision. I could only manage a grunt. All the exhaustion of the trip pressed down on me. The days on the road without sleep. The terror at being caught, at being found out. The fear of finding this woman who now leaned over me . . .

The more things change . . .

I passed out.

EXCERPT FROM "ON DRACI AND REVOLUTION"
(REDACTED)

It was once said that the true power of the draci lay in the fear that they engendered. They kept a vicious balance. Who dared start a war when the retribution would likely raze all your cities to the ground? Who dared start a revolution when it could be swallowed in searing flame? Nothing burned so bright or so hot as dragonfire. Nothing.

10

I woke inside the tower. Night outside – again or still, I wasn't quite sure. White bandages were wrapped about my shoulder, and by the lightness that spread now through my body I guessed that I was probably on painkillers. I touched the wound tentatively. It seemed that bullet had only grazed me. Another scar.

Attia. Had that been her, truly?

I pushed myself upright and fought a spell of dizziness. I swallowed the vomit that rose in my throat. I stood and stumbled out into the night.

She sat at the bottom of the slope, by a low fire, tending it with a stick. My heart lurched. She sat hunched and lost in thought, her brow furrowed. She looked up at me when I emerged from the tower. She smiled.

"You're awake," she said.

I didn't move. I didn't get any closer. "What is going on?" I said.

Attia bit her lip, her smile faltering. "Come," she said. "Sit down."

I hesitated. The strain between us was palpable. What had I expected after all these years? I made my way slowly down to the firepit. A beaten metal pot rested among the coals, and steam poured from it. I noticed then that Song's body was gone. As I sat I saw that beside Attia was a metal chest, about the size of a suitcase. The clasps were firmly shut and "GA-239" had been etched on the smooth surface. "I suppose we have a lot of catching up to do," she said.

"I waited three days for you," I whispered.

She exhaled loudly. "I know."

"What happened?"

She prodded the fire with the stick. "I was arrested," she said. "Not long after we split up. I thought I was going to be killed." She shrugged. "Apparently they thought I was too valuable to waste away in the labor camps. They wanted me to work for them. Weapons research."

So she *had* been arrested.

"After all they did. All our friends they killed." I didn't even feel angry anymore. Just tired and confused. "You could have said no."

"I was ready to die rather that work for them," she said. I could hear the anger in her voice. "Until they told me that they'd found you. That they knew where you were. They even showed me fotos of you sitting in the kaffahouse where we'd agreed to meet."

I remembered suddenly the fotos that the Commissariat major had shown me in the hotel. Those fotos from all those years ago. A slow realization bloomed inside of me.

"They said that they would leave you alone if I worked for them. They said that if I didn't do what they wanted, if I tried to talk to you, then they'd kill you." She looked up at me then, tears in her eyes. "I did terrible things Gaius. I did them to protect you. Because I loved you."

I was stunned. I couldn't begin to wrap my head around what she'd said. "All these years, I'd thought . . ."

"I know," she whispered. "I'm sorry."

All those years on the run, hiding, alone. I remembered every relationship I'd tried to forge, how they had all been poisoned by the bitterness that I carried within me. I thought of the image I'd made of Attia, the coward, the betrayer. The woman who had cast me away for the sake of her work. The one who had left me alone and ruined my life. I'd made a story in my head, a story of my own life, that of a man wronged and cast aside. But the opposite was true. The self-pitying narrative I'd crafted, the one that had controlled my life, was a lie.

She'd loved me enough to throw away her life, to go against everything she'd believed. And in return I'd hated her.

"Attia," I said. I was beside her. In her blind spot. Her face had shifted, contracting like it did when she worried over an unsolved problem. I reached out and brushed her arm lightly. She was so close. She smelled like the fire and lavender soap.

I stood. "Look at me Attia."

She did.

I reached down and pulled her to her feet. In those mismatched eyes I saw my own pain, mirrored back at me. *Look what they've done to us.* I reached for her with both arms, one good and one bad. She staggered forward into my embrace. Her body felt so familiar against mine. I hugged her tight, and didn't care about the pain that arced through my shoulder. I held her, and hugged her, and then I started crying. As I wept I felt as though she was the one holding me, but then her body began to shake with tears and we were holding each other.

We stayed like that for a long time.

Afterward we fell back to the ground around the fire and sat with our arms about one another, silently staring at the low flames.

"I worked for them for years," she said after a time, her words muffled into my chest. "In their labs and universities. I thought of you. I dreamed of running away, finding you, and escaping. But I was watched too closely. I couldn't risk it.

Then, several years ago, agents of the Primary Directorate came to me. They said they wanted me to defect to the Mandate, to supply them with information on their weapons programs. I did what they wanted. I came here, worked with the best scientists in the Mandate, feeding the Commissariat secrets all the time. I helped them build a weapon."

"The Dragon's Egg," I said, looking at the chest beside her.

Attia frowned. "That's what we called it, yes. When it was completed I stole it. I went into hiding. I told Song that they could have it. If they brought me you."

I shook my head. "You wanted to trade me for the Egg."

Attia nodded. "But I knew that as soon as they had it they would kill us both. Once you were here I had to get you alone. I planted that message in the kaffa tin, hoping you would find it."

"In the museum," I said. "Was that you?"

She nodded. "I got desperate. I needed to see you. I was hoping to pull you away, but Song was too close. I couldn't get you alone."

"So what now?"

"We'll go south. Into the disputed territories in India if we can."

"Will that work?

She shrugged. "I don't know. I feel like our chances are better together though."

But they're still impossibly long, I didn't say.

Silence stretched between us then, accented only but the occasional pop from the fire.

I rubbed a hand through my hair. Dust shook free. I looked askance at the metal chest. "I still don't understand. Why so much trouble for a dragon's egg?"

"It's not a dragon's egg."

"What?"

"Come here," she said.

She took me by the hand and led me into darkness. Holding my hand in hers, she knelt down and pressed it against the metal box.

"Open it."

I was almost afraid to. What was she trying to show me?

I reached down and released the clasp. I swung the chest open, and frowned. Inside the chest, resting in a wood frame, was a perfectly round sphere of silver-white metal. I reached out and pressed my hand against it. It was just slightly warm to the touch. I didn't pick it up, but I could *feel* the denseness of it. "I don't understand," I said.

"Gailium," she said.

I stared at her blankly. Nothing made any sense.

"I would have called it Arturium if I'd known you liked your new name," she said sadly. "A new metal, one made in a laboratory. Remember when I said that if I ever found a new element I'd name it after you? I did it."

"This is the Dragon's Egg?" I said dumbly.

"All spies have codenames." She laughed then, though the frown never left her face. It made her look sad and afraid at the same time. "The dragons are dead. They wanted to replace them. You can't remake the past, but you can create something new." She glanced at her watch, and then the sphere. "Not long now," she said. "You'll see soon enough. We'll be safe here."

She closed the lid of the chest and took me by the hand. We scrambled up the rock slope toward the tower, her helping me balance with my bandaged arm. I could feel that widening gulf in my understanding again. This whole ordeal had felt like I was stumbling from one dark room to another. Was she just rambling?

We reached the top of the hill from which the tower emerged, and instead of climbing inside we skirted around the base until we looked over the desert to the East. The moon swung low through the sky and it illuminated a smattering of sandstone ruins below. They were so old and covered in desert that in my mind's eye they manifested as labyrinthine canyons as much as anything manmade.

"I don't understand."

She pressed her finger to my lips. "Just watch. Wait."

The specter of death still hung over us. She had dragged me into the most dangerous situation of my life. More dangerous, even, then Aelia Capitolina. Maybe I should be mad at her, but when I studied her face all I felt was a thrill.

"I love you," I said.

The wind whipped through the ruins below. "You don't understand," she said. "What I've done . . ."

What was she—

And then, far in the distance, a flare of light. Attia, the salt-flats, the stone city below, were all illuminated as bright as day. I squeezed my eyes shut and turned away. Even through eyelids, and then my hand, the white light shone over everything. When it faded I opened my eyes and blinked in the direction of the light. An incandescent column of smoke and fire, brighter than the ten thousand stars, rose up into the pre-dawn sky. And then there was a low, rumbling boom. A heaven-shattering explosion.

"You see now," Attia said. "You see what they made me do. What I did for you." She made a sound and I wasn't sure if she was laughing or crying.

The more things ch— No. This wasn't merely a replacement. We had lived too long in the shadow of our history. I found her hand and squeezed it tight. *Make something new.*

The horizon shone white with the fire from a second sun. One brighter than dragonfire.

Mountains of Green

Catherine Schaff-Stump

Kayo sharpened the corners of the sheet she folded into a perfect square, just so. Even though it was laundry to be done, Mrs Sasa preferred the customer to have a neat impression of her service. Kayo folded, her eyes on bleached cotton. She did not look at him, although she felt him looking at her, his blue eyes skimming her smooth black hair like he was using his hands, caressing her ears, and touching her long braids. She kept her face as smooth as the white sheet.

She also felt the other set of eyes, like *kami* were watching her, in the distance, hovering over the scene. She wondered if the spirits of Japan liked the Occupation. The eyes of the *kami* watched her hands pluck a second sheet from the pile of dirty laundry, watched Private Quill and his *gaikokujin* face, pulled outside, looked down onto the converted city hall, now American barracks, and hovered over cars and bicycles in the narrow streets, the rubble and the makeshift buildings in the neighborhoods of Hakodate.

Quill said something to her in English and left. Kayo exhaled, slowed her breathing, unclenched. His footsteps faded away, and she turned toward Quill's desk. Quill always left presents for her. Today he had left her three things, and two were useful. There was half a bag of rice, much too dear for her to afford, and a chocolate bar, which she would not care for, but which she would pass along to her little brother Isao, who would sell chunks of it to the boys he played with. The third thing was a pair of nylons.

Kayo had no need for nylons. Since the war had ended, she wore pants, rolled up at the ankles, too large, but right for her now that she worked long, hard hours scrubbing clothes. Even if she wore skirts, she would never wear nylons. She was only thirteen years old.

She would give them to Isao as well. He was a natural sales-man. Surely, one of these Hakodate women would want something like this at a good price. With a little effort, even a troubling gift like Quill's nylons could find some use.

Kayo stacked the last sheet into the basket. She tucked the chocolate, the nylons and the rice around the sheets and followed Quill down the hallway, past the commander's office and toward the exit. The office door was closed, and she heard language gobbledygook on the other side.

That meant she would have to wait outside before she could return to the laundry, to collect the money for the order she had delivered today. She went outside and sat on the concrete steps and placed the basket on the ground. These Americans never took off their shoes, and she didn't in the barracks either. Wearing shoes inside just wasn't natural.

"Kayo!" Isao ran toward her. He was dressed in a dirty pair of black shorts. His knees were covered with smut from the streets, his white tennis shoes were gray, and his stomach gaped through a hole in his striped shirt. Maybe she should ask Quill for a needle and thread. If he was going to leave her gifts, they might as well be useful gifts.

Kayo tried out the stern look that her mother would have given Isao under the circumstances, but she couldn't sustain it. Thinking of her mother made her think about crying. She knew she was failing Isao when she didn't scold him for skipping school. "What are you doing here?"

"Working," he said. "Like you. Did the *gaijin* give you anything today?"

Kayo produced the nylons and the chocolate. "See what you can do with these."

Isao let the nylons dangle from his hand. They floated in the air like *bonito* flakes. "Hunh," said Isao. "These don't seem very sturdy."

"It doesn't matter. Women will want them. You should take them to the Comfort Center, see if any women want them there."

Isao shook his head. "They closed it, remember?"

Kayo's lips thinned. "Yes. Now I remember. Well, someone will want them."

"Maybe you should keep them, and see if anyone at the laundry wants them. Maybe old Mrs Sasa wants to look sexy. Or she wants to give them to one of her girls."

She cuffed Isao, and he winced. "That is for disrespecting your elders," said Kayo. "If Mrs Sasa didn't give me work, you and I would starve." Kayo thought. "Should I give them to her as a thank you present?"

"No!" Isao shoved the delicate nylons into his pocket. "We live in the new Japan. It's all about money and democracy. There are no more gifts without motive. You need to be more ruthless. Like a fox. Like an American."

"But Mrs Sasa—"

Isao's voice lowered. "She would fire you on the spot if she knew we were *hibakusha*. They believe that we are freaks because of the bomb. Don't paint her as our savior. She uses young girls to make a killing off GI Joe's laundry. Don't let her talk you into doing anything else."

Kayo wanted to scold Isao, to remind him of who was the oldest, but he had learned so much. He could speak English. He could make money out of dust. She said nothing.

The door to the barracks opened. Kayo dusted off her baggy pants. As she stood, one long, skinny braid whipped over her shoulder. The American commander had an envelope for her, written in English letters. "*Kane*," he said, massacring the Japanese word for money. It didn't matter. She took the envelope.

Out the door behind him came a strange man. She'd never seen his like. Her first thought was *akuma*, a demon. This man was black, with hair that clung to his skull in black and gray whorls. He dressed like an American army officer, the same army uniform, but different patches than the rest of them. Not taking her eyes off him, Kayo stumbled down the steps next to her basket. She gathered Isao to her side. Isao's mouth gaped open.

The man towered over the commander, a full head taller. "Hey Isao," said the commander. "Glad you're here. Dr Marsh needs someone to help him, and I thought about you."

"They're talking about you," said Kayo. "What are they saying?"

"They want me to help that man. He is a doctor."

The *akuma* man knelt so he could look Isao in the eye. Kayo looked away, as direct eye contact was rude. She was ashamed that Isao met the man's gaze without flinching. "Hello," *akuma* man said in accented Japanese.

"Hey Joe," said Isao in English. He went on into a strange patter that Kayo recognized as his merchant talk.

"No," said *akuma* man in better Japanese than Kayo expected. "I don't want to buy anything from you. I need a guide. I hear you know what I'm looking for."

"What are you looking for, Marsh-*sensei*?" Isao couldn't pronounce the "r" and the word was Ma-shu. English had some stupid sounds.

"I'm a biologist. I focus on the effects of radiation."

Kayo's stomach tightened. Were they looking to study people? His Japanese was good, but she didn't know what his words meant. There were already scientists in Nagasaki and back in Hiroshima, studying people with their hair falling out and their skin sagging off their faces, burns and sickness and death. So far, Kayo and Isao had not been sick, but every day she lived in fear of it. She did not want to be alone in the world. She didn't want to die.

Isao shook his head. His smile sparkled. "Marsh-*sensei*, you are in the wrong city."

"I've heard there's something outside of town. You could help me look."

Kayo shook her head. She had heard about it too. They talked about it at the laundry. Some sort of mutated animal, a fantasy, they said. But she didn't think so. She thought that when the Americans came with their poisonous bomb, that Japan's guardians would not let this pass, and now they were awake. Maybe that was also her fantasy, one that kept her moving forward.

Isao had that gleam in his eye, the one that sealed a deal. "You want me to guide you?"

"Yes. I need someone who knows the area to help me."

"I am afraid," said Kayo, studying her feet, "that my brother and I are new here. Perhaps another boy would be better."

Isao pulled himself up, and pointed at himself, middle finger to nose. "I'm your guide," he said. "We may be new here, but I've been everywhere."

Kayo winced inside. Did he ever go to school at all? She hoped her parents would forgive her.

"That's what they tell me," said Marsh. "Then tomorrow we'll get started."

Kayo's hands were becoming red and scaly from the harsh soap of the laundry. She wrapped strips of cloth around them when they weren't in the water. She and Isao sat in the tiny room they occupied, eating dinner by a dim lantern. Isao took the small bowl of rice from her and dug in, chopsticks flashing like blades.

"Not so fast," said Kayo. "That's all you get tonight."

"Soon," said Isao, "we'll have more. I'll take that American everywhere. Except where he could find anything." He picked a grain of rice off his upper lip and popped it in his mouth.

"There's nothing to find," said Kayo. "Don't you feel ashamed, taking advantage of that man?"

"No," said Isao. He uncrossed his legs and poured her a small cup of hot water. They could not afford tea. "We must take advantage of them. Besides, there is something out there. He doesn't need to find it right away, that's all."

"One of the guardians?" Kayo smiled. She sipped the water. The Americans had brought clean water and, tea or not, it was a blessing to have it.

Isao nodded. "Not the *kirin*, the dragon, or the phoenix. They all flew away when the bomb came. But the turtle. Now, the turtle is slow. The turtle wants vengeance for Japan."

Isao would pick the turtle. He loved them and had kept several over the years. "For our family," said Kayo.

"For our army," said Isao.

"If you found the turtle," said Kayo, "I would not be displeased."

Her *kami* eyes failed her when Quill touched her shoulder. She sprang away from him, putting a bed between him and her. "It's okay," said Quill. That much English she understood. His freckles made him look like a spotted salamander and his red hair repulsed her. He spewed out some English and started toward her.

She slipped past him and ran into the hall, past the commander and Marsh. The commander asked her something in a concerned voice, but she didn't stop running until she was outside. She ran to the laundry without the basket, without the sheets and without the payment for the last load, her throat coated with the metallic taste of fear.

The laundry was a swampy quagmire of humidity, like a hot Hiroshima day in the summer. Old women stirred a giant vat of clothes, scrubbed clothes on washboards, and toted baskets of clothes to drying racks. Coming down the stairs from Mrs Sasa's office, two young women wearing Western dresses blew kisses at their boss. Mrs Sasa walked from station to station, supervising the work of her employees. She noted Kayo's appearance.

"What is it, Kayo-*chan*?" She placed a solicitous hand on Kayo's shoulder, her nails like the talons of a dragon.

Kayo shook her head. She had no idea what to say.

"Where's the money for the order?"

"I forgot it."

Mrs Sasa puckered her lips. "That's not like you."

"I'm sorry," she said.

"You come into my office," said Mrs Sasa.

The noise of the laundry diminished a little as Mrs Sasa slid her door shut. She tapped her finger on her chin. "What is this about?"

"Nothing," said Kayo. "I saw a mouse in the barracks. I was afraid."

Mrs Sasa laughed. "There isn't a woman in Japan afraid of a mouse anymore. Try again, little liar."

Kayo shifted and listened to the floorboards creak.

"Was one of the GIs mean to you?"

Tears rimmed in Kayo's eyes. "No. Not mean."

Mrs Sasa could afford tea. She poured Kayo a cup, sat at a low table, and patted the *tatami* beside her. "Kayo," she said, "I don't know what happened, but I think I can guess. How old are you?"

"Thirteen."

"And you are not a woman?"

"No. Not yet."

"I feel sorry for you. I know you have no mother. You mustn't feel ashamed of a man being attracted to you. You must take advantage of it."

"I can't."

"A soldier gives you gifts. Isao told me when he tried to sell me nylons last week. You accept these gifts."

Kayo nodded.

"You must," said Mrs Sasa. "It is a very practical thing to do in your situation, but you must know that any American wants something in return for their investment. They aren't like us. Give this man what he wants. There will be more gifts, better gifts."

"I can't do that," whispered Kayo. "I can't."

Mrs Sasa's hand covered the top of Kayo's. "I am only giving you advice. It is such a little thing to give for such a good return. After the first time, you will feel no fear." She laughed. "You will only be bored. Get pretty things for yourself, get food for your brother."

"I can't."

Mrs Sasa shrugged. "I can only give you my opinion. What you do is up to you. Now, I need you to go back to the barracks and get my money."

"Can someone else go?"

"No," said Mrs Sasa. "That will remain your job."

The eyes of Private Quill followed her whenever he thought there were no officers looking. Kayo avoided his eyes and didn't go into any room with him unless someone else was there. Quill stopped leaving her gifts. That was fine as long as Isao led Marsh around the countryside, but the money that Isao made from cigarettes, chocolates, and the other knick-knacks was essential. They could never afford rice without Quill.

One night Isao bought home fish. Kayo scolded him. "We need to save our money."

"We need fish," said Isao. "Just this once."

"No," said Kayo. "Quill doesn't give me gifts to sell anymore."

"Well, Marsh-*sensei* keeps giving me money." Isao lifted bits of fish to his mouth. "I like him. He's been teaching me about genetic mutation."

"What's that?"

"Sometimes when you are irradiated, it can change you."

Kayo had bad dreams about that. "It has not changed you or me."

"You," said Isao.

"What do you mean?"

"I mean that I've mutated into a rich man."

"So, he thinks that this creature you're looking for is a mutation? Not a turtle?"

Isao shrugged. "If an animal mutates, it could become anything. You know, a dog or a *tanuki* could have two heads or something." Isao puffed as he chewed the hot fish. "With Marsh-*sensei* in my pocket, we don't need Quill. Besides, I think I could convince the *sensei* to take us to America."

Kayo clucked in disgust. "Marsh-*sensei* will leave. There is no mutated monster and he will make science somewhere else." She chewed on her lower lip. "We need Quill."

"Why did he stop giving you gifts?" said Isao. "Did you make him mad?"

"In a way," said Kayo. She made up her mind. She pushed her fish away.

"Don't you want it?"

"No. You can have mine. Come with me tomorrow. I need you to translate some English for me."

Kayo brushed her hair and left it out, black, smooth and glossy. She borrowed a dress from one of Mrs Sasa's girls, belted at the waist to hide how baggy it was on her. Mrs Sasa offered some lipstick, suggesting that it would make her look more adult, but Kayo didn't want to look more adult. Part of her hoped that if she looked thirteen, Quill would go back to the way things were before.

He didn't though. When she entered the barracks with her laundry basket and Isao, he watched her as though she were laid on a small ceramic plate with *wasabi* and ginger especially for his eyes. When she explained to Isao what she thought Quill wanted and what she needed his English for, they had argued. In the end Isao had agreed to speak for her, but he was angry and ashamed.

Isao's narrow eyes were like a microscope, boring into Quill. "My sister says that she doesn't mind if you date her. As long as you give us a full bag of rice and enough money to buy good food each month."

Quill pinched Kayo's hair between thumb and forefinger, and rattled off something to Isao. "He says that he'll do that." Isao gestured with his hands as he and Quill negotiated. Kayo knew were talking about the exact amount of yen that Kayo would be worth a month.

Then it was done. For a bag of rice and money for fruit and fish, she was a prostitute to an American. They wouldn't go hungry. She was nauseous.

"He says tomorrow night. Come here. I know a place in the country he can take you."

Quill disappeared and returned with two envelopes, one for the laundry, one with some yen for her. He outlined her jaw with a finger, kissed her on the forehead and they left. Outside, she hugged herself with her hands to stop shaking.

Isao plucked the envelope away from her. He counted the money. "This is more than we've seen in a month, Kayo. More than Marsh-*sensei* gives me." He put it in the dirty pocket of his shorts.

"Give it to me," said Kayo. "I need to buy our dinner."

"No," said Isao. His face was hard. "I keep the money."

She raised her hand to slap him, but she put it down again, and she didn't look at him. Her tears splattered in the dirt, her fists clenched at her sides. Kayo's tears blinded her as she made her way back to the laundry.

Before meeting Quill, Kayo let Mrs Sasa use rouge and lipstick to paint her face. Mrs Sasa began to talk about how Kayo might like to date other men, to make more money. She could arrange things, and keep a small fee. Kayo said no. It was bad enough that there was the fact of Quill. She would not sink that low. Mrs Sasa helped Kayo pile her hair upon her head, like a

Hollywood starlet. Kayo felt very unlike herself, which made her feel better about everything. She thought about the woman she looked like on the outside. This woman was not Kayo. She was someone else.

At the barracks, she navigated the stairs unbalanced, teetering in borrowed pumps. Quill leaned on a counter, scowling. He said something in English and pointed at his watch. Kayo knew she was late. He grabbed her wrist. Tonight he looked like a hungry tiger, and she knew that while she would walk through her life for the rest of her years, tonight Quill would eat the piece of her that was alive.

They drove an American jeep out to a farm in the country, an old-fashioned house with torn paper jagged in the *shoji* doors. She and Isao had stayed here on their way from Hiroshima to Hakodate. No one was here now, the house too far from town, too old to be of use to the Americans.

Quill spat out a wad of gum. He had also gone to some effort to look nice, his hair slicked back, and his uniform brushed and straightened, like he was some Joe taking his girl to the movies. He reached for her across the seat and pulled her in from the small of her back, and he kissed her. His tongue pushed into her mouth like a snake, a swollen thing that made her gag. She squirmed to get away. He clenched her to his body. She froze like a rabbit, only her mind active, screaming the word "no" over and over.

He stopped and said something in English, sharp and mean. There was only hunger in his eyes. He had paid. They had a deal. With shame, she began unbuttoning the top three buttons of her dress, her fingers clumsy, her hands trembling. She thought about what she needed to do to make sure that she and Isao survived. Rice. Water. Fish.

Quill placed a hand down her bra, over a tiny budding breast. She winced and closed her eyes. His fingers played with the hooks, and he leaned her back on the car seat. She riveted her eyes shut. He was everywhere.

Then abruptly Quill disappeared.

Kayo opened her eyes. Marsh dangled Quill by the collar of his shirt, his fist cocked back, ready to strike Quill like a temple bell. The *akuma* man stood a foot over Quill, dangerous. No, not a demon. An avenging *bodhisattva*.

Behind them, Isao rocked on his feet, a satisfied cat, sunning itself in the light of success. He opened the jeep door and helped her out. "Run, Kayo. Not toward the house."

The ground shook with the tremor of an earthquake. Kayo jumped out of the rocking car and onto the side of her ankle, just as she had feared because of the pumps. She abandoned the shoes. The ground shook again, jarring. Over the tree line, part of mountain moved, a hill of green.

"See," Isao yelled over the roar that filled the night like an air-raid siren. "Good value for the money, *sensei*." Isao stared at the creature, and it turned in their direction. Kayo knew then. He was controlling the monster. At least she thought he might be. Both of them what Marsh called mutations.

Marsh dropped Quill, who jabbered some frantic English and raced toward the house. A dome, a giant green-shelled turtle, blended into the pines of the mountain so that when it slept, the people of Hakodate would not see it.

Now the turtle was awake. Isao stared at it, standing his ground. "You are the protector of children!" he yelled. "That man is yours!"

Marsh grabbed Kayo's arm and they swerved out of the monster's path. The turtle lumbered on stalky pillars. Its tail leveled trees, and its shell plowed the ground as it plodded toward Quill.

Quill bee-lined for the dilapidated house. He scrambled into the crawl space. She imagined his screams drowned out by the air raid siren of the *kaiju*'s shrieking roar.

Kayo heard Isao shout, or it might have been in her head. "Protect my sister. Protect Japan."

The turtle stamped the house in its path flat. It exploded into splinters, frames, mats and rot. Kayo couldn't look at another explosion, more destruction. Crumbling and crunching crescendoed and died. The night became silent. The turtle turned back to Isao, who touched its beak as it bent down. Then it plodded back to the mountains, back to its sleep.

Isao pulled Quill's money out of his pocket, dropped it, and ground the white envelope into the grass with his dirty tennis shoe. "We will never spend a penny of that money," he said.

"You will tell Mrs Sasa you are not interested in any more of her ideas, and you will quit the laundry."

Kayo shook her head. "How will we live? I must do something. I must take care of you."

Isao took her hand. "We've managed before. We'll do so now."

Kayo kissed his forehead, and he wiped glossy red lipstick off with the back of his hand.

Marsh spoke in Japanese. "Kayo, are you okay?"

Kayo clutched her dress across her chest and bowed. "Thank you very much, *sensei*."

"Don't worry about it. Isao told me tonight we'd find a monster. We did, but we got here in time." He crossed his arms and studied Isao. "You've been holding out on me."

Isao put his hands up in the air and smiled at Marsh. "No, I haven't. I promised you we'd find your mutation. What will the commander say when you tell him Quill is dead?"

"That Quill wasn't the only monster here." Marsh ran a hand over his head. "I mean, that was an accident. That would never happen again, right?"

"No," said Isao. "Never."

The turtle once again tucked into the mountains. Kayo watched the pines shift on the mountains behind it and felt Isao's eyes watching her, and the sleepy eyes of the turtle. She felt protected. She felt safe.

The Wings The Lungs, The Engine The Heart

Laurie Tom

As Karl scrubbed his hands in the small allotment of water he could afford, he could hear the muffled scraping of Mueller pulling the heart-box out of storage on the opposite end of the operating room. Tarps dropped with a dull thud, and tiny wooden wheels wobbled as they rolled on the uneven floor.

Karl shook his hands dry and glanced at his cane, resting against the wall beside the washbasin. Sometimes he needed it after a long day's work, but he was fresh this afternoon, and the last thing he wanted was to be berated for his human frailties should he decline the operation.

"Do we have enough of the right blood?" he asked Mueller.

"I believe so, Dr Huber."

That did not inspire confidence in Karl, but there was little help for that. Blood transfusion was still a very new thing, and this ramshackle facility was a building apart from the rest of the infirmary. It had a special operating room for a unique purpose as ordered by the Kaiser.

Mueller placed sheets of paper on a tray beside the operating table, depicting the means by which Karl was to connect the heart-box to his patient. He had looked over those sheets far too many times, all in preparation for this.

The door to the operating room opened with a bang as Ostermann entered the room. "They're almost here!" His orderly handed a set of hastily scrawled notes to Karl, who glanced at them perfunctorily before passing them on to Mueller. Mueller set them down by the heart-box instructions.

Karl was not happy, but at least now he would be given the chance to do his job. He would have gladly operated to save the life of a soldier, regardless of whether or not he had limbs, but the army would not bring any such man here.

Instead he had to deal with Dr Steinfeld's monstrosity. The good doctor would not risk his neck out so close to the front, where Allied bombing could conceivably blow him into his next life. Instead Karl and a handful of others were dispatched like jackals along the Western Front, each with a godforsaken contraption to use when a suitable candidate was found.

He needed a soldier who was dying or newly dead, but with a body that was intact enough to perform after resuscitation. And therein lay the problem. Soldiers in trenches frequently died after being blown to pieces or blistered by gas, and that was if sickness and disease did not claim them first.

The wait had made Karl idle, and frustrated.

Ostermann held open the door, ushering in a pair of men carrying a body on a stretcher. They moved their cargo smartly to the table, their movements quick and oddly reverent.

Karl took command, calling for his staff to remove their patient's clothes and wash him down; then he spoke with the men who had brought his candidate.

"What killed him? He looks already dead."

"Believed to be a single bullet through the torso. He seems to have bashed his chin against the butt of his machine gun when he landed, but that should not have been fatal."

Karl glanced over his shoulder at the bruised face of the young man on the operating table and agreed. That would heal. *If* he got up again. He had hoped for someone who was dying rather than dead. He did not know how long after death Steinfeld's heart-box would work, assuming it did at all, but aside from being already dead, he could hardly have asked for a better candidate.

"Landed?" he asked.

"His triplane, sir. Please," and now the soldier's voice wavered, "you've got to bring him back. A lot of men died to retrieve him."

Karl grimaced. "Who in God's name is this that men would be sent to die just to bring a body back?"

"*Rittmeister* Manfred von Richthofen. High Command wants . . ."

Karl had heard enough. Oh, he knew what High Command wanted, but he did not have to be happy about it.

He ordered the soldiers out and looked at his staff, who had wheeled the heart-box over and were ready to begin. The loathsome thing was almost as wide as a soldier's bed and tall enough to reach a man's waist. Mueller cranked it up and it thrummed as the orderly checked the medical notes left by the soldiers and added the first pints of blood. This would be Karl's first attempt to connect the monster, but he knew the steps. Steinfeld had gone over them far too many times. The man did not trust him.

Karl scowled at the body on the table as he came alongside. Reaching out a gloved hand, he prodded it lightly. So this was Manfred von Richthofen. It would be his bad luck to get him. The body was cooling, but not cold. And if it was High Command that wanted Richthofen resuscitated, eyes would be on every detail if he failed. He wasn't sure resuscitation would even be possible anymore, and throwing good lives after bad; sheer folly. What was one pilot in the grand scheme of things?

The way High Command paraded him around one would think *der Rote Kampfflieger* was single-handedly winning the war. Even the British had a name for him: "the Red Baron". Richthofen was worth more than a hundred men as far as propaganda was concerned, but how many of those men did they send to retrieve a body that may never walk again?

Certainly he had a friendly grin and an enviable kill record, making him the face of the best Germany had to offer. People at home could rest easy knowing men like *der Rote Kampfflieger* were fighting the Allies in the West. He was also an arrogant noble who thought so highly of himself that against all common sense he was willing to paint his plane completely red so enemies and allies alike would know when he took to the air.

He probably would have lived longer if he hadn't been flying red.

But work was work.

Karl didn't expect to resuscitate him, given how long he must have been dead, but he and his staff might learn something from the attempt. He expected he would get reprimanded by the military for failing to save an already dead man, but honestly what worse could they do to him? He was already working in a hospital in spitting distance of the Allied bombers.

Richthofen recuperated with an orderly on duty in his room at all hours of the day and the heart-box ever whirring at his side. For days he did not regain consciousness and the machine pumped blood for a heart that no longer beat. The bullet that had claimed Richthofen's life had entered beneath his right armpit, punctured one lung, clipped his heart, and exited just above his left nipple. He had probably remained conscious for only moments after, and despite himself Karl was impressed to know that Richthofen had managed to land at all before succumbing to such a wound.

The man had a way of defying the odds. Karl knew this was not the first time that Richthofen had been shot down. He had been in the hospital previously after having been shot in the head and again the man had managed to land his plane.

Karl checked on his patient at least twice daily, more frequently when Richthofen regained consciousness, though the man was addled as though from a fever and would not remember him six hours later. As Karl waited for his patient to change one way or the other he paged through *Der Rote Kampfflieger*, Richthofen's autobiography. Mueller had brought it for his own reading, but pushed it onto Karl, telling him that he might like his patient a bit better if he understood him.

Karl only accepted it out of tedium. It was foolish for a man in his twenties to think he had a life story worth telling, but Karl supposed it was all for propaganda. People loved to know their heroes. Karl used to, but Steinfeld had turned out no hero. Famous people never lived up to being the picture that others had painted.

Ten days after Richthofen's arrival, he greeted Karl upon his entrance and said, "I am told that I have you to thank for reviving me."

Karl pulled up a chair beside him and said, "There is nothing to thank. You have an inhospitable road ahead of you."

The heart-box thrummed beside the bed across from Karl, a box of pumps and tubes, four of which ran to the harness around Richthofen's torso and from there into his back. The moment the machine stopped, Richthofen's life would end.

And the young man seemed well aware of that, because his eyes traveled to the box on hearing Karl's words.

"I must confess," he said, "I don't know entirely what this is about."

"There is a medical researcher, Dr Hermann Steinfeld, who has been working on a mechanical heart to keep people alive when their own stops working. The Kaiser agreed to provide funding, believing that such a machine could be invaluable to the military. He thinks Steinfeld might eventually be able to create a device that would allow a previously killed soldier to return to combat. But for now, all we can hope for is to prevent someone from dying. We need physically healthy candidates to test the machines with, to rule out any complications due to weakness of the body, and since we can hardly ask for someone who is not dying to volunteer . . ."

"You pick from the fallen, who would otherwise die."

"Healthy in all ways aside from the bullet that would kill them."

"So what is to become of me?" And in his voice, Karl heard a challenge.

"I don't know," said Karl. "To my knowledge, you are the first success we've had. Truthfully, I did not expect to save you at all. I suppose the next step is to see how long you last."

He would probably be reprimanded if word of his bedside manner left the room, but his orderly said nothing, well acquainted with Karl's disposition, and *der Rote Kampfflieger* simply nodded. "I suppose you are right. I shall have to ask though, is it possible that I will eventually be disconnected from this machine?"

Karl inhaled and said, "We expect that based on our observations of you and others we will eventually be able to improve on the design, but we could not repair your heart, nor do we expect that it will regain its function on its own. The machine beats for you, and I'm afraid you will remain connected to one for as long as you live."

Disappointment flashed across Richthofen's face, but only for a moment and then it was gone again. Karl knew from his autobiography that he had been an active man: an avid horseman, a gymnast as a boy, and possessed a love of hunting. He would do none of that now, not with a machine that had to be wheeled on a cart, and charged and cranked every day.

Karl felt a twinge of sympathy, but then he remembered this was a man who had hunted men with the same precision and thrill as hunting game.

"What day is it?" Richthofen asked.

"May second, your twenty-sixth birthday."

Richthofen sighed. "I don't suppose I'll eventually recover enough to fly again, will I?"

"I don't see how that would be possible," said Karl.

But for the second time, Karl was wrong.

Over the coming weeks, members of Jagdgeschwader 1, Richthofen's fighting wing, came to visit him. The news given to the general public was simply that *der Rote Kampfflieger* had been shot down, but was recuperating. It was not unheard of, or even unusual, for pilots to emerge alive from downed aircraft, so there was no reason for anyone to think there were facts hidden beyond any official statement.

Richthofen's wing was another matter entirely. They had dearly wanted to visit their commander as they had the last time he had been shot down, and it was only out of concern that pilots on leave would share conjectures with friends and family that the military bureaucrats finally allowed a few of the officers to visit.

But they had restrictions, and Karl had been the one to relay them to Richthofen.

Do not tell them that the heart-box cannot be removed. Do not tell them you will never fly again. Do not let them worry. They must know you are recovering for the sake of the Fatherland.

"I am tired of lying," he said to Karl, "so I decided to do something about it."

Richthofen had lost weight since his resuscitation, though once he had been able to get out of bed he had begun daily calisthenics, as best he could manage on such a short leash. And when he was not exercising, he was writing. Writing letters home, orders to his men – Karl did not know, but Richthofen had kept both Ostermann and Mueller running to the dispatch carriers every other day. He was a stubbornly busy patient for a man who could not leave his own room without assistance.

"I am alive and grateful," said Richthofen, "so do not misjudge me. For now, you even let me out of bed, but I cannot go more than two meters before the cords go no further. I should like to tear them out, but we both know where that would take us."

"You will not have to face a military investigation if you die," said Karl.

"Is that a jest?"

Karl shrugged. "Maybe. I tend to find myself in a black sense of humor. I know many people will be unhappy with me if you die. I may end up unhappiest of all."

"And yet your manner does not indicate that you place a priority on my well-being." There was a thin smile on Richthofen's lips. The man was not stupid. Whatever injury the earlier bullet had done to his skull, it certainly hadn't dulled his perception.

"You will have to forgive me if I am less than excited that one soldier should be given special treatment over another, especially since we do not expect you to fly again."

"They will want to give me an administration job for certain." Richthofen grimaced. "I turned one down, you know. They did not want to lose me on the battlefield. I am worth more as an ideal than as a pilot, no matter how many planes I shoot. I could be the greatest pilot in history, and still they would put me behind a desk, only to wheel me out when they want to show off a war hero."

Karl said nothing, but he did not believe Richthofen would ever have such a job. The machine, his heart-box, would have to be carried everywhere he went. The public would not want to see Richthofen as a cripple. There would be no tours of the countryside, no waving to the people who believed in him. He might still be useful for propaganda, but not as a man to stand before the masses.

Germany still had a few aces though. Wilhelm Reinhard, who was leading JG 1 in Richthofen's absence, was no laggard, having recently bagged three planes in a single day. Even Richthofen's younger brother, Lothar, was quite the pilot himself. The only thing that made *der Rote Kampfflieger* unique was that over time he had downed more aircraft before dying than other pilots.

"I thought of something else I can no longer do," said Richthofen, reclining on his bed. He stuffed a pillow under his back, so he could lay a little more comfortably, but true comfort would never be possible with the tubes behind him. "I was trying to think of a way to exercise in here and I remembered my old gymnastics classes at the academy. I can still stretch, and if I'm careful I can even cartwheel," – Karl cringed, trying not to picture what a tangle of tubes Richthofen could have made – "but the thing I miss the most, is the horizontal bar."

"I remember reading about that in your autobiography."

Richthofen rolled his eyes and shook his head. "I wrote that under orders and they edited me terribly. I am not that person anymore. I wish I could fix it. Maybe now I will have the time."

The door opened and Mueller stepped inside. He nodded respectfully to Richthofen and then handed a telegram to Karl. Karl opened it and frowned.

"Bad news?" said Richthofen.

Karl shook his head. "No, but it looks like you will not have to worry about being carted all over Germany to wave at civilians anymore."

Richthofen's face crumpled, and he looked to the large box by his bed, still churning for all it was worth. Karl pitied him, just a little, knowing that he must be coming to a terrible conclusion about his future, but he could not in good conscience allow the mood to remain.

He sighed and said, "You are a real devil, if you have not been told already. Now I know what all those messages were for. You know what they want and still you push . . ."

"Then it can be done?" said Richthofen. He lifted his head, his bearing returning. "You told me the heart-box was a test, to see if you could revive soldiers and send them back into combat."

Karl nodded and handed him the telegram. "High Command has consented, with Dr Steinfeld's encouragement. He agrees that the box would be a real bother to wheel everywhere you go, but there's no reason it could not be installed into one of the biplanes. High Command has set aside one of the new Fokker D.VIIs, and they are customizing it just for you."

Much to Karl's dismay, as Richthofen's attending doctor he and two of his orderlies were assigned to accompany him, which meant they had to be ready to pack up and move every few days so that Jagdgeschwader 1 could focus on where the fighting was heaviest.

The modified version of the Fokker D.VII arrived in late June, specially rebalanced to allow the heart-box to be stowed in a space behind the pilot's chair. The life-giving tubes would run through slots in the backboard of the seat, which was inserted between pilot and machine after Richthofen was seated. It did not allow for an easy entrance or egress for the pilot; indeed, he could not manage without a team of three men to aid him, but Richthofen was flying again.

A part of Karl did not like to see a man who was clearly still a patient flying alone in the air, but the men of JG 1 were clearly pleased to have him back. They barely gave a thought to the box behind him and Richthofen downplayed the danger. Whether he had a heart-box or no, the risk of being fired upon was the same as always.

After a day's dogfight, Richthofen would retire to his quarters in whatever facilities Karl and his team had available to them. On this particular day, it was an abandoned farmhouse, and Karl had set Richthofen up in the master bedroom.

Ostermann wheeled the heart-box beside the bed and a weary Richthofen lay down, careful not to damage the tubes that sprang from his back.

"You know," he said to Karl, "it is so much different flying than it is here on the ground."

"I suppose it has always been that way."

"No. I do not mean different as in anything an ordinary man would feel. Do you know how they connect the heart-box to the biplane?"

"I saw the schematics and read Dr Steinfeld's notes."

Karl had only had been present for Richthofen's initial "installation" into his plane, to ensure the life of his patient was not in danger, but beyond that he saw attending as a pointless exercise. He could not be there every time Richthofen flew, and it was best that his ground crew be the ones familiar with the procedure since in the event of an emergency they would be the first ones available to extract him.

"The Fokker itself powers the heart-box when I am in the air," said Richthofen. "It's more powerful than the box alone. I can feel the blood rushing through me, I can feel excited again. This box . . . it only beats at the pace it likes, and it's not enough for a fighting man in the sky, but together with the Fokker I can feel the wind in my lungs again."

"I am glad it is working out for you."

"Is there a way we can get a Fokker's engine to permanently power the heart-box?"

"Only if you never want to move again outside of an airplane."

Richthofen frowned, but his voice was wistful. "I barely move outside of one already. I don't know . . . How do you deal with it?"

"Deal with what?"

"Mueller told me that you used to be a gymnast as well. A good one."

"Used to be. I broke my ankle and it didn't heal well." Karl tapped his cane against the floor. "I can manage walking just fine, standing long enough for surgeries most days, but no tricks anymore. I'm not lucky enough to break the same bone twice and still be pronounced fit for combat duty."

Richthofen laughed, a soft sound. "I broke my collarbone and you your ankle. One of them still allows a man some maneuverability, the other does not. Still, you have my sympathies."

Karl did not see what for. He hadn't cared about gymnastics in years. With two children and an anxious wife far away in Bonn, all he wanted was to survive this job and see himself home again. It wasn't as though he had ruined his only means of living. His ankle was nothing compared to what so many soldiers had lost.

"Our supply lines are struggling," said Richthofen. "I don't like to talk about it in front of the men, but you, my skeptic friend, must have noticed. We're not going to hold the land we gained this past spring."

"It was bound to happen," said Karl. "This whole war has been a mess, what it has done to our country, to our people, to soldiers like you."

"I have downed ninety planes now. Clearly Germany could not be better off. Shall I shoot a hundred? Then perhaps the Allies will turn tail and run home."

"I doubt that will happen."

"And then we will lose the war. Can you tell me something, good doctor? I know you will not mince words. Right now my life is bearable because I am among good company and I can stretch my wings in my Fokker and feel like an eagle again, but what will happen to me when the war is over? Will I ever fly again?"

Karl did not know.

It was late September, 1918, and Karl could feel the war was ending. The Allies were making their push, forcing the Germans back to the Siegfried Line. Men talked about an armistice in hushed tones, as though too fearful to believe. Germany could no longer hold on, and yet the men of the Imperial German Air Force still flew sorties. So long as Allied bombers threatened the men on the ground, JG 1 would fly.

Karl entered Richthofen's room to find the man performing push-ups. It was difficult for the already lean pilot to keep muscle on his body. They had constructed a rudimentary treadwheel for him outside, a little something they could haul around in trucks along with their tents as they moved from battle to battle, but he could only go in good weather and if Mueller or Ostermann were free. One time one of the cart wheels had fallen into a rabbit hole and nearly dislodged the heart-box from its cradle. Richthofen had turned a pasty white, but he did not stop his requests to go, and reluctantly Karl had allowed him to continue.

If Richthofen was not fit he could not fly, and if he could not fly, then what purpose did he have as anything other than a test subject for Steinfeld's machine?

"Here is the checklist from the mechanics," said Karl, handing him a few sheets of paper.

Since Richthofen could not reasonably inspect his plane himself, he had to rely on his ground team to perform to his satisfaction. Part of that involved filling out the list he had created to make sure nothing was overlooked. It was supposedly for his peace of mind, but Karl did not think that it actually helped. Richthofen took the checklist, glanced at all the marks made, and set it aside on the stand by his bed.

"The plane looks fine," said Karl.

"It looks fine, but it never flies fine," said Richthofen. "The balance is different with the heart-box inside. Fokker did an admirable job trying to adjust the plane for me, but I can tell the difference."

"You haven't been downed a third time."

"I was never the kind of pilot who becomes one with his machine, just a man who knows how to use a tool he's been given. I can compensate for some things."

He sat down and sighed.

"It feels very odd to say this, but I am not looking forward to the end of the war."

"The end will be a good thing."

"It will be, for most people, and I am not selfish enough to wish to prolong it when there are so many good things that will come from its end, but I am still saddened by the thought." Richthofen looked at the heart-box beside him. "This device works so well. Sometimes I wonder that it does not jam like our guns. It is not natural. We should have you doctors building our weapons instead of the engineers that we have."

"The heart-box is not without its flaws," said Karl. "We have fitted other patients with them since. You have been lucky, but others have not, and we've been able to address issues in yours before they have become a problem. Even though it has never stopped, we have still replaced parts, turning off one pump while the other remains active, so it is not as though it has never worn down."

"I try to picture myself going home, seeing my mother, with

this blasted contraption behind me, and the image never works. I do not know whether she would be sad or grateful. Do you have family you will be returning to when this is over?"

"Yes. In Bonn. My children are still young, the eldest ten and the youngest six. My wife has been very good, looking after them while I am gone."

"Girls I had never met would write me proposals for marriage," said Richthofen, with a sad smile. "Though I am still young and still a war hero, do you think they will when I come home?"

Karl refused to answer such a question. "Self-pity doesn't become you. Crippled or no, you are still the highest scoring ace this entire war."

"That is high praise, coming from you."

"It is not praise, just a fact. With the heart-box you are doing more for the Fatherland than most soldiers could ever hope. You are not just a name for propaganda purposes. You are still *der Rote Kampfflieger.*"

Richthofen looked out the window and said, "I suppose so, but I cannot win this war single-handedly. What are a hundred planes to the battles in which thousands die in a single day? The best I can do is fly my red Fokker at the head of my hunting wing and bring some relief to the men below, so that at least for one day they can fight without worry of bombs dropping on their heads."

Outside, Karl could see a Great Dane bounding around the airfield. Moritz. He was Richthofen's dog, but the pilot could only approach him with caution after the rascal had nearly severed his tubes from the heart-box without understanding better. Moritz was a pleasant dog, normally well mannered, whose only vice was the common want of something to chew.

"A part of me still cannot believe that Loewenhardt is gone," said Richthofen. They had lost the Jasta 10 squadron leader earlier this month. Parachutes were more common now, but his had not opened when he jumped. "Everyone is gone. Wolff, Voss, and Schaefer last year. Now Udet's mind is so broken we've had to send him away and Lothar is in the hospital due to his injuries – again. Wenzel isn't much better. Reinhard is dead, not from our enemies, but from a simple accident. We've lost every single one of JG 1's squadron commanders this month, and yet there is still me, and I would have died last April."

Karl had met a few of them, and they had been fine men, nearly all of them aces of the highest order, and many of them dead or incapacitated by the age of twenty-two. Only Richthofen had died clean enough to recover. This heart-box had been a good idea, but Karl did not think it was as useful for returning soldiers to war as Steinfeld had promised.

"I am not going to give up," said Richthofen. "You do not need to worry. I think if we were down to the last plane in Germany I'd still fly . . ."

In the silence that followed, Mueller appeared in the doorway.

"Dr Huber, an enemy fighter wing has been spotted and the men are scrambling. If you deem *der Rote Kampfflieger* healthy, his ground crew will be ready."

"He is," said Karl.

Mueller nodded and jogged off to relay the message.

"It is time to fly." Richthofen stood, the smart and confident grin on his face completely at odds with how Karl had seen him only moments before. This was the hero, this was *der Rote Kampfflieger* that people believed in. "Seeing as Ostermann is not here, would you be kind enough to help me move my machine?"

Karl wrapped his hands around the handlebar of the cart and pushed as Richthofen carried the gathered tubes in his arms so there was no risk of running them over. They rolled out the door and down the short hall to the front door.

The ground crew was ready by the time they arrived. One of the men had Moritz under leash and Richthofen risked giving the dog an affectionate scratch on the head while someone else held his tubes.

Karl watched the crew hoist the heart-box into the plane, the tubes just barely long enough for Richthofen to stand on the ground while the box was fitted into the body of the Fokker, then the crew lifted the man himself. For a former gymnast, who would leap into his plane as easily as he would over a vault, it must have been agonizing. Karl remembered the pain in his bad leg and turned away as they lowered him in.

"Huber!" shouted Richthofen.

Karl looked up.

The crew was fitting the backboard of his seat between him and the heart-box. Richthofen leaned forward over his control stick to give them room, but he also looked over the edge of the cockpit at Karl.

"You're still here!" said Richthofen, with a smile. "Usually you don't stay."

"I need to take the cart back when they're done," he said, waving at the heart-box's erstwhile cradle. The crew had placed the toolkit for the machine back in the cart. "Since you had me come out instead of Ostermann or Mueller."

Richthofen grinned as though he knew better. He seemed inclined to say more, but then the seat backing was set and his crew jumped down to get ready for flight. Everyone on the ground stepped back, and the moment passed.

Der Rote Kampfflieger settled back against his seat, the only time he could rest his back against another object without feeling the pressure of the tubes between them. The propellers spun, kicking up dust as the plane rolled forward. Moritz whined.

Then the plane lifted into the air, a bright red eagle taking to the sky to join the many colorful planes of JG 1, the hunting wing that their enemies called the Flying Circus. But it wasn't a circus to Karl. There was nothing entertaining about the show they had to perform.

Late that evening, Mueller entered Karl's room and said, "Richthofen has not returned. He is the only one unaccounted for from today's sortie. The men think we've lost him. One of them spotted a red biplane landing in no man's land."

Another lucky landing. Karl grunted and said, "Then the army can send another detachment to retrieve him. If they hurry like last time they'll have him in our bunker in time to hook him up to a new machine. If he's still alive and the heart-box undamaged, it should keep pumping for a few more hours."

And even if he died again, he might just be lucky enough to be resuscitated again.

But though they waited, no rescuers came.

Perhaps the war *is* ending, thought Karl, and so High Command had decided they no longer needed *der Rote Kampfflieger*. Why throw good lives away after one that had already ended, when there was no longer a purpose to fighting?

He should have been pleased that High Command would be so sensible. Instead he found himself outside in the cold September air, smoking a cigarette in the dark where no one would see.

Days later, Jagdgeschwader 1 moved on without them. Days after that, the battered remains of Richthofen's plane were carted over to the empty airfield. Karl counted no less than forty bullet holes on the left side alone. The heart-box was still installed behind the pilot's seat, but Richthofen himself was gone. Karl was told that his concern was the box, not the man, and that the body was no longer worth looking at for research purposes, given the time that had passed.

He did not believe that.

Karl did not know enough about planes to tell whether this shot or that would have brought the eagle down, but he knew the heart-box. Mueller and Ostermann removed it for him and he found it almost entirely intact. Certainly it was scuffed and battered about its protective casing, which was only natural given the roughness of combative flight, but the mechanics on the inside were no worse for wear. The heart-box was no longer running, certainly. The batteries would have drained within hours once fuel from the plane stopped coming, but he saw no reason the heart-box shouldn't work the minute they refueled or recharged it.

But then Karl held up the tubes that had led from the box to Richthofen's body and frowned. There was blood on their ends, of course, as the blood circulated from his body to the machine and back again, but . . .

"Mueller, did you say the army only retrieved his plane after JG 1 had moved on?"

"Yes, Doctor."

Richthofen's blood should have congealed long before the time the army retrieved him, so why was there blood on the outside of the tubes unless Richthofen had been separated from them while he was still alive?

He stood up and climbed the ladder beside the plane, leaning over to peer inside the cockpit. It didn't appear as though any bullets had penetrated the interior. There were no perforations, no blood.

Richthofen had likely been alive, possibly bruised, but not bleeding, when he landed.

Karl looked down at the seat back, which lay on the ground where they had placed it after removing the heart-box. There was a tiny splash of blood right where Richthofen's back would have rested, but no damage.

He jumped from the ladder to the ground, pondering. Could Richthofen have been so unlucky that a bullet had shorn the harness that held the tubes to his body? It would explain a hasty landing, and the outside blood, but the odds of that happening were astronomical.

And the army had taken his body.

Had Richthofen himself disconnected the tubes? Was that why they had taken him? For Germany's highest scoring ace to commit suicide . . .

Karl could well imagine the frustration of being trapped between enemy and allied lines, unable to move, realizing that help would never come. But he frowned, unsatisfied.

"Did you find something, sir?" asked Mueller.

"By any chance did anyone say whether Richthofen's body was found inside the plane?"

"Do you mean whether he fell out?" Sometimes in the violent death spirals of a plane, the pilot would be ejected. "I don't think that would have been possible. The ground crew always straps him in tight before letting him go, and his seat-belts seem to be fine."

So they were.

Karl tried to remember if Richthofen had been wearing them when he had taken off, but he knew he had not been paying attention.

"Yes, you're right," he muttered. "Richthofen would have been in his plane when he landed."

They had denied him a body.

But Richthofen would not have killed himself. No. Karl could not believe that. If he had disconnected himself, there had been a reason, and if he died perhaps it had been with the anticipation that he would be found and revived again.

Karl wanted to believe that.

But all he wrote in his report was that the heart-box had survived intact, and did not appear to have been a contributing factor in the pilot's death.

In another two months, the war was over. Karl would be heading home, and he could give up on thinking about the heart-box and waiting for a suitable young candidate to land on death's door. His family would be waiting. It was almost his eldest's birthday, though he knew with the country's food supply so low he could not afford to give her the kind of dinner she really wanted.

Karl carefully packed his tools and his few personal possessions in preparation for his journey home, among them a simple black-and-white commemorative postcard, in memory of *der Rote Kampfflieger*.

He stared at it before placing it in his bags, until he no longer saw the man in the photo at all. Karl could not help but remember his own time as a boy in gymnasium, when he would practice on the horizontal bar. Release. Twist. Catch. Release. Flip. Catch. Every catch he missed he risked pain and agony below, but nothing would have stopped him from letting go. All he could think of when he took to the air was: this must be what it's like to fly.

Acknowledgments

"Rolling Steel: A Pre-Apocalyptic Love Story" © 2009 by Jay Lake and Shannon Page. Originally appeared in *Clarkesworld Magazine*. Reprinted by permission of the estate of Jay Lake and by Shannon Page.

"Don Quixote" © 2012 by Carrie Vaughn, LLC. Originally published in *Armored*. Reprinted by permission of the author.

"The Little Dog Ohori" © 2015 by Anatoly Belilovsky. Original to this volume.

"Vast Wings Across Felonious Skies" © 2015 by E. Catherine Tobler. Original to this volume.

"Instead of a Loving Heart" © 2004 by Jeremiah Tolbert. Originally published in *All Star Zeppelin Adventure Stories*. Reprinted by permission of the author.

"Steel Dragons of a Luminous Sky" © 2015 by Brian Trent. Original to this volume.

"Tunnel Vision" © 2015 by Rachel Nussbaum. Original to this volume.

"Thief of Hearts" © 2015 by Trent Hergenrader. Original to this volume.

"In Lieu of a Thank You" © 2008 by Gwynne Garfinkle. Originally appeared in *Strange Horizons*. Reprinted by permission of the author.

About the Contributors

Born in the Caribbean, **Tobias S. Buckell** is a *New York Times* bestselling author. His novels and over fifty stories have been translated into seventeen languages. He has been nominated for the Hugo, Nebula, and John W. Campbell Memorial Award for Best New Writer. He currently lives in Ohio.

Jay Lake was a winner of the John W. Campbell Award for Best New Writer, and a multiple nominee for the Hugo, Nebula and World Fantasy Awards. He lived in Portland, Oregon and lost a six-year battle with colon cancer on June 1, 2014. Jay was a prolific writer and editor, and blogged regularly about his cancer at his website jlake.com. His books for 2013 and 2014 include *Kalimpura* and *Last Plane to Heaven* from Tor Books and *Love in the Time of Metal and Flesh* from Prime Books. His work has been translated into several languages including Czech, French, German, Hebrew, Japanese, and Russian.

Shannon Page is the author of several dozen short stories; her first two novels were *Eel River*, in 2013; and *Our Lady of the Islands* (co-written with Jay Lake), named a *Publishers Weekly* Best Book of 2014. She also edits and proofreads at home in Portland, Oregon, and her website is shannonpage.net.

Carrie Vaughn is the author of the *New York Times* bestselling series of novels about a werewolf named Kitty. She has also written a handful of stand-alone fantasy novels and upwards of seventy short stories. She's a graduate of the Odyssey

Fantasy Writing Workshop, and in 2011 she was nominated for a Hugo Award for Best Short Story. She's had the usual round of day jobs, but has been writing full time since 2007. An Air Force brat, she survived her nomadic childhood and managed to put down roots in Boulder, Colorado, where she lives with a fluffy attack dog and too many hobbies. Visit her at carrievaughn.com.

Anatoly Belilovsky is a Russian-American author and translator of science fiction with over twenty-five publications in *UFO*, *Nature*, *F&SF*, and other markets. He was born in a city that went through six or seven owners in the last century, was traded to the US for a shipload of grain under the Jackson-Vanik amendment, and learned English from *Star Trek* reruns. He blogs at loldoc.net.

E. Catherine Tobler has been a finalist for the Theodore Sturgeon Award. Her fiction has appeared in *Clarkesworld Magazine*, *Strange Horizons*, and *Beneath Ceaseless Skies*. And her first novel is *Rings of Anubis*. Follow her on Twitter @ECthetwit and her website is ecatherine.com.

Jeremiah Tolbert is a writer and web developer living in Northeast Kansas with his wife and son. His short stories have appeared in magazines such as *Lightspeed Magazine* and *Asimov's*.

Brian Trent's science fiction and dark fantasy has appeared in numerous publications. He is a 2013 winner in the Writers of the Future contest and his work regularly appears in *Analog*, *Daily Science Fiction*, *Apex*, *Clarkesworld Magazine*, *Escape Pod*, *Cosmos*, *Strange Horizons*, *Galaxy's Edge*, and much more. He lives in New England.

Rachel Nussbaum is a young writer and artist living on the Big Island of Hawaii. She enjoys experimenting with different genres and has previously written science fiction, urban fantasy, and horror stories. Currently, Rachel is attending university, studying English, art, and animation. One day she hopes to write and illustrate her own novels and comic books.

Trent Hergenrader is an English professor at the Rochester Institute of Technology, where he teaches creative writing workshops as well as courses on literature, media, and games. His short fiction has appeared in *Fantasy & Science Fiction*, *Weird Tales*, *Best Horror of the Year: Volume 1* and other fine places.

Gwynne Garfinkle lives in Los Angeles. Her fiction and poetry have appeared in such publications as *Strange Horizons*, *Interfictions*, *Mythic Delirium*, *Apex Magazine*, *Shimmer*, and *Goblin Fruit*. She is working on a couple of novels, as well as a book of poems inspired by classic films, TV, and pop culture.

Genevieve Valentine's first novel, *Mechanique: A Tale of the Circus Tresaulti*, won the 2012 Crawford Award. Her second, *The Girls at the Kingfisher Club*, is out now from Atria. Her short fiction has appeared in *Clarkesworld Magazine*, *Strange Horizons*, *Journal of Mythic Arts*, *Lightspeed*, and others, and the anthologies *Federations*, *After*, *Teeth*, and more. Her nonfiction and reviews have appeared at NPR.org, The A.V. Club, and io9.

Joseph Ng is a contemporary writer of stories. He has written in multiple genres for the page, the screen, and the stage. His ebook, *Death and Other Things*, was published in early 2013; and his short story, "Prose and Koans", was featured in *Esquire* (Malaysia) magazine's March 2014 issue. He currently resides in Kuala Lumpur, and can occasionally be seen wandering its streets in search of inspiration, meaning, and really nice cheesecakes.

A. C. Wise is the author of numerous short stories appearing in publications such as *Clarkesworld Magazine*, *Shimmer*, *Year's Best Weird Fiction Vol. 1*, and *Imaginarium: The Best Canadian Speculative Writing* (2012 and 2014), among others. In addition to her writing, she co-edits *Unlikely Story*. Find her online at acwise.net.

Kim Lakin-Smith is a science fiction and dark fantasy author of adult and children's fiction. Kim's short stories have appeared in numerous magazines and anthologies. Her diesel-punk novel, *Cyber Circus*, was shortlisted for both the British Science Fiction Association Best Novel and the British Fantasy Award for Best Novel 2012.

Nick Mamatas, the son of a diesel mechanic, is the author of the novels *The Last Weekend* and *I am Providence*. His short fiction has appeared in *Best American Mystery Stories*, *The Mammoth Book of Steampunk*, and many other anthologies and magazines.

Tony Pi is a Canadian writer with many short story credits in fantasy and science fiction, including translations into Polish and Chinese. He was a finalist in the Prix Aurora Awards and the John W. Campbell Award for Best New Writer.

Costi Gurgu's fiction has appeared in Canada, the United States, England, Denmark, Hungary and Romania. He is the author of three books, *Recipearium*, a novel, and short story collections *The Glass Plague* and *Chronicles from the End of the Earth*, and over fifty stories for which he has won twenty-four awards.

Cirilo S. Lemos was born in Nova Iguaçu, Rio de Janeiro, in 1982. He dedicates his time to writing, teaching and preparing his children for the inevitable machine rebellion. Author of the novel *O Alienado*, about stories, realities and bureaucracy, he likes horrible dreams, predictable realities and family photos, almost all the time.

Erin M. Hartshorn lives in Pennsylvania with her husband, two kids, and English cocker spaniel. A member of SFWA and the Garden State Speculative Fiction Writers, Erin has had fiction published in *Clarkesworld Magazine* and *Daily Science Fiction* as well as in various anthologies. She blogs at erinmhartshorn.com/blog and is on Twitter @ErinMHartshorn.

Dan Rabarts was the recipient of New Zealand's Sir Julius Vogel Award for Best New Talent, 2014. He co-edited the multi-award-winning flash horror anthology *Baby Teeth: Bite-sized Tales of Terror* with Lee Murray, and his short stories have appeared in numerous anthologies, magazines, ezines, and podcasts. Learn more at dan.rabarts.com.

Mark Robert Philps is a writer and freelance videographer who lives and works in Vancouver, BC. He attended the Clarion workshop in San Diego, and his fiction has appeared previously in *AESCIFI: The Canadian Science Fiction Review*. His home on the internet is markrobertphilps.com.

Catherine Schaff-Stump writes for children and adults. She finds she has greater success publishing when she writes about turtles. She lives with her husband in eastern Iowa and has the requisite author quota of cats. More information about her and her work is available at cathschaffstump.com.

Laurie Tom has wanted to learn about World War I ever since she read *All Quiet on the Western Front* in high school, and is impressed that men once flew in planes that were little more than canvas and wood. Her short fiction has appeared in publications such as *Strange Horizons*, *Galaxy's Edge*, and *Crossed Genres*.